Sins
of the
Fathers

Susan Howatch

 Simon and Schuster / *New York*

Contents

PART ONE

Sam: 1949

Chapter One

SOON AFTER my return from Germany in that troubled spring of 1949, my boss asked me if I would marry his daughter. It was, as I at once realized, a unique occasion. Although I was approaching middle age and not unsophisticated, I had never before been proposed to by the father of a would-be bride without either her knowledge or her consent.

"Well?" said Cornelius encouragingly before my speechlessness could become an embarrassment to us both. "What do you say?"

I knew exactly what I wanted to say. The Germans had a phrase for it. *"Ohne mich,"* I had heard them say again and again during my recent trip. "Count me out." And those terse words had soon symbolized to me all the exhaustion and disillusionment of postwar Europe.

"Ohne mich!" I now responded automatically, too appalled to be diplomatic, but luckily Cornelius knew no German. As he looked blank it occurred to me that I had just bought myself a few precious extra seconds and I at once used the time to pull myself together. As soon as he had said coldly, "Pardon me?" I replied without hesitation, "That means 'What a happy suggestion!'" and gave him my warmest smile. The twenty-three years I had spent working as an investment banker on Wall Street had perhaps overdeveloped my talent for survival.

We were sitting in his office at the bank, and beyond the French doors the sunlight of early evening slanted across the patio. The bank, a huge Renaissance-style relic of the nineteenth century, stood at One Willow Street on the corner of Wall, but the senior partner's office at the back of the building might have been a hundred miles from the noisy streets of downtown Manhattan. In the patio the magnolia tree was in full bloom, reminding me of summers irretrievably lost, the summers in Maine on the estate where my father had been the head gardener, the summers in Germany in those sunlit days before the war. The beauty of the magnolia blossom suddenly seemed unendurable; I had to avert my eyes. But when I glanced around the room I saw the bleak furniture, the violent primary colors in the painting above the fireplace and, beyond his desk, the anxious little man who occupied the senior partner's chair.

"You'll do it, Sam?" He seemed about to collapse with relief. "You'll fix it?"

I thought of all the times he had asked me those questions in the past, and when I glanced past him again into the patio I saw not the magnolia tree but the high wall black with city filth and the doorway, long since bricked up, which had once led into Willow Alley.

"Now, wait a minute!" I protested, laughing. "Don't rush me—this is a big occasion! It's not every day a hardened bachelor of forty-one receives such an unexpected proposal from his boss!"

"Sam, I know—I just know—that this is the only solution to the problem—"

"And don't think I don't understand your problem and sympathize with you. It must be harrowing in the extreme to have an eighteen-year-old daughter who's just tried to elope with a beachboy. However, as one of your oldest friends and certainly your most loyal partner, I owe it to you to point out that I may not be the best candidate for the role of son-in-law. Of course I appreciate the big compliment you're paying me—"

"Oh, for Christ's sake!" said Cornelius, exasperated. "Let's be honest about this! What does a man do when he has a beautiful daughter who's heiress to a fortune? If he's got any grain of moral responsibility he marries her off to someone he can trust before some goddamned gigolo can ruin her life!"

"Yes, but—"

"The trouble is, there are very few people I trust; in fact, the only people I trust one hundred percent today are my three friends who knew me back in the days before Paul left me all his money. And since Jake's married and Kevin's queer, that leaves you. Goddamn it, Sam, I can't think why you're dragging your feet about this! You've

5

been saying for years that you wanted to get married, and you know very well that I'd make this marriage worth your while in more ways than one. What's your problem, for Christ's sake?"

There were several replies I could have made, but any attempt to be honest would only have had the effect of prolonging the conversation and I could now see the conversation had to be terminated immediately. Cornelius needed time to calm down. Clearly Vicky's escapade with the beachboy had propelled him into a big panic, but if I gave him the chance to recover his equilibrium he would soon realize his wild matrimonial pipe dream was best forgotten. Clearing my throat, I reluctantly prepared to abandon the truth and lie my way out of trouble.

"There's no problem," I said soothingly. "I'm not a man to miss my opportunities, but give me a couple of days to adjust to the idea, won't you? I'm a human being, not a robot programmed to give the correct response whenever someone presses a button!"

"Why, Sam, I'd never think of you as a robot, you know that—and I hope you'd never think of me as a mad scientist bent on pressing all the wrong buttons!" He gave me one of his most attractive smiles, the boyish one which made him look so innocent, and rising nimbly to his feet, he held out his hand. His gray eyes were brilliant with affection. "Thanks a million, Sam," he said. "I knew you wouldn't let me down."

Before we could shake hands, the white telephone rang on his desk to indicate a call coming through on his private line. "That'll be Alicia," said Cornelius, immediately tense again. "She said she'd let me know if the trays of food left outside Vicky's door had been touched. If you'll excuse me, Sam . . ."

I escaped.

II

IT'S NOT easy to work for someone the same age as oneself. Nor is it easy to work for one's closest friend, particularly when the friendship has spanned twenty-four years. Cornelius and I, both forty-one, had first met when we were boys of seventeen in 1925, but despite the fact that our work created a common bond, the bank paradoxically both united and divided us. It compelled us to share huge segments of our lives, yet since Cornelius was the boss, the sharing was never on equal terms. I respected Cornelius and we got along well, but sometimes (since I was only human) I couldn't help resenting my subordinate position, and I had never resented it more than I did that evening when he tried to push me into marrying his daughter.

It was Cornelius' uncle, Paul Van Zale, who had first brought us together. Immensely rich, immensely powerful, with his own Wall Street investment bank, his beautiful showpiece wife, and his mansions on Fifth Avenue in New York and at the summer resort of Bar Harbor in Maine, Paul had a profound influence on me when I was growing up. I was the son of German immigrants; my parents, working as gardener and housekeeper, took care of Paul's summer home for him in the long intervals between his visits, and since I was only his servants' son, I hardly expected him to pay any attention to me when he came to Bar Harbor on vacation. However, when I was seventeen he invited me to live as a guest in his home in order to be one of the three companions he was seeking for his great-nephew who was due to visit him that summer from Ohio. Cornelius was Paul's only male relative. Having no sons of his own, Paul had decided it was time to discover if his great-nephew was tough enough to sustain the burden of the Van Zale fortune and eventually succeed him at the bank.

At first I didn't know what to make of Cornelius. I didn't know what to make of the two other boys either. Paul seemed to have selected an odd quartet of protégés, and although we were all the same age, seventeen, we appeared to have nothing else in common. Kevin Daly was the son of a rich Irish-American politician and attended a famous Eastern Seaboard education establishment a world removed from the high school I attended at Bar Harbor; Jake Reischman came from New York's German-Jewish aristocracy and lived in a Fifth Avenue palace which I, brought up in the lodge at the gates of the Van Zale estate, could hardly begin to imagine. Kevin seemed overpoweringly extraverted and self-confident; Jake seemed incredibly debonair and sophisticated. I felt very conscious of my social inferiority in their presence, and had it not been for the fact that Cornelius was even more overwhelmed by them than I was, I might well have flunked the golden opportunity for advancement which Paul was offering me, and retreated in despair to the lodge.

However, Paul soon bound us together. At the end of that summer we were all united in our hero worship of him and unanimous in our desire to be as dazzlingly successful in life as he was, and when he recalled us in 1926 for a second summer as his special protégés, we were all excited by the prospect of our reunion.

But our reunion was short-lived. Paul was killed soon afterward. In those days wealthy men in his position were so vulnerable to assassination by Bolshevist fanatics that he had always employed a bodyguard, but the men who conspired to murder him were sophisticated enough to overcome this routine precaution against disaster. The world, stunned by his death, was stunned too by his will; Paul had named Cornelius as his heir. This was the first public indication Paul had given that he considered his great-nephew tough enough to take on such a considerable responsibility, and as time passed everyone slowly realized that his confidence hadn't been misplaced.

Cornelius had delicate health and a frail appearance. At the age of eighteen he also had a face like a choirboy's, a respectful way of talking to his elders, and a smile which apparently gave women an irresistible desire to mother him. No one could have looked more harmless, and no one, as Paul once remarked dryly, could have been more adept at employing that vampire's trick of going straight for the jugular vein.

It took Cornelius some years to establish himself as senior partner at the bank, but by the time he was thirty his life was mirroring Paul's with uncanny precision. He had his Wall Street bank, his showpiece wife, his mansions on Fifth Avenue and at Bar Harbor; he had all Paul's wealth and success and fame.

I wasn't doing so badly myself. After Paul had died in 1926 I went to New York because Cornelius, always a realist, had known he would soon need a loyal ally, while I, always an opportunist, was determined not to pass up the chance to fulfill my classic American dream of achieving wealth and success. Of course none of the Van Zale partners had taken us seriously. They had thought we were just a couple of schoolboys playing at being bankers, and so they had laughed, writing us off by assuming our dreams were inevitably doomed to failure.

I often thought of those men at the bank who had laughed at us back in 1926.

They were all dead now.

When we had first begun to work at the bank, the most powerful man on the premises had been Paul's favorite partner, Steven Sullivan, a man some twenty years older than Cornelius and myself. Huge, shrewd, flamboyant, Steve had at first terrified us both, yet right from the start we had both known this was the one man we had to oust from the bank if Cornelius were ever to sit in that coveted senior partner's chair.

"Of course it'll be difficult to eliminate him," Cornelius had said, summoning all his talent for long-range planning, "but there's no reason why we shouldn't fix the elimination in the end. Where there's a will there's a way."

We fixed it. We ousted him. Later he died. We were indirectly responsible for his death too, although Cornelius would never admit it, saying it was hardly our fault that Steve had driven his car into a tree after drinking the contents of a bottle of Scotch. Cornelius never admitted anything was his fault. He always just said: "I was driven to do what I had to do," and then he would start talking about something else. He seemed to have an inexhaustible talent for shutting out the past he had no wish to remember, and it was a talent I often envied, for it would have been such a relief if I could have walled off not only my guilt about Steve Sullivan but my guilt about being a German-American who hadn't fought in the war.

I had only just returned from my first postwar vacation in Germany. I had been thinking of it ever since I had arrived back in New York, and I knew the memories would continue to haunt me with unbearable clarity: the ruined cities, the terrible peace of the shattered countryside, the Allied soldiers laughing in the streets—and finally the G.I. at my side who had whistled "Lili Marlene."

It occurred to me, as I escaped from the senior partner's office on that April evening in 1949, that when compared with the nightmare of my German vacation Cornelius' idiotic suggestion that I should marry his daughter could almost be classed as a joke. However, my moment of humor was short-lived. My position was potentially too awkward, and as I ran up the stairs from the back lobby I knew I was breathing hard not only from the sudden exertion but from my extreme tension as well.

I entered my office. On my desk I found a pile of letters awaiting signature, six pink notes recording telephone messages, and a long memo from my personal assistant, but I ignored them all, fixed myself a double Beefeater martini on the rocks, and reached for the phone.

The bell rang eight times before Teresa picked up the receiver.

"Hi," I said, "it's me. Are you busy?"

"I'm cooking jambalaya for Kevin's dinner and wondering if he'll ever have the nerve to eat it. How are you?"

"Just fine. Can I see you tonight?"

"Well . . ."

"I lied. I feel terrible. How about a quick drink? I'll sit in the kitchen while you cook."

"Okay, come on over."

"You're the best girl in all New York. I'm on my way."

III

I HAD MET Teresa at my friend Kevin Daly's house four months ago. Kevin's annual Christmas parties had become the only occasion on which he, Jake Reischman, Cornelius, and I met under one roof; we were all a long way now from our summers as Van Zale protégés at Paul's Bar Harbor home.

"The Bar Harbor Brotherhood!" Kevin had exclaimed exuberantly when the four of us had been reunited after the war. "Or should it be the Bar Harbor Mafia?"

It was true that the word "brotherhood" was too sentimental a description of the ties which still existed between us, and even the word "friendship" could no longer be used to describe our association accurately. Jake and I never met unless we had business to discuss, and since Jake had become head of his own investment-banking house, he preferred to deal solely with Cornelius. Cornelius saw Kevin regularly at meetings of the board of the Van Zale Fine Arts Foundation but seldom saw him socially, while I, having no interest in the arts, had all but lost touch with Kevin before I met Teresa. To an outsider it might have seemed that Cornelius and I were the two who were closest, but I often suspected Cornelius was closest to Jake. They met on equal terms. Cornelius was always ready to swear, particularly after a glass of champagne, that he regarded me as a brother, and he was always, even without the champagne, careful to softpedal his power over me by insisting how indispensable I was to him, but both of us had no illusions about our true status. It was the dark side of our relationship which we tacitly accepted but could never bring ourselves to discuss. No one is ever indispensable. I knew that just as I knew that Cornelius would always be the boss and I would— if I were sensible—always be the right-hand man, but I wasted no time dwelling on it. It was just a fact of life to be accepted sensibly without a fuss.

"You bankers!" said Kevin when we occasionally got drunk enough to reminisce to him about the less-publicized events of our shared past. He made no secret of his contempt for Wall Street but he followed our careers with the vicarious interest of a writer perpetually on the lookout for new material. In 1929, when Kevin had abandoned Harvard Law School to live in New York, he had intended to be a novelist, but only one novel had ever been written. For years now he had written plays, the early ones enjoyable, the later ones increasingly puzzling, and had long since left his fashionable Greenwich Village garret to live in a fashionable Greenwich Village brownstone west of Washington Square.

Kevin loved his house. Cornelius had once suggested that the house was a substitute for the family who had never forgiven Kevin for leading a life which they could only regard with disapproval, and even if this theory remained non-proven, there was no denying that Kevin had spent large sums of money on creating a showpiece home for himself. Hating to leave the house unattended, he even went to the trouble of converting the top floor into a studio apartment for a caretaker. His caretakers lasted about six months. Young, attractive, invariably blond, and always female, they were either writers or painters or sculptors; musicians were prohibited because they made too much noise. The girls were delighted to have a rent-free apartment and an uncomplicated relationship with an employer who had no interest in beating a path to their bedroom door, but the inevitable quarrel always came when Kevin refused to lend them money. Kevin could be tough. I heard young male guests had been ejected from the house with similar incisiveness, although Kevin seemed to prefer to live alone.

He was living alone—apart from the current caretaker—when he had invited me to his party the previous Christmas, and as it turned out, I was the only one of his three Bar Harbor friends who accepted the invitation. Jake was away in California, and Cornelius, who had not enjoyed the previous Christmas party, made some excuse not to go.

"Don't know why you want to go and mingle with a bunch of queers," said Cornelius, but I just laughed. Other people's sexual tastes were of no interest to me, and besides, Kevin gave the best parties in town.

When I arrived at his house, about forty people were screaming elegantly at each other beneath the crystal chandeliers in Kevin's large old-fashioned living room. Kevin served the usual cocktails to cater to conventional American taste, but the hallmark of a Daly party was that the guests had the opportunity to get drunk on champagne.

Unfortunately, a grateful client had given me a surfeit of champagne earlier that day at lunch. "I'll take a Scotch on the rocks," I said to the hired butler, and was just eyeing a dish of caviar when someone exclaimed behind me, "You must be jaded! What kind of a guy turns down free French champagne?"

I swung round. A plump young woman with wild curly hair, a large nose, and a wide mouth was smiling at me. She wore a scarlet dress which fitted badly, and a gold cross on a chain around her neck. Her eyes were very narrow, very bright, and very dark.

"You can't be anyone from show business!" she added, laughing. "They *always* drink champagne!"

"No kidding, I thought they took baths in it. Are you an actress Miss . . . ?"

"Kowalewski."

"Pardon me?"

"Teresa. I'm the new caretaker."

I was greatly surprised. This girl could hardly have been more different from the willowy well-educated blonds whom Kevin usually employed.

"What happened to Ingrid, the Swedish girl?" I asked, saying the first thing that entered my head.

"Ingrid went to Hollywood." By this time she was looking at me with as much surprise as I was looking at her. "You're not one of Kevin's regular crowd, are you? Would you be his lawyer or something?"

"Good guess. I'm a banker."

"A what? Jesus, the noise is awful in here! I thought you said you were a banker!"

"I did. And what's your line, Teresa?"

"I paint. Gee, are you really a banker? You mean you stand in a teller's cage all day long and dole out the dough?"

I was entranced by her ignorance. Later I realized she was entranced by mine.

"You've never heard of Edvard Munch? You've never heard of Paul Klee?"

"No," I said, "but I'm more than willing to learn."

After a couple of dinner dates I told her a little about my work.

"You mean I can't come into your bank with a ten-dollar bill and open an account?"

"Our commercial bank, the Van Zale Manhattan Trust, deals with that kind of client. P. C. Van Zale and Company is an investment bank. We raise money for the big corporations of America by floating issues which the public can buy as an investment."

"I don't believe in capitalism," said Teresa firmly. "I think it's immoral."

"Morality's like mink," I said. "It's great if you can afford it." And although she laughed, I did not mention my work to her again.

Meanwhile she was still refusing to tell me about her painting, and even when she eventually took me up to her studio, I found the canvases were stacked facing the wall because she felt they were too bad to be displayed. Once when she was taking a shower I nearly raised the cloth which covered the half-finished work on the easel, but I was afraid she might realize the cloth had been disturbed, and I liked her too much to put our new relationship in jeopardy. I liked her lack of pretentiousness and the way she always said what she thought. Although she was shrewd and by no means naive, she had managed to retain a simplicity which reminded me of girls I had dated long ago when I had been growing up in Bar Harbor. I wanted to take her out to the smart midtown nightclubs, but she said she preferred the little ethnic restaurants in the Village. I wanted to give a big dinner party so that she could meet my friends, but she said she preferred our evenings alone together. I wanted her to spend more time at my apartment, but she said the servants made her nervous. For some time I had postponed inviting her to my apartment because I found it hard to believe she was as indifferent to money as she appeared to be, but eventually in February I took the risk and invited her to hear some records from my collection.

We listened happily to the phonograph, watched our favorite television shows, and read the New York Sunday *Times* together the next morning.

"Imagine being ashamed of being rich!" she said affectionately when we went to bed again on Sunday night.

"I'm not ashamed of it. It's my own money, I earned it and I'm proud of it, but I've met too many women who have ended up finding my bank account more attractive than they found me."

"Sam," said Teresa, "no matter how often we start a conversation on an interesting subject, we always wind up talking about money. Have you noticed? I can't understand it. I'm not even interested in money. Why do we keep talking about it?"

I smiled, apologized, and at last allowed myself to believe she meant what she said.

Teresa might not have been interested in money, but she had some strong ideas about earning it. Although she accepted my free dinners and the occasional modest gift, she refused my offers of financial assistance and said she had always believed in "paying her own way." To provide herself with the bare essentials of life she used to take temporary jobs as a waitress and quit as soon as she had saved up enough money to keep herself for a few weeks. She seemed to have no interest in a regular job or a normal life, and yet despite this unabashed bohemianism (which fascinated me), she was still conventional enough to enjoy cooking, try her hand at dressmaking, and maintain her old-fashioned ideas about taking money from well-meaning men. This odd mixture of the conservative and the eccentric became increasingly beguiling to me; although I disapproved of her attitude toward a regular job, I respected her dedication to her painting, and although I could not approve of her place in the drifting population of the city, I admired her ability to fend for herself in New York and live by the rules she had set herself.

Eventually the moment came when I was unable to resist mentioning her to my friends.

"A new girl?" said Cornelius vaguely. "That's nice. Why don't you bring her to dinner with us?"

"She wouldn't be interested in dining in a Fifth Avenue palace with a bunch of millionaires."

"All women," said Cornelius, "are interested in dining in a Fifth Avenue palace with a bunch of millionaires." But when I just laughed, he decided my attitude sprang from the fact that Teresa was unpresentable, and after that he lost interest in her.

Cornelius himself had been married twice, first to a society hostess fourteen years his senior who had married him for his money before giving him something no money could buy—his daughter, Vicky—and second to a society beauty two years his junior who had married him for love and presented him with two stepsons, the children of her previous marriage. Vivienne, the first wife, now lived in Florida and I had not seen her for many years. The second wife, Alicia, I saw frequently in her role of Mrs. Cornelius Van Zale, wife of the well-known millionaire and pillar of New York society. There were no mistresses. Cornelius did not approve of an unconventional private life, and although he had never expressed the opinion that I should marry and settle down, I knew he would automatically disapprove of a bohemian mistress like Teresa.

By this time I was becoming increasingly annoyed by Teresa's endearing but absurd refusal to accept money from me. I enjoyed giving presents; I had no sinister motives and I objected to being treated as if I had. I felt her attitude demeaned our relationship, particularly since all I wanted was to make our lives run more smoothly along their shared groove. Of course some cynic could have made an unpleasant comment on my offer to set Teresa up in a smart apartment only two blocks from my Park Avenue home, but the truth was, I was tired of creeping about Kevin's house at all hours of the night and suspected Kevin was equally tired of this continuing nocturnal invasion of his privacy.

"Look," I said at last to Teresa in yet another effort to persuade her that the situation needed improving, "we're lucky! I have enough money to make our affair twice as enjoyable! It's a bonus, not a millstone round our necks! Why fight it? Why suffer if you don't have to? It's illogical! It makes no sense! It's an inefficient use of our precious leisure hours!"

I was glad when this had the desired effect of making her laugh, but I soon realized that ridiculing the situation was still not going to change it.

"I've nothing against living in a midtown apartment," she said. "In fact, I sure hope I'll live in one someday, but when I do, I'm the one who's going to be paying the rent."

I was so exasperated I wanted to slap her. I even lost control of myself sufficiently to accuse her of holding out in order to win an invitation to move in with me, but I knew this was nonsense even before she looked scornful and told me what I could do with my precious penthouse; I was well aware that she felt uncomfortable in my home and disliked going there. At first I had been hurt by this, but later I felt relieved. Despite my current frustration, I was neither infatuated nor ingenuous and I knew very well that a man in my position can hardly install his bohemian mistress in his apartment in full view of the world and still keep that world's wholehearted respect. However, this inescapable truth only made me the more determined to keep her as close to me as possible in circumstances which my world could regard with its customary indulgent indifference.

I reconsidered my position. I was doing well, but obviously I had to do better if I were to extricate her from that house in Greenwich Village. I decided now was the time for a long weekend in some idyllic location. I knew from past experience that long weekends, introduced into the affair at the right moment, could prove highly successful, and feeling cheered by the prospect of success, I began to consider suitable destinations. Maine, Cape Cod, North Carolina, Florida . . . My mind ranged swiftly up and down the Eastern Seaboard and even made the trip to Bermuda before the obvious answer occurred to me: Europe. Teresa, daughter of Polish immigrants, had never been there and had always longed to go. Glamorous, romantic, irresistible Europe . . . two weeks . . . and everyone said Paris had been barely touched by the war.

Staging a candlelit dinner *à deux* in her favorite French restaurant, I ordered champagne and proposed that she should accompany me on my upcoming European vacation. I didn't tell her my reservations had been made for hotels in Germany. Reservations could be canceled and itineraries could be reorganized. Besides, I had never talked to her about Germany beyond telling her right from the start that although I was a German-American I had no German connections. I had even lied and told her I had been born in the States.

"Paris!" breathed Teresa, greatly tempted.

I scented victory. "We can go first class all the way and have ourselves a ball!"

She sighed. "I'd sure like to go . . ."

"Great! Then it's settled! I'll call my travel agent!"

". . . but I can't. It's no good, Sam. If I let you buy me once, you'll buy me over and over again until before I know where I am I'll be living in a penthouse overlooking the East River with a checkbook in my purse and a mink round my shoulders and a lover who owns me lock, stock, and barrel. Don't get me wrong—I know you mean well and I appreciate it, but my independence means more to me than a dozen trips to Europe, and I'm not giving it up, even for you."

"But I'd respect your independence, Teresa!"

"I wouldn't if it could be bought."

We quarreled. It was because I was so disappointed. I almost canceled my vacation, since I hated the thought of two weeks without her, but then I told myself I was behaving like an infatuated young kid and needed time on my own to cool off. I had a long serious debate with myself to decide whether I had fallen in love with her, but logically I don't see how I could have. Then I had another long serious debate with myself and admitted I had drifted into a situation where logic had no part to play; I was crazy about her and I would be crazier still if I tried to deny it.

Having the guts to face up to this disturbing reality certainly represented some kind of a triumph, but my triumph was short-lived when I realized I was at another dead end with no idea what to do next. I couldn't live with her publicly. Apparently I couldn't even persuade her to live with me privately. My logical mind, still functioning sporadically despite such illogical circumstances, told me that left three further courses of action. I could give her up. I could preserve the unsatisfactory status quo. Or I could marry her.

Giving her up was unthinkable. Preserving the status quo was already exasperating me. Marriage was as impossible as living with her openly. Or was it? Yes, it was. Marriage wouldn't work. The harsh truth, which I somehow had to face squarely if I wanted to preserve my sanity, was that Teresa would never fit into my world. If we married, either she would have to make some changes in her life or I would have to make some changes in mine, and I could hardly embark on a proposal which ran: "Say, I'd like to marry you but you've got to make a lot of changes before I lead you to the altar." I did wonder if perhaps I might try to make some changes in my life, but I soon gave up that idea. I liked my world just the way it was, and any radical alteration was inconceivable.

But then I went back to Germany, and as I set foot again on my native land for the first time in ten years I forgot everything—Teresa, Van Zale's, my entire American life—in the ordeal of my repatriation.

I had thought I was well prepared. I had read interminable reports and talked to people who had been there. I had waited four years after the end of the war because I had wanted to be sure I could accept whatever chaos I might find on my return, but when I did return I found not only that the reality was so much worse than I had imagined, but that I had no idea how to cope with it. No newspaper report, no photographs in *Life* magazine, no conversations with eyewitnesses could ever have prepared me for those ruined cities and my shattered illusions and the G.I. who had whistled "Lili Marlene."

"How was Europe?" said Teresa brightly when I returned.

"Just fine." I could say nothing about Germany, but I did try to tell her about Paris. I drew on my memories of my visit there before the war.

"How was Germany?" said Cornelius casually later.

"Not so bad." But I knew, as soon as I returned to Willow and Wall, that I could no longer go on pretending nothing had happened. If I was ever going to live at peace with myself, I would have to make some far-reaching changes in my personal and professional life.

I wanted to call Paul Hoffman of the Economic Cooperation Administration, who was at that time recruiting investment bankers to help rebuild the economy of Europe. I even got as far as lifting the receiver to ask for the ECA's number in Washington, but I replaced the receiver because I knew that before I talked to Paul Hoffman I had to talk to Cornelius. There was no question of my resigning from Van Zale's. Van Zale's was my life, the symbol of my success, the embodiment of that classic American dream which had nurtured me for so long. But I wanted a leave of absence, and only one man had the power to give me what I wanted.

Unfortunately the prospect of the unavoidable interview with Cornelius was far from appealing. Cornelius was an isolationist, although in theory he had broken with the doctrine after Pearl Harbor in order to conform with official American policy. He had never been able to offer me a rational explanation of his dislike of Europe, but dislike it he did and I knew that he would balk at giving me a leave of absence that would enable me to work for European reconstruction. It made no difference that he agreed in theory with the economists who argued that America's own welfare depended ultimately on the generous use of Marshall aid; in practice he grudged every dollar spent propping up the countries which had so unforgivably dragged America into a second world war.

In addition to this incurable chauvinism I knew I would also have to deal with his reluctance to dispense even temporarily with my services. Although I had never fooled myself I was indispensable to Cornelius at One Willow Street, I was well aware that none of my other partners could match me as a confidant and collaborator. As Cornelius himself often said, there were few people he trusted com-

pletely. In the circumstances it was just my bad luck that I happened
to be one of them.

I had thought my position could hardly be more awkward, but I
was wrong. It took a sharp turn for the worse when Vicky Van Zale
tried to elope with her beachboy and Cornelius conceived his preposterous matrimonial pipe dream. Far from wanting to unlock the
handcuffs of our shared past, which had shackled us together for so
long, he was now apparently eager to throw away the key, and as I
drove up to Kevin's house that evening to see Teresa, I wondered in
despair how I was ever going to extricate myself from that golden
cage Cornelius was busy reinforcing for me at Willow and Wall.

I got out of my Mercedes-Benz. "You needn't wait, Hauptmann,"
I said. "I'll take a cab home."

As the car drove away I glanced down the tree-lined street and up
at the pastel sky. It was a beautiful evening, and suddenly against all
the odds my despair receded and I even smiled at the memory of my
last meeting with Cornelius. Had he seriously thought he could bribe
or blitz me into marrying his pampered little daughter? He must have
been out of his mind. I was going to marry Teresa. Of course I was
going to marry Teresa. That was why the idea of marrying anyone
else seemed so absurd, and I knew then that I had wanted to marry
her for some time but had suppressed the truth from myself. However, now I could openly acknowledge how much I loved her because I no longer had to tell myself that she would never fit into my
wealthy New York world. My world was going to change and I was
going to change with it. With my leave of absence secured by some
brilliant diplomatic stroke which I could not yet imagine, I'd go to
Europe, commit myself to the idealism of the Marshall Plan, and
fight at last as a loyal American for the Germany I had loved so
much before the war.

And later? Later the anticipated postwar boom would be in full
swing and I would somehow persuade Cornelius it was in his best interests to open an office of Van Zale's in Europe. . . . My new life
stretched ahead of me as far as the eye could see, and Kevin's front
door swung wide to welcome me as I ran up the steps. She was there,
smiling at me, and when I saw her my heart felt as if it were about to
burst not only with happiness but with relief, as if I had finally succeeded in resolving all the conflicts that had tormented me for so
long.

It was a brilliant seductive illusion. But I shall never forget how happy I was on that April evening in 1949 when I saw Teresa smiling at me and I ran up the steps into her arms.

"Hi, honey!" she said, kissing me. "Leave your latest million bucks at the door, come on in, and I'll fix you a martini which would stop even General Sherman dead in his tracks. Gee, you look almost as exhausted as you sounded on the phone! Just what the hell's been going on?"

Chapter Two

I

TERESA HAD a smudge of dirt on her unpowdered nose and scarlet lipstick on her full-lipped mouth. Her dark hair streamed wildly in unexpected directions, as if defying the law of gravity. Her turquoise dress, worn with a white belt which matched her high-heeled sandals, looked as if it had been punished at the laundry, for the seams were strained around her hips and the buttons barely met across her bosom. As usual she wore her gold cross but no other jewelry.

"You're looking wonderful!" I said, kissing her again. "Where did you get that sexy dress?"

"In a street market down on the Lower East Side. Now, don't avoid answering my question! Why did you sound so desperate on the phone?"

I had no wish to embark on an explanation of my tortuous relationship with Cornelius. "Well, there's this big corporation called Hammaco who want to float a ninety-million-dollar issue—"

"Oh, God. Let me fix those drinks. Are you sure you don't mind sitting in the kitchen? I'm just making the rice for the jambalaya."

"Where's Kevin?"

"He's not back yet from rehearsal." She led the way down the hall to the back of the house.

Kevin's kitchen was the masterpiece of his perfect house, and represented all the qualities I liked about his home. The room was simple and uncluttered, but it had that uncluttered simplicity which only money can buy. The kitchen, a replica of a room Kevin had admired in a New England farmhouse, was large and airy. An old-fashioned range, installed for ornamental purposes, gleamed black beneath a partially exposed brick wall. The closets were solid maple. A sturdy rectangular table stood in the middle of the room with four matching wooden chairs. Herbs grew in pots on the windowsill, copper pans hung on the wall, and the warm red-tiled floor glowed in the soft light. Kevin employed both a cleaning woman and a daily housekeeper to maintain his home in the immaculate order he demanded and which one meal cooked by Teresa promptly destroyed.

"Sorry everything's in such a mess," said Teresa, clearing a space at the table. "It's the housekeeper's day off and I offered to cook this meal for Kevin because he gave me five dollars to buy a pair of shoes. The soles finally dropped off the other pair and the little guy around the corner said they couldn't be fixed anymore. . . . That's odd, I'm sure I had some olives for your martini. I wonder what I did with them."

"Kevin lent you money?"

"No, it was a gift. He never makes loans."

"That's what I thought. Well, if you can accept money from Kevin . . ."

"I can't. That's why I'm cooking him this meal in return. I guess I'll have to look around for another job now my savings have run out. . . . Sorry, honey, but I can't find those olives, maybe the cat ate them. Two ice cubes in the martini?"

"Thanks. Teresa, you don't have to go looking for another job. I've just had this great idea—"

Without warning she turned on me. "I've had just about enough of your great ideas! And I've had just about enough of you talking about money! I'm sorry, but I'm in a filthy mood today because my work's going so badly. That's why I've got to get back upstairs to the canvas as soon as I've presented Kevin with his dinner."

"Hey, wait a minute!" I was thrown mentally off balance by this totally unexpected attack and could only stammer in protest, "What I've got to say's important!"

She slammed down the packet of rice. "So's my work!" she shouted at me. "You think it's just an amusing hobby because I don't make any money at it—money, money, money, that's all you think about, day in, day out! Or *do* you think of anything else? I'm damned if I know. I've known for some time now that you don't understand the first thing about me, but now I'm beginning to wonder if

I understand the first thing about you. Oh, you talk and talk and talk on a surface level, but what really goes on beneath all that big-time charm and sexy savoir faire? I can't make up my mind whether you're a nice decent guy or a real bastard. I guess you have to be a bastard if you're prepared to waste your life in a corrupt, materialistic, repulsive profession like banking, but—"

"Just a minute." I had pulled myself together by this time and knew exactly what to say. I did not raise my voice but I altered my tone, just as I did whenever a client became truculent and had to be painlessly put back in his place. "Let's get this straight. Banking's a fine profession. You may not think it's as much God's gift to humanity as painting pictures, but if you knew a little more about banking and were a little less busy assimilating some fallacy-ridden Marxist crap, you'd see that bankers perform a necessary service for the economy—and therefore for the country as a whole. So quit pushing me this 1930's fable about the bankers being the bad guys, okay? Just pause to think for a moment. What's happening right now in 1949? It's the bankers who are going to put Europe together again after all the soldier-heroes and politicians have blown it to bits! And that brings me to what I wanted to talk to you about. I've seen how I can use all my training and experience as a banker in the best possible cause—"

"Oh, forget it. That kind of rat race is all so meaningless, so futile—"

"For Christ's sake!" I was now very angry. "Don't you try to hand me some garbled philosophical junk about the meaning of life! Who the hell knows what it all means? In the long run isn't it just as meaningless to paint a picture as to make a buck? I guess you think I've always been too busy making money to ask myself the usual fundamental questions, but I'm not the money-making robot you seem to think I am and I've often wondered, particularly lately, what life's all about. Is there a God? It seems inconceivable, but if there is, his managerial skills would appear to be pretty damn poor. Is there a life after death? Again it seems inconceivable, but if it exists and God has a hand in it, it's bound to be a lousy mess. Personally I'm not interested in fantasy, just in hard facts which I can organize into a coherent order. We live in a capitalist society, and it's not going to change in our lifetime. Money keeps that society going. You need money to live, you need money to do the things you really want to do, you need money to do good—which brings me to what I came here to say. In Europe right now—"

"Europe!" blazed Teresa. "I don't give a damn about Europe! All I care about is us and where we're going! At least I've tried to accept you as you are, banking and all. But when have you ever made any effort to accept me as *I* am, Sam? When are you ever going to stop trying to buy me and turn me into some kind of domesticated mistress?"

"Jesus Christ!" I shouted, finally losing my temper. "I don't want to turn you into a domesticated mistress! I want to turn you into my wife!"

Far away at the other end of the hall the front door clicked open. "Hey, Teresa!" called Kevin. "Guess who's just picked me up in a Rolls-Royce the size of a beer truck at Forty-second and Broadway!"

In the kitchen we were motionless, staring at each other. Teresa's lips were parted and the little gold cross had disappeared between the curves of her breasts. I wanted to make love to her.

"I'll wait for you upstairs," I said in a low voice. "I don't want to talk to Kevin."

"No."

"Teresa . . ."

"I'm sorry, I know I'm being mean to you, but I can't help it, I just can't help it. . . . My life's in such a mess. If only I could work —I've got to try to work tonight or I think I'll go out of my mind."

"But I must talk to you!"

"Not tonight. I can't. I've got to be alone. I must work, I must."

"But I love you—I'll help you sort everything out."

"You just don't even begin to understand."

The door of the kitchen was flung wide as Kevin made a grand entrance in the best show-business tradition.

"Teresa, my angel! What's that extraordinarily sinister aroma emanating from the stove? Why, hullo, Sam—no, don't go! Why are you looking as flustered as if I'd caught you *in flagrante delicto?* You know I permit my female staff to receive gentlemen callers!" And as I sank down reluctantly on the nearest chair, he exclaimed, laughing as if he could wipe the tension from the room with his exuberance, "Christ, those asinine actors have driven me clean up the wall! It's a wonder I'm not dead of apoplexy!"

Kevin looked younger than forty-one. Dark and six feet tall, just as I was, he had, unlike me, kept both his figure and his hairline. His frivolous air was deceptive. Like Wall Street, Broadway was a tough world and only the fittest survived. The dimpled chin, claimed by many to be the source of his appeal to both sexes, was set in a hard unyielding jaw.

". . . and now look who's here!" he was saying, gesturing toward the threshold with the air of a conjurer about to produce six white rabbits from a hat, and glancing past him, I saw Jake Reischman in the doorway.

Immaculate as always, surveying the world with his habitual expression of infinitely sophisticated cynicism, Jake had paused on the threshold of the kitchen to inspect his new surroundings much as an experienced traveler might have paused at the gateway of some forbidden city. Kitchens were no doubt a novelty for Jake, since he would so seldom have had the opportunity to see one. Unlike Cornelius, who had been born on an Ohio farm and had grown up in middle-class surroundings near Cincinnati, Jake had lived all his life in the upper reaches of New York's German-Jewish aristocracy.

Our glances met. He never hesitated. His mouth curved in a formal smile, although his eyes remained a clear chilly blue.

"*Guten Tag,* Sam."

"Hullo, Jake."

We did not shake hands.

"Jake, you know Teresa, of course . . ."

"On the contrary," said Jake, "I've never yet had that pleasure."

"No?" said Kevin, surprised. "But I distinctly remember . . . Ah, but that was Ingrid, of course. Well, let me introduce you: this is Teresa Kowalewski, Jake. Teresa, this is Jake Reischman, yet another of my notorious banking friends."

"Miss Kowalewski," said Jake smoothly, again producing his formal smile as he held out his hand. His instant mastery of the Polish surname was so dazzling that for a moment we all stared at him in admiration.

"Hi," said Teresa shyly at last, wiping her hand hastily before offering it to be shaken.

"Now, what are we all drinking?" said Kevin sociably. "Jake, I've got this magnificent Southern hooch which Teresa introduced me to—she brought a bottle all the way from New Orleans to New York, and now I order it direct from Kentucky by the case. Have you ever tried Wild Turkey bourbon?"

Jake shuddered. "I'll take some Scotch, please—Johnnie Walker Black Label, if you have it. No soda or water. Three rocks."

As he spoke, the rice began to erupt stealthily over the stove, and Teresa with an exclamation of dismay rushed to attend to it. Kevin had already left the room in search of the Scotch, and I watched, Jake indolently removed an onion ring from the nearest chair in order to sit down opposite me. I looked away; I was trying to think how I would escape from the room but could find no excuse that would not imply I was snubbing Jake by making a quick exit, and at last in an awkward effort to appear friendly I said, "How are things with you?"

"Moderate. Let's hope the FRB's cut in the price for stock purchases will help the market out of the doldrums. I became so tired of listening to Truman talking of the danger of inflation, when it was so patently obvious all danger of inflation was past. . . . I hear you're only just back from a European vacation?"

"Yes." I wanted to say more, but no words came.

"How nice," said Jake, unperturbed. "Incidentally, did you see the *Times* today? Groups wearing jackboots and singing 'Deutschland Über Alles' were parading in the streets of north Germany . . . how little life seems to change sometimes! But no doubt you found Germany very changed. You did go to Germany, didn't you?"

"Yes." I tasted the martini but could not drink it. I put the glass back on the table just as Kevin walked back into a silent room.

"How's Neil, Sam?" he said cheerfully, referring to Cornelius. "Has that daughter of his succeeded in giving him a nervous breakdown yet?"

I just managed to say, "She's still working on it."

"Poor Neil! Of course I saw it all coming a mile off. If I were Vicky, entombed like Rapunzel in that antediluvian architectural relic which Neil calls home, I'd certainly have let down my hair to the first young man who came along. God knows no one's fonder of Neil and Alicia than I am, but frankly I think they've no idea how to bring up an adolescent girl. When I think of my four sisters—"

"When I think of my two daughters," said Jake, who had three children approaching puberty, "it seems clear to me that Neil and Alicia have always made the best of a very difficult job."

"Well, we all know what hell it is being a parent," said Kevin, who had given Jake his Scotch and was pouring gin generously into my half-empty glass. "Shakespeare knew what he was doing all right when he wrote Lear's part. . . . Teresa, is that really jambalaya? It looks like some unmentionable organ of goat, an ethnic dish undoubtedly, probably Turkish or perhaps Lebanese."

"Thanks a lot, pal." Teresa was still scraping furiously at the burned rice at the bottom of the pot. "Do you want a salad?"

"Lovely, darling. Well, as I was saying . . . Sam, why are you getting up? You can't possibly waste all that gin I've just lavished on your glass! What do you want to run away for?"

The front doorbell rang.

"Now, who can that be," mused Kevin, casually adding a dash of vermouth to my glass. "Maybe it's one of the actors stopping by to apologize for the attempted rape of my play."

"Can someone please answer the door for me?" said Teresa, who was looking more harassed than ever. Having billowed out of the pot, the rice had stuck fast to the stove.

Jake looked around as if he were surprised there was no butler—or at the very least a uniformed maid—to attend to the door.

"Teresa," said Kevin, "don't we have any olives for Sam's martini?"

The doorbell rang again.

"Will one of you goddamned millionaires get off your backside and answer that door!" shrieked Teresa.

For the first time Jake looked at her with considerable interest, but I was the one who left the room as the bell rang for the third time.

Confused thoughts slowed my progress down the hall. Why had I tried to leave? Of course I had to stay. I could hardly leave my conversation with Teresa on such an unfinished note. If there were problems, they had to be talked out. The work could surely wait until the problems were solved . . . but what kind of problems were they? And was Teresa right in saying I just didn't begin to understand?

In a haze of exhaustion and acute anxiety for the future I pulled open the front door and found Cornelius on the doorstep. We stared at each other in disbelief.

"What are you doing here?" I said stupidly.

"I thought Kevin might be the one person in all New York who could cheer me up. What are *you* doing here? I thought you and Kevin hardly ever met nowadays!"

"I had a date with Kevin's caretaker."

The kitchen door swung open as Teresa glanced down the passage.

"Bring him in, Sam, whoever he is, and maybe he'll eat some rice.

I seem to have made enough to feed the entire Allied forces in Europe."

For lack of anything better to say, I replied, "Teresa, I'd like you to meet Cornelius Van Zale."

"Hullo," said Teresa. "Do you like rice? Come on in and have some Wild Turkey bourbon."

"Some what?" Cornelius whispered to me as Teresa retreated.

"Southern liquor."

"Good God. Is it very strong?"

"I believe it's about a hundred and one proof."

"That sounds exactly what I need."

We went into the kitchen. Enthusiastic greetings followed, coupled with tactful inquiries about Vicky.

"I would have called you yesterday when you arrived home with her," said Jake, "but I figured that if you wanted to talk, you'd call."

"Thanks, Jake, but I was beyond speech. I couldn't even get to the office today until noon."

I was moving around the edge of the room to the stove, where Teresa was stirring the jambalaya, but before I could reach her, Kevin raised his glass and said, laughing, "Well, it's not often all four of us are together in one room! Let's drink to the Bar Harbor Brotherhood. May we continue to prosper by worshiping at the altar of Mammon just as our great benefactor—ah, Mephistopheles!—would have wished!"

I reluctantly picked up the drink I did not want just as Cornelius retorted acidly, "Forget the altar of Mammon. As anyone who's ever been rich knows, money doesn't guarantee you one damn thing except problems. Do you think this disaster with Vicky would have happened if she hadn't been heir to the Van Zale fortune?"

"It might have," said Kevin. "She's very pretty. Incidentally, what happened to the beachboy who caused all the trouble?"

"I paid him off, of course." Cornelius was drinking his bourbon almost as fast as his host.

"How much?" asked Jake with interest.

"Two grand."

"For a beachboy? You were too generous!"

"They didn't quite make it to Maryland, did they?" said Kevin, more interested in the unsuccessful elopement than in its financial consequences.

"The police picked them up at the state line." Cornelius drained his glass, which was promptly refilled.

"The press coverage was disgraceful," said Jake. "What kind of aides do you have? Couldn't they have bought off the editors and issued a single dignified press release?"

"I've fired my chief aides."

"I should think so, too! When you hire people to pick up after you, you don't expect to be deafened by the noise of the bricks they drop."

Teresa was no longer making a conscious effort not to look at me. She had forgotten my presence. I saw her listening round-eyed, the unshredded lettuce poised in her hands.

"What do you think of all this, Teresa?" Kevin said kindly, drawing her into the conversation. "You're the only one of us who's had practical experience of running away from home at eighteen."

Teresa looked shy again, as if she had peeked through the curtains of a lighted room and glimpsed an obscene yet titillating tableau. I had a moment of immense anger and automatically took a large mouthful of my martini.

"Well," she said awkwardly with an embarrassed glance at Cornelius, "I'd say Vicky was lucky that she had a father who cared enough to run after her and bring her back."

Cornelius looked shocked, as if it had never occurred to him that some fathers might sanction their daughters' elopements. "But what happened to you when you left home?" he demanded with the air of a man who feels compelled to ask a question no matter how little he wants to hear the answer.

"I went to a big city—New Orleans—met a man I liked, moved in with him, and started to paint."

"Jesus Christ!" said Cornelius.

"Oh, the guy wasn't keeping me!" said Teresa hastily. "I got a job waitressing and we shared the household expenses fifty-fifty. Of course I'm not suggesting your daughter should follow in my footsteps, but—"

"—but a little sex never did anyone any harm," said Kevin comfortably.

"I categorically disagree one hundred percent," said Cornelius, very pale.

"Hell, it never seemed to do you much harm! When I think of those wild parties you and Sam used to give back in 1929—say, Sam,

` do you still have that great record of Miff Mole and his Molers play-
ing 'Alexander's Ragtime Band'?"

"You're missing the point, Kevin," said Jake. "I'm with Neil all
the way on this one—every man wants his daughter to be a virgin till
she marries. You'd better get Vicky married off as soon as possible,
Neil. Surely you can arrange something? It doesn't matter if it only
lasts a couple of years. Even a short marriage would give her the experience to cope with the fortune hunters who'll close in after the divorce."

Cornelius immediately assumed his most neutral expression and
took care not to look in my direction.

"You're missing the point too, aren't you, Jake?" said Kevin. "If
Vicky's no longer a virgin, why should Neil bother with this antiquated solution to the pragmatic marriage? Why not just let her go
her own way, make her mistakes, and learn from them?"

"Don't be ridiculous," said Jake. "How can you possibly let a girl
go her own way when she's heiress to several million dollars? It
would be criminal negligence! And who said Vicky was no longer a
virgin? She thought she was going to be able to marry the beachboy
after twenty-four hours in Maryland, didn't she? Or course she would
have saved herself for her wedding night!"

"Well, if you believe that," said Kevin, "you'll believe anything."

"*Stop!*" shouted Cornelius so suddenly that we all jumped. "This
is my daughter you're discussing, not a character in one of Kevin's
plays! Of course Vicky's still . . . well, there's no question about it,
none whatsoever." He pushed away his empty glass and levered himself to his feet. "I've got to get home. Kevin, can I use your phone to
tell Alicia I'm on my way?"

"Sure, use the extension in my study."

"Gee, he was real upset, wasn't he?" said Teresa in a hushed voice
after Cornelius had left the room. "I almost forgot he was a famous
millionaire. He was just like a regular guy."

I was at once immensely angry again. I also could not understand
why Teresa, normally unimpressed by wealth, should have been so
entranced by this fleeting glimpse into a rich man's muddled domestic
life, and I felt humiliated on her behalf when I saw how amused Jake
and Kevin were by her naiveté.

"I can see you don't know much about millionaires, Miss Kowalewski!" said Jake, suddenly producing a social overture so polished
that it was hard to believe any woman could have found such

artificiality attractive. "Let me buy you a drink sometime and widen your horizons!"

"Forget it, Jake," said Kevin. "Sam's been teaching Teresa all she needs to know about millionaires. Teresa, how's that old Lebanese goat in the pot shaping up? Jake, stay and have some jambalaya with us!"

"Unfortunately, I'm dining out tonight, so like Neil, I must be on my way. . . . Good-bye, Miss Kowalewski—no doubt we shall meet again. Good night, Kevin—thanks for the drink." He turned to me, old money facing new riches, a Fifth Avenue aristocrat confronting a provincial immigrant, one German-American facing another German-American across six million Jewish corpses and Europe's six years of hell.

"*Auf Wiedersehen,* Sam," he said.

I experienced an unbearable longing for something valuable which had been lost, and for a second I saw not the remote head of the House of Reischman but the friendly youth who had exclaimed to me with such enthusiasm long ago at Bar Harbor: "Come and stay with us—we'll make you proud to be German again!" And I remembered how I had felt when I had visited his Fifth Avenue home; I remembered how I had drunk German wine and heard his sisters playing German duets on the grand piano and listened to his father talking to me in German of German culture in the golden days before 1914.

"Jake . . ." I said.

He stopped and looked back. "Yes?"

"Perhaps sometime we might have lunch . . . I'd like to talk to someone about my vacation, someone who would understand. . . . You know how impossible Neil is about Europe."

"I'm afraid Europe has no interest for me at the moment," said Jake politely. "Paul Hoffman's been trying to recruit me for the ECA, and I had to tell him frankly to look elsewhere. Unlike people such as yourself, who preferred not to fight Hitler, I was away from home for four years and now all I want to do is stay in New York and let other people sweep up the European mess. And now, if you'll excuse me, I really have to be going. Kevin, I'll see you at the next board meeting of the Van Zale Fine Arts Foundation—or the first night of your new play, whichever is sooner."

"That's assuming I survive rehearsals! I'll see you to the door, Jake."

They left the room. I finished my martini in a single gulp and waited. I didn't have to wait long.

"Christ Almighty, Sam!" whispered Teresa, shocked. "Were you a Nazi sympathizer?"

I threw my empty glass at the wall. Of course I had had too much to drink. I realized that as soon as the glass shattered, and taking a grip on myself, I said rapidly, "I'm sorry, I'm not mad at you—I'm mad at Jake. Back in 1933 I visited Germany and was impressed by the way Hitler was pulling the country back onto its feet. A lot of people were similarly impressed at the time, and yet just because I made one casual pro-Hitler remark, Jake immediately turned against me and spread the story that I was a Nazi from one end of Wall Street to the other. I'll never forgive him for that. I'm a loyal American. I totally reject the propagandist view that any German who wasn't Jewish was automatically pro-Nazi. I was rejected from the services because of my eyesight, not because I was a fascist fanatic with a load of swastikas in the closet!"

"It's all right, Sam," said Teresa, embarrassed. "It's okay. I understand."

But I was unable to let the subject rest. "I know I was opposed to America getting into the war before 1941," I said, "but so were a lot of other good loyal Americans—and I *am* an American. I'm not a German. I'm not a Nazi. I never was. Never."

The door opened as Kevin returned to the room. "Well, that's that," he said. "Jake's purred off in his Rolls, Neil's swooped away in his Cadillac, and we're all back to normal again—or are we? Sam, you look as if you could use another drink. What on earth possessed you to bring up the subject of Germany with Jake? Hasn't it been patently obvious ever since Jake returned home in 1945 that he's even more mixed up than you are about the goddamned war?"

I stood up unsteadily. "I've broken one of your glasses. You must let me replace it. I'm real sorry about all the mess."

"Oh, stop talking bullshit and sit down again, for Christ's sake. Teresa, I've got two scenes to rework, so if you'll serve me up some of that old goat on a tray, I'll retire to my study and leave you two free to make love on the kitchen table or do whatever you feel is necessary to exorcise all the heavy Teutonic angst."

"Sam won't be staying, Kevin," said Teresa. "I just have to work tonight. Nothing went right for me today."

"Teresa . . ." I could barely speak.

"Sam, I'm sorry. I did try to explain—"

"You explained nothing!"

"Oh, stop arguing with me, stop persecuting me, just stop, stop, *stop!*"

"Okay. Sure. Sorry. I'll call you." I hardly knew what I was saying. I groped my way toward the door. "So long, Kevin. Thanks for the drink."

When I was halfway down the hall I heard Kevin mutter to Teresa, "Go after him, you fool! Can't you see he's at the end of his rope?"

"He's not the only one," said Teresa.

The front door banged shut behind me and I stumbled down the steps into the street. For a moment I stood still while I wiped the mist from my glasses, and then I began to walk blindly uptown.

II

As A result of a strike, over half the city's cabs were off the streets, and on Sixth Avenue I boarded a bus for the ride north. The rigors of the subway were more than I felt prepared to endure.

Behind me two businessmen began to discuss Germany, and I wondered in despair how long I would have to wait before Germany ceased to be a topic of obsessive interest. Even now, four years after the war, Germany prostrate seemed to fascinate Americans as much as Germany rampant.

"Even if they lifted the prohibitions against investing in Germany, who would want to invest? The country's still occupied, there's nothing back of the German currency, and besides, there are too many open questions—the Ruhr, for example. If the Ruhr industries are dismantled . . . yes, I know the ECA are against dismantling, but just tell that to the French. Keep the German bastards on their knees, they say, and who can blame them?"

Unable to stand the conversation a second longer, I left the bus and started to walk. I cut crosstown to Fifth and past Madison to Park, and all around me I sensed rather than saw New York, rich, gleaming, intact, a world away from those other cities with their shabby ruined streets. Memories flickered through my mind, the smoky cafe in Düsseldorf where the rouged hostesses had danced with the black marketeers while the band played "Bei Mir Bist Du Schön," the American soldiers chewing gum in the wrecked streets of

Munich, the English tourist who had got drunk with me and said, "Let me tell you where I went sightseeing today. . . ."

I suddenly realized I had reached my apartment building. It was eight-thirty. Behind me traffic was still roaring down Park Avenue, and in front of me the doorman was holding open the door for me with a smile.

"Good evening, Mr. Keller. . . . Sir, there's a lady waiting in the lobby for you."

I was still so deep in thought that I only stared at him blankly, but before he could speak again a voice from the past called, "Sam!" and when I spun round I saw a petite, voluptuous, well-remembered figure tip-tapping across the lobby toward me. Jet-black hair (formerly chestnut-brown) cascaded softly around a perfectly lifted face; sparkling blue eyes regarded me with an unabashed interest which failed to hide her air of desperation.

"It *is* you, isn't it, Sam?" she said, hesitating unexpectedly, and I realized that I had probably changed far more than she had in the eighteen years since she had divorced Cornelius.

"Vivienne!"

"Darling! You remembered!"

"How could I ever forget?"

The doorman, who had been listening to this inane dialogue with approval, gloated as Vivienne glided into my arms.

"Darling, how perfectly heavenly to see you again after all these years! Now, Sam sweetie"—I was released after an accomplished kiss —"forgive me for waylaying you like this, but—"

"Is this about Vicky?"

"You bet it's about Vicky! That little bastard Cornelius has given orders that I'm not to be admitted to his Fifth Avenue shack, but I'm telling you, darling, I'm telling you here and now that I'm not leaving town until I've seen my daughter, and if that son of a bitch of an ex-husband of mine thinks I'm going to stand by doing nothing while he mismanages Vicky's entire life . . ."

I saw the doorman's hypnotized expression and automatically attempted to silence Vivienne by steering her toward the elevator.

"You'd better come up," I said with reluctance, and was at once whipped back into the maelstrom of the Van Zale family's domestic problems.

III

MY PENTHOUSE was on the twenty-eighth floor. It was too big for me but I enjoyed the views south past the Chrysler, the Empire State, and Metropolitan Life to the misty towers of downtown Manhattan. The forty-foot living room was useful for parties, the dining-room table could effortlessly accommodate sixteen, and the servants' rooms were comfortable enough to ensure I had no trouble keeping a first-class couple to act as my housekeeper and chauffeur.

I lived mainly in one room, the den, which had been described by the realtor as the library. It was a large sunny room and I had furnished it with my favorite recliner, a goose-neck reading lamp, and an old leather couch which my mother had tried to give to the junkman after I had bought her a three-piece suite some years ago. I had no books in the room except for twenty years of *The New Yorker* bound in leather, but I had my record collection, two phonographs, three tape recorders, a television, and a radio. In the closet, which I kept locked, were my German memorabilia: my cousin Kristina's watercolors of the Siebengebirge, the albums of photographs taken at the little house in Düsseldorf, the souvenirs of visits to Berlin and Bavaria. On the walls hung framed photographs: my parents, the dog I had once owned, two turn-of-the-century shots of Wall Street, and a panoramic view of Ocean Drive near Bar Harbor.

I loved my den. I kept it very neat and very clean all by myself, since I liked to think that there was at least one part of my home where the servants were never allowed to go. I used to vacuum the carpet on Sunday mornings when my housekeeper was at church. Cornelius had laughed at this eccentric behavior, but I liked vacuum cleaners—in fact, I liked all machines, and the more efficient they were, the more I enjoyed them. At that time my favorite hobby was dismantling and reassembling my television set. I liked the little wires and the gleaming metal and the system's exquisite logic and precision. When I was working with my hands and using the electronic knowledge I had acquired over the years, I could tune out the rest of the world and forget the pressures of my life at Willow and Wall.

The rest of my apartment had been furnished by a fashionable interior decorator and was exactly the kind of home a man in my position has to have to impress his clients, his friends, his enemies, and all the other people who know he started life as an immigrant in a blue-collar home. I was not snobbish, merely practical. Since I dealt continuously with influential men, it was essential that I could present a domestic front they could respect. It was a fact of life which my benefactor Paul Van Zale had taught me long ago at Bar Harbor.

"Darling, what a heavenly apartment!" exclaimed Vivienne as I led her into the living room. "And what a marvelous jungle you've managed to grow on that enormous terrace! Oh, I just love modern paintings—is that one over the desk by Picasso?"

"No, it's by some guy called Braque. Neil gave it to me on the twentieth anniversary of our partnership. He said it would be a good investment." I thought of Teresa gasping: "Jesus . . . a Braque!" and subsiding weakly onto the couch. With an abrupt movement I opened the cocktail cabinet. "Drink, Vivienne?"

"Darling, I'd adore a martini. The very mention of Cornelius' name makes me want to hit the bottle in the biggest possible way."

As I mixed her drink she told me she had taken the first train to New York from Florida as soon as she had read in the press of Vicky's elopement, and had made repeated efforts, all unsuccessful, to gain admittance to the Van Zale mansion to see her daughter.

"I've called and called on the phone, of course," she added, "but all I ever got were the aides and the secretaries. Then finally I remembered you. You're the one man in all New York who can always get Cornelius to the phone, and I was wondering . . ."

"Vivienne, forgive me, but would it really serve any useful purpose if you spoke to him? It seems to me—"

"Sam, I've got to talk to him—it's for Vicky's sake, not mine! Do you think I'd give a damn if I never spoke to Cornelius again? My God, when I think of the way he treated me! Oh, I know I married him for his money, but I was very fond of him and I'd been a good wife, and there I was, pregnant with his child—"

"I remember, yes." I had been trying to restrict myself to soda water, but the occasion was just too much for me. I got up to add a shot of Scotch to my glass.

". . . and then he finds out he'd been married for his money . . . Okay, so I was stupid to let him find out, but if he hadn't been eavesdropping . . ."

"Vivienne, believe me, I remember all this much too well!"

"I'll bet the little bastard never told you how he cut me off afterward! 'It's finished,' he says, cool as dressed crab, 'it's over. I have nothing else to say.' Can you imagine! What a way to terminate a marriage to an affectionate, faithful, pregnant wife! And then he even had the nerve to complain when I sued the pants off him for divorce and got total custody of Vicky!"

"Well, that's past history now, Vivienne. I know you had custody of Vicky originally, but Cornelius has had complete custody since she was ten years old, and he's not going to welcome any interference from you either now or at any other time."

"Of course he won't welcome it, but the hell with him! I can't just sit back and let him mess up my little girl's life! Look, Sam, I want Vicky to come and live with me while she gets over this disaster. I know Cornelius thinks I'm poorer than white trash just because I had the guts to remarry and turn my back on all his million-dollar alimony, but my husband—my last husband, I mean—left me a little money when he died, and I've got the cutest little house in Fort Lauderdale now. Oh, I know it's not Palm Beach, but it's *nice,* Sam, and I know some lovely people there. Don't you see—I could give Vicky a *normal* home! Oh, Sam, you know what happens to all these heiresses—the fortune hunters, the gigolos, the fake Russian princes, the drink, the drugs, the breakdowns, the suicides . . ."

"Vivienne, Neil's just as anxious as you are that Vicky should have a normal, happy life!"

"Cornelius," said Vivienne, "has lived for twenty-three years in a Fifth Avenue palace with fifty million dollars for pin money, his own Wall Street bank, and all the aristocracy of the Eastern Seaboard sashaying up his driveway in their Cadillacs to tell him hello. He wouldn't even recognize normality if he met it eyeball to eyeball at high noon."

"Nonsense! The Van Zales have the quietest, happiest, and least pretentious family life of any people I know!"

"Well, if that's true," said Vivienne fiercely, "why does Vicky run away from home at the very first opportunity she gets? I'm not calling you a liar, darling, but I think there's a screw loose in that household somewhere, and I want my little girl back." To my amazement she began to weep, and her bosom, which Cornelius had once confessed had given him more wet dreams than any other piece of anatomy he had ever encountered, rose and fell with mesmerizing precision. It was miraculous how well she had retained her figure, almost as miraculous as her success in looking younger than I was when she was fourteen years my senior.

"Have another drink," I said, wishing I was in bed with Teresa, and tried to think clearly. I had the strong feeling that despite my reluctance to be involved, the situation could be turned to my advantage. The fact was that I was already involved; if I wanted Cornelius to grant me that leave of absence from Van Zale's, I had to persuade him to abandon his matrimonial pipe dream, and in order to achieve that, I had to provide him with an alternative solution to Vicky's problems. Beneath Vivienne's stagy weeping and phony mannerisms I sensed a genuine concern for her daughter, and I thought it could be argued, not unreasonably, that Vicky would benefit from a long vacation in Florida. Whether Cornelius would accept this argument was debatable, but I could try. What did I have to lose? I rose to my feet, moved to the phone, and picked up the receiver.

"Okay, I'll get him on the line."

"Oh, Sam . . . *darling* . . ." Vivienne, trembling with gratitude, was teetering across the floor to kiss me on the cheek.

A Van Zale aide answered the phone.

"Keller," I said. "Is he there?"

"Darling!" breathed Vivienne again, stretching out her hand to take the receiver, but I stepped backward away from her.

"I'll handle this, Vivienne, if you don't mind. . . . Neil? Yes, it's me. Can you take some upsetting information without getting upset? I've got Vivienne here with me. She wants to invite Vicky down to Fort Lauderdale for a while to give everyone a breathing space, and personally, I don't think that's such a bad idea."

"Are you out of your mind? She hates the bitch!"

"Maybe, but what's the harm in letting Vivienne at least talk to her to issue the invitation? The world won't fall apart any farther than it's fallen already, and who knows, Vicky may even be grateful to you later."

"Let me have a word with Vivienne."

"No. You'd fight. I'm staying on the line until you transfer this call to Vicky's room."

"Oh, shit!" said Cornelius, but I heard him tell his aide to transfer the call.

I waited. Eventually I heard the bell ring again, but nobody answered. "Neil?" I said tentatively at last.

As I had guessed, he was listening in.

"Yes, I'm here," he said heavily. "Well, you'll just have to tell Vivienne that Vicky's not picking up the phone."

"Would it be too much to ask you to go up to her room and let her know her mother's on the line?"

"Yes. It would. But maybe I'd better check on her anyway to see if she's okay." He set down the receiver and I heard a door close in the distance.

While I waited, I told Vivienne what was happening.

"My God, Sam, do you think she's all right? She hasn't been suicidal, has she?"

"Just mad at the world in general."

We went on waiting. I tried not to think of Teresa in her cheap turquoise dress with the little gold cross slipping into the hollow between her breasts, but the next moment I was remembering when we had last made love. I had had a shade too much to drink and the occasion had been only moderately successful, although Teresa had sworn everything had been fine. Later, when I was working for the ECA in Germany and my problems had been straightened out, I was going to give up cigarettes and hard liquor and drink only the occasional glass of wine.

The line clicked. The pristine future dissolved, leaving me enmeshed in the clouded, chaotic present. "Sam?" gasped Cornelius. "She's gone!"

"What!"

"I had the guys force the door. The window was open. She'd let herself down onto the terrace by knotting some sheets into a rope. Oh, Christ, Sam . . ."

"Is there anything I can do?"

"Yeah, keep that bitch Vivienne off my back," said Cornelius, voice shaking, and hung up.

I stood looking at the receiver in my hand while Vivienne demanded to know what had happened. Finally I recovered sufficiently to say, "Vicky's run away again."

She looked first shocked, then incredulous. "You don't expect me to believe that, do you?" she demanded furiously. "That little bastard's just spinning you that yarn to get rid of me!"

"Not this time. This was genuine. My God, I hope I never have an eighteen-year-old daughter!" I slumped down exhausted on the couch.

"Well, what's he going to do, for God's sake?" Vivienne shouted at me in a frenzy of frustration. "What's he going to do?"

By this time I knew I had had as much of Vivienne as I could take. Ringing the bell briefly twice, my signal which indicated that I wanted my chauffeur to have the car waiting at the curb, I said shortly, "Neil has an army of people working for him, and the police commissioner's a personal friend. He'll find her. And now, if you'll excuse me, Vivienne . . ."

"But I can't go now! I must wait for him to call you back with further news!"

"I'll call you as soon as I hear anything."

" 'Anything to get rid of the old bag,' he thinks! Why the great rush to get rid of me, darling? Are you expecting someone?"

"No."

"Sure? Incidentally, are you still dating those fluffy little blonds who live in outrageous places like Brooklyn, or do you feel less socially inferior nowadays and set your sights a little higher?"

"My chauffeur will drive you back to your hotel, Vivienne. I'll see you to the door."

"I guess that's why you've never married," she said idly. "You only feel at home with that kind of girl, but that kind of girl wouldn't feel at home here. Or would she?" Her glance flicked cynically over the living room. "Rich men can make a girl so adaptable."

"You married for money," I said before I could stop myself. "You should know."

She laughed. "Yes, darling," she said without a second's hesitation, "but I'm not the only one in this room who knows how it feels to be owned lock, stock, and barrel by one of the richest men in town."

There was a silence. Then without a word I walked into the hall and held open the front door for her.

"You'll call me, won't you, as soon as there's any news?" she said after telling me the name of her hotel, and the question reminded her that it was in her best interests to part from me on a friendly note. When I remained silent, she somehow managed to produce a smile and a seductive tone of voice. "Come on, Sam! What happened to that nice all-American boy I used to know with the innocent smile and the Down East accent and the cute old-fashioned manners? I'm sorry I was so bitchy—I was just so disappointed not to talk to Vicky. I'm sure you make out just fine in your private life! All that success, all that money—so sexy!" She sighed, took my hand in hers, and eyed me mistily. "We *are* friends, darling, aren't we?" she murmured, applying a light pressure to my palm with her fingers.

"Why, of course, Vivienne!" I said, matching her insincerity ounce for ounce, and finally managed to get rid of her.

I went back to my den and sat down. Presently my housekeeper knocked on the door to say that my dinner was waiting for me on the serving cart in the living room, but I went on sitting on my couch in the den. Vivienne's jibe was still drifting deeper and deeper into my consciousness like a feather falling from a great height, and for the first time in my life I was wishing I had never met Cornelius, wishing Paul Van Zale had passed me by when I had been clipping that hedge in his garden long ago.

I could so clearly visualize the life that might have been. By this time I would be living in a new split-level house on the outskirts of Bar Harbor, or maybe Ellsworth, but no, the sea at Bar Harbor would be nicer for the kids—for of course I would have kids, probably four or five, and a pretty wife who was a wonderful cook, and we'd have barbecues on weekends and be friends with all our neighbors and go to church on Sunday. There would have been no visits to Germany, because naturally with my growing family I couldn't have afforded the trip to Europe, so I would have remained the all-American patriot, someone who would have volunteered for the army in 1941 without waiting to be drafted, someone who would have despised the German-Americans who secretly angled for exemptions, someone who could not have conceived of a situation in which a millionaire had arranged an exemption for his best friend by making a single phone call to someone in Washington who owed him a favor. . . .

The doorbell rang.

Looking out of the den in surprise, I found my housekeeper hovering uncertainly in the passage. "That'll be Miss Vicky, Mr. Keller," she whispered, troubled. "The doorman just buzzed from the lobby to say she was on her way up. He said she ran straight past him into the elevator before he could stop her."

"Miss Vicky?"

"Yes, sir, Miss Van Zale."

The doorbell rang again, and this time did not stop. Abandoning the den, I moved swiftly past my housekeeper, crossed the hall, and pulled open the front door.

"Vicky . . . Jesus Christ!"

"Uncle Sam!" cried Vicky as if I were the last man left on earth, and hurtled across the threshold into my arms.

Chapter Three

I

"UNCLE SAM, I've come to you because you're the only sane person I know," said Vicky, clasping my hand as if it were a piton riveted to the face of a cliff. "In fact, you're the only person who can save me, so please don't just pat my head and send me back to Daddy as if I were a stray poodle. If you do, I think I'll jump off the Brooklyn Bridge."

"Gee whiz," I said, "excuse me while I get out my suit of armor and my shining white horse. Have a drink of mead or something—or better still, how about something to eat? I haven't had dinner yet, and if I'm going to save you, I've got to be well-fed."

I took Vicky into the den, rescued the serving cart from the living room, and asked my housekeeper to bring an additional place setting. Back in the den I found a tape I had made of several Glenn Miller records and threaded it into my recorder. The music, dreamy and soothing, filtered into the room as I offered the wine decanter to my guest. "Do you want to try some of this?"

"Is it like that California Kool-Aid Daddy serves at home?"

"No, this is French wine from Bordeaux."

"Oh, Uncle Sam, you're so wonderfully European and civilized!" She smiled at me radiantly, a schoolgirl on a disagreeable but not unexciting spree, and it occurred to me that although her troubles were genuine, she was unable to resist the adolescent urge to dramatize them. I smiled back, trying to see beyond the schoolgirl to the woman she might one day become, but all I saw was the teenage uniform of pleated skirt, bobby socks, and the sloppy pink sweater. Her long thick wavy golden hair was brushed back from her face and secured at the nape of her neck with a pink bow. She had her mother's pert nose and Cornelius' brilliant black-lashed gray eyes, her mother's neat oval chin and Cornelius' stubborn mouth, which looked so deceptively tranquil in repose, and as I wondered how I would have dealt with her if she had been my daughter, I came to the uneasy conclusion that I would probably have coped with the responsibility no better than Cornelius.

"Do you want some sauerbraten, Vicky?" I said, after my housekeeper had brought the extra place setting.

"Gee, I don't think I could possibly . . . Well, yes, it does smell kind of good. I haven't eaten for ages."

With the food and drink liberally distributed, we settled ourselves on the leather couch.

"Well, now," I said, "what do I have to do to save you?"

"You can help me get away from home."

"Again? So soon?"

"I've just got to get away. Oh, Uncle Sam—"

"Vicky, if you're old enough to elope to Maryland, you're old enough to stop calling me 'Uncle.' Just 'Sam' will do fine from now on."

"But I like to think of you as an uncle! I'll always think of you as an uncle!"

I resisted the urge to say, "Thank God," and instead asked, "What's the problem at home? I know there was a fuss when you dropped out of that art-appreciation course at Christmas, but—"

"Oh, God, yes, that was awful! The trouble is, Daddy just won't *listen* to me. I'm never allowed to do what *I* want. It's always what *he* wants. As soon as I graduated from Miss Porter's last summer, I wanted to go to junior college in Europe, but Daddy wouldn't have it, said Europe was decadent and I could learn all I had to learn right here in America. Then I wanted to go to college right away, and he says no, I'm too young to leave home and I must 'fill in' a year first. So then I wanted to go to Europe on vacation and he wouldn't let me go on my own and insisted I go with Aunt Emily, who drives me crazy, and those two cousins of mine who drive me crazier still. After that came the art-appreciation mess. I never wanted to do it in the first place! As I've said to him over and over again, all I really want to do is go to college and major in philosophy, but—"

"Philosophy?"

"Sure, it's the only subject I can ever imagine being seriously interested in. I mean, you grow up taking everything for granted and then suddenly you think: Why am I rich when most of the world is poor? And then you think: And what kind of a world is it anyway? And you read people like Marx and that gets you thinking, and then you discover that political philosophy is just one aspect of a vast subject. . . . Of course, Daddy thinks I'm nuts. He thinks philosophy is just a hobby for social failures. He wants me to major in something useful, like Spanish, or feminine, like English literature."

I thought it was about time someone gave Cornelius credit where credit was due. "But he does agree that you should go to college. He's not being entirely an ogre."

"He says he wants me to go to college, yes. But . . ." She put down her fork and stared at her glass of wine. Finally she said, "Recently I've come to believe he's changed his mind. I think he's just stringing me along. That's one of the reasons why I got so desperate. I think . . . Uncle Sam, please don't laugh at me, I know it sounds crazy, but I think he's going to try to pressure me into getting married."

I was acutely aware of my own fork poised in midair over my bowl of salad. Pulling myself together, I speared a slice of cucumber.

"Of course I want to get married," said Vicky hastily. "I want to be a wife and mother just like any other girl who's not abnormal. But I want to go to college first before I settle down."

"Sure, I understand. What I don't understand is why you should think your father wants to marry you off."

"I've suspected it for some time, but it was the big row over Jack that convinced me."

"Jack? The beachboy?"

"Don't call him that. It makes him sound like a gigolo, and he wasn't. He was nice."

"Sorry. Tell me just what happened so I can be sure I've got my facts straight. You met him down in the Caribbean a couple of months ago, your father told me."

"Yes, I'd never gone along with Daddy and Alicia before on their annual Caribbean vacation—I'd always been in school, but when I dropped out of the art-appreciation course Daddy said I must come with them because he couldn't leave me on my own in New York with nothing to do. Well, that was okay. I hate New York in February. So there we were in Barbados and I met Jack on the beach. He was a lifeguard employed by one of the hotels, but it was just a temporary job. He was going back home to California to college this fall. Of course I was staying on Daddy's yacht, but I used to go ashore every day, meet Jack for a swim, and have an ice cream while we talked about movies. He was just crazy about Betty Grable. He showed me his Betty Grable pinups once. He said my legs reminded him of her. He was so sweet."

"Uh-huh."

"Well, we had a lovely time, nothing serious, just a kiss now and then—gee, it was romantic!—and then Daddy said it was time to go to Antigua, so that was that. But I gave Jack my address and he promised to write, and suddenly last week—wham! There he was on the doorstep. I was so thrilled. He said he'd hitched a ride on a banana boat to Miami, where he'd snuck on a freight train heading north. He said he'd been thinking of me nonstop ever since I left Barbados. Well, gee, it was so sweet of him to come—what else could I do but invite him to stay for a few days? But then Daddy goes berserk and says no, never under any circumstances, and Jack can get the hell out. My God, how rude can you get! I was so embarrassed I could have died. After Jack had gone to the YMCA, Daddy and I had this huge row, and that was when . . ." She stopped.

"When he said something like, 'I wish to God you were safely married and out of my hair'? You shouldn't have taken him so seriously, Vicky! People often say silly things in the heat of the moment, and your father's no exception."

"It wasn't like that at all. You see, for some time now he's been pushing the doctrine that a woman's only true fulfillment in life lies in being a wife and mother. Well, okay. I'm sure he's right. But he kept saying it when he didn't have to say it, like someone dropping a huge hint, and I was already so tired of him dictating to me that this sort of *sotto voce* marriage commercial was just the last straw. I felt I wanted to make some big gesture to shut him up—to remind him that it was my life and that it was about time he stopped all this massive interference. So I decided to—"

"—demonstrate your independence by eloping with Jack."

"Poor Jack! It was mean of me—I wasn't in love with him and I never really had any intention of marrying him or even going with him . . . sleeping . . . you know." She blushed. Tears sprang to her eyes unexpectedly, but she blinked them back. "I know I behaved badly, but I was so desperate . . . I thought it would solve something . . . but it just made things worse. There was another ghastly scene when we got back to Fifth Avenue, and that was when I realized I couldn't—*couldn't*—stay there any longer."

"Did Neil start pushing his wife-and-mother line at you again?"

"Oh, it was much worse than that! He said that if I was so keen to get married, he could easily find me a suitable husband. And then Alicia said . . . Alicia said . . . Alicia said . . ." She went dead white. I was no longer eating. At last she managed to say, "Alicia said why didn't I marry Sebastian."

I laughed. "Good God, now I've heard everything! Poor Alicia, I wonder how long she's been cherishing that little pipe dream!"

"Uncle Sam," said Vicky in a shaking voice which made me want to kick myself for my insensitive response, "this is no laughing matter. This is very serious. This is life and death."

"I'm sorry, honey, I didn't mean to . . ."

"You see, what Alicia wants, Alicia gets. Daddy's so crazy about her that he always bends over backward to accommodate her, and that's why when she came right out and admitted she wanted me to marry Sebastian, I was absolutely terrified. It's obvious, of course, why she wants me to marry him. She feels guilty because after she married Daddy she found out she couldn't have any more children, but she's figured out that if Daddy's daughter by his first marriage marries her son by her first marriage, she and Daddy will at least have mutual grandchildren." She shuddered, but it was no affectation. Her pallor now had a greenish tinge. I even wondered if she was about to vomit. "I loathe Sebastian," she whispered. "I just loathe him."

I decided that the best way of handling the conversation was to be as sensible and down-to-earth as possible. Melodrama can seldom thrive in an atmosphere of candid common sense. "What's so terrible about Sebastian?" I said. "I know he's shy, but he's not a bad-looking guy, and he's smart enough to be doing well at Harvard."

She was unable to reply. I began to be seriously perturbed. "Vicky, does your father know exactly how you feel about Sebastian?"

"No," she said. "There was a scene four years ago, but we were all supposed to have got over it. We've all promised never, never to refer to it again."

I felt more perturbed than ever. "That's all very well, Vicky, but I think Neil would be horrified if he knew this incident, whatever it was, is still very much alive for you. But at least on one point I can put your mind at rest. Your father has no intention of encouraging you to marry Sebastian. In fact, I can promise you Sebastian just doesn't figure in his plans for your future at all."

Her relief was painful to see. "Are you sure?"

"Very sure. In fact, I couldn't be more sure. I can't reveal confidential conversations, but I give you my word of honor that you've been jumping to the wrong conclusions."

"But Alicia . . ." She broke off with a start as the buzzer sounded in the hall. "Who's that?"

"I don't know. My housekeeper'll get it. Vicky, Alicia's little pipe dream is her problem. But it's not yours."

A faint tinge of color was returning slowly to her cheeks. "I'd still like to get away from home for a while. . . . Uncle Sam, would you take me to Europe?"

"Europe! *Me?* What a great idea! However, I doubt if your father would approve of me taking more time out from the office when I've been away so recently. Look, why don't you go down to Florida for a while and stay with your mother? Your mother's in town right now, as a matter of fact—I was talking to her earlier this evening, and I was impressed by how concerned she is for your happiness."

"That old hag? Concerned about me? You've got to be kidding! She's concerned about nothing except how to hold on to her latest lover! Why, I'd rather take a vacation on the Bowery than in Fort Lauderdale with my mother!"

My housekeeper tapped on the door and looked in. "Excuse me, Mr. Keller, but Mr. and Mrs. Van Zale are on their way up."

"No!" shrieked Vicky.

"God help us all," I said in German.

The doorbell rang in the hall.

II

"I CAN'T face them!" sobbed Vicky. "I can't!"

I gripped her shoulders and gave her a short sharp shake. "Calm down at once, please. That's better. Okay, I'll talk to your father in the living room, but I want you to stay right here in the den. Can I trust you to stay here and not run away? I'd hate to have to lock you in."

She said in a small voice, "I'll stay."

"Good. Now, just remember this: fantastic though it may seem to you, all your father wants is your happiness. And remember this, too: no one can force you into marriage. All you've got to do is say no—or at the very worst, keep your mouth shut when you're expected to say 'I do.'"

"Yes, Uncle Sam," she whispered. Her great gray eyes, shining with unshed tears, regarded me as devoutly as a true believer might gaze on a minister declaiming the word of God from the pulpit, and for a brief moment I thought again of all the children I had never had in the split-level home which had never existed on the outskirts of Bar Harbor.

"Right," I said abruptly, giving her hand a quick squeeze. "Now, just you keep your promise and stay here. No eavesdropping." Turning up the volume of the music, I escaped into the hall and opened the front door just as Cornelius rang the bell a second time.

They were standing side by side in the corridor, Cornelius looking pale and exhausted, Alicia looking pale and bored. I knew Alicia well enough to guess that the bored expression was an affectation masking other, more disturbing emotions, and I knew Cornelius well enough to realize his exhaustion was no affectation. He was wearing the black suit he had worn at the office, a plain indication of his domestic chaos, since he always changed into casual clothes as soon as he arrived home. Alicia was faultless in mink and diamonds.

"She's here, isn't she?" said Cornelius. "One of my security guards saw her climb out of the window, and rather than restrain her by force, he followed her here before reporting back to me."

"Come in."

I led them into the living room. They looked around expectantly.

"She's in the den listening to Glenn Miller," I said. "Neil, Vicky seems very sure she wants to get away from Fifth Avenue for a while, and I'm becoming increasingly convinced that she's right. I think the best thing she can possibly do at this point is to take a long vacation so that the dust from this explosion has time to settle. Do you think your sister could help? If Emily were to invite Vicky to Velletria . . ."

"I think it's time Vicky stopped running away," said Alicia in her most expressionless voice. She was straightening the seam of her glove and not looking at me. "Anyway, she detests the Midwest, and Emily's girls drive her crazy."

I had a brainstorm and remembered Paul Van Zale's widow. "Maybe Sylvia in San Francisco—" I began.

"Sylvia," said Alicia, still inspecting her glove, "is away on a cruise."

"Sam," said Cornelius unevenly, "did you tell Vicky that Vivienne wants her to go down to Fort Lauderdale?"

"Yes. She wasn't interested."

"Thank God! We couldn't have approved of that, could we, Alicia?"

"Definitely not," said Alicia.

"Besides, I don't want Vicky to go away!" cried Cornelius as I opened my mouth to prolong the argument. "Let me talk to her. I want her to know I didn't mean to upset her . . . I want her to know that everything'll be all right and we love her and want her to come home!"

"Yes, but that's not solving anything, can't you see? That's just pretending the problem doesn't exist!"

"What problem?"

The door clicked open. Vicky, her face tearstained, peered in. In the distance the Glenn Miller orchestra was playing "Moonlight Serenade."

"Vicky . . . honey, we've been out of our minds. . . . How could you do this to us? . . . Vicky, we love you! Please, sweetheart, please forgive us and come home!"

Alicia took a cigarette from her purse and lit the tip with a small gold lighter encrusted with emeralds. I had never before seen her smoke in Cornelius' presence. Cornelius was asthmatic.

"Oh, Daddy . . ."

She ran into his arms and stuck there. The Glenn Miller orchestra went on playing "Moonlight Serenade."

"Daddy, I'm sorry, I didn't mean to hurt you. . . . Oh, Daddy, I love you too . . ."

Alicia went to the mirror and examined one of her diamond earrings. Her glance met mine but was instantly averted. After smoothing a strand of her dark hair, she adjusted the diamond ring on her wedding finger.

"Sweetheart, we'll work this out, I swear it—just say what you want and I'll fix it right away."

"Cornelius."

He turned to face his wife. "Yes?"

"Nothing. . . . Perhaps if Vicky's feeling better we should go home now. I think we've all imposed long enough on Sam's hospitality."

"Daddy," said Vicky, ignoring her stepmother, "I want to go to Europe for a while."

"Whatever you want, sweetheart. Europe? I'll take you myself just as soon as I can make arrangements to leave the office."

"No, no, that wasn't what I meant at all! Darling Daddy, I know how you loathe Europe, and I wouldn't dream of dragging you back there! I want to go with Uncle Sam."

Cornelius and Alicia swiveled to look at me. I cleared my throat and gave an apologetic laugh, but before I could disassociate myself from this proposal, Alicia said sharply, "Don't be ridiculous, dear. Sam's a busy man. He doesn't have the time to chaperon you around Europe, and even if he did, the idea would still be totally unsuitable. If your father really feels he can sanction another trip to Europe, I'll ask your Aunt Emily if she can take you—in fact, maybe it would be best if Emily came to New York right away to help us sort out this situation, and if Sam will let me use his phone, I'll call her right now in Velletria. Now, run along with Daddy, please, and let's have no more melodrama tonight. Cornelius, perhaps you and Vicky could wait for me in the car while I make the call."

"Sure." Cornelius turned obediently to his daughter and took her hand in his. "Come along, sweetheart, we'll work this out, I promise you."

Vicky looked back over her shoulder at me, and when I smiled at her encouragingly, she smiled back. "Thanks for listening, Uncle Sam," she said before allowing herself to be led from the room. The last words I heard her say before the front door closed were: "Daddy, *please* let me go to college and major in philosophy!"

In the silence that followed their departure, Alicia and I looked at each other wearily.

"My God," she said, "get me a drink, would you please, Sam? Sherry will do, but make it a double. I feel ripe for the sanatorium."

I murmured something sympathetic and hunted for the Tio Pepe.

"I still think it's a mistake for her to run away to Europe, but with Cornelius promising her the sun, moon, and stars, what choice did I have but to agree to the idea? Personally, as I've already said,

I'm dead against her running away anywhere. She's got to learn to stand her ground and cope with her mistakes, or else she'll always be an immature little girl."

I poured the sherry into a glass. "Ice?"

"Please. I don't believe in this European fad of drinking everything lukewarm. And talking of Europe, why on earth does she want to go back there? And why on earth does she have to go on and on and on with this stupid idea of majoring in philosophy? She knows Cornelius thinks it's crazy—why can't she pick a subject which pleases him? Anyway, I don't see the point of girls going to college, particularly girls like Vicky, who are obviously destined to be wives and mothers. It seems a complete waste of time."

I said noncommittally, "Maybe some European finishing school would be more suitable."

Alicia shuddered, though whether at the thought of Europe or of a finishing school was hard to tell. "Possibly," was all she said, "but at best it could only be the most temporary solution to the problem of Vicky's future." With the glass of sherry in her hand she moved to the phone. "I'd better call Emily—excuse me using your phone, Sam, but I feel I have to talk to her without Cornelius trying to listen in on an extension. . . . Hello? Operator? I want to call Velletria, Ohio, person to person to Mrs. Emily Sullivan. . . . Thanks." She gave the number and then sat sipping the sherry fastidiously, like a cat sampling cream from an unfamiliar bowl. Her green eyes, which slanted over high cheekbones, accentuated this feline impression. Although she was thirty-nine, her smooth pale, unblemished skin made her look younger, and her slender figure reminded me of the photographs on the fashion pages of the New York *Times*.

"Of course," she said as she waited, "it would all be easier if only Cornelius wasn't so hopeless with her, but as you and I well know, he's spoiled her ever since she entered the world. I've done my best to introduce some sort of normality into our family life, but I never got total care of Vicky till she was ten, and that mother of hers was a disgrace—she even let Vicky wear lipstick at eight! Obscene! Poor little girl. Anyway, I've tried to be a good mother to her, God knows I've tried, Cornelius knows I've tried, *I* know I've tried, but . . . Hello? Emily? This is Alicia. Emily, can you please come to New York as soon as possible? I hate to sound as if I'm passing the buck, but I just can't cope anymore, and of course the situation's quite beyond Cornelius. . . . Bless you, Emily, many, many thanks, how soon can you . . . you'll come right away? Emily, I can't tell you how much I appreciate this—look, let me call you back to discuss the details. I'm at Sam's place at the moment, and . . . No, she's not here, but when I get home and call you back, of course you can speak to her. All right. . . . Thank you, darling. . . . 'Bye."

She replaced the receiver. "Thank you, too, Sam. I hate to involve you in all our sordid trials and tribulations. Can you please give me another glass of sherry? I feel I must sit down for a moment before I go out to the car. I feel totally exhausted."

I took her glass and moved back to the cocktail cabinet. Although I was more than willing to be supportive, I was beginning to feel uneasy. In all the eighteen years since Cornelius had married his second wife, Alicia and I had remained no more than polite acquaintances, and I suspected that once she had recovered her customary reserve, she would regret having been so frank with me. Our formality did not mean we disliked each other; on the contrary, I admired her looks and her style and respected her unquestioned fidelity to Cornelius, particularly since fidelity was not common in the society in which the Van Zales moved, but Alicia's reserve was intimidating, and the iciness of those severe, expensive, well-bred good looks was sufficient to preclude all thought of a less formal friendship. Even if she had had no connection with Cornelius, it would never have occurred to me to go to bed with her.

I had often speculated to myself about the Van Zales's intimate life, just as one so often speculates idly—and futilely, since such facts are ultimately unguessable—about the private habits of people one knows well, but could reach no obvious conclusions beyond the fact that since their marriage had lasted eighteen years with no hint of infidelity on either side, they had to be doing something right. I often wondered what it was, for I sensed that the marriage was not always happy, but Cornelius never spoke to me of any difficulties, and I, of course, never asked. When we had been young men sowing our wild oats, he had often discussed his women with me, just as I had discussed mine with him, but with his second marriage that sort of conversation came to an end, so that now, years later, I would no more have dreamed of discussing Teresa with him than he would have dreamed of discussing Alicia with me.

"Now, Sam," said Alicia, as if uncannily sensing my thoughts, "I know we've never been more than polite acquaintances, but I'm so desperate I'm going to ask you to level with me. Has Cornelius discussed his plans with you?"

I looked suitably blank. "Plans?"

"For Vicky. Oh, God, of course he must have discussed them with you—he's probably been pouring out his heart to you ever since the elopement! You *must* know he thinks the only hope of avoiding disaster is for Vicky to marry as soon as possible!"

"Hm," I said. "Well . . ."

"The truth is," pursued Alicia, barely listening, "that I can't help feeling ambivalent about the idea. I do agree that marriage is the only solution, but on the other hand, I've had firsthand experience of marrying young and living to regret it. I was only seventeen when I married my first husband, and Vicky's no more mature now than I was then. I believe she should wait until she's at least twenty-one before she attempts to cope with the demands and responsibilities of marriage, but the trouble is, I don't think Cornelius and I can take another three years of this. We've hardly begun yet, Sam! This is just a little episode over a beachboy with the brains of a louse, and look at us, we're in pieces. What's going to happen when the first really smart playboy comes along? The entire prospect's a nightmare."

I made several rapid deductions. Alicia might want Vicky to marry her son Sebastian, but Sebastian himself was only twenty and probably no more ready for marriage than Vicky was. Obviously Alicia preferred the idea of a mature twenty-one-year-old Vicky marrying an eligible twenty-three-year-old Sebastian who had graduated from Harvard and was safely launched on his career at the bank. Meanwhile Cornelius was busy pushing the idea that a three-year wait would be disastrous and suggesting that I could save everyone from a nervous breakdown by arriving on the scene with a wedding ring in my hand. Alicia's dilemma seemed clear; torn between her natural desire to champion Sebastian's cause and her natural dread of future crises centered around her stepdaughter, she was now anxious to hear my views on the situation in the hope that they might help her see a clear solution to the problem.

I wondered what line to take. Logically I should combine forces with Alicia to champion Sebastian's cause; anyone who favored an alternative husband for Vicky should be encouraged. But it was impossible for me to forget Vicky's revulsion toward Sebastian, and I was convinced she would never marry him. Or was I? Young girls did change their minds. And Alicia could make a useful ally. . . .

Expediency triumphed. I took a deep breath. "Well, Alicia," I said with care, "I certainly sympathize with your situation; it's a big problem. But whether Vicky marries now or later, the job of looking after her is going to be no marital sinecure, and frankly, as I'm going to have to tell Neil, it's not a job I'd care to handle."

Her eyes widened. I felt as if I were riding in a plane that had just hit an air pocket—or as if the mire into which I had been floundering since my interview with Cornelius that afternoon had finally closed over my head.

"You?" said Alicia incredulously. "Cornelius suggested that *you* should marry Vicky?"

Too late I saw that Alicia's dilemma was not whether Vicky should marry Sebastian. She had merely been unable to make up her mind whether they should marry now or later. I said rapidly, "Neil was just exploring various possibilities. Of course we both realize Sebastian's far more suitable."

Alicia put down her glass of sherry and began to pull on her gloves. Her face was ivory smooth. "Cornelius has never cared for Sebastian," she said. "I might have guessed he'd try to double-cross me like this."

"Alicia—"

She whirled round on me. "You'd do it too, wouldn't you?" she said, her voice trembling. "You'd marry her! All Cornelius has to do is make sure he cracks the whip hard enough—but on second thought, no, why should he need to crack a whip? You're being offered a beautiful young girl, access to the Van Zale fortune, and the prospect of your children having all the social advantages you never had! It would take a better man than you, Sam Keller, to turn that kind of offer down!"

I felt the heat throbbing behind my skin, but I kept my temper. I said in my politest voice, "I'm in love with someone else and I plan on marrying her soon. Vicky has no appeal for me, Alicia. Other people may see her as the most eligible heiress on the Eastern Seaboard, but to me she's just a mixed-up little schoolgirl who calls me Uncle Sam."

"So Cornelius will have to crack the whip after all. What does it matter? The end result will be the same. You'll marry her," said Alicia, and walked out, slamming the door in my face.

For a moment I stood listening to the distant whine of the elevator, but at last I wiped the sweat from my forehead, returned to the den, and removed the Glenn Miller tape from the silent machine.

III

I WANTED to call Teresa, but I was too afraid of interrupting her work and making her even angrier than she had been earlier. I wanted to drink to numb the sexual tension that was making me restless, but I knew I had already had too much to drink that evening. I wanted to stop thinking of the life I might have had if Paul Van Zale had passed me by, but I was so depressed that for a long time I could only sit slumped on the couch while I wallowed futilely in my dreams of provincial domesticity.

I told myself I sentimentalized domesticity because I was a bachelor, but that very obvious explanation did not make my dreams less attractive. Then it occurred to me that I might be sentimentalizing domesticity because I was a German, and at once the dreams lost their power to charm. I reflected how odd it was that different nationalities picked different subjects to sentimentalize. The British were sentimental about animals. The French were sentimental about *l'amour*. The Americans were sentimental about violence, glorifying the Wild West and now World War II in a steady stream of Hollywood movies and Broadway shows. I thought of Rodgers and Hammerstein unerringly touching that sentimental streak in the vast American subconscious by producing first *Oklahoma!* and now—starting tomorrow—*South Pacific.*

I made a mental note to look for the tickets I had bought long ago for the coming Saturday night. I had planned to surprise Teresa. I would still surprise her. My depression began to lift at last. After all, everyone knew that a successful love affair was seldom one long upward curve on the graph of happiness, but tended to fluctuate, like the stock market; just because the Dow Jones Industrial Average slipped occasionally, nobody automatically assumed the economy was heading for disaster.

I was just planning how I would propose again to Teresa over a champagne supper following a show-stopping performance of *South Pacific,* when the phone rang.

I grabbed the receiver. "Teresa?" I said breathlessly.

"Who? No, this is Vivienne. Is there any news, Sam?"

I was amazed by how completely I had forgotten her. "Vivienne!" I said. "Gee, I was just about to call you. Yes, Vicky's fine—she's back home again now, so there's no need for you to worry anymore."

"Has anyone told Vicky I'm in town?"

"I told her myself, but she doesn't want to go to Fort Lauderdale right now—she's set her heart on going to Europe with Emily. I'm sorry, Vivienne, I did my best to push your cause."

"There's only one cause you push, Sam Keller," she said bitterly, not believing me, "and only one master you and your hatchet serve!" And she slammed down the phone as violently as Alicia had slammed the door in my face.

I went to bed and dreamed of a world in which I was my own master. I went to bed and dreamed of a world without Cornelius. I went to bed, and in my dreams I moved back through the looking glass to the blue skies and bluer seas of Bar Harbor. I went to bed and dreamed . . .

IV

I DREAMED the nightmare which had disrupted my sleep at regular intervals since the outbreak of war in 1917. It had changed over the years to encompass certain new experiences, but it always began with the same true incident from my past: at the age of nine I had walked into my school classroom to find that someone had written on the blackboard: "HANS-DIETER KELLER IS A NO GOOD GERMAN PIG." Then a gang of older boys had beaten me up and I had run crying all the way home.

At this point in my dream the truth and I parted company and fantasy began. The fantasies varied but the theme remained the same; I accepted Nazism in order to have my revenge on those who had hurt me, and then I rejected it for destroying so much that I'd loved. The rejection scenes were always accompanied by violent images, swastikas stained with blood, bulldozers shifting mounds of corpses, cities incinerated by fire-bombing, but that night as all the familiar appalling pictures streamed through my mind, my dream led me down a terrible new path. Without warning I was walking again across the polluted earth near a small town in Germany, and as I thought again of all those who had died, I heard the G.I. at my side whistling "Lili Marlene."

I awoke gasping, switched on all the lights, and groped my way to the den. My fingers somehow managed to put a record on the phonograph. I had to play a tune from the past to negate the end of that nightmare, a happy tune from a happy past, so I picked the record which recalled all my most carefree memories of the summer of 1929, when Cornelius and I had given wild parties together and celebrated our twenty-first birthdays with illegal champagne.

Miff Mole and his Molers began to play "Alexander's Ragtime Band."

After I had played the record three times I felt calmer, calm enough to recall the past truthfully without emotion. Anti-German sentiment had been common in 1917 and my family had probably suffered less than other German-American families, since my father had refused to be intimidated. After the incident in the classroom, he had hung a large American flag on our front porch and announced to the principal of my school that my constitutional rights as an American citizen would be violated unless steps were immediately taken to reprimand my assailants. The principal, a fair-minded man, had responded satisfactorily and the rest of my schooldays had passed without incident. It was my father who had suggested that it would be better if I had an American name. He had favored Hank, since it was similar to Hans, but I had insisted on Sam, the cowboy hero of a popular comic strip.

I devoted the following years to becoming thoroughly American. My father insisted that there need be no conflict in my conscience, since Germany had done nothing for us while America had given us everything. His remaining family in a small town near Berlin had been wiped out in 1918, but he refused to speak of his loss. My mother lost two brothers in the war, but one sister in Düsseldorf survived to remarry in 1920, and I often had to make secret journeys, not to the post office in Bar Harbor, but to the post office in Ellsworth, in order to mail food parcels to Europe. Once it took me ten minutes to summon the nerve to enter the post office because I was so ashamed to betray any German connection.

I became a very good American. I got straight A's in high school and took the prettiest girl to the junior prom and I figured out a way to work my way through law school by doing summer gardening on the Bar Harbor estates. I ate turkey with cranberry sauce on Thanksgiving and set off fireworks every Fourth of July and sang "The Star-Spangled Banner" louder than anyone else on every patriotic occasion. I even started speaking English when my parents and I were alone together, but my father put a stop to that because he said it was a great advantage to be bilingual and that I must on no account let my German lapse.

He did not like his employer, Paul Van Zale, but being a practical man, he had no trouble accepting the benefits which Paul could offer his employees. My parents were well-paid in their positions as gardener, housekeeper, and caretakers at the Van Zale summer home, and when Paul selected me to be his protégé, my father was the first to shake my hand.

"This is what being an American's all about, Sam," he said to me. "This is your big opportunity. This is every immigrant's American dream." And he told me I should go down on my knees and thank God I was a citizen of the finest country in the world where even the poorest man could become rich and successful.

I became rich. I became successful. I lived on Park and dined on Fifth and dealt daily with the Eastern Seaboard aristocracy who inhabited that palace at Willow and Wall. And then one day in 1933 I stepped out of the all-American world of my all-American dream, and later, when I stepped back, nothing was ever the same again.

I went back to Germany. I saw my native land again for the first time since I was two years old, and I found an odd little Austrian with a toothbrush mustache was saying it was no shame to be German. I found too that Germany was beautiful, more beautiful than I had ever imagined, and far more beautiful than my parents had ever dared to tell me in their efforts to abort their homesickness and bring me up as a good American. By the time I found my German relatives who had survived the war, America already seemed far away, a view glimpsed fleetingly through a thickening mist, and all the time the funny little Austrian was telling me I should be proud to be German, until at last—at long last—I was proud.

People probably think me such a practical, down-to-earth, hardheaded businessman; they probably never realize that despite my iron grasp of reality—or perhaps because of it—I have to have my dreams, my American dream, my German dream, even my sentimental dream of domestic bliss. War propaganda has fostered the image that the Germans are mindless machines, but no machines built those fairytale castles in Bavaria and no machines wrote some of the world's finest literature and no machines cheered the Berlin Philharmonic over and over again in the thirties whenever they played Beethoven's

Ninth. I shall never be the fascist robot my enemies want to believe I am, never. My dreams are too important to me. Even now, when my German dream was dead and my American dream was dying before my eyes, I had still managed to find a European dream to sustain me. Once more I pictured working for the ECA, and my last coherent thought before I fell asleep was: thank God it's not too late to start again.

However, once the sun woke me at seven the next morning, I had no choice but to put my new dream back on ice until the circumstances were more favorable. I dragged myself off the couch in the den where I had fallen asleep. I forced myself to go through the ritual of showering, shaving, dressing, and eating. And finally, when no further postponement of the inevitable was possible, I summoned my Mercedes-Benz and set off downtown once more to the bank at Willow and Wall.

V

As soon as I reached my office, I buzzed for my personal assistant, greeted and dismissed my secretary, sampled my first cup of coffee, hung up my hat, glanced at the mail, scanned the headlines of *The Wall Street Journal* and moved to the mantel to adjust the Dresden china clock which had once belonged to Paul Van Zale. The knock on the door came just as I was opening the glass face.

"Come in!" I shouted.

The door opened. I saw him in the mirror, tall as his father had been before him, but spare and dark, his eyes bright in his pale thin face.

"Yes, come in, Scott," I said abruptly, and glanced back at Paul's clock. It was one minute slow.

"Do you want the correct time, Sam?" said Steve Sullivan's son, always so anxious to help, always so eager to please.

"No," I said. "It doesn't matter." Snapping shut the glass face, I turned my back on all reminders of Paul. "What's the latest news on the Hammaco bid?"

"Bridges McCool have definitely dropped out of the bidding, but the other syndicate's still in the ring with us—I just checked to make sure. Oh, and here's the market report you wanted."

"Thanks. You're looking very disheveled! Have you been up all night?"

"No, Sam, I fell asleep at my desk by mistake at two this morning."

"Well, never let me see you show up for work like this again! You'll impress no one, least of all me, by looking as if you'd just walked out of a Bowery flophouse!"

"I've managed to get hold of a razor—"

"I'm not interested in how you plan to improve your appearance. Just fix it, and fix it pretty damn quick."

"Yes, Sam," said Scott, faultlessly obedient, utterly respectful, and withdrew.

I immediately regretted my abruptness. Scott had a special place in the Van Zale family; he was the stepson of Cornelius' sister, Emily, and since 1933 Cornelius had shared with Emily the responsibility for his upbringing. Scott's mother had died in 1929, his younger brother, Tony, had been killed in the war, and his father, once a senior partner of Van Zale's, was also dead, so it was only natural that over the years he had drawn close to his stepmother and her family.

I thought of his dead father, Steve Sullivan, who had fought Cornelius for control of the bank back in the thirties. I thought of Cornelius saying long ago: "Of course it'll be difficult to eliminate him. . . ." And I thought of my role in that elimination.

I had told myself afterward I had had no choice but to obey orders, but the war trials had long since put that unattractive defense in its proper place, so to ease my conscience all I could now do was attempt to forget the entire incident. However, this had proved impossible. Even if I had had the talent for forgetting what I didn't want to remember, Scott's presence at the bank would always have prevented me from perfecting this idyllic state of amnesia.

To admit that I disliked his presence at the bank would have been to admit my guilt about the past, so I had always tried to conceal my feelings. In fact, I made a great effort to like him and up to a point I succeeded, but the truth was he made me uneasy, and my uneasiness not only persisted but increased over the years. Just why he made me so uneasy was hard to pin down. It was too simple to say he reminded me of a part of my past which I preferred to forget; this was undoubtedly true, but human beings tend to adjust to adverse circumstances, and I had long since reached the point where I did not automatically remember Steve Sullivan's death whenever Scott walked into the room. It was a help that Scott bore no obvious resemblance to his father. He neither smoked nor drank, nor, as far as anyone knew, had a steady girlfriend. He worked late every night and was often at the bank on weekends. He dressed conservatively, charmed the clients with his well-informed conversation, and sent his stepmother, Emily, flowers every year on Mother's Day. No young American's behavior could have been more exemplary, as Cornelius was always telling me with quasi-paternal pride, but I was beginning to wonder if perhaps this was in fact the reason why Scott made me so uneasy: he was just a little too good to be true.

With his latest market report still in my hand, I sat down and flipped the intercom. "More coffee."

My secretary's secretary came running on the double. I picked up the red phone which connected me directly to the senior partner's office below.

"Mr. Van Zale's wire," said one of Cornelius' aides.

"Keller. Is he there?"

"No, sir, he's not in yet."

I hung up. My secretary arrived with some interoffice mail. The phone rang.

"Hold all calls." I skimmed the new batch of papers, shoved them aside, and turned to Scott's report. The phone rang again and kept ringing. I flipped the switch on the intercom again. "Pick up that phone, for Christ's sake!" The noise died. Returning to the report, I found it was immaculately written, and leaning forward, I reached again for the intercom.

"Sam?" said Scott a moment later.

"Get in here."

He arrived clean-shaven. I held up the report. "This is very good. Thank you. Now, let's discuss how we're going to get a line into the rival camp to see how their bid's shaping up. We've got to win this Hammaco bid, Scott. A ninety-million-dollar issue isn't a two-bit crap game. Do we have a complete list of the other side's syndicate?"

He had brought it with him. I was impressed but said nothing, just glanced down the list of names, but for a moment I was back in those far-off days before the Crash when I had stood where Scott was now standing and his father had been sitting in my chair. The memories snowballed. The silence lengthened. I went on staring at the list in my hand.

"Sam?" Scott said nervously at last. "Is something wrong?"

"No. No, it's just fine. I was trying to figure out which of these firms is the weak link we can snap to find out what's going on. Let me see . . . Bonner, Christopherson—maybe we could work out something there. Cornelius got Bonner himself out of trouble with the SEC recently in order to make up for screwing Christopherson over the Pan-Pacific Harvester merger back in forty-three. Christopherson's dead now, of course, and Bonner wants to get back alongside us next time Harvester launch an issue. Call Bonner. He's a tough customer, but lean on him. I think he'll know which side his bread's buttered on."

"Bonner himself isn't involved in this syndicate, Sam. It's his son-in-law, Whitmore."

"That's better still. I've known Whitmore for years, and he's got as much backbone as a jellyfish. In fact, it was he who got Bonner into such hot water with the SEC. You call Whitmore, and don't just lean on him—squeeze him till the pips squeak, to use the immortal words of that British bastard Lloyd George. I want a line into that rival camp today, Scott. I don't care how you do it, but get it in."

"Right, Sam. Will that be all?"

I sighed, moved restlessly to the window, and looked down at the magnolia tree in the patio. "I guess so. . . . But how times change!" I added impulsively. "When I was a young kid on Wall Street, we all sat around like gods and waited for clients to come crawling to us for money. Now the clients sit back and let us fight each other for their business. Competitive bidding! My God, Paul Van Zale must be turning in his grave!"

Scott smiled but made no comment, a respectful young man tolerating the nostalgia of an older generation.

"Okay," I said abruptly. "That's all. Check back with me when you've talked to Whitmore."

"Yes, Sam." He departed.

I reached for the red phone again.

"Mr. Van Zale's wire," droned the aide.

"Christ, isn't he in yet?" I hung up and summoned my secretary. "I'm going to have to chair the partners' meeting. Get me the major file on Hammaco."

In the conference room I found a dozen of my partners lounging around the table and gossiping about golf. In the old days at Van Zale's, long before I had joined the firm, the half-dozen partners had sat at huge mahogany desks in the bank's great hall while the senior partner alone had been secluded in the room which now belonged to Cornelius, but later, when the bank had merged with another in 1914, the great hall had been assigned to the syndicate division and the partners had been given their own individual rooms on the second floor. Now that the bank had expanded, the space had again been rearranged; Cornelius had kept the senior partner's office on the first floor, and the six partners who had been longest with the firm had kept their rooms on the second, but the remaining partners had returned to the great hall, still known as "the sin bin" in commemoration of the syndicate division. The syndicate men themselves had moved to Seven Willow Street, the adjacent building, which we had acquired during our expansion after the war.

Cornelius had chosen his partners with typical shrewdness. First came the window dressing, six men in their sixties who could provide not only solid experience but a solid, respectable front. Then came the six men in their fifties, men who might be somewhat less orthodox but who had all resigned themselves to the knowledge that they would never sit in the senior partner's chair. That left the three men in their forties, and these had to be watched with scrupulous care in case they acquired delusions of grandeur and attempted to annex more power than they could be trusted to handle.

Cornelius and I were, as always, the youngest. Cornelius had not yet faced the day when he felt obliged to hire a partner younger than himself, although now we were both past forty we knew he should give the partnership a shot of youth before it became senescent. However, Cornelius disliked thinking of young ambitious men one rung below him on the ladder. People thought this was odd and said most men in his position would have welcomed the opportunity to impose their power on younger men, but I understood Cornelius' reluctance all too well. Cornelius and I knew better than anyone just how dangerous ambitious young men could be.

As I entered the conference room, the partners straightened their backs and stopped talking about golf. I smiled warmly at them. They smiled warmly back. Cordial greetings were exchanged as one of the Van Zale aides passed around the coffeecups, and then we all settled down to our traditional daily discussion.

In fact, the partners' meetings were a waste of time, and I favored cutting them back to one a week. The purpose was to keep each other abreast of our different projects and to have consultations about policy, but the partners in the sin bin always knew what everyone else in the sin bin was doing, and the select six partners upstairs with the exception of myself were all too old to be involved in work of any importance. Through various informants Cornelius and I were also well aware of what went on in the sin bin, so we would hardly have lacked information if the daily meetings had been abandoned, but like all wise dictators, Cornelius wanted to maintain the formal trappings of democracy. The daily meetings persisted under the fiction that we were all deciding what was best for the firm; occasionally we even took a vote, which Cornelius would quietly ignore if it turned out to be contrary to his wishes. Sometimes partners became annoyed, but not for long. Cornelius did not like being surrounded by discontented people, and any partner who complained was gently advised to move to another firm.

"For, after all," Cornelius would say solicitously, "the last thing I want is for you to be unhappy."

The surviving partners learned their lesson and took care to appear well content in Cornelius' presence. Cornelius had a controlling interest in the partnership, with absolute authority to hire and fire whom he pleased, so it was only sensible to be on the best possible terms with him. Also, every partner knew he was far from irreplaceable. Van Zale's was a great investment-banking house with a history that stretched far back into the nineteenth century, and there was never any shortage of good men who wanted to work at Willow and Wall.

"What's the news on Hammaco, Sam?" asked a partner, one of the forty-five-year-old mavericks who had to be watched with care.

"Good," I said. "The bidding closes tomorrow. Everything's shaping up well."

"What exactly is this Hammaco business?" said one of the silver-haired veterans who had just tottered back from a vacation in Florida.

"This is a ninety-million-dollar issue for the Hammer Machine Corporation, who are planning to expand into the armaments business. With the cold war hotting up, this is obviously good business, particularly for a corporation like Hammaco. The bidding conditions were tough—I'll have a copy of the terms of sale, the preliminary prospectus, and the proposed purchase statement routed to you in the interoffice mail. We've had the 'due-diligence' meeting at the Hammaco offices, and also a preliminary meeting of our syndicate.

The main price meeting is tomorrow morning, with a final price meeting at two tomorrow afternoon."

"How's the rival camp?" said another maverick. Those mavericks always enjoyed keeping me on my toes.

"I've got a line on them. As soon as I know what they intend to bid, I'll make damned sure we outbid them. I see no problem." I turned to the two partners from the sin bin who were supervising the syndicate division's spadework on the Hammaco bid. "I'd like a word with you guys after this meeting."

There was a knock on the door, and Scott slipped in. "Sam, an important call."

I glanced at my partners. "Excuse me a moment, gentlemen." In the corner by the phone I murmured to Scott, "Is it Neil?"

"No, the president of Hammaco."

"Christ!" I picked up the receiver and found the president wanted to invite me to lunch. I accepted. "Cancel my lunch date," I said to Scott as I hung up, "and find out if by some miracle our rivals couldn't stand the pace and have thrown in the sponge." I was just moving back to the conference table when the phone rang again, making me jump.

"Keller," I said, picking up the receiver.

"I want to see you," said Cornelius in a voice of ice, and severed the connection as violently as a guillotine severing a criminal neck.

I did not stop to think what I had done. Sometimes it's better not to think, in case one loses one's nerve imagining disasters which have never happened. I got a cigarette alight, politely asked the eldest partner to chair the meeting, and then, unable to stop myself fearing the worst—whatever the worst was—I ran downstairs to the senior partner's office and prepared to face the lion in his den.

Chapter Four

I

CORNELIUS, LOOKING as exhausted as if he had just suffered an asthma attack, was sitting huddled in his swivel chair behind the enormous desk. I almost inquired anxiously about his health, but when I saw the brutal line of his mouth I decided to keep silent. With reluctance I at last allowed myself to speculate about the unknown mistake which had roused his wrath.

"If I asked you a very simple question," said Cornelius in a tired patient voice, the one he regularly used before losing his temper, "would it be too much to hope that you might give me a very simple answer?"

I was being invited to take the bull by the horns. "What's wrong?"

"I mean, if I asked you if you were in the habit of repeating confidential conversations conducted with me in this room, you wouldn't go into some rambling evasive explanation that I'd find embarrassing, would you? I'd hate to be embarrassed by you, Sam. I'd be very upset."

"Cut it out, Neil. You know damned well I don't go broadcasting our private conversations to all and sundry."

Cornelius immediately jumped to his feet, leaned forward with both hands on the desk, and shouted at me, "Then why the hell did you tell Alicia that I wanted you to marry Vicky?"

"Because she gave me the impression she already knew all about it." My reflexes for warding off attack were so finely developed that it was only after I had spoken that the shock made my heart thump painfully in my chest. I clasped my hands behind my back, took a deep breath to steady myself, and then made the classic move from defense to counterattack. "And why the hell didn't you tell me," I demanded angrily, "that Alicia thought you shared her view that Vicky should marry Sebastian? How do you think *I* felt when Alicia and I ended up talking at cross-purposes and she realized you were trying to double-cross her? I don't like being embarrassed by you either, Neil, and don't think you have the monopoly on getting upset by your friends."

Cornelius slumped back in his chair. Long experience of dealing with him had made me aware that when he was angry with himself he often tried to deflect his anger onto others, and long experience of dealing with me had taught him I was adept at absorbing his anger and neutralizing it by remaining unintimidated. Now his anger was spent, I saw that only the misery remained. He began to breath unevenly, and I turned away as he produced the pills which warded off his asthma. He hated anyone to see him when he was unwell.

"Neil, believe me, I'm sorry if this has resulted in trouble between you and Alicia, but—"

"I'm not discussing my marriage with you, either now or at any other time," he said, but as he paused to swallow the pills, it occurred to me that he longed to discuss it but was held back by complex emotions which I could not understand. "And talking of marriage," he said, still breathing badly but unable to stop a second rush of anger, "Alicia tells me that you, quote, were going to have to tell me, unquote, that you couldn't marry Vicky. That sounds like an interesting decision, particularly since you implied to me yesterday that you were willing to consider the idea. Can you possibly bring yourself to tell me more about it? I just hate having important decisions relayed to me secondhand."

Now I was really in deep water. Flicking a speck of dust from the seat of the client's chair, I sat down leisurely in order to give myself a few precious seconds to plan my strategy. Should I lie, stall, or tell the truth? I decided that the situation was so far beyond redemption that an outright lie would be pointless, but I could not make up my mind whether to tell the whole or the partial truth. Finally, unable to decide how partial the partial truth should be, I gave up any idea of stalling and resigned myself to unvarnished honesty.

"Well, Neil," I said with the smile one friend might reserve for another in very adverse circumstances, "don't think I wasn't tempted

by your suggestion. And don't think I wouldn't normally do everything I could to help you, but I'm afraid that right now I'm not in a
normal situation. I'm very much in love with Teresa—Kevin's caretaker—and I've made up my mind to marry her."

He stared at me blankly. His delicate classical features might have
been sculptured in marble. Then he tried to speak, but his asthma had
worsened and the words were lost in his sporadic gasps for breath.

To give him privacy, I moved to the concealed bar behind the
bookcase and filled a glass of water from the little sink. I knew better
than to show alarm or summon help. When the glass of water was in
front of him, I moved to the window, and keeping my back to him as
if nothing had happened, I said levelly, "I know you'll have trouble
understanding why I should feel this way about a penniless Polish-
American girl from a coal-mining town in West Virginia, but my
mind's made up and I'd be lying if I let you believe that either you
or anyone else could alter it. I'm fond of Vicky; she's very pretty and
very cute, but she's not for me, Neil, and if I married her I wouldn't
be doing anyone a favor, least of all Vicky herself."

I stopped to listen. His breathing seemed fractionally better, as if
the pills were already doing their work, and I decided to risk turning
around. "Would you prefer that we continued this discussion later?" I
said, giving him the chance to get rid of me and complete his recovery in private.

"Yeah," he whispered. "Later. Lunch?"

"I'm lunching with Fred Bucholz of Hammaco."

Cornelius visibly revived. His breathing quieted, and as a barely
perceptible color returned to his face he looked me straight in the eye
and said, "Win that bid and we'll forget about everything else. Even
Vicky."

It was most unlike Cornelius either to give up so easily or to
reverse himself for no apparent reason. The Hammaco bid was important but hardly crucial to the firm's welfare, and as I eyed him
skeptically he saw my suspicion and smiled. "You know me too well,
Sam!" he said, all anger forgotten at last. "Yes, Hammaco's just a
side issue. The truth is, I've changed my mind about Vicky. Alicia
succeeded in convincing me last night that (a) it's a mistake for girls
to marry too young and (b) it would be a mistake for Vicky to
marry you, no matter how old she was. So we'll forget all about it.
I'm sorry if I put you in an awkward position."

I knew that Alicia had great influence over him, but I knew too that Cornelius tended to cling obstinately to his more perverse ideas, and I still could not quite believe he had abandoned the scheme. "Okay," I said. "Let's forget it." I moved toward the door.

"You'll have to explain to me sometime about Teresa," said Cornelius. "Maybe when you become officially engaged. I always enjoy your engagements. Do you realize you would have had at least three wives by now if you'd succeeded in coaxing all those fiancées to the altar?"

I smiled back at him. "This time I've no intention of letting history repeat itself! I'll check back with you later, Neil, to report on the Hammaco lunch."

"Good luck."

The door closed. The back lobby was dim and cool. I allowed myself a moment to savor my relief, and then, still aware of a weakness in the pit of my stomach, I returned to my office to recuperate from the interview. But the phone rang before I could relax. The representative of one of our syndicate's leading investment banks was on the line.

"Sam, I'm getting worried about this Hammaco business. With the price of zinc still falling, and steel showing no signs of recovery—"

"I have inside information from the Treasury that there'll be no slump in spite of all the talk of deflation."

After I had calmed him down, I got rid of him and summoned my secretary.

"Get me the Treasury."

I wanted a drink, but it was only ten o'clock. I lit another cigarette instead, but five minutes later, with the inside information from the Treasury no longer a figment of my imagination but a trump card firmly embedded in reality, I felt sufficiently cheered to call Teresa.

"Hi," I said when she picked up the phone. "Tell me right away if I'm calling at a bad moment, but I just wanted to know how you are."

"I'm okay." But she sounded uncertain. "I'm sorry I was so mean to you last night, Sam. It was just that I was so depressed."

"Sure, I understand. That's okay." Since it was a medical fact that women were moodier than men, I made a big effort to be considerate. "I'd sure like to get together with you tonight or tomorrow," I said, "but why don't I give you a little more time to straighten out those work problems of yours? However, I'm going to come and get

you on Saturday night even if I have to carry you off by force! I've
got tickets for *South Pacific*."

"Oh, great."

There was a pause while I tried to suppress my baffled disappointment.

"Sorry, Sam, did you say *South Pacific?* Gee, that would be *wonderful!* How did you ever manage to get tickets? What a great surprise!"

I felt much better. "We'll make a big evening of it," I said, "an
evening to remember." Then I blew a kiss into the phone, replaced
the receiver, and feeling in excellent spirits, summoned Scott to resume the battle of the Hammaco bid.

II

"SAM, I'M out of my depth," said Scott. "The other side are definitely still in the running, so I called Whitmore at Bonner, Christopherson, but he refused to talk to me, and it's hard to squeeze
someone till the pips squeak when they have their secretary perpetually geared to say they're in conference."

"The son of a bitch! And to think I helped put that bastard where
he is today when I let Bonner's in for a slice of that railroad pie back
in '35—he'd never have got to marry his boss's daughter without that
kind of success under his belt! Okay, get on the extension, Scott, and
take a lesson in how to fillet a fickle fish."

There followed one of those conversations with which I had become all too familiar during my years as Cornelius' right-hand man.
In fact, the technique of bending an opponent gracefully into an ally
was so familiar to me that I might have conducted the conversation
in my sleep. I called the offices of Bonner, Christopherson. Whitmore
again tried to hide behind his secretary, much to my disgust. I despise cowardice in businessmen who should have the guts to make at
least a token attempt to brazen their way out of a tight spot.

"Tell Mr. Whitmore," I said to the secretary, "that I'm calling to
do him a favor. I've just received private information from the SEC."

He came gasping to the phone.

Leaning back in my swivel chair, I idly watched the sunlight playing on the mellow mahogany furniture and listened to myself talking
very soothingly in a steady stream of clichés. When I had been young

and had fallen back out of sheer nervousness on the use of ingratiating clichés, I had noticed with surprise that my opponents nearly always wilted beneath the hypnotic cumulative effect of so many banal phrases uttered in a honeyed voice. It was a lesson I had never forgotten.

"Well, hello there, Frank! Long time no see! How are you doing? How's your wife . . . and children . . . gee, that's just wonderful! I'm real happy to hear it. . . . Say, Frank, I'm calling because you're one of my oldest, dearest friends and I want you to know that I can do you a favor. I never forget my friends, Frank. If there's one thing I can't stand, it's a man who forgets his obligations to his friends. . . ."

I went on like this for some time. Briefly translated from the crap, I reminded him that Bonner, his father-in-law, wanted Van Zale's to include his firm in the next Pan-Pacific Harvester syndicate. I reminded him that Van Zale's was always besieged with firms who wanted to participate in a syndicate where the pickings were guaranteed to be opulent, and that inevitably some firms had to be disappointed. I reminded him that even though the relationship between Van Zale's and Bonner, Christopherson had recently improved, I could imagine circumstances in which it could go rapidly downhill again, with the result that Bonner's would be excluded from the new syndicate.

". . . and your wonderful father-in-law—how is he, by the way? Great! . . . Yes, your wonderful boss would be real disappointed, and if there's one thing that makes me feel sad, Frank, it's the thought of a nice guy like Mr. Bonner being disappointed . . ."

And so on and so on.

". . . so I thought maybe you and I could get together, you know, nothing official, just a quiet little drink someplace this evening . . ."

"Six-thirty at the University Club?" said Whitmore faintly.

"The Metropolitan Club," I said, "and make it six sharp."

I hung up and went on watching the sunshine streaming through the window. Presently Scott returned to the room.

"Congratulations, Sam!" he exclaimed with enthusiasm. "You nailed him cold!"

I looked at him. There was no reason why I should doubt his sincerity, but I did. The doubt existed for no more than a second, but I immediately recognized it as a symptom of that uneasiness which I found so hard to explain. As usual my uneasiness was followed by guilt that I should distrust him, and to make amends for my inexplicable suspicion, I was careful to spend a minute being nice to him before I sent him back to his desk.

When he had gone, I was about to recall my secretary when a glance at my calendar told me Good Friday was only a week away. To underline his Episcopalian upbringing, Cornelius gave his employees a holiday on both Good Friday and Easter Monday, and I always took advantage of the long weekend to visit my mother in Maine. I decided to call her to confirm that I was coming, and automatically as I picked up the receiver I pictured her in the hideous little frame house which I had bought for her after my father died. It was not the kind of home I would have chosen for her, but my mother had been insistent. She did not want a new house on the outskirts of town with a view of the sea. She wanted a property within walking distance of the stores and the church. She did not want a car. I gave her presents for the house, but afterward she put them away because she felt they were too good to use. I had given up inviting her to stay with me in New York because I had now accepted that she would never come. The idea of air travel terrified her, she disliked trains, and she regarded my offer of a chauffeur-driven limousine as too intimidating to be seriously considered, while beyond this fear of travel was the unswerving conviction that she would be either robbed or killed if she were ever to set foot in New York City. My father, much more adventurous, had been proud to visit me once a year, but neither he nor I had ever been able to prise my mother loose from Maine.

During my visits home I saw little of my mother, since she spent all day in the kitchen cooking me my favorite dishes. Usually I would go walking on Mount Desert. If I happened to meet anyone I knew, I would at once invite him to join me for a beer so that no one could complain to my mother that I was now too grand for my old friends, but otherwise I made no attempt to be sociable. I was willing enough to listen to an old acquaintance complaining to me about his wife, his mortgage payments, and how hard it was for him to get by on a salary of three thousand a year, but unfortunately there was little I could say about my own life without arousing my companion's incredulity, envy, and resentment.

My mother and I watched television together in the evenings. Television was a blessing because it demanded both visual and aural attention. In the old days we had felt obliged to make some comment whenever our glances met during a radio program, but now we could watch the screen secure in the knowledge that no comment was needed until the program had finished. My mother was proud of her television, which I changed for her every year, and I was relieved that I had at last found a present she could use as well as appreciate.

"Hi," I said as she picked up the phone. "How are you doing Down East?"

"Good. The weather's terrible, so cold. My rheumatism's bad again, but the doctor just says take aspirin—five dollars he charges, and all he can say is take aspirin. Mrs. Hayward died, and they had a nice funeral. Marie Ashe and her husband split up—drink—I always said he was no good. The TV's still going nicely. There's no other news. Are you coming in next week? What do you want to eat?"

We discussed food. Finally my mother said in a brisk voice to hide her excitement, "It'll be nice to see you. How's New York?"

"Just fine."

"Good." My mother never asked about girlfriends, never suggested I should get married, never complained that she had no grandchildren. Once long ago she had asked me about my private life, and my father had been furious. "Don't you persecute that boy with goddamned women's questions!" he had shouted at her. "Don't you realize that if you make him uncomfortable he won't come back and see us anymore?" And when I had protested, he had been equally furious with me. "Do you think I'm stupid? Do you think I don't understand?"

The fragility of our relationship terrified my mother and made me think often of the ordeal of parenthood. How could parents endure to labor for years, to sacrifice themselves so that their children should have nothing but the best, and to discover in the end that it had all been for so little, for a quick visit on national holidays and a few hours spent in front of the television set in a silence neither side knew how to break? I wished my mother could enjoy all the presents I wanted to give her to assuage the guilt I felt. I wished there were some magic words I could use to alleviate our constraint. After my father died I did manage to say to her: "Has it all been worth it?" but she had not understood, and when I had tried to explain she had said simply: "Of course. If you're happy."

"I'm glad you're happy, Hans," my mother was saying on the phone as I watched the sunlight slanting across the carpet of my office. The German name had been slipping out more often since my father's death. "I'm glad everything's going well for you in New York."

"It'll be good to get home again," I said, and immediately the words were spoken, I felt a great sadness, for of course, as my parents and I had known for years, I could never go home again. I was a victim of that classic dilemma which probably exists in other countries but which I always thought of as peculiarly American: I had left my home to pass through the looking glass into the land of milk and honey, only to find later that the looking glass was a one-way mirror and that no matter how hard I tried, I could never go back again to the country I could so clearly see beyond the glass wall. The milk might go sour and the honey might run out, but the glass would never crack. I was an exile in the world I had chosen for myself, a prisoner serving a life sentence which no one could cut short.

It was a subject Teresa and I had once discussed. "You must amputate your past," she had said firmly. "You're falling into the trap of all exiles and looking back at home through rose-colored glasses. At least I'm not tempted to make *that* mistake! I can remember my home town all too well—the coal dust and the filthy shacks and the mean streets and the children without shoes and my father getting drunk and my mother always being pregnant . . ."

"But it was home, wasn't it?" I had said. "It's still part of you."

"I amputated it," she had insisted. "It's gone."

I had wanted to ask her more questions, but she had changed the subject and it never arose again. Yet I often wondered how successful her amputation had been, particularly since I could see that despite her bitterness she still clung to the symbols of her early life, the little gold cross which represented the church she had long since left, the Polish cooking which she favored whenever she had not volunteered to produce a creole dish for a special occasion, the frugal habits acquired during years of poverty, and finally, most important of all, the blend of pride and dignity which prevented her from living off men and stooping to pick up any financial favors that came her way.

Eventually it occurred to me that her belief that she had amputated her past was an illusion. The past was still with her, and she was still on the other side of that looking glass. She was living far from home, but somehow, through some process I could not guess, she had managed to maintain contact with her early life. Although she had blended into the background of New York, she had remained untouched by its corruption, and when I realized this, I realized too why it was so necessary for me to win her. I had this deepening conviction that Teresa could lead me back through the looking glass; I felt increasingly sure that once I had Teresa, I could at last go home again.

The sunlight was still slanting onto the carpet of my office. "There's just one more thing," I said impulsively to my mother.

"Yes?"

"I've met this girl and I'd like to bring her with me next weekend to meet you. Her name's Teresa. She's twenty-five. She was brought up as a Catholic but she doesn't practice anymore. She's only been in New York for a few months. She's just spent seven years in New Orleans, but she comes from West Virginia. She likes to cook."

"Oh!" My mother sounded in despair for fear she should say the wrong thing. Huge excitement battled with the knowledge that she must remain calm to avoid annoying me. "Teresa, you said?" she murmured tentatively. "Would that be Italian?"

I had been prepared for this question and had decided to be frank from the start in order to give her time to adjust to the idea. "No," I said. "She's Polish."

There was a silence. "Well," said my mother rapidly at last in a frantic attempt to repair the gap in the conversation, "I'm sure there are a lot of very nice Polish people in America. Yes, do please bring her here. I'll . . . I'll spring-clean the guest room for her . . . and get out those new sheets you gave me—the ones which were too good to use . . ."

"Fine, but don't make too much fuss. Teresa's like the girl next door. She's no Eastern Seaboard princess."

My mother, on the verge of expiring with excitement, somehow managed to bid me good-bye.

After concluding the call, I did not immediately return to my work but sat thinking in my chair. I knew my mother had always hoped I would marry someone high-class, but I knew too she would feel far more at ease with Teresa than with some expensive product of the Anglo-Saxon Protestant aristocracy. It was unfortunate that Teresa was Polish, but once my mother was presented with grandchildren, she would soon forget her prejudices, and although I suspected Teresa might be ambivalent about the prospect of maternity, I felt sure she would want children once she realized they need not interfere with her painting. I intended to hire a live-in nurse so that she could paint whenever she liked. I knew how much her painting meant to her, and besides, I thought it was a good thing for a woman to have a hobby in addition to her domestic duties. Cornelius had remarked lately that since her two boys had grown up, Alicia often had trouble finding ways to occupy her time.

A warm glow enveloped me as I thought of my mother happily spring-cleaning the guest room. I was glad I had made her happy. I was going to make her happier. It was a good feeling.

With a sigh I turned my thoughts back to the office, and after dictating as many letters as possible in the limited time at my disposal, I left the building and was chauffeured uptown to the Colony to lunch with the president of Hammaco.

III

I WAS satisfied that the lunch had been a success, but my satisfaction was jolted on my return when Scott told me the president had lunched the previous day with the account manager of the rival syndicate.

"The bastard!" I said. "Trying us both on for size! If he just wants to pick the side he likes best, why put us through the hoops of this goddamned competitive bidding system? He should either go the fancy-lunch route or else he should have nothing to do with either of us until the sealed bids are delivered. The trouble with clients nowadays is that they think they're God. It makes me laugh when I see the reports of the current antitrust case and read how prosecuting counsel is bleating about the all-powerful conspiracy of investment bankers that's terrorizing American big business. Here I am, slugging it out to the death with our rivals, and prosecuting counsel is saying there's no competition in the investment-banking industry! Sometimes I think it's too bad the Justice Department didn't name Van Zale's in the antitrust suit. I'd have told Judge Medina a thing or two!"

"I'll bet you would, Sam," said Scott, adept as always at the respectful response.

I abruptly changed the subject.

IV

I GAVE Whitmore the number of my private line and told him to call me immediately his syndicate's final price meeting finished the following afternoon.

"Sure, Sam, no problem, no problem at all." Whitmore looked white but somehow produced a fond smile, and we parted with a long, lingering handshake.

When I reached home I called Scott. As usual he was working late. "We're all set for tomorrow," I said. "Whitmore'll sing all the details of our rivals' final bid as sweetly as a canary. Are you working on that final market report?"

"Of course," said Scott, ever perfect.

I hung up.

V

I HAD brought the Hammaco files home with me, and I worked till midnight as I went over the details and calculated the best price we could offer. Then I went to bed and snatched a few hours' sleep before riding downtown for the final battle. When Scott met me at my office at eight we went through the final market report and updated my pricing.

The morning meeting of the syndicate's price committee took place at ten, and the final meeting was scheduled to take place at two. I expected to hear Whitmore's news at three, which meant I could make any necessary adjustment with the committee before the bid was submitted at four. It was a tight schedule, and my nerves were on edge as I chaired the final price meeting and gave the report on market conditions, the status of recent offerings of similar size and quality, and the extent to which institutional buyers had expressed interest in Hammaco. The next order of business was to decide upon the public offering price of the issue and the price to be paid to the issuer. As the account manager, I put forward the proposal relating to this "cost of money," and my proposal was discussed for some time by the entire group before several pollings succeeded in fixing our final prices. No one dropped out at the last minute, so there was no panic while shares were reapportioned.

"Okay, gentlemen," I said at last. "And now, if you'd all care to wait a few minutes, I'll check with my sources to see if I can come up with a little inside information." I turned to my two partners from the sin bin. "You can get the boys in number seven to start wrapping up the paperwork. I don't anticipate any major adjustments."

I sped back to my office. "Get Whitmore on the phone for me," I said to Scott as soon as the door was closed, but Whitmore was still out of his office. Evidently our rivals' price meeting was still going on.

I fixed myself a Beefeater martini, very dry, on the rocks with two olives, and sat drinking it while I waited.

The red phone rang.

"Any news?" said Cornelius.

"Not yet."

The white phone rang. It was my private line. I hung up on Cornelius and grabbed the receiver.

"Sam?" said Whitmore.

"Go ahead."

He gave me the news. I hung up on him too and fixed myself another martini, even drier, straight up. Then I called Scott. "Get in here." I called the syndicate division at Seven Willow. "Hold everything." I drank my martini very fast and had just got a cigarette alight by the time Scott arrived on the double.

"They've undercut us."

"My God! But how?"

"They must be really paring down the spread. There's no way they could come up with that kind of figure and still make a respectable profit."

"What do we do now?"

"See Neil."

We ran downstairs. Cornelius was talking to two of his aides, who were immediately dismissed as soon as I appeared in the doorway. As the door closed, Cornelius said sharply, "Well?"

I gave him the news. Cornelius took it calmly. "Well, there are two possibilities," he said, leaning back in his chair. "Either our illustrious rivals have gone out of their minds, or Whitmore's lying."

"Jesus!" I was appalled. "If he's been lying to me I'll—"

"Of course," said Cornelius soothingly. "Of course we will. However, meanwhile . . ."

"Neil, I doubt if I could get more than half our syndicate to undercut those figures, and if we took up the slack ourselves, it would wipe out our profit."

"I think Whitmore's double-crossing you," said Cornelius, "but not by choice. He doesn't have the guts. I think you scared him so shitless that he's run to his boss and confessed, and now Bonner's giving him orders. I know I got that firm out of trouble with the SEC the other day because I thought it might be useful to have them in our hip pocket instead of perpetually snarling at our heels, and I know Bonner acts as if he wants to be friendly and grab a piece of the next PPH syndicate, but maybe Bonner still hasn't forgiven us for screwing Christopherson over the Pan-Pacific Harvester merger back in forty-three; maybe in spite of PPH he just can't resist this golden chance to screw us back."

"That's possible."

We thought about it. I was aware of Scott standing quietly by the door.

"Bonner knows that if we undercut that kind of bid we'd be cutting off our nose to spite our face," said Cornelius. "He wants to make us look like fools. Let's hold fast to what we've got, and I'll bet you we'll still win the damned bid hands down."

"Right." I turned to Scott. "Give the go-ahead to the boys in Number Seven and tell them to wrap up the paperwork right away."

"Yes, Sam," said Scott.

VI

THE CALL from the president of Hammaco came through at three minutes after six. I was drinking black coffee and lighting another cigarette.

"Sam!"

"Hi, Fred . . . how was the bid?"

"Well, Sam, it was a real close call, and I just hate to have to tell you, but . . ."

The expression on my face must have altered, although I was unaware of moving a muscle. I looked across the desk at Scott, and as I saw him realize what had happened, I thought with a clarity which shocked me: he's glad. The knowledge, expressed in words yet somehow beyond verbal expression, radiated powerful emotions which I neither stopped to analyze nor attempted to control.

I did not speak. After replacing the receiver, I stood up, walked to the window, and stared silently down into the patio.

At last I heard Scott say, "I'm sorry, Sam. I guess I must feel almost as badly as you do. We all worked so hard."

I turned slowly to face him. "Maybe our rivals had a line into our camp," said my voice, "just as we had a line into theirs. And maybe Whitmore was playing a double game and relaying information in both directions."

Scott looked blank. "I guess that's possible, but it seems unlikely. Would our rivals use that kind of tactics? And who on our side would have given Whitmore his information?"

I knew at once he was innocent. A guilty man would have made a much neater comment to terminate my suspicions, but perversely the very knowledge that my doubts about him remained impossible to justify only pushed me further toward losing my self-control. Before I could stop myself I said bluntly, "Did you talk to Whitmore today?"

Comprehension burst upon him. His habitual pallor vanished as the color flooded his face. "If you mean what I think you mean by that question, Sam," he said, somehow keeping his voice level, "I must ask you not only to withdraw the question but also to apologize. Otherwise I shall go to Cornelius and tell him I can no longer work with you."

For the first time in my life I saw his father in him. It was as if the curtain had gone up on a performance which long ago I had seen time after time: Steve under pressure, Steve turning the tables, Steve knifing his way out of trouble with a couple of terse sentences which had sent Cornelius and me backing into the nearest corner. I had forgotten until that moment how frightened we had been of Steve Sullivan. I had forgotten the relief which had mingled with the guilt when I had heard of his death. I had taken such care to forget, because those memories were better suppressed, but now they were all coming back to me; now I could remember them far, far too well.

I took off my glasses and began to polish them with my handkerchief. Amidst my shock—and I was profoundly shocked—I was furious with myself for making the foolish accusation which had laid me wide open to such a successful counterattack. I didn't see how I could conclude the interview without a loss of face.

At last I managed to say: "I'm sorry—I'm not myself. Losing that bid was a big disappointment to me." Cornelius would be furious if he heard I had lashed out at an innocent Scott. He would think me neurotic. Whatever happened, I had to smooth over the incident. "Of course I withdraw the question," I said rapidly, "and of course I apologize. Thank you for all your hard work on the bid. I appreciate your loyalty and support."

He did not move, but I sensed him relax. "Thank you, Sam. That's okay. I realize you were very upset."

"And now, if you'll excuse me . . ."

"Sure."

He left the room. I made a great effort to pull myself together quickly, but it took me a full minute before I could face picking up the red phone.

"Yes?" said Cornelius.

"We lost."

"Come right down."

I found him drinking Coca-Cola out of a cut-glass tumbler, but when I entered the room he moved at once to the concealed bar.

"Want some?" he said, producing a bottle of brandy.

"That's a humane and generous gesture in the circumstances. But I don't want to drink alone."

Cornelius produced two glasses the size of thimbles and carefully poured a couple of drops of brandy into each.

"Well?" he said after I had swallowed my drink in a single gulp.

"I'm sorry, Neil. What else can I say? Of course I accept full responsibility."

"No, the responsibility's mine. I was the one who said we should ignore Whitmore. We should have adjusted the bid—not as much as Whitmore and Bonner hoped we would, perhaps, but some adjustment should still have been made. . . . Well, so much for postmortems. Everything's going wrong at the moment, isn't it? First Vicky, now Hammaco. I wonder what the next disaster will be. They say trouble always runs in threes. . . . Sam, you're looking terrible. You know how much I disapprove of drinking at the office, but I think you'd better have some more brandy."

Cornelius was being so nice to me that I began to feel nervous. "No, I won't drink any more," I said. "I'm okay. Neil, once again,

I can't apologize sufficiently for not arriving at a winning formula . . ."

"Oh, forget the apologies, Sam, and tell me what's really bothering you! I'm worried. You're drinking and smoking too much—incidentally, please do me a favor and put out that goddamned cigarette—and now you look as if you're about to fall apart. What's your problem? It's not just Hammaco, is it? Is it this girl you're so crazy about? Is she at the bottom of it all?"

"Hell, no! She's the one bright light on the horizon!"

"Then what is it? There *is* something else, isn't there?"

"Well . . ."

"Come on, Sam, remember the old days. When one of us made a mistake or got into trouble, the other came to the rescue; we had to operate that way in order to ensure we both survived here. Now you've obviously got problems, and if you fall apart there'll be a big mess, so you've damn well got to talk to me. It's your moral duty as a Van Zale partner."

I knew better than to argue with Cornelius once he started talking about moral duty. This was obviously the moment when I should tell him I wanted to go to Germany to work for the ECA, but although Cornelius seemed to be in an exceptionally sympathetic mood, I couldn't help thinking the moment was hopelessly wrong. To reject his daughter, lose the Hammaco bid, and then ask for a prolonged leave of absence would surely be begging for trouble . . . or would it? On reflection it occurred to me that perhaps the reverse was true, and now was the perfect time to ease myself away from the wreck of the battlefield. I decided to take the chance and confide in him.

"Well, Neil, I've been feeling kind of screwed up about everything lately. When I was in Germany—"

"Oh, Christ," said Cornelius. He returned to the liquor cabinet, took out two large glasses, and poured us both double brandies. "I wish to God you'd stay away from Europe," he said. "You know how it always upsets you. I can't think why you had to go back to Germany last month. If I didn't know you so well, I'd say you had masochistic tendencies."

I had a moment of acute loneliness. I realized then how isolated I was, unable to communicate my most private feelings to those around me. I wanted to talk about Germany, to unburden myself of the memories of my recent visit—even to confess every detail of the ordeal of growing up German-American during and after World War

I—but no one wanted to listen. Cornelius became exasperated every time I mentioned the word Germany; Jake had long since turned his back on me; Kevin was a stranger. Even Teresa, the one person I most wanted to confide in, had inexplicably distanced herself from me by retreating behind her work.

I groped for the words which would communicate my feelings without alienating him further. "Germany means something very special to me, Neil," I said with difficulty at last, "just as America means something very special to you. Do you remember how upset you got in the Depression when you found out people were living in caves in Central Park? Well, people are living in air-raid bunkers in Germany. The port of Hamburg's closed and thirty thousand men are unemployed. And all through the Ruhr—"

"Yes, yes, yes," said Cornelius. "It's terrible, of course it's terrible, but we'll fix all that. The Americans will patch up Europe as usual, and maybe we'll have a few years of peace and quiet before World War III—"

I saw my opportunity and grasped it. "That's exactly the point I want to make, Neil. The Americans are going to rebuild Europe, and I want to be a part of that. In fact, I've got to be a part of it—it's my moral duty, if I may use your own favorite phrase against you."

"Trash," said Cornelius, who was much shrewder than his fondness for ingenuous moral platitudes would suggest. "It's not your moral duty. It's your guilt."

"Okay, it's my guilt! That doesn't make my desire to take a leave of absence from Van Zale's in order to work for the ECA any the less real! Don't you see, Neil? Can't you understand? This is a very special opportunity for me to work in a just, meaningful cause, and if I let it pass me by—"

"Christ, you're talking like some idealistic kid of eighteen!"

"I wasn't allowed to be an idealistic kid of eighteen," I said. "Maybe it would have been better if I had been. Maybe it would have been better if I'd never met Paul, never come to work here, never got involved in a life where I spend my time blackmailing and cheating and lying—no, don't interrupt me! You asked me to tell you what was bothering me, so let me have my say! This Hammaco bid simply underlines everything that's wrong with my life, Neil. Twisting Whitmore's arm, trying to screw our rivals, being counterscrewed by them in return—and all for what? So that Van Zale's can bank another million bucks! So that Hammaco can go into the armaments business and step up the cold war! Can't you see how wrong it all is? Can't you see it's empty? And what the hell does it all mean anyway? Don't you ever ask yourself that sort of question? And don't you ever have that kind of doubt?"

"Never," said Cornelius. "I enjoy my work, I enjoy my position in life, and I'm entirely happy with no regrets, no misgivings, and no morbid introspection of any kind."

"Oh yeah?" I said, drinking my brandy too fast. "Then let me ask you a couple of questions. Do you never think of Steven Sullivan? And do you never remember Dinah Slade?"

VII

I HADN'T intended to ask those questions. Nowadays Cornelius and I seldom mentioned our old enemy Steve Sullivan, and we never under any circumstances referred to Dinah Slade.

It was now over twenty years since Cornelius had first clashed with Steve. Although barely out of our teens, we had by our hard work at the bank since Paul's death acquired a certain confidence, and Cornelius had begun to feel he could no longer tolerate his most powerful partner's indulgent, patronizing contempt. However, when he first suggested that we might try "persuading" (his word) Steve to abandon the New York office in order to run the London branch of Van Zale's, I thought he had gone mad.

"How could we ever force him to do that?" I was scared as well as horrified. The idea of us kicking Steve out of One Willow Street conjured up a vision of two kittens trying to deprive a lion of his dinner by hauling him away by the tail.

"Don't be dumb, Sam," said Cornelius, always astonished by the naiveté which even after two and a half years at the bank I still occasionally displayed. "Have you really forgotten what happened when Paul died?"

To protect the bank after Paul's murder in 1926, Steve had been driven to conceal the true facts of the crime from the police and pursue his own private, ultimately successful vendetta against the murderers. Cornelius now proposed the time had come for us to use this technical obstruction of justice as a lever to oust Steve from Willow and Wall.

"But that's blackmail!" I said, appalled.

"No, no, no," said Cornelius soothingly. "There's no extortion of money involved. I'm just going to point out a few facts, apply a little logical persuasion. What's wrong with that? Salesmen do it all the time."

I wasn't present at Cornelius' interview with Steve. I just sat in my office and waited dry-mouthed. I didn't think he could possibly succeed in twisting Steve's arm, but I admired him very much for having the guts to try.

Eventually he rejoined me. He looked a little white around the mouth, but his smile was radiant.

"You did it?" I gasped.

"Sure." Cornelius tried to sound nonchalant and failed. We laughed, and after I had shaken his hand with enthusiasm we hurried home for a celebration drink. I remember thinking as we scampered up the steps of Paul's Fifth Avenue mansion and yodeled "Yippee!" exuberantly in the hall, that Cornelius was the most remarkable person I had ever met and that I was very lucky to have him for a friend. I knew it was in my best interests to like him, since my future success as a banker lay in his hands, but I could never have worked for any man I despised. Nowadays, when Cornelius has such a reputation as a despot, many people find it hard to believe how generous he was to me when we were young, sharing his home and his wealth readily with me, never taking advantage of our disparate financial and social positions, as willing to stand by me as I was to stand by him during our early struggles to survive at the bank. He was loyal and straightforward with me always, irreproachably honest, untiringly considerate and good-natured. He was also—and nowadays plenty of people might find this hard to believe too—great fun. We had a lot of laughs together in the old days, particularly during that golden summer of 1929 after we had ousted Steve Sullivan from New York, and I'll never forget my twenty-first birthday when we threw a huge party, drank illegal champagne, and danced with our favorite girls to the music of "Alexander's Ragtime Band."

We were not alone in enjoying the summer of '29. Far away in London Steve Sullivan had become involved with the young woman who had been Paul's mistress, Dinah Slade. Since we knew it was only a matter of time before he fought back to reestablish himself in New York, we regarded this new alliance with extreme suspicion.

Dinah was more than just Paul's former mistress. She was also one of his celebrated protégés, and in 1922 he had set her up in her own

London cosmetics business. She was seven years our senior, evidently competent, obviously ambitious, and although we had never met her, Cornelius had long regarded her as a threat to his peace of mind. His antagonism was probably rooted in jealousy; she had been very close to Paul and highly regarded by him. She had even borne Paul a son, Alan, who was later killed in the war. Cornelius, who had set his heart on being Paul's heir, not unnaturally disliked the idea of this illegitimate son's existence, and it had been a great relief to him when the child had been omitted from Paul's will.

"If Steve's messing around with Dinah Slade," he said to me in 1929 when rumors of Steve's exploits reached us from London, "he's up to no good."

"At least she may keep him securely anchored in London!" I suggested hopefully, but I was wrong. The Wall Street crash brought Steve back to New York, and once he was home he soon bulldozed himself into an impregnable position at Willow and Wall. It took the 1933 government investigation into investment banking to drive him back to Europe to avoid testifying before the committee (Van Zale's, like so many other eminent investment-banking houses, had lived recklessly before the Crash), but once he was back on the other side of the Atlantic, our troubles with him began in earnest. Leaving his wife, he renewed his old ties with Dinah Slade. Later he married her, confirming our suspicion that the two of them had formed an unbreakable alliance, but before they could attempt to reestablish Steve's control over the bank, Cornelius had moved to outflank them. The senior partner in New York was "persuaded" to retire (a routine income-tax-evasion problem had been uncovered by us some time before), and when Cornelius assumed control of the New York office, he also assumed the whip hand over Steve. Steve had a free rein at the London office, but ultimately London was answerable to New York. All we now had to do was set Steve up in a tight corner. Then we could cut him down when he tried to break out.

"This time we've got him," I observed with relief, but I was wrong, for now it was Steve's turn to outflank us. Resigning from Van Zale's, he used the money from Dinah's cosmetics business to found his own London issuing house, and soon our best European clients were leaving Van Zale's to follow him. Although Steve was no longer a Van Zale partner, it seemed the war was far from over; on the contrary, as Cornelius remarked, incensed, it had entered a new, even more virulent phase.

"What are we going to do?" I said in despair.

"Well, of course," said Cornelius, "he'll have to be stopped. He's annihilating our London business. The survival of our entire European office is at stake."

"But how can we possibly stop him?"

"When attacking the enemy," said Cornelius, "always aim for the Achilles' heel."

"His drinking problem?"

"What else? We'll let it be known that he didn't resign from Van Zale's. We'll say all the partners combined to force his resignation on account of his alcoholism."

"But that's slander!"

"Then let him sue! Let him get up in a witness box and try to convince a jury that he's taken the pledge!"

I was disturbed. "But are we morally justified in cracking his reputation like that?"

"What's morality got to do with it? This is survival! We have to protect our interests in Europe!"

This was undeniable. I clamped down on my doubts, and the rumors began.

Soon afterward we heard Steve had been admitted to a private nursing home which specialized in the treatment of alcoholics, and we realized he was making a serious effort to overcome his drinking problem.

"Okay," said Cornelius, "this is where we move in for the kill. I'll broadcast from one end of Wall Street to the other that Steve's been hospitalized for DTs, and you'll go to London to spread the news around the City. Oh, and while you're there, make sure you fix him. And I mean *fix* him. For good. I want all the world, not just the financial community, to know that he's a drunken has-been."

"But short of forging a photograph of him at this place and getting it printed in a national newspaper, I don't see how—"

"Exactly. Do it."

"But—"

"Sam, I want that man to see that newspaper and know that he's *finished*. Got it? Look, this guy's been persecuting us for years. He's done untold damage to Van Zale's, and if we let him crawl away from this mess now, he's sure to try to stab us in the back as soon as he's recuperated. We've got to finish him now, Sam. We must. What choice do we have? It's his fault—he's forcing us to take this action. We're just victims acting in self-defense."

"Neil, you don't really believe that. You can't."

"Oh yes, I do!" said Cornelius fiercely, and then he said in a very polite voice, "I hope we're not going to quarrel about this, Sam. I hope you're not going to try to tell me what I should do for the good of my firm."

I looked at him and he looked at me. I knew at once that I was being presented with a reality that I couldn't afford not to face, the reality that my best friend was first and foremost my boss, who could and would fire me if it suited him. It was a bleak, bare, bitter moment of truth.

I thought, though of course did not say aloud: You've changed. Things shouldn't have to be this way between us. We should still be the friends we were long ago back in the twenties at Bar Harbor.

And when I thought of Bar Harbor, I remembered Paul saying to us all: "If you boys want to get on in life, don't waste your time yearning for the way things ought to be. Just concentrate on dealing with the way things really are."

"Well?" said Cornelius.

I stood up and turned away from him. "I'll have my secretary book a passage to England right away."

I arrived in London.

I obeyed my orders.

Steve died.

He had been on the wagon for some time by then, but when he saw the forged photograph, he drank a bottle of Scotch and tried to drive from Norfolk to London to see me. His car crashed into a tree somewhere near Newmarket. There was no other car involved in the accident. He died later in the hospital.

"Tell Cornelius I'll never forgive him," wrote Dinah to me in reply to my formal letter of sympathy, "and I'll never forget."

"That's a declaration of war if ever I heard one!" said Cornelius at once when I relayed the message. "Okay, this is where I take care of that lady once and for all."

I'd met Dinah in London and liked her. I was feeling sickened by the part I had played in Steve's death, and amidst all my guilt I was conscious of revulsion. "I think we've done enough, Neil. Let her be."

"I'm not asking you to do anything but sit on the sidelines! I'm going to settle this score in person!"

"Neil, Dinah loved Steve. She's suffered enough—"

"Shut up. Stop trying to give me orders."

"I've no intention of giving you orders! I'm just trying to point out—"

"Forget it! That woman's been nothing but trouble for years and years. She tried to stop Paul making me his heir—of course she always wanted her son to get the Van Zale fortune. She broke up my sister's marriage to Steve, and you know as well as I do that Emily's never been the same since that bastard walked out on her. She gave Steve the money to set up his own banking business in order to smash Van Zale's in the teeth—naturally he'd never have been able to do that without her backing. And now . . . *now* she's got the god-almighty nerve to declare a new round of hostilities! I'm sorry, Sam, but my patience is exhausted. I'm going to teach that woman a lesson she'll never forget."

But in the end it was Dinah who did the teaching; in the end it was Cornelius who received the lesson he never forgot.

By a malign combination of circumstances, he had the legal means to deprive her of her home, Mallingham Hall, and now he decided to embark upon his revenge by evicting her. He went to England himself in 1940 to administer the coup de grace, and although I saw no possibility of Dinah turning his inevitable triumph into a defeat, I found later I had underestimated her. She outwitted him by burning the house; she destroyed her ancient family home rather than let it fall into Cornelius' hands, and by that act of destruction she proved to him that there were some things no money could buy, no power could extort, and no man, not even Cornelius, could corrupt. She didn't even give him the chance to get even with her. On the day the house was destroyed, she sailed to France to take part in the historic rescue of the British Army at Dunkirk, and when she failed to return, it was as if she had outwitted him yet again. She died a heroine's death, putting herself beyond his reach once and for all; he lived on with the memory of her indisputable victory.

"So she won," I said to him when he eventually returned to New York. I had to say that. It was a mistake, but I couldn't resist it. I suppose I knew then that I too often wanted to turn the tables on Cornelius but suspected I would never have the courage to do so.

He just looked at me. Then he said: "I refuse to discuss that woman with you either now or at any other time. I never even want to hear her name mentioned again." And he turned his back on me before I could reply.

I kept my mouth shut after that. Day after day, month after month, year after year I never raised the subject with him, but at last on that April day in 1949 when my guilt and my self-disgust and my unbearable isolation were driving me far beyond the barriers erected by my common sense, I heard myself put to him the two questions which I knew should never be asked:

"Do you never think of Steven Sullivan? And do you never remember Dinah Slade?"

VIII

CORNELIUS' EYES assumed their remotest expression. He sipped his brandy and looked out of the window. "I hardly think the subject of Steve Sullivan and his last wife is germane to our present discussion."

"But I think it is! I think the Sullivan affair shows as clearly as this Hammaco mess what kind of lives we've been leading since you gained control of this bank back in the thirties, and I think you should be reminded occasionally that we ruined Steve Sullivan and drove him to his death!"

"As far as his death was concerned, I disclaim all responsibility. He got drunk and drove his car into a tree, and that was that."

"He would never have got drunk if you hadn't ordered me to—"

"I did what I had to do. He left me no choice. Sam, do please stop trying to drown yourself in your own misplaced remorse! I happen to find these neurotic displays of guilt very tiring."

"Okay, maybe you can argue that Steve left you no choice but to fight him to the very end of the line. But what about—?"

"I'm not interested in discussing Dinah Slade. It was hardly my fault that she sailed off on a suicide mission! I categorically deny all responsibility for her death!"

"Then why did you take care of Steve and Dinah's three little kids after Dinah was killed? Why did you bring them back here for the duration of the war? You were shamed into it by your guilty conscience! You were shamed into it because she died a heroine's death after wiping the floor with you and making you look cheap and small!"

"This is pure fantasy, Sam. Obviously you must have had too much to drink. It wasn't my decision to bring those children to America in 1940. Emily insisted on it. Of course it was typical of Emily to volunteer to look after her ex-husband's children by the woman who had usurped her."

"Was it? Are you sure Emily didn't take care of those kids because she's your sister and she felt in some degree responsible for the wrong you'd done?"

"Now you appear to be suffering from some sort of persecution mania. There's nobody alive today who knows exactly what happened back in the thirties when Steve and I were fighting for control of this bank. Certainly Emily herself knows virtually nothing about what went on."

"But do you think she isn't smart enough to have figured out what happened? And tell me this, Neil: do you honestly think Scott hasn't figured it out as well?"

Cornelius swiveled round in his chair. "Scott and I understand each other."

"Are you sure? Neil, that's what I meant when I said that maybe you should take time out occasionally to remember Steve Sullivan; maybe you shouldn't just keep on telling smug lies to yourself about how you've no guilt and no regrets; and maybe, just maybe, if you think hard enough about it, you'll see that it's not me but you who's slipping out of touch with reality. I think Scott's trouble, Neil. I know his story has always been that he hated his father ever since Steve walked out on Emily to chase after Dinah Slade; I know your story has always been that he's more devoted to Emily than he was to his own mother and that he's as close to you as a kid brother. But the plain fact is that neither you nor Emily is related to him by blood and that when all's said and done he's the son of the man you ruined. Don't get me wrong—I like him. But I don't trust him. I think he's a time bomb ticking quietly away under our feet. When the time comes, don't offer him a partnership. Help him into a partnership in some other house, if you're so fond of him, but whatever you do, get him out of this bank at Willow and Wall."

Cornelius had quietly picked up the receiver and was dialing Scott's number on the interoffice phone. I stopped speaking. At the other end of the wire Scott picked up the receiver.

"Scott," said Cornelius politely, "could you please come down here right away? Thank you."

He hung up. We waited. Neither of us spoke, although I knew what was coming. In trying to tell him how to run his firm, I had made a huge mistake, which Cornelius was quite unable to stop himself compounding. Any challenge to his authority always compelled him to make some gesture which would unequivocally underline his power.

Scott slipped quietly into the room and closed the door. "Yes, sir?"

"Sam and I were very pleased by how hard you worked over the Hammaco bid," said Cornelius courteously, "and I think the time has come to offer you a partnership."

"Cornelius!" He smiled radiantly and his black eyes shone.

I looked away as they shook hands, but finally I too had to offer my hand in friendship. "Congratulations, Scott!" I said. "Nothing could please me more!"

"Thank you, Sam!" His handclasp was firm and unhurried.

Cornelius said they would discuss the details later, and after Scott had withdrawn exuberantly I sat down again without a word. The remaining brandy in my glass tasted bitter.

"Now, Sam," said Cornelius mildly, "I've come to the conclusion you're seriously overwrought, so I've decided you need a little extra vacation. I'll put through a call to La Guardia field right away and have my private plane placed at your disposal for the weekend. Why don't you take Teresa down to Bermuda?"

I managed to say, "Thanks, but we've got tickets for *South Pacific* tomorrow night."

"You have? Wonderful! That should help you forget your problems for a few hours! And talking of those problems, I think it would be better if we didn't discuss the future anymore right now—it wouldn't be fair to you in your present state."

"Neil—"

"Oh, don't think I don't understand! I understand absolutely! You're suffering from a crisis of confidence, the kind of thing which usually overtakes men of fifty, not men in their prime like you and me, but you'll get over it, Sam. You just need a little time to recover from this visit to Germany, but once you've recovered, you'll be viewing things from a sane, rational point of view again and then you'll see very clearly how foolish it is to talk of taking a leave of absence in order to pander to some unfortunate obsession you have as the result of being a German-American."

"But—"

"Relax! Don't you worry about a thing, Sam! And don't you think I won't stand by you through this crisis. Believe me, I'm not going to let you mess up your life by doing something you'll regret later! After all, you're not just my partner, are you? You're as good as my brother, so in the circumstances I consider it my moral duty to look after you and save you from yourself—"

"Neil, I can't take that moral-duty crap from you right now, I'm sorry. Just cut it out."

Cornelius sighed. "I thought it was appropriate, since—unless I've misunderstood you—you've just been trying to lecture me on the subject of my moral standards. Sam, I don't want to get too tough with you when you're in such a low state, but maybe I'd better tell you I'm not too interested in listening to you preach sermons. If I want to hear a sermon, I'll go to church. 'Render unto Caesar the things that are Caesar's and unto God the things that are God's,' said Christ, meaning churches and banks should be kept separate, and that was damned smart advice. Now, I know I'm no saint here, but outside these walls I've always tried my best to live a decent life, and if God's doing any kind of accounting at all, he'll see at a glance that my life's like a double-entry system—and I think he'll realize too, once he tots up the debits and credits, that there are far worse guys than me around. . . . Do you understand what I'm saying?"

"I ought to. I've heard it often enough."

"Then do me a big favor, would you, and apply what I've just said to this business of Scott. Maybe it's possible to criticize me for my handling of the Sullivan affair, but if I was ever at fault, I've made amends through Scott. I've brought that boy up since he was fourteen years old. I've done everything I possibly could for him, and he's a good boy, Sam. Get that into your head, and do please try not to be so neurotic about him in future. I'm proud of the way Scott's turned out, and if you think for one moment that he isn't grateful to me for picking up the pieces after Steve had made such a disgusting mess of his paternal obligations—"

The intercom buzzed, and when Cornelius flicked a switch we heard his secretary say, "Mr. Van Zale, I have your sister on the phone, and she wants to speak to Mr. Keller. Is Mr. Keller still in conference with you?"

Cornelius and I looked at each other, both equally surprised.

"Yes, he is. Just a moment," said Cornelius abruptly, and leaning forward, he handed me the receiver of the phone so that I could take the call from Emily Sullivan.

Chapter Five

I

"I WANTED to talk to you about Vicky," said Emily Sullivan at lunch the next day. "Cornelius has told me everything. He finally broke down and confessed."

"He did? Uh . . . pardon me, Emily, but could you possibly . . . ?"

"Elucidate? I'm referring, of course, to this thoroughly misguided suggestion that Vicky should marry you."

Almost twenty hours had elapsed since I had received the disastrous news from the president of Hammaco, and Emily and I had just finished lunching at my apartment. It was two o'clock on Saturday afternoon.

I had thought it odd that Emily had wanted to see me, but the idea that she might discuss some topic other than her niece was one I had never seriously considered. Like Alicia, Emily had always been on good terms with me, but over the years our relationship had remained formal.

Emily was forty-three and looked it. She had not kept up with feminine fashions, and in consequence her clothes seemed dowdy. She had become plump, and although not plain, she somehow managed to look nondescript. Twenty years ago any stranger would have noticed the family resemblance between Emily and Cornelius, but now it was possible to look at them without realizing they were brother and sister. Cornelius had effortlessly held on to his good looks; Emily, apparently just as effortlessly, had let hers slip away.

Yet still there were moments when she reminded me of him, and sometimes I thought that the more dissimilar they became in looks, the more alike they became in personality. Emily, a ruthless administrator, dominated numerous civic committees in Velletria, the wealthy Cincinnati suburb where she had grown up, and according to Cornelius her days were filled with charitable duties which required hard work, determination, and an outstanding ability to ride roughshod over any obstacles which stood in her way.

"As soon as Cornelius confessed his scheme to engineer a marriage between you and Vicky," said Emily, toying with the glass of hock which she had hardly touched during the meal, "I knew it was vital that I should talk to you."

"But, Emily," I said, "you can relax! Neil himself has assured me that he's abandoned the idea, and even if he hadn't, I wouldn't go along with it. I'm very much involved with someone else."

Emily visibly sagged in her chair with relief. "Thank you, Sam. That's exactly what I wanted to find out. I wasn't sure how far to believe Cornelius when he said he'd given up the idea, and knowing that he's more than capable of manipulating people to the altar under the mistaken conviction that it's in everyone's best interests, I felt I couldn't rest until I'd spoken to you. I'm sure I don't have to remind you of the part Cornelius played in promoting my own marriage to Steve, and what horrified me so much about this latest matrimonial meddling of his was how easily such a marriage could happen if you were a willing accomplice. It would only take the minimum of effort on your part to make Vicky fall in love with you."

"Well, I . . . . Emily, aren't you exaggerating a little? I'm flattered, of course, by the implied compliment, but—"

"Come, Sam, false modesty doesn't suit you. I don't think Cornelius, being a man, has any idea how attractive you could be to a young girl like Vicky if you put your mind to it. Vicky's by no means a stupid girl, but she's very young still, and her upbringing has, to put it mildly, left a lot to be desired. She's wide open to the attentions of a smart sophisticated man of her father's age whose celebrated professional charm has been legendary for years."

"Why, Emily, how very unpleasant you make me sound!"

"That wasn't my intention. I was just trying to be honest, and besides, I happen to believe that fundamentally you're a decent man who wouldn't want to hurt Vicky in any way. The answer to Vicky's problem, of course, is education. There's a long tradition in our family that the women should be well-educated, and if Vicky is taught how to think properly, she'll be able to cope with the difficulties inherent in her position as an heiress. She must go to college. Then maturity will follow, as night follows day."

I refrained from reminding Emily that her own studies at Wellesley had not saved her from the mistake of marrying Steve Sullivan.

"You don't share Alicia's view," I said tentatively, "that education is a waste of time for a girl whose obvious destiny in life is to be a wife and mother?"

"Well, I'm devoted to dear Alicia," said Emily, finishing her hock with an effort, "but one really cannot expect useful comments on the education of intelligent girls from a woman whose favorite occupation appears to be listening to soap operas on the radio."

"I think Neil also has doubts about whether college is the answer to Vicky's problems."

"Cornelius," said Emily, "should pause to examine his past. It was a pity *he* never went to college! If he hadn't been so severely undereducated as the result of his asthma, perhaps *he* wouldn't have got in such a mess when he was young! That disastrous first marriage to Vivienne, and then . . ." Her lips pursed at the memory of Cornelius' scandalous elopement with Alicia. "Cornelius was never the same after Uncle Paul started paying him all that attention," she said. "My dear mother often remarked upon it when she was alive. Cornelius changed . . . but he was such a dear little boy when he was young, and so sweet-natured!"

I raised my eyebrows wryly, but she wasn't looking at me. "Education," she repeated with a severity no doubt intended to counterbalance this unexpected display of sentiment, "is the answer. With a college education, Vicky will be better equipped to settle down, marry, and have children, just as all women should. . . . No, I won't have more coffee, thank you, Sam. I must go back to Fifth Avenue. I promised I'd take Vicky shopping this afternoon to buy clothes for Europe. The passages are booked for Wednesday, so there's very little time."

"I'm glad your girls will be joining you tomorrow. Remember me to them, won't you? I doubt if I'd recognize Lori now! Fourteen, is she, or fifteen?"

"Almost sixteen. And Rose is eighteen."

"You don't say! Well, how time flies. . . ."

We said good-bye with polite relief, and I was just retrieving the unfinished bottle of hock from the dining room when the telephone rang.

"Sam," said Teresa, "I hate to tell you, but I'm calling with bad news. . . ."

II

I THOUGHT of Cornelius saying: "Trouble always comes in threes."

"Why, what is it, honey? What's the problem?"

"I've got some kind of virus and I'm feeling like Mississippi mud. I don't see how I can make it to *South Pacific* tonight. I'm very, very sorry."

There was a pause. I could not immediately master my disappointment, but at last I said, "I'm sorry as well. That's too bad." A picture flashed through my mind of Teresa lying on her bed, the canvases stacked along one wall beyond the easel, the sunlight slanting through the skylight onto her tousled hair. "I hope you feel better real soon," I said in a friendly, concerned voice, and suddenly remembered Emily referring to my "professional charm" as if it were a pair of gloves that could be pulled on and peeled off at will.

"Well, I've just taken three aspirin, and with any luck I'll pass out for a few hours and wake feeling better. . . . I'll call you tomorrow, honey, okay?"

"Sure." I stared blankly at the forty-foot living room designed, decorated, and furnished for the man I was supposed to have become.

"I must see you," I said suddenly. "I must."

"Of course. We'll get together just as soon as I can stand up without feeling like I'm dying. Now, Sam honey, I don't want to hang up on you, but . . ."

"I understand. You just rest up and take care of yourself, and we'll talk later."

I hung up and sat for a long time looking at the silent phone. After I had finished the wine I threw the tickets for *South Pacific* in the trash basket, but halfway through my next cigarette I retrieved them. The thought of all the trouble I had taken to get those tickets made me reluctant to throw them away, and I started calling my friends to see if they had made plans for the evening. Everyone seemed to be busy. Finally, exhausted by the effort of making polite conversation after the offer of the tickets had been declined, I abandoned my friends and tried to think of an acquaintance who would not care if I sounded unsociable. Immediately I remembered Scott, and decided that after my disastrous show of hostility it might well be politic to make a friendly gesture in his direction.

"Hello?" said Scott, picking up the receiver in his East Side apartment.

"This is Sam. Could you use a couple of tickets for *South Pacific* tonight?"

"Thanks, but Broadway musicals just aren't my ball game. I'm sure someone else would appreciate the show far more than I would."

"Can you think of anyone? I'm about to throw the tickets away."

"Let me see." Scott applied himself to the problem as if it were some difficulty that had arisen at the office. "Could Cornelius go with Vicky?" he suggested finally. "It might take their minds off their joint troubles for a couple of hours."

"I happen to know Cornelius and Alicia are going out to dinner tonight. You wouldn't want to be noble and take Vicky yourself, would you, Scott?"

"I'm dining with Emily. Why don't *you* take Vicky? Or are you the one who's had to cancel this date?"

"No, it was the other party who canceled."

"Then there's your answer. Take Vicky and do everyone a favor, including yourself! You don't want to miss this show, do you?"

"I guess not," I said. "No, I don't. Okay, thanks for the suggestion —I'll think about it."

I fixed myself a highball and sat listening to my Glenn Miller tape as I considered the situation. I had nothing to lose by following Scott's advice. Since Vicky was due to leave for Europe within days, no one could suspect me of embarking on some sinister seduction campaign if I took her out, and unlike the various other women whom I might have asked to take Teresa's place, she would not expect me to go to bed with her. It would be an unemotional evening free from sexual pressure. I thought I could just about tolerate it. It seemed the right thing to do.

Picking up the receiver, I started to dial.

III

SOUTH PACIFIC.
Rodgers and Hammerstein.
The curtain rose on Mary Martin. The curtain rose on Ezio Pinza. The curtain rose on actors dressed in American uniforms, and suddenly I was no longer part of that packed house west of Broadway. I was three thousand miles away in the quiet peaceful countryside near Munich, and in a terrible fusion of my conflicting nationalities, the G.I. at my side was whistling "Lili Marlene."

IV

MY GERMAN relatives were all killed in the war. In 1940 my cousin Erich, a pilot in the Luftwaffe, was shot down in the Battle of Britain. In 1942 I heard from friends in Zurich that the family's little house in Düsseldorf had been bombed and my aunt was dead. In 1943 my uncle's factory was destroyed. He was taken to a hospital but did not survive. Kristina, my favorite cousin, was the only one who lived till the end of the war. I had no communication from her, but after V-J Day I received a brief letter saying she was working in a hospital in Munich; she had requested a transfer from the army hospital in Düsseldorf after her mother's death, and one of her best friends had been transferred with her. It was this friend who wrote to me three months later to say that Kristina too was dead, killed accidentally in some shooting incident. I wrote back at once for further details, but when I received no answer I knew I would eventually have to summon the nerve to find out exactly what had happened.

It took me four years to summon that nerve. Men came home from Europe and described appalling conditions, and it was not until 1949 that I thought matters might have improved sufficiently to make a visit bearable. I flew to Europe in mid-March.

I had no trouble tracing the girl who had written to me, since I had met her before the war in Düsseldorf and I was able to contact her through her family. Having returned to Düsseldorf, she had given up nursing and was working as a hostess in one of the new nightclubs which served black-market smoked salmon at twelve dollars a head to the hoods who could afford it. She did not want to talk to me, but I insisted that she have a drink with me at my hotel.

It took me an hour of steady questioning before she told me what had happened. There had been a party. Kristina had left late, and when she was only halfway home she had been shot. She had walked into a trap set for a gang operating on the black market, and the military police had opened fire without realizing she was innocent.

"Military police?" I repeated, to make sure I had not misunderstood.

"Yes. They were soldiers." And the girl had looked me straight in the eyes and said in English, "*Your* soldiers. They were Americans."

I somehow got out of Düsseldorf. I went to Bonn and Cologne before I realized I had to get out of the entire Rhine valley. I headed south, an anonymous tourist who spoke perfect German; I looked down from the hill at Nuremberg on the ghastly ruins of the old city, and I walked among the shattered streets of Munich where Kristina had spent her final days. I saw the American soldiers in the streets but I did not speak to them, and they, thinking I was German, did not speak to me. I remained alone, locked up in the isolation of my grief, until one night at my hotel I met a foreigner whose German was as flawless as my own, and we began to drink together.

He was an Englishman.

Eventually he said, "You wouldn't recognize the City of London now—and did you ever go to Coventry when you were in England before the war?" But when I said I could understand that he must hate the Germans, he just laughed and said, "No, the English hate the French. We've had hundreds of years of experience in perfecting that particular art, but we're still novices at hating the Germans."

It was hard to tell how serious he was, for he was very drunk and the English have such a curious sense of humor, but I was very drunk myself, so I just said, "I've now reached the point where I don't hate anyone. Hatred makes things worse. Hatred stops one coming to terms with all the horror and grief. And one must come to terms with it. Somehow."

"Ah, the horror, the horror, the horror!" said the Englishman rapidly, and now I could detect the understated black humor he was using to soften the starkness of our conversation. "Let me tell you about the horror I found when I went sightseeing today. Thought I'd get out of Munich for a quiet day in the country. Found myself at a little place called Dachau. Of course they don't advertise it as a tourist attraction, but the G.I.s on duty there will show you around."

I said, "Don't tell me about it. I don't want to know."

But as soon as the words were spoken, I knew I had to know every detail.

The young man I had been before the war had danced to a German tune but had been forced to leave the dance floor before the music ended. The older man I had become had studied the music in manuscript and knew in theory how the tune finished, but he still had to hear those final bars. He had to have no doubt whatsoever in his mind what tune he would have danced to if he had been permitted to remain on the dance floor till the party's end.

I went to Dachau.

There are some things which cannot be spoken about. I once met a man who told me he had spent three years as a prisoner of war, but when I found out that his captors had been the Japanese, the conversation ended because I knew there was nothing else that could be said. If someone had asked me after my return to America, "What place in Germany made the deepest impression on you?" and I had answered, "Dachau," that admission too would have precluded further conversation. I could not have spoken of it. Perhaps I might have said it was a mild springlike day when I went there and everywhere was very quiet and peaceful, but I could not have spoken of the photographs of the piles of bodies being moved by bulldozers; I could not have spoken of the fingernail marks raking the ceilings of the gas ovens; and I could never have spoken of how I felt afterward when I walked back across the polluted earth to the gates, and the G.I. at my side whistled those last lingering bars of "Lili Marlene."

V

MARY MARTIN was singing "I'm Gonna Wash That Man Right Outa My Hair" and the audience was loving it. I looked around at the happy, rapt faces of those who had survived the war to live in a country untouched by destruction, and although I was one of them, I felt cut off, isolated by my survivor's guilt. It was then I knew that if Cornelius continued to refuse me a leave of absence I would resign from Van Zale's, because no man, not even Cornelius, was going to stop me from following my conscience and wiping out the guilt I could no longer endure.

Mary Martin had finished washing her hair onstage and the audience was shouting for an encore.

I thought again of my unique opportunity to wash away my guilt by working for the ECA. By working for both America and Germany simultaneously, I could make amends to Germany for the killings of the American soldiers and yet also make amends to America for my refusal to fight the Nazis. It was the one valid solution to my dilemma, my one chance to escape forever from the painful conflicts of my past, and suddenly as I sat in that Broadway theater my position seemed clearer than ever before; I felt as if I had been marked for survival in order that I might make my own special contribution to the postwar world, and although I was not a superstitious man I was convinced then that if I ignored this role which had been assigned to me I would not long survive in the empty world I had built for myself in New York.

Mary Martin was singing an encore. The little girl at my side was watching with shining eyes. The show went on . . . and on . . . and on. . . .

VI

"Wasn't that a great show, Uncle Sam?" said Vicky with enthusiasm.

Her pale blue evening frock had a full skirt, a high neckline, and no sleeves, while her hair, coiled in a knot, was pinned on top of her head to make her look grown-up. She was wearing the minimum of makeup, and her fair delicate skin had the bloom of a peach which some gifted master gardener had been tending with infinite care.

"Of course musicals are very low-brow," she was saying brightly, "but I guess even composers like Wagner enjoyed a beer-garden singsong in between writing episodes of the Ring. Do you like Wagner, Uncle Sam?"

"Who?" I said, teasing her, and we both laughed.

"I thought you might have enjoyed the Teutonic ambience! Of course he had a lot in commin with Nietzsche."

We were at the Copacabana, and the band, taking a break from the new craze for the rumba, was playing a waltz. A passing waiter refilled our champagne glasses.

"Oh, I feel so much better!" Vicky exclaimed. "I wish life was always like this—the theater, the Copa, waltzes, and champagne! I can't thank you enough for taking me out, Uncle Sam—it's just such a wonderful change from everything that's been happening lately."

Unexpectedly I remembered Emily saying in a rush: "Cornelius was such a dear little boy and so sweet-natured!" I smiled at her. "I'm grateful to you for accepting my invitation," I said readily. "It would have been a real waste of a ticket if you'd stayed home."

I started to think of Teresa again. Was she really ill or was she in such a state of depression over her work that she had been unable to face a night out on the town? I resolved to call her as soon as I returned home.

"Do you have any records of this band, Uncle Sam? Tell me more about your record collection."

I began to talk about my records, but as I spoke of the music of Louis Armstrong, Kid Ory, and Miff Mole, I could think only of that other music, the rustle of discarded clothes, the creak of the bed, the harmony of sighs, the polyphony of pleasure. I drank my champagne and murmured to Vicky about nothing, but all the while in my mind I was with Teresa, my beautiful Teresa, and in my mind's eye I could see her lying naked among the tangled sheets, the little gold cross slipping out of sight between the curves of her breasts.

". . . Uncle Sam?" said Vicky.

"I'm sorry, honey—what did you say?"

"Can we dance, please?"

"Why, sure!" I said, feeling guilty that I hadn't issued the invitation myself, and escorted her at once onto the dance floor.

Her hand touched my shoulder. Her body brushed mine. I was with Teresa yet not with Teresa, in bed yet out of bed, in heaven yet down on earth at one and the same time.

I felt the instinctive reflex in my groin and recoiled from her. My voice said, "Excuse me just one second . . ." and then I was moving fast, edging past the other couples on the floor, and heading blindly for the men's room. The pivacy came as a sickening relief.

Later, after I had washed my hands, I wiped the sweat carefully from my forehead with a handkerchief and polished my glasses. My vision cleared. Looking in the mirror, I saw with relief that my face was empty of tension, and making a great effort, I summoned the energy to return to the dance floor.

I found Vicky sitting stiffly at our table while she watched the dancing. The band was playing a fox-trot.

"Hi!" I said smoothly with my easiest smile. "Sorry about that! I ate something for lunch which . . ." I stopped. I had noticed how pale she was, and now I saw that she was unable to look at me. I had stepped back quickly on the dance floor, but evidently not quickly enough, and in one disastrous moment a lighthearted evening had been transformed into the stickiest of social morasses.

I knew at once that some sort of acknowledgment would have to be made if we were to meet in the future without embarrassment, so I sat down, forcing myself to remain casual, and said in my most relaxed voice, "Why, you must be so tired of all males exhibiting the same unoriginal behavior on the dance floor! And to think I wanted to be different from the average kid in a tuxedo out on his first date! Say, I know it's a lot to ask, but could you possibly find it in your heart to treat my unbelievably juvenile reflex as a compliment? I assure you I'm not usually so overcome whenever I ask a lady for a dance!"

She looked at me with great searching gray eyes. I waited, holding my breath, but evidently she found what she needed to find in my expression, for she was able to say without difficulty, "Okay. Thanks for the compliment."

We made no effort to dance again, but we had some coffee while I told her about a recent business trip to Los Angeles, and there was no awkwardness between us. It was only when we left the building that she said shyly, "It's just as well you're not really my uncle, isn't it, or your compliment would have been kind of awkward."

"You bet!" I agreed, striving to maintain my relaxed tone of voice, but the Western slang sounded unpleasantly strained in my ears.

She said nothing else. As my chauffeur opened the door, she slipped into the back of the Mercedes while I, taking great care not to touch her, followed her inside.

"It was a lovely evening," she said politely as we drove through the gates of her father's house. "Thanks again."

"My pleasure—it was fun." That sounded much too smooth. My casual manner was being shredded by the razor edge of my tension. "Well, so long," I said rapidly as I helped her out of the car and gave her hand the briefest of clasps. "Have a wonderful time in Europe, and don't forget to send me a postcard!"

She stared down at her gloved hands.

"Vicky?" I said sharply.

"I . . . I feel all confused . . . upside down. I don't even know if I want to go to Europe anymore."

Above us the front door opened and Alicia, immaculate in an unadorned black dress, swept down the steps to the driveway.

"Hello, dear, did you have a nice time? Good, I'm so glad. Thanks so much for being kind enough to give her a treat, Sam. I'm sure we all appreciate your generosity. Do you want to come in for a drink? We had to cancel going to the dinner party—Cornelius had an emergency meeting of one of the foundation subcommittees, and in fact he's still out, but of course if you'd like a quick Scotch . . ."

Evidently she was doing her best to restore normal diplomatic relations after her harsh words to me the previous Wednesday, and I smiled to show her I was equally anxious for a truce. "Thanks, Alicia, but I have to be getting home," I said, taking care to sound regretful, and then I glanced once more at Vicky. "Europe's the best place for you now, believe me," I said. "Once you're there, you'll get a fresh perspective and then you'll be able to sort out everything far more easily than if you'd stayed in New York."

"I . . . guess so."

"I know so. 'Bye, Vicky. *Bon voyage.*"

"Thanks." She did not move, and although I looked back at her over my shoulder, the light from the hall was behind her and I could not see her expression. It was only when she spoke again that I knew our relationship had entered a new and irreversible phase.

"Good-bye, Sam," she said.

Chapter Six

I

As soon as I reached home, I dialed the number of the house in Greenwich Village.

"Tom?" said Kevin, pouncing on the phone. "Where the hell have you been?"

"Sorry, Kevin, this is Sam."

"Who?" said Kevin blankly.

"Sam, you crazy guy! Sam Keller! Say, how's Teresa? Is she feeling better?"

There was a pause. Then: "Just let me focus for a minute," said Kevin. "God, what a relief to forget about my private life and concentrate on someone else's! Teresa? She's still locked up in the attic with the aspirin bottle, Sam. She asked not to be disturbed."

Now I was the one who hesitated. "She *is* there, isn't she?" I said suddenly. "You're sure she's there?"

"Christ, yes! Don't be ridiculous! Sam . . ." He stopped.

"Yes?"

"I'm just emerging on the wrong side of a hideous love affair. If you're at a loose end, why don't you come out and get drunk with me?"

Kevin and I weren't drinking companions. For a second our different worlds bumped together awkwardly and were still.

"For God's sake, Sam, I'm not trying to proposition you! What filthy minds you heterosexuals have!"

"Well, I didn't for one moment suppose . . ."

"I'll meet you at your apartment in twenty minutes," said Kevin, "and we can go and hit the bottle someplace midtown."

He hung up. I sat exactly where I was for ten seconds. Then I blundered downstairs into the damp dark April night and grabbed a cab downtown to the Village.

II

THERE WERE two entrances to Kevin's house, the front door and the basement door, which had once been the servants' entrance. I had often wondered why Kevin had not set the basement level aside for his caretakers, but supposed the attic's north light would be more attractive to artists than the gloom below street level.

Like Teresa, I had the key to the servants' entrance. The back stairs began in the basement and coiled upward to the attic past the doors which opened into the first- and second-floor hallways.

Above the basement I opened the first of these doors and looked out. The lights were on but everywhere was silent. "Kevin?" I called in a low voice.

There was no answer. Checking his study at the front of the house, I found he had abandoned his work not merely in the middle of a scene but in the middle of a sentence. I went to the kitchen. Amidst the debris on the crowded kitchen table I found two dirty plates, two empty wineglasses, and a half-finished bottle of California red, while on the stove the remains of filé gumbo, one of Teresa's favorite creole dishes, clung pungently to a large pot.

I remembered Teresa was supposed to be too ill to cook. I remembered Kevin had been waiting for a friend and had probably planned on being out that evening. The next moment I was back on the attic stairs.

On the second floor I had to stop to get my breath. The stairs were lit below me, but above my head the last flight of stairs remained in darkness, and I made no attempt to turn on the light. Leaning against the wall, I listened to my heart thumping against my chest and wondered if I were on the verge of making some disastrous mistake, but I knew that even if I were, there was nothing I could do to avoid it. I could not now walk away. I had to go on.

I had just put my foot on the first step of the final flight when I heard Teresa cry out. The cry appalled me. I knew exactly what it meant, and as the blood rushed to my face I clawed my way up the remaining steps in a haze of rage and pain.

In those last seconds I saw it all and remembered everything, the casual arrogant conversation between Jake and Cornelius the previous Wednesday, Teresa gazing fascinated into their rich privileged world, Jake taking notice of her and idly asking for a date. Violence welled up in me. Of course Jake would have got a kick out of taking my girl. I was still a Nazi in his eyes, and the Jews were never going to forgive the Nazis, never, never, never. . . .

I flung open the door of the attic, punched on the light, and stopped dead in my tracks.

There was a flurry from the bed, but I paid no attention because all I saw were the paintings. The canvases were lined up neatly along the wall like pictures in a street exhibition, and even the cloth was gone from the half-finished work on the easel.

No one said anything. The bed was in shadow in the corner behind me, and because I knew what I would find there, I felt no curiosity, only an instinctive urge to postpone the pain of that final confrontation for as long as possible. The paintings gave me the excuse I needed, and mesmerized I moved closer to the canvases.

I saw pictures, neat, bright, and obsessively detailed, of small-town American life. I saw the little white frame houses, the row of stores, and the corner bar all clustered beneath the shadow of an enormous slag heap, and in the distance were the mountains and a little white Polish church on a hill. Exquisite care had been lavished on every detail of that scene, and as I understood the intense yearning which lay behind that representation of a past recaptured, my throat ached, for I saw that Teresa in her art had achieved the impossible. She could move freely between one world and another. The looking glass was no barrier to her. By drawing on the vital living entity of her past, she had conquered the rootlessness of the present and triumphed over the American dilemma which had defeated me.

"He'll never understand," I said to her. "Never."

There was no answer. I turned slowly to face them, and saw with a shock that wiped my mind clean of all emotion that the scene was even more appalling than I had imagined.

The man with Teresa wasn't Jake. It was Cornelius.

III

TERESA WAS rigid with fright. Her fingers clutched the sheet tightly across her breasts, as if she had forgotten I was accustomed to her nakedness, and her eyes, reflecting the horror of my presence, were wide and dark. She tried to speak, but of course there were no words which could adequately have expressed how she felt.

I was still looking at her when he slipped softly from between the sheets and stooped to recover his clothes from the floor. They were casual clothes, a rich man's clothes for bumming around, white pants, open-necked checked shirt, loafers, a corduroy jacket. He looked so young, but young and tough, not young and vulnerable, his hard mouth set in its firmest line, his fine eyes downcast, his movements rapid and economical. When he was dressed, he turned his back on her to look at me, but I still felt nothing, no violence, no pain, no rage. I felt lobotomized by the shock. I just stood there dumbly, and as I stared, he walked right up to me and said with his familiar iron nerve, "It was wrong. I'm sorry."

"Take her," said my shaking voice. "She's yours, you bastard."

And before another word could be said, I left them and stumbled out of the house.

IV

IT WAS raining. I walked to the corner of the block and paused, unable to remember where I was. There were no cabs in sight. The Village was a blurred mass of bright lights and shiny windows and people trying to dodge the rain. Later I seemed to be on Eighth Street west of Fifth Avenue, although I had no memory of walking east from Kevin's house. A prostitute accosted me. I could not understand what she wanted. The sound of one of Frank Sinatra's songs was drifting through an open window nearby.

Later I realized I was on the subway in a train crashing dizzily uptown, but I struggled to the surface at Herald Square because I knew I was going to be ill. I vomited into the gutter, stumbled forward a dozen paces, and vomited again. People looked at me as if I were a Bowery bum, but presently another prostitute accosted me and I had to cross the road to get rid of her. Standing shivering by Macy's amidst the brilliant city lights, I felt as if I were part of some huge sordid canvas, the antithesis of Teresa's paintings, a hell on earth bounded by concrete and great barred doors marked "No Exit."

I somehow got hold of a cab.

"Park Avenue and . . ." I could not speak properly, and the vomit had left a bitter taste in my mouth. As the car rocketed along Thirty-fourth Street, I looked up as if searching for a glimpse of the natural world in the wet night sky, but all I saw was the glazing hulk of the Empire State Building and beyond it the glow of manmade light canceling the darkness of nature.

At my apartment building I paid off the cab and groped my way into the lobby.

"Sam . . . at last!" It was Kevin. I had forgotten about him, and as I stopped, my eyes mechanically recorded the details of his appearance, the figure which made casual clothes look smart, the fine lines at the corners of the eyes which needed no glasses, the fighter's jaw which marred his matinee-idol looks. It was only then, as I watched him with a stranger's detachment, that I realized what a stranger he was to me. We might have shared all the usual adolescent confidences long ago at Bar Harbor, but in later life we had never had one single conversation on any meaningful subject.

He took one look at my face and saw what had happened.

"You fool," he said. "I tried to head you off."

"You tried too damn hard."

Some indefinable change in his expression dissolved the mask of his exuberance, and for the first time in my life I saw him not as the boisterous extravert who gave the best parties in town but as the enigma who wrote plays in blank verse which I did not understand.

"Let me come up to your apartment," he said, "and I'll fix you a drink."

"I've got to be alone."

"No. Not just yet. Better not."

I had no strength to argue with him, so we rode the elevator together in silence to my penthouse. In the den I slumped down on the couch while he poured out the brandy, but it was only when he sat down opposite me that I realized how grateful I was that he had stayed. Violent emotions were struggling at last to the surface of my mind, and the violence frightened me. I wouldn't have wanted to be alone.

"What a mess I made of that phone conversation," he said. "I guess it was because I was so upset."

"Tell me—I want to know exactly . . ."

"He turned up at eight. Teresa had been cooking, and when the doorbell rang I assumed it was you. I don't mind her using the kitchen for an important date so long as I'm out, and I was supposed to have plans for the evening—but I was stood up. That's why I was there when he arrived. He was very embarrassed when I answered the door, and even tried to embark on some explanation, but I cut him off, told him I didn't want to listen because I had problems of my own. Then I shut myself up in my study and tried to work. Needless to say, I couldn't."

I drank my brandy. Kevin poured me another.

"Listen, Sam," he said at last, "this is a disaster of catastrophic dimensions, I realize that, but if you and Teresa really have something going for you, for God's sake see if you can't still work things out—no, listen to me! Just listen! The one fact to focus on in this mess is that the situation's not just horrific, it's inexplicable."

I looked at him blankly. "Inexplicable?"

"Yes—totally incomprehensible! Just think for a moment. We both know Neil well enough to realize that, incredible though it may seem, he's not your usual run-of-the-mill millionaire like Jake, who routinely goes around screwing whoever catches his fancy. He's a one-woman man. Have you ever known him to be unfaithful to Alicia before?"

"No, I . . . never have."

"Okay, so you can concede that this is extraordinary behavior for him. But it's extraordinary behavior for Teresa, too. Given her absorption in her work, she just doesn't have the time, let alone the inclination, to practice bed-hopping on a grand scale."

I tried to sort this out, but it was too difficult for me. "What are you getting at?"

"I'm trying to say that I think tonight's episode is more likely to be a freak accident than the opening scene of some grand passion."

"I think you're wrong," I said. My lips were stiff and it was still hard to form my words properly. "I think she's fallen for him in the biggest possible way."

"Why?"

"She showed him her pictures." I could hardly get the words out. My hand reached automatically for the glass of brandy.

"Jesus Christ!" said Kevin in disgust. "Couldn't she see that Neil's the world's biggest philistine? He can only define art in terms of a checkbook and a balance sheet!"

In the hall the buzzer sounded, making us both jump. Brandy slopped onto the table as the glass jerked involuntarily in my hand.

"Stay where you are," said Kevin. "I'll deal with this."

But I followed him to the hall.

"Yes?" he demanded, picking up the receiver of the intercom. There was a pause. I could hear nothing, and I was just moving closer when Kevin said tersely, "Take my advice and beat it. You've caused enough trouble for one night."

I grabbed the receiver from him. "Teresa?" I said.

Down in the lobby Cornelius cleared his throat.

"Come up," I said, and severed the connection.

Kevin looked skeptical. "Are you sure you can handle this right now?"

"Yes. I want to kill him, but I won't. I'm glad now I was too shocked even to beat him up in the attic. I think you're right, Kevin. There's got to be some sort of explanation. I just can't believe . . ."

I paused to wipe the sweat from my forehead, but at last I was able to say evenly, "I'm not working anymore at Van Zale's. That's finished, along with my friendship with Neil. But if I could only take Teresa with me to Germany, maybe—"

"Take Teresa to Germany?"

"Yes, I'm going to work for the ECA. They're recruiting investment bankers to help rebuild the German economy. I'm going to work for a new Europe. I'm going to put everything right."

"But, Sam . . . Sam, Teresa would never be able to work if she were removed from America and isolated in some country where she couldn't speak the language!"

"But she wouldn't be isolated! I'd marry her—of course I'd marry her! We'd have a nice new home with one of those modern kitchens where she can practice all those creole recipes, and we'd have three or four kids, and . . . Why are you looking at me like that?"

The bell rang, and turning abruptly away from Kevin, I unlatched the door.

Cornelius, looking chilled and delicate, walked past me without a word and halted beneath the center light in the hall. His fists were shoved deep into the pockets of his pants. He was huddled in his corduroy jacket as if the temperature outside was below zero.

"Sam, can I see you alone, please?" He did not look at Kevin.

"No."

"But—"

"*No,* goddammit! Stop arguing and get into the den!"

We went into the den.

"Have some brandy, Neil," said Kevin.

"No, thanks. Kevin, how the hell did you get in on this act?"

"I might ask you the same question! Sam and I have just agreed it's inexplicable that you and Teresa should have ended up in bed together. How did it happen?"

Cornelius swung to face me. "Sam, do we really have to air our most private troubles in front of someone who isn't interested in women and therefore can't understand a single word we say?"

"I'm very interested in women," said Kevin, getting up to leave. "Probably more interested than you are. But I agree I'm not interested in seducing my best friend's girl. I leave that kind of pastime entirely to men like you."

"Stay where you are, Kevin," I said abruptly. "He's only trying to get rid of you because he's planned the entire conversation on the basis that there would be no third party present."

Cornelius sat down very suddenly on the edge of the couch, and without a word Kevin brought a third glass from the living room and poured out the brandy. We all drank in silence, and when I saw Cornelius was drinking fastest of all, I felt better. As soon as my nerves were steady I said, "Okay, I'm listening. Talk. But tell me the truth, because if you start lying to me, I'll—"

"Okay," said Cornelius rapidly. "Okay, okay."

I waited. Kevin waited. Cornelius looked increasingly miserable but finally said, "It was all kind of an accident. I was feeling upset. Personal problems. But I'd like to make it clear that I love my wife, and if you think I'm on the verge of divorce, you couldn't be further from the truth."

No one argued with him. We went on drinking and waiting.

"I had to talk to someone," said Cornelius, "but I didn't know anyone suitable. Maybe I should have gone to a call girl, but I didn't think I wanted sex, and anyway I don't approve of that kind of thing. Finally I decided to go to see you, Kevin, because you always seem to cheer me up if I feel depressed."

"Make up your mind," said Kevin. "One moment you're behaving as if my sexual preferences make me some kind of moron, and the next moment you're saying you were craving my company."

"Oh, hell! Listen, I'm sorry—"

"Okay, forget that. Go on. You wanted to talk to me . . . so you arrived at my house and asked for Teresa. Let's hear you talk your way out of that one."

"I only asked where she was because I wanted to talk to you on your own! But you were in such a filthy mood that you gave me no chance to explain anything!"

"This is all so unlikely," said Kevin, "that I suppose it just has to be true. But can you please explain why, if your visit was so spontaneous, Teresa had spent at least two hours cooking dinner for you?"

"I don't think she was cooking specifically for anyone. She said cooking was therapy—she liked to cook when her work wasn't going well. She said she was depressed about everything, so depressed that she'd canceled a big date with you, Sam—"

"—so the two of you sat down in the kitchen," I said, painfully remembering the abandoned filé gumbo and the bottle of California red, "and had dinner."

"That still leaves you a long way from the attic," said Kevin cynically to Cornelius. "What happened next?"

"Well, I didn't feel like talking, but I was grateful to her for being hospitable, so I felt I ought to make an effort at conversation. I asked her if she'd seen the Braque retrospective at the Museum of Modern Art, and we talked about modern art for a time, and I told her about the Kandinsky I've just bought for my office—"

"All right, we get it. You gossiped about art. And then I guess she invited you upstairs to see her pictures."

"Wrong," said Cornelius. "She didn't. She tried to hand me some garbage about how her paintings weren't good enough for anyone to see. Of course I was fascinated. Jesus, when I think of all the artists in New York who try to ram their stuff down my throat . . . and here was this girl behaving as if she'd rather die than let me look at her work. 'It's just junk!' she kept saying. 'Only junk!' 'So what?' I said. 'I see a lot of junk in the art world. Junk holds no terrors for me, none at all.' And I set off up the stairs to the attic. She ran after me, and all the way upstairs she kept saying she was no good, useless, a fifth-rate Norman Rockwell. I thought it was cute she should be so shy . . . Anyway, I got up to the attic and took a look at the pictures, and they weren't bad at all, in fact some of them I liked very much. The style is American primitive, of course, but she's got strong classical overtones in her draftsmanship. I said, 'Your work reminds me of Breughel,' and she said, 'That's the most wonderful thing anyone's ever said to me,' and suddenly . . . well, I don't know . . . she looked so sweet and earnest, and . . . the bed was right there and . . . it happened."

He stopped. When nobody said anything, he drained his glass of brandy. "Of course it was unforgivable," he said at last. "I won't make excuses for myself except to say that I was very upset, emotionally unbalanced by my private problems—"

I lost my temper and sprang to my feet. "Are you trying to tell me that's the whole story?" I said, my voice shaking with rage. "Do you really think I'm going to believe this fairy tale?"

Kevin's eyes widened. Cornelius looked sick.

"I told you not to lie to me!" I shouted. "I warned you—"

Kevin stepped between us. "Take it easy, Sam. What makes you so sure he's lying?"

"He's telescoped two separate occasions into one!" I elbowed him aside. "You first slept with her the very night you both met, didn't you?" I shouted at Cornelius. "You slept with her last Wednesday! That was the night you had your big row with Alicia as the result of my revealing to her that you wanted me to marry Vicky. And it was the next morning—Thursday—that you nearly passed out with asthma in your office when I told you I planned to marry Teresa. She'd given you the impression that her affair with me was over, and you'd assumed it was as much my decision as hers—you were horrified when you discovered my feelings for her were far stronger than you'd been led to believe! In fact, you were so bursting with remorse that ever since you've been bending over backward to be nice to me, telling me to forget about marrying Vicky, telling me not to worry about the Hammaco disaster, offering me your private plane for a weekend in Bermuda—"

"Right," said Cornelius. "Right. Absolutely right. Yes, that was the way it was. It was all her fault for giving me a false impression of the way things really were. I'd never have deliberately taken Teresa away from you, Sam, I swear it."

"Then if that's the way it was, you son of a bitch, *why did you go back to her tonight* when you knew beyond any shadow of doubt how I felt about her?"

"She invited me," said Cornelius.

Kevin had to restrain me from hitting him. Words streamed from my mouth, but I was speaking German and no one could understand. I groped for the right words, but my vocabularies were inextricably mixed and at last I gave up, slumped down on the couch, and put my head in my hands.

"I didn't want to tell you that," said Cornelius, "because I knew you'd be hurt. That's why I tried to make out that last Wednesday's scene happened tonight. Last Wednesday happened just as I've described, except that you'd gone to bed, Kevin, by the time I got back to your house, and Teresa, who was clearing up the jambalaya in the kitchen, invited me to have some coffee instead of some filé gumbo. As I said, it was all a sort of casual accident which I'd made up my mind was never going to be repeated. And then late last night at the office—after you'd gone home, Sam . . ." He stopped.

"Go on," said Kevin when I still could not speak.

"Teresa called me and invited me to dinner tonight. I said, 'You've got one hell of a nerve,' but she couldn't see it. 'No man owns me,' she said. 'I'll do what I like. I'm sorry for Sam,' she said. 'He's a nice guy. But he's not for me and never will be.' 'Okay,' I said, 'if that's the way you feel, so be it, but you'd better damn well straighten things out with Sam so that he knows where he stands.' 'Oh, sure,' she said, 'but I'm fond of Sam and I don't want to hurt him more than I have to—I've got to find the right moment to tell him.' 'Find it real soon,' I said, and hung up. Then I sat around and thought about the situation. I knew I was being stupid. I knew it would be much better to leave her alone. But you see, I had these problems . . ." He stopped again. "I can't explain any further."

There was a silence. I suddenly felt very, very tired, so tired that even my rage toward him was impossible to sustain. I myself might have made his mistakes if I had been laboring under similar misapprehensions, and I believed him when he said he had only lied to save me from further unhappiness. It would have been so much easier for me to have thought of him as the aggressor, with Teresa the reluctant victim. The thought that their roles had been reversed was intolerable to me.

"I won't go back to her," said Cornelius at last. "I couldn't. Not after this."

I repeated the words I had spoken in the attic. "Take her. She's yours."

Kevin said strongly, "I think you should talk to Teresa before you make any final judgment on the situation."

"Kevin, can't you see that I've been given the gate in the biggest possible way? If it hadn't been Neil, it would have been someone else. Teresa was evidently ready to move on. Perhaps I've subconsciously known that ever since she started inventing excuses not to see me."

"Yes, but . . . ." Kevin pushed back his hair in a distracted gesture. "There's a lot I still don't understand about this," he said finally. "We now know Neil had certain unspecified personal problems which made him act out of character, but what we still don't know is why Teresa acted out of character—why she ditched you in the worst possible way by two-timing you with your best friend. I just don't understand that at all."

I was so exhausted I could barely shrug my shoulders. "Neil can talk art to her. He's better-looking than I am. Isn't it just a question of trading in last year's automobile for a newer, more exciting model?"

There was a slight pause before Kevin said gently, "Sam, are you sure you've ever really known Teresa? She's not just a facile girl who'd carelessly trade you in for a better-looking partner who can talk art with her! She's a complicated woman who's apparently decided—for reasons I can't begin to fathom—that Neil can help her sort out her problems better than you can." He set down his glass and moved toward the door. "You go to Germany, Sam," he said, still speaking gently but no longer looking at me, "and you find one of those famous women who think of nothing but *Kinder, Kuche, und Kirche*. Believe me, you'd never be happy with someone like Teresa. You can't recognize the conflicts arising out of her work, and even if you could, I doubt if you could cope with them. . . . Come on, Neil, let's go. I think it's time we gave Sam a chance to recover."

Cornelius lingered in the hall. "Sam, we'll get over this, won't we? I know it's a terrible thing to have happened, but—"

"Oh, for Christ's sake, get the hell out and leave me alone!"

Cornelius trailed away, a small forlorn figure with a pinched expression.

When they had gone, I remained in the hall until I heard the whine of the elevator descending to the lobby, but at last, when the ensuing silence became too great to endure, I headed blindly back to the brandy bottle to put myself beyond the reach of my pain.

V

SHE CAME to see me the next day. She wore a neat black coat and skirt, a frilly white blouse, and a little black hat with a feather in it. I hardly recognized her.

I was hung over and not thinking clearly. When I heard her voice on the intercom, my first thought was that she wanted me back. It was only when I saw the formality of her clothes that I realized the affair was not to be resurrected from the grave.

"Hi," she said awkwardly, her hands twisting the strap of her purse. "It was nice of you to let me come up. I promise this won't take long."

Unable to speak, I opened the door wider, and as she passed me I had a strong urge to take her in my arms. But before I could move, she said in a low voice, "I came because I owed you two things: an apology and an explanation."

I pulled down the shades of my personality so that my pain would remain private, and suddenly I saw my so-called "professional charm" for the defense that it was, a suit of armor protecting me from the rigors of the life I had chosen for myself. I tried to discard the armor, but no discarding was possible. It was as much a part of me as a skin graft, and if I tore it away I knew I would bleed to death.

"Well, I guess I could use an apology!" I said, smiling at Teresa good-humoredly. "Thanks!"

Teresa said in a polite voice, "I wasn't going to apologize for sleeping with Cornelius."

No suit of armor is impregnable. I turned away in retreat. "Come into the living room and have a seat," I said, somehow keeping my voice calm and courteous. "Excuse me looking like a hobo—I'll have to start getting up earlier on Sunday mornings! Can I fix you some coffee?"

"No, thanks."

We went into the living room and I lit our cigarettes with a steady hand. Outside, rain was falling again. I could see my plants gleaming wetly on the terrace and swaying in the cold wind gusting up Park Avenue.

"I was going to apologize for not leveling with you," said Teresa.

"I wanted to apologize for fobbing you off with excuses instead of telling you the truth. I was such a coward, Sam. I'd like to think I couldn't face telling you because I was genuinely fond of you and I knew you cared so much. That was certainly one of the reasons for my cowardice. But there was another reason. I couldn't face the truth about myself. We all live with our little illusions, don't we, and sometimes it's not so easy to cast aside those defenses and face the world stark naked."

"I understand."

"Do you? I wonder. This is where we get away from the apologies and into the explanations. It would be so easy to say: 'Oh, you've never understood me!' but the situation's not as simple as that. I think in theory you understand me very well—the problems of a European-immigrant, blue-collar background, the drive to make it in New York, the continuous pressure to compromise one's principles in order to get ahead . . .'' She checked herself before continuing levelly, "You understand all that. But you're like a child trying to do a sum before he's been taught math. You can recognize all the figures but you can't add them up."

"I'm not sure I follow you."

"Let me give you an example. You know in theory how important my work is to me. Yet in practice you continue to treat me as if I'm capable of leading a normal life, and you're quite unable to accept me as I am. When you proposed marriage, you weren't proposing to *me*—you were proposing to the woman you were determined I should become."

"But that's not true! I would never have tried to change you, Teresa, I would never have asked you to give up your painting! I've always respected your career!"

"Oh, you say that so glibly, Sam, but Jesus, you just have no idea what that means! You respect my career—oh, sure! But it would always have to take second place to *your* career and what *you* wanted and what *you* thought would be best for our marriage!"

"Well, naturally, in any marriage there have to be certain priorities . . ."

"I only have one priority, Sam. My work. That's why I'm not interested in living with anyone or being domestic or trying to put a husband's interests first as a good wife should. Perhaps you can have some idea of what I'm trying to tell you if I say that my drive to work is stronger than my drive for sex. I like sex—there's no substitute for it, and I'd certainly miss it if I didn't have it, but if I had to be celibate I'd survive somehow. But I couldn't survive without my work. That's why I've been so miserable lately. I've been so confused about my personal life that I've been unable to work—I find it impossible to be creative if I'm in a state of mental disorganization. But I've straightened myself out now by facing up to the kind of person I really am—and don't think it was easy. It wasn't."

"I don't understand. Are you saying—?"

"I'm saying it's easier to conform and pretend one's just like everyone else, marking time until Mr. Right comes along to ring the wedding bells and wave the magic wand which will make everything take second place to married bliss—I'm saying it's much easier to pretend one's potentially as sweet, selfless, and domesticated as the ideal woman's always supposed to be. But I'm not sweet, selfless, and domesticated, Sam, and what's more, I never could be. I'm not going to change, and once I'd faced up to that truth, I had to accept that I just didn't want someone like you. I thought I did. I *wanted* to want you. But I can't cope with a nice guy with normal domestic inclinations. I need someone who recognizes that he'll always take second place to my work, someone who already has a wife to give him the family life I can't provide, someone who'll offer sex, but on a strictly part-time basis, someone, in other words, who's just as selfish as I am. I need someone like Cornelius."

After a long while I stood up and went to the window. The rain was still streaking down, and clouds obscured the summits of the skyscrapers. Staring through the mist toward Wall Street, I said at last, "I want to know exactly what happened."

"I don't think I can discuss Cornelius with you."

"I'm not interested in his performance in bed. I just want to know how you arrived there." I took off my glasses and started to polish them. "You and I may be finished," I said, "but I've still got to come to terms with this situation before I can move on to someone else, and I can't come to terms with it unless I know the whole truth. I'm beginning to believe what happened was inevitable, but I've got to be sure, can't you see? Please . . . I wouldn't ask you to speak of it unless I felt it was important."

"Well, I . . . can I have a drink?"

"Sure." I checked the clock and was surprised to see the hands pointing to noon. "What can I get you?"

"You wouldn't have any Wild Turkey bourbon, would you?"

We laughed politely, two strangers sharing a distant memory.

"How about a martini?"

"Okay."

I fixed two Beefeater martinis, very dry, with plenty of ice and three olives apiece. I had no inclination to drink, but I knew it would be the best cure for my hangover, and I wanted to think clearly.

"You remember I refused to invite you up to the attic last Wednesday evening," said Teresa.

"I remember."

"Well, after you'd gone, I did go back upstairs and try to work again, but it was useless. Finally I gave up and went down to clear up the mess in the kitchen, but as I struggled with the cleaning up, I just felt worse than ever. I sat down and thought: Here I am, twenty-five years old, penniless, going nowhere. I couldn't even claim I was starving for my art, because the truth was that although my savings had run out, I was being temporarily kept by Kevin. That morning he'd given me two weeks to get a job and pay my own way, but the fact remained that at that particular moment I was living off him. It made no difference that he was homosexual. If anything, it made the situation worse, since I was taking money from him and giving nothing in return. And I thought: What a fraud I am! What a hypocrite, boasting to you of my independence but taking money from Kevin whenever your back was turned. . . . And I despised myself.

"Then Cornelius arrived. It was kind of late by that time, but when I told him Kevin had gone to bed he said it didn't matter and could he please have a cup of coffee in the kitchen. I couldn't figure him out at all. He seemed to be in some sort of emotional state which prevented him from speaking—he just sat at the kitchen table and drank coffee. It was eerie. In normal circumstances I'd have been embarrassed, but I was so upset I just thought: Oh, screw him, and I didn't bother to make conversation. Then, right out of the blue he said, 'Do you like that Braque Sam keeps in his living room?' and I said, 'I've seen better.'

"We talked about art for a time. I don't know why Kevin has this idea that Cornelius is a philistine, because although Cornelius may be incapable of holding a paintbrush, he seems to have a good eye for art—he certainly talks more sense about it than most people one meets. Anyway, eventually he asked about you, and I said—admitting it out loud for the first time—that it was useless and I intended to break up with you.

"Then he said, 'Great! Can I see your pictures?' and we both laughed because of course it was such a cliché, a variation on the old line about etchings. When I told him he wouldn't like my paintings, he said, 'Try me.' I can't describe how he looked, but suddenly I had this intuition that he was just right for me, so I said, 'Okay,' and took him upstairs. I was talking all the time because I was so nervous, but he wasn't fazed at all, and then I realized that the feeling was mutual, that he—for whatever reasons—had decided I was just right for him.

"He was nice about my paintings . . . very nice. I . . . . it's hard to explain, but he was honest. I couldn't have taken it if he'd been insincere."

After a moment I said, "I see."

Crushing out her cigarette clumsily, she stood up. "There's nothing more to tell and I've got to be going. . . . Forgive me, Sam. I know I've treated you badly and I'm very sorry that I've hurt you like this. I hope you find someone else real soon."

I stood up too to escort her to the door. "I'd like to ask you for a parting favor," I said evenly. "May I buy one of your pictures? I'd like the one of the street with the slag heap in the background and the little white church on the hill."

The silence was absolute. Turning to look at her, I saw she was motionless, and I thought dispassionately how odd we must have looked together, she so tidy in her trim black suit, I so uncouth in my crumpled bathrobe.

Suddenly she began to cry. The tears filled her eyes and spilled down her cheeks, but she didn't speak.

I said, "Is it sold?"

She nodded, scrabbling for the handkerchief in her purse.

"How many did he buy?"

"All of them."

"When's the exhibition?"

"In the fall . . . his gallery . . . he's getting together a collection of American primitives."

"Uh-huh. Congratulations."

"Oh, Sam . . . honey . . ."

"Don't worry," I said, "I won't ask if he promised you the exhibition before or after he'd gone to bed with you. Good-bye, Teresa. We may not both have ended up in the same bed, but we've certainly ended up in the same boat. If the sea gets too rough, just give me a call and I'll do what I can to help. Believe me, anyone owned by Cornelius Van Zale needs all the help they can get."

VI

HE HAD bought her.

I showered, shaved, and dressed carefully in my best gray suit, a crisp white shirt, and my favorite dark blue tie.

I could have forgiven him if the relationship had been triggered by some unexpected mutual compatibility, such as their interest in art. I could have forgiven him if he had been overtaken by an improbable but not impossible catastrophe such as love at first sight. I could even have forgiven him if he had discovered some magic formula not available to him elsewhere for happiness in the bedroom. But Cornelius was rich. He was handsome. He could have had any woman he wanted to gratify a sexual impulse which his wife was apparently unable to satisfy. There was no need for him to have taken Teresa, smashed the standards which had made her so special, and transformed her into an awkward embarrassed woman in black whom I hardly recognized.

The truth was, he had seen her, she had amused him, and he had acquired her, much as he had acquired the Kandinsky painting which hung over the mantel in his office. I was reminded of Paul Van Zale, satisfying his obsession with power by writing his cynical opinions on the blank slates of his protégés' impressionable young minds, and I saw then what a fool I had been, drawing her into Paul's tainted world and expecting her to remain unchanged. It was ironic to remember that for a long time I had been unable to consider marrying her because I had felt she could never fit into that world. Now, thanks to Cornelius, she fitted in far, far too well.

I knotted my tie. I brushed my hair, parting it to make the best of my hairline, and when I had finished, I surveyed myself carefully in the mirror. I was perfectly dressed, perfectly groomed, in perfect harmony with my perfect penthouse, and leaving the bedroom, I returned to the living room to finish my drink.

It had stopped raining. The clouds had lifted from the shining spire of the Chrysler Building, and for a moment I stared out of the window as if I were staring backward into the past for a glimpse of the young man I had been once at Bar Harbor. But the young man had been lost long ago, my early life was just an imperfect memory, and the road back to my other world was wholly blocked by the filth I had waded through in the pursuit of my American dream. The past could never now be recaptured. I might have recaptured it with Teresa, but Teresa was gone, swallowed up in the filth, and I knew at last beyond any doubt that no matter how many times I returned to Bar Harbor in the future, I would never go home again.

The past was sealed, like a tomb. That left the future.

I had one thought, and one thought only. I said aloud to the Chrysler Building, "He's not going to get away with this." And to myself I said, "I'll make him pay."

Germany could wait. I'd get to Germany in the end, and I'd make amends for the past, just as I knew I must, but I wouldn't turn to the ECA to underwrite my dreams; I'd turn to Cornelius Van Zale.

I thought of Cornelius declaring on numerous past occasions: "When dealing with an enemy, always aim for the Achilles' heel."

I thought of Cornelius' Achilles' heel. I thought of it for some time.

Of course I wouldn't hurt her. How could I? It would be a pleasure to look after someone so cute and pretty and sweet-natured, and I would do everything in my power to ensure she was the happiest little girl in New York. She could have a beautiful home, plenty of servants, a charge account at Tiffany's, and a baby every other year, and everything would be moonlight and roses. It would be good to be married at last, and with a young wife like Vicky I'd be the envy of all my friends. I pictured my mother's expression when she saw her first grandchild for the first time. I pictured a honeymoon which I took infinite care to ensure was idyllic. I pictured dining by candlelight every year with my wife on our wedding anniversary, and giving her diamonds and furs and everything she could possibly want. . . .

I stopped, reminded myself that I was a practical man, and surveyed the situation from a more detached point of view, but the conclusion I reached was the same. I had had enough filth in my private life. I had had enough of women who left me, sold out, and slept with other men. I wanted innocence now, I wanted purity, I wanted a decent normal happy home with a pretty young wife, four bright promising kids, and a beautiful home in the suburbs—first the New York suburbs, then the suburbs of Bonn. . . .

Cornelius would hate it, of course, but what could he do? I'd write my own ticket. I'd have him by the balls.

I moved to the phone, and when the English butler picked up the receiver in the Van Zale mansion, I never hesitated.

"This is Mr. Keller, Carraway," I said in my most charming voice. "May I please speak to Miss Vicky?"

PART TWO

Alicia: 1949

Chapter One

I

"SAM'S MARRIED Vicky!" gasped Cornelius. He could hardly speak. His breathing was erratic.

I allowed myself three seconds to register this monstrous news before I paid full attention to his condition. "I'll get your medication," I said, slipping out of bed. "Lie down."

He was standing in the doorway that connected our bedrooms, but when I spoke, he obediently groped his way to my bed and subsided among the pillows. He was a bad color and in considerable discomfort.

In his bathroom I found the vial, removed two tablets, and filled a glass of water. I had lived with him too long to be frightened by his asthmatic seizures, but I was upset because I knew how much he hated me to see him in such a humiliating condition.

Half an hour passed with agonizing slowness. I wanted to send for the doctor, but the suggestion was rejected. Cornelius was an expert at diagnosing the severity of each attack, and just as I was on the point of overruling his decision, he became better. Even so, it was still another twenty minutes before he attempted to speak. His first words were: "This is the worst day of my entire life."

"Now, calm down, Cornelius, or the asthma will come back."

"*Sam's married Vicky!*" he shouted at me.

"Yes, dear. I can't imagine why you should be so upset. Wasn't this exactly what you wanted?" I stooped to straighten the bedclothes.

Rolling over, Cornelius buried his face in the pillow with a groan. His bright hair curled on the white linen, and taking advantage of his averted face, I sank down on the bed and touched the nearest strand. Since hair has no sensory nerves, he felt nothing, but I still held my breath for fear he should be aware of me.

I had just withdrawn my hand reluctantly when he flung himself over onto his back again, and the abrupt movement pushed the bed-clothes below his waist. His pajama jacket, which I had unbuttoned at the start of the attack, was open, and I saw he was still faintly sun-burned from our Caribbean vacation in February. Below the crisp golden hairs which covered a neat oval in the middle of his chest, I could see the fine bones of his ribs and the hard smooth masculine texture of his skin.

"I heard the phone ring," I said at last. "Where were they calling from?"

"Annapolis. They were married this afternoon in Elkton, Maryland, after fulfilling those token residence requirements. Apparently the story Vicky handed us about staying with an old school friend at Chevy Chase was a complete fiction, and Sam met her off the train as soon as she arrived in Washington from Velletria."

"I don't understand," I said politely, watching the clumsy knot in the cord of his pajamas but averting my gaze before it could rest on the shadowy lines beneath the material. "Why did they feel they had to elope?"

"Sam knew I'd turned right against the idea of him marrying Vicky."

"You had? Why didn't you tell me? I never knew!"

"The whole subject had caused us such problems that I didn't want to drag it up again."

"But what made you change your mind?"

"I . . . got myself into a mess. Accidentally. And I didn't trust Sam not to compound it."

"What on earth are you talking about?"

"The operative words are: 'I didn't trust Sam.' I only wanted Vicky to marry a man I trusted one hundred percent."

"But—"

"Forget it. I don't want to talk about it any more."

Hearing the abrupt note in his voice, I tried to change the direction of the conversation before he could terminate it by returning to his room. "Well," I said briskly, "what amazes me is not that they decided to get married. After all, Vicky's very lovely, and Sam, though plain, is far from being an unattractive man. Of course I doubt if it would have occurred to him to marry her if you hadn't put the idea in his head in the first place, but that's neither here nor there. No, what amazes me is that Emily could have let this happen. Vicky's been under her nose for two whole months—six weeks in Europe and now these last two weeks in Velletria. Surely she must have suspected something was going on! Sam must have been in touch with Vicky, there must have been letters and phone calls . . ."

"Not necessarily. He probably sewed the whole thing up when he made that surprise trip back to Europe at the end of April. I never really believed his story that one of our clients wanted to expand into the international market."

"But he was only in Paris for a week!"

"Alicia, Sam could take a corporation, analyze it, dissect it, restructure it, merge it, parcel the shares out among the selling syndicate, and bank the profits all within the space of forty-eight hours. Don't tell me he couldn't sew up his own marriage in a week!"

There was a pause while he sipped some water. He was leaning on his right elbow with his back to me, and I was conscious of the gap between the pants of his pajamas and the jacket. Stretching out my hand, I let my fingers stop a millimeter from the skin.

"What are you going to do?" I said mechanically, withdrawing my hand as he set down the glass.

"What can I do? He's got me by the balls." This crude figure of speech, quite unlike the language he usually used in front of me, both revealed the degree of his distress and made him more aware of his surroundings. He buttoned his jacket, surreptitiously checked the fly of his pants to make sure it was closed, and thrust back the bedclothes. "Let's both get some sleep," he said, leaving the bed and moving to the communicating door between our rooms. "It's after midnight."

"But, Cornelius . . ." I had been so hoping that he would spend the rest of the night in my room that I automatically tried to delay his departure.

"Perhaps it won't be such a disaster after all," I said quickly. "Sam's fond of Vicky, and despite what you say, I'm sure you can trust him to do his best to be a good husband. Of course it's a pity Vicky hasn't married a man who truly loves her, but—"

"Oh, Christ, don't start on your obsession with Sebastian again! It's so downright unhealthy!"

"Not nearly so unhealthy as your fixation about your daughter!" I blazed, and then flinched as he slammed the door behind him without bothering to reply.

I sank down trembling on the edge of the bed. Time passed, but I did not move.

I had just resigned myself to my isolation when he slipped back into the room. He had reknotted the cord of his pajamas, but his pants still sagged at the waist because he was so slim. Sitting down on the bed beside me, he put his hand over mine.

I sat looking at his beautiful hands, which should have belonged to an artist, and for a moment pictured them drawing some exquisite picture or perhaps playing a Chopin nocturne. But Cornelius played no instrument and nowadays consigned nothing to paper except his signature. I had received only two letters from him in my life; he had written to me in the hospital after I had given birth to the second child of my first marriage. I had kept the letters, and now, eighteen years after Andrew's birth, I occasionally reread them to remind myself of a time when communication, even by the written word, had been easy and direct.

After the silence between us had persisted for a full minute, I said levelly, "I'm sorry to detain you by making such a stupid remark. You really should lie down and relax now, or the asthma will get worse again."

Without hesitation he climbed into my bed, and when I turned out the light and lay down beside him, his fingers at once intertwined with mine. We lay like that for some time, joined yet separate, he with his thoughts, I with mine, and just as I felt I could no longer endure the tension, his hand relaxed in mine as he slept.

I waited till I was sure he was sleeping deeply. Then I drew his hand against my body and pressed as close as I dared to him in the dark.

II

HE AWOKE at dawn. I felt his fingers curl involuntarily against my thigh, and in a flash I too was awake, panic-stricken for fear he would realize I had placed his hand where I most wanted him. Pretending I was still asleep, I moved fractionally so that his hand could slip free.

We were still. With relief I thought he had fallen asleep again, but then he said quietly, "Alicia," and when I did not answer, he switched on the light.

The glare dazzled us both. When I could open my eyes, I saw he was still shading his face with his hand, and I had three seconds to watch the line of his arm and shoulder before he let his hand fall. I quickly looked away.

"Alicia . . ."

"No, don't let's talk, Cornelius. How are you going to get through a day at the office unless you have more sleep? This is the wrong moment for talking, and anyway, there's nothing to talk about."

"My God," he said, "sometimes I really do think we'd be better off divorced."

It was no longer possible to speak dispassionately in a cool voice while I pretended I was half-asleep. Sitting bolt upright, I shoved the hair blindly out of my eyes and shouted at him, "Don't say that! How dare you say that! You must never, never say that again!"

"But I can't bear to see you so unhappy." He was in despair. His eyes were bright with pain. "I love you so much I can't bear it. I thought that after last April we'd found some sort of solution, but . . ."

"Cornelius," I said, somehow recapturing my crispest, most sensible voice, "I think it would be the greatest mistake to choose this moment, when we're both so overwrought, to review the decision we reached last April, but just let me say this: our decision was the only possible one in the circumstances, and I've been most relieved to see that it seems to have been working out well. You now have a satisfactory mistress. I'm delighted. Nothing could please me more. I know for the moment I've chosen to remain alone, but that's my own personal decision and there's no need whatsoever for you to worry about me. Please rest assured that I'm perfectly happy, and although of course I regret that we're no longer as close as we once were, you should know that I've completely accepted our new relationship and remain thoroughly contented with our marriage."

He lay motionless in bed. He was watching some distant point above the picture on the far wall. "But if you've accepted it and I've accepted it," he said slowly, "why aren't we at peace?"

"These things take time. One can't turn from a sexual to a platonic relationship as easily as flicking a light switch. Now, Cornelius, you must stop treating this situation as if it were in any way odd or unusual. Most couples don't sleep together anyway after they've been married for eighteen years. It's nothing out of the ordinary."

"I wonder what would have happened if—"

"That's the most dangerous phrase in the English language. Please don't use it. I hate it. It's always the prelude to some pointless reminiscence which is best forgotten."

"But I don't see why we should have to suffer like this!"

"There's no suffering. We're extremely fortunate and happy. We have money, we've kept our looks, and although your health isn't always good, it hasn't stopped you from having a successful, satisfying career. We have three wonderful children, and although I admit your daughter often drives me to distraction, I'm at heart as devoted to her as I know you are to my two boys. Of course it's sad that we have no children of our own, but if I've accepted it totally—as I have —then I think you should too. There's no need for you to feel guilty, Cornelius. I've been saying this to you now for so many years, but I'll say it again if there's any chance that this time you can finally bring yourself to believe me. What happened, happened. You didn't choose to get sick back in 1931. It wasn't your fault. It was like an act of God."

"Acts of God come and go. They don't go on and on and on."

"This is sheer self-pity, Cornelius. I know it's difficult for a man to come to terms with the fact that he can't father children, but think how much more difficult life would be if you were not only sterile but permanently incapable of intercourse. In one of my soap operas the other day, the hero got polio and now he's paralyzed from the waist down, with the result that his wife—"

He groaned. "Please! Isn't it enough that we have to cope with real life? Do we really have to cope with imaginary people's imaginary problems as well?"

I laughed, and when he saw I was amused, he was able to laugh too. The tears were burning behind my eyes. Turning my head sharply away from him, I saw our reflection in the mirror across the room, a happy handsome couple relaxing in an elegant sumptuous suite.

"I love you very much," he said. "You're the most wonderful woman in the world."

"I love you too, darling."

The mirror seemed to absorb our words and make them as unreal as our reflection. I thought of all the magazine stories I read about true love, marital bliss, and happy endings, and suddenly the reflection in the mirror was a mere blur, as if reality had triumphed at last over the dreaming images of the mind.

"Alicia . . ."

I should have stopped him, but I did not. I was weak as well as foolish, clinging to him as he started to kiss me, and so it was together that we wiped out all the painful progress we had made toward achieving a peaceful platonic relationship. We were back where we had started before the catastrophe of our quarrel the previous April, and nothing had changed, least of all the grief and the acute unendurable frustration.

When the failure could no longer be ignored, he said to me, "Let's do what we did before we were married . . . when you were still pregnant . . . when we couldn't . . . when I couldn't . . ."

I had been weak and was now paying for the weakness by being forced to witness his immense humiliation and shame. For his own sake, even more than for mine, I was now determined to be strong.

"No," I said.

"But I wouldn't mind, I swear it—I'd do anything to make you happy!"

I knew very well he secretly hated any deviation from a sexual pattern which he considered to be normal. During the first year of our marriage, when our physical relationship had been perfect, I had marveled that such middle-class conservatism, heavily swathed in puritan beliefs, could prove so erotic, but when I was older I realized that Cornelius was erotic to me not in spite of his puritanism but because of it. I was reminded of stories of Victorian men who, accustomed to women encased from the neck to the feet in elaborate garments, would swoon at the glimpse of a feminine ankle. The sight of Cornelius discarding not only his shirt but his prim Midwestern upbringing was still sufficient even now after years of marriage to stimulate me to a fever of excitement.

The excitement hurt. Smothering it behind my most impassive expression, I said neutrally, "If you'd do anything to make me happy, Cornelius, then let's please revert to the agreement we reached last April. I know that you love me better than anyone else, and the knowledge itself is enough for me. There's no need for you to dem-

onstrate that love physically, so you mustn't feel under any obligation or compulsion to do so."

He at once got out of bed and moved rapidly to the door.

"Cornelius . . ."

"It's okay," he said. "I've been stupid. I'm sorry I bothered you.
Good night."

The door closed and I was alone again. Immediately I turned out
the light so that I could not see the empty space where he had slept
beside me, but beyond the window the dawn was breaking, and when
I could no longer ignore the deserted bed, my courage failed me and
I began to cry.

III

SOMETIMES I laugh at the soap operas when they present a grand
passion as glamorous, creating an exciting but serene world filled
with the music of soaring violins and the vistas of never-ending
golden sunsets. Grand passions aren't like that at all. They're terrifying and destructive, razing homes, smashing lives, and ripping apart
all semblance of civilized behavior, and beneath the gleaming veneer
of compulsive passion is the dark sordid stratum of other people's
suffering and loss.

I married my first husband, Ralph Foxworth, when I was seventeen in order to escape from an unhappy home. When I was twenty
and five months pregnant with my second son, I met Cornelius.
Three days later I went to live with him, and by the time Andrew entered the world I had already embarked on my new marriage.

I was still very young. I thought that if Cornelius and I loved
each other enough the golden sunsets and soaring violins would still
be waiting for us when we emerged from the shadow of my divorce. I
thought I could bear losing both my sons to Ralph in the custody
battle once I began having more children, and I thought that so long
as I had Cornelius we would easily survive any misfortune which
might overtake us in the future.

But there was no golden sunset. The violins played lusciously for a
short time and then were still. I see life very differently now.

I am not a religious person, although of course I go to church at
Easter and Christmas when the event is an Episcopalian social occasion, but I have come to believe that there are certain natural laws

which operate in human affairs, just as there are natural laws which regulate the world around us. When I was small I learned that the sea is governed by tides; if the tide comes in, it must also go out. When I was older I learned that grand passions too operate under similar implacable laws; if you exchange your husband and children for paradise, you should not be altogether surprised if paradise turns out to be more—or in my case very much less—than you bargained for.

It took me some time to realize this, since the first two and a half years of our marriage were exquisitely happy, marred only by my private grief that I never saw my sons, but on September 7, 1933—the anniversary of that day never passes without me feeling ill with the weight of past unhappiness—Cornelius was informed that he had become sterile as the result of an attack of mumps suffered two years earlier. We were hardly surprised when this discovery affected our intimate life, and we accepted that we would need time to adjust to the situation, but it never occurred to us that our marriage was to be permanently crippled. We stumbled on awkwardly for a while. At last Cornelius overcame his difficulties, but before long, inexplicably, they recurred. He saw various doctors, all of whom told him that there was no physical reason why he should not have a normal sexual relationship with me, but this unanimous diagnosis failed to result in the disappearance of our troubles. Cornelius became increasingly awkward, I became increasingly nervous, and even on those rare occasions when we managed to consummate the marriage, the moment was always too brief and too burdened with anxiety to give us more than a tantalizing glimpse of the pleasures we had taken for granted in the past.

Realizing that our childlessness was at the root of the problem, we discussed the possibility of adoption, but the idea was discarded when Ralph remarried and gave me generous access to my boys. Soon afterward Cornelius won better access to Vicky too, so that we were able to see all three children at Christmas and Easter as well as during the month of August, which we always spent at Bar Harbor. In 1938 I was just telling myself severely that it was unreasonable to want to see the boys more often when I was already so fortunate, when Ralph was killed in the airship disaster at Lakewood, New Jersey, and Sebastian and Andrew, now aged nine and seven, came to live with us permanently.

Matters at once improved out of all recognition. I was so happy to have the chance to be a full-time mother at last, and Cornelius, perhaps feeling that I no longer minded our childlessness, overcame his difficulties for a time. We never recaptured the perfection of the early days, but we probably managed as well as the average husband and wife who had been married for seven years, and the grinding awkwardness between us had dissolved. Then in 1941 Cornelius succeeded in winning sole custody of his daughter and Vicky came to live with us.

I can think of a number of reasons why Vicky dislocated our marriage, but I can never decide which reason is correct. Perhaps the damage was caused by a combination of these reasons, but whatever the cause, the one indisputable fact was that our marriage once more entered difficult times.

Perhaps the main trouble was that I had not anticipated how difficult Vicky was going to be. I knew her well by that time, but when she had visited us in the past she had always been on her best behavior. Once she came to live with us, matters were very different. Of course one cannot expect children to be on their best behavior all the time, just as one cannot expect a stepmother's job to be easy, but I had underestimated the time, patience, and sheer mental effort required to help a troubled ten-year-old settle down in a new environment. Vicky was pert, rebellious, and determined to dramatize her situation by classing me as the wicked stepmother. I was equally determined to make allowances for her, since the custody struggles had been bitter, and the mother, an irresponsible nymphomaniac, had obviously no idea how to raise a child properly, but my nerves became frayed and I soon found I was under considerable strain.

I wanted to love Vicky. I had always longed for a daughter, particularly a little girl who looked like Cornelius, so it was a great disappointment to me when Vicky proved so different from the ideal daughter I wanted so much. Naturally I concealed my disappointment; I thought I had concealed it perfectly, but perhaps Cornelius sensed my feelings and resented them. Or perhaps he felt guilty that he had imposed another woman's daughter on me instead of giving me a daughter of my own. Or perhaps the strained atmosphere in the family caused subconscious tensions in his mind. As I have already said, I can think of more than one reason why Vicky should have dislocated our marriage, but whatever the reason was, the dislocation now showed signs of becoming not merely a temporary but a permanent feature of our domestic landscape.

It was hard to cope. My one preoccupation was to present a normal front to the children so that they should remain untouched by our problems, but in 1945 came the incident which almost terminated our marriage. Vicky was fourteen and a half, Sebastian sixteen. I cannot describe this incident except to say that I was and still am convinced of Sebastian's innocence. Vicky was maladjusted about sexual matters, thanks to that disgraceful mother of hers, and although I tried to talk to her sensibly about male behavior in certain circumstances, she was too hysterical to listen. Cornelius was useless; he was incapable of being sensible where Vicky was concerned, and in a flash he was siding with her against me when I tried to defend Sebastian. Since I could not forgive him for some of the things he said about my son and he could not forgive me for some of the things I said about his daughter, it was hardly surprising that we became estranged and for a whole year made no attempt to sleep together.

But then he came back to me. He said he had been so miserable that he had asked Jake Reischman to lend him one of his mistresses—it was typical of Jake that he should have had more than one to offer —but the incident had been so sordid that he couldn't repeat it. He said he loved me and wanted me back. I went back to him.

We were happy for a little while, but it didn't last, I guess we both knew it wouldn't last, but oh, the pain, I can't be cold and crisp and detached anymore, it's beyond me, I'm so unhappy. I can't describe the pain, it was there all the time, soaking through me, and when I could bear it no more, I went to the doctor and said please, *please* give me some tranquilizers, and when he asked me why I was so upset, I didn't say: "My husband can hardly ever make love to me." I said: "My husband and I have no children."

"But Mrs. Van Zale!" he said, amazed. "You have three children, your two sons and your stepdaughter!"

"I mean the other children," I said. "All the children we never had." But I could not describe the loss to him. I could not tell him that Cornelius and I had planned to have seven children—yes, seven— one daughter and six sons ("One more than the Rockefellers!" we had often said, laughing), and we had planned their birthdays and named them and plotted their careers. "Oh, it was just a game," I said to the first psychiatrist, "just a way of making me feel better because I missed my boys so much." "No, it wasn't a game," I said to the second psychiatrist. "It was real, they were all real, I knew what they looked like, and then suddenly one day they were gone and I didn't know—still don't know—how to bear the loss, I still miss them so much, whenever I think of them I can't endure their nonexistence."

The psychiatrist was kind, but he didn't really understand.

"I was so good at having children," I said as I watched him write me a new prescription for tranquilizers. "I'm not a very special person, not clever or gifted, but when I gave birth to Sebastian, I felt for the first time in my life that I was *someone*, a real person, Alicia Blaise Foxworth, talented, brilliant, successful. I would have felt like that when Andrew was born too, except that I knew I was going to have to give him up, so I tried hard not to be emotionally involved in the birth. But I was. I cried and cried when I was parted from Andrew, but I had to stop because I didn't want Cornelius to know. I had to shut up all my grief inside me and pretend not to mind. Sometimes I think I've been doing nothing else all these years except shutting up the grief and pretending, pretending, pretending. . . . I must never let Cornelius know I mind, you see, because it would hurt him so much, I love Cornelius, I couldn't bear to hurt him, I'd rather die than let him know how much I mind our childlessness."

But that was a lie. I lived and I let him know. On April 6, 1949, the unthinkable happened, my self-control broke down, and the fragile relationship we had preserved with such difficulty for so many years was finally wrecked beyond repair.

IV

THE TROUBLE began when Vicky, bent on melodrama as usual, embarked on a ridiculous elopement with a beachboy and the quiet facade of our troubled family life again cracked wide apart. Cornelius could do nothing but ask in despair where we had gone wrong, and when he looked at me as if I were the cause of Vicky's selfish irresponsibility, I had trouble restraining myself from pointing out that the entire disaster had arisen because he had spoiled her from the cradle to compensate himself for all the children he had never had. However, I think this home truth must have been obvious even to him. Certainly the situation seemed to fuel his guilt toward me, and we were already on the borders of a vast new estrangement when I discovered that he was secretly planning to marry Vicky to Sam Keller.

Sam was so like a brother to Cornelius that I always thought of him as my brother-in-law. Since he was a man who never let a woman feel unappreciated, I found it easy to be friends with him, but I knew very well that the charm he lavished on me was due entirely to the fact that I was Cornelius' wife. If Cornelius had ever divorced me, Sam would never have given me another glance because Sam defined the world only in terms of what was important to Cornelius. He was one of those men who gravitate instinctively to sources of great wealth and power; though born to neither wealth nor power themselves, they have an infallible instinct for latching on to the right patrons and sticking with them through thick and thin. Too clever to be merely a lackey and too shrewd not to take every possible advantage of his friendship with Cornelius, Sam was no mere sycophantic hanger-on but a formidable force in his own right.

Of course he was the wrong husband for Vicky.

I knew he could not love her, just as I knew he was capable of marrying her to please Cornelius. I am deeply opposed to men marrying girls they don't love. My first marriage taught me in no uncertain way about the misery waiting for a girl in a loveless relationship, and although I secretly longed for Vicky to leave home, I found myself unable to sanction the idea of Sam as a husband for her, particularly since there was someone else far more suitable who could offer her all the love she would never receive from Sam.

Sebastian had always loved Vicky. There was nothing unnatural about it. They were not related by blood, and although my marriage to Cornelius had made them stepbrother and stepsister, they had not been brought up together from the cradle. Personally I thought it was more unnatural for Sam to marry Vicky, since she had been taught from birth to regard him as an uncle.

Sebastian was steady and quiet. He would have provided the perfect foil for Vicky's exuberance. He was also clever and more than worthy of her self-conscious intellectual affectations. It was true that Vicky was set against him, but that attitude just sprang from the perversity of adolescence, and once she was fully mature, I felt sure she couldn't fail to appreciate him as he deserved.

However, if I'm honest with myself, I have to admit that I did not want them to marry just because I felt they were well-suited. In fact, under normal circumstances I might have thought Vicky was unworthy of Sebastian and hoped he would recover from the calf love which had afflicted him in adolescence, but of course unfortunately my circumstances were so very far from normal.

I wanted them to marry because I felt it would remove Cornelius' guilt and heal our crippled marriage. I felt that if his daughter and my son could give us grandchildren to replace those children who had remained unborn, our loss would be wiped out in the joy of our mutual gain. Gradually over the years I had come to believe that this marriage was the only cure for a marriage which was becoming too great a strain to endure, and by that April in 1949 the strain had brought me close to breakdown. I found it difficult to pretend I still wanted him sexually when I had come to dread the nights so much; I dreaded the agony of wondering whether he would touch me, I dreaded the probability of his impotence, and I even dreaded the rare occasions when he was successful because I resented that he could be satisfied when satisfaction was always beyond me. I was angry too after the incident of Jake Reischman's mistress, although Cornelius had sworn he had been unable to make love to her. I thought he had no right to go to another woman when I had tried so hard to be a good wife to him. I could see no reason why I should have to be penalized just because I knew, as no other woman knew, that he felt less of a man because of his sterility. My anger grew. I clamped down on it but could not stamp it out, and eventually it combined with all my dread to annihilate the desire for him that I had always taken for granted.

It was at this point, when our marriage was at its lowest ebb and I was clinging more fiercely than ever to my dream of Sebastian marrying Vicky, that I discovered Sam had been marked for the role of Vicky's keeper.

"I must talk to you, please," I said politely to Cornelius after we had rescued Vicky from Sam's apartment on that Wednesday evening early in April. "It's important."

"Let me just see Vicky to her room." As usual he was smothering her with paternal love and as usual the little minx was tugging at his heartstrings for all she was worth. "Wait for me upstairs," he suggested as an afterthought. "I want to change out of these goddamned business clothes just as soon as I've got Vicky settled."

I did not argue with him, but went to my bedroom to wait. It was an hour before he reached his room next door and another five minutes before he had changed his clothes, but I spoke not one word criticizing him for the delay. I assumed he had been chatting away to her without noticing the time, but this was nothing unusual. I always had to take a backseat when Cornelius was absorbed with his daughter.

"I must talk to you," I repeated as he entered the room. I was wearing my nightdress and peignoir by that time, although I had not removed my makeup.

"Oh, God!" he groaned, not listening to a single word I said. "Poor little Vicky! What the hell am I going to do?"

My last ounce of patience evaporated. "Well, don't pretend you don't have it all arranged!"

He stared at me. "What do you mean?"

That was too much. I could tolerate his genuine concern for his daughter's welfare, but not his feigned ignorance or his conspiracies hatched behind my back. "I mean that you've lied to me!" I blazed. "You always implied you shared my hope that Vicky would marry Sebastian someday, yet now Sam tells me you've made this secret deal with him behind my back! Of course he said he was going to have to tell you he couldn't marry her, but if you think for one moment I believed him, you couldn't be more wrong! He'll do whatever you say, of course, but I think it's disgraceful. I don't know how you could do this to your own daughter! How can you marry her off to a man who cares nothing for her while all the time, right here in our own family, is a young man who worships the ground she—"

"Oh, for Christ's sake!" He sprang to his feet. Every muscle in his body seemed to harden with rage. "Don't hand me all that feminine romantic crap—as if Vicky would ever consider marrying Sebastian! Alicia, you've become highly neurotic about that boy. I haven't said anything before because I haven't wanted to hurt you, but I can see we've now reached the stage where something has to be said. This blind adoration of Sebastian is highly unfair to Andrew and very bad for Sebastian himself!"

"You've never liked Sebastian," I said. "Never."

"That's quite untrue and shows how neurotically you view the situation. Now, listen, Alicia. You just must be sensible about this. It's not healthy to live vicariously through Sebastian and Vicky by manufacturing a dream world where your son marries my daughter and produces half a dozen children you can pretend are the children of our marriage. You've got to come to grips with reality and realize that this dream hasn't one hope in hell of coming true."

"But I truly believe . . . in time . . ."

"No. I'm sorry. Please don't think I'm unsympathetic, because I'm not; we have a central tragedy in our marriage, and I recognize that. But we must cope with it as best we can. In some ways it's easier for me, because I have the world of my work at Willow and Wall, but you have your world here on Fifth Avenue and you could do so much more than you do at present to lead a full, rewarding, interesting life. Instead of wasting so much time with your soap operas, why don't you get out, see more of your friends, maybe get involved in one or two new charities? Once you were occupying your time more meaningfully, I'm sure your life would seem less frustrating, so please—make an effort to get out of this rut you're in! I don't want to come home from work one day and find you're in the middle of some neurotic breakdown."

"If I have a breakdown," said my voice in fury, "you'll have only yourself to blame. It's not *my* fault we never had any children."

All the lights in the bedroom were on. There was no darkness to hide our expressions. For a moment we stood motionless, as if hypnotized by so much blinding clarity, and then Cornelius took a small step backward. His face was white as bone.

"Why shouldn't I spend my time enjoying soap operas?" said my voice. "It's better than sitting around thinking of all those children you never gave me. And it's certainly better than thinking of a husband who's never any good in bed."

In the silence that followed, I told myself I had thought the words but not spoken them aloud. I couldn't have spoken the words aloud because I was incapable of being so wicked.

Cornelius took another step backward. His eyes were brilliant with pain, and I knew then that the words had been spoken and that nothing could wipe them out.

There were no more words. I looked at his dear familiar face and saw it was stricken beyond recognition with his grief. He went on backing away until he blundered against a table, and then he turned, opened the door, and stumbled out into the corridor.

"Cornelius!" I found my voice, but it was too late. I ran after him down the long corridor, down the yards of red carpet to the head of the grand staircase, and all the time I was crying his name. I saw him cross the hall, but he did not look back. The stairs seemed endless. My slippers whispered frantically on the vast marble floor. "Cornelius!" I sobbed. "Cornelius!" I dashed out of the front door, and halfway across the forecourt I reached him and clung to his arm.

He wrenched himself free. "Stop that screaming," he said sharply. "Stop it at once."

"Cornelius . . ."

"I have nothing to say to you. Let me be."

He walked away from me to the gates, and when I tried to cling to him again, he shoved me away so violently that I fell. The cobbles were like lumps of ice. Lights were going on inside the house as the servants responded to the noise, and in shame I crept back up the steps to the porch. I had just reached the sanctuary of the library when the security men streamed into the hall.

I waited in case he returned for his bodyguard or one of his cars, but he did not, and at last when the house was quiet I tiptoed upstairs and sat down in his bedroom to wait.

He came back at dawn.

I was still waiting up for him, but I had taken three tranquilizers and was calm.

When he entered the room, he did not look at the chair where I was sitting, but went to the window, drew back the drapes, and stood staring across Central Park. Finally he said, still not looking at me, "I just can't think why we've struggled on so senselessly for so long."

"Cornelius . . . darling . . ."

He spun round. "Please! No more of your scenes! I've had enough of them!"

I groped for composure. Evidently I could only lessen his pain by pretending to be calm. I was not to be allowed any emotion. He could not cope with my grief as well as his own.

"Did you go to anyone?" I said in my most colorless voice.

"Yes." My new manner seemed to reassure him. He still could not look at me, but he sat down on a chair nearby and started to pull off his shoes.

"Did you . . . ?"

"Sure. It was just fine. As if I'd never been sick." He chucked the sneakers across the room and stared after them.

"A call girl?"

"God, no! You may not think I'm much good, but I haven't yet sunk so low I have to pay for it."

"Then who was she?"

"No one you know. Her name's Teresa something-or-other. She's got some godawful Polish name I can't remember. She's Kevin's latest caretaker."

"Kevin has a Polish girl? I thought she was Swedish." The conversation was becoming almost sociable. As I listened to my casual remarks I watched him undo the top button of his shirt.

"Ingrid went to Hollywood."

"Oh."

We were silent. He undressed no further but picked up his tie from the floor and sat fingering it.

"Of course you'll want a divorce," he said politely at last.

I groped for words again, and when I spoke, my voice sounded more distant. "Because of the adultery?"

He stared at me. "We can use the adultery as the legal excuse, of course, but I was really thinking of . . . well, I fail to see why you should want to stay married to me in these circumstances. Now that I know exactly how you feel, I can't think how you endured the marriage all these years—or why you should have wanted to endure it. I guess you pitied me and felt you had some kind of obligation to stay, but that needn't detain you now. On the contrary, the obligation's on me to let you go without delay."

I could not speak.

"Unless . . ." The tie was taut in his hands.

I nodded, but he was staring at the tie and did not see me. "Unless despite everything you still feel . . ." He looked up at last and saw the expression in my eyes.

The chair fell sideways as he jumped to his feet and stumbled across the room into my arms.

A long time passed while we held each other, but when we were calmer we sat hand in hand on the edge of the bed and conducted a conversation in that peculiar brand of verbal shorthand which many married couples develop over the years.

"I still can't believe . . ."

"Don't be ridiculous, Cornelius. If you love someone, you love them, and that's that."

"You're not secretly longing for . . ."

"No. Are you?"

"Never. Divorce is for other people."

"I hate myself so much for making you think . . ."

"No, it was good you spoke out."

"All those wicked hurtful things I said . . ."

"They cleared the air. I see now we've let things drift too long. All my fault."

"No . . ."

"I mean, the way I reacted. Christ, Alicia, can you ever forgive me for . . . ?"

"She doesn't matter. In fact, it might even be best if—"

"Yes, but only if you agree."

"Well, so long as she's suitable—no fuss, no mess . . . Is she . . . ?"

"No. Not pretty or beautiful. Believe me, she'll do. I'm just ashamed I didn't have the guts to set up such an arrangement years ago and spare you from all the . . ."

"No, I would have minded very much earlier. Now it seems right. I can't explain."

"But we've got to discuss it, work it all out, and put an end to this needless suffering. We've both of us suffered long enough."

There was a pause while we arranged our thoughts and dredged up the strength to go on. I went on holding his hand tightly. Beyond the window, the sky was growing paler over the park.

"Let's start with the obvious," said Cornelius at last. "One: no divorce. We love one another, and the thought of not being married is inconceivable. Two: no sex. It's clear our sexual relationship's shot, and if we can accept this, we'll both be much happier. Three: no fidelity. It would hardly be facing reality if we were to expect celibacy from each other in the circumstances, particularly since I'm only forty-one and you're only thirty-nine."

I was so busy thinking of him with another woman that I missed the wider implication of this remark. "Cornelius, I'd almost rather you had a string of casual women than one special mistress who might fall in love with you."

"There's not the remotest chance this woman could fall in love with me. She's one of these egocentric artists totally in love with her work, and if she ever did make difficulties for me, I could buy her off. That's why she's so suitable and that's why I'd rather have one regular woman. It makes the situation easier to manage. Besides, to have a string of women would be shoddy, degrading to both of us. Now, as far as you're concerned . . ." He took a deep breath but found he could not go on.

"Oh, I shall be all right, Cornelius, if we can find happiness together again."

"That's just wishful thinking. That's not facing the facts. Of course I'd like to think that you were some kind of saint who could sit waiting for me at home in tranquil celibacy while I went out and slept with my mistress, but, Alicia, I didn't get where I am in life by dealing with fantasies! Of course you must take a lover. It's the only practical solution."

"But I can't imagine ever wanting anyone else!"

"And I shouldn't enjoy thinking of you with anyone else, but that's not the point. The point is that if we're ever to make this new arrangement work, we've got to start with equal rights or else I'll wind up feeling more guilty than ever and you'll be even more angry and frustrated than you are now—yes, be honest, Alicia! Admit it! We've got to be honest with one another!"

"Yes, we've suffered too much by pretending."

"Exactly." He sighed with relief. "This is all going to work out for the best," he said presently. "Marriage should be a dynamic relationship, growing and changing to reflect the growth and change of the partners. We'll be okay—in fact, I feel much better already. Sitting down and discussing our problems frankly like this has to be the smartest thing we could have done."

"Yes, I feel we're much closer now. Like the old days."

"We used to have such good talks, didn't we?"

"And such peaceful silences. Do you remember I said to you once how much I loved our silences?"

"I remember, but I'd forgotten. Our silences have been so tense for so long." He kissed me on the cheek. "But it'll all be different now, won't it?" he said, smiling at me. "We'll be happy again. . . . Now I think we should try and get some sleep before the sun rises any higher. You must be as tired as I am." And kissing me again, he told me he loved me.

"I love you too," I whispered, clinging to him in a rush of happiness, and it was then, as I felt his body at last pressing against mine without constraint, that the long-forgotten desire blazed through me and I knew that our problems, though changed, remained unsolved.

Chapter Two

I

OUR NEW intimacy soon evaporated. A different tension sprang up to replace the tension we had neutralized, and I was forced to withdraw again behind my coolest facade in order to preserve the new arrangement we had so painfully evolved.

It seemed a terrible irony that once the burden of our sexual relationship was lifted, the stress which had dulled my desire disappeared and my physical need for him revived. I was conscious of little except my intense longing, and in an attempt to deflect my thoughts from Cornelius, I became more enrapt than ever with my daytime serials and confession magazines. I even found myself dreaming of sex. At first I was disturbed, believing only men could have such vivid fantasies, but I came to long for the dreams because they provided a release from tension.

Neither of us had anticipated that he would feel it necessary to distance himself from me, as if he dared not come too close for fear of reviving the specter of our old relationship, and soon I found myself missing not merely the sex but the casual loving gestures, the pressure of his fingers intertwined with mine, the comfort of his arms around me in a brief embrace, and the touch of his mouth on mine as he paused for a brief kiss. In theory we should have been so much more relaxed with each other that the casual gestures increased, but in practice we found that any physical exchange now created awkwardness. I was aware of losing him again, and in my distress I saw him with such clarity that I noticed details I had overlooked for years, the inflections of the Midwest still strong in his speech, his graceful gait, his radiant smile which was all the more dazzling because his face in repose was so set and still. I noticed too his sculptured profile, the straight nose, the firm chin, the masculine mouth, the elegant line of his forehead below his fair curling hair. And last I noticed how short he was, barely taller than I, but his height was unimportant because he was so beautifully built, his bones fine but strong, his skin unblemished, his muscles carefully exercised by regular swims in the pool.

I saw him less and less. He worked increasingly late at the office, as if despite all that had been said, his guilt remained unexorcised, and I assumed that on some of those nights he stopped at Kevin's house in Greenwich Village. I told myself over and over again how lucky it was that he had found someone suitable, but this statement, which in April had seemed arguable, now only underlined the intensity of my unhappiness whenever I knew he was with another woman.

I did make a great effort to consider my situation rationally. I could not confide in Cornelius or he would try to make love to me and throw us back into the old abortive cycle of guilt and frustration. Besides, after the wicked way I had rejected him in April, I did not think I had the right to disrupt our new arrangement. I decided that the onus was on me to adjust to the situation, but adjustment seemed impossible, because despite all Cornelius had said on the subject, I could not imagine consoling myself with another man.

It was true I had considered the idea in theory. During our worst times in the past I had occasionally wished I could turn to someone else, but I had always rejected the possibility at once. This was not only because Cornelius was my whole life and I could not imagine either leaving him permanently or abandoning him temporarily for a little hole-in-the-corner adultery. Nor was it only because other men, sensing my devotion to my husband, made no attempt to proposition me. Nor was it just because my pride told me it was humiliating for a woman to offer herself to some man she didn't love in order to ease a physical need. It was because my sexual desire, though intense, was riveted implacably to Cornelius. No other man aroused any desire in me whatsoever, and in fact I could hardly see other men from a sexual point of view because my desire for him was so strong.

The problem had now become so all-consuming that I could hardly concentrate on performing my daily household duties, and when I lay in bed on that June morning after Vicky's wedding night I found it difficult to summon the will to face the day ahead.

However, I finally got up when I realized that Cornelius' asthma attack gave me the excuse to enter his bedroom and ask how he was feeling. But at the door I hesitated. Perhaps he would be too embarrassed to want to see me. With shame I remembered how weak I had been, encouraging him to make love to me the previous evening when I should have spared him the humiliation of his inevitable failure, and as soon as I acknowledged my shame I knew I had to try to repair the damage caused by my selfish behavior. I waited till I was calm and then nerved myself to open the communicating door. Perhaps the awkwardness would dissolve more easily if I pretended the disastrous scene had never taken place.

I glanced into the room. Cornelius was still sleeping, but as I watched, not daring to go too close, he stirred, stretched, and opened his eyes.

"I just wondered how you were feeling this morning," I said in a voice a nurse might have used in some well-run hospital. "Are you well enough to go to the office?"

He sat up as abruptly as if I had cracked a whip. I saw then that I had been wasting time worrying about his embarrassment. His only thought was for his daughter. "My God—Vicky and Sam! Oh, Christ . . ." He flung himself back on the pillows with a groan and put his hands over his face as if he could hide from the memory. Then he sat up again and ran his fingers distractedly through his hair. "Alicia, should I call her? I don't know where they're staying in Annapolis, but I could find out. If I called now, I could catch them before they left for their honeymoon."

"Cornelius"—on this subject at least I could be sensible—"I should leave them well alone."

"But supposing Vicky's unhappy? Supposing she needs me?"

"Well, dear, I hardly think she can have forgotten your phone number. If she needs you, she'll call you, and meanwhile, I'm sure it would be a mistake for you to worry about her when she's probably in the seventh heaven of marital bliss. Now, about your asthma . . ."

"Forget the asthma. I've got to issue a press statement." He was back to normal, racing into action with all his other troubles forgotten. After ringing for his valet, he picked up the receiver of the white telephone. "Taylor, get Hammond. I want to dictate a press statement about my daughter's marriage—yes, marriage. M-a-r— That's right." Slamming down the receiver, he turned to the black phone but hung up before dialing. "Christ, I can't face Emily. Alicia, could you . . . ?"

"Yes," I said. "I'll tell her."

"And call Sylvia in San Francisco. Oh, God, poor little Vicky . . ."

Fortunately at this point his valet arrived, and returning to my room, I rang for coffee before facing the telephone.

I wanted to break the news first to Paul Van Zale's widow, Sylvia, but since San Francisco was three hours behind New York, it was too early to call her. Cornelius was devoted to this great-aunt of his although they had seen little of each other since she had settled in California before the war. Sylvia, who was by no means as old as the title "great-aunt" implied, had remarried in 1939 after a lengthy visit to her San Francisco cousins, and her new husband was a lawyer with a wealthy practice in the Bay Area.

My coffee arrived. I could postpone the moment no longer, and gritting my teeth, I summoned the energy to inform my sister-in-law that she had proved to be a hopeless chaperon.

I did not like Emily and Emily did not like me but we always behaved with great affection toward each other so that Cornelius should not be upset. Priggish by nature, Emily had condemned me for leaving my first husband while I was still carrying his child, and since I suspected she was undersexed, I was hardly surprised when she appeared incapable of understanding the force of a passion which had driven me to give up my children in order to remain with the man I loved. Emily talked a great deal about exercising Christian charity, but like so many regular churchgoers she did not practice what she preached. However, even if she had been an atheist, she would probably still have been incapable of sympathizing with me, because she had long since decided that her mission in life was to martyr herself for children—either her own or other people's—and so she consistently put the interests of those children before her own welfare. I suspected that during her brief marriage her husband had been ruthlessly relegated to a subordinate role in the family, but unfortunately she had picked the wrong man to be an audience for her saintliness. Steve Sullivan had had little time for women whose sexual tastes were not as frank and florid as his own.

"Darling," I said as Emily picked up the phone in Velletria, Ohio, "it's Alicia."

"Alicia darling, what a lovely surprise!" Emily, always up early in order to make a prompt start on the day's good works, sounded tiresomely bright and cheerful. "How's everything in New York?"

"Disastrous. Vicky's just eloped with Sam."

There was a shattered silence. If the news had not been as distasteful to me as it obviously was to her, I might have taken an unforgivable but human pleasure in her stupefaction.

"That can't be true," said Emily at last in a hushed voice. "I don't believe it. When did this happen?"

"The wedding was yesterday. Sam called Cornelius last night from Annapolis."

"*Annapolis?*"

"Annapolis, Maryland."

"I am well aware," said Emily coldly, "that Annapolis is in Maryland. I just don't understand how Vicky could have got there."

I briefly outlined the few details I knew of the elopement. "I can't think why you didn't realize what Vicky was up to, darling," I added, unable to resist responding to her chilliness by pointing out a few home truths. "You were with Vicky when she saw Sam in Paris, and young girls can never hide an infatuation—they always have to talk about the man endlessly to anyone who'll listen."

"Are you implying that Cornelius blames *me* for this debacle?" said Emily in a voice of ice.

"No, of course not, Emily dear, but—"

"Because it's not *my* fault if Vicky felt compelled to marry a man twice her age in order to get away from home!"

"Emily, can you conceivably be suggesting—?"

"I'm suggesting nothing except that I refuse to accept any blame for the disaster. Moreover, I strongly resent your accusations that I'm responsible when all I did was try to help you out after you yourself admitted that the problem of Vicky was beyond you!"

"I never meant to imply—"

"Oh, yes you did. May I speak to Cornelius, please?"

"He's drafting a statement for the press."

"Very well. I'll speak to him later when I've calmed down. Meanwhile, you can tell him from me that I hope he's happy now that he's ruined his daughter's life."

"Emily, Cornelius didn't want her to marry Sam—he'd changed his mind! This news was a dreadful shock to him!"

"What trash! You don't believe that, do you?"

"Emily!"

"Do you think I don't know my own brother? And do you think I don't know Sam Keller? My God, I could tell you some stories from the past . . . but I won't. That's all finished now, and I mustn't resurrect it. I'll just say that it couldn't be more obvious to me that Cornelius has planned this from start to finish with ample help as usual from his . . . No, I won't dignify Sam by describing him as a friend. He's always been a bad influence on Cornelius. If Sam hadn't been there, always willing to obey orders so efficiently, Cornelius would never have dreamed of attempting any of his more questionable schemes. Oh, I've no illusions about Sam Keller! I don't want to sound prejudiced, but when all's said and done, he's a German, isn't he, and we all know nowadays what the Germans are capable of!"

"Why, what a very unchristian thing to say!" I exclaimed, not because I had any desire to defend Sam but because I was unable to resist the compulsion to dent her air of righteous indignation. "Aren't we supposed to forgive our enemies? Or do we just sit back and leave that to God?"

Emily hung up. I poured myself some more coffee and considered the mess I had made of the interview, but I came to the conclusion that I'd been provoked beyond endurance. With any luck Emily would call back to apologize once she realized how unfairly she had behaved, and we could stitch our relationship together again without Cornelius knowing we had quarreled.

I did wonder idly what dark past misdeeds she had been referring to, but supposed with a yawn that she had been making some reference to her late husband, Steve Sullivan, who had died a self-ruined alcoholic back in the thirties. Emily's canonization of the husband who had left her for another woman was really becoming very boring, and her hint that Cornelius and Sam had not always behaved like choirboys struck me as being not only stupid but naive. Steve had tried to push Cornelius out of the bank, which belonged to Cornelius by right. Everyone knew that. Of course Cornelius had had to defend himself, and of course he had probably been driven to use tough measures, but big business, like war, does not operate according to normal civilian standards, and I for one could not blame Cornelius for doing whatever was necessary to ensure his survival at the bank. Anyway, his world at Willow and Wall did not concern me. How could it? I cared nothing for banking. It was a man's world and I wanted no part of it. All that mattered to me was that I had a husband who loved me and who, regardless of what had happened at the bank, had always been a devoted family man.

As my thoughts returned to the family, I saw it was still too early to break the news of Vicky's marriage to Sylvia, but I decided instead to call Sebastian in Cambridge, Massachusetts. Sebastian had just concluded his second year at Harvard, where he was majoring in economics, but so far he had not let me know when he would be returning home for the summer vacation. Several times during the past week I had almost given in to the urge to call him, but Sebastian did not like me calling unless I had important news, so I had somehow summoned the determination to wait until I heard from him.

It occurred to me as I picked up the receiver again that the one positive aspect of Vicky's elopement was that it gave me the perfect excuse to ask Sebastian when he was coming home.

"Darling, it's me," I said nervously when he came on the line. "Were you sleeping?"

"Yes."

"Oh, I'm sorry. I—"

"What is it?"

"Well, it's about Vicky—bad news. I wanted to tell you before you read it in the papers. She's eloped again."

There was a silence.

"She got married in Maryland yesterday to Sam Keller. Cornelius and I were flabbergasted but of course there's nothing we can do. We'll just have to make the best of it."

The silence continued. My heart ached for him. Finally I said in a rush, "Darling, I'm so very sorry—"

"Don't be. Okay, thanks for calling." The line went dead.

"Sebastian . . ." I still had no idea when he was coming home. I debated whether to call him back but decided I must leave him alone to come to terms with his shock and disappointment. I felt depressed. Evidently I was destined to be a failure on the phone that morning, and concluding that the news was so bad it could only be satisfactorily communicated by letter, I rang for my maid, dressed in my smartest black frock to negate the image of Vicky dressed in white, and went downstairs to write to Andrew.

156

II

I LOVED my second son, but he had never needed me. That too must have been the result of one of the natural laws governing human relationships; if you give up a baby at birth in order to pursue a grand passion, you should not be surprised later when your child automatically turns to his nurse for maternal love and regards you merely as an agreeable stranger who tries to kiss him too often.

However, although I felt sad that I had missed the best years of Andrew's childhood, I was not bitter because Andrew was obviously unmarred by being abandoned in early life. Not only had he been his father's favorite, but his excellent nurse had brought him up with as much love as if he had been her own child, so although in theory he had been deprived, in practice he had always basked in a wealth of security and affection. It was Sebastian who had been deprived, because Sebastian had been old enough to miss me when I left home. Sometimes I thought that no matter how much love I lavished on Sebastian, I would never be able to compensate him for putting Cornelius first long ago.

Once I had tried to explain to the boys how mesmerized I had been when Cornelius had first burst into my life, but neither of them had been much interested. "I didn't want to leave you," I had said, the words tumbling out awkwardly because the subject still made me feel so distressed. "It nearly killed me to leave, but I was so helpless, as if I had no will of my own. It was like being hypnotized. I couldn't have acted in any other way."

"So what?" Sebastian had said carelessly. "You got us in the end. What does it matter now? Why go raking up the past and making yourself upset all over again?"

And Andrew had said, "Gee, Mom, that's just like the movies!"

I had wondered then if I would have found it easier to communicate with daughters, but my experience with Vicky had soon disabused me of that particular fantasy. I always seemed to have difficulty expressing myself to my sons, perhaps because my separation from them had left an indissoluble legacy of shyness or perhaps because I wanted so desperately for them to love me despite all I had done. Caught between my desire to smother them with affection and my fear that Cornelius might look upon any overindulgence as a sign that I was compensating myself for the unborn children, my manner toward the boys ranged uneasily from warmth to reserve.

"Dearest Andrew," I wrote that morning after nibbling the end of my pen for ten minutes. I never found letter-writing easy unless I was writing to Sebastian. To help me choose the correct words, I pictured Andrew, who was finishing his last semester at Groton. What would he be thinking about? Games probably. Andrew was so straightforward. I visualized his green eyes bright with the spark my eyes had always lacked, his dark hair flopping forward across his forehead, his mouth curved in a cheerful smile. He was every mother's dream of a happy, normal, well-adjusted eighteen-year-old son. I was so proud of Andrew. I could not imagine why I found it so hard to know what to say to him.

"I guess you will be astonished to hear that Vicky has just got married," I wrote after two false starts. "She has married Sam. Cornelius and I were very surprised but wish them well. Don't believe any lurid stories you may read in the papers, because the journalists will be sure to muddle up the news somehow. If you wish to congratulate Vicky by writing to her, I'm sure she'd be very pleased.

"I do hope school is going well—not long now before you come home! No doubt you'll be sad to leave, but what a happy time you've had there and how well you've done. Longing to see you, darling, all my love . . ."

I seldom wrote long letters. I acted on the principle that a boy at school would prefer to get short letters regularly than long letters sporadically, and neither of the boys had ever complained.

A great longing for Sebastian swept over me, and as soon as Andrew's letter was sealed I pulled a fresh sheet of paper toward me and wrote impulsively: "Darling, I'm so sorry about this stupid marriage of Vicky's. I know how hurt you must be, but don't be angry with Cornelius, because he truly didn't sanction this. When he got the news, he was so horrified that he had a bad attack of asthma. I'm angry with Sam for making such an exhibition of himself with a young girl, and I'm *livid* with Vicky for being so irresponsible, although of course she's only eighteen and very immature and I should make allowances. Now, darling, I know you must be so depressed, but do please take an optimistic view if you can. At least Sam is a known quantity and we can be sure he'll take care of Vicky in style— it's not as if she'd married that beachboy whose only knowledge of civilized life consisted of a shack in a California subdivision tract.

There's also another point which is obvious to me but may not be so obvious to you: *this marriage won't last.* I give it five years at the most, and just think: by that time you'll be twenty-five and established at the bank and the whole situation will look very different. All my love, darling . . ."

After rereading the letter twice, I sealed it with meticulous care and then nerved myself to write the necessary letter to Vicky. After three drafts, two cups of coffee, and four of the cigarettes I so rarely smoked, I produced a letter which read:

"My dearest Vicky: I was, of course, surprised to hear of your marriage but nonetheless send you my very best wishes for the future. It does help that we all know Sam so well and are more than aware of those attractive qualities which made him one of the most eligible bachelors in New York. I'm sure many girls would envy you in your new role.

"Your father is wholly reconciled to the news and you can be sure that we'll both give you a warm reception when you return to New York. Meanwhile, please let me know if there's anything I can do to help smooth your passage from one world to another. I too married young, as you know, and I often wished I had an older woman to talk to occasionally about the more unfamiliar aspects of married life. I know we have had our differences in the past, but please understand that I have always been deeply concerned for you and that as your father's only child you have a very special place in my affections. With fondest love . . ."

I felt so exhausted after this protracted effort that I hardly had the strength to pick up my pen again, but I was determined not to shirk the last letter. Having ground my cigarette to pieces in the ashtray I wrote firmly:

"Dear Sam: I have no wish to give you advice, when you obviously have the whole matter so totally in control, but may I suggest you stop by here with Vicky as soon as you return to New York? Poor Cornelius is determined to accept the situation, but he does need to be reassured that his daughter is well and happy. I doubt if you need my good wishes for the future, but you are certainly welcome to them if you think they will improve family relations. Sincerely, Alicia."

I mailed my last two letters to Sam's Park Avenue apartment, and a week later on a Friday evening the butler announced that Mr. and Mrs. Keller had arrived to see us.

III

SAM LOOKED slimmer, smarter, and very bright-eyed. The celebrated Keller charm was much in evidence. Vicky, ravishing in a little pink dress with a matching ribbon tying back her fair curls, clung to his arm and gazed up at him adoringly. I had expected some semblance of marital harmony, but this overpowering bliss stunned me so much that I was speechless. In panic I turned to Cornelius, but saw with dread that he too was tongue-tied.

Fortunately Sam—as usual—produced exactly the right words to help us all gloss over the awkwardness, and within minutes I was able to say sincerely to Vicky, "You look wonderful, dear. I've never seen you look prettier."

"Isn't she beautiful?" sighed Sam.

Some unpleasant emotion which could not be named made my fingers curl tightly into the palms of my hands. I watched him slip his arm around her as they sat down on the couch, watched her immediately lean closer to him as she smiled up into his eyes.

"I can't think why Carraway's taking such a long time with the champagne," I said rapidly to Cornelius as I stood up. "Shall I . . . ?"

"Yes, ring the bell." Cornelius, mysteriously, was also rising to his feet as if he could no longer remain seated. We looked at one another without comprehension and sat down again. To my horror I realized I had forgotten to ring the bell.

"Is there an ashtray, Alicia?" said Sam casually, opening his cigarette case.

I took advantage of the new excuse to rise to my feet, but when I brought Sam the ashtray, I gave him a hard look to see whether he had deliberately staged the excuse to save me embarrassment. It was impossible to tell. He was smiling at Vicky again and seemed unaware of the ashtray I placed on the table in front of him.

"Well, honey, open up your purse and let's show Neil and Alicia all those wonderful photos we took in Bermuda!" He turned to toss an explanation in our direction. "I chartered a yacht which picked us up in Annapolis the morning after we were married."

"Oh, it was so romantic!" said Vicky dreamily. "And when we got to Bermuda, we found this beach which was just gorgeous, and—"

"You're not going to smoke, Sam, are you?" said Cornelius, betraying he had been unaware of the preceding conversation. "My asthma's been very bad lately."

My nails dug deeper into the palms of my hands. I suddenly knew that I had to treat Sam and Vicky with the greatest possible warmth, although why I should have felt this was so important, I had no idea. "Oh, don't be ridiculous, Cornelius!" I exclaimed. "Of course Sam must have a cigarette! I'll adjust the air conditioning to extract the smoke. Yes, Vicky dearest, do show us all your lovely photos—I can't wait to see them! Did you have good weather? Bermuda's such heaven—I remember it's one of your favorite places, isn't it, Sam?"

Sam began to talk in his deep leisurely voice about Bermuda while Vicky passed around the photographs. I was just trying for the third time to take an intelligent interest in the conversation when Carraway entered with the champagne.

"Well!" I said frantically as we all raised our glasses. "Here's to a very happy marriage!"

"Our best wishes to you," added Cornelius politely, and to my relief I realized he was recovering his nerve.

"Why, thank you!" said Sam with his warmest, most captivating smile. "We appreciate that, don't we, honey?"

"Mmmm . . . oooh, what lovely champagne!"

I noticed that we all drank equally fast.

"And here's to you two!" said Sam, finally unleashing the full force of his charm to bend the scene to his will. "Thanks for giving us such a truly great welcome and for being so magnificently generous and understanding—no, I mean it! I truly do! Now I owe you wonderful people an apology, so I'm going to go right ahead and apologize for temporarily wrecking your peace of mind—well, I did, didn't I? Let's call a spade a spade!—but bearing in mind all the water that had previously flowed under the bridge, I just didn't see that I had any alternative except to play Romeo and elope. I knew you'd both oppose me if I went to you and said: 'Well, it's a funny thing, but I really do want to marry your unique, beautiful, enchanting daughter'—and be honest, Neil, you still doubt my sincerity, don't you? Well, you needn't. I love Vicky and she loves me, and we're going to be the happiest couple in all New York."

The most extraordinary part of all was that I believed him.

IV

AFTER THE Kellers had gone, Cornelius retired to the library to work, but later from my bedroom window I saw him slip out of the house with his bodyguard. He wore casual clothes, a white tennis shirt, sneakers, and blue denims, and I knew he was on his way to the woman in Greenwich Village. The Cadillac crawled away; the courtyard gates swung shut, and turning abruptly from the window, I left my room and began to walk.

The house was very large and I walked a long way. Situated on the corner of a Fifth Avenue block, the house overlooked Central Park although the main entrance into the forecourt stood on the intersecting crosstown street. Paul Van Zale had built the place for Sylvia after their marriage in 1912, and on his death in 1926 the mansion had passed to Cornelius, together with the rest of the Van Zale fortune. The irony was that although Cornelius secretly disliked the house—the heavy European-style architecture was hardly in accord with his modern tastes—he obstinately refused to sell it. For him it was a symbol of his power, a fitting counterpart to the magnificent Renaissance-style building at Willow and Wall, and so we went on living there, even now the children were grown up. I did not mind. I had always lived in huge gloomy houses filled with antiques. My father, Dean Blaise, a contemporary of Paul's, had also been an investment banker with a grandiose taste in houses, and even after I married Ralph my surroundings had changed little. My father had given us a mansion filled with antiques in Albany when Ralph had embarked on his political career.

Walking on and on down the corridors of the Van Zale mansion, I at last found myself in the deserted nursery. Cornelius' first wife, Vivienne, had designed the nursery when she had been pregnant, but since she and Cornelius had separated before Vicky's birth, the room had remained unused until I had begun my life with Cornelius. Then Sebastian had occupied the nursery for a few weeks until the judge had declared me to be an unfit mother and awarded custody to Ralph. Years later I had tried to turn the nursery into a playroom, but the children had preferred the games room with the French doors that opened into the garden. The nursery had always been a failure, and now with disuse it had become shabby and forlorn.

I sat down on a little stool by the rocking horse and thought for some time. Perhaps I should arrange for the nursery to be redecorated. Vicky was sure to have a baby within the year.

I rose to my feet automatically, just as Cornelius and I had risen to our feet at the unbearable sight of another couple effortlessly achieving the harmony which lay beyond our reach. I could now identify the unpleasant emotion I had gone to such lengths to hide. It was jealousy. I was jealous of a woman whose husband could prove his love so positively that she had been transformed into the most radiant bride I had ever seen.

Immediately I hated myself for being jealous. Then I found I was hating Vicky for making me give way to such a destructive, shameful emotion. I pulled myself together. The truth was not that I hated Vicky, but that I did not understand her. I did not understand why she had never accepted me as a mother when her own mother had been such a failure. I did not understand why she should have felt unhappy at home when I had bent over backward to be kind and patient. I did not understand how she could have looked twice at Sam Keller when Sebastian loved her so much. I understood nothing about her. I was being made violently unhappy by an enigma, a puzzle I seemed destined never to solve.

With a great effort I made a new attempt to be sensible. I had done my best for Vicky in the past, and one can't do more than one's best. As for the future, we would probably get along much better now that she had left home. In fact, if only I could conquer my stupid, humiliating jealousy, there was no reason why we shouldn't be on the best possible terms.

I knew I was jealous because Vicky was underlining to me how empty my life was. I knew too that the obvious solution was to take steps to make my life less empty, but that was easier said than done. What could I do to make my life more interesting? My annual charity fashion show was always widely praised, but fundamentally I disliked charity work because I was too shy and lacked the necessary militant organizational skills. My secretary, who was very efficient and who no doubt stayed with me because I interfered with her as little as possible, had carte blanche to deal with all my charities as she saw fit. I was not clever, so there was no point in taking a little morning course in French conversation or perhaps afternoon lessons in bridge. I was not musical, and although I drew well I didn't see how I could improve my life by spending more time sketching. I supposed I ought to meet more people, but in my role as Cornelius' wife I met a great many people regularly and devoted much of my time and energy to living the social life my position required. I wondered dimly what it would be like to meet people who saw me as myself, not merely as Cornelius' wife, but the thought seemed remote, bordering on fantasy. I *was* Cornelius' wife. I was good at being Cornelius' wife, and that was all I wanted to be.

But Cornelius had someone else. And my life with him was empty. I had to build a life of my own somehow, and that was so difficult when I had always defined my life in terms of other people. I had been my father's daughter, Ralph's wife, Sebastian's mother, Cornelius' wife . . . and now obviously I must be some man's mistress. It was no use shirking the idea anymore. I'd been cowardly in refusing to face the conclusion Cornelius had so sensibly reached the previous April, and it was very clear to me now that for everyone's sake I must put an end to the loneliness which was making me increasingly neurotic and embittered.

I said to myself calmly, as if it were the most natural thing in the world: I'll have an affair. Then I said fiercely: *I must.* But when I thought of Cornelius, slim and supple in his blue denims, the voice in my head cried in despair: I can't, I can't, I can't. . . .

V

"ARE YOU all right?" said Cornelius.

"Oh, yes! Just fine. I had a call from Sebastian today. He's coming home tomorrow."

"Uh-huh. Great. Well, if you'll excuse me . . ."

It was such a relief to have the opportunity to escape from my insoluble problems. I decided I would only think of them again later, at the end of the summer when we returned to the city after spending August at Bar Harbor. Meanwhile I was busy, excited, and happy. I had something to look forward to at last.

My first husband had thought Sebastian was slow-witted because he had talked late and had at first been backward with his lessons, but when I had better access to my boys I bought special books to help Sebastian with his letters and numbers, and that was when I found out he was clever. Other people found out later, but I found out first. As a child he had a squint and protruding teeth. Cornelius thought he was plain; he never actually said so, but I noticed how often he was complimentary about Andrew's looks, while Sebastian was never mentioned. But I found the best doctor in New York to operate on that "lazy" eye and the best dentist to make sure those teeth grew straight, and when Sebastian was suffering from the skin troubles common among adolescents I did not say, as Cornelius said: "Oh, he'll grow out of it!" I took Sebastian to the best skin specialist instead, and now he was six feet tall with a clear skin and arresting dark eyes and a smile which displayed perfect, even teeth. I still marveled at how big and strong and grown-up he was. Sometimes when I saw him after a long separation I could hardly believe in the miracle which had enabled me to give birth to him, but there he was, my son, the living reminder of that unforgettable time when I had felt *someone*, Alicia Blaise Foxworth, talented, successful, special.

On the morning he was due to arrive home I had my hair freshly set and dressed in my new white linen suit with the new black-and-white polka-dot overblouse. The skirt, tighter and shorter than last year's fashion, flattered me and made me glad I had taken such trouble to stay slim. I wasn't so happy with the overblouse, but one can't expect to like every detail of the latest fashions. After selecting a small black pillbox hat, I found my smartest black purse and gloves and set off to the station in Cornelius' new primrose-yellow Cadillac.

The train was ten minutes late. I stood coolly by the ticket barrier and even when the train arrived I tried to conceal my excitement because I lived in dread of embarrassing Sebastian by some unwise display of affection.

Sebastian was not demonstrative.

When I saw him walking toward me I raised my hand in acknowledgment, smiled casually, and took a small insignificant step forward. My heart felt as if it were about to collapse with happiness. He was wearing a shabby crumpled summer suit, his favorite tie, which looked overdue for a visit to the cleaners, and no hat. The battered old suitcase in his hand must have been heavy, but he carried it as easily as a woman would carry a purse.

"Hello, darling," I said offhandedly. I knew it was always better to err on the side of coolness. "How are you?" I had to stand on tiptoe to kiss him because he was so tall.

"Okay."

We went out to the car in companionable silence.

"Christ," said Sebastian when he saw the Cadillac, "what a god-awful color."

"Cornelius loves it. *'Chacun à son goût!'* "

"Don't think much of his *goût*. Why the hell doesn't he buy a decent Rolls-Royce?"

"Darling, you know how Cornelius likes to patronize American industry."

"I thought the general idea nowadays was to pour money into Europe. God, what an awful place New York is—look at it! Just look at it! Look at all the dirt and the mindless people and the mean streets! What a junk heap!"

"It would be worse in Philadelphia," I said, making a New York joke.

"Where's that?"

We laughed, and when we were both sitting in the car I could not resist leaning over to give him a second kiss.

"It's lovely to see you again, darling."

"Uh-huh. What's scheduled? The usual? No hope of Cornelius canceling the big xenophobic July Fourth family saturnalia and migrating early to Bar Harbor?"

"Oh, darling, you know how Cornelius loves his American traditions!"

"Emily and the gang coming?"

"For July Fourth? Yes, of course."

"And Scott?"

"I guess so."

"Thank God. At least there'll be one person who's interesting to talk to."

"Darling, you really shouldn't say things like that!"

"Anyone else coming?"

"Well . . ."

"Sam and Vicky?"

"Yes. Oh, darling—"

"Forget it. I don't want to talk about her."

The journey continued in silence. I wanted to squeeze his hand comfortingly but I knew that would be a mistake. On our arrival home Sebastian immediately went to his room, closed the door and began to play *Tannhäuser* on his phonograph, and it was six o'clock before I could summon the nerve to disturb him.

"Cornelius is back, darling," I said, tapping on the door. "Won't you come down and say hello?"

Sebastian emerged grumpily and without comment tramped downstairs to the Gold Room, where Cornelius was glancing at the *Post*.

"Hello, Sebastian!"

"Hi."

They shook hands. They looked incongruous together, Cornelius so fair and fine-boned, Sebastian so dark and heavily built. Sebastian was the taller by several inches.

"How are you?"

"Fine."

"Good journey?"

"Yep."

"Harvard?"

"Okay."

"Great!"

Silence. I pressed the bell. "What would you like to drink, Sebastian?"

"Beer."

"All right." We waited. With relief I thought of something to say. "Darling, do tell Cornelius what you think of the economic situation—what was that remark you made at the station about Marshall aid?"

The evening passed without too much awkwardness, and at nine-thirty Cornelius excused himself, saying he wanted an early night.

"How impressive you were with your knowledge, darling!" I said to Sebastian as soon as we were alone. "Cornelius was so impressed, I could tell."

"Maybe." He fidgeted impatiently. I wondered if he wanted to retire to his room again to listen to *Tannhäuser*.

"Do you want to go to bed, darling?" I said, feeling I ought to give him the opportunity to leave if he wanted to. I did not want to be clinging or possessive.

"No. Please stop calling me darling the whole time. Since you gave me such a godawful name as Sebastian, the least you can do is use it."

"Of course! Sorry. It's funny how these stupid endearments become automatic." I smiled at him and thought: So much love but no one to give it to. I looked around the room blindly as if I could find some recipient waiting in the shadows.

"Are you okay, Mother?"

"Yes, of course. Why?"

"You seem pretty tense."

So even Sebastian had noticed. It seemed the crowning humiliation.

"I'm all right," I said evenly, but I saw then more clearly than ever that the day was fast approaching when I would have no choice but to reconsider those problems which still seemed so far beyond solution.

VI

"ARE YOU all right, Alicia?" said Kevin Daly.

We were sitting on the terrace of Cornelius' summer cottage at Bar Harbor two months later. Cornelius had not inherited Paul's summer home but had later acquired a similar property half a mile down the road. Styled in the manner of a Mediterranean villa, the house had thirty rooms, all with extensive views, and ten landscaped acres of garden which sloped downhill to the sea. Every summer I stayed there with the children while Cornelius spent as much time with us as his work permitted, and every summer Emily would travel from Ohio with her two girls to share our vacation. Since her daughters had been left fatherless at an early age Cornelius considered he should take a special interest in his nieces, and they in their turn had been brought up to regard him as a substitute for the father they could not remember.

As Cornelius always enjoyed being with children, and as it was obviously right that he should give all possible assistance to his sister, I did not object to this situation—although a whole summer of Emily frequently reduced me to exhaustion—but I was surprised when Cornelius took an equal interest in Emily's stepchildren. Emily's renegade husband, Steve Sullivan, had continually dabbled with marriage, and her daughters were only two of the children he had fathered over the years. There had been two sons from an earlier marriage; the younger, Tony, had been killed in the war, but the older, Scott, was a great favorite with Cornelius and even worked at the bank.

"And why not?" said Cornelius. "Why should I be prejudiced against him on account of Steve?"

I made no attempt to argue with him, but personally I was much impressed by this true Christian forgiveness and sheer generosity of spirit. We all knew Cornelius had had good reason to hate Steve, and a lesser man would surely have washed his hands of all Steve's children except the ones who were related to him through Emily. However, Cornelius continued to be charitable, and in 1940 he even took charge of the three children of Steve's last liaison, his marriage to the English businesswoman Dinah Slade. In fact it was Emily who looked after them for the duration of the war, but Cornelius always did his best to be agreeable toward them. Why he bothered, I could not imagine, for the children were unattractive and difficult and I suspected even Emily, with her talent for martyrdom, was glad when they were old enough to return to Europe to complete their education at English boarding schools. For the first two years after the war they had continued to spend their summers with us at Bar Harbor, but since the twins, Edred and Elfrida, had celebrated their eighteenth birthday in January 1948 they had not visited America and the checks which Cornelius had sent them so generously had been returned to him.

"I guess they think they've imposed on me long enough," said Cornelius, but I could tell he was hurt.

"I think it shows a disgraceful lack of gratitude," I could not help saying to Emily, but all Emily said was, "Growing up isn't always easy, particularly if you lose both parents at an early age."

In contrast to the English Sullivans, the American Sullivans were all devoted to Cornelius and quick to display their affection and gratitude toward him. At that moment, as I sat on the terrace at Bar Harbor with Kevin, they were all playing tennis with Andrew on the court below. Andrew was partnering Emily's elder daughter, Rose, and Scott, who had arrived from New York for a long weekend, was playing with Lori, the younger girl. Of the rest of the family, Sebastian had gone off by himself somewhere as usual, Emily was visiting the local branch of the Red Cross, and Cornelius had just been called away to the phone, so I was alone with Kevin on the terrace. He was staying with friends at North-East Harbor and had driven over to visit us for the day.

"Yes, I'm fine, Kevin. Nothing's the matter at all. . . ."

Kevin was the same age as Cornelius, and good-looking in a way which I, never having been to Ireland, was probably mistaken in thinking was Irish. He had thick dark hair, bright eyes, and a wide winning smile. Twelve years ago he had ceased attending social occasions with a succession of pretty girls and had let it be known that a young actor was living with him at his house in Greenwich Village. The actor had lasted no longer than the pretty girls, but all New York now knew about Kevin Daly's private tastes, and poor Cornelius, who was fond of Kevin but naturally disapproved of homosexuals, had been much embarrassed by the incident.

Nowadays we seldom saw Kevin socially, but I admired his beautiful home and I enjoyed myself when we were invited to dinner there once a year. I liked the plays he wrote, too, although when I read the reviews afterward I wondered if I had truly understood what the plays were about. Kevin wrote in blank verse but I didn't mind that because the actors were so clever and made the lines sound just like ordinary conversation. The plots were usually sad, but I enjoy stories which involve me emotionally. The women were very well-drawn.

". . . at least . . . well, no, Kevin, nothing's the matter. Not really. Nothing."

I liked Kevin the best of the three men whom Paul Van Zale had chosen long ago to be Cornelius' summer companions. I had never entirely trusted either Sam's charm or Jake Reischman's sophistication, but Kevin's spontaneity had always put me at ease.

"It's just that I've so much enjoyed the summer here with the children," I said, making an effort to answer his question in a way which would not increase his suspicion that something was wrong, "and I'm just dreading the return to New York."

"No kidding!" said Kevin agreeably, helping himself to more bourbon and offering me the sherry decanter. "I always feel I'm going mad if ever I'm away from New York for too long. I feel kind of mad at the moment, as a matter of fact. I hope to God the house hasn't burned to the ground. I think I'll call Mona as soon as Neil's through with the phone."

"Mona?"

"My current caretaker. Oh, you must meet Mona—she's such fun! She's got these two hopelessly immoral goldfish who . . . Say, Alicia, are you sure you won't have some more sherry? No? I don't blame you, it looks just terrible. Have you ever tried Wild Turkey bourbon? It's wonderful if you feel the slightest bit depressed."

I somehow managed to laugh, but as soon as I laughed I wanted to cry. It was because he was genuinely concerned. I thought it was so kind of him to spare a moment to worry about someone who was just the wife of an old friend.

Making a great effort to match his casual tone of voice, I said lightly, "I was always brought up to believe that gentlemen drink Scotch, Southerners drink bourbon, and ladies—if they drink at all—drink sherry or, if they're very fast and live in New York, cocktails with a gin base." But even as I spoke I was wondering painfully how long Mona had been in residence as his caretaker. I realized that Cornelius must have given the Polish woman an apartment as soon as I had sanctioned the arrangement, and suddenly the world looked gray to me, while the laughter from the nearby tennis court seemed cruel and mocking. I was going to be quite alone when I returned to New York. Sebastian would return to Harvard, Andrew was due to go into the air force to pursue his ambition to be a pilot, and Cornelius would spend most of his time at Willow Street. I was going to be utterly alone with nothing to do, nowhere to go, and no one, no one, *no one* I could possibly turn to . . .

"Oh, Kevin!" I exclaimed in despair, but could say no more.

"Life's frightful sometimes, isn't it?" said Kevin. "Do you ever feel you'd like to grab a hatchet and smash everything in sight? I'd like to, but unfortunately there'd be nothing to smash. My personal life at the moment's like Hiroshima after the bomb."

"I . . ." I wanted to speak, but again nothing happened.

"Of course, if I were you, the first thing I'd smash would be that ghastly house of yours on Fifth Avenue. I always felt so sorry for you, marrying that mausoleum when you married Neil! Now that all the kids are grown up, can't you persuade him to sell it so that you can choose a home of your own? Think what fun you could have picking out a nice house, and how great it would be to ditch all the priceless antiques and have exactly the furniture you want! I think you deserve some sort of reward, Alicia, for being such a superb Mrs. Cornelius Van Zale all these years—I think it's time *you* came first for a change. It should now be *your* turn to express *your* self— and when I say *your* self I don't mean Mrs. Cornelius Van Zale's self, I mean the self that belongs to *you*, Alicia . . . what was your maiden name?"

"Blaise."

"Alicia Blaise. *You.* You're still there, aren't you, buried alive in that godawful tomb on Fifth Avenue? God, if I had the dynamite, I'd blow the whole place sky-high myself to set you free!"

I laughed. My eyes were full of tears, but he never saw them because I was taking such care to stare down at my hands. More laughter came from the tennis court below us, but I barely heard it. Even when Cornelius returned to the terrace and Kevin excused himself in order to use the phone, I was hardly aware of them, for I had just seen my problems from an entirely different angle and the vision mesmerized me.

I saw now that I didn't have to become some man's mistress in a sacrificial gesture made solely to make life more tolerable for myself and those around me, and that contrary to what I had always supposed, I wasn't on the brink of some last resort which required me to abandon my self-respect. For the truth was, Mrs. Cornelius Van Zale didn't have to debase herself by inaugurating a new era of self-effacement as some man's mistress; instead, Alicia Blaise could assert herself by taking a lover.

That was quite different.

In taking a lover, instead of becoming a mistress, I would have an active, not a passive role. I would define myself, not be defined by someone else, for this step was one I could take not only for myself but *as* myself, and I would have to take it all on my own without any help. I would have to choose the man myself. I would have to manipulate the first meeting with him. I might even have to seduce him if he balked at seducing me. It was a terrifying landscape, but it was *my* landscape, the landscape of my own creation, and it would belong entirely to me.

I thought in panic: I can't do this, I can't stand alone with no one to help me, I don't have the courage.

But then I thought of Kevin saying: "Isn't it *your* turn, Alicia?" and I thought: Yes, why should I be miserable when everyone else is happy and content? Why should I? And that first faint spark of anger gave me the courage I needed to go on.

For the first time, I began to think not of some man who might condescend to take an interest in me for his own amusement, but of a man who could adequately assume the role I needed so much to assign to him.

Chapter Three

I

As EVERYONE knows, it's easy for a man to find someone to sleep with him. He just has to walk up to any of the numerous willing candidates and ask. But for a woman, particularly a woman such as I was, the situation is far more difficult.

New York society was notoriously loose. The cynical joke that the only way to be sure that a couple were sleeping apart was to establish that they were married did in fact have a strong root in reality, but I was not by nature promiscuous and my two husbands had been the only men in my life. It was true I had retained my looks, but I knew very well that my appeal to the opposite sex was limited by my reserve, which often made me seem cold and aloof. I was not and never would be one of those scintillating women who could ensnare a man just by lighting a cigarette.

As I took a bath before changing for dinner that evening, I saw clearly that there were two separate problems which had to be overcome. The first was that both my temperament and my scanty past experience placed me at a disadvantage in initiating an affair, and the second was the old difficulty that there was no man I wanted. I decided to tackle this latter problem first by making a determined attempt to visualize someone suitable. Obviously he would have to be someone of my own social level; I wasn't about to throw all discretion to the winds by seducing a servant, a mailman, or a store clerk at Macy's. Obviously, too, since I wanted someone as firmly anchored to his domestic situation as I was to mine, he would have to be someone's husband, but the only husbands I knew well were the husbands of my friends, and I refused to treat my friends shoddily. In fact, I had no close friends—my shyness has always made such friendships difficult—but there were a number of women I liked and I was determined that they should continue to like me as much as I liked them. That left the husbands of my more casual acquaintances, and the idea of approaching strangers was inconceivable.

I added more hot water to the bath and lay back in despair, but gradually as I persisted with my train of thought I found the situation became clearer. I asked myself why a stranger should seem so ineligible when most women would surely have preferred a lover who had no connection with their everyday life, and I realized that I was distrustful of strangers not merely because I was afraid they would gossip about me but because I was afraid they would gossip about Cornelius. No one who hasn't suffered from the pens of the gossip columnists can imagine how fanatical a victim can become to avoid their attentions, and ever since I had left Ralph to live with Cornelius I had placed the highest value on a private life which remained private under all circumstances. The gossip columnists kept a sharp eye on us because we were very rich, we were still moderately young, and we were the parents of one of America's prettiest heiresses, and although our quiet family life had provided the minimum of fodder for these columns, I was always aware that the vultures were ready to pounce if we ever put a foot wrong. Vicky's elopement with the beachboy had been made twice as unpleasant by the fact that the news had been plastered all over the tabloids.

So because I was in a different social position from most women, my options too were different. In fact, I had no options, because there was only one course I could safely consider. I had to find a man who would not only keep quiet about me to his friends but a man who would somehow be able to resist saying in the men's room of the Knickerbocker Club: "Say, Cornelius Van Zale sure has problems!" The picture of my lover slipped into focus at last. He was going to have to be not just a friend of Cornelius but an ally who would always be loyal to him, and of course, as I well knew, there were only three men in all New York whom Cornelius trusted absolutely. Sam was ineligible. Kevin couldn't help me.

That left Jake Reischman.

I scrambled out of the bath, upset my dusting powder over the carpet, and huddled myself deep in the folds of the largest towel I could find, but later, sitting at the vanity while my maid brushed my hair, I was able to think of Jake again. His great advantage was that I felt I could trust him as absolutely as Cornelius did. He was a man of the world, yet he had been married for fifteen years and maintained a rigidly respectable home life. Obviously such a man would not only share my horror of gossip but would know just how to conduct an affair with the maximum of taste and good sense.

Of course, he was Jewish, but I wouldn't think of that.

I thought about it. For a moment my Eastern Seaboard upbringing among the Yankee aristocracy overcame me, but then I remembered where the road to anti-Semitism had led Germany, and I was ashamed of myself. A Jew was a man, not some alien species of animal life, and anyway, Jake was fair, like Cornelius. If I put aside the degrading prejudices which had been instilled into me in childhood, I thought he was one of the few men I knew whom I might be able to find physically attractive.

The next hurdle, I thought as I dismissed my maid and hunted through my jewel boxes for a necklace, was to engineer an opportunity to speak to him alone. Whenever I saw him, he was usually with his wife—a very dreary woman whom I had never liked—and I thought it would be unwise to call or write to him at his home. To contact him at his banking house was out of the question. I would have to plan the next move very carefully. There must be no mistakes, no mess.

I went down to dinner.

II

"AND WHEN is your next major exhibition at the Van Zale Art Museum, Cornelius dear?" inquired Emily, daintily picking at her roast duck.

"It opens on the Monday after Labor Day. I've got together a collection of American primitives—several well-known artists and one or two newcomers."

"What a pity I can't stay in New York to see it!" said Emily. "But I'll be in the middle of my fund-raising drive for the displaced persons of Europe."

"I loathe American primitives!" exclaimed her daughter Lori, a tall noisy girl of sixteen with glossy dark hair and bright blue eyes. "I like huge florid pictures by Rubens of men with no clothes on!"

"Lori!" said her sister Rose, in disgust. "Do you have to be quite so vulgar?"

"Surely Rubens' specialty was naked women?" said Scott, amused. "You're confusing Rubens with Michelangelo, Lori!"

"Oh, I can't bear Michelangelo! His angels look like hermaphrodites!"

"That's enough, Lori dearest," said Emily sharply.

"Angels *are* hermaphrodites, surely," said Scott to his half-sister.

"Angels don't exist," said Sebastian, munching duck.

"Nonsense!" said Scott. "They exist in the mind."

"That doesn't make them real!"

"Reality is only what the mind perceives."

"But—"

"Oh, I can't bear these intellectual discussions!" said Lori. "Pass the salt, please, Andrew."

"You're so intolerant, Lori!" exclaimed Rose.

"No, I'm not! I know what I like, that's all, and what I don't like are American primitives. Why are you interested in them, Uncle Cornelius? I thought you only liked those awful blobs of red paint in messy black lines by Picasso!"

"Aren't you confusing Picasso with Kandinsky?" said Scott.

"I thought Kandinsky played for the Cincinnati Reds," said Andrew. "And just what is an American primitive anyway?"

"Oh, God," said Sebastian.

"Andrew's joking!" said Emily with a little silvery laugh.

"Fat chance," said Sebastian.

"Cornelius," I said, "when did you say the opening of this exhibition is? I don't recall seeing it on my calendar."

"Well, it must be there! My secretary told your secretary . . ."

"I like American primitives," said Rose. "They have such pure innocent lines."

"Enchanting," agreed her mother, "and I must say I do like a painting which is *representational*."

"Is there going to be a big reception for the opening?" I said to Cornelius.

"Yes, of course. All the New York art world will be there."

"And all the board of the Van Zale Fine Arts Foundation?"

"Sure."

So Jake would be there. I pictured the crowded reception, the cigarette smoke, the chance for a quick word in a quiet corner. But how was I ever going to detach him from his wife, who always clung to him like a limpet at all large social occasions? My problems once more seemed insuperable.

When I again became aware of my surroundings I found that the footmen were removing the plates of the main course before bringing in the dessert.

"What did you make of that chess problem in the *Times* last Sunday?" Scott was saying to Cornelius.

"It was interesting, wasn't it?" Cornelius immediately brightened at the prospect of a chess discussion, and as he gave Scott his peculiarly radiant smile, I realized, not for the first time, that Scott had a relationship with Cornelius that neither of my boys had been able to achieve. For a moment I watched Scott closely but saw only his neutral good manners and his pleasant easy smile. I supposed some women might have found him attractive, but he did not attract me; there was some quality about his appearance which I found repellent. It was as if his black hair and black eyes were the outward manifestations of an opaque, closed personality, and I couldn't understand why Cornelius found it so easy to behave paternally toward him. But perhaps Cornelius' attitude was more fraternal than paternal. There was only eleven years' difference in their ages, and Cornelius had once said to me how much he wished he could have had a brother. They also had various interests in common: the bank, Emily and her girls, chess . . .

"I hate chess!" said Lori. "All those little figures on a board—what's the point?"

"But chess is like life, Lori," said Scott, smiling at her. "We're all a lot of little figures trying to edge our way across the board."

I began to think again of Jake Reischman.

III

"I HAVE TO warn you," said Cornelius to me a week before the exhibition opened, "that this woman I . . . that Teresa Kowalewski is one of the artists whose work will be on display and that she'll be at the opening. Of course there's no need for you to meet her. I've already asked her to arrive late, so she won't be there at the beginning when we meet the other artists."

"I see." My image of the unknown woman became clearer; she was a woman ambitious enough to sleep her way to success. I passed no judgment but merely noted with relief that Cornelius had probably been correct in assuming she would never fall in love with him.

Cornelius was pretending to read the paper. It was evening and we were having a drink together in the Gold Room of our home on Fifth Avenue.

"Well, I've certainly no wish to meet her," I said, "but if I want to avoid her later, how will I know who she is?"

"She's about my height and she has curly dark hair which always looks untidy. She'll be wearing a red evening frock."

"How can you be so sure?"

"Because she only has one evening frock."

"Oh."

We did not say anything else. He turned a page of his paper, Carraway announced dinner, and as we rose to our feet to go to the dining room, I resumed my elaborate plans to detach Jake Reischman from his wife.

IV

I SAW HIM enter the long crowded room, a tall man, heavier than he used to be, his hair not only fairer than Cornelius' but straighter and thinner at the crown. His eyes reminded me of a clear sky on a winter's morning. As I watched, he worked his way toward us with effortless expertise, a word here, a word there, a light pat on the back, a professional smile, a step forward, sideways, forward again.

He was alone.

At first I could not believe it, and then as I grasped the fact that my elaborate plans were no longer necessary, I felt for the first time that fate was on my side and luck was at last beginning to run my way.

He reached us. "Good evening, Neil . . . Alicia." His professional smile touched those wintry blue eyes briefly in acknowledgment that he was among old friends.

"Hello, Jake . . . where's Amy?" said Cornelius naturally.

"She had to have a wisdom tooth removed today—an abscess developed last night, great crisis. She sent her apologies and said how disappointed she was not to be able to come. . . . Why, Vicky! Mrs. Keller, what a vision of loveliness! How's married life?"

"Oh, Uncle Jake, what an old flatterer you are!" said Vicky, hugging him warmly.

"Skip the 'uncle,' my dear, and drop the 'old.' You're forgetting I'm just as young as your husband! Hello, Sam, how are you? Art exhibitions surely aren't in your line!"

"Vicky's trying to educate me—I keep telling her it's a hopeless task, but she won't take no for an answer!"

We all laughed, and realizing in panic that I had to contribute to the conversation to prevent Jake moving on, I said quickly, "How are the children, Jake? Has Elsa settled down at her new school?"

"She likes the food, but I foresee she'll be no happier at this school than she was at the last, unless she makes up her mind to diet. She should lose thirty pounds and become svelte and soignée—like you, Alicia my dear," said Jake, smooth as midwinter ice, and smiled at me to signify a formal detached approval.

"Thank you!" I said, my mouth dry.

Sam and Vicky had already drawn away to speak to someone else, and at that moment another millionaire buttonholed Cornelius. I could hear talk of endowments for art scholarships and the setting up of another major trust fund.

"Perhaps I should escape before they ask me how the capital should be invested," murmured Jake. "Excuse me, Alicia."

My heart almost stopped beating. I felt faint.

"Jake . . ."

He paused politely.

"Jake, I . . ."

"My God, what a noise there is in here! Neil's invited too many people. Step over here, my dear—I can hardly hear you."

We moved to a quiet corner behind a block of sculpture. I smoothed my hands frantically against my formal black gown as if I could somehow wring all the poise I needed from those elegant folds, but when I tried to speak, I found to my horror that I had forgotten the careful opening sentence I had endlessly rehearsed for the occasion.

"Alicia? Is something wrong?"

I found my tongue. "No, nothing's wrong," I stammered, "nothing at . . ." I ran out of breath unexpectedly and had to pause to regain it. I felt as if I were in the midst of some violent punitive exercise. ". . . at all. I just . . . Jake, may I see you sometime, please? There's something I'd like to discuss with you. I know you're very busy, but . . ."

"I always have time for my friends. When would you like us to meet?"

"Oh, I . . . well, I . . . I thought maybe you could stop by at our house after work one evening for a drink."

"Yes, of course—I'd be delighted. What evening did you have in mind?"

"I thought . . . perhaps next week . . . Thursday. . . . Of course, if it's not convenient . . ."

"Thursday would be fine. But won't Neil be away in Chicago?"

"Yes. But this is something very confidential, Jake. You mustn't tell Cornelius. Or anybody else."

"My lips will be completely sealed, I promise you!" He looked both bemused and intrigued. "I hope there's nothing seriously wrong?"

"Oh, no," I said. "Nothing. Thanks so much, Jake."

"Till Thursday," he said, raising his hand casually in farewell as he drifted away into the crowd. "I'll be looking forward to it."

I stared after him, and the noise in the room seemed to increase, until I felt dizzy. Leaning back against the wall, I tried to breathe evenly, but my body was bathed in sweat and I felt more ill than ever. I felt unclean, too, as if I had been contaminated by some disgusting disease.

The compulsion to turn to Cornelius for comfort was overwhelming, and when my dizziness had passed I edged my way blindly through the crowds to the place where we had separated. The journey seemed to take an immense time. I felt as if I were moving in that familiar nightmare where the person one wants is always just beyond one's reach.

"Cornelius!"

I found him at last. He turned, and as I swayed with relief, the woman at his side stopped talking. I stared at her. Nobody spoke. It was as if the whole room had fallen silent, although the roar of conversation still pounded sickeningly in my ears.

"Alicia," said Cornelius in a voice devoid of expression, "this is Teresa Kowalewski. Some of her pictures are here, as you know. Teresa, this is my wife."

The woman wore a shiny red dress and red shoes. The two shades of red were a bad match. She was taller than Cornelius and looked large and awkward beside him.

"Hi," she said, looking larger and more awkward than ever.

"Good evening." I wished I could think of some annihilating phrase. In my daytime serials the best wives could always cut the mistresses down to size.

For a second I still could not believe she was the woman who went to bed with Cornelius. I knew that there was a Polish-American woman somewhere in Manhattan called Teresa who painted pictures and had only one evening frock, and I knew that Cornelius had for various reasons been seeing her regularly, but I had never comprehended the enormity of her role in his life. No doubt I had preferred not to face the truth; perhaps, loving Cornelius as I did, I had been incapable of facing it. But now the magnitude of the whole appalling hurtful mess burst violently upon me and there was no avoiding it. This vulgar, coarse, garish girl went to bed with my husband. Somewhere in New York there was a bed where they lay naked together and practiced all the physical intimacies I was denied. She knew how he kissed. She knew how he made love. She possessed a whole world of knowledge which should have belonged only to me and which she had no right to share.

I looked at Cornelius and for the first time felt totally betrayed.

"This is just the most exciting day of my life!" the woman was saying in a rush. "In fact, I'm so frightened I can hardly speak!"

"Oh."

"Teresa's frightened of the critics," said Cornelius unnecessarily.

"Oh."

"Why, there's Kevin!" exclaimed the woman. "Excuse me, but I just must . . ." She flew off thankfully.

After a pause Cornelius said, strained, "I'm very sorry. I can't think why you came over to us. I did warn you."

"Yes. It doesn't matter." I looked around blankly for someone to talk to. Yet another millionaire buttonholed Cornelius.

I wondered what Jake would be like in bed.

V

I WAS WEARING my smartest black dress and trying to decide how much makeup to use. I disliked makeup, but once one's fortieth birthday was on the horizon one could hardly pretend one's natural appearance was the most flattering. At last I powdered my face lightly, applied an unobtrusive lipstick, and gave my eyelashes a careful brush with mascara. Then, turning to my jewel boxes, I passed over the diamonds which Cornelius liked me to wear, ignored the rubies, sapphires, and emeralds which I secretly detested, and selected an unadorned gold pin.

By six o'clock I was downstairs in one of the reception rooms—not Cornelius' favorite, the Gold Room, which was small and cozy, but the Rembrandt Room, where gloomy Rembrandt self-portraits gazed down upon the exquisite furniture of eighteenth-century England. I drank a very large martini and ordered another. By that time I was wondering in panic if the Versailles Room would have provided a less depressing atmosphere, but I did not think I could have faced seeing myself reflected in all those gilt mirrors. Besides, the furniture was too rococo. Jake deserved the effortless elegance of the English furniture, and perhaps, as he was so accustomed to living with the Reischman art collection, he would barely notice the introspective Rembrandts on the walls.

"Mr. Reischman, madam," announced Carraway grandly in his richest British accent.

As I rose to my feet, I discovered that the unaccustomed martini had made me lightheaded, and I rested my fingertips unobtrusively on the nearest table to steady myself. Under the circumstances it seemed not only a nominal but a hopeless attempt to maintain my equilibrium.

"Alicia!" said Jake, moving smoothly into the room. "How are you? I hope I'm not late." He held both my hands for a second and released them. The physical contact, arid and meaningless, was over before I could register any emotion, even dread. I noticed for the first time that he had square, workmanlike hands with short fingers.

"No, no, of course you're not late! Do sit down. What would you like to drink?" I tried not to sound like an actress reading an unfamiliar script.

Jake glanced at my empty martini glass and then said casually as he sat down opposite me, "I'll take some Scotch on the rocks. Johnnie Walker Black Label, if possible."

We made small talk about the opening of the exhibition until Carraway returned with our drinks. Jake was relaxed, polished, imperturbable. I was concentrating so hard on maintaining the conversation that it was hard for me to notice the details of his appearance, but I was aware that his dark suit was perfectly cut and that his plain shirt was fastened at the wrists by gold cufflinks.

". . . and how lovely Vicky was looking!" said Jake. "Marriage evidently agrees with her."

"Yes, we're all so relieved."

Carraway withdrew. Jake picked up his glass of Scotch. "Here's to you, Alicia!" he said with a suave courtesy any diplomat might have envied. "Thank you for inviting me. Now, what's this confidential matter you mentioned? I have to admit I hardly know how to contain my curiosity!"

It occurred to me that if he had had any inkling of what I had in mind he would have been far less flippant. "Well . . ." I drank some more of my new martini and began again. "It's just . . ." I stopped.

"Is it about Neil?" said Jake, still suave but mercifully direct.

"Yes," I said, drinking very fast again.

He offered his cigarette case to me.

"No, thank you, Jake, I hardly ever smoke nowadays. Cornelius' asthma—"

"I'm not Cornelius and I think you should have a cigarette to calm you down."

I took the cigarette. As he lit it for me he said abruptly, "Is Neil in some kind of trouble?"

"Oh, no!" I said rapidly. "Everything's fine. It's just that, well, we've decided to . . . to live a little differently, that's all. I mean, it's entirely a mutual decision, and our marriage is intact, but . . . well, it's all a bit different now from the way it used to be."

After a pause Jake said, "I see," and lit his own cigarette.

"No, I don't suppose you do, because I'm explaining myself so stupidly. Cornelius has a mistress, Jake. I mean, it's not like that time when you . . . it's not just one night here and there with anyone who happens to be available. There's a woman he sees regularly. I guess you probably know all about it."

"No," he said. "I didn't know."

"Oh. I somehow have this idea that you, Cornelius, Kevin, and Sam know all each other's secrets."

"My dear, those days are long gone—we're all a hundred light-years away now from those Bar Harbor summers with Paul. How did you find out about this mistress?"

"Oh, Cornelius told me," I said, "of course."

There was another pause before Jake said, "Of course."

"For various reasons—I needn't bother you with them—Cornelius and I have decided not to sleep together anymore. We've discussed the whole thing calmly and sensibly and agreed that he should take a mistress while I should . . . should . . ."

"Take a lover? Neil surprises me. I wouldn't have thought him capable of being so civilized. Does he feel extraordinarily guilty toward you for some reason?"

I heard myself say quickly, "I don't want to go into his motives, Jake."

"And I'm not sure I want to hear them. Well," said Jake, sitting back comfortably in his chair with his glass in one hand and his cigarette in the other, "so you're looking for a lover."

"Yes." Unable to look at him, I finished my martini and listened to a calm sensible woman who could not possibly be me talking nonchalantly about the difficulty of committing adultery. "Of course, it's very awkward. I've got to be totally discreet, and that's why I can only choose someone who would be loyal to Cornelius. You may think it absurd—even bizarre—that I could only ask someone loyal to Cornelius to do something which would appear to be the ultimate disloyalty, but . . ."

". . . but what more loyal gesture could one imagine? If the man looked after his friend's wife when the friend himself was apparently unwilling to do so, wouldn't he in fact be doing everyone the greatest possible favor?"

"Exactly!" An enormous burden seemed to dissolve amidst the relief that such perfect understanding made further explanations unnecessary. "Yes. Well . . . you can see how awkwardly I'm placed. There are so few men I can rely upon absolutely, and since Sam's married to my own stepdaughter and Kevin wouldn't be interested . . ."

"My dear Alicia!" Jake put down both glass and cigarette and sprang to his feet. "What an enormous compliment!" Without the slightest hesitation he took my hand and raised it to his lips before sitting down beside me on the couch. "I'm immensely flattered! Thank you very much. However . . ."

"You're not interested." I did not know how I was going to endure my humiliation. My face was already hot with shame as I stared down at my hands, but just as I was wondering in despair how I was ever going to face seeing him again, he said wryly, "You underestimate yourself. If you were any woman but Cornelius Van Zale's wife, I assure you I wouldn't have waited all these years for an invitation."

His left hand moved. I could see with great clarity the blunt square nails and the solid flesh around the joints, and when that hand covered mine I found those thick powerful fingers had a firm comforting clasp. Then I noticed with equal clarity that the dark material of his suit was stretched tight across his thigh as he leaned toward me, and for a second I had a vivid impression of the strong solid flesh beneath. My glance traveled farther up his thigh and then stopped, although the image I now saw existed only in my imagination.

I felt hot, but the heat no longer sprang from embarrassment. I heard myself say in a low voice, "I know you'd never deceive Cornelius under ordinary circumstances, Jake, but these circumstances are quite different. After all, Cornelius has given me his full permission to have an affair with whomever I choose."

"Alicia," said Jake, "let me give you a word of advice. Neil may sincerely believe he can regard your adultery with equanimity. He may honestly and truly believe it. But the fact is, there are very few men who can tolerate their wives' adultery, and I doubt if Neil would ever be able to take his place among those select few. It's all very well to say that you've both discussed this in a civilized fashion, but the truth is, there *is* no civilized way of discussing adultery. It's a primitive subject dealing with primitive emotions, and the people who get into the worst messes are always the people who think they're operating under these so-called civilized agreements. Never, never tell him if you're unfaithful to him, and make very, very sure you're never found out."

I felt chilled. "You think it would be too dangerous for you to become involved with me."

"No, I didn't say that." Satisfied that I had taken his warning seriously, Jake seemed to relax. With his free hand he reached for his cigarette. "I think if we were careful," he said, "there'd be a ninety-nine-percent chance that we'd never be found out. It's only in the canons of literature that adultery inevitably has disastrous consequences. However, there would always be that slight risk, and frankly it's a risk I just can't afford to take. I do a lot of business on Wall Street with Neil, and his goodwill is vital to me. And besides . . ." He fell silent.

"Besides," I said bleakly, concluding the sentence for him, "no matter what one says to the contrary when one's trying to be sophisticated, a man just doesn't go to bed with his best friend's wife."

"Nonsense, it happens all the time! Anyway, men like Neil and myself don't have friends in the accepted sense of the word. We have the three A's instead: allies, aides, and acquaintances. Or in other words: those we barter with, those we buy, and those we acknowledge because it suits us to do so." I must have looked shocked by such cynicism, for he added quickly, "But yes, I'm fond of Neil and I respect him—although that's irrelevant to what I'd intended to say, which was this: I have trouble believing that I'm the best solution to your problem. Surely the answer is to wait until Neil recovers from this temporary madness and comes back to you? What the hell's he doing, with this other woman anyway? It's *you* he's crazy about! You've no idea what a shock you gave me just now when you said he had a regular mistress."

"He can't help it—it's not his fault . . ." To my distress, I began to cry.

Jake's hand tightened on mine. "Can you try to explain the problem to me?"

"No, I mustn't . . . not fair to Cornelius . . . no one must know."

"Are you sure it wouldn't be better to tell someone? And don't you think in retrospect that your main reason for inviting me here was that you were at your wits' end and needed someone to confide in?"

"Perhaps." I had pulled my hand away and was scrabbling for a handkerchief.

He crushed out his cigarette. "I don't think you want a lover at all," he said, reaching for his Scotch. "I think you just want someone to talk to."

My voice said at once, "It's not as simple as that."

"No?"

I shook my head violently and watched the Scotch glint gold-brown as the glass was replaced on the table.

"I must go before I do something very foolish," said Jake, rising abruptly to his feet.

I said nothing.

He did not move. Several seconds passed. I could not look at him.

"It's not that I don't want to help you. I only wish I could come up with some helpful advice."

"Please go, Jake."

"But I want you to know . . ."

"It's all right. I understand."

There was another silence before he said politely, "We must meet again, of course. Unless you'd prefer . . ."

"Yes. I want to go on as if this meeting had never happened."

"As you wish." He moved toward the door. "Forgive me, but I'm sure this is the wisest course for both of us."

I nodded, my head bent over my clasped hands, and waited for the noise of the closing door. The wait seemed interminable, but at last I heard the soft click of the lock signaling to me that I was alone.

"Oh, God!" I cried aloud in despair, and the tears streamed through my fingers as my whole body shook with sobs.

His hand touched my shoulder.

I gasped. The shock was so great that it transformed that delicate gesture into an electrifying act of violence.

"I locked the door," he said, and took me in his arms.

Chapter Four

I

I COULD think only how different he was from Cornelius. Cornelius'
mouth was always so firm, even when he was kissing softly, but
Jake's kisses were somehow more pliable, less easily defined. His lips
were thin but subtly shaped; his tongue was hard yet tentative as he
sought to explore the mouth I could not open; I was aware of complex emotions stirring behind that polished surface, emotions which
would have been alien to Cornelius' straightforward expression of
physical desire, and although I tried to part my lips for him, my
reserve intensified to defeat me and I knew I was frightened of the
unknown.

Jake paused. I felt his arms relax around my waist. He had not
moved his hands during the embrace, yet I had been acutely aware of
those strong fingers pressing insistently against my spine. I felt frightened again, lost, muddled.

I saw him glance swiftly at the door as if he wished we could retreat upstairs to less formal surroundings, but of course that was impossible, as some servant would have been certain to see us. Finally,
in an attempt to make the room less inhibiting, he said in a low
voice, "Shall I draw the drapes?"

I nodded, and presently the drapes swung shut to mute the early-
evening light, but although it became darker in the room, I could still
see him clearly. When he slipped off his jacket, I noticed that although he was so much bigger than Cornelius, he was far from being
so well-proportioned. I thought of the perfect line of Cornelius' neck

and shoulders, and suddenly I longed for him, not just for his physical presence but for his simple direct uncomplicated attitude to passion, which had always pierced straight through the armor of my reserve and effortlessly allayed my most private fears.

Jake pulled off his tie and undid the top button of his shirt.

When he took me in his arms again I could feel the increased heat of his body, and aware in panic that I could not now withdraw without alienating him forever, I managed at last to open my mouth to his. His manner at once altered. The deliberate, sensual restraint which had made his kisses so oddly flexible and so wholly foreign merged into a darker, more aggressive sexuality directly at odds with the urbane mask he presented to the world, and as I had my first glimpse into the rough, angry, bitter reaches of his personality, I realized with horror that I was about to give myself to a man I had never known.

I could no longer make a conscious effort to adopt the right responses. As his hands began to move and I felt the strength of the pressure building in his body, my nerve failed me. I went rigid with tension, then struggled to be free.

He at once released me and stepped back. His eyes were a hot violent blue. I was terrified.

"I'm sorry . . . forgive me . . . I don't understand . . . I wanted you so much . . ."

"You wanted him." I saw him swiftly conceal all trace of the mysterious primitive personality he had revealed. Producing a handkerchief, he carefully wiped the sweat from his forehead and buttoned his shirt rapidly to the neck. Then he picked up his glass of Scotch, drained it, and reached in the pockets of his discarded jacket for a cigarette. When it was alight, he inhaled once and left it in the ashtray while he knotted his tie.

"Jake, I hardly know what to say. I feel so embarrassed and ashamed . . ."

"Don't be absurd. If anyone has to feel embarrassed and ashamed, it should be me. I can't think why I was naive enough to imagine a complicated problem could ever be solved so simply. Here, have some of this." And he passed me his cigarette while he slipped on his jacket.

I put the cigarette to my lips but could not inhale. I was feeling lost again, not knowing what to do, but then he took charge of the situation, made me sit down beside him on the couch while we shared that cigarette, and put his arm around me as I edged nearer to him for comfort. After a moment I had the courage to say, "Are you very angry?"

"No. Disappointed, yes—I'm only human! But not angry. How about you? Do you feel better or worse?"

"I'm not sure, I feel so muddled. Is it possible that I could feel better after making such a mess of everything? Isn't this the moment when I should go completely to pieces?"

He laughed. "I wish it was—I'd like nothing better than to put you together again! Now, tell me what's at the root of this problem. Don't you think I've earned the right to know?"

I told him everything. It took a long time. Afterward Carraway brought us sandwiches and coffee; I had no desire for food, but Jake was insistent, so I ate half a chicken sandwich. The coffee was rich and at last I began to feel stronger.

"It's an interesting idea of yours," Jake was saying, "that the situation would be improved if Vicky were to marry Sebastian, but I doubt that you're right. I think Neil needs a much stronger jolt than that to set him back on the rails."

"What do you mean?"

"Well, he's got everything out of proportion, hasn't he? He's got all his priorities screwed up. Any balanced man would see that so long as he has you it doesn't make a goddamned bit of difference that he's sterile. God, if I had a wife like you . . . However, I don't want to wander from the point. What Neil needs is some kind of blinding reminder of the vital facts of life, but I must admit I don't see how he's going to get it. Has he seen a psychiatrist?"

"Oh, no!" I said, appalled. "He'd never consider such a thing! I've seen two or three psychiatrists myself, but—"

"You! My God, you're the one who's normal!" Jake set down his coffeecup, flicked a crumb from his cuff, and stood up. "I must go or there'll be a row with Amy when I get home. Listen, my dear, we must, of course, meet again. I usually work till six-thirty or seven, but at least one night a week I always arrange to leave the office at five. Which day next week would suit you?"

"It's difficult. . . . You see, Cornelius will be back from Chicago by then."

"Oh, I wasn't going to suggest we meet here! I have an apartment in the East Fifties. Why don't we meet there a week from today?"

"Well, I . . . yes, I'd like to, but—"

"We'll just talk. That's all you need right now."

"But would that be fair to you?"

"Why not? Would it be any fairer to either of us if I insisted you went to bed with me when all you wanted was to go to bed with someone else? Do you imagine I'd enjoy that any more than you would?" Without waiting for an answer, he wrote down the apartment's address and gave me one of a pair of keys which he extracted from his key ring. "There's a doorman in the lobby," he said, "but if he stops you, just say you've come to see Mr. Strauss."

I took the key and folded it carefully in the paper recording the address. As we walked to the door, I wanted to say so much to him, but the words were too difficult to choose. I even found it hard to say a simple thank-you and good-bye.

In the hall a footman opened the front door as Carraway hovered by the stairs, and Jake and I paused, two actors playing their opening scene before their first audience.

"Good night, Alicia. Thank you for the coffee and sandwiches."

"You're very welcome, Jake. Good night," I said politely, and stood watching from the porch as his car slipped away into the twilight.

II

"I'VE COME to see Mr. Strauss," I said a week later to the uniformed doorman of the modern apartment building on East Fifty-fourth Street.

Evidently this was an unremarkable event in the doorman's daily life. With a smile he gestured toward the elevators and said, "Number 6D, ma'am."

Trying to behave as if I were well-accustomed to meeting Mr. Strauss at his apartment, I entered the elevator, pressed the button, and wondered how many other women had held the key which I now took from my purse. Jake suddenly seemed unreachable, walled off from me by years of extramarital experience. No doubt he was only interested in me because I presented more of a challenge to him than the women whom he was accustomed to seducing without effort, and feeling deeply depressed, I fitted the key in the lock and opened the door.

"Jake?" I called nervously.

There was no reply.

Closing the door, I tiptoed across the little hallway into the spacious living room beyond. Long low couches upholstered in dull crimson lay limpidly on an enormous Persian carpet. The couches were peppered with plump cushions covered in a heavily embroidered material which matched the thick luxurious drapes, and the walls were hidden beneath the coordinating dull crimson of the flocked wallpaper. The room's three paintings, all showing elaborately detailed scenes of Venice, looked as if they might be Canaletto originals borrowed from the Reischman art collection, while the three low brass tables, which added an Oriental touch to the room's sumptuous atmosphere, reminded me that Jake, as well as being a German-American, was also a Jew.

Feeling further removed from him than ever, I took off my hat and coat and put them away in the empty closet by the front door before I searched my purse for a cigarette. My lighter refused to work. I found a little kitchen, but there were no matches there, so, taking a deep breath, I entered the bedroom. The huge bed was canopied with yards of crimson silk, and again I was reminded not of Europe but of the Middle East. Moving across another exquisite Persian carpet, I ignored the full-length French Impressionist nude which was the room's only picture and opened the drawers of the nightstands on either side of the bed. One nightstand was empty. The other contained a slim volume of cartoons reprinted from *The New Yorker,* a book of untranslated poems by Goethe, and three packets of male contraceptives.

"Alicia?" called Jake as the front door opened in the distance.

Guiltily ramming shut the drawer, I hurried back to the living room.

"I'm sorry," I said incoherently, "I was just . . . Why, what have you got there?"

Jake was carrying a large brown paper bag. We kissed as casually as if we had been meeting every week for twenty years, and then he moved past me into the kitchen.

"I haven't used this place in a while," he said. "I just stopped for a few of the necessities of life." Opening the bag, he extracted a bottle of Johnnie Walker Black Label, a jar of olives, one lemon, four bagels, half a pound of cream cheese, and several slices of lox. "There's already gin and vermouth here," he said. "Can I fix you a martini?"

"Well, I don't usually drink martinis, but perhaps . . ."

"Wait a minute." He was hunting in the closet below the counter. "The last incumbent of this place seems to have walked off with two bottles of vermouth and one and a half bottles of gin. God, how shoddy! Would you object strongly to drinking Scotch?"

"I've never drunk Scotch before. I shall feel very decadent! My father had old-fashioned ideas about what women should drink."

"I'll call up the liquor store."

"No, no—let me try the Scotch! But make it very weak."

"Sure." He began to fix the drinks. "Do you like bagels?"

"I . . ."

"You've never had one!" He was smiling at me, his eyes bright with amusement but also with wariness, as if I were as much an unknown quantity to him as he was to me.

"Of course I've had bagels before!" I said defiantly. "Why not? You don't have to be Jewish to eat bagels!"

When he laughed, the faint tension between us immediately dissolved. "Good! But let's get to the food later. Can I give you a light for that cigarette?"

We went into the living room and sank down on one of the crimson couches. It was wickedly comfortable.

"What do you think of this place?" said Jake before I could start to feel nervous again.

I did not know what to say, because his taste was obviously so different from my own. I like light pretty rooms full of pastel colors and elegant furniture, rooms which give an impression of uncluttered space. "It's very striking," I said cautiously.

"But not in accordance with the best white Anglo-Saxon Protestant standards of the Yankee aristocracy!" he said, amused, but before I could look as embarrassed as I felt, he raised his glass in a toast. "To us both," he said. "I'm very glad to see you."

I was still feeling overwhelmed by our differences, but I managed to return his smile, raise my glass to his, and murmur, "Thank you." The Scotch tasted odd, but softer than a martini. Replacing my glass on the table, I tried desperately to think of something to say, and as if he sensed my panic, he at once began to speak.

"It's unfashionable now to talk about the aristocracy, isn't it?" he said casually. "But do you remember how it was in the old days when everyone talked so freely of Our Crowd and Yours? The Jewish and Yankee aristocracies, the twin pillars of New York society, the parallel lines that never met!"

"I don't think we should talk about . . ." I said rapidly, and then found the gulf between us impossible to name.

"But yes, we must!" said Jake at once. "We should discuss the subject endlessly until we're bored to death with it, or it'll be nothing but a millstone round both our necks!"

"I . . ."

"Let me start by telling you how much I've been admiring your courage."

"Courage?"

"The courage to step outside the conventions we were both taught to respect."

"You mean . . ."

"Parallel lines are never supposed to meet. You reached out and bent them. Perhaps it would be hard for someone who wasn't raised in either Your Crowd or Mine to realize the courage that took."

"No, it wasn't courage, it was just . . ." I struggled to explain how unimportant the differences had seemed in the circumstances. "Of course, one can't pretend the differences don't exist," I said at last, "but now only the similarities seem important—the fact that we both come from the same world, even though that world has two such separate halves. I feel that despite everything, we must still talk the same language."

"Ah, but talking's so difficult!" said Jake. "It's so easy to say the same old words and never say anything new. That's why I'm so convinced we should say all the things we've never said to each other in all the years since we first met—how many years is it? Twenty? Well, never mind how long we've pretended to know each other, that's not important now, and there are other questions I'd prefer to ask. For instance, what was it like growing up Dean Blaise's daughter, a little white Anglo-Saxon Protestant princess in the heart of Old New York?"

"Jake!" I had to laugh at the appalling description, and suddenly the gulf which separated us no longer seemed unbridgeable. "You can't really want to know about that!" I protested. "You can't!"

"Ah, you mysterious Anglo-Saxons!" he exclaimed, laughing with me as his fingers closed tightly on mine. "You'd suppress the whole world if you could, in the name of your so-called good breeding and good taste! Well, I prefer to acknowledge the absurdities of the world frankly, and even laugh at them if I choose. If one really stopped to think about the insane way the universe is arranged, one would go mad in no time, so now and then it's good to laugh, it's therapeutic, it dilutes the pain. . . . Now, please . . . tell me about your early life. I have this amusing suspicion that despite our differences, it was far more like mine than either My Crowd or Your Crowd would be willing to believe."

III

I TALKED to him through several meetings. We met always on Thursday, always at the same time, always for no more than an hour. I told Cornelius I was on the committee of a new charity, and he said he was glad I had found another interest to occupy my time.

During all our meetings Jake never suggested that we should adjourn to the bedroom. We kissed casually when we met and kissed warmly when we parted, but otherwise there was no physical intimacy between us. Yet the intimacy which did exist became increasingly important to me. We would sit drinking his favorite Scotch, and while I talked I would watch the way his fingers gripped the glass and notice the angle of his profile when he raised the glass to his lips. The curve of his fine elegant mouth became familiar to me, as familiar as his high forehead, his thin nose, and the solid line of his jaw, and as the days shortened and I saw him only by artificial light, I noticed the way his straight thinning hair seemed no longer pale but the subtlest shade of gold.

Whenever we met he would bring something different to eat. The bagels with lox and cream cheese were followed by pastrami, which I could not eat, and then by potato pancakes which I found delicious. It was only when I arrived with some caviar, which he refused to eat, that I realized he was enjoying all the food he never had at home. The cuisine at the Reischman mansion on Fifth Avenue was much too grand to acknowledge the existence of bagels and pastrami.

In fact, Jake and I ate little at the apartment. I developed a taste for Scotch, although naturally I was careful to continue drinking sherry at home in case Cornelius started wondering where I had acquired my new drinking habits. I also smoked more than usual, but I never felt guilty about that because Jake was a chain smoker, lighting one cigarette from the butt of another. Sometimes I wondered if he smoked so much because it was a strain to listen to me, and sometimes I wondered if he smoked so much to take the edge off his sexual appetite, but I did not know and could not guess. Instead I went on talking. I talked about my isolated childhood with a stepmother who disliked me and a father who was absorbed in his work, and Jake smoked and listened but remained an enigma. I talked about the boarding schools, the dreadful summers when I had been exiled to Europe with a succession of governesses, and Jake nodded and was sympathetic but unfathomable. I told him how I had married Ralph to escape from home, I tried to describe now I had felt when I had been someone special, giving birth to my sons, I recounted the whole sorry history of my first marriage with its disastrous conclusion, and Jake listened and encouraged me to talk, though for what purpose, I did not know.

Yet I talked. I went on talking to this stranger who was outwardly beginning to seem so familiar to me, and then one day, halfway through our sixth meeting, our roles slowly reversed themselves, and he began to talk to me.

IV

"OF COURSE, I always knew we were different," said Jake. "I always knew we were special. When I was a little boy I thought we were royalty, the cream of Old New York. My father was like a god. Everyone bowed and scraped to us. There was a horde of lesser relatives, all reinforcing my childish belief that we were the center of the universe. It would be hard for you to imagine how protected I was, but perhaps not so hard for you to imagine what a shock I had when I finally went out into the world and encountered prejudice. Nothing had prepared me for it. My father had had a little talk with me when he had conceived the heretical idea that I might go to Groton, but since I never got as far as the gates, I never got the chance to mix with boys from the other world. The powers at Groton put my father very politely in his place by saying they just didn't think Groton was quite the right school for me; they didn't think I'd be happy there.

"At first I couldn't believe I'd been rejected. Then I was very hurt, but finally I realized that the only thing to do was to be very debonair and say 'So what?' Sometimes I think I've been acting debonair and saying 'So what?' ever since.

"God, how I hated Your Crowd.

"Then Paul came into my life and everything changed. You know Paul's background—you know he was a Yankee aristocrat who had been trained in a Jewish banking house. He spanned both worlds. He and my father were as close as Sam and Neil are today. I can't remember a time when I didn't know Paul, but I never knew him well because most of the time I was just a kid, and children didn't appear at the extraordinary social occasions when my parents entertained the Van Zales at dinner. But Paul must have noticed me, because he invited me to Bar Harbor that summer when I was seventeen.

"I was very nervous. I admired Paul but I was in awe of him. I was also scared of the three Gentile boys he had invited to his summer home, and I was scared too of Bar Harbor, the haven of all the most blue-blooded Yankee aristocrats who thought Newport had gone down in the world and who believed all the Jewish resorts on the New Jersey shore were far beyond the pale. So when I arrived for the start of my vacation, I was very, very debonair and very, very grand, and the first two days were hell.

"Then Paul dragged us all out of our shells, and I realized with amazement that the others were just as nervous as I was. He used to make us debate set subjects after dinner, and the first subject he chose was what it meant to be an American. Of course it meant something different to each one of us. I had to explain what it was like to be a Jewish boy from Fifth Avenue, Kevin had to explain what it meant to come from an Irish-American Catholic family heavily involved in politics, Sam had to tell us what it meant to be a German immigrant, and Neil had to tell us what it was like to be a cloistered Midwesterner from a Cincinnati suburb. Paul forced us to know each other, and once the barriers were down, we saw how alike we were, four bright ambitious boys, perfect material for Paul to influence as he pleased.

"I stress this Bar Harbor experience because I want you to understand what a turning point it was in my life; I want you to understand what I owed to Paul, and why, when the time came, I let myself be influenced by him. Paul did for me what the gods of Groton had refused to do: he introduced me to that other world, and it was a gold-plated introduction, because as Paul Van Zale's protégé I found all kinds of doors were immediately opened to me. But Paul did more than that. He treated me exactly as he treated the others, and the others, taking their cue from him, treated me as an equal. It was an environment devoid of prejudice, and it gave me the self-confidence I so badly needed.

"That was the positive side of the Bar Harbor experience. But there was a negative side, too. It's debatable how far a cynical man of the world like Paul Van Zale should be allowed to take over a bunch of adolescent kids, particularly kids who were not only insecure, but mixed up—and I was feeling very mixed up at the time, because I'd just realized I didn't want to be a banker.

"Of course, I hadn't dared tell my father. My father was a tyrant, and we were all terrified of him. Like your father, he was absorbed in his work, so to our relief we didn't have to see him much. It was true he was indulgent with my sisters, but with my brother and me . . . Did you know I once had an older brother? He could never measure up to my father's standards, poor bastard, and my father kept beating him and beating him until one day he just ran away and never came back. He died in an automobile accident in Texas in 1924. God knows what he was doing down there, and nobody ever dared find out. My father said his name was never to be mentioned again, and meanwhile, of course, I'd become the son and heir. . . .

"During the second summer I spent at Bar Harbor—the summer of '26, when Paul was killed—I finally nerved myself to seek Paul's advice. But when I confessed I couldn't face telling my father I didn't want to be a banker, Paul just said, 'If you really hated the idea, you'd tell him.'

"I couldn't help wondering if the situation was that simple, but Paul told me in no uncertain terms to pull myself together. He said, 'You're ambitious, aren't you?' and I said, 'Yes, I am.' Then he said, 'And don't you want to spend the night of your fortieth birthday thinking how successfully you've doubled your father's fortune?' and I said, 'Yes, I do—but shouldn't there be more to life than mere worldly success?'

"He just laughed. He patted me on the shoulder as if I were some pathetically innocent small child and said kindly, 'For God's sake, go into the bank or you'll spend the rest of your life regretting your lost opportunities!' And he added, 'You're at an idealistic age, but when you're older you'll see more clearly that ideals are nothing but a millstone around a man's neck. The moralists may decry worldly success, but the truth is, mankind is so vain and so petty that it finds worldly success the only kind worth chasing. If you want to get on in life, Jake, you won't waste your time worrying about the way things ought to be. You'll concentrate on learning to deal with the way things really are.'

"Well, I went into the bank, and I doubled my father's fortune, but I didn't have all those happy self-satisfied thoughts on the night of my fortieth birthday. I took my wife out to dinner and tried to pretend I had something to say to her, and then, after I'd got rid of her at home, I went out again to a woman I kept—no, not here, it was over on the West Side—and I got drunk and when I awoke next morning with my hangover, all I could think was: I wonder what it would have been like if I'd stood up to my father. I wonder what it would have been like if I'd never listened to Paul Van Zale.

"My secret dream had nothing to do with making money on a large scale—nor, to tell the truth, with any idealistic vision of serving mankind. It was just something I wanted to do. I wanted to own a hotel—oh, a grand hotel, of course! Five stars in all the best guidebooks! I wanted to own a hotel in Bavaria. Just as well I never did. God, that animal Hitler. I can't describe how I felt when I got back to Germany in 1945 and saw where the Nazis had led the country. . . .

"I was one of the interpreters when they started interviewing the war criminals. I couldn't take it, but when I angled for a transfer, I ended up in Munich just as they were sorting out Dachau. There were sights I saw—things that can't be spoken about, and yet they must be spoken about, they must, or people will forget. . . . Eventually I managed to get home, get away from all those ruins—yes, it was the ruins I couldn't bear, the ruins and the G.I.s swaggering around chewing gum—it was all such a nightmare, like watching a multiple rape with Germany the victim and everyone, the Nazis, the Allies, just everyone, doing nothing but ravage, brutalize, and destroy. . . . And Germany was lovely, so beautiful. I'll never forget how much I wanted to live there long ago before the war.

"My wife never felt at ease in Germany, although her family is just as German as mine. She won't speak German either, and pretends she's forgotten it. I can't think why I married her—no, that's not true. I know. I was dating this Gentile girl—not seriously, but I was twenty-five, and I guess my father thought he'd turned a blind eye long enough. He said he thought it would be a good idea if I started seeing Amy occasionally. He was mild about it, but I knew an order when I heard one. Amy was very suitable, naturally, one of Our Crowd, nineteen years old, brought up like my sisters to be a lily of the field . . . but she was prettier than my sisters. At first I thought she was cute. God, it's a terrible mistake to marry when you're only half in love. . . .

"I'm fond of my kids and I'd fight to the death to protect them, but I never know what to say when we're together. I don't see them much—too busy at the bank—and I know now that this is exactly the situation I wanted to avoid when I was eighteen, the whole cycle repeating itself with me standing in my father's shoes. I never wanted to end up like my father. But I have, and there's nothing I can do about it now—except, perhaps, not to stand in my son's way if he decides he can't face the future I can't resist planning for him.

"Yet if David rebels and decides not to go into the bank, it'll be the end of Reischman's as we know it, and I can't help feeling sad about that. The Reischman family's dying out too. Demographers never seem able to explain why families rise and decline, but it must surely be part of a built-in biological pattern. My great-grandfather came to America with three brothers, and they produced twenty-one sons, yet now, three generations later, David is one of only two male Reischmans in his generation. If he doesn't go into the bank, I'll incorporate it to preserve the name and retire as chairman of the board, but it seems a pale anticlimax of an end to a colorful family history. Probably we won't even be living on Fifth Avenue by that time either—the real-estate speculators seem to think of nothing nowadays except tearing down as many private houses as they can get their hands on in order to build apartment houses and stores. The old order changes, as Tennyson pointed out, and gives way to the new. . . .

"But I don't like the look of the new order. It seems to render my order not only obsolete but meaningless. Yet what can I do? Do what I've always done, I guess: act debonair and pretend I don't give a damn. But I do. I care very much. I live in my family home knowing its days are numbered; I work in my family firm knowing that too will probably come to an end as a private banking house; I live with a woman I don't love for the sake of children I can't talk to and rarely see; I have mistress after mistress, but any idea of love seems increasingly remote. And what does it all mean? What's the point? I guess the point must be that there's no point. I tried to talk about this to Neil not long ago, but he refused to discuss it seriously. Perhaps I scared him by raising issues he himself isn't yet able to face, but he'll have to face them one day—one day he'll have to say to himself: 'Just what the hell am I doing, and what's the goddamned point?' and then I'd like to know what kind of answer he's going to dig up to soothe himself.

"Yet Neil's very different from me. He's got this wonderful trick of seeing everything in black and white and believing firmly that God's always on his side—a masterpiece of Anglo-Saxon self-deception! Or does he really think that? Can anyone with Neil's brain—and he's certainly no fool—possibly be that simple? Sometimes I think he puts up that Anglo-Saxon front to protect himself. Sometimes I think he's too frightened to contemplate a world where God doesn't exist or a world where God, if he exists, is hostile. . . . But now I'm getting too metaphysical. I must stop. Have you understood what I've been trying to say, Alicia, my dear, or have I merely been talking gibberish?"

I poured us both some more Scotch, took his hand in mine, and said gently, "Tell me more about your beautiful hotel."

V

IT WAS on the morning after this conversation that Vicky came to see me. I had finished glancing through the day's mail and had handed it to my secretary to be answered; I had approved two menus which my housekeeper had submitted for coming dinner parties, and I had written my weekly letter to Sebastian. After ordering coffee to be brought to the upstairs sitting room where we kept the radio and television, I finished my flower arrangement in the Gold Room and prepared to relax for half an hour with a daytime serial.

The footman admitted Vicky as I was crossing the hall.

"Alicia!" she exclaimed. "Are you busy? I just thought I'd stop by."

She looked lovelier than ever. Her hair had been freshly set and she was wearing a new blue coat which I had not seen before. There was a faint flush to her cheeks. Her gray eyes sparkled with happiness. I suddenly felt old and drab.

"Why, how nice to see you, dear!" I said. "You'll have coffee, won't you?" I turned to the footman. "I've just ordered coffee—see that there's enough for two, and bring it to the Gold Room, please."

"I was going to save the news till this evening when Daddy came home," Vicky was saying buoyantly, "but I just couldn't wait! So I called Daddy at the bank and told him, and he was just thrilled to pieces, but one of the first things he said was: 'Sweetheart, do call Alicia—she'll be so pleased!' So I was going to call you, and then I thought, no, I'll go over to Fifth Avenue and surprise you . . ."

I wondered what was happening in my daytime serial. Would the heroine's sister's pregnancy finally be established today, and would the paternity of the heroine's own baby be confirmed beyond all possible doubt? It occurred to me dimly that real life was so much less interesting. Girls always seemed to know exactly when they got pregnant, and the proud father was usually all too easy to spot at fifty paces.

". . . so anyway, I just rushed out of the house and zoomed into a cab . . ."

As we entered the Gold Room I noticed that the Sèvres clock had stopped again. I felt annoyed. I had particularly instructed Carraway to remind the new footman to wind it daily.

"This all sounds very exciting, darling," I said. "Am I to understand . . . ?"

"Yes! I'm having a baby! Oh, Alicia, isn't it just the most wonderful news you could ever imagine!" said my radiant stepdaughter, and flung herself into my arms.

"That's lovely, darling!" I looked at the silent clock. Time was rushing forward for Vicky in a heady pulsating whirl, but for others time had stopped long ago and the world was quiet beneath the glass case which protected them from dust. "I'm so pleased," I said. "Congratulations! When . . . ?"

"Next April!"

"Perfect! Spring christenings are always so nice. I must look for the family christening robe." I thought I was saying all the right things, but it was hard for me to be sure, because I could no longer think clearly. "And how's Sam?" I said, just remembering him in time.

"*Thrilled!* In the seventh heaven!"

"Yes, of course. Yes, he would be." Out of the corner of my eye I saw Carraway himself entering with the coffee. "Carraway," I said. "The Sèvres clock has stopped again. I'm very displeased."

"Stopped, madam? I shall attend to it personally at once. Perhaps a slight overhaul or cleaning . . ."

"Winding's all it needs, Carraway, as you well know. No, don't do it now. I'm busy with Mrs. Keller. Come back later."

"As madam wishes." Carraway withdrew with an air of worldly resignation, as if he were missing the British aristocracy he had served in England before the war. I despised myself for such a petty display of anger, but fortunately Vicky hardly noticed; as usual she was totally absorbed in herself.

I drank my coffee, listened to her chatter with a smile, and tried not to think of those magic times long ago when I had been someone special, Alicia Blaise Foxworth, talented, successful, unique. But of course I thought of them. The pain was suddenly as sharp as a butcher knife. I hated myself for not being able to keep the knife sheathed, and the more I hated myself, the more unbearable the pain became.

"Darling, I hate to rush off," I said. "I'd just love to talk to you for ages, but I have a lunch date."

Vicky jumped up readily. "Oh, of course! I only intended to stop by for a few minutes anyway, but please . . . come over this evening with Daddy and let's all have a very special family dinner together!"

"Thank you, dear, that would be lovely. About seven?" I had no idea what Cornelius and I were supposed to be doing that evening, but I could sort that out later. My most important task now was to get rid of Vicky before she could think I was cold or uncaring, and after walking with her to the front door, I gave her the warmest embrace I could manage.

"Good-bye, dear. . . . Thanks so much for stopping by . . . I'm so happy for you . . . thrilled . . ." My voice broke. I turned away.

"Why, Alicia . . ." Vicky sounded both awed and amazed. With relief I realized she had diagnosed my emotion as sheer feminine sentimentality and was touched.

"Till this evening." I was already running up the stairs, and although she called something after me, I did not look back. Somehow I managed to shut myself in my room before I burst into tears, but the more I cried, the more I despised myself, and the more I despised myself, the faster the tears flowed. My only thought as I struggled for self-control was that if anyone were ever to guess how disgracefully jealous I was, I would surely die of shame.

But no one would find out. No one came near me anymore. I was a relic from a dead world, like the Sèvres clock, a relic which people admired occasionally but never touched, a relic separated from the world beneath a glass case which nowadays no one ever bothered to remove.

I looked around for a hammer to smash the glass, and saw the telephone by the bed.

My tears stopped. Dragging the phone directory from the drawer of the nightstand, I hunted through the pages for the letter R.

Reischman & Co. 15 Willow.

I dialed the number. I was calm now. My cheeks were dry but stiff, a sign that the tears had mingled disastrously with my makeup.

"Reischman and Company. Good morning, may I help you?"

"I want to speak to Mr. Reischman." I was peering into the mirror to see the extent of the damage. All my mascara had run.

"Mr. Reischman's office . . . good morning."

"Is he there, please?"

"I'll just check to see if he's in conference. Who shall I say is calling?"

I started to tremble. "Mrs. Strauss."

"One moment, Mrs. Strauss." There was a click as she pressed the hold button, and I went on trembling, wondering how I had had the nerve to disturb him at work. I must have been insane. What a terrible error. Maybe if I were to hang up . . .

"Mrs. Strauss!" said Jake in his most casually sophisticated voice. "What a pleasure! How may I help you?"

I gripped the receiver. My voice, sounding impossibly cool and remote, said, "Good morning, Mr. Reischman. I was hoping I could arrange an appointment to see you."

"But of course! When are you free?"

"I . . ." My nerve deserted me. I closed my eyes tightly, as if I could blot out the nightmare of my desperation.

"I have a lunch date I can cancel," said Jake carelessly.

"Oh. Well . . ."

"Twelve-thirty midtown?"

"Yes, thank you. I'll be there." I hung up. For one long moment I sat transfixed on the edge of the bed, and then I moved swiftly to the vanity to repair my appearance.

VI

I REACHED the apartment early because I wanted a quick Scotch to calm me down before he arrived. I was terrified of losing my nerve and making some messy scene which would make him regret his invitation. I supposed he would arrive with food for lunch. I would have to pretend to eat, but perhaps I would feel like eating later; perhaps when I saw him I would feel better.

I left the elevator at the sixth floor, ran all the way down the corridor to apartment 6D, and scrabbled frantically in my purse for the key.

"Oh, God," I said when I couldn't find it. "Oh, *hell* . . ."

The door swung wide.

"In a hurry?" said Jake, smiling from the threshold.

"But you're early!" I said idiotically after my gasp of surprise.

"I was in a hurry too."

"You mean you haven't got much time?"

"I mean I've got all the time in the world," he said, taking me in his arms, "and I didn't intend to waste any of it."

The door closed behind us. The light seemed different in the apartment, but that was because I had never before been there at noon. The luxurious living room was shadowed, but the rich sumptuous furnishings no longer seemed alien. I felt as if I were moving into a country which I had never previously visited but which was familiar to me through hours of painstaking research.

His arms held me firmly. I was now used to him being so much taller than I was, and as I raised my face to his, I closed my eyes, not because I was reluctant to look at a stranger but because I did not want a close friend to see that something was wrong.

"It's so lovely to see you!" I whispered, telling myself over and over again that I wasn't going to make a scene. "I wanted so much to see you . . ."

"But you're not looking!"

I opened my eyes with a smile and felt the tears spill down my cheeks.

"Alicia . . ."

"Oh, it's all right," I said in a rush. "I'm fine. Everything's wonderful. Nothing's the matter at all."

"Ah, you mysterious Anglo-Saxons!" he said, laughing. "The self-control! The discipline! The ruthless stiff upper lip!"

I laughed too. I was still crying as I laughed, but now I no longer cared, because my unhappiness wasn't important anymore. We sat down on the couch, and gradually my tears stopped. There was no longer time to cry, because I was kissing him, and when he kissed me, I no longer wanted to grieve. For I was someone special again at last, not just a discarded woman of no use to anyone, but Alicia Blaise Van Zale, very talented, very successful, utterly unique, and one of the most dynamic men in all New York had fallen in love with me and wanted me for his own.

PART THREE

Cornelius: 1950–1958

Chapter One

I

HE WAS very small and had minute features set in a pale oval face. His eyes were closed. He was wrapped in a white hospital blanket and looked like one of the wax dolls my sister Emily used to play with long ago in Velletria. It seemed impossible to believe that he was a living, breathing being, someone who would grow up to discuss the stock market with me, but for a second I pictured him as an adult, tall like Sam but otherwise looking exactly like me, sitting in my chair at the office, laying down the law at every partners' meeting, running my Fine Arts Foundation, dictating junk to the press, ordering his new Cadillac, and making some pretty woman miserable; Paul Cornelius Van Zale III (for of course he would take my surname later), investment banker, philanthropist, patron of the arts, my pride and consolation in some remote era when I was just a shriveled-up old man with no hair, no teeth, and less life in some grisly retirement palace I had concocted for myself in Arizona.

"We're going to call him Erich Dieter," Vicky was saying, adjusting the unreal bundle in her arms. "Eric for short. Oh, nurse, do take him away, would you? Thanks. Oh, and bring another vase for these new flowers, please, when you get the chance." Subsiding onto the pillows, she absent-mindedly toyed with one of the carnations crowding the bedside table. "Well, as I was saying . . ."

"Erich Dieter?" I said.

"Wait, nurse," said Alicia sharply. "Vicky, perhaps your father would like to hold the baby for a moment."

"Heavens, Alicia, men aren't interested in that sort of thing! As far as they're concerned, newborn babies are only damp little bundles which leak at the wrong moment!"

"*Erich Dieter?*" I said.

"Vicky, there's no need to affect such a repulsive modern cynicism toward what is, after all, one of the miracles of this world."

"Oh, God, when do we get a break for the soap commercial?"

"ERICH DIETER?" I shouted.

They all jumped. The nurse nearly dropped the baby.

"Give him to me, nurse," said Alicia, scooping the bundle out of the nurse's arms and adjusting it with great competence. "Leave us now, please. There's nothing else Mrs. Keller requires at present."

"Stop!" shouted Vicky in a voice almost as loud as mine. "I never said you could hold him! I refuse to let the two of you commandeer him—he's mine, not yours to dispose of as you think fit!"

Sam chose that moment to walk into the room with an armful of yellow roses.

"Oh, God!" cried Vicky, bursting into tears. "I can't stand more flowers—I'm beginning to feel I don't exist except as some sort of machine which has to be fueled with bouquets! Take them away, for goodness' sake, and leave me alone—all of you! *Go away!*" And while we gaped at her, she slid farther down on the pillows and pulled the covers over her head.

"Please leave," said Alicia politely to the crimson-faced nurse.

I was helplessly patting the heap under the bedclothes. "Vicky, honey . . . forgive us . . . please . . . we didn't mean to upset you . . ."

A shadow fell across the bed. "I think you'd better go," said Sam.

"But—"

"Come along, Cornelius," said Alicia in the schoolmarm voice I detested.

Muffled sobs made the bedclothes shudder.

"Vicky . . . sweetheart . . ." I was struggling ineffectually to pull down the sheet. "It's okay—of course you can call him Erich Dieter . . ."

Sam's hand closed on my wrist. "Out, Neil."

"But—"

"She's my wife, not yours. Out."

"What a fucking stupid thing to say!" I was so upset that I lost control over my vocabulary, and Alicia's expression reminded me that in all the nineteen years we had been married, I had never before uttered such an obscenity in her presence.

The bedclothes were thrust back. "If you don't stop fighting and using disgusting language," cried Vicky, "I'm going to get out of this bed and walk out of this hospital and have a hemorrhage and die!"

The door swung open as two doctors and the head nurse blazed into the room. "What's going on in here? What's all this noise? Who's upsetting the patient?"

"I want to be alone!" wept Vicky. "I can't stand them fighting over him any longer!"

The senior doctor looked at us with a cold, bleak, jaundiced eye. "You will all leave, please. I must be alone with my patient."

We slunk away into the corridor, Sam still holding the yellow roses, Alicia still holding the baby.

"I hope you're proud of yourself," said Sam, white with fury.

"That was a disgraceful scene, Cornelius," said Alicia in a voice of ice.

I turned my back on them and walked away.

II

TELLING THE chauffeur to wait for Alicia, I dismissed my bodyguard and walked crosstown from the hospital, which was on the East Side. Ahead of me I could see the cool dark trees of the park, but they were farther away than I had anticipated, and finally, losing patience, I jumped aboard a bus. For a moment that took my mind off my troubles. I had not been on a bus since I was eighteen, and at first I enjoyed the novelty of clinging to the strap alongside my tired, shabby fellow travelers, but then I realized I was as lonely on the bus as I would have been with Alicia in the back seat of my Cadillac, and on the other side of the park it was a relief to elbow my way out onto the sidewalk.

Central Park West was a roaring mass of rush-hour traffic. I walked downtown slowly, my hands thrust deep into my pockets, and tried to identify the different models of automobile which crawled past me. I liked cars, although I seldom drove; a man in my position just doesn't go bucketing around behind the wheel of his own automobile if he wants to cut the right image with those who work for him, but sometimes I used to drive out to one of the new highways with only my bodyguard for company, and give my favorite Cadillac some exercise. I liked the power of the accelerator and the thrust of the engine and the submission of the steering wheel to the slightest pressure of my fingers, although of course I never said so, even to my bodyguard. It might have seemed childish, and a man in my position has to be very careful to do nothing which might lay him open to ridicule. Nothing deflates a powerful facade quicker than mockery; that was a fact of life I had learned long ago when I had been stripping power from other people in order to survive in a hostile world.

Reaching the Dakota, I took the elevator to Teresa's sixth-floor apartment, which faced east across the park.

"Hi!" she said, startled, emerging from her studio just as I removed my key from the front door. "What a surprise! I thought you'd be all tied up holding the baby and drinking champagne!"

"Forget it." I stepped past her without a kiss and trudged into the kitchen. As usual it was in chaos. Plates were stacked high, dirty pots littered the stove, the table was a mess of unidentifiable food that smelled ripe for the garbage. The huge furry brown cat which Teresa somehow managed to love was chewing something in a corner. The floor was dirty.

"Honey, don't go in there—it's a pigsty. Come and sit in the living room."

"I was looking for a drink."

"Why didn't you say so? I'll fix you something right away!" She was wearing a stained beige smock over skintight black pants, and her feet were encased in an old pair of slippers punctured at the toes to display the chipped red paint of her toenails. Her hair looked as if it had had an accident at the beauty parlor. As her dark eyes regarded me shrewdly, I noticed that her full lush mouth was unmarked by lipstick, an indication that her work had been going too well to allow her to pause to put on makeup before rushing to the studio at the start of the day.

"Sorry I look like a Polish joke," she said later, giving me a glass of Scotch and water. "I'll go and shower while you relax."

As soon as I heard the bathroom door close, I moved noiselessly into the studio for a look at the new work. It seemed to be a picture of some kind of funeral, though it was hard to be sure. Whatever it was, it still needed a lot of work. I decided I did not like this drift of Teresa's toward postimpressionism. It was too derivative and there was no money in it; if people are going to spend money acquiring that kind of junk, they want the real thing, not a third-rate imitation, and anyway Teresa's talent was wasted in this inexplicable pursuit of a postimpressionist ambience. Her natural pristine style, which she had temporarily abandoned (And why? Guilt? Did she unconsciously associate it with selling out? God only knew, I certainly didn't), was directly at odds with this new blurry groping for artistic effect, and as I moved from the studio to the bedroom, I wondered, depressed, if she were on the brink of peppering her canvases with little dots, like Seurat. I'd have to say something if she did; I wouldn't be able to keep my mouth shut, but I was always very careful what I said to Teresa about her work, and although I was honest, I was never destructive. Paintings are like an artist's children, and you don't go telling a mother to her face what a godawful job she's made of bringing up her child.

Shying away from all thought of children, I quickened my pace to the bedroom.

The bed was unmade, the vanity awash with trash from a dozen dimestores, stockings scattered over the floor, clothes flung haphazardly over a chair. Another cat snoozed on a pile of dirty washing. Below a poster of Lenin, looking fierce, the works of left-wing writers were stacked in piles on the mantel, and I thought again, as I had thought once or twice before, that Teresa was going to have to shed her casual interest in communism. There was no future in the arts nowadays for anyone with un-American leanings, and if she wanted to remain alive and well and exhibited regularly in New York, the poster of Lenin would have to go, to be replaced perhaps by a poster of Clark Gable dressed as Rhett Butler. *Gone with the Wind* was as American as apple pie.

Without moving his position, the cat opened his yellow eyes to stare at me from his pile of dirty washing. I sipped my Scotch and stared back. I outfaced him. He had just closed his eyes again when Teresa, clad in a hideous striped towel, emerged from the bathroom, slumped down on the tumbled sheets beside me, and stretched her arms luxuriously above her head as she tossed the towel aside.

I set down my glass, shed my clothes, and took her.

The cat watched us occasionally with his blank yellow eyes.

"Like another drink?" said Teresa when it was over.

"No, thanks."

We lay side by side. I was feeling as I had felt on the crosstown bus, surrounded by shabbiness, in close proximity with other human life, but totally separate, utterly alone.

"Want to talk?" she said.

"Not much." I suddenly remember my first wife, Vivienne, complaining how offensive it was when a man lacked even the most rudimentary postcoital good manners, and with an immense effort I pulled myself together. If I was fool enough to treat Teresa as if she could be rented, I might wake up one morning to find she had torn up our rental agreement and hired herself out to someone else.

"I'm sorry," I said, kissing her on the mouth and letting my hand rest for a moment on her breast. "I know I'm behaving badly, but it's been a rough day."

She kissed me back, gave my hand a squeeze, and slid out of bed. "Let's eat something—I haven't eaten all day, and I'm starved. I'll fix you something nice. What would you like?"

"A hamburger."

What I liked best about Teresa was that she never pestered me with stupid questions. She just asked what I wanted and got on with the job of providing it. At her best she never even asked; she diagnosed my state of mind and wrote her own prescription. I was sure she liked me, but underneath that sluttish exterior the mind that produced those well-ordered paintings was essentially detached. Of course I was never fool enough, despite all the things she said when I was inside her, to believe that she loved me.

"Ketchup," she muttered, hunting around the kitchen closets.

"Over there on top of the cat food."

Artists are strange people. Kevin often regaled me with that fatuous remark attributed to Scott Fitzgerald: "The very rich are different from you and me." But I'm on Hemingway's side. The very rich are no different; they just have more money. The real difference in this world is not between the rich and the poor but between those who create and those incapable of creation. I'm Cornelius Van Zale, forty-two years old, and in common with numerous blue-collar workers making some pittance a week, I'm proud of my family, I work goddamned hard Monday through Friday, and I like drinking an occasional glass of beer and playing a game of checkers and watching baseball whenever I get the chance. But although Teresa Kowalewski, twenty-six years old, may enjoy cooking, going shopping, and all the other typical feminine pursuits as much as any Westchester housewife, when that canvas calls, all these occupations become a blinding irrelevance, and if they persist in cluttering the landscape, some emotional disaster is sure to follow. Sometimes I think artistic talent must resemble a malign mutation of the human brain. It's scarcely conceivable that a person can inhabit both the outer world of normal people and the inner world of the creative and still stay sane. No wonder Van Gogh went to pieces and Munch painted screams and Bosch was fixated with hell. Imagine living with such scenes in your mind and then going out to buy bread from some fool who chatted about the weather.

Sam thought I owned Teresa, but he was wrong. No man owned Teresa, because no man, not even the richest man on earth, could ever buy her away from her art. I know about artists. I've studied them with the same interest as an anthropologist who studies some culture utterly different from his own. I'm fascinated primarily by how artists can make something out of nothing. It's power, of course —not my kind of power, but still power, something which in certain circumstances can far outdistance my kind of power, a mysterious force, an enigmatic miracle, a wrestler's lock on eternity.

I made a renewed effort to be pleasant and sociable. "The baby was very cute," I said, watching the ketchup drip glutinously onto my hamburger, "and so small it was hard to believe he was real."

"It must be odd to have a baby," said Teresa, unable to imagine any creative urge which did not involve paint, but willing to concede the experience could be memorable. "Is Vicky okay?"

"They told Sam when he saw her this morning that it was an easy birth, but she was very overwrought tonight. In fact, she was quite unlike herself. Vicky's always so sweet and bright and nice-natured, but tonight . . . well, she seemed real upset. She even cried."

"Postpartum blues."

"Do you think so? Is that what it was?"

"Sounds like it. But don't worry, honey, postpartum blues are very common, and they never last long. She'll be her old self again in a day or two, you'll see. . . . Coffee?"

"Thanks." Now that I realized there was a simple medical explanation for Vicky's behavior, I felt much better. "Sam and Alicia seemed to think it was all my fault that she cried," I said on an impulse, "but it wasn't. I was just surprised because they're giving the baby a German name."

"Trust Sam to wave the German flag!" said Teresa, offering me milk for my coffee.

"Well, they're going to anglicize the name by calling him Eric, but personally I think he should be called after my great-uncle, the one who left me all the money. After all, Paul picked Sam out when Sam was just a gardener's boy clipping a hedge! Sam owes him everything."

"Sam owes you a lot, too. The baby should be called Paul Cornelius."

"Well, I know most people don't like the name Cornelius." I fidgeted with my hamburger. "But personally," I said, again deciding to confide in her, "I've always liked it. It's different. Special. That's why I've never let anyone except Sam, Jake, and Kevin call me Neil —and they only call me Neil because Paul told them to. He thought Cornelius was a difficult name for an adolescent boy to handle, and I was too shy of Paul in those days to say how it had always given me confidence. Neil's just ordinary, but Cornelius is a great name."

"Maybe the next one will be Paul Cornelius. Anyway, honey, I shouldn't worry about the trouble tonight—it'll blow over. Don't forget, it was a big event, and emotions were running high."

"Right. And talking of emotions running high, I wish Sam would stop behaving as if he'd found the secret of eternal youth. It's getting irritating—almost as irritating as Alicia talking about my *grandson* the whole damned time. Christ, just because my daughter has a baby, I don't see why everyone should treat me as if I'm ripe for an old folks' home!"

"Eat up your hamburger, old man, and let's go hit the sack again."

An hour later, in bed, when we were drinking more coffee and Teresa was snacking pound cake, I dusted the crumbs off my chest and glanced reluctantly at my watch.

"Guess I'd better be getting back."

"Stay longer if you want. I shan't work anymore tonight."

"No, I have to go and make my peace with Alicia."

"Was she really that tough at the hospital? Jesus, I think you're a saint to stand it! Most other men would have divorced her long ago and followed in Sam's footsteps—wedding bells, a pretty young wife, and a baby before the first anniversary!"

I got out of bed without a word and began to pull on my clothes. The room now seemed intolerably squalid.

"Sorry, honey, I goofed. I practically bust a gut trying never to criticize Alicia, but sometimes the gut busts and I spill over. Don't take any notice of my bitchiness."

"You're not jealous of Alicia, are you?"

"Hell, what would I want to be jealous of her for? She's welcome to her empty life!"

"Are you sure?"

"Honey, you know I love you and think you're great in bed and more handsome than a film star, but can you seriously imagine what I'd be like if I was transplanted to your Fifth Avenue palace? I'd be stark staring mad within twenty-four hours! Anyway, what possible motive could I have for wanting to step into Alicia's shoes? I don't want children, and having a wedding ring wouldn't make me paint better pictures."

In the end, everything still centered on the painting. Wedding rings, children, and Fifth Avenue mansions were all unreal shadows trying to impinge on the brilliant surface of the canvas. I knew Teresa, and Teresa knew herself. I was safe.

"Good night, honey," she said, kissing me at the door. "Take care."

"Paint well, Teresa."

Outside, it was dark, and turning up my collar against the chill spring wind, I hailed a cab and was jolted back across the park to that other world on Fifth Avenue.

III

WHENEVER I came home from Teresa, I always had a shower. This had nothing to do with the level of hygiene in her apartment. At the beginning of our affair I had showered before leaving her, but I still found that as soon as I reached home I felt compelled to shower again. I spent much time pondering on the significance of this fanatical quest for cleanliness, but concluded I was responding to the need to keep my life in two strictly sanitized compartments. The shower was an attempt at purification akin to the old Roman custom of *lustratio* which my Bar Harbor summer tutor had once mentioned to me; the Romans always made acts of lustration after celebrating some pagan rite and before returning to the normality of their civilized routine.

I was heading swiftly up the main staircase for my rendezvous with the shower when Alicia called my name from the hall. I didn't stop—the pull of the shower was too strong—but I did turn my head to look at her. She was wearing a gray dress with a diamond clasp at the shoulder, and diamond earrings below the smooth dark curves of her hair. She looked matchlessly beautiful. My pace automatically quickened up the stairs.

"Cornelius . . . wait!"

"Give me five minutes, would you?" I fled to the bathroom, locked myself in, stripped off my clothes, and bundled them into a heap out of sight behind the trash basket. Then with enormous relief I stepped into the shower.

After counting slowly to one hundred and eighty, I turned off the water and dried myself vigorously for a further sixty seconds. It was soothing to follow the familiar routine. Feeling much better, I knotted my towel carefully around my waist and made sure my genitals were hidden. This was a very important part of the routine, because no one, not even Teresa, was ever allowed to see me naked from the front. It was true that Teresa had once been exposed to this view by accident on a long light summer evening when we had kicked off all the bedclothes, even the sheet, which I always took care to keep drawn up to my navel, but she had made no comment, so I had kept calm and pretended I didn't care. Perhaps she had noticed nothing unusual. Human beings came in all shapes and sizes, and for all I knew, small testicles were a dime a dozen, equally common among those who have suffered from mumps and those who have no idea what the word "orchitis" means. Perhaps at a casual glance my testicles even looked normal. To my eyes they looked deformed, but since I knew exactly how deformed they were, it was hardly surprising that to me they should seem so hideously abnormal. I often wondered what Teresa thought of my eccentric modesty, but knowing Teresa, I guessed she would have shrugged her shoulders and accepted it long ago. Teresa concentrated on the basic issues. So long as the rest of my sexual equipment felt and acted as if it were in first-class condition, she wasn't about to bother to find out why I went to bed with my shorts on and only wriggled out of them when I was safely under cover of the sheet.

With the towel around my waist I unlocked the bathroom door and with shock discovered that Alicia was waiting for me in the bedroom. My hands flew at once to my waist to make sure the towel was secure.

"Please excuse me for bothering you like this," she said, and I noticed suddenly how tense she was, "but there really is an immediate problem. Vivienne's here. Apparently as soon as she heard the news about the baby from Sam she got the first flight out of Miami, and now she wants to know why Vicky's receiving no visitors. She says she won't leave here till she's spoken to you in person."

"Christ! How did she get in?"

"She arrived when we were at the hospital, and the new footman admitted her. I've reprimanded Carraway for not instructing him properly, but—"

"Okay, let me fix this." I pressed the bell by my bed and kept my finger in place until my valet arrived on the double to bring me fresh clothes. Then I picked up the house phone. "Hammond?" I said to my chief aide. "I want my ex-wife out of this house. Give her money, buy her a meal, do whatever has to be done, but get her out." I hung up, switched phones, and dialed Sam to suggest that since he was responsible for Vivienne's invasion of New York, it was his duty to ship her right back to Florida, but the housekeeper at the Kellers' new home on East Sixty-fourth Street told me that Sam was out to dinner.

"Vivienne seems to believe that you bribed the doctors to keep her out of the hospital," said Alicia tentatively after I had reemerged from the bathroom with my shorts on.

"Christ!" I fought my way into a clean T-shirt and grabbed the sweater my valet was offering me. "Well, all I can say is," I said, wrenching on my pants, "that if that woman thinks she can bust into the hospital and upset my little girl—"

I was interrupted by loud voices shouting in the corridor, and almost before I could button my fly, the bedroom door was flung open as Vivienne, hotly pursued by Hammond and his two henchmen, burst across the threshold.

"How dare you order your punks to manhandle me!" she screamed. "I'll sue you, you bastard!"

"So sue me. I'll wipe you off the map." I turned to my aide. "Hammond, you're fired. Get out." I had managed to step into a pair of loafers before anyone had noticed I was barefoot. A man may just possibly be able to exercise power without socks on, but without shoes he can only look ridiculous.

"Now, you listen to me, you son of a bitch—" Vivienne was shouting at me.

"Be quiet!" I blazed, discarding my neutral expression and level voice so abruptly that everyone in the room jumped. "How dare you burst in here as if you were still mistress of this house with the right to come and go as you please! And how dare you harass my wife by creating these disgusting scenes!"

"I want to see my daughter! I want to see my grandson! What right have you to keep them from me? They're mine as well as yours!" Vivienne suddenly collapsed in a heap on the bed. She was wearing a powder-blue suit, very high heels, and a load of gold jewelry which clinked when she walked. Her tears were making deep furrows in her makeup. She looked wrecked, raddled, and revolting.

"Cornelius," said Alicia in a quiet, composed voice, "I know Vicky can't receive any more visitors tonight, but couldn't Vivienne at least see her own grandchild for a few minutes?"

"Oh, for God's sake, don't keep mentioning that word 'grandchild'! Do you think Vivienne wants to be reminded she's nearer sixty than fifty these days?"

"Isn't he a bastard?" said Vivienne to Alicia. "He's not even proud to be a grandfather! You'd think he'd go crazy over this grandson, wouldn't you—particularly since he's never been able to produce a son of his own!"

I wanted to vomit. I even turned aside for fear I might begin to retch, but before I could take a step toward the bathroom, Alicia said with the most exquisite dignity, "Please, Vivienne—it's a great disappointment to me that I've failed to give Cornelius the children he would certainly have had with someone else. You may not care what you say to him, but as one woman to another, I must ask you not to intrude in a private matter which is so full of sadness for me. Now, as far as the present problem's concerned, I'll personally take you to the hospital and make sure you're admitted—if Cornelius gives his permission. May I have your permission, please, Cornelius?"

I did not look into her eyes for fear of the pity I might find there. I just walked over to her without a word, took her hands in mine, and kissed her on the cheek. Then I kicked off my loafers, sat down, and pulled on my socks. My eyes felt hot. I was dumb with the humiliation that she had felt obliged to tell such a lie on my behalf. I wanted to retch again when I realized how pathetic she obviously thought me.

"Wonderful!" Vivienne was saying sarcastically. "I just adore cozy little marital love scenes! Well, now that you've shown me you're still capable of kissing your current wife, would it be too much to hope that you'll fall in with her offer to take me to the hospital?"

"You've caused Alicia enough trouble for one night," I said, stepping back into my shoes. "I'll take you."

"Thanks, but I'd rather go with a sympathetic woman who understands how disgracefully I've been treated!"

"You'll go with me and like it," I said, and set off ahead of her down the corridor.

IV

"WHAT A lot of time we've spent screaming at each other in the past," said Vivienne, powdering her nose in the back of my new azure Cadillac. "Looking back, I can see what a waste of energy it all was. I've got news for you, darling. When you get old—truly old like me—you form quite different ideas about the kind of things that are important. The most important thing for me now is to reestablish my relationship with my daughter and see as much of my grandson as possible. Wasn't it just the craziest piece of good luck that we produced Vicky? That honeymoon in Palm Beach at Lewis Carson's gorgeous château—God, I can hardly believe it happened, so much has happened since. Remember how you'd given up smoking and used to munch chips in bed after we'd made love? It's funny, but I can hardly believe that you and I, now two strangers sitting side by side in this heavenly car—darling, what divine upholstery!—were once two lovers wrapped up in the most torrid affair in town! Doesn't it seem just the teeniest bit fantastic?"

"Fantastic, yes. But we were different people then."

"I guess we were. But in some ways you're even more attractive now than when you were just a cute little kid with an angel face and fifty million dollars! It's sweet you're still so fond of Alicia. Do you screw a lot of other women in your spare time?"

"Mind your own fucking business." This was evidently destined to be the day when I was hounded into using obscenities in front of the opposite sex.

"*I* remember when you were just a nice well-brought-up little boy who never used that kind of language in front of a lady!"

I somehow refrained from making the obvious comment. If we were ever to survive the visit to the hospital without coming to blows, I had to ignore all her attempts to needle me with her idiotic chatter.

It was nearly ten o'clock by that time, but I had no trouble gaining admittance to the hospital, which in its efforts to accommodate its rich patients was run on the lines of a deluxe hotel. The head nurse on the fourth floor confirmed that Vicky was not to be disturbed, but a junior nurse took us to the nursery, where Eric Keller was sleeping in the company of three other infants.

"Oh!" said Vivienne thrilled, as the baby was brought out of the nursery for our inspection. "Isn't he *lovely!* Can I hold him?"

She held him. The nurse smiled indulgently. Sam's son slept on serenely, eyes closed, little pale oval face unmoving.

"Isn't it exciting?" whispered Vivienne. "Just think, Cornelius—our grandson! Ours! Isn't it wonderful?"

All I could think was that I was with an oversexed bitch whom I detested and that she was trying to tell me Sam Keller's son was some kind of a miracle. The depth of my misery startled me. Groping for a more conventional response, I stared down at the baby in an effort to share the emotion which was transforming Vivienne's hideously artificial face, but I felt nothing. I was back on the crosstown bus again, surrounded by people yet remaining in isolation.

"Yeah, he's great," I said. I wondered vaguely if I was jealous of Sam, but I didn't see how I could be. The baby had to have a father, and what better father could I have wished for him than my best friend?

I wondered if Sam was still my best friend. I was almost one hundred percent sure he was, but twenty-four years of surviving in a world where the most unexpected people became insane enough to believe they could double-cross me with impunity had given me somewhat cynical views on friendship. However, my fears for Sam's sanity had receded considerably since he had married Vicky the previous June. I had no doubt now that he genuinely loved her; certainly he seemed so wrapped up in marital bliss that I thought it unlikely he would upset Vicky by stabbing me in the back for snitching Teresa—assuming, of course, that he still held it against me for snitching his mistress when she herself had regarded the affair as dead as a doornail.

I shuddered as I remembered the circumstances surrounding my acquisition of Teresa. How could I have known she'd misled me about Sam's feelings for her? And how could I possibly have guessed that Sam, who had always chased blond glamor girls with no talent, no brains, and no hope of luring him to the altar, should have fallen so crazily in love with Teresa that he had even talked of marrying her? I had sailed blithely into the biggest possible mess and had been damned lucky to scrabble my way to safety without getting my throat cut, but occasionally I still fingered my neck warily and had nightmares about blades flashing in the dark. Perhaps I should have played safe and given up Teresa, but she was such an ideal mistress for me and when Sam, out of pride, had insisted that I keep her, it had almost seemed less awkward to keep her than to give her up. Certainly Sam's later devotion to Vicky had helped convince me that he no longer cared whether or not I had once annexed his girl.

Or did he still care? I didn't like him choosing those German names. It was like a gesture of defiance, a hostile act reminding me that he had the power to name the baby and I had no power at all. I didn't like any situation where my power quotient was nil, and I very much disliked Sam reminding me how powerless I was on this particular occasion.

Erich Dieter. My God.

"Oh, I feel so happy!" said Vivienne with a little sob as the baby was borne back to the nursery. "Darling, let's go somewhere and have a little sip of champagne!"

"Forget it." A second after I had spoken, I realized that my behavior with Vivienne that evening was the clearest possible giveaway of my misery. If I wanted to prevent anyone guessing how disappointed I was that Eric's father obviously had no intention of sharing him with me, if I wanted to ensure that no one realized my pitiable fancies of the last few months had come so abruptly to an end, I had to make an effort, and make it fast. The one nightmare of my life was that everyone would secretly think me pathetic because I had no sons of my own.

"I'm sorry," I said rapidly. "Yes, of course I'll buy you some champagne, but will you excuse me, please, if I don't drink with you? The fact is, I've been feeling lousy all day—it's the new medication I've been given for my asthma. Where would you like to go to celebrate?"

"The Plaza. You don't have a suite there by any chance, do you?"

"No. Do you want one?"

"Oh, darling, that *would* be heaven! I'm sorry I said all those horrid things to you earlier—you're now reminding me of how adorable you used to be when you were twenty-two!"

"Have you got enough money to tip the bellhop?"

"Darling, I thought you were never going to ask! Could you possibly . . . ?"

In the Cadillac I phoned the Plaza to ensure they had a suite available, and wrote her a check for a thousand dollars.

"Well, Vivienne," I said as the car drew up in front of the hotel, "order up whatever you like from room service, and have a good time. You'll excuse me if I go home now, but—"

"Cornelius."

Her hand gripped my arm, and taken by surprise, I swiveled to stare at her. In the bright light which streamed from the hotel lobby, I saw her eyes were very blue and for the first time that evening I was able to connect her with the woman I had married long ago.

"I must talk to you," she said in a low voice. "Please come in with me."

After a pause I said "Okay" in a voice without expression and followed her out of the car. We had already picked up Vivienne's bags from the small drab hotel near Grand Central, and as the bellhop carried them into the lobby of the Plaza, we walked together to the reception desk. Vivienne checked in. We still did not speak to each other, and even the ride upstairs in the elevator passed in silence. In the suite I absent-mindedly tipped the bellhop five dollars and moved to the phone to order the champagne.

"Will California do?" I said, glancing at the room-service wine list.

"No, Cornelius, it won't. We used to have this conversation in the old days when we debated what wine to serve at dinner parties—I'm surprised you don't remember. I guess Alicia just gives in to this fad of yours about not consuming anything made outside of America. I'll have some Heidsieck, please, and make it vintage."

"Caviar?"

"Yes, and make it Russian."

I gave the order, hung up, and turned to face her. She was watching me. Her face was pale but calm.

"Yes?" I said politely.

"Cornelius," she said, "we've got to come to terms with one another. I've decided to move to New York to be near Vicky and the baby—oh, I can't afford Manhattan, of course, but that's only one of the five boroughs, isn't it? I'm going to get a little place in Queens. I used to think the world would end if I was reduced to living in Queens, but now I can see the world would end if I stayed away."

There was a pause before I said carefully, "I can understand that Fort Lauderdale isn't what you've been used to in the past. Perhaps if I bought you a house in Palm Beach . . ."

"Cornelius, it's just no good trying to bribe me to remain in Florida. I've made up my mind to return to New York, and if I'm going to be living in the same city as you, I think we owe it to Vicky to make some attempt to be friends."

"I think we owe it to Vicky to keep a thousand miles apart! Be realistic, Vivienne! Of course it would be better if we were devoted friends shedding rays of sunshine whenever we crossed Vicky's path, but that's not going to happen, is it? You detest me and I detest you, and whenever we meet, we fight. That's the reality of the situation, and I only deal in realities!"

"Okay," she said, "you only deal in realities. Then deal with this one: why did Vicky marry Sam? Wasn't she running away not just from me but from you too—wasn't she looking for some wise, all-powerful parent who could take care of her where we'd failed? Cornelius, so long as Vicky's a little girl running away from us, she'll never grow up, but if we could change, be nominal friends instead of undisguised enemies . . ."

"Spare me the amateur psychology! You were the parent who failed Vicky, not me! You were an unfit mother—why, Vicky begged the judge to let her come and live with me!"

"You bribed the judge!"

"I goddamned well did not! Jesus, Vivienne, look at us, we're fighting again! Now, listen to me. If you want to come and live in Queens, there's nothing I can do to stop you, but don't be surprised if Vicky doesn't want to know you, don't be surprised if Sam gives you a cool reception, and don't be surprised if I do my best to see as little of you as possible. The truth of the whole matter is—as we both know—that you're estranged from your daughter and you have only yourself to blame. 'We reap what we sow,' as my mother used to say back in Velletria—"

"And when are you going to reap what *you* sowed? You only wanted to take Vicky away from me because I'd outwitted you by marrying you for your money, and depriving me of Vicky was your idea of revenge!"

"That's bullshit. My one concern was for my daughter's welfare."

"If you'd really been concerned for Vicky's welfare, you wouldn't have wrecked the happy home I'd made for her!"

"Yes—the happy home where you slept with one man after another and wound up with a Las Vegas gangster—some example for a little girl!"

"But I *married* Danny Diaconi! Oh, get out, damn you, get out and leave me alone! There's just no way we can talk to each other, no way at all!"

I got out with relief. In the corridor I passed a waiter carrying a tray of champagne and caviar, but I never looked back. Making a great effort to shut out the sordid thought of my ex-wife camping on my doorstep and inevitably disrupting my tranquil family life, I rode the elevator down to the lobby and trudged wearily outside to my Cadillac.

It was time once more to go home to Alicia.

V

"Has my wife gone to bed, Carraway?" I asked the butler when I arrived home.

"No, sir, she's in the Gold Room."

"Bring me a Scotch and soda there, please." I spoke in the polite neutral voice I reserved only for Carraway. I did not like English servants with their talent for making their American masters feel inferior, but this one happened to be a masterpiece of his species, and I always respect the best. Carraway in turn respected my respect. Prior experience of employment in my country had taught him about the horrors awaiting in households where the employers had only the crudest idea how to behave toward their servants, and he knew when he was well off.

We had five reception rooms on the first floor in addition to the library, the dining room, and the ballroom, but as a rule we used only the Gold Room, which was small and intimate. Vivienne had originally chosen the gold decor, but later under Alicia's orders the golden drapes had been removed, the golden furniture had been reupholstered, and the golden carpet had been dispatched to the attics. The predominant color in the room was now pale green.

When I opened the door, Alicia and Sam jumped as violently as if I had caught them in an adulterous embrace.

"Hi," I said, breaking the awkward silence. "I've just unloaded Vivienne at the Plaza and I feel I've earned a drink. Good to see you, Sam. Sorry about all the trouble at the hospital. Did you see Vicky again after I left?"

"No, I thought it better not to." He sat down again uneasily, a big man in an expensive suit, his eyes wary behind his glasses. "I apologize too, Neil, if I was too abrupt."

"What the hell, you were right! She's your wife, not mine! Let's forget the whole mess, shall we?"

"Sure, I'd be glad to."

Carraway glided in with my Scotch and soda. He looked as if he had been born with a silver salver in his hand.

"Thank you, Carraway."

"Thank you, sir." The English never say "You're welcome," only endless thank-yous. It keeps them in control of situations which would otherwise degenerate into friendly fireside chats. The English are masters of the minor power plays, those tricks of speech which can be used to dominate any difficult scene. Sam and I were no novices at the game either. One of the ironies of any rare confrontation between us was that we each knew exactly what the other was going to do.

"Well!" I said agreeably when Carraway had gone. "What were you two plotting when I caught you in the act?"

I could see Sam thinking: Hostile question, taking the bull by the horns. Neutralize immediately.

He laughed and stretched out his long legs to give the impression he was relaxing. "You flung open the door so abruptly it was small wonder we both jumped! It was nothing, Neil—we were just discussing the baby's names again. To tell the truth, I'm having second thoughts about calling him after my cousin. Sure, I was fond of Erich, but Vicky never knew him and the name means nothing to her. I think it would be more appropriate if we called the baby Paul Cornelius after you and Paul. It would be more meaningful for Vicky as well as for myself."

"Well!" I said, thinking: Sickly-sweet reassurance. Destroy with light acerbic touch. Keep smiling. "That's an interesting suggestion! You want my honest opinion?"

"Why, sure!" said Sam, wanting nothing of the kind.

"I think it would be a mistake to feel sentimental about Paul, who always despised sentimentality, and as far as I'm concerned, I'm all for something original—I'm not interested in echoes from the past. No, you stick with Erich Dieter. I admit I was surprised at the hospital, but I was under the mistaken impression Vicky wanted to call him Sam after you."

That was a bad error. I had made a statement which was obviously untrue. In the pause which followed, I watched Alicia gazing in embarrassment at the unlit logs in the fireplace, and my fingers bit into the palms of my hands as I clenched my fists behind my back.

"Well," said Sam thinking: Got to defuse this somehow, Christ, how awkward, "if you're sure . . ."

"Hell, Sam, it's nothing to do with me! I'm just the grandfather, as Alicia never ceases to remind me!" Another bad error. I sounded both angry and jealous beneath my lighthearted manner. The sweat of humiliation trickled down my back. I had to get out. "I feel about seventy, and aging fast!" I said, trying to make a joke of it and only succeeding in making us all feel more embarrassed than ever. "I think I'll go to bed and rejuvenate myself. Don't rush off, Sam. Alicia, have Carraway bring Sam another drink."

I left the room, closed the door firmly, took six paces down the corridor, and then padded back to listen. On the other side of the panels Sam was saying, "Damn! He was upset, wasn't he? And I thought I was handling it well."

"Well, don't persist now with 'Paul Cornelius' or you'll make everything worse . . ."

I crept away.

Retreating upstairs, I dismissed my valet, sat down on my bed, and interlocked my fingers tightly as I reviewed the situation. I did not understand how I could have mishandled the scene so badly. Perhaps I was emotionally upset. But no, how could I be? I had sorted myself out long ago. The trouble had arisen because *they thought* I was emotionally upset, and it was their suspicions, not the facts themselves, which I found upsetting. I hated them thinking I was neurotic, someone to be handled with kid gloves, when I knew without doubt how well-adjusted I was. I had known for sixteen years now that I would have no son—sixteen years, seven months, and five days, to be accurate—and if one can't come to terms with an unfortunate fact of life after sixteen years—sixteen years, seven months, and five days—just what the hell can one come to terms with, for Christ's sake? Of course I would have liked a son, but one can't have everything in this life, as my mother used to say back in Velletria, and since I had damned near everything else, how could I complain? I didn't complain, that was the answer, but Alicia kept trying to stuff her own soap-opera emotions into my head and make out I was suffering from some sort of deprivation. Of course I felt sorry for Alicia, because it was obvious she would have liked more children, but she had her two boys and I'd given her a stepdaughter, so why should she complain either? I refused to feel guilty when we were all one big happy family with so much going for us. Why should I? I didn't believe in guilt anyway. Guilt was for maladjusted neurotics who could not cope with life. God dealt out the cards, and one played the hand as best one could, and that was that.

Sixteen years, seven months, and five days. It sounded like a jail sentence. September 7, 1933, and the sky was a steaming hazy blue. . . . That was when everything had come to an end, my dreams of a large family, my perfect physical relationship with my wife, my hero worship of Paul, who had filled the void left by a father I could hardly remember—and even my sister's marriage had come to an end, leading me into an open breach with my brother-in-law, that son of a bitch Steve Sullivan . . .

I was taking another shower before I remembered I had had a shower only a short time earlier. I must be going out of my mind. I tried to figure out what the new shower meant. Another act of lustration? Perhaps I was trying to wash away the memory of the humiliating scene in the Gold Room. I always had good clean cheerful thoughts under the shower.

Putting on my pajamas, I got into bed and was just opening a book when I heard the door of Alicia's room open. I switched off my light immediately and lay motionless in the dark.

Perhaps if she thought I was asleep she would slip into bed with me and put my hand between her thighs. She had done that once out of pity for me, and later when I had been impotent she had pitied me enough to refuse my offer to make love to her in a less conventional way. She knew I disliked such practices, and no doubt she thought it was pathetic that I should offer to do something I disliked in order to please her. I sweated at the memory but then reminded myself that I was indulging in unnecessary torment. Our sexual relationship was dead. It had taken me a long time to realize how great a hell I was putting her through by persisting in my selfish efforts to recapture our past happiness, but once I had understood how much she was suffering, I had ended the relationship at once.

I would have done anything for Alicia, anything at all. When I had first discovered we would have no children, I had offered her a divorce so that she could have children by someone else, but she had chosen to stay with me—and not just because I was rich; Alicia had her own fortune and her own inherited place in New York society. No, this unique, beautiful woman had chosen to stay with me in adverse circumstances because she had thought I was the one man who could make her happy. It was small wonder that since then I had done everything in my power to ensure her happiness. She had wanted me to love her sons; I had bent over backward to treat them as my own. She disliked charity work; I had taken great care that she should never be bothered by any of my charitable interests. She needed, naturally, the very best home I could provide for her; I maintained Paul's Fifth Avenue home, which I loathed, specially for her benefit. She had wanted to end our sexual relationship; I had ended it. If she had wanted a divorce, I would somehow have found the strength to give her that too, though I didn't see how I could have survived without her. I had even told her to take a lover because I had realized it was better to be a complaisant husband than a deserted one. I loved her. I wanted her more than any other woman in the world, and often when I was making love so effortlessly and emptily with Teresa my impotence with my wife did indeed seem like a jail sentence—sixteen years, seven months, and five days of imprisonment in some police state where torture was rife and justice nonexistent. Every day I woke shouting inside my head: "I've suffered enough! Let me go!" and every day my faceless jailer would remind me that he had thrown away the key of my cell. Whoever was dealing the cards of life had tossed me an ace of spades to ruin my royal flush in diamonds, and sometimes I thought that single black spade was digging my grave.

The glow of light beneath the door which linked our bedrooms was extinguished, but nothing happened. I waited alone in the dark.

I was on the crosstown bus again, but it was an empty bus without a driver, and the loneliness was more than I could bear.

Slipping out of bed, I padded to the door and listened. Nothing. In an agony of indecision I moved away again and tried to think logically. Could I make some excuse to knock on the door? No, I couldn't think of one. Could I be honest and just ask directly if she would object if I lay down beside her for a while and held her hand? No, I couldn't. Her immediate reaction would be: Poor Cornelius, impotent as ever, I'd better humor him, but how pathetic. Yet the hideous irony of it all was that I wasn't poor Cornelius, not by a long chalk. I was rich, successful, powerful Cornelius with a mistress who had told him that very evening how great he was in bed. So if I was a failure, I was a failure in one place only, and that place was the mind—Alicia's mind, of course, not mine. There was nothing wrong with my mind. But Alicia thought I was a failure, so I was. I'd worked that one out long ago. All these stupid people who waste fortunes on psychiatrists should try a little clear-eyed self-analysis occasionally. They might save themselves some money. Anyway, I don't believe in psychiatrists. They're for women and queers.

I got back into bed.

Thinking of queers reminded me of Kevin, and thinking of Kevin reminded me how few people I could talk to anymore. I would never have dreamed of revealing any of my most private troubles to anyone I had met since I had inherited Paul's money, for the whole point about power is that people must think you're impregnable or else they lose the respect which your power extracts from them. I was hardly about to reveal my problems to anyone I didn't trust, but I trusted very, very few people.

I trusted my sister, but we had drifted apart over the years, particularly when she had returned to live in that dump Velletria after the war. I trusted Paul's Sylvia, whom I had always greatly admired, but she lived three thousand miles away. My mother had died in 1929. My stepfather, whom I had never liked, was dead. My own father, an Ohio farmer whom I was supposed to resemble, had died when I was four. Even Paul himself, the great-uncle who had adopted me in his will, had been dead for twenty-four years—and had never cared much for me during his lifetime. The knowledge of his indifference still hurt, although since I was the only person who knew the indifference had existed, it was easy for me to bury the knowledge along with all my other past memories which I was determined never to resurrect. In fact I made a cult of respecting Paul's memory, so that no one would ever guess how much I resented him for that casual indifference, which might, if he had lived, have been translated into active dislike.

However, there was no doubt that despite Paul's antipathy he had given me everything I wanted, and so I supposed it was right that I should respect his memory. Certainly I was glad I had been a Van Zale protégé. Would I have made it to the top without Paul's help? Almost certainly yes, but it would have taken me longer. Paul's backing had provided an invaluable shortcut to me as I set out along the road to power, although that hardly mattered now, because it was all so long ago. All that mattered at the moment was that Paul was dead and couldn't help me with my problems.

Apart from my family, there remained only the three friends who had known me when I was nobody, just undersized, underestimated Cornelius Blackett from Velletria, Ohio. Sam I was no longer one hundred percent sure I trusted. Kevin amused me, but it would never have occurred to me to have a serious conversation with a homosexual, while Jake . . . But yes, I trusted Jake. He lived my kind of life and had my kind of business problems. Jake was probably the one true friend I had left, but the fact remained that we had no communication on a personal level. We talked about finance, politics, and art but never about our families, and I knew why. A man who loves his wife and believes strongly in marital fidelity can have little to say to a man who hasn't slept with his wife in years and lays as many women as possible in his spare time. I would never have criticized Jake; I was hardly in a position to criticize him after I began my affair with Teresa, but the difference in our private lives continued to present a barely perceptible but ever-present barrier between us.

I turned on the light again to let Alicia know I was awake. Then I turned it off and waited. Still nothing. Obviously she was asleep. Lucky Alicia. I wondered if she had ever followed my advice and taken a lover, but it seemed unlikely. Alicia was not promiscuous, and as everyone knows, only promiscuous women enjoy extramarital sex. Women don't have erotic thoughts the way men do anyway. When they see a man they don't picture him naked and calculate the size of his erection. They imagine him wearing a tuxedo and giving them two dozen red roses while the violins in the background play "The Blue Danube." Women are romantic. They dream about love, not sex, and Alicia wasn't in love with anyone else. If she was, I would have known.

Anyway she was sick of sex, that was obvious. I didn't blame her either, after all I'd put her through.

I got up again, went to the bathroom, used the toilet, flushed it, and wandered aimlessly back to the bedroom. At the window I looked out over Central Park and thought of all the hundreds of people I knew in the city, the acquaintances attached to my business and social life. Surely there must be someone I could talk to! It didn't

have to be a deep meaningful conversation. Just an informal chat would take the edge from the discomfort of insomnia.
I went downstairs to the library.
I had five address books. Number one contained the names of people I liked enough to invite to small dinner parties, number two covered larger dinner parties, number three cocktail parties, number four dances, and number five exhibitions. My personal secretary had cross-indexed them in a card file which was kept meticulously up to date, and every six months Alicia herself revised the books, shuffling people into different categories, bringing new people in and dropping old people out. Alicia always knew whom I wanted to see and how often I wanted to see them.

I was halfway through address book number one when I realized it was much too late to call anyone in New York. I went on flipping over the pages while I debated whether to call Sylvia in San Francisco, but I knew Sylvia would want to talk about the baby and I felt I had had more than enough of little Eric Keller for that day.

The S page fell open beneath my fingers and I saw the entry "Sullivan."

For one split second I was back, back in the past, back with Steve, back knowing he'd wipe me out if he could, back with blood, murder, and mayhem, back at Emily's frightful wedding, back, back, back into the appalling past, back to Steve quitting Van Zale's but still trying to smash me in the teeth, back to the schemes and the machinations, back to his death on that English country road, back to the woman who'd backed Steve to the hilt, broken up Emily's marriage, and turned Paul against me, back to *Dinah Slade* outwitting me with the grand suicidal gesture which had destroyed her, back to all those deaths, all that blood, all that guilt, but no, my hands were clean, I'd washed them and washed them, and now I knew there was no guilt, I knew I'd been driven to do what I did, I knew the past was dead and there'd be no resurrection, never, never, *never.*

I heaved the concrete slab of my will over the grave of my memories and obliterated all thought of the past from my mind.
Sullivan, Scott. 624 E. 85, NYC.
I relaxed. Scott was *my* boy, not a son exactly, because he was only eleven years my junior, but perhaps a much younger brother. Steve had tossed him aside sixteen years ago—sixteen years, seven months, and five days ago, the same day I had discovered I would

have no son of my own. That was the day Steve had walked out on Emily to chase after Dinah Slade. He had had two sons by an earlier marriage, but he had junked them as if they were of no importance, just as he had junked his two daughters by Emily. The younger son, Tony, had always been a problem to me, but I had not seen him again after 1939, when he had gone to live in England, and in 1944 he had been killed in the war. However, Scott had survived the war and Scott was quite different from both his brother and his father; in fact, I never even thought of Steve and Tony when I was with Scott.

Scott was no boisterous wheeler-dealer, tossing off God knows how much liquor a day and seducing every woman in sight. Scott was low-keyed. And Scott was smart. He knew about all kinds of interesting things. Scott was quiet but he could put on a good social manner which the clients liked, just as he could put on a tough front which made the clients respect him. Scott *was* tough. I liked that. Men who don't drink, don't smoke, and (maybe) don't have sex are usually degenerates with all their perversions buttoned up, but Scott was normal—I was sure he was normal because I had spent so much time with him and I would have sensed if something had been seriously wrong. I had looked after him all the way through adolescence, and I was proud of the way he had turned out. In fact I liked him far better than either of my stepsons, although I had always gone to extraordinary lengths to conceal this from Alicia.

Scott was a night owl, often up till two in the morning reading his latest highbrow book. I normally have no time for highbrows, but Scott never made a fetish of all that useless knowledge, never showed off, never looked down on anyone who wasn't as well-educated as he was. Besides, one could talk to him for hours and never realize he was a highbrow, because he could deal with realities as ably as he could deal with some high-flown intellectual theory. I respected Scott's grasp of the realities of life. The reason why Sam was neurotic about Scott was that he totally failed to understand how realistic Scott was. Scott hated his father and had long ago written him off. Scott liked me. I had cared for him, taken trouble over him, done everything possible to ensure he would have a fine career—and that meant something to Scott. In fact, it meant everything. If we had been characters in one of Kevin's plays, Scott would have been harboring some huge grudge against me for ruining his father, and retribution would be hovering in the wings, but that only goes to show what junk even the best literature can be. Scott wasn't waiting to nail me. He was too fond of me, and anyway, even if he had hated my guts, his grasp of the realities of life was so firm that he would have abandoned all hope of revenge. There are some men who just can't be nailed. They're too powerful—and that, in the final analysis, is what my kind of power is all about. I'm communicating with people. I'm flashing out a message which tells people they have to get along with me and treat me with respect, and Scott had got that message long ago, received it loud and clear, and now I knew I was free to enjoy my friendship with him without any neurotic fears and anxieties. In fact, I secretly relied very much on my friendship with Scott. My world would have been a far lonelier place without him.

I picked up the phone.

"Yes?" said Scott on the first ring.

"Hi Scott! Cornelius. Are you sleeping?"

"No, I'm reading the Venerable Bede."

That was what I liked about Scott. Every other person in New York was probably sleeping, making love, getting drunk, or watching television, but Scott was doing something truly stimulating.

"Venerable who?" I said, already enjoying myself.

"Bede. He was a very literate eighth-century monk who lived in the north of England. I'm just reading his history of the Anglo-Saxon church."

"Not exactly a book-club selection!"

"Maybe it should be. He's talking about matters of universal human interest."

"Such as?"

"The brevity of life and the ignorance of man."

"My God! Say, Scott, come on over and tell me all about it—I'll send a Cadillac."

"Spare the chauffeur. I'll take a cab."

I sighed with relief. The emptiness of the night was dissolving, and for a brief time I could forget my troubles by pondering with Scott on the wafflings of some poor old monk. Hurrying upstairs, I flung on a pair of pants and a sweater, laced up my sneakers, and then returned to the library to wait for him.

VI

HE ARRIVED ten minutes later, a tall, spare man of thirty-one with black hair cut very short and black eyes set deep in a pale, tough face. He had that look of someone who ought to be reckoned with. I liked it. I did not underestimate it—I never underestimated the dangers of restless ambitious men bent on carving out a comfortable niche for themselves—but I had had nearly a quarter of a century's experience in dealing with such people and I knew how to keep them in line. I never mind the successful people unless their dreams of grandeur get so far out of control that I'm put in the unenviable position of having to wake them up. It's not success I despise. It's failure.

"Hi, Scott," I said, smiling as I offered him my hand to shake.

"Hi!" He gripped my hand and smiled back, projecting both confidence and common sense along with his friendliness. "Are you nuts or something? What's the idea of hauling me over here at one in the morning to discuss the Venerable Bede?"

"Hell, you know what millionaires are like! They'll do anything for kicks, as the scandal sheets are always telling us. . . . Say, after you've told me about Bede, can we play chess?"

"I might have guessed Bede was just the bait to lure me crosstown!"

In the library I went to the little liquor cabinet I kept tucked away behind the far bookcase and uncapped two bottles of Coca-Cola. "Okay," I said, handing Scott his Coke and sitting down opposite him across the chessboard. "Tell me Bede's views on the brevity of life and the ignorance of man."

"Well . . ." Scott offered me a stick of chewing gum, and as we sat chewing companionably together I thought how odd it was that the two of us, living in a country Bede had never heard of, should be discussing his views twelve hundred years after his death. The immortality of artists and thinkers struck me again, and once more I felt restless at the thought of a power which had passed me by.

"Bede's telling a story," said Scott, still chewing, "about the conversion to Christianity of one of the great English kings, Edwin of Northumbria. Edwin was conferring with his thanes—his aides—about whether he should take the plunge and turn Christian. Well, there they are, sitting around in the Witenagemot—the boardroom—and trying to figure out their options. It's a big decision, because if Edwin turns Christian, all the rest of them have to turn Christian too, but finally one of the guys says, 'Look, let's try the new religion—what have we got to lose? We don't know a damned thing. Human life is like the flight of a sparrow when the sparrow flies into a lighted hall in the depths of winter, pauses for a moment in the warmth, and then flies out of the door at the far end into the night again.' Or, to put it baldly: We don't know where we come from, we don't know where we're going, and our time in the lighted hall of life is just a brief flash in comparison with the vast darkness of eternity."

I tried to concentrate on the essentials. "Did Edwin turn Christian?"

"Sure. They all figured any religion which offered increased enlightenment was worth a try."

"And what happened to Edwin?"

"He got wiped out by his great heathen enemy Cadwalla, and the English relapsed into paganism."

"So it was all a waste of time."

"But was it? We can't know that for sure. Obviously there were people who turned Christian, because of Edwin's conversion, and remained Christian, despite Cadwalla's victory. Don't forget, Christianity triumphed in the end."

"That can't have been much consolation to Edwin when he got wiped out!"

"How can you be so sure? Edwin died for something he believed in, for a belief he thought would ultimately prevail."

"Yes, but that doesn't alter the fact that he died a failure!"

"Doesn't it? Doesn't that depend on how you define success and failure? Doesn't that depend on what things you consider important? And aren't you assuming death always represents failure, although that's not necessarily so?"

I immediately thought of my enemy Dinah Slade dying for her country at Dunkirk after a successful, satisfying life.

"Can't think why you read all this depressing ancient history, Scott. Let's play chess."

We began to play. After a while I said, "Do you really believe that, Scott—that life's no more than a sparrow's flight through a lighted hall?"

"Don't you?"

"Well . . . makes life seem kind of senseless, doesn't it?"

"Life *is* senseless," said Scott. "That's why it's so interesting to read the philosophers who try and shape the world into some kind of order."

"Why bother? God invented the world, and that's that."

"But do you believe in God, Cornelius?"

"Of course. All sensible people do. There must be a starting point in creation, and that point's God." I casually captured a pawn. "Your move."

"But that's what's so interesting, Cornelius. Not all sensible people do believe in God. Before the advent of Buddhism, for instance, the Chinese had no concept of God at all. In other words, a quarter of the human race lived and died for centuries without feeling the need to believe in a supreme being."

"Well, the Chinese are odd, of course. Everyone knows that." I poured myself some more Coke. "Personally," I said after he had made his move, "I don't think life's so senseless at all, in fact it seems very well-arranged to me. I certainly know what *my* life's all about. I've been put in charge of great wealth and I have a moral duty to use it to benefit as many people as possible. This I try to achieve through my Fine Arts Foundation and my charities."

"Fair enough."

"I have a wonderful family, I love my work, and I lead a successful, rewarding life. I'm very fortunate and happy."

"That's great," said Scott warmly, "but personally I think it's a waste of time to ask yourself if you've led the good life, because few people can be objective enough about the facts to reach any valid conclusion. I think the great question a man should ask himself is not: Gee, just how wonderful am I? but instead: Has it all been worth it?"

"Okay." I thought it was time to turn the tables on him. "You've been leading an ascetic life for years, Scott—has it all been worth it?"

Scott laughed. "Sure! I decided long ago that I wasn't interested in transient pleasures. They're not important. I wanted to study the supreme achievements of the human mind so that when I ask myself: Has it all been worth it? I can give an unequivocal Yes. The world only really exists in the intellect, so if you refine the intellect, you refine the world you're forced to live in."

"You've lost me, Scott. All this intellectual garbage is beyond me. Your move."

Scott edged his knight away from my bishop. "Okay, forget me—let's turn to you. Has it all been worth it, Cornelius?"

"Of course! I'd do it all again! I've always done my best to lead a decent productive life, and one can't do more than one's best."

"Indeed one can't! Your God must be pleased with you, Cornelius!"

"Yeah . . . well, to tell the truth, I don't see God as a father figure peering over my shoulder the whole time. I see God as a force —a form of pure power." I saw a brilliant opening for my queen, but it was three moves ahead. "I see God as kind of impersonal," I said, debating whether to knock off his knight. "Like justice."

"Ah, justice!" said Scott. "Yes, justice is a fascinating concept. Your move."

My fingers closed on his knight. "You mean revenge?" I said casually, very casually, the chessboard wiped clean out of my mind. "Old Testament justice? An eye for an eye, a tooth for a tooth—that kind of thing?"

"No, I'm not interested in Old Testament justice, and I find revenge intellectually boring. To chase one's enemy with a meat ax presents no challenge to the mind at all. Revenge is man playing God. I'm more interested in God playing God—or, to put it in nontheological jargon, in natural justice."

"How do you mean? Are you talking about so-called 'poetic justice' —'we reap what we sow' and all that garbage?"

"Cornelius, I'm just as ignorant as King Edwin and his thanes—it's no good looking to me for enlightenment! I guess what I'm saying is that I'm interested in finding out more about the meaning of life—like a medieval knight on the great allegorical quest for the Grail. Do you know anything about the Arthurian legends, Cornelius?"

"Yeah, wasn't there a movie with John Barrymore? You know, you ought to get married or something, Scott. All this talk about Holy Grails makes me think you're getting as eccentric as what's-his-name, the guy who went looking for it—Galahad. Wasn't there something wrong with him?"

"He was celibate. In the Middle Ages chastity was supposed to give a man superhuman strength."

"A nervous breakdown more likely. You're not really celibate, are you, Scott?"

"Are you asking me if I'm a virgin?"

"Not exactly. I'm sure you've . . ."

"Tried sex? Of course. Doesn't everyone?"

"With girls?" I said in a sudden panic.

"What extraordinary questions you ask sometimes, Cornelius! Yes, with girls. Why shove a key down a crack when it'll fit in the lock?"

I relaxed, smothering a gasp of relief. That was my boy talking at last, sane practical normal Scott with his firm grasp on the realities of life. I got nervous when he became too highbrow to make sense.

"I kind of worry about you sometimes, Scott," I said, smiling at him.

"Yeah?"

"Yeah." I looked down at the board and saw he had blocked the brilliant move I had planned for my queen. "But I don't have to worry about you," I said, glancing up sharply at him, "do I?"

"No, Cornelius," he said, returning my smile. "You don't have to worry about me."

There was a long silence while I studied the mystery of the board between us, but finally I heard myself say, "I may seem sometimes to be sentimental, Scott, but basically I'm a practical man. You do understand that, don't you?"

"Why, of course!" said Scott, looking surprised that I should ask such an inane question. "Like Byron, you're interested in 'things really as they are, not as they ought to be.'"

"Byron said that?"

"In *Don Juan,* yes."

"I never thought a poet could be that smart!" I said, fully relaxing at last, and shot my bishop sideways to win the game.

Chapter Two

I

IT TOOK us some time to settle down again after the drama of Eric Keller's arrival in the world, but we managed it in the end. The central character in the drama grew out of his first set of clothes, ate, smiled, and did what he was supposed to do. All the women in the family made regular pilgrimages to the crib, Sam wore out a camera taking photographs, and Vicky imported an English nurse to change the diapers while she bought herself a new wardrobe of clothes and began to read detective stories. She claimed these books were full of social significance, although this seemed unlikely; I suspected she just said that in order to back down gracefully from her earlier pose of being an intellectual, but as I told her on more than one occasion, she didn't have to convince *me* that Raymond Chandler was more fun to read than Jean-Paul Sartre.

"Women weren't meant to be intellectuals anyway," I observed later to Teresa. I was thinking less of Vicky than of my mother and sister, both of whom had inherited intellectual tastes. "You can educate them to the hilt, but all they truly want to be is wives and mothers—unless they're artists, of course. Artists are the exceptions that prove the rule, but they're not normal."

"Thanks a lot!"

"Well, what I mean is—"

"Stop right there, honey," said Teresa good-naturedly, "before I slug you over the head with the ketchup bottle."

I obediently kept quiet, but I couldn't help thinking what a relief it was that Vicky had turned out like Emily. Supposing by some freak of nature Vicky had turned out to be an artist like Teresa! Or supposing—and this was much more likely—Vicky had turned into a nymphomaniac like Vivienne! I shuddered at the thought. However, even Vivienne had felt the urge to be a wife and mother in the end. It hadn't lasted, of course, but it proved my point that all women except artists were instinctively attracted by domesticity.

I had one thing in common with my sister Emily: a talent for raising children. I knew I had probably been too indulgent too often with Vicky, but at least she had always known I was intensely concerned about her welfare, and children not only have to be loved, they have to feel their parents care enough to take positive action on their behalf. Vicky might have had her troubles in the past, but as I could see for myself and as everyone nowadays was always telling me, she had turned out wonderfully well. I had also had trouble in the past with my stepsons, but now they too were a credit to me. Sebastian had graduated *summa cum laude* from Harvard and Andrew was already an officer in the air force. Of course we had all had our occasional difficulties, but our family life with its stresses and strains alternating with long periods of happy tranquillity was probably very normal, and having applied myself successfully to the challenge of being a good father, I was more than willing to apply myself to the task of being an affectionate but sensible grandparent.

I was determined not to make a fool of myself. The scenes after Eric's birth had taught me a lesson, and nowadays I took scrupulous care to behave well in the nursery. It was true I did call at the Kellers' house two or three times during the working week, and it was true I always brought some sort of little gift with me, but I never stayed more than ten minutes and I never spent more than five dollars. On alternate Saturdays Eric visited us at Fifth Avenue, but I never made a big fuss over the occasion, and if the visit had to be canceled I just said, "Well, that's too bad," and never referred to it again. I took a few photographs, but not many; I played with him in the nursery, but not too often; and when Alicia said kindly, "Isn't he cute!" I just said, "Yes, he's okay."

On the Saturdays when Eric didn't visit us he went to see Vivienne, now established, not in Queens, but in a plush apartment complex in Westchester. Sam had told Vicky that it was in Eric's best interests that Vivienne should live in a high-class neighborhood, and Vicky hadn't argued with him. Neither had I. I never interfered, never complained, although I knew the mere sight of her mother always upset Vicky. But Sam was the boss. It was his family, and Vivienne was his problem. I just went right on being the model grandfather and took care to keep well out of Vivienne's way.

In April 1952 Eric celebrated his second birthday. He was tall for his age, and sturdy. He had fair curly hair which Vicky allowed to grow too long, but again I never criticized or interfered. His dark eyes made him look more like Sam than he really was. He talked coherently. Of course he was very smart. I bought him a huge stuffed giraffe, a tank with a rotating gun, and one of those toys with wooden pegs which you have to smash through a holed board with a hammer. I knew I should have brought only one present, but a second birthday was an important occasion, and besides, I had been behaving so well that I thought I could indulge myself for once.

Vivienne was at the birthday party. She brought six presents, all useless, and cooed over the little kid until I wanted to vomit. Alicia and I left early.

The party was on a Sunday. On Monday morning at nine o'clock Sam came to my office and suggested we have a drink together that evening to work out the family problem.

"What problem?" I said blankly.

He looked at me as if he found it hard to believe I was serious. All he said was, "I have a meeting midtown this afternoon. I'll meet you in the King Cole Bar of the St. Regis at six."

Automatically I gave the natural friendly response. "Come and have a drink with me at home!"

"No, Neil," he said. "I think it would be best if we met on neutral ground."

I felt as if an earthquake had blasted through my office and split the ground beneath my feet. This was a power play. Sam was slipping me into a vise.

"Okay, sure," I said casually, and pretended to return to work.

I spent the whole day trying to figure out what was coming. Three times I nearly called Vicky, and three times I decided against it. It was just possible that Vicky knew nothing about this so-called problem, but if she did, I might upset her by any cross-examination, and once I upset Vicky, I would be playing into Sam's hands.

I tried to clamp down on my panic, but horrific thoughts were already crawling out of the darkest corners of my mind into the light of day. Was this perhaps the long-delayed stab in the back for snitching

Teresa? No, that was surely impossible, since Sam was still crazy about Vicky, and Teresa had long since ceased to be important to him. But in that case, what the hell was he up to?

I went on sitting at my desk, and occasionally, about every ten minutes, I groaned. I had an absurd longing to rush upstairs to Sam's office, grab him by the sleeve, and plead, "Don't do it, Sam! Whatever it is, don't do it!"

I thought to myself: I wish I was back in the old days again. I wish I was back in the summer of '29 when Sam and I sowed our wild oats and got drunk on bathtub gin and danced to "Alexander's Ragtime Band."

I pulled myself together. Nostalgia would get me nowhere. To be sentimental would be to play a losing game. I had to pussyfoot forward stealthily with my eyes skinned for trouble, and if Sam tried a swipe at me I'd disarm him at once and cuff him for being such a fool.

But Sam wasn't a fool. He wouldn't try a swipe at me unless he was sure he had me by the—

"Oh, God!" I said, and headed for the liquor cabinet, but I never fixed myself a drink. This was not the time to go hitting the bottle. I could do that later, after Sam had revealed his hand, and his hand was probably just some gripe about how I was giving Eric too many presents. I was being neurotic, trying to turn my best friend into some kind of assassin and imagining I had a guilty conscience. My conscience was clear. Teresa had been through with Sam. I had sincerely believed Sam was no longer interested in her. Teresa had more or less invited me to go to bed with her. I had been the seduced, not the seducer, the victim of a gross misunderstanding.

Just who do you think you're kidding, Cornelius! That was the way things ought to have been, but was that the way things really were?

"I guess you've been to my art gallery, Teresa."

"Sure. The exhibitions there are great."

"Well, of course I'm very careful whom I exhibit. I have to think very highly of an artist before I consider exhibiting him . . . or her. . . ."

The truth was that I had had power and used it. Teresa, flat broke, emotionally muddled, and worried sick about her work, hadn't stood a chance.

"I'm sorry, Cornelius—I didn't mean to tell him about the exhibition, but he wanted to buy one of my pictures. . . ."

I hadn't wanted Sam to know about the exhibition so soon. I had wanted a decent interval to elapse to blur the connection between the bedroom and the exhibition hall, but there had been no interval, only an unpleasant progression from one sordid fact to the next. Sam could have drawn only one conclusion from such an unpalatable set of facts, but he had said nothing, and even later at the exhibition he had given no hint that he resented what I'd done. Afterward I'd wished he had. I'd had a set speech well prepared. "Because of my personal troubles, I wanted her very much and this was the only way I felt I could reach her—by appealing to her through her art." That statement would have made my acquisition of Teresa seem less like a commercial transaction and more like the foolish muddled act of a man distracted by misery; that statement, nauseous though it might still have seemed to Sam, at least had the virtue of being true.

However, no excuses could alter the fact that I had made a seamy proposition which hadn't been refused. Would Teresa have slept with me if I hadn't made her that irresistible offer? Maybe. But maybe not. Since she and I had now been good friends for three years, I had thought the origins of our affair no longer mattered, but perhaps I'd been wrong. Maybe they did still matter. Maybe Sam had been far more hurt by my ill-timed acquisition than I had ever wanted to believe.

At half-past five, feeling as if the day of judgment was about to dawn, I left the office, crawled into my new Cadillac, which was appropriately as black as a hearse, and headed uptown to the St. Regis.

II

THE KING Cole Bar of the St. Regis Hotel is a huge, well-lit room ideally suited to be a neutral meeting place for two bankers who would normally drink together at the Knickerbocker Club. The enormous bar snakes along one wall beneath the famous murals of King Cole by Maxwell Parrish, and the tables are set well apart so that eavesdropping is difficult even when the room is quiet and uncrowded. Sam had picked his battleground well.

I had planned to be ten minutes late, but to my great annoyance I was still the first to arrive, and not wanting to lose face by sitting around waiting for him, I headed immediately to the men's room. The first person I saw when I walked in was Sam. He was washing his hands, like a surgeon preparing for a big operation, and glancing at his watch. We laughed when we saw each other, and I thought: First round a draw.

"What are you drinking?" he said when we were finally seated at a table and the waiter was hovering nearby.

I had already decided that I had to signal my complete lack of nervousness. "I'll have a tomato juice," I said, smiling, and thought: That'll rattle him.

"One tomato juice, one gimlet," he said to the waiter, and I knew the second round had gone to me. He couldn't face me without a shot of gin.

However, by the time the drinks arrived, I was wishing I had ordered a lime juice on the rocks so that I could have switched drinks with him while he was looking the other way. I was sure my need for gin was greater than his.

"So what's the problem, Sam?" I said after he had finished telling me about his afternoon meeting with the president of Hammaco, a huge corporation which had foolishly slighted us in the past, only to discover the enormity of their mistake. I took a sip of the thick sickly juice in my glass and wondered if any vegetable could be drearier than a squeezed tomato. "Let's have it!" I said encouragingly. "Cards on the table!"

"Vicky's at the end of her rope," he said promptly, and lit a cigarette. He knew I hated people smoking in close proximity to me. Third round to him.

"Vicky? At the end of her rope?" Of course he was exaggerating. "But why?" I said. "I don't understand."

"She says she can't stand the tug-of-war any longer."

"Tug-of-war?" I said, suppressing the instant recollection of Vivienne's lavish presents coupled with my gifts from F. A. O. Schwarz.

"Don't be dumb, Neil," said Sam, no longer smiling. "You're not scoring any points by acting ignorant."

Fourth round to him. I pulled myself together. At least all this had nothing to do with Teresa. "Can you conceivably be referring to Eric?" I said cheerfully.

"You bet I am! You and Alicia on one side, Vivienne on the other, and the three of you always in and out of my house, spoiling my kid rotten, and trying to tell Vicky how to bring up our son."

"Sam, Alicia and I have never—"

"The point isn't whether or not the three of you actually dictate orders. The point is that Vicky believes that you do. Vicky feels intimidated and miserable. Remember, she's still little more than a kid herself, and she can't cope with all these adults muscling in on her territory with, quote, helpful, unquote, advice."

"Don't pretend you haven't got your own ax to grind too, Sam! This isn't just Vicky's problem, is it?"

He flinched. I scored. Fifth round to me.

"Okay," he said. "I'll admit it. I don't like you trying to take over my son and treating him as if he was yours. It would be different if you were a regular old grandpa of sixty-plus and I was a young kid in my twenties. Then I'd just say: Gee, the poor old senior citizen, I've got to give him some pleasure in life. But we're the same age—and not only the same age. We've got this whole shared past which has shackled us together more tightly than any blood tie. Sometimes I think you're like my doppelgänger, and that's eerie, I don't like it, I can take seeing you every day at the bank, but I don't want to see you constantly in my own home as well. In other words, I want you to get the hell out of my private life, Neil. You're being too goddamned intrusive, and let's be honest, let's voice a truth we both know: since I married Vicky, you don't own me anymore."

The nerves jangled in the pit of my stomach as all my most nebulous nightmares assumed the rock-hard rigor of reality. Trying to calm myself, I thought: Sixth round to him. I sipped my tomato juice again and tried to look friendly.

"Hell, Sam!" I said good-humoredly. "What's all this sinister German talk about doppelgängers? Now, let's not get overemotional about this. The most important thing is obviously Vicky's happiness, right? Okay, well, if we're driving her crazy, we'll cut down on our visits for a while."

He said abruptly, "That's not good enough."

I finished my tomato juice and signaled the waiter. "It isn't?" I said with a little smile to show him I was still prepared to be good-natured despite all his efforts to provoke me.

"No, it's not. The fact is, we want another child, but Vicky flatly refuses to have one while the three of you are hovering around her like vultures ready to devour whatever she produces."

"Yes, sir," said the waiter at my elbow.

"Give me a martini," I said, "straight up."

"Give me the same," said Sam, finishing his gimlet.

I gave the waiter one second to turn his back and then wiped the good-natured expression off my face as I slammed into the attack. "Now, look, Sam—"

"Believe me," he interrupted, outshouting me yet still managing to sound soothing as he picked up the nice-guy expression I had discarded, "I want to be reasonable about this. You three are the grandparents, and you have certain rights, and I want to be humane. But I've got to put Vicky first. You'd agree with that, Neil, wouldn't you? That's what you've just said, isn't it? Vicky's got to come first."

I knew I was being steered into some blind alley to be beaten up. I back-pedaled rapidly, nodding my head in agreement and saying in my meekest, most reasonable voice, "Sure. Right. But it strikes me Vicky's being just a bit neurotic about this, I mean, like a schoolgirl, you know, sort of hysterical. Couldn't you be a bit firmer with her, take a tougher line? Couldn't you say—?"

"Neil," he said, "are you trying to tell me how to run my marriage?"

"Hell, no!" I said. "Of course not!" I looked around for my drink, but the bartender was still shaking the cocktail pitcher. "Just a minute," I said. "I've got to go to the men's room. Excuse me."

I went to the men's room again, looked at my white face in the mirror, used the urinal, washed my hands, and looked again at my white face. My mind was as blank as a wiped slate.

Returning to the martini, I drank half of it in two gulps and set down my glass.

"Look, Neil," said Sam kindly, as if he were thinking: Poor old Neil, no sons of his own, I mustn't get too rough, "this is not an uncommon problem. It happens all the time in small towns across America. Daughter gets married and lives on her parents' doorstep. Husband eventually has to take her away to preserve her sanity."

Rage burst through me, but I never altered my expression. Any display of temper would only make him sorrier for me, and I was determined not to lose control of the interview. Every word now counted, and every sentence was a weapon.

"You want to leave New York," I said.

"Yes."

"Where do you want to go?"

"That depends on you, Neil!" Sam was smiling again, paying out the rope which had snapped taut between us, so that we had additional room to maneuver. "Naturally, I don't want to leave Van

Zale's, and it occurred to me that this might well be the ideal moment to open a European office. With the postwar European economies showing signs of gathering strength at last . . ."

"Whereabouts in Europe?"

"Germany."

I felt the prick of the knife between my shoulder blades, but I didn't stop to examine the knife, take its measurements, or marvel at its efficiency. My first priority was to take defensive action.

"That's a wonderful idea, Sam!" I said enthusiastically, manipulating the slack on the rope into the best noose I could manage. "A European Van Zale's again to cash in on the postwar boom! But I'm afraid I see no point in opening an office unless it's in the financial center of Europe, and besides, the German political situation is still unstable, thanks to the Russians. We'll base the office in London."

"But my German contacts, my bilingualism . . ."

"Stick to speaking English, Sam. I've had enough trouble with your pro-German sympathies."

"But I've no affinity with England!"

"Get one. Or quit."

The rope strained between us as I watched him pick over his options. He could quit without fear of me crucifying him later, because he knew I would do nothing to upset Vicky. Yet he had a big stake in Van Zale's, bigger than he would ever get anywhere else, and if I dropped dead, he could scoop the bank into his hip pocket. He disliked England, but he'd survive. He would use his charm to insist that he was one hundred percent American, and most of the time it would never occur to the British that Keller was a German name. And even if they did get around to wondering how German he was, they would probably assume that with his dark complexion and his adopted first name he was not only German but Jewish too.

I smiled at the irony. Umpteenth round to me.

"Okay!" he said, looking generous to give the impression he had conceded victory voluntarily on this point, although we both knew I had wrung the concession from him. "England, here I come!"

We smiled at each other. I felt ready to collapse with relief. I'd won. I still had the whip hand. He hadn't dared push me too hard. I had saved my grandson from being raised as a German, and I was still indisputably the boss despite this unprecedented attack on my authority.

"We'll make it a two-year assignment in London," I said genially, "and then you can hand over to someone else and bring Vicky back." I now had time to examine the knife at my back, but before I could complete the job of disarming him, Sam took a deep breath and stabbed me all the way up to the hilt.

"Gee, Neil," he said, "I can see I haven't made myself clear. We won't be coming back to New York."

I didn't say anything. It was impossible for me to say anything. It was barely possible for me to breathe.

"I'm willing to compromise with you by starting in London," said Sam reasonably, "because I can see that from a business point of view this would be best. But as soon as the London base is operating smoothly, I'm going to start an office in Germany. This is what I've wanted for a long time, and this is what Vicky wants too, Neil, make no mistake about that. Vicky wants what I want, and she wants to be where I want to be, and you wouldn't want to upset Vicky, would you, Neil? You love Vicky and you wouldn't want to distress her by being less . . . shall we say flexible? . . . than you should be."

There was another terrible silence, and as we stared at each other I saw at last the way things really were: not Vicky's husband and father focusing single-mindedly on her welfare, but two men whose friendship had been irrevocably dislocated, two predators stalking one another in a nasty brutish world dense with jealousy and revenge. I saw too that the truth was neither black nor white but a murky mixture of the two. Sam did love Vicky. He did want the best for her. But over and above all else he was using Vicky to get what he wanted, and what he wanted was not only an independent life in Germany away from my long doppelgänger's shadow but repayment with interest for that night when he had found me in Kevin's attic with Teresa. He was going to take my daughter and my grandson away from me as absolutely as I had taken Teresa away from him, and there was nothing I could do to stop him. If I fired him, he would still go to Europe to work; if I tried to keep him in New York, he would resign and still put the Atlantic between us. He might prefer to stay with Van Zale's, but if the chips were down, he'd quit and walk into another top job somewhere else. His ambition and his revenge meant more to him than the sentimental ties of a twenty-six-year-old partnership.

I looked on the shattered fragments of our friendship and heard my voice say painfully, "Sam . . . what happened to those two kids who danced to 'Alexander's Ragtime Band'?"

He had discarded the mask of his charm. As his face hardened, he said brutally, "The record wore out and we found other games to play." He finished his martini and stood up. "I'd better be getting back to Vicky or she'll be wondering what's happened to me. And I don't want to miss Eric's bedtime."

He had won the final round. I remained seated in front of my empty glass.

"So long, Neil. Glad we've got this straightened out."

I waited until I was sure he had gone, and then I ordered another martini and tried to figure out how I could stop Alicia pitying me as soon as she heard the appalling news.

<h1 style="text-align:center">III</h1>

"I FEEL so exhausted," said Vicky, "and I think it's because I'm trying to be too many things at once—the perfect wife, the perfect mother, the perfect daughter, the perfect stepdaughter. So I've got to cut down on all these roles and settle for the ones that are most important."

"So you've chosen to be the perfect wife and mother? Well, that's fine, sweetheart, that's all I've ever wanted for you anyway, but—"

"It's not that I don't love you, Daddy. It's just that I've got to get right away from being a daughter. I'm not a little girl anymore, and I want to grow up, but somehow when I see you and Mother fighting over Eric, it puts me right back in the past again—"

"Yes." I turned away.

"—and I want to make a clean break with all that. Sam understands. I just want to be with Sam."

We were in the living room of the Kellers' house on East Sixty-fourth Street the morning after my meeting with Sam. Most of the furniture had come from Sam's Park Avenue penthouse and had that impersonal look of luxury which only furniture in the most expensive hotels achieves. The Braque I had once given Sam hung above a small walnut desk and was a bad companion for the early Picasso which I had donated as a wedding present. Outside it was raining. I wandered over to the window and looked into the patio, where Sam's plants, transferred from his penthouse terrace, exhibited their unlikely enthusiasm for city life. On the table near the window was a book entitled *Heute Abend,* and when I opened the cover I found it was a German textbook.

"Don't be angry, Daddy."

"I'm not angry. All I want's your happiness, you know that. It's just that I don't quite see . . ." I closed the cover of the book and turned to face her again. "Why Germany?" I said. "Why Europe? Wouldn't you be happier in America?"

"I know you hate Europe. I don't expect you to understand."

"I don't hate it. It's just that it has no message for me, like a canvas by Rubens. Vicky, if I thought you'd be happier in America, I could have Sam open a branch office in Boston or Chicago . . ."

"No. I want to go to Europe. I want what Sam wants. I just want to be with Sam."

Sam seemed to have turned himself into some kind of Svengali. "Look, Vicky, you've got to be honest with me. Is Sam forcing you to go to Europe against your wishes?"

She looked at me as if I'd taken leave of my senses. "Of course not! Oh, Daddy, don't be so silly! Sam wouldn't force me to do anything! He's sweet to me!"

"You're truly happy with him?"

"*Of course!* What a question! Daddy, do please stop worrying about me! Sam looks after me just as well as you ever did."

"I see," I said. I thought about that. Then I said, "And you think going to Europe will make you feel more grown-up?"

"I'm sure of it."

"Then you must go." I saw with great clarity that if Vicky wanted to be more grown-up, I should be the last person to stop her quest for maturity. Mature women with minds of their own were far more likely than girls utterly dependent on their Svengali-type husbands to form their own ideas about where they wanted to live and what kind of life they wanted for their children.

A glimmer of hope flickered dimly on the horizon. The odds were that time was on my side. At the moment, the balance of power was weighted in Sam's favor, but if I hung on, kept the peace, and played the part of the saintly, resigned, long-suffering boss who would accept any indignity for his daughter's sake, the day might eventually dawn when Vicky would tire of Europe, and then the balance of power would tilt in my favor again. My main task now was obviously to stage a reconciliation with Sam, because it would never do if he resigned in a fit of pique and went straight to Germany. So long as I was his boss, I would in theory retain my power to drag him back across the Atlantic, and one day I might be in a position to dispense with theory and put that power into practice. I detested waiting games. I detested the thought of letting Sam walk all over me while I smiled and did nothing. And I detested the prospect of Vicky and Eric disappearing into Europe. But I was a survivor. Heaving a sigh, I scraped together all the cunning, the patience, and the iron determination which I had acquired over the years, and said in my meekest, mildest voice, "Don't you worry about anything, sweetheart! I understand the situation much better now, so you go to Europe with Sam, just as you want, and don't you feel guilty about it for one minute. I'm sure it'll all be for the best in the end."

IV

I PLAYED my part to perfection until the Kellers left for Europe, but as the *Queen Mary* steamed off down the Hudson, I felt more depressed than I had ever felt in my life. I felt I had to be alone, yet paradoxically I couldn't bear the thought of solitude.

"Would you like to go out to dinner, Cornelius?" said Alicia, trying to be nice to me.

"No, thanks." I knew she was feeling sorry for me, and I couldn't bear it. Making some excuse, I retired upstairs and later slipped out of the house to see Teresa, but I got no farther than the lobby of the Dakota. I was so depressed that I had no sexual desire, and there seemed no point in seeing Teresa unless we went to bed. I couldn't have discussed the situation with her; any explanation involving Sam's motives would inevitably have led us back to the one subject which mutual embarrassment always forbade us from discussing: the night at Kevin's house, my irresistible offer, the seamy start of an affair which should never have started at all. Anyway, I didn't want Teresa to know that Sam had got the better of me. It was important that she should believe there were no chinks in my armor, and I didn't want to betray that I could be vulnerable.

"Yes, sir?" said my chauffeur as I returned from the Dakota seconds after leaving the car.

I thought quickly. I had to talk to someone, but whom could I possibly confide in without losing face? I was back with the old problem that there were so few people I could trust. This time I couldn't even talk to Scott or Jake; I couldn't let anyone who worked on Wall Street know that Sam had wiped the floor with me. Perhaps Kevin . . . Kevin might cheer me up, although of course I couldn't have a serious conversation with a homosexual. But at least he knew the circumstances surrounding my acquisition of Teresa, so I wouldn't have to embark on long explanations of Sam's behavior.

The thought of no explanations was immensely appealing.

I set off for Greenwich Village.

V

KEVIN'S KITCHEN was warm and cozy, reminding me of the farm where I had been born. I could just recall sitting on my Negro nurse's lap in front of the kitchen range while Emily played with her dolls, and my mother, her needlework forgotten, browsed through a huge book which I later assumed was the Bible and later still found out was a novel in French by Balzac. I always felt very secure in kitchens, and was pleased when Kevin invited me to drink, not in his formal living room, but at the kitchen table.

"It's the ultimate compliment I pay my guests!" he said, laughing as he uncapped the Wild Turkey bourbon. "Drinks in the kitchen is the Kevin Daly equivalent of Louis XIV giving audiences on the john!"

Kevin was a tall slim, dark man who looked as normal as those guys Sears Roebuck pick to model denims for their catalogs. When he wasn't smiling, he could look both obstinate and tough, the sort of person who might start a fight in a bar after a few drinks, although in fact Kevin abhorred violence and as a conscientious objector had spent the war years working for the Red Cross. He drank too much, but then, he was an artist, so I made allowances for him. His plays were getting more obscure, but then, he would insist on writing that blank verse, which I privately thought was an intellectual affectation. You don't go to the theater to hear poetry—unless the play's by Shakespeare, and any impresario can tell you that Shakespeare's bad box office. However, the critics thought highly of Kevin, and since the critics can make or break a play in this town, his plays usually did well. A couple of the early ones, written before he had developed the unfortunate taste for blank verse, had been filmed successfully, and certainly I had always done everything I could to support his work, even now when it was becoming less commercial.

". . . and imagine Sam screwing you like that!" he was saying, sounding sympathetic but not one bit surprised. "No wonder you look exhausted! Have another drink."

"Thanks." I was feeling better. It made all the difference to be able to talk frankly to someone. "The worst part," I added in a fresh burst of confidence, "is not that I'll be cut off from Vicky and Eric. There'll be regular visits, and I think that if I'm smart, I'll get them back in the end. The worst part is that I've lost Sam for good. It's probably hard for you to understand how much my three Bar Harbor friends mean to me, but . . ."

"It must be a question of relaxation."

"Right, Sam was the one person I could relax with at the office. I didn't have to play the role of big tycoon with Sam, but that's all finished now. It's going to be lonely at Willow and Wall in future, and I'm going to feel very . . . isolated. Yeah, that's the word. Isolated. Hell, I feel isolated already! I feel so cut off from people."

"Your position at the bank must surely make a certain amount of isolation inevitable. But what about your private life? You've still got your wife to talk to. And your mistress."

I thought of myself retreating from Alicia that evening. I thought of myself being unable to face Teresa. The silence lengthened. I looked at Kevin, but he was gazing at the picture of the wild turkey on the bottle of bourbon. A lump of anguish hardened in my throat, and suddenly my depression seemed no longer diffuse but concentrated, a despair which demanded immediate verbal expression. "Kevin . . ."

"Uh-huh?"

But I didn't know what to say.

"Things are okay with Teresa, aren't they?" said Kevin carelessly as the silence lengthened again. "Or are you getting tired of her?"

"Hell, no! It's just . . . I don't know. Nothing. At least . . ."

"Christ, communication's hard sometimes, isn't it?" said Kevin. "It's like being in a pit and shouting for help but finding you've lost your voice. Or it's like getting lost and asking the way and finding no one speaks your language. Or it's like climbing into a suit of armor to protect yourself and then finding you can't get out."

"Suit of armor?"

"Yes—God, it happens all the time! We all try to hide from one another. I think it's because life's so fantastically complicated that we all get scared shitless and can't face it without a suit of armor—or at the very least a nice old-fashioned mask. But it's terrible to get trapped behind a mask. I've been there. I know."

"What do you mean? When were you ever trapped?"

"When I was pretending to be a heterosexual, of course! When did you think! The worst part was not being able to have an honest conversation with anyone. It's difficult enough to talk anyway about a personal problem, but when that problem's sexual in origin . . ."

I thought incredulously: He knows. He understands. No, he can't possibly understand. And how can he possibly know? Shall I talk to him? No, I can't. How can I talk to a homosexual? But I *am* talking to a homosexual. No, I'm not. I'm silent. There's nothing I can bring myself to say, nothing. I'm trapped, just as he said. Trapped behind my suit of armor, trapped behind my power.

"Kevin . . ."

"Uh-huh?"

"My personal life's all mixed up. Alicia's the one I love. She's the one I really want. I only go to Teresa because . . ." I stopped. I felt as if I'd sprinted a hundred yards at top speed. I'd run out of breath.

"In that case," said Kevin comfortably, as if it were the most natural thing in the world, "I guess you go to Teresa because for some reason you can't have Alicia."

"Yes. But . . ." I found some more air, breathed it, picked up my glass, and gulped the rest of my bourbon. "But none of this is Alicia's fault," I said rapidly. "That's why it's such a nightmare. None of this is Alicia's fault. I don't mean . . ." I put the glass to my lips again, but it was empty. "I don't mean I'm impotent. Of course I'm not. I can get it up as well as any other guy. Teresa proves that. I mean, what I'm trying to say is . . ."

"I understand."

"What I'm trying to say is, I'm all right, I'm okay, I'm fine. It's just . . ." To my horror I found I couldn't go on. I couldn't tell more lies and I couldn't tell the truth. I was aware of the bottle of bourbon, but I dared not reach for it in case my hand shook and I betrayed how upset I was. Kevin would think me pathetic. A homosexual pitying *me!* God, what a nightmare. I had to pull myself together, had to . . .

"Jesus, isn't sex hell sometimes!" exclaimed Kevin suddenly. "Impotence, frigidity, premature ejaculation, adultery, sodomy, and lust

—how on earth do we all tolerate it? I think I'll write my next play about how wonderful it is to be a eunuch. Have another drink."

I nodded. Fresh bourbon glinted in my glass, and there was a splash as he added an ice cube.

"Of course, any psychiatrist would tell you," said Kevin, "that these problems are all stupefyingly common. It's because no one ever talks about them that one assumes one's going through some uniquely horrific experience."

I drank half my bourbon straight off. Then I said cautiously, "Do you believe in psychiatrists?"

"I guess they may help some people. But like God and the pope, they've never been much use to me."

"You mean they couldn't tell you why you're homosexual?"

"Oh, they told me! They told me in excruciating, interminable, conflicting detail! All I can say is, Neil, that after hours wasted confiding in priests and fortunes wasted talking to psychiatrists, I'm not convinced there's any one reason for my sexual preferences. And I'll tell you this, too: contrary to what all the smart people think on the cocktail circuit these days, Freud doesn't have all the answers. I suspect the human mind is like a version of the street directories of the five boroughs, and that although Freud plowed his way through Manhattan and the Bronx, he never reached Brooklyn, Queens, or Staten Island."

"Hm," I said. "Well, I've never believed in psychiatrists myself, of course . . ."

"One good thing you can learn from observing them is how to listen. Do you listen, Neil?"

"Listen?"

"Yes, do you listen to Alicia? Do you listen not only to what she says but to all the things she leaves unsaid? Do you know exactly what's going on in her mind?"

"I thought it was *my* mind that was important here!"

"But don't you see," said Kevin, "that what goes on in your mind depends on what you think is going on in hers? Have another drink."

"Thanks. No, I'd better not. I don't want to arrive home drunk." I was thinking of Alicia's crushing pity and rigorously suppressed contempt and her loss of sexual desire for me. I knew what went on in her mind, all right. It was no mystery. It was all too painfully obvious. "Well, like I said, Kevin, I don't truly believe in all this psychoanalysis crap—it's just like a religion, and how can a religion ever work for you unless you've got faith in it? Anyway, there's no miracle cure for this situation, I just have to live with it, I'm powerless to do anything else. . . . Powerless. Yes, that's it. That's why I get so upset. It seems so wrong that I should have so much power at my fingertips, yet in this one area of my life . . . It's all a question of power, isn't it? Power's communication. Do you remember Paul saying that to us once at Bar Harbor?"

"Ah, Mephistopheles!" said Kevin, dividing the dregs of the bourbon between us. "How could I ever forget Paul Van Zale and all his dangerous crypto-fascist bullshit!"

"Kevin!"

"Ah, come on, Neil! Don't tell me you still have any illusions about Paul!"

"I've no illusions, but I still respect him. He made a success of his life."

"I think he wasted it. I think he was a deeply dissatisfied, perhaps even a tormented man. Has it never occurred to you that it was a damned odd thing he did, appropriating the four of us like that and converting us to the Van Zale way of life? In retrospect, I think it was not only extraordinary but sinister. I'm surprised our parents allowed it. Well, my father was probably glad to get me off his hands for the summer, and Sam's parents were no doubt blinded by the prospect of social advancement, and Jake's father was as bad as Paul, but I wonder what the hell your mother thought. I'll bet she had mixed feelings."

"She didn't want me to go. But, Kevin, why should you think Paul's habit of picking out protégés meant he was dissatisfied and tormented? He just liked to do it because he had no sons of his own."

"That was the excuse he allowed to be circulated, but I don't believe it, not now. I think the whole thing was an exercise in power and also an attempt to justify himself. If he could convert a bunch of bright young men to his way of thinking, then maybe his way of thinking wasn't so goddamned rotten as he secretly suspected it was."

"But—"

"Don't get me wrong. In many ways I liked Paul, and I certainly enjoyed my time at Bar Harbor. But a lot of what he said was not only nonsense, but dangerous nonsense. For instance, 'Success at any price' is certainly an attractive slogan. But *his* idea of success? And at *any* price? I tell you, Neil, that's not a recipe for real living! That's a prescription that puts you in hock till you die. Shall I open another bottle of bourbon?"

"No. Oh, hell, okay, why not? Let's get drunk. Kevin, I know what you're trying to say about Paul, I'm not dumb, but you see, Paul's philosophy was never meant to apply to someone like you. You're an artist. You've got your own special power which sets you apart and makes you independent of the kind of power Paul was talking about. When Paul talked about power and success, he was really talking to people like me—and Sam and Jake too, of course, but especially to me, because he knew I'd never be happy until I'd made his world my own—"

"And are you happy, Neil?"

"Sure I am! Oh, I know I have a problem or two, but only a fool would expect life to be a hundred percent perfect. I'm really very happy indeed. Life's great."

"Wonderful! In that case you can sit back and look smug while I tell you how I'm currently sunk in gloom and think life's fucking awful."

"Is this something to do with—?"

"No, relax, this has nothing to do with my sex life! It's all about being what you're pleased to call an artist. If you'll keep your mouth shut for a minute, I'll try to explain what it's like to be a successful American playwright who's nearly cutting his throat because he's not as good as Eliot and Fry."

"I'll bet you make more money than those two put together!"

"But can't you see that's the crowning awfulness? If I had the guts to write the kind of play I really want to write, nobody would touch it. But sometimes I think I'd rather be a first-rate failure than a second-rate success."

"But you're not a second-rate success! I like you better than Eliot and Fry. I never understood *The Cocktail Party,* and as for *The Lady's Not for Burning—*"

"Neil, you're wonderful. Come and drink here more often."

Some unknown time later I heard myself say emotionally, "Kevin, I'm sorry I was such a son of a bitch to you after you let everyone know you were a homosexual. I'm sorry I took you out of address book number one and put you in address book number five and wouldn't go to your parties. I'm very, very sorry—yes, I truly am—but I want you to know, Kevin, that I'm not a son of a bitch, not really, not underneath."

"Yes, you are," said Kevin, "but that's okay, because if you can accept me as I am, then I can accept you as you are, even though you're a son of a bitch."

We shook hands very solemnly and swore eternal friendship.

It's funny how simple and straightforward life seems when you're drunk.

Less than six weeks later we were no longer on speaking terms.

Chapter Three

I

THE TROUBLE began when Kevin received a subpoena to appear before the House Committee on Un-American Activities. We were moving toward the end of 1952, and in the Senate McCarthy was at his zenith. Afterward I blamed the whole disaster on McCarthy. If it hadn't been for his questionable success in winkling the communists out of the woodwork of government, the House committee might have remained as it had been before those fatal years of the late forties and early fifties, a backwater for political has-beens with racial prejudices.

However, with McCarthy on the rampage in the Senate, the House committee saw the opportunity to increase their power and by 1952 they had turned their attention to people in the arts, either communists or radicals, who could provide them with information about the hidden reds in America. Kevin had never been a communist, but like so many writers and artists, he had had radical views in the past and had often mixed with people whose political views could be considered questionable. So it was not surprising that the committee, scrounging around for new sources of information, should select him to testify on the subject of his past and present acquaintances.

In spite of this, it was still a shock when one evening Teresa met me with the news that Kevin had received his subpoena. And it was an even bigger shock when she added that he had every intention of taking the Fifth Amendment and refusing to testify against his friends.

I went to see Kevin at once. I pointed out that any attempt he might make to take the Fifth would result in him being blacklisted; no one would dare to produce his plays, and his career would be ruined.

"You could even be jailed for contempt," I added. "Look what happened to Dashiell Hammett—a writer who refused to testify! Kevin, your only hope of saving yourself is to tell the committee everything they want to know. It's done all the time nowadays, and your friends will understand that you've got no choice."

"But Neil," said Kevin, "the whole point is that I do have a choice. Is it really so impossible for you to see that?"

We argued for some time but got nowhere. He claimed that unless someone took a stand against the committee, the government might soon decide to start chasing Jews and homosexuals as well as communists. I claimed that the inauguration of Eisenhower as president would see the initiation of a new approach to the cold war, with the result that communist persecution would no longer be politically necessary. "So whether or not you sacrifice your career for idealistic liberal principles, it won't make one blind bit of difference to the future of America," I concluded. "It'll be irrelevant. If you ruin yourself, you'll have ruined yourself for a cause which exists only in the minds of you and your fellow intellectuals."

But he couldn't see it. We continued to argue until at last he said, "Neil, I don't want this to degenerate into a serious quarrel. You go your way and let me go mine. It's my life, after all, and my career. Not yours."

I said no more, but of course I was determined not to give up the fight on his behalf, and two days later I invented some business excuse, stepped aboard my private plane, and was flown at top speed to Washington.

Luckily I didn't have to go as far as the Oval Office, although I would have gone there if it had been necessary. I just went to my favorite congressman, the one most heavily involved with the Committee on Un-American Activities, and after reminding him who had recently helped extricate him from a budding scandal (why are politicians always so reckless about graft?), I said it would be sad if his little problem were to surface again so soon after his reelection. I then remarked that it would make me very happy if the committee could forget all about the New York playwright Kevin Daly, who had never been a card-carrying party member and whom I personally knew to be a good loyal American, and I'm glad to say the congressman was very understanding about the whole matter, so understanding that after a round of handshakes I was assured I had nothing left to worry about.

Feeling very pleased with myself, I flew home to New York and went straight to Teresa to announce that Kevin's problem with the committee had been unequivocally solved.

In delight Teresa phoned Kevin, but he hung up on her. I thought that was odd, but supposed he was too overcome with relief to speak, and when I later found him waiting for me at my home on Fifth Avenue, I naturally assumed he had come to celebrate his reprieve. His towering rage, which exploded as soon as we were alone together in the library, was such a shock that I nearly dropped the bottle of Wild Turkey bourbon which I stocked specially for his visits.

"You goddamned interfering son of a bitch, how dare you try to play God with my life!"

"Kevin! What do you mean? You had a problem, and I fixed it, that's all! Why are you so angry?"

"I didn't ask you to play fairy godmother!" Kevin yelled. "I didn't ask you to go waving the magic wand of your corrupt political influence! I asked you to leave me alone so that I could take a good hard slam at the committee—I had lawyers who were willing to help me, I had liberal backers, I had people from the press on my side—"

"You'd all have come to grief, and anyway, I consider I had a moral duty to stop you from wrecking your career!"

"If I want to wreck my career, I'll wreck it! It's no goddamned business of yours!"

"Well, okay, but you might at least be grateful that I—"

"*Grateful!* I'm supposed to be grateful because you get a kick out of waving your power around as if it were a Colt forty-five . . . or any other phallic symbol I could name?"

"Look, pal," I said, setting down the unopened bottle of bourbon with a crash, "get this straight, and save the psychological crap for one of your dumb plays. At great trouble and expense and even risk to myself I did you the biggest possible favor, and if you think I got some kind of degenerate sex kick out of it, you must be out of your perverted pro-communist mind!"

Without a word Kevin turned and walked to the door.

"Kevin!" My legs were moving. There was cold sweat on my back. Something was happening to my breathing, but I paid no attention because I was so upset. "Kevin . . ." I just managed to grab his arm before he opened the door, but he shoved me away.

"Fuck off! If you were any other guy, you wouldn't still be in one piece!"

"But, Kevin, I'm your friend!"

"Not anymore," said Kevin violently, and slammed the library door in my face.

II

". . . AND HE slammed the door in my face," I said to Jake half an hour later. I was three blocks north of my home in the library of the Reischman mansion. Vast olive-green drapes covered vast ugly windows. A dim light in the ceiling far above us shone limpidly on the untranslated German classics and the masterpieces of English literature. Jake and I were sitting facing each other in leather armchairs poised on either side of an immense fireplace. Jake was drinking Johnnie Walker Scotch. I had by that time progressed to neat brandy.

"God, I feel so mad!" I said, trying to sound angry but only succeeding in sounding miserable. "I mean, how ungrateful can you get? I only wanted to help him!"

"Come, Neil," said Jake, giving me one of his thin smiles, "you're not really that naive."

"I only wanted to help him!" I repeated stubbornly, but I knew what he meant. My misery broadened to encompass my shame. "Oh, hell, okay, maybe I did do it to impress him. I certainly enjoyed impressing Teresa. Maybe I did it because I wanted to prove something to him—that I wasn't vulnerable . . . not someone to be pitied . . . No, forget I said that, I take it back. But I did do it too because I wanted to help him, Jake! My motives weren't all bad. I did mean well, I swear it!"

"Well, never mind your motives now. The important thing is that you should learn from your mistakes. You do realize, I hope, what your mistakes were? Number one: never put your friends in your debt by a naked display of power. Your friends are only your friends because they like to kid themselves that underneath all those millions you're as ordinary as they are, and you let them kid themselves because you want to think that you have friends who like you in spite of the money. But if you go around manipulating their lives, no matter how altruistic your motives, you destroy this mutual illusion, with the result that neither of you can continue to live comfortably with the truth. And the truth is, of course, that you're not ordinary, you have a surplus of the commodity most men secretly want—power—and you have more control over them than they can psychologically stand."

"Yes. Right. Oh, God, how could I have been such a—"

"Your second mistake," said Jake, lighting a new cigarette from the butt that was dying between his fingers, "was your failure to grasp Kevin's own attitude to his dilemma. Just because you can't understand it doesn't mean it's some kind of grand intellectual delusion, yet you behaved as if he'd proved himself certifiable. No wonder Kevin got so angry. What you were really doing was insulting his view of life—or reality, if you prefer—by imposing your will on his."

"Hell, yes, I guess I was. But I didn't mean to! All I wanted—"

"Yes, we know what you wanted. Your third mistake—"

"Christ, is there another?" I felt close to complete despair.

"—was to rant on like a fundamentalist preacher from the Bible Belt about your so-called moral duty. Try to be a little more sophisticated, Neil! My God, twenty-five years in New York and you're still capable of acting like a farmboy from Ohio!"

"But I was sincere when I talked about moral duty!"

"Sincerity is nearly always undiplomatic and very often disastrous. Anyway, I question your sincerity. Maybe you should too. Your talk of moral duty was just an excuse for interfering, and you've already admitted that your motives for helping Kevin weren't as pristine as you'd like to believe."

"Yes, but . . ." I sighed. I felt tired and muddled and dispirited, and Jake, seeing this, stood up, patted me on the shoulder, and refilled my glass of brandy.

"Relax, Neil. No one ever acts for the purest possible motives. You tried to do what you genuinely believed to be right, and an impure motive or two doesn't alter that basic fact. You were misguided, the result was a disaster, but I accept that you were fundamentally well-intentioned."

"And you sympathize?"

"Of course. I know how fond you are of Kevin. I know how much it means to have a friend who's known you from the beginning."

I experienced an enormous surge of relief and gratitude. When all was said and done, there was no friend as close to me as Jake. He alone understood the problems of wealth and isolation because his position was so similar to my own.

"How can I make it up with Kevin?" I said at last, worrying over the problem. "Shall I write him a letter? If I call he'll just hang up." I had an inspiration. "I could write him a letter *by hand*. That would show him I was sincere. He knows my correspondence is always typed by secretaries."

"I should leave him alone. Any move you make toward a reconciliation will probably encourage him to think you're exercising your power again, and he'll stay hostile. The first move's got to come from him."

"But it may never come!"

"Possibly, but if you make big mistakes, you must expect to pay for them."

"'For every wrong someday you'll pay'?" I said, quoting a Hank Williams song. "You don't truly believe that, do you, Jake?"

Jake thought for a moment. "No."

We laughed together, two cynical New Yorkers with an unusual amount in common.

"How's Vicky?" said Jake as I stood up to go.

"Just fine, judging from her letters. How are your kids?"

"Okay." Jake never seemed interested in his children, and as the conversation veered at last toward our domestic lives, I felt that strange slender barrier rise between us to sever our lines of communication.

"How's Amy?" I said, mechanically completing the ritual of family inquiries.

"Fine. . . . How's Alicia?"

"Oh, she's just great! She's taking much more of an interest in life these days with her charities and that flower-arranging course she gives to the Junior League. I'm very pleased. I was worried about her around the time Vicky got married. It's hard for women when all the kids have left home."

"Sure."

He came out with me to see me off. Leaving the library, we traversed a huge gloomy atrium and our footsteps echoed eerily on the marble surrounding the ornamental pool. The gilded pipes of the organ were lost in the shadows of the domed ceiling.

"What do you think of the latest shenanigans of the antitrust

case?" he said. "Judge Medina must be on his knees by this time."
I responded automatically to his move to restore the communication lines. "It's my one regret Van Zale's wasn't named as a defendant in the case along with the other seventeen investment-banking houses," I said. "I'd have told prosecuting counsel a thing or two!"

"Think of the legal bills you'd have to pay. And the time you'd have to waste."

"True." We paused by the mock-medieval front door and shook hands.

"Thanks a lot, Jake. You're a true friend. I appreciate it."

"Good night, Neil. And remember: soft-pedal the power in front of your friends, reserve the phrase 'moral duty' for discussions with your local minister, and try not to act all the time as if you strongly suspect God is a white Anglo-Saxon Protestant."

"I don't suspect it, I know it!" I retorted, feeling very much better, and heard his laughter ring out behind me as he gently closed the door.

III

I WAS still estranged from Kevin six months later when Vicky gave birth in London to a second son, who was promptly named Paul Cornelius. Sam and Vicky both phoned to invite me to England for the christening, and although I did not want to appear as if I were seizing the excuse to visit them, I promised that Alicia and I would cross the Atlantic in August. I was careful to stress that we would stay in a hotel. Sam had bought a house overlooking Hyde Park, and I had no doubt it was spacious enough to accommodate us, but I was anxious not to put too great a strain on his hospitality. I didn't want to upset Vicky by aggravating the tension which was certain to be present in any reunion between myself and her husband.

Vicky seemed to have settled down well in London. She had registered for a course in German but had abandoned it when she became pregnant, and anyway, she was too busy organizing her new home to pay serious attention to studying. Her letters described her struggles with the English interior decorators, Eric's first day at his English nursery school, the difficulties of living up to the expectations of British servants (I thought of Carraway and sympathized), the miraculous quality of English radio and television, and the ever-present fascination of the queen, the coronation, and the weather. Occasionally she mentioned a new movie or imported American musical which she and Sam had seen in the West End, but they were too busy entertaining Sam's new clients to go out much on the town.

Several times every week I spoke to Sam on the phone to make sure everything was progressing satisfactorily in London, and although I knew he resented my breathing down his neck, I was determined to keep him on his toes by regularly reminding him who was boss. Under the circumstances it seemed the least I could do to restore the correct balance of power between us and a small price for him to pay for his new life in Europe. However, I was careful to keep our conversations friendly, and no one eavesdropping on us would have guessed that our good-humored exchanges masked bitterness on my part and probably exasperation—to say the least—on his.

"So how are the British, Sam?" I said on the first working day after the coronation in June. "I hope you enjoyed yourself drinking the queen's health and listening to everyone declare that the spirit which conquered Mount Everest was the spirit which won the war!"

"Well, I'm all for giving credit where credit is due," said Sam placidly, "and why shouldn't I drink the queen's health? I like the royal family. They're all German anyway."

That was one of our milder exchanges, I reminding him that living in Europe wasn't all moonlight and roses and he rebuffing me by bragging about how well he was handling a potentially hostile environment. But our most acrimonious conversations arose over the kind of image I wanted the new Van Zale's to present in London.

Van Zale's had had a London office for some sixty years, but I had closed its doors and withdrawn our capital from Europe before the outbreak of war there in 1939. Banking had changed greatly over those sixty years. Originally we had specialized in letters of credit and loans to foreign governments, but after World War I that business had died and by the time Steve Sullivan went to London to be the resident partner in 1929 we had become interested in putting American money into English business—not an easy task, as British businesses often raised the money for their needs without the help of issuing houses. However, Steve had done well in adverse circumstances and our London house had shown a profit until the impending war had cast a shadow over European finance. Now times had changed yet again; the shadow was gone, American corporations were spearheading an economic invasion of Europe, and it was natural for them to turn for help to an investment-banking house with the best transatlantic connections.

"We must make it clear we're an outpost of America," I said firmly. "After all, this is economic war. I know the British feel sentimental about Americans because we beat Hitler for them, but the economic reality is very different from that political fantasy which the politicians are pushing to convince the Russians that the West is totally united. The economic reality is that we're fighting for control of Britain, the empire, Europe, and the world. Forget the politicians talking about friendship. The future lies in the presence of the American bottle of ketchup on the English breakfast table. I want the most modern office you can get, the most modern equipment, and whenever possible, American staff. I want a portrait of the president in the lobby and the Stars and Stripes flying right alongside the Union Jack—"

"Neil, you're dreaming. Wake up. The British don't feel that sentimental about us. They don't even admit we won the war for them. In fact, they haven't forgotten how we left them to fight the Battle of Britain alone, and if there's one thing they resent nowadays, it's Americans like you who think America can muscle in and convert England overnight into a U.S. satellite. We must soft-pedal the American image. We've got to be quiet and discreet and gentlemanly."

"Is there a law which says we can't be quiet and discreet and gentlemanly—Jesus, how godawful that sounds!—in modern offices with modern equipment?"

Our old office in Milk Street, a dark dismal relic of the Victorian era, had fortunately been bombed to pieces, so there was no question of going back there. I was glad. We needed a new image, and anyway, I'm not sentimental about old buildings. One can get very, very tired of sordid plumbing.

However, Sam told me that the right location was more important than modern conveniences, and presently I was informed that he had taken a floor of a building off Lombard Street.

"How old's the building?" I said suspiciously on learning that it had survived the blitz.

"New by English standards. It was built in 1910."

"*Nineteen-ten!* Christ, are you sure there's not a demolition order on it?"

Sam tried to tell me that since much of the City of London was still in ruins, we were lucky to find decent office space at all, but I cut him off.

"God, I sometimes wonder why we're bothering with this European office," I said. "Can it be worth it? I reckon Europe's washed up anyway. This economic boom will never last."

"Your trouble, Neil, is that you've never lived in Europe, you're God knows how many generations removed from any ancestor who grew up there, and you just don't understand it. Forget your simplistic American vision of Europe as a washed-up continent. Europe's always being washed up—it means nothing. The Romans washed it up, Attila washed it up, Napoleon and Hitler washed it up, but the point is that Europe doesn't wear out, no matter how often it's sent to the cleaners. Europe survives. Invest in it. And for God's sake give me carte blanche to do what I know is best for Van Zale's—I realize it's hard for you, but just try not to be such a backseat driver!"

We laughed coolly at the joke. I gave him the carte blanche. We hung up seething.

"I wish you'd make the effort to come over here," Sam said after his new son was born. "I think you'd stop worrying so much about the London office if you could see for yourself how well we're doing."

"It's not a question of making an effort," I said, although it was. It's always an effort to go to a place where you know you've no hope of feeling at home. "Of course I'll make the trip! Do you think I'd want to postpone meeting the latest member of the family?"

Sam laughed, but I wondered if he had been secretly hoping I'd never summon the will to leave America. I wondered too, despite the fact that he seemed pleased to be a father again, how he really felt now that he had two little kids screaming at the top of their lungs, giving their nurse hell, and calling him Daddy. I supposed he was enjoying the novelty, although like Jake he had never seemed interested in children. It all seemed kind of a waste to me.

Meanwhile I had decided I was ready for a vacation, even a vacation which had to be spent in Europe. Since Sam and Vicky's departure I had kept myself very busy, following the activities of the oil lobby in Congress, launching several large flotations to improve the nation's highway system, and attending numerous meetings of the Van Zale Fine Arts Foundation. I had welcomed Eisenhower's arrival at the White House, cheered the collapse of the marathon antitrust case involving investment banks, and invested in a painting by

271

Kokoschka which no one, not even Teresa, liked. The end of the Korean mess was imminent, and I foresaw record peacetime demands for funds; it certainly seemed the right time to take a break before the economic pace stepped up and we all reaped the benefits accruing from the new administration, but when I finally faced the prospect of an overseas vacation, I nearly flunked it. Europe was such a long way away. I couldn't decide how to get there. Should reservations be made on one of the Stratocruiser Speedbirds which flew daily to London? I decided I didn't care for flying unless I knew the pilot personally. Alicia suggested that a sea trip might be pleasant, so I told my aides to fix passages on a transatlantic liner, and when they had done that I told them to buy me all the latest guidebooks on England. I knew I had to be well prepared for this trip. No European was going to think *me* an ignorant American barbarian who was incapable of approaching a foreign country with respect. I studied hard, and often read far into the night.

"I'm not looking forward to this trip one bit," I confessed at last to Alicia. "Wish we were going to Bar Harbor as usual."

"But, Cornelius, think how exciting it'll be for you to see Vicky again!"

"Yes," I said, "but nothing good ever happened to me in England." I thought of my one previous visit to Europe in 1940 when I had been outwitted by my old enemy Dinah Slade. "I've got this feeling," I said, "that as soon as I set foot on English soil, something disastrous will happen."

"Nonsense!" said Alicia firmly, and began to talk about the suite which had been booked for us on board ship. She seemed to be looking forward to the vacation, although I knew she liked Europe no better than I did, and she was clearly excited about the voyage.

"So you're sharing a cabin with your wife!" said Teresa when I finally disclosed some details of my departure to her. "Great! And I'm supposed to step aside gracefully and cheer, I guess, while you sail away on a second honeymoon!"

"Nothing like that's going to happen!" I protested, much gratified by this display of possessiveness. "Of course we've got to share a suite to keep up appearances, but there'll be separate beds."

"Oh, yeah?" said Teresa. "Well, have a good time, and if you don't come back here panting to jump into bed with me, I'll smell the biggest possible rat!"

"I'll remember that!" I promised, feeling more gratified than ever, and thought how lucky I was that we still got along so well after more than four years together. Occasionally I did wonder if she were unfaithful to me, but I was reassured by her chronic untidiness, which would have made it impossible for her to conceal infidelity for long. Certainly she always behaved as if she liked me. I had become increasingly fond of her as the years passed.

"So long, Teresa," I said on the evening before my vacation began. "Be good."

"You too, angel face. No screwing around."

We kissed with commendable passion and parted.

I sighed. Europe loomed ahead, as cold and uninviting as an iceberg, and trying not to feel as if I were as doomed as that notable iceberg victim the *Titanic,* I trudged home to Fifth Avenue and went to bed with the latest copy of the London *Times.*

Chapter Four

I

ALICIA TRAVELED only with her maid, but I brought with me two aides as well as my valet and my bodyguard. I like to be protected from all the more unpleasant aspects of travel, and with my aides dealing with the tiresome details, my valet ensuring that my clothes were always immaculate, and my bodyguard preventing any unwelcome intrusion from the press, the needy, or the just plain curious, my journey to Europe was uneventful.

It was also unembarrassing. I had been worried in case Alicia privately regretted having to sleep in the same room as me in order to keep up appearances, but the suite was so large and the twin beds so far apart that we both quickly relaxed. Soon I even felt happy; after years of separate bedrooms it was painfully exciting to sleep so close to her again. Of course I knew I must never upset her by any thoughtless proposition, but I would surreptitiously watch her brush her hair or apply her makeup, and think how lovely she was. It was as if I were seeing her again after a long absence, and the farther we traveled from New York, the more fantastic it seemed that I should find it easy to go to bed with another woman. Fortunately the liner docked at Southampton before my fantasies of a miraculous reconciliation could overwhelm my common sense, but I think Alicia sensed my happiness in being near her again, because her habitual cool politeness eased into a warmer, gentler manner which was far less formal.

I had told Vicky there was no need for her to meet the ship, since

Southampton is some way from London, but of course she was there with Eric, Nurse, and the new baby. Paul Cornelius Keller was dark and glum. I turned to Eric with relief. He was three years old now and looked more like Vicky than ever, but he seemed to have become very shy, and it was difficult to get a word out of him.

"It's just a phase he's going through," said Vicky, embarrassed.

"Sure! I understand," I said, but I had expected an effusive welcome and couldn't help feeling disappointed. "How's Sam?"

"Oh, Sam's fine! He said he was so sorry not to be here to meet you, but he had this very important meeting . . ."

"Well, of course business must come first!" I said, but I didn't like Sam sidestepping the chore of meeting me.

My aides had arranged for two limousines to transport us to London, but I traveled in the inevitable Keller Mercedes-Benz with Vicky. Sam used their other car, a Daimler, to impress his English clients in the City.

I took a cautious look at England from behind the stout glass windows of the Mercedes, and as we left Southampton and rode smoothly deep into the Hampshire countryside, I felt that well-remembered tension rise within me to set my nerves on edge. The best way I can describe it is to say that it felt like a kind of nakedness—the nakedness of an unarmed soldier advancing toward heavy artillery lined up on some appalling battlefield. I looked at the pretty fields and the quaint little villages and felt not only foreign but stripped of the identity which nurtured me in New York. In New York I was someone special: Cornelius Van Zale, the well-known banker and philanthropist. But here I was no one, just an exile in a land as alien to me as the far side of the moon.

I was back in my teens again suddenly, overwhelmed by feelings of inferiority, terrified that people would laugh at me, dreading their casual contempt. The anger returned too, the anger I could remember so clearly from my youth. The same voice in my head said: No man laughs at me and gets away with it. And as we passed through a little town, I looked out of the window at the British and thought: I'll show them.

"Isn't England lovely?" said Vicky with a sigh. "Isn't it nice to think most of our ancestors came from here?"

"Yes," I said, but I couldn't imagine my ancestors being at home in any country except America. I couldn't even imagine my ancestors. The only ancestor I've ever been interested in was my father, and I only got interested in him because I was going through such hell in the present that for once the past seemed to have something to offer. I was wrong. There was nothing there. My father might have been tenacious enough to build a small homestead into a large prosperous rural fiefdom; he might have been bold enough to marry out of his social background, and tough enough to withstand the Van Zale family's disapproval; he might well have been the kind of guy I could have got along with. But what use was that to me, since he had died when I was four and I now had no way of communicating with him? Before the war I had bought the farm he had owned in the hope that it would somehow bring me closer to his memory, but I had been wasting my money and my time. The past is dead. It's wound up and plowed under, and to believe anything else is self-indulgent fantasy.

"Do you truly like England, Vicky?"

"Oh, *yes,* Daddy! Everything's so civilized, and I just love all the pageantry and the tradition and the . . ."

I somehow kept my mouth shut, but I felt unutterably depressed. I had hoped Vicky would already be restless in her new environment, but evidently I had hoped for too much too soon.

My depression deepened when we reached London. There's something nightmarish about that city, those gray streets sprawling endlessly in all directions, those huge haughty buildings, those fanatically well-tended parks, those hostile inhabitants talking English with a whole range of unintelligible accents. London's like some elaborate maze designed for a Minotaur whose desire for formality borders on obsession. I thought of New York, of cozy bunched-up Manhattan teeming with color and vitality, chockablock with gleaming skyscrapers and glimpses of glittering water, crammed with vistas ravishing in their geometrical simplicity, and by the time we arrived at the Savoy Hotel I was so homesick that I could hardly drag myself out of the car.

I pulled myself together. It was now important that I make a good impression, since in the eyes of the staff of the Savoy I was just another American tourist who might or might not know how to behave in public. I felt thankful that I was traveling in a convoy of two Rolls-Royces and a Mercedes-Benz together with five servants, a beautiful wife, and a mountain of the best-quality leather luggage. The English could plainly see I was no carpetbagger from California or, worse still, some jumped-up Texas cattle baron in a ten-gallon hat.

I checked my black suit, dusted my cuffs, concealed my nervousness behind my most impassive expression, and prepared to represent my country with as much dignity as possible.

My aides had been working hard. On reaching the lobby I was welcomed effusively and ushered upstairs to a gargantuan suite overlooking the river. There were flowers everywhere. A complimentary magnum of champagne stood in a silver ice bucket. I was introduced to the floor waiter, who promised to do everything necessary to ensure my gastronomic comfort.

"Thanks very much," I said, keeping my face expressionless so that they would all think I was an old hand at touring the grand hotels of Europe, and nodded to my aide to start distributing tips.

By this time I was feeling better. The Savoy had acknowledged that I was a visitor of consequence, and I began to feel that my New York identity might possibly be within my reach again. I saw the phone and picked up the receiver. That made me feel better too, and as I started to dial I knew that although my power had been temporarily switched off, like an electric current, it was now starting to flow smoothly again.

"I'll leave you to get settled in," said Vicky after I had spoken to Sam and replaced the receiver, "but do come on over as soon as you can, won't you? Eric can't wait to show you his nursery!"

I made a couple more calls to business acquaintances in order to jack up the voltage of my electric current, and afterward felt so completely recovered that I was reluctant to leave the phone.

"Get that last letter I had from my sister," I said to my aide, on an impulse.

The aide came running, the letter in his hands.

"Who are you calling now, Cornelius?" called Alicia from one of the bedrooms.

"I promised Emily I'd call those English stepchildren of hers. I may as well get it over so that I can enjoy the rest of the trip." I found the Cambridge telephone number and told the aide to start making the call.

Alicia was in the doorway. "I guess we ought to see them while we're here."

"No, why the hell should we? They haven't been in touch with us for years. I didn't like to complain to Emily, who always makes out she's so fond of them, but I was kind of disgusted by their lack of gratitude."

"You should have told Emily. *She* may enjoy playing the long-suffering martyr who dotes on her husband's children by another woman, but I don't see why you should have to follow in her footsteps."

"It's bad enough Emily and I never seeing eye to eye with each other about her canonization of Steve's memory. I couldn't make matters worse by arguing with her over those kids as well."

"The number's ringing, sir," said my aide. Then: "Hello? Mr. Cornelius Van Zale is calling Miss Elfrida Sullivan—is she there, please? Thank you, will you hold the line?" He passed me the receiver.

I assumed a neutral voice. "Elfrida?"

"Yes." The monosyllable was bleak and uncompromising.

"Hi, how are you," I said, still maintaining my neutrality, but with increasing difficulty. "I'm vacationing in London, and Emily asked me to give you a call. How are Edred and George?"

"Well."

"Good. Any special news that I can relay to Emily?"

"None."

I suddenly realized I was in the middle of a highly unpleasant interview.

"Seen anything of Vicky lately?" I said. "She didn't mention you, but I assume you've been in touch."

"No."

"Oh. Any special reason?"

"Yes."

"Oh? What's that?"

"You killed my father," said Elfrida Sullivan, and hung up.

II

OF COURSE I'd done nothing of the kind. Steve Sullivan's death was an accident. When I gave the final order to Sam in 1939, I didn't say: "Kill him." I just said . . . Well, my exact words didn't matter. Steve had been persecuting me for years, and I had had no choice but to ensure he emerged from our struggles with his career in ruins. It wasn't my fault if he had found he couldn't live with himself after Sam and I had proved to the world he was an unstable drunk who had been hospitalized in one of London's best-known nursing homes for alcoholics.

"Fix him," I had said to Sam. "And I mean *fix* him."

I remembered Sam's shaken voice later on the transatlantic phone. "When Steve saw that photograph and knew he was finished, he drank a bottle of Scotch and set off in his car to confront me. . . ."

But there was no one now alive who knew exactly what had happened to Steve in 1939, no one except Sam and myself—and, apparently, Elfrida Sullivan.

The full implications of this appalling fact suddenly streamed through my mind. *How* did Elfrida know? How long had she known? And who could possibly have told her?

"How was Elfrida?" I heard Alicia call from the bedroom.

"Fine." I was in such a state of shock that I could hardly speak. Making a great effort, I sat down and started to arrange the known facts into some kind of coherent order.

It was possible that after Steve's death his wife, Dinah, had broadcast the unsavory facts to all and sundry, but all the evidence suggested she had told very few people. If she had made a fuss, I would have heard about it, but I had heard nothing and had concluded that she had been too upset to magnify her bereavement by making unpleasant public scenes. Perhaps her grief had been such that she had had difficulty discussing Steve's death even with those closest to her, but that remained mere speculation; the one fact I did know was that after her own death at Dunkirk in 1940 only two people appeared to know the whole story. One was Alan Slade, the product of her famous liaison with Paul Van Zale back in the twenties, and the other was Tony Sullivan, Scott's younger brother and Steve's second son.

I was in England at the time and met them both in London. Emily had cabled that she was willing to look after Steve and Dinah's three young children, and because Alan and Tony themselves were hardly more than schoolboys who were going to find it difficult to care properly for their young half-sister and half-brothers, it was obviously best for them to accept Emily's offer. Alan was reluctant. He disliked the idea of the children going off with me to America. However, Tony, who like Scott had been brought up by Emily after his mother's death, had convinced him of Emily's unrivaled talent as a stepmother.

Despite our final agreement, it had been a hostile interview, and even after the agreement had been reached, Tony had still wanted to tell the children that I had been responsible for their father's death. A most unpleasant scene then ensued, which was only terminated when I pointed out sensibly that the children would hardly consent to go off to America with me if they thought I was a murderer, and that it would be far better to leave the subject of their father's death well alone. Tony (in many ways a stupid boy) continued to insist mulishly that at ten years of age Edred and Elfrida were old enough to hear the truth, but Alan (who was undoubtedly intelligent) saw the logic of my statement, and in the end they agreed to keep quiet for the time being.

Both Alan and Tony were killed in 1944, and as far as I knew, they died without having breathed a word against me to either Edred or Elfrida or George. The children, brought up by Emily with her usual skill, remained civil to me for the duration of their stay in America, and even after they returned to England they were willing enough to spend their next two summer vacations at my Bar Harbor summer home. But on the twins' eighteenth birthday in January 1948 they returned the check I had sent them as a present, and since then I had received no communication from them. At the time, I had been puzzled by this rudeness, but frankly I had always found the children difficult, and anyway, eighteen is an age at which many adolescents behave eccentrically. The thought that they might have uncovered the truth about their father's death did cross my mind, but I dismissed the idea because I was sure no one could have told them. It was impossible.

Yet it had happened.

I roused myself sufficiently to summon my aide. "Get me my sister in Velletria, Ohio."

It took some time to reach Emily by phone, but at last the receiver was put in my hand.

"Cornelius? Darling, why are you calling? Is something wrong?"

"Emily, just what did you tell the English Sullivans after the war about my quarrels with Steve?"

"Your quarrels with . . . Why, nothing! I've never told them anything that wasn't common knowledge—I just said you two had disagreements which led to Steve leaving Van Zale's and setting up a new business in London. Cornelius, what *is* all this? You sound very upset. What's happened?"

"Elfrida's just accused me of murdering her father."

There was an absolute silence.

"Of course it's a slander," I said, "and I'm trying to find out who's at the bottom of it. Elfrida seems to have formed this opinion at the time of her eighteenth birthday, but by January 1948 there would have been no one left alive who might have felt inclined to give her such a perverted version of the facts. Unless, of course, you yourself drew some unfortunate conclusions about the past and then, without telling me, wrote to the twins on their eighteenth birthday—"

"I did no such thing!"

Before my bewilderment intensified, I had a moment of profound relief.

"I'll write to Elfrida," Emily was saying strongly. "I'm very distressed. Hatred is so self-destructive. She must be very unhappy."

This was typical of Emily. As usual she had missed the whole point and got bogged down in the moral angle. I wasn't concerned with the consequences of hatred. I wasn't even concerned about being hated by Steve Sullivan's three youngest children. What did concern me was that Steve had been Scott's father as well as theirs. If someone had given Elfrida a brand-new view of the past, what was to stop her passing it on to her half-brother in New York? And what was to stop Scott believing her and turning against me? Of course, I had brought Scott up with my view of the past, but supposing he were to find out . . . I cut off all thought of what I didn't want Scott to find out, and wiped the sweat from my forehead. "Emily, you don't understand. Listen, Emily—"

"I'll do my best, I promise you, to persuade Elfrida to forgive you. You might have done wrong in the past, but you've done your best to make amends, and besides, it's not for us to pass judgment on our fellowmen. That must be left to God."

I was so horrified that I couldn't even hang up and cut myself off from all this theological drivel. "What the *hell* do you mean?"

Emily, unfazed, started quoting the Bible. " 'Judge not, that ye be not judged—' "

"No, no, not that! What did you mean about the so-called wrong I've done in the past? For Christ's sake, has someone turned you against me too? I did no wrong, Emily! Steve and I had a rough fight, I admit it, but he initiated it. I only acted in self-defense."

The transatlantic connection hummed emptily between us.

"Emily!"

"Yes, dear."

"Look, what's been going on? Who's been talking to you? Who's been slandering me? Who—?"

"If you're so innocent, why are you working yourself into such a panic?"

"I'm not in a panic! I'm just . . . well, to tell the truth, I'm concerned about Scott. I don't want him bothered by Elfrida's hysterical accusations. You know how fond I am of him, and how fond he is of me. This could be very embarrassing to us both."

"Oh, you don't have to worry about Scott," said Emily, and as if she felt this statement needed an explanation, she added after a slight pause, "Your relationship with Scott shows you at your very best, Cornelius. I'm proud of the way you took charge of him when he was such a disturbed, difficult boy of fourteen and brought him up with such complete success. You can be proud, too. That episode does you nothing but credit."

Shame gripped me so unexpectedly and so violently that I was speechless. I thought: That's the way things ought to have been. But was that the way things really were? And then I thought with a terrible, unbearable clarity: What an appalling mess I've made of my personal life. Christ, I've been so unhappy. Christ, I *am* so unhappy.

I blocked that thought out, pulled the shutters down over such unspeakable consciousness, switched on the lights of my self-protective reflexes, and prepared to settle down once more in the steel-lined cell I had built for myself so carefully over the years.

"Yes, I *am* proud of the way I brought up Scott," I said. "To be frank, I'm proud of my whole past. I've done nothing to be ashamed of. God deals out the cards of life, and you play the hand as best you can, that's all. It's not my fault if I occasionally found myself with a lousy hand."

"Yes, dear," said Emily. She cleared her throat. "Give my love to Sam and Vicky, won't you? And the little boys too, of course! Tell Vicky I can't wait to see some pictures of Paul! I hope there wasn't too much disappointment that he wasn't a girl."

I didn't bother to answer. Who could be disappointed by having two sons? I said good-bye and hung up before it occurred to me that I still had no idea who had been talking to Elfrida about the past.

I couldn't stop thinking about it. I considered every angle of the mystery over and over again, until at last, inevitably, my thoughts began to focus on Tony Sullivan; I was remembering how strongly he had insisted that the children should be told the truth.

I had taken charge of Tony in 1933 when I had taken charge of Scott, but Tony and I had never got along, and eventually he had turned his back on me and sailed off to England to live with his father's last family; Steve was dead by that time, but Dinah had given Tony a home with Alan and the three little kids at Mallingham in Norfolk, where her family had lived for centuries. Scott, staunchly loyal to me, had quarreled with Tony at about this time, and after Tony went to England, the brothers remained estranged and never met again. This had, of course, been a great relief to me. I knew what kind of stories Tony would have heard about me as soon as he had begun his new life at Mallingham.

I went on thinking of Tony. I felt no emotion. That had all been spent long ago. Back in 1931 Tony had given me mumps, that stupid kid's disease which was to mar my whole life, and once I had found out I was sterile, I had never been able to look at him without remembering and remembering and remembering. . . . I didn't blame him, exactly—after all, it was hardly his fault—but I just remembered. He was a reminder. He also looked like Steve. That made me remember, too. He was a reminder of too damned much. I also had this odd feeling that he was destined to be my permanent nemesis. It's a strange fact of life that certain people's paths intersect periodically with one's own, sometimes with beneficial results, sometimes with a disastrous aftermath, and for me Tony Sullivan had always provided the catalyst for disaster.

As I lay awake worrying that night, I thought: Tony's at the bottom of this somehow. But how? He died in 1944. Or did he? Perhaps he survived . . . prisoner of war . . . amnesia . . . only just recovered . . . returned to Mallingham . . .

Sleep mercifully put an end to these neurotic fantasies, but the next morning I woke up and began to worry all over again. Throughout the day I told myself repeatedly: The past is dead. The past can't touch me anymore. But then came the bombshell.

Elfrida herself arrived at the Savoy and demanded to see me.

III

I WAS dressing for dinner at the time. Sam and Vicky were due to take us out that evening to a show.

"There's a Miss Sullivan downstairs, sir," said my aide. "She wants to know if she can come up."

I opened my mouth to say no, but the words which came out were: "Let me talk to her." I had to get to the bottom of this mystery before I left England. It was all very well to reassure myself by saying that nobody could prove anything and that Scott would always take my word against Elfrida's, but I just didn't want Scott upset. Taking the receiver from my aide, I said pleasantly into the mouthpiece, "So it's you again! I hope you're not still playing at being prosecuting attorney. What charges do you want to press today?"

"I want to talk to you about Mallingham," said Elfrida.

Dinah Slade's old home had found its way into Paul's hands in 1922, and when he had died four years later, the property had devolved to me as his heir. The house was a charred ruin, but the land was still mine. I had had some vague idea of transferring it to the National Trust, since the acreage was in an area which they wanted to preserve, but I had never been able to summon the mental energy to issue the necessary orders to my lawyers. I always tried not to think of Mallingham, since it inevitably reminded me of Steve and Dinah and a whole series of events I knew it was wiser to forget. I didn't want to think of it now.

"Look, Elfrida, I'm a busy man and I don't have the time to waste raking over the past with you—"

"I want to talk about the future."

I supposed she wanted her old home back. To my relief, I suddenly saw how I might appease her and neutralize the danger she represented. "Okay, come up," I said, and abruptly severed the connection.

IV

SHE WAS a tall girl, large-boned and masculine, her curly hair cut short. She wore no makeup and her clothes were unflattering. Her eyes were a bright light blue.

I had taken a couple of pills for my asthma and was breathing evenly. I had dismissed everyone from the suite except Alicia and her maid; I could hear them talking to each other in the far bedroom as I went out into the hallway to open the door.

Elfrida was twenty-three years old. She had taken a degree in English at Cambridge University and had afterward spent a further year obtaining a teaching diploma before applying for a position in a private school near Cambridge. Her twin brother, Edred, taught music at the same school, but according to Emily, was trying to get a job in an orchestra. The younger boy, George, had finished his last year at boarding school and was scheduled to go to one of the newer English universities in the fall. Emily had told me what he intended to study, but I had forgotten. I wished I could forget all the English Sullivans, all Europe, and indeed everything and everyone east of the state of Maine.

Opening the door, I told Elfrida to come in.

"Right," I said, leading the way into the sitting room but not inviting her to be seated. "I'm about to go out, but I guess I can spare you a minute or two. You should have called for an appointment. Now, what's your problem? Do you want the Mallingham lands back? I'd planned to give them to the National Trust, but if you like, I'll donate them to you instead. I would have offered earlier, but after you and Edred deliberately cut yourself off from me—"

"Thank you," said Elfrida neatly, "I accept the offer. How kind of you. And while you're about it, you can write me a check for a million dollars."

That rocked me. It was not simply the request for money; I was well accustomed to such requests from the indigent. Neither was it simply the ridiculous amount involved; I was well aware that the indigent often lose touch with reality. What shocked me was the hint of extortion, the implication that I owed her a huge sum in order to compensate her for a great loss. What shocked me was the buried past erupting out of its sealed coffin and even threatening bizarrely to repeat itself. Her mother, Dinah Slade, had once asked for ten thousand pounds from my great-uncle, Paul Van Zale.

"A million dollars?" I said. I knew I should laugh and exclaim: "You're kidding!" but all I could say was, "What the hell are you talking about?"

"I want to start a school," said Elfrida, still the picture of serene self-confidence. "I've decided to rebuild Mallingham Hall, restoring it as far as possible, and turn it into a boarding school for girls. I shall name it in memory of my mother. She was very interested in education for women."

"I see." I got a grip on myself. "How very commendable!" That sounded too silky, too insincere. I groped for a better tone, a more even tone, the tone of a philanthropist who believed in encouraging worthy schemes. "Well," I said mildly, "I am, as you know, a charitable man, and for many years I've set aside a certain portion of my wealth for my educational trust. I see no reason why I shouldn't help you, but of course we must approach this project in a sensible manner. I can't just sit down now and write you a check for an amount which sounds to me totally excessive."

"You owe me every cent of it!"

"I think not," I said, still very mild. "I did my best for you when you were orphaned, and despite your recent efforts to insult me, I'm prepared to do my best for you now by putting you in touch with the Van Zale lawyers in London and my educational trust in New York."

There was a pause. I made a quick calculation. Of course it would all be deductible. My accountants would be very pleased, and so would I. The net loss to me would be minimal, and I would have the satisfaction of knowing I had permanently muzzled the most dangerous of the English Sullivans by smothering her with Christian charity. Even Emily would approve.

Elfrida was looking suspicious. Although inexperienced in the ways of the world, the girl was clearly no fool. "I want all that in writing," she said.

"Of course—on the understanding that you stop announcing to all and sundry that I killed your father. If I ever hear that you've been behaving so irresponsibly again, I shall withdraw my financial support."

She gave me a look which reminded me of her father. There was amusement mingled with the scorn, irony with the contempt. "Just give me the money," she said, "and spare me the exhibition of guilt."

I laughed. I produced my most radiant smile. "But of course you can have the money! I'm happy to give it to you. I just wanted to make sure we understood each other, but I'm really not the ogre you believe me to be! Oh, and talking of what you believe . . . just who's been trying to persuade you that I was responsible for your father's death?"

Elfrida's head jerked up. Her expression puzzled me. She looked thoroughly bewildered. "Don't pretend you don't know!" she said automatically.

I had a sharp premonition of disaster. I kept my face impassive, but my hands interlocked tightly behind my back. "Of course I don't know! If I knew, I'd sue the bastard for slander!"

"You can't sue a dead man."

I stared at her. She stared back, still skeptical of my ignorance, but finally she wrenched open her purse and pulled out a tattered envelope.

"I did bring the letter," she said, "but I hardly thought I'd need to remind you of its existence."

I knew I was on the brink of some appalling abyss, but I knew too I could not stop myself toppling into it. I went on staring at her. Then I realized I was staring at the letter. The ache of tension started to twist in my lungs.

"Don't tell me no one's ever shown you Tony's letter!" Elfrida burst out incredulously. "Don't tell me no one's ever confronted you with it and demanded an explanation!"

"Tony," I said. "Yes. I knew it was him. It had to be Tony, always Tony . . . Tony wrote a letter?"

"He wrote it in 1944 just before he went to Normandy. Alan had been killed, and Tony wanted to be sure that if he were killed too, Edred, George, and I wouldn't grow up in ignorance of how our parents died."

"Nineteen-forty-four. He wrote the letter in 1944."

"Yes. He typed it and made two copies."

"Copies. Did you say copies?"

"Yes, he put all three copies in separate envelopes and left the lot with my mother's solicitors in Norwich with instructions that the top copy should be held there until Edred and I were eighteen. Didn't you wonder why you never heard from us again after January 1948? That was when we got our copy of Tony's letter."

"And the other two copies . . ."

". . . were posted to America as soon as Tony was killed in 1944. One went to Emily. Tony felt guilty that he had abandoned her home to live at Mallingham, and he felt he owed it to her to explain just why he had turned so completely against you. And then of course the last copy of the letter went to—"

"Scott," I said.

"Who else?" said Elfrida.

V

I was breathing very carefully—in, out . . . in, out . . . in, out. I had to think about my breathing. I could not afford an asthmatic scene. In, out . . . in, out.

"Tony wanted Scott to know everything too," Elfrida was saying. "He was upset that they'd become estranged, and he hoped that if Scott read the whole story in a posthumous letter he might at last be able to believe the truth. Of course Tony planned to see Scott after the war and make another effort to convince him, but he was taking no chances. That letter was his insurance that the truth would survive."

I couldn't think of Scott. I wanted to, but I knew it would upset me too much. I wanted to tell Elfrida to stop talking, but I didn't dare speak. I had to wait. I must do nothing that might disturb the rhythm of my breathing. Did I dare hold out my hand, or would even that small physical exertion prove fatal? In, out . . . in, out. No, I had to risk it. I had to know.

I held out my hand. She gave me the letter. For one long moment I stood listening to my labored breathing and then I sat down, opened the envelope, and stepped right onto the roller coaster that swooped back into the past.

VI

I read the letter. Afterward it was so hard to know what to say. I knew in my mind how I felt, but it was so hard to find the words to express myself. Since I'm not an intellectual, I don't have that intellectual trick of dealing in metaphysical abstractions as if they were concrete facts. The language of philosophy is foreign to me, and although I can talk of morality as fluently as any man who has had a religious upbringing, it occurred to me now that that language too was foreign to me, my fluency learned parrot fashion and useless in any intellectual argument. Anyway, I had always distrusted intellectual arguments. They only clouded one's view of reality. It was far more practical to see a situation in stark black and white without any colors that could confuse the issue. One made better decisions that way. And of course, to get on in life and be a success, one had to make good decisions.

But now someone else was using my technique against me. Tony Sullivan was seeing the past in black and white, but his blacks were my whites, and his whites were my blacks, so his view of the past was the opposite of mine. I wanted to say that to the girl before me, but I knew that wouldn't be sufficient comment; I had to persuade her that Tony's landscape, with its absence of color, even of grays and off-whites, was no more valid than my own stylized view of the past which had sustained me for so long, but truth was such an abstract subject and I was incapable of saying what I wanted to say.

I suddenly thought of Kevin remarking when we were discussing why people hid behind masks: "I think it's because life's so fantastically complicated."

"Life's so complicated," I said at last, "so confusing. Everyone sees the truth differently. The truth is different things to different people. Eyewitnesses can give different stories of the same set of facts. I respect Tony's view, since he's obviously so sincere, but what he says in this letter just isn't the whole story."

"Oh?" said the girl bitterly. "Do you deny that you were so obsessed with power that you did everything you could to smash my father's career and ruin my mother's life?"

I was careful not to snap back a brutal reply. Instead I thought hard and struggled again for the right words, for the words which came closest to reflecting the truth. "I don't believe," I said slowly at last, "I was any more obsessed with power than your father was. But perhaps the truth was that it was more necessary to me than it was to him. He was a big tough guy with an attractive personality, and he didn't really need power, he just enjoyed it. He had other ways of making people notice him, you see. Power wasn't his sole means of communication."

"*Communication?*" She looked at me as if I'd gone mad. Perhaps I had. I wished again I could express all these abstract ideas better. I wished there were some hard facts I could use, but there was only the truth, slippery and shadowy, and my knowledge that for once I had to confront it instead of retreating behind a shield of comforting clichés. I thought of those clichés—"I did what I had to do," "I was more sinned against than sinning," "I considered it my moral duty"—and the familiar phrases, usually so comforting, echoed emptily through my consciousness. Suddenly I felt very, very tired. I wanted so intensely to withdraw into my familiar black-and-white world, but there was the letter, my black-and-white world turned inside out against me, the accusations filling line after line after line.

"Cornelius forced Dad out of Van Zale's, but that wasn't enough . . . hounded him . . . tried to smash his new business . . . rumors about Dad's drinking fostered on both sides of the Atlantic . . . Sam Keller forged a photograph . . . Dad knew he was ruined . . . driving . . . empty road . . . even then Cornelius wouldn't let Dinah alone . . . persecuted her . . . but she fooled him . . . she won. . . ."

She won.

"Please go now," I said to Elfrida.

"But is there nothing more you can say?" she said in a shaking voice. *"Nothing?"*

"What more can possibly be said? I could spend about five hours telling you my life story and trying to explain why I acted as I did, but what's the point? You're not truly interested in me or even in the whole truth about what happened back in the thirties. You're interested primarily in yourself. You're trying to anesthetize the pain you feel about your parents' deaths by blaming someone, and of course I'm tailor-made for the role. Okay, go ahead. Blame me. I don't pretend to be a saint. I don't pretend I haven't done things I've later regretted, and I don't pretend I haven't made mistakes. But does that make me a monster? No, it damn well does not. It makes me a human being, and maybe when you're a little older and a whole lot wiser and more tolerant, you'll have some glimmer of the hell your father put me through time after time with his sneers and his jeers and his . . . But no, I'm not going to say any more. I'm going to stop right there. Nothing I say now can alter the past, so why discuss it? The past is over, the past is done."

"But we all have to live with it," said Elfrida. "The past is never over. The past is present."

"That statement has no reality," I said, speaking too loudly. I supposed I was very upset. My chest was hurting. I knew I was going to be ill. "That statement is an intellectual delusion. That statement," I said, "that statement . . . is not . . . acceptable . . . not acceptable to me either now . . . or at any other time."

I left her. I had to. I somehow got to the nearest bathroom, where I sat down on the edge of the bath. I was gasping for breath, fighting and sweating for it, but I kept calm and bent my whole will toward subjugating the suffocating pressure in my chest. For a while I thought I was going to be all right. My breathing became more regular and the pain eased. Eventually I found I could move. Using the towel rail, I groped my way to my feet, paused for a moment to make sure there was no relapse, and then very slowly eased myself back into the sitting room.

Elfrida had gone. Alicia, fully dressed for the evening, was watching television as she waited for me.

"Cornelius, are you ill?" she said as soon as she saw my face.

"My asthma. Don't think I can make it. Tell Sam and Vicky I'm very sorry."

"Was it Elfrida? I heard you shouting at each other, and I wondered—"

"I don't want to talk about it."

She stood in silence, her gloved hands gripping her jeweled evening purse tightly, and I longed for her so much, even though I knew she was far beyond my reach.

"Kevin was right," I said more to myself than to her. "Trying to reach people . . . so hard . . . yet no one wants to be alone. Being alone's like being dead. Alicia . . ."

"Yes?" She was pale with anxiety now, distressed by my obvious ill-health. I saw her twist the little jeweled strap of the purse in her hands.

"Do you remember last week . . . in the paper . . . report of how the last of the Stuyvesants died?"

She was obviously bewildered but made an effort to respond. "Yes . . . poor old man! He was the last of such a famous old New York family, and he'd been a recluse for years. It was all rather pathetic, wasn't it?"

"He died alone," I said. "One of the richest men in New York . . . all by himself in his Fifth Avenue mansion . . . and *he died alone.*"

"Cornelius, sit down and I'll call a doctor this minute. Have you got your medication, or is it in the bathroom?"

"He was absolutely isolated," I said. "He had no communication with anyone . . . no communication. . . . It's all a matter of communication, you see. Elfrida didn't understand, but it's all a matter of communication. I've got to have power, I've got to communicate, how can I communicate without power? Nobody would take any notice of me. Steve Sullivan . . . never took any notice . . . but I made

him notice. I communicated. Only way . . . for someone like me
. . . but why doesn't it work better? Why am I so isolated? Alicia,
do you hear me? Do you hear what I'm saying?"

"Yes, dear, but don't talk any more. It's so bad for you when
you're breathing like this. . . . Operator? I want to call a doctor at
once. It's an emergency."

"Alicia, you're not listening. Alicia, you've got to listen. Alicia . . ." My breath finally gave out. The iron band closed around my
chest, and the last thing I saw before I lost consciousness was Alicia
rushing toward me yet at the same time receding eerily into the distance.

VII

LATER, WHEN I had recovered, I was embarrassed by the memory of
that scene, but fortunately Alicia must have been as embarrassed as I
was, for she never referred to it again. Ranting about the last of the
Stuyvesants, rambling on and on about communication—I shuddered
at the memory of such demented behavior and decided that I had
been temporarily unhinged by shock. I was still shocked by Elfrida's
revelations, but I had made up my mind not to think about them
while I was sick. My first priority was obviously to struggle back to
health.

I had had to be taken to a hospital. I had not been hospitalized for
my asthma since I was a child, and I had forgotten how much I hated
hospitals.

"Get me out of here!" I said to Alicia as soon as I dared expend
precious breath on a conversation. "Get me out of this country! Just
get me out!"

We left in early September, curtailing our vacation, and as soon as
Europe disappeared over the horizon I felt better. Now I no longer
lay awake at night and wondered where my next breath was coming
from. Now instead I could allow myself to dwell on that terrible interview with Elfrida. And now at last I had no choice but to grapple
with the enigma which was Scott.

I couldn't think why Scott had never confronted me with Tony's
letter. Emily's case was different. I knew exactly why Emily had
never shown the letter to me. She'd been too ashamed. She had practiced what she preached and forgiven me as best she could, but I saw

now why she had moved away from me back to Velletria, and I understood why, whenever we met, there always seemed so little to say.

Emily was easy to figure out.

But Scott remained an enigma.

I thought of Scott with his self-confessed interest in justice, a latter-day knight in search of a mysterious Holy Grail which he had never defined with precision, and the more I thought of him, the more clearly I could see him: smart, tough, capable Scott, always so *interesting;* pleasant, sociable, respectful Scott, always such a *comfort* to me, always there when I wanted him, always the perfect antidote to isolation.

I thought: Of course I'll have to get rid of him. After this, I'd be insane to do anything else.

VIII

"HI, CORNELIUS!" exclaimed Scott a week later. "How are you?"

I noticed at once how fit and relaxed he looked. He was wearing a lightweight pale suit to combat the September heat, and the color emphasized his suntan. His black eyes sparkled.

"I'm just fine," I said. "How was your vacation?"

"Wonderful!" Scott was always secretive about his vacations, which I had begun to suspect were spent sampling the delights of the flesh as extensively as possible. "I took a boat to Alaska. My, you should see that Inside Passage!"

"Hm."

"And how was your own vacation, Cornelius? I hear you had to cut it short."

"The English air didn't suit my asthma."

"That's too bad! I'm sorry."

"Yes, it was a pity. . . . By the way, I saw your half-sister when I was in London. Have you heard from her recently?"

"No, we're only in touch at Christmas. How is she? You're looking very sober! I hope there's nothing wrong."

"On the contrary, Elfrida and I are launching a project together. She wants to found a school at Mallingham in memory of her mother. I'm donating the land and backing her through the Van Zale Educational Trust."

"What a great idea! And how nice that the two of you could get together like that!"

"Yes. . . . But Elfrida seemed under the impression she was extracting some kind of revenge."

"She did?" Scott seemed to find this genuinely amusing. He even laughed. "How naive!"

"What do you mean?"

"Well, it won't cost you a cent, will it? It'll all be deductible."

I got up without a word and walked away into the other half of the room. I was at my office. Outside, the sun was beating down upon the patio, but indoors the air conditioning was keeping the room as cool as an icebox. I walked to the fireplace to examine the digital clock before pacing back to the fireplace by my desk to stare at the Kandinsky above the mantel. Scott seemed unfazed, although by this time it must have been obvious that something was seriously wrong. The interview, littered with my tense silences and expressionless comments, was far removed from our usual relaxed conversations.

I turned to look at him. He raised his eyebrows quizzically and smiled at me. "What's the trouble?" he said in the most natural voice imaginable. He must have had nerves of iron.

I said abruptly, "Elfrida showed me Tony's letter."

"Oh, yes?" said Scott sociably. "I always wondered when that old skeleton was going to crawl out of the closet. I suggested to Emily at the time that we should show the letter to you, but she wouldn't hear of it, and out of respect for her I didn't argue. She seemed to think it might upset you. I can't think why. You must have been well aware that Tony hated your guts, and it's always seemed clear to me that his version of the past was unlikely to either surprise or disturb you. I hope I wasn't wrong."

I did not answer directly. I was too overcome with admiration for the way he was handling the conversation. But perhaps he had had his responses prepared for years. The chance had always existed that I would see the letter eventually.

I decided I didn't quite dare to feel relieved. Not yet. Not until I was one-hundred-percent sure that relief was justified.

There was a pause. Then I said, "What did you make of the letter?"

"Not much," said Scott, as if we were discussing a somewhat sub-

standard article in the New York *Times.* "Like Elfrida's bid to extract revenge, it struck me as being naive."

"Oh?"

"Well, sure! Come, Cornelius, I'm not a baby, and I know how
the world's arranged. You and my father had a power struggle. Such
things are very common in big business. They happen all the time.
You won. Almost certainly my father made the mistake so many
people have made in the past and underestimated you. That's tough.
Bad luck, Dad, but you really should have been a little smarter. So
what does my father do next to restore his fortunes? He goes to England. He then has a wonderful opportunity to make a big comeback,
but does he make the best of it? No, he doesn't. He throws all his
chances away because he can't leave the bottle alone. He dies. Again
that's tough, but alcoholics always die, usually sooner rather than
later. That leaves you alive and well and in full command at One
Willow Street. Do I expect you to be a saint? No, I do not. Saints
don't occupy the senior partner's chair at One Willow Street. You're
a powerful, dangerous, and unscrupulous despot, and anyone who
works here and doesn't know that has to be some kind of mental defective. I'm not a mental defective. I . . . Shall I go on? I don't want
to bore you by spelling all this out unnecessarily, but perhaps under
the circumstances . . ."

"Go on." I couldn't stand any longer. I was too weak with relief. I
sat down rather suddenly in the senior partner's chair. "You were
saying you weren't a mental defective . . ."

"I'm not a mental defective. I'm ambitious, as you well know, and
I want to get to the top in banking, as you also well know, and I'll
take every opportunity I can get, as must be abundantly clear to you
by this time. Why should I bother to deny it? And why should you
bother to get flustered when you've always had and always will have
total control over my career at Van Zale's?"

"Why indeed?" I hardly knew what I said. The relief was so enormous by this time that I even wondered in alarm if I were on the
verge of tears.

"So I ask you," said Scott, "what's the big deal about this goddamned letter? Tony may have enjoyed presenting you as some kind
of Count Dracula in modern dress, but to be honest, I don't give a
shit. I'm no more interested in the way you *might* be—a latter-day
Dracula—than the way you *ought* to be—a golden-haired angel with a
halo and wings. I'm interested in the way you really are. And you

know why I'm only interested in the way you really are, Cornelius?"

"Tell me." I was getting stronger with every passing second. I even managed to smile at him.

"I'm interested in the way you really are because you're my boss and you hold the key to my future—and believe me, Cornelius, I'm only interested in the future. Why should I crucify myself over what might or what might not have happened in the past? What good could that possibly do me? You've taught me to be a pragmatic survivor, Cornelius! Look at me and congratulate yourself on the way I've turned out!"

I burst out laughing. He laughed too, and suddenly I felt so happy again, as if I had lost a pot of gold but had finally located it after a long agonizing search. My loneliness and misery vanished abruptly. I wished only that we were at home so that we could have a game of chess and chat about eternity as usual.

"So I've made you in my own image, have I, Scott?" I said humorously. "Powerful, dangerous, and unscrupulous—weren't those the words you used?"

"Right!"

"That scares me! I'm not sure I like it."

"Oh yes, you do! You wouldn't have me any other way."

We laughed again, and all my fears seemed so irrational, so irrelevant to the affection which existed between us. It occurred to me that I had been more severely disoriented in England than I had realized at the time. I must have been out of my mind. This was *my boy* still, nothing to do with Steve, and the past was all sealed off, just as it should be.

"Of course I ought to get rid of you!" I said, thinking how ridiculous the idea sounded as soon as it was voiced aloud.

"Well, that would be very aggravating," said Scott frankly, "and I don't mind admitting I'd be very hurt, but as I've already said, I'm a survivor, and I don't think I'd have much trouble walking into a top job somewhere else."

"Hell, I'm not letting my best man go!"

"Thank God. You had me worried for a moment. I thought you were just about to cut me up and feed me to the pigeons in the patio."

"I wouldn't do that! I'm too fond of those birds! Say, Scott, talking of birds . . . what was the name of that guy who wrote about the sparrow in the lighted hall?"

"Bede."

"Come round to Fifth Avenue tonight and tell me more about him. I'll get in some Coke and dust off your favorite chess set."

Scott said he'd be looking forward to it.

Later, when I was alone, I sat at my desk for some time while I doodled on my blotter and summed up the situation with a cool, practiced, rational eye. My last thought before I pushed the buzzer to summon my secretary was: Yes, I do trust him. But I shouldn't.

Chapter Five

I

I DID not see Emily again until the following spring. Usually she joined us for Thanksgiving, but that year some minor ailment kept her in Velletria, and although I reissued the invitation for Christmas, she said she was committed to running a big holiday party at the local orphanage. Her elder daughter, Rose, had graduated from Wellesley that summer and was helping Emily with the local good works while she decided what to do with herself. Meanwhile, Lori, who admitted frankly that good works "bored the pants off her," had bucketed around from Foxcroft to a Swiss finishing school and was now idling away some more time by completing an advanced-cooking course in nearby Cincinnati. She wanted to live away from home, but Emily, rightly in my opinion, refused to agree to this while Lori was under twenty-one. Young girls need looking after, particularly young girls like Lori, who wore tight sweaters and had a pinup of Marlon Brando tacked to her bedroom wall.

"I think Lori's just great!" said Andrew to us presently. "Boy, did they finish her off at that Swiss finishing school! When I first visited Velletria after her return from Switzerland, I could hardly believe she was the same person as the little pest who broke the strings of my tennis racket at Bar Harbor. She was sitting on the couch with her legs crossed like Rita Hayworth, and she had her hair flopping over one eye like Lauren Bacall, and she was smoking a cigarette with her eyes half closed like Marilyn Monroe, and when I gaped at her like some hillbilly from hicksville, she said, 'Hi, gorgeous! Love your uniform.' I just reeled! It was wonderful! Somehow Aunt Emily's living room is the last place you'd expect to find a torrid sex symbol!"

"Emily's going to have trouble with that girl," I forecast to Alicia, but I was wrong. In the end, Emily had no trouble at all, because Lori not only decided to get married but decided to marry someone of whom we couldn't possibly disapprove. She picked Andrew. I doubt if Andrew himself had much say in the matter. In the summer of 1953 when I was in Europe he was transferred to an air-force base near Cincinnati and would often spend his leave with Emily and the girls. By Christmas he and Lori were engaged and announcing their plans to marry in the spring.

"And just think, Cornelius!" said Alicia, her eyes shining, although she had never much cared for Lori, "my son will be marrying your niece!"

"Hm," I said, but I felt no kinship with Lori, whose noisy vitality all too often reminded me of her father, Steve Sullivan. "I hope she'll behave herself when Andrew's up in the clouds flying the planes. They say life on those air-force bases can be pretty wild."

Alicia said nothing more on the subject, but I sensed she was disappointed, and I realized she had been hoping this marriage might prove to be a viable substitute for her old soap-opera dream that Vicky should marry Sebastian.

I liked Andrew much better than I liked Sebastian, although we had no interest in common beyond a fondness for watching baseball. He was straightforward and good-natured, a clean-cut all-American boy. His slight physical resemblance to his mother made it easy for me to feel affectionate toward him, and although his extravert's nature was entirely different from hers, I had no trouble remembering that this was the son of the most important woman in my life, a boy who deserved the best paternal care I could offer. He was no match for Sebastian intellectually, but he was intelligent and, better still, articulate. I foresaw success for him in his chosen career, and although I had no interest in planes, I backed him up to the hilt when he decided to enter the air force. Since I knew he would never make a banker, it had been a relief to me when he had selected such a respectable, patriotic way of earning his living, and having survived the Korean war with honors, he was now angling for a transfer to Germany, since Lori thought a spell in Europe would be "so glamorous."

"That girl's going to boss Andrew around until he won't know whether he's coming or going," I said to Alicia shortly before the wedding.

"Andrew says he loves to be organized."

I said nothing, but I believed wholeheartedly that a man should be the boss in his own home. I strongly disapproved of pushy, domineering women with minds of their own and wills to match. If God had wanted women to be that way, he would have made just one sex, men, and arranged for reproduction by some kind of scientific splitting in two, like amoebas.

However, I forgot my disapproval of Lori as soon as Vicky arrived home for a visit in order to attend the wedding. Sam came later, spending only a few days in America before flying back to London to attend to his business commitments, but Vicky and the boys spent the whole month of May with us.

To my despair I found she was still enamored of Europe. To my horror I found she was now studying German in earnest. And to my rage I found Sam was starting to push me to open a German office.

"Two years in London," I said to him. "That was the agreement."

"Yes, and next year is 1955 and the London office will be two years old. If we don't start planning for the German office now, it'll be 1956 before I get to Germany."

That would give Vicky another year to return to her senses and become prostrated by homesickness for America.

"You've waited so long to get to Germany," I said to Sam. "What's one more year?"

"Look, Neil—"

"I refuse to be rushed on this. I sanction the German office in principle, but I don't want to tackle the expansion into Europe before we're ready for it. Aren't I allowed to be prudent and sensible when your beloved Germany's at stake?"

He just looked at me. If looks could kill, I would have suffered an immediate cardiac arrest, but I went right on smiling sympathetically and even offered him my hand to shake. I saw he was tempted to quit there and then, but of course he didn't. It was worth waiting out the extra year and remaining under the lucrative Van Zale umbrella with a happy, untroubled Vicky at his side. Sam was playing for high stakes, and he wasn't about to abandon them unless I flatly refused to send him to Germany.

He somehow managed to shake hands with me, and we parted friends in an atmosphere thick with hostility.

After such an exhausting interview, it was almost a relief to leave New York for the wedding in Velletria, the Cincinnati suburb where I had eked out my life amidst stupefying boredom from the age of five till the age of eighteen. I am by nature unfitted for life in a prosperous Midwestern suburb which numerous decent commendable citizens find delightful. Not even God had performed a greater service when he had rescued the children of Israel from Egypt than Paul Van Zale had performed when he had rescued me from Velletria, Ohio, and drawn me east to New York.

The wedding took place at the Episcopal church where I had endured countless dreary sermons throughout my childhood, and Emily held the reception at the country club. It was a successful wedding even though Lori wore a skintight dress which reminded me of a mermaid. I wondered if she could possibly be a virgin but thought it most unlikely. Emily cried throughout the service, probably with relief. After I had given the bride away I gazed vaguely at the stained-glass windows and wondered what my mother would have thought of it all. My mother had been a forceful woman who had ruled her second husband, if not her first, with formidable domestic efficiency. I had had repeated struggles to prevent her from smothering me, and since my will had been stronger than hers, I had won, but nevertheless I had been fond of my mother and had felt genuinely bereaved by her death. Bossy and opinionated though she was, she had loved me and done her best for me, and one can't expect more of a mother than that. In fact, so sentimental did I feel that day about my mother that I jumped at the opportunity to sit up late with Emily that night and reminisce nostalgically about our shared past.

As I reminded myself later, there's no bigger mistake one can make than to give way rashly to sentimental impulses.

"Oh, it was such a lovely wedding!" said Emily, dabbing away with her handkerchief again.

"Lori looked very pretty," I said generously, putting my arm around her and giving her a squeeze. I really was in a dangerously sentimental mood.

"Dear Steve would have been so proud!" whispered Emily.

"He'd probably have been in a wheelchair. How old would he have been by this time? Seventy?"

"Sixty-seven," said Emily coldly. "How small-minded you are

sometimes, Cornelius, how utterly lacking in generosity of spirit. I'd have thought that tonight of all nights—just for once—you could have found it in your heart to be charitable toward Steve."

"But I didn't say anything against him! I just made a comment about his age!"

"You implied a debilitated senility. Cornelius, for years and years I've put up with your snide remarks, your acid comments, your—"

"Now, wait a minute! You can hardly expect me to follow your example and canonize Steve's memory!"

"I haven't canonized Steve's memory. I should never have married him, and he made me very unhappy, but at least I have my two wonderful girls—and at least I have the Christian decency to remember his good points as well as his bad points, and to forgive him for all the wrong he did! However, I've long ago given up expecting you to show any Christian spirit. Paul wiped all that out when he ruined you with his wealth. Sometimes I feel glad poor Mama died when she did. I consider it a mercy that, unlike me, she was spared all knowledge of your later activities."

"Oh, Christ, Emily, what garbage you talk! Just because Tony Sullivan writes one melodramatic letter—"

"Who told you about Tony's letter?"

"Elfrida showed it to me when I was in London last August. I was horrified and appalled. Why have you never confronted me with it? Why have you brooded over it in secret all these years? Don't you think you had a moral duty to hear *my* side of the story before you silently sat in judgment on me and decided I was every bit as bad as Tony said I was? You knew Tony hated me. Why you should automatically accept the word of a biased, hotheaded young man without even deigning to hear the word of your own brother, I have no idea, but all I can say is I feel very hurt. I wasn't going to mention the subject, but since you've brought it up . . ."

"It was you who mentioned Tony's name—no doubt out of guilt. I always thought it was a disgrace the way you treated that boy. You hardly ever spoke to him—it was always Scott this, Scott that, Scott, Scott, Scott! I guess it was because Tony looked like Steve, while Scott had inherited Caroline's looks—Scott was the only one you could look at without feeling overcome with remorse!"

"That's not true. Listen—"

"No, you listen to me! It's true I've held my tongue for years and years, and yes, maybe that *was* the wrong thing to do—maybe I should have spoken up long ago to save you from yourself!"

"Oh, my God!"

"Give up that bank, Cornelius. It's the root of all your present problems and past disasters. Give it up and devote yourself to your Fine Arts Foundation and your Educational Trust. That would be worthwhile and meaningful."

"Banking's worthwhile and meaningful! And why in God's name should you think the foundation and the trust offer the equivalent of a religious order to which I can retreat in order to lead a pure, un-sullied business life? Jesus, you should come to some of the board meetings and see all those millionaires jockeying for position—that would disillusion you pretty damned quickly!"

"I see that you're deliberately choosing to misunderstand me. Let me try again. Cornelius, now that you're middle-aged—"

"Thanks, but I consider I'm still very much in my prime!"

"—you should reassess your life and question your values. Do you ever pause to question your values, Cornelius? Or has your wealth put you so out of touch with reality that you're no longer capable of getting your priorities right?"

"You're the one who seems to be out of touch with reality here! The trouble with you, Emily, is that you live such a cloistered life here in this godforsaken dump that you've no idea what goes on in the world. Why don't you remarry or take a lover or lose twenty pounds or dye the gray out of your hair or go on a cruise or do something interesting for a change? All these endless good works and a single bed at night are enough to drive any sane woman off the rails!"

"Well, of course," said Emily, rising to her feet to terminate the in-terview, "I always knew you were obsessed with sex."

"And I always knew," I shouted, rising to face her, "that you're sublimating your sex drive by acting like a religious crank!"

Like so many violent quarrels, the element of the absurd mingling with the shafts of rage gave an additional savage twist to the explo-sion. I think Emily and I both realized this, and for one long moment we stood stock-still as if we were trying to make up our minds whether to embrace with laughter or part estranged. But there was no reconciliation. Emily just said coldly, "Poor Mama must be turning in her grave to hear us quarrel so disgracefully. I apologize for at-tempting to speak to you so frankly, and I hope you'll forgive me when I explain that I acted only out of love and concern. Whatever you do, you're still my brother, and I'll never speak one word against you to anyone, but don't think my loyalty represents a condonation either of your opinions or of your way of life. Now, we'll set this scene behind us, if you please, and never refer to it again."

She swept out of the room. I laughed to try to convince myself I hadn't been outfaced, but I knew I had. Later I went to bed and lay awake for a long time in the dark, but before I slept I had made up my mind what to do, and the next morning I said humbly to Emily, "Say, I'm real sorry about last night. You know how fond of you I am and how much you mean to me. I'd like to take back all those stupid things I said."

"The subject is closed," said Emily, terminating the conversation with a ruthlessness which shattered me. "Apologize if you wish, of course, but I myself have nothing else to say."

I saw the wintry look in her gray eyes and knew I'd lost her. But perhaps in fact I'd lost her long ago when I had encouraged her to marry Steve Sullivan so that I could gain some temporary security for myself at the bank.

"Emily . . ."

"Yes, dear?"

"Nothing—it doesn't matter," I said, sick at heart, and abruptly turned away.

II

TEN MONTHS after Andrew and Lori's wedding Vicky gave birth to a daughter, but this time not even my desire to see my family could coax me aboard a ship to Europe. The baby was named Samantha. I made no comment on this execrable name but merely sent the required christening present from Tiffany's. However, the thought of a small granddaughter just like Vicky attracted me, and I had just written to suggest that the Kellers should visit us at Bar Harbor in August when my attention was diverted by a crisis which blew up over Sebastian.

I did not dislike Sebastian, but he was very, very difficult. My task as a stepfather would have been easier if he had resembled Alicia, but I always found it hard to believe she could have produced such a son. However, since he *was* her son, I had been determined to establish a good relationship with him, and logically this should have been easy to achieve; Sebastian had an excellent academic record, he had never wavered from his early decision to be a banker, and he had been working hard at Van Zale's since he had finished his army service under the draft (I had secretly used my influence to keep him out of Korea).

During his childhood he had required little paternal discipline. Andrew had always been bouncing in and out of scrapes, but Sebastian, prowling around by himself, had needed only an occasional reprimand to keep him on the rails. It was true I often wanted to hit him, but that was because he exasperated me and not because I found his behavior insulting.

The trouble with Sebastian, on paper the ideal stepson, was that he was totally charmless. Reserved and morose, he sat like a great hulk at the dining table and exuded a miasma worthy of any fabled death's-head at a feast. I wanted to like him, but my efforts never seemed to get us anywhere. His desperately unattractive personality also made me worry about his future at the bank. There's more to being a banker than working out an issue with financial flair and parceling it out to the public. A banker must take his clients to lunch and inquire tenderly after their families as well as their credit, and I had begun to doubt that Sebastian would ever be capable of more than a formal greeting, a few apelike grunts, and endless awkward silences.

He was a continuous source of anxiety to me. The situation was complicated by the fact that Alicia idolized her son, and I lived in dread that if I somehow alienated him irrevocably I would also alienate her. The rockiest days of our marriage had not been when I had begun my affair with Teresa; the nearest we had ever come to divorce was that time in 1945 when we had quarreled over Sebastian.

To put the whole sordid matter in the smallest possible nutshell, I can only say that he had indecently exposed himself to Vicky during one of our family summers at Bar Harbor. By a superhuman effort I had sufficiently controlled my rage and revulsion to send him to his Foxworth relations without laying a finger on him, but Alicia and I had quarreled almost fatally, and for months afterward I had been afraid of coming home from work in case she'd walked out on me. But she had stayed, and gradually by another superhuman effort I had taught myself to look back at the incident with detachment. Many adolescent boys find their new sexuality hard to handle, and

Vicky was an exceptionally attractive young girl. The two of them were unrelated by blood. They had never even lived beneath the same roof until both were approaching puberty, and adolescence must have added to the awkwardness of a situation already rendered tense by adult squabbles over custody. Under the circumstances, I had decided I should feel sorry for Sebastian. I had to feel sorry for him anyway, because it was in my best interests to be sympathetic, and I was, as I reminded myself over and over again, always mindful of my best interests in adverse circumstances; I was essentially a pragmatic man.

After Sebastian had been discharged from the army, he lived at home for a time, but shortly after the wedding in Velletria he moved into a gloomy apartment in Murray Hill. When we were grudgingly invited to visit him, we found black carpet on the floor, black fabric on the chairs, and a black coffee table in front of a black leather couch. Two prints by Hieronymus Bosch adorned the walls, and some horror by Dali (painted before he turned soft and started painting Madonnas) defaced a corner of the hall. God knows what was kept in the bedroom.

I spent anxious moments wondering if these tastes indicated some form of sexual perversion, but although I checked Freud's entry in the *Encyclopaedia Britannica,* Freud's views seemed such garbage that I didn't bother to read to the end of the summary. No wonder Kevin had felt that Freud had never reached Staten Island, Brooklyn, or Queens in his journey through the psychological equivalent of the street directories of the five boroughs! Personally I thought Kevin was being generous in suggesting Freud had even made it through Manhattan and the Bronx. My knowledge of Freud's theories had previously been confined to the intriguing hearsay guaranteed to stimulate a flagging cocktail party, but I saw now how wise I had been to keep my knowledge limited. All that talk about the id, the libido, and phallic symbols was enough to make any sane man look askance at himself.

"Why do you like black so much?" I asked Sebastian in curiosity after Freud had failed to provide me with an answer, but Sebastian just said, poker-faced, "Because it's dark."

I gave up, telling myself I had done all a father could to raise a normal well-adjusted son, and if Sebastian was odd, it could hardly be my fault. Having myself lacked even the most basic paternal advice from my own stepfather, I had made very sure my stepsons had gone out into the world knowing one end of a condom from the other and aware that VD wasn't a reference to some Allied victory in World War II.

When the crisis blew up over Sebastian, it was the spring of 1955. The weather was beautiful, the stock market was booming, and I had just bought a new milk-white Cadillac with pale blue upholstery. In fact, I was in such good spirits that I even stopped after work to buy a bottle of champagne for Teresa, but when I arrived at the Dakota I found her in a sour mood. Her painting was going through a bad patch. I had successfully steered her away from postimpressionism, but now she had been seduced by the current craze for the American abstract, and the malign influence of Jackson Pollock was leering at me from every canvas. I had told her politely that I thought she should return to her earlier pristine style. She told me she wanted more from life than the reputation of being a second Grandma Moses, and why the hell couldn't I mind my own business. Our sexual relationship had become unpleasantly mechanical. Once I had even asked her if she wanted to end the affair, but she had said "No, thank you" very politely and on my next visit had cooked me a magnificent steak with béarnaise sauce. Later she had asked me if I myself wanted to end the affair, and I had said "No, thank you" equally politely and had given her a gold bracelet from Cartier's. I had hoped that this would mean we could be more relaxed with each other, but when I arrived at the Dakota that evening I was told that menstruation was on, sex was off, and the new picture was a disaster. She was right. It was, and declining her halfhearted offer of a hamburger, I left the champagne in the refrigerator and set off home in my Cadillac.

As I entered the hall, the first person I saw was Jake Reischman.

"Neil!" he exclaimed at once. "Thank God you're here! I was on my way over to the Dakota to get you. Does Teresa usually leave the phone off the hook at this hour?"

I was unsurprised by these references to Teresa; he met her every time I exhibited her work and had known for years that I kept her at the Dakota. But I was confused by his presence.

"What are you doing here?" I said stupidly.

"Alicia called me in a panic. She tried to call you, but you'd left the office, and when you didn't come home she turned to me as one of the old Bar Harbor Brotherhood, someone she could rely on in a crisis—ah, here she is! Yes, it's all right, Alicia, he's here." He took

me by the arm and propelled me into the library. "Sit down and I'll
fix you a drink. Alicia, would you like me to tell Neil what the police
said? You should go and lie down."

Alicia looked like death. "I couldn't, Jake," she said, "but do
please stay and explain to Cornelius." She sat down stiffly on a hard
chair near the door.

Jake had already moved to the liquor cabinet. "Scotch, Neil?"

"Okay. But what the hell—"

"Let me just get the drinks. I can promise you we all need them."

"Okay, but . . . wait, Jake, Alicia doesn't drink Scotch."

"Oh, I do drink it nowadays, Cornelius," said Alicia mechanically.

Jake said at once, "You were drinking Scotch when I arrived. I assumed—"

"Oh, yes, of course. Yes, I'd like another Scotch. Thank you,
Jake."

"For Christ's sake, why the hell are we all wasting time discussing
Alicia's drinking habits!" I was almost tearing my hair with exasperation. "Jake, what's going on? Why were the police here? Has there
been a robbery?"

"No, Neil, it's Sebastian. He's in trouble. The police allege he beat
up some woman on the Upper West Side."

I knocked back my Scotch, grabbed the phone, and streamed into
action. "Middleton, get the police commissioner." I depressed the
phone and dialed another digit. "Schuyler, get my lawyers over here
right away." I hung up the house phone, got an outside line, and
dialed the number of Sebastian's apartment.

"Hello?" said Sebastian laconically.

"Sebastian, what the hell's going on? Are the cops there?"

"Yeah. They've made some crazy mistake. I've called my lawyer."

"Don't say one syllable without him. I'm coming right over."

I hung up. The phone rang beneath my fingertips. "Yes?"

"I have the police commissioner for you, sir."

"Put him through. Hello? Yes, this is Cornelius Van Zale. What
the hell are you doing persecuting my stepson? . . . What? You
know nothing about it? Then may I suggest you find out right away?
My stepson's name is Sebastian Foxworth, and some of your men are
harassing him right now at one-one-four East Thirty-sixth Street, I
repeat, one-one-four East Thirty-sixth Street. You get hold of your
precinct captain and tell him I sue automatically in all cases of

wrongful arrest." I hung up. The phone immediately rang again. My personal lawyer was on the line.

"What's going on, Cornelius?"

"How much does it cost to beat an assault rap?"

Alicia bent over as if she were about to faint. Jake moved across to her automatically but then stood around like a tailor's dummy as if he couldn't decide what to do.

"For Christ's sake, Jake!" I snapped, interrupting my lawyer, who was giving me some unspeakable drivel about bribery. "Get Alicia onto the couch and ring for her maid, can't you?"

Jake obediently tried to make himself useful. I hung up on my lawyer and ordered a car to the door.

"I'll go over right away," I said to Alicia, giving her a kiss. "Don't worry, I'll fix this, no problem. Jake, I'll call you. Thanks for your help."

And I rushed over to Sebastian's apartment to make good my promise.

It was extremely awkward, since the injured woman, a West Side prostitute, had in her possession Sebastian's wallet, which contained his driver's license with the address still made out to his old Fifth Avenue home, but the woman turned out to be most reasonable when she saw the color of my money, and the police needed little encouragement to be persuaded that she had been hit by her common-law husband after he had discovered her with Sebastian. No one wants to waste time prosecuting a petty assault case when there are cases of murder, rape, and arson on the books waiting to be solved.

When I was finally alone with Sebastian I said to him, "We may as well get what sleep we can now, but I want you in my office at nine o'clock tomorrow morning, and if you're one second late, you're fired."

"Okay," said Sebastian.

I looked at him. I never spoke, but after five seconds he stopped slouching against the wall, and after ten seconds he reddened and muttered, "Yes, sir."

I turned on my heel and left him.

III

HE KNOCKED on the door at nine o'clock, and rising from my desk, I took him into the other half of the double room where I worked. In Paul's day the room that opened onto the back patio had been furnished as a library, while beyond the archway the far room had been used as an elegant sitting room where a few select people had gathered every afternoon to drink tea. I had dispensed with nine-teenth-century tradition. The main room was now designed as an austere study, while the far room, as I had once heard a junior part-ner whisper, had become the chamber of horrors. This was the place where I fired people, clubbed them into line, or conducted interviews with clients who thought their long-suffering investment banker was in business solely to hold their hands while their paths automatically paved themselves with gold.

"Sit down, Sebastian," I said to my stepson, who was already unhealthily pale.

He sat down awkwardly on the couch, while I remained standing before the fireplace, one hand resting on the bleak marble mantel.

"Well?" I said abruptly.

He cleared his throat. The sound reverberated on the ash-white ceiling and unadorned walls. The carpet in the room was steel-gray. Behind my shoulder the digital clock flickered scarlet, time's life-blood oozing away into infinity.

"Well, Sebastian?" I said again as he struggled to compose him-self.

"Thanks for clearing up the mess, sir. I'm sorry you were in-volved. I apologize for all the trouble."

That was a long speech for Sebastian, but I made no acknowl-edgment. The silence lengthened. I never moved a muscle, but he be-gan to shift on the couch.

"I'm still waiting, Sebastian."

"I'm sorry, sir, I don't understand . . ."

"I'm waiting for your explanation."

"Oh." He shifted again, trying to find a comfortable position, but as I well knew, the modern couch, backed only by a single teak rail, precluded all hope of comfort.

"I want to know," I said without expression, "why an intelligent young man, well brought up in a happy home with every conceivable advantage which wealth can provide, has to behave in this sordid and incomprehensible manner."

He said nothing. I felt my temper begin to rise. Moving so suddenly that he jumped, I abandoned the fireplace to position myself in front of the window. "Has it never occurred to you," I said, "to date a nice girl, buy her dinner, take her to a movie?"

"No, sir."

"Why not?"

"I'd rather have dinner and go to the movies by myself."

"Why?"

"I don't like talking to stupid people."

"Then why don't you date someone intelligent?"

"Intelligent girls aren't interested in me."

"Why not?"

"Because I'm fundamentally uninterested in their brains, and they're intelligent enough to find this insulting."

Conversation ceased. Sebastian, sitting on the edge of the couch, was glowering at the carpet. I was aware with exasperation that instead of crumbling into abject loquacity he was hardening into rebellious silence.

Moving back to the fireplace, I prodded the screen gently with my toe.

"Sebastian," I said, showing him my back but watching him in the mirror, "you must, please, cooperate with me in getting to the bottom of this. Can't you see that if we don't solve this problem, it's going to happen all over again? Now, just give me the facts. There's no need to be afraid of shocking me, because I assure you I'm quite unshockable. Let's start with the obvious question: why did you hit this woman?"

Sebastian looked up. His dark eyes were hard with hostility. "Why don't you try reading the Marquis de Sade?" he said.

He had shocked me. Gripping the edge of the mantel, I told myself that this was Alicia's son, that I had brought him up from the age of nine, and that he was—had to be—at heart a good, decent boy.

"You mean," I said slowly, "it gave you a sexual thrill to beat up this woman."

"That's right."

My mind, fine-tuned to lies after twenty-five years of survival under trying circumstances, at once sensed a false note in his voice.

"This is a pose, Sebastian," I said coldly. "Please don't waste my time like this. It can only deepen the contempt I already feel for your behavior."

He reddened and refused to look at me.

Since severity was apparently leading me nowhere, I switched my mood, sat down beside him on the couch, and put an arm around his shoulder.

"Look," I said, "tell me the truth. I'm your father and I want to help you."

"You're not my father." He got up and walked away.

My fists clenched. I sprang to my feet, but before I could speak, he mumbled, "She said something stupid and I lost my temper. I hate stupid people." He began to roam around the room, sometimes pausing to scuff up the carpet by shoving his heel into it. "She said I hurt her," he muttered. "She said it as though I meant to hurt her. What annoyed me was that it was such a dumb thing to say. What was I supposed to do—shrink? And she said it at such a stupid time, just when I . . . And then she tried to pull away, and I got mad and goddamned well shoved her away from me and she fell backward out of bed and slammed her head against the nightstand and her nose started to bleed and she started to scream and it was all so *stupid*, I wished I were a million miles away. I got away as quickly as I could, but in the fuss I left my wallet behind and as soon as she saw my Fifth Avenue address, of course she couldn't resist trying to make something of it. . . . I'm sorry, Cornelius, but you can see how it was, it was all just a stupid accident and won't happen again. You don't need to worry about me, you truly don't."

"But I worry about you very much, Sebastian," I said before I could stop myself. I forgot my exasperation, forgot the chill of the interrogation room and the clinical choreography of power. I was with an unhappy young man who was my responsibility, and for his mother's sake I had to give him all the help I could. Knowing he would shy away from any display of affection, I said carefully in my most reasonable voice, "I think you should try to form some sort of . . . socially acceptable relationship with a member of the opposite sex. I can't believe you derive any"—I paused again for the right words—"sustained benefit from these very transitory episodes. I think you should look for an intelligent girl who attracts you physically, and then—after a trial period—propose marriage. You're twenty-six years old and I think you should consider containing your very natural physical requirements in a structure which is regarded, both by convention and by modern sociology, as a suitable sexual framework."

"It doesn't contain your physical requirements very well, does it?" burst out Sebastian. "And who are you to criticize me for going to whores?"

I walked right up to him and struck him across the face.

We were both trembling. I hated him for making me lose my temper when I had wanted only to be kind. He hated me for reasons which I preferred not to analyze but which probably sprang from the fact that I had deprived him of his mother when he was young. Now my apparent rejection of her gave him another cause for grievance.

"Sorry, Cornelius, but—"

"Be quiet!" I blazed. "Now, get this straight: I don't go to whores. For the past six years I've had one mistress, and one mistress only, in order to spare your mother from an aspect of our marriage which she now finds distasteful. Now, you listen to me, and you listen well. If you want to get on in this bank, you'll make some changes in your private life. I don't pick my partners from maladjusted neurotics who are incapable of leading normal lives. If you're set against marriage at present, you can certainly leave it till later—I'm not strong-arming you into proposing to the next girl you meet. But you damn well find a steady girl by the end of the year or you'll be out on your ass looking for a job. Okay? Got that? Am I making myself quite clear?"

He looked frightened. Of course he had no idea I was bluffing him. I could never have faced Alicia with the news that I had fired her son, but Sebastian did not understand my relationship with his mother, and he had grown up in a house where my word was law.

"Yes, sir," he whispered.

"Right. Now, get the hell out back to your work."

He stumbled away, and I sank down exhausted in the nearest chair.

It took me some time to recover from that scene with Sebastian, but when I reviewed it afterward I thought I had given him good advice. It would certainly do him no harm to go steady with a girl, and although I assumed he would always retain his preference for whores, I was practical enough to realize this was a trait I was unlikely to change. Some men preferred such women for some mysterious reason, which was perhaps part of the New York street directory which Freud had never reached—Queens, perhaps, or maybe Staten

Island. I had never been to Staten Island and often thought vaguely that anything was capable of happening there.

However, my most significant achievement was that I had clearly spelled out to Sebastian how important it was to present a normal domestic front to the world, and I presumed that eventually, perhaps when he was around forty, he would for the sake of his career pick a suitable woman to be his wife. Meanwhile, he remained a constant worry to me, but that was nothing new; I was used to that particular burden and had long since learned to live with it.

With a sigh of resignation I heaved my anxiety aside, called Jake, and thanked him for looking after Alicia so well during the trauma of the previous evening.

IV

SEBASTIAN DROPPED the bombshell on me two months later in June. He arrived on a Sunday at noon when he knew Alicia and I would be having lunch together, and informed us casually, without any warning or even a tactful preamble, that he was getting married.

"Married!" Alicia and I were both transfixed. We were eating outdoors on the terrace, a large flowered umbrella shading our white wrought-iron table from the sun. Before us the garden stretched tranquilly to the distant tennis court. A sprinkler was watering the lawn, the birds were singing on the balustrade, and only the drone of traffic beyond the high brick wall reminded us that we were in the heart of a city.

"Yes. Married." Sebastian looked in the pitcher on the serving cart. "What's this? Tom Collins?"

"But, Sebastian . . ." Alicia rose to her feet, only to sink down again into her chair.

"Is this a pitcher of Tom Collinses?" said Sebastian again.

"No, lemonade." I tried to make a speedy recovery. "Are we by any chance allowed to know the name of your fiancée?"

"Elsa." He turned to the nearest enthralled footman. "Bring me a Tom Collins, would you?"

"*Elsa?*" Alicia and I repeated in voices loud enough to be heard in the Reischman mansion three blocks away.

"Yes. Jake's daughter. The fat one." He found a spare plate and helped himself to eggs Benedict.

I flicked my wrist at the servants, who reluctantly retreated indoors. Alicia looked wildly at me for help. Her eyes were a dull shocked green. I was so angry I could hardly speak. To calm myself I poured fresh coffee into my cup and picked up a soft roll. "I didn't know you'd been dating Jake's daughter," I said in the friendliest voice I could muster. "How long's this been going on?"

"A couple of months. I've been taking her out every Friday night to a drive-in movie in New Jersey."

If he had told us he had taken her to the far side of the moon we couldn't have been more amazed. We stared at him in stupefied silence.

"I like New Jersey," said Sebastian, drawing up a chair and dumping himself in it. "I like all the hamburger joints and the billboards and the plastic-looking shops on Route 22, and I like that bit of the turnpike when you go by all the oil refineries. It's surreal. So are the road stops," he added as an afterthought. "I like the way you drive and drive and the restaurants always produce identical food. It's like a science-fiction movie."

"I see," I said. "So you've only been seeing Elsa once a week."

"Hell, no, I've seen a lot more of her than that! She used to come downtown and meet me on my lunch hour and we'd ride the Staten Island ferry together."

"Staten Island?" I shouted.

Sebastian looked up from his eggs Benedict. "What's wrong with Staten Island?" he said, astonished. "I like the way the ferry pulls out and you see the whole weird Manhattan skyline drawn up like a row of dinosaur's teeth. It's a great way to spend a nickel."

"Uh-huh," I said. I suddenly realized I was speechless. "Uh-huh."

"Darling," said Alicia, very white but regaining her immaculate self-control, "do the Reischman's know you've been seeing Elsa?"

"Of course not! Why go looking for trouble? Elsa told them she was staying Friday nights with Ruth in Englewood."

Ruth was the Reischmans' newly married elder daughter.

"Staying . . . Friday nights . . ."

"Sebastian, are you trying to tell us . . . ?"

"It's okay," said Sebastian comfortably. "Ruth swore she'd give Elsa an alibi—in fact, she said she only wished someone had been around to give *her* an alibi when she was looking for ways to bust out of her chastity belt. . . . Say, I wish to hell Carraway would bring my Tom Collins." He looked crossly over his shoulder before attacking the eggs Benedict again.

"Cornelius . . ." said Alicia faintly.

I took charge of the situation. "You're telling us," I said, enunciating every word clearly to make sure there was no mistake in communication, "that every Friday night for the past two months—"

"One," said Sebastian. "The first month we were just friends, but after that, yes, we checked into a motel near the turnpike." Abandoning his eggs Benedict, he laid down his fork and looked me straight in the eyes. "I did just as you told me," he said. "I took your advice down to the last letter. I found an intelligent girl who attracted me physically, I took her out a number of times, and then—after a suitable trial—I proposed marriage. Wasn't that just what you advised?"

Carraway emerged from the house, his silver salver glittering in the sunlight. "Your Tom Collins, Mr. Foxworth."

"Great. And bring us a bottle of champagne too, would you? I just got engaged."

"Congratulations, Mr. Foxworth!"

"Thanks." He drank half his Tom Collins and resumed munching his eggs Benedict. "Say, isn't it about time you two followed Carraway's lead instead of cross-questioning me about my dating habits?"

"Cornelius," whispered Alicia, "did you truly tell him . . . ?"

"I never, never told him to—"

"Oh yes you did!" said Sebastian fiercely.

I shot to my feet, but Alicia grabbed my arm and said rapidly before I could speak, "That's enough, Sebastian. Don't talk to your stepfather like that—and *stop eating, sit up straight, and look at me when I talk to you!*"

Sebastian clenched his fork, straightened his back, and stared at some point past her left shoulder. "I'm sorry, Mother, but—"

"And don't interrupt!" I had never before seen Alicia so angry with him. "How dare you behave like this—as if we hadn't already had enough of your sordid escapades! I've never been so ashamed of you in all my life! You've taken the daughter of one of Cornelius' oldest friends and treated her exactly as if she were no better than some cheap prostitute!"

"But he—"

"And don't you dare say Cornelius advised you to do so!"

"Pardon me, Mother, but he told me to have sex with the girl I intended to marry, and frankly, I think that's good advice. I wouldn't dream of marrying a girl I hadn't slept with. I'm sorry if you find that offensive, but—"

"You can't possibly want to marry Elsa!"

"Oh yes I do!" said Sebastian, mouth turning down stubbornly at the corners.

I managed to get a word in. "Alicia, I'm afraid Sebastian's trying to pay me back for a very unpleasant conversation we had after the incident with the police."

"You couldn't be wider of the mark," said Sebastian. "I thought your advice was pretty good. In fact, I was just thinking I'd be stupid not to follow it when I met Elsa midtown one day outside Korvette's. Well, I said hi and she said hi and suddenly I thought: Maybe she'll do, so we went into the nearest coffee shop and had a couple of malteds. She was shy, so we didn't talk much. I asked her if she had a boyfriend and she said no, she guessed men thought she was too fat. I thought she was cute. I like fat girls. Anyway, when we got talking, I found she was kind of interesting. She's studying design at art school, and later, when she showed me some of her designs, I thought they were great—surreal. She gave me one to hang up in my apartment. Then we talked about Dali's pictures and went to the Museum of Modern Art. Why have you never bought any of Dali's work, Cornelius? I wish I could paint like Dali or design patterns like Elsa. Anyway, on our next date I said, 'Now I'll show you something *truly* surreal,' so we drove out along Route 22 and saw a real deadbeat film about a werewolf. It was fun. Then a couple of weeks later —it was after we'd checked into the motel for the first time—"

"Cornelius," said Alicia, "we don't have to listen to any more of this, do we?"

"—we found a Coke machine looking just like a surreal robot, and oh boy, we sure laughed! Anyway, we got our Coke and went to bed and it was very nice, and afterward we switched on the TV and watched a rerun of *I Love Lucy*—and boy, did we laugh again! It was one of the funniest *I Love Lucy*'s I've ever seen—maybe you saw it? It was the one where Ricky says to Lucy—"

The terrace doors opened as Carraway, flanked by two footmen, made a grand entrance with the champagne.

"—and then Lucy says to Ricky—"

I watched, riveted to my chair, while Carraway opened the bottle. The entire scene was quite beyond my control.

"—and then Fred and Ethel get in on the act—"

The servants finally managed to tear themselves away.

"Oh well, here's to Elsa and me!" said Sebastian, diverted at last by the champagne, and raised his glass to his lips.

Neither Alicia nor I attempted to drink.

"Sebastian," said Alicia, surprising me again by taking the lead in the conversation, "I'm sorry . . . I do understand you've had a pleasant time with Elsa, but I can't possibly approve of you marrying a plain fat Jewish girl with no poise or charm when you could do so much better for yourself."

"And my God, Sebastian," I added with a shudder as I hastened to give her support, "if Jake ever finds out you've been sleeping with his daughter, he'll not only break you in two, he'll probably break me in two as well!"

"No, he won't!" said Sebastian, dark eyes suddenly hard and bitter. "Why shouldn't I sleep with his daughter if he runs around with your wife?"

Nothing happened. It was quiet. Then a bird hopped lightly across the balustrade, trilled sweetly, and flew away into the shrubbery. Sweat started to trickle down my back.

Alicia's face was like carved ivory, smooth, inscrutable, exquisite. "You will leave this table, please, Sebastian," she said without raising her voice. "I can see exactly why you wanted to hurt me by inventing such a wicked lie, but perhaps when you're calm enough to consider my reasons for disapproving of your plans, you'll see fit to apologize. Now, please go."

Sebastian drained his glass, grabbed the bottle of champagne, and made off with it in the direction of the summerhouse.

"Alicia," said my voice, "are you . . . ?"

"Don't be ridiculous, Cornelius," she said. "Can you imagine me ever having an affair with a Jew?"

I couldn't. I wiped the sweat off my forehead. "But what the hell gave Sebastian such an idea?" I said, puzzled.

"God only knows! No, wait—it must have been that time . . . Oh, but how stupid! Jake came here once when Sebastian was still living at home, Cornelius—it must have been shortly after Sebastian had left the service. You'd gone away somewhere—Boston, was it? I don't recall. However, Jake thought you were due to leave the following morning, and so he stopped by after work to see you about some matter connected with the Fine Arts Foundation—don't you remember? I told you all about it afterward."

"Yes, I think I do remember. But why should Sebastian . . . ?"

"Naturally I invited Jake to have a drink, and Sebastian discovered us in the Gold Room while Jake was telling me some long story about one of his daughters. If Sebastian thought that scene was an illicit rendezvous, he must have been out of his mind, but I'm sure the only reason he made that insane remark was that he was livid that I don't want him to marry that huge flabby girl who's as plain as a pumpkin and never has a word to say for herself. Oh, God, Cornelius, what on earth are we going to do?"

Carraway, who was certainly working overtime that Sunday, reopened the French doors.

"I beg your pardon, sir, but Mr. and Mrs. Jacob Reischman—"

The Reischmans streamed past, setting him aside with the efficiency of Old Money accustomed to treating servants like pieces of furniture.

"Good afternoon, Neil," said Jake, pale with rage. "Good afternoon, Alicia. Please excuse us for interrupting your meal."

We rose as one to our feet.

"Good afternoon, Jake. Good afternoon, Amy," I said.

"Good afternoon, Amy and Jake," said Alicia.

"Good afternoon, Cornelius and Alicia," said Amy.

"Please sit down," I said politely. "May I offer you a drink?"

"Thank you, no. We will, however, sit down. Sit down, Amy."

Amy, a large overdressed woman with graying hair locked up in the tightest of permanents, sat down obediently on the chair which Sebastian had abandoned, while I pulled up a fourth chair for Jake. As I sat down, I managed to press Alicia's foot under the table and point to my chest to indicate she should leave the talking to me. Despite the Reischmans' obvious wrath, I had a shrewd suspicion they knew less than we did; Elsa would surely have cut her own throat rather than confess to her parents that she had lost her virginity in a New Jersey motel before a gala performance of *I Love Lucy*.

"I presume you have been informed, as we have just been informed," said Jake, "that your son has been seeing our daughter on the sly and making what can only be described as clandestine assignations?"

"You mean he's been dating her," I said.

"He never asked our permission!"

"Jake, this is 1955. Which century are you living in?"

"Your son persuaded our daughter to concoct some outlandish alibi with her sister so that we wouldn't discover he was taking her to a series of New Jersey drive-ins!"

"Jake, I'm not responsible for your daughters. You are. And what's so wrong with a drive-in movie?"

"Such vulgarity!" whispered Amy with a shudder. "So immoral!"

"Be quiet, please, Amy. I'm sure we're all aware of what goes on at drive-in movies. Just why Sebastian couldn't give my daughter a respectable night out, I don't know. Wasn't my girl good enough to be properly entertained? The whole situation would be different if he had taken her openly to Carnegie Hall or the Met, but to sneak off with her to a New Jersey drive-in is, I consider, nothing short of an insult to my daughter's background, family, upbringing—"

"Oh, forget it, Jake!" I said good-humoredly. "Try to remember what it was like to be young! I know it sounds crazy to us to go to a drive-in movie in New Jersey, but is it really so different from that time in 1928 when you and I and our favorite girls snuck off to ogle Mae West in *Pleasure Man* before the police closed the show down?"

"Did you really, Jacob?" said Amy with interest.

"Be quiet, please, Amy. Now, listen to me, Neil. Don't pretend you don't know what I'm talking about. I have an eighteen-year-old daughter, and she's going to be a virgin when she marries, and I'm not letting her run around the New Jersey drive-ins with a man who, I think you'll concede, is very far from inexperienced."

"I can't think why you're saying all this to me," I said. "Sebastian's over twenty-one and his own master. Why don't you say it all to him?"

"You know very well why. Because the four of us have got to unite against this crazy idea that Sebastian and Elsa should marry after a two-month courtship punctuated by visits to drive-in movies."

There was a pause while the four of us sagged in our chairs with relief that we were to remain friends despite such adverse circumstances.

"Naturally," resumed Jake, "I'm opposed, as no doubt you are too, to the principle of marrying out of one's religion and culture. Marriage is difficult enough at the best of times. To begin marriage with such a handicap can only be sheer folly. I speak, of course, without cultural or religious prejudice. I'm just stating the facts."

I listened with half my mind to this predictable tirade, but with the other half I was remembering how happy I had been as a young man with Alicia. I recalled an occasion long ago in a California hotel when she and I had laughed together over a bag of peanuts; there had been no television in those days, but we had lain on the decadent circular bed, I with my crossword puzzle, she with her confession magazine, and life had been good and warm and happy. Nostalgia overwhelmed me. I thought of Sebastian and Elsa ingenuously enjoying television together, and for the first time in my life I found myself wholly in sympathy with my stepson. Maybe I hadn't found him easy to understand, maybe I had made mistakes, but now at last I saw I was in a position to make amends for my shortcomings.

I said, "Jake, just stop for a moment and listen to yourself. I'm not going to accuse you of racial prejudice, but just think back over what you've said and see if you can't revise it. I don't like this attempt to discriminate against my son."

"I wasn't discriminating against your son!"

"Oh? Are you sure? Look, Jake, the days are long gone when the twin aristocracies sat side by side in New York like oil and water and never mixed. Why shouldn't you have a Gentile in your family, and why shouldn't I have a Jew in mine? We're New Yorkers, aren't we, living in the world's most cosmopolitan city, which is perhaps the nearest modern equivalent to ancient Rome, where all races met and mingled. Remember what we learned long ago at Bar Harbor during those godawful Latin tutorials! There was an Etruscan aristocracy as well as a Latin aristocracy in ancient Rome, but did they remain separate forever? No, they did not! They merged to become a single Roman elite!"

"I'm amazed by your retentive memory. However, even if we set aside all the cultural and religious objections to this marriage, the fact remains that Elsa and Sebastian are totally unsuited—"

"Are they?" I said.

"Cornelius!" Alicia could contain herself no longer. "You're surely not in favor of this—you can't be!"

"Look," I said to her and to Jake and even to the subservient Amy, who was watching me round-eyed, "let's strip aside all this myth and prejudice and stultifying middle-aged outlook and examine the situation as it really is. Sebastian's not easy to know, and he's had his difficulties in the past, but he's a good boy who's doing well in life and is going to do better. He's never taken a serious interest in a nice girl before because he's always felt too shy, but now that he's made the effort, you can be sure he'll be far more appreciative of Elsa than the young men who spend their time propping up the New York debutante dances every season. He wants to settle down and be a good husband—and for his wife he's chosen your daughter, who's also shy and who's never had a boyfriend before and who—dare I be this honest?—is never likely to win the title of Miss America. Admit it, Jake! Sebastian's a good catch for Elsa. Amy, you'll admit it even if Jake won't!"

"Just a moment, please, Amy," said Jake automatically as Amy opened her mouth. Taking a handkerchief, he mopped his forehead. "Neil, I can't believe you're serious."

"He isn't serious, Jake," said Alicia.

"But I am! Darling"—I was careful to choose an endearment I hadn't used in years in order to signal to her that I was sincere—"I've just seen this could be the making of Sebastian. Remember California, December 1930, and how happy we were?"

"Sebastian *is* nice-looking, Jacob," said Amy tentatively. "Clever, too. Will he be head of Van Zale's one day, Cornelius?"

"Amy, who am I to foretell the future?"

"Sebastian won't get the bank, Amy," said Jake. "Neil will take over one of the little Kellers and train him up to be Paul Cornelius Van Zale III. Blood's always thicker than water."

"I'm sorry," said Alicia to Amy, "but I don't think they should marry. It's got nothing to do with prejudice. I just don't think Sebastian's in love with her. I'm sure he likes her very much, but—"

"I entirely agree," said Jake. "Elsa's not in love with Sebastian, either. It's just a young girl's infatuation."

"Of course the children would be brought up Jewish," said Amy to me.

"Amy, I'm sure Sebastian and Elsa will work out some acceptable arrangement!" I turned to her husband. "Come on, Jake!" I said pleasantly. "Face reality! If you persist in burying your head in the sand, Sebastian and Elsa may well decide to graduate from their New Jersey drive-ins to a New Jersey motel!"

"My God." He shuddered, found a clean glass on the serving cart, and poured himself some lemonade. "Is this a Tom Collins?"

"No. Carraway!" I called.

He was on the terrace in seconds. Of course he and the footmen had been straining their ears at the nearest window. I felt like Aladdin rubbing the magic lamp.

"Bring another bottle of champagne, please."

"I oppose this marriage," said Jake. "I oppose it."

"You can't stop a girl marrying if she's put her mind to it, Jake," I said mildly. "I've had personal experience of that painful fact, and if you keep acting as if it's 1855 instead of 1955, you too could have a daughter marrying at some city hall in Maryland."

"Oh, Jacob," said Amy, "we must give Elsa a wonderful wedding! It would kill me if she wasn't a proper bride!"

"Amy, can't you understand? She's not in love with him!"

"Yes, but, Jacob, she may never get another chance to marry someone who's not after her for the money—you may be ruining your daughter's whole life! And Sebastian's such a good-looking boy, so tall and virile. It's like a dream come true for Elsa. You don't know how miserable your daughter was, crying and crying every night because she was so fat and so homely and had no boyfriend—"

"Stop!" shouted Jake.

"But, Jacob, you want your daughter to be happy, don't you?"

Jake looked at the pitcher of lemonade as if he wanted to hurl it through the window. "I don't think Sebastian would make her happy!"

"I think the marriage would be a disaster," said Alicia, "but the trouble is, Jake, that nobody's going to listen to us. It's also very hard to disagree with Cornelius' view of the reality of the situation. Sebastian's determined to marry her, I can tell, and Elsa's probably more than capable of following in Vicky's footsteps to Maryland. In the old days we might have worked out some scheme to keep them apart, but nowadays children do as they please, and to hell with the parents."

Jake gritted his teeth. We all waited. Finally he said, "A year's engagement."

"Oh, Jacob!" said Amy. "Girls can't wait a year nowadays, and neither can young men!"

"Well, perhaps there *is* something to be said for premarital sex," I began mildly.

"Absolutely not!" said Jake fiercely. "Not where my daughter's concerned! All right, nine months."

"A spring wedding!" said Amy, pleased, and out of the corner of my eye I saw Carraway sweeping majestically toward us with the champagne to seal the deal.

V

THAT EVENING when I was alone working in the library on some cost projections for my new arts magazine, Sebastian knocked on the door and looked into the room. I had not seen him since he had stalked off the terrace with the bottle of champagne, although Alicia had called him at his apartment after the Reischmans had departed and asked him to come back.

"Hello," I said warily. "Come on in."

He ambled across the floor, folded himself into a chair on the other side of my desk, and regarded me gloomily. His expression, half-sullen, half-mutinous, indicated that his mood had returned to normal after his lunchtime euphoria. He said dourly, "Thanks."

"What? Oh, yes, that's okay, Sebastian. I do sincerely believe this marriage is the right thing for you."

The usual awkward pause ensued. Making a desperate effort at conversation, I said lightly, "I didn't know you were an *I Love Lucy* fan!" and I at once suffered a pang of guilt. I felt I should have known.

"Yeah, *Lucy's* great."

Silence fell again. He shifted in his chair. "Cornelius . . ."

"Yes?" I said, willing myself to be patient .

"I'm sorry." He swallowed. "Truly sorry."

"Uh . . ." I tried to figure out why he was apologizing. "That's all right, Sebastian," I said hastily. "Don't worry about it."

"I know Mother never would."

For a second I was back on the terrace with the little bird trilling sweetly on the balustrade. I sat motionless in my chair.

"I was just so mad at her," said Sebastian, "calling Elsa a plain fat Jewish girl with no poise or charm. That was bitchy."

"It was certainly tactless," I said cautiously, "but don't forget your mother had had a big shock. Sebastian . . . just out of interest . . . what exactly prompted you to make that extraordinary remark about your mother and Jake?"

"It was nothing. I just found them having a drink together one evening when you were away, that's all."

"Yes, your mother mentioned that. She even told me about it at the time. But what made such an unremarkable incident so unusual that you not only remembered it but served it up with such a twist months later?"

"I don't know," said Sebastian. He drew his eyebrows together and looked contemplative, like the little plastic figures in novelty stores of apes looking at human skulls, and then, just as I had decided it was useless to expect a logical explanation of such illogical behavior, he said suddenly, "I guess it was because Mother was drinking Scotch."

Chapter Six

I

THE ROOM was silent, but in my memory I heard my voice from the recent past ring in my ears: "For Christ's sake, why the hell are we all wasting time discussing Alicia's drinking habits?"

The memory expanded. It was automatic, unstoppable. The small trivial incident reran itself effortlessly before my eyes.

"Alicia doesn't drink Scotch, Jake."

"I do now, Cornelius."

"You were drinking Scotch when I arrived. I assumed—"

"Oh, yes, of course, Jake . . ."

I saw them as actors, Alicia fluffing a cue, Jake prompting her with the right line, Alicia glossing over the error so quickly that I, in the audience, enrapt by the drama unfolding offstage, had paid no attention to the hidden drama flashing briefly before my eyes.

I stared at Sebastian. He was talking again. I struggled to concentrate on what he was saying, and all the while part of my brain said: Not true, can't be true, jumping to conclusions, being neurotic, don't believe it, can't believe it, won't believe it, sick fantasy, going out of my mind.

"Yes," Sebastian was saying meditatively, "that was probably it. You know Mother's got all those funny old-world ideas about what women should drink. You know she never drinks anything except sherry—unless there's a crisis like that time at Bar Harbor when Andrew broke his leg and you fixed her a martini. Well, when I looked into the Gold Room that evening and Mother asked me to join them for a drink, I noticed right away that Jake was drinking Scotch. I particularly noticed because there was a bottle of some very good Scotch, Grant's or something, no, Johnnie Walker Black Label, on the table by the ice bucket, not that plebeian stuff you yourself like, and I was tempted to have some. Then, to my astonishment I saw that there wasn't a sherry glass in sight and Mother had the same drink as Jake. Well, I guess there's no reason why Mother shouldn't take to Scotch in her old age, but that's probably why the scene stuck in my mind, because I thought: Gee, that's fast living for Mother, swilling Scotch with a man who's not her husband! Stupid, wasn't it? I mean, if there's one thing we all know about Mother, it's that she never would."

"Yes. Right."

"Christ, I never realized how anti-Semitic she is!" He heaved himself out of the chair and plodded off to the door. "Guess I'd better be going. 'Bye, Cornelius. Thanks again."

"Good night, Sebastian."

He left. I went on sitting at my desk. Then it occurred to me that there was probably a very simple explanation and that if I were to ask Alicia what it was, she would tell me and I would feel much better. I tried to phrase the question. "Excuse me, Alicia, but how come you've been drinking Scotch in secret for months and Jake is fully aware of this habit while I'm not?"

Absurd. Foolish too. Once I revealed to Alicia that I knew, she would be sure to pity me, and our relationship, nowadays so tranquil, would immediately grind into an awkwardness so horrific that my mind refused to contemplate it. Whatever happened, neither she nor Jake must find out that I knew.

And what did I know anyway? It was no big deal. Six years ago in 1949 I had told my wife to take a lover, and sometime during those past six years she had taken one. That was very sensible of her and fully in accordance with the agreement we had worked out. She had even chosen the one man in all New York who could be totally trusted to keep his mouth shut and not use his victory to laugh at me whenever my back was turned. I marveled at her good sense. I sighed with relief at the thought of Jake's perfect discretion. I told myself what a practical man I was, effortlessly sanctioning pragmatic solutions for life's more awkward problems. All three of us were so civilized and sophisticated. Everything was going to be just fine.

There was a photograph of Alicia on my desk, and after a while I realized I was looking at it. I saw her smooth shining dark hair and her gray-green eyes slanting above her cheekbones, and suddenly I was remembering with searing clarity her unblemished skin, her small round firm breasts, her . . .

I wanted to kill him.

Blundering to the liquor cabinet, I slopped something into a glass, I don't know what it was, it tasted of nothing, all my senses were numbed, I was blind, deaf, and dumb with the pain. I tried to pull down the shutters as usual over such unendurable consciousness, but the shutters were jammed, I couldn't get a grip on them, I couldn't block that pain out. It streamed through my shattered mind and shaking body, and all I could think was: I can't bear such pain, I can't live with it, I don't have the *power* to live with it. . . . And the word "power" ripped through my torn consciousness until I felt I was bleeding to death.

There was a knock on the door.

I was standing by the liquor cabinet with an empty glass in my hand. A bottle of Canadian rye was uncapped. I picked it up and poured myself another measure.

"Yes?" I said.

The door opened. "Cornelius . . ."

I couldn't look at her. I picked up my glass and drank. My hands were still shaking.

"Excuse me, but I just wanted to make sure Sebastian stopped by to apologize before he left."

"He did. Yes." I kept my back to her as I returned to my desk. My cost projections lay where I had left them, like an archaeological relic from a lost world.

"Good. Oh, Cornelius, I'm so depressed about this marriage! I know I must pull myself together and be a reasonable mother-in-law, but it's very hard to be reasonable when I just don't understand what Sebastian can possibly see in that girl."

"Yes."

"Well, can *you* understand what he sees in her?"

"No."

There was a pause. "Cornelius, is anything wrong?"

"No. How long have you been drinking Scotch?"

"What?"

"I said, how long have you been drinking Scotch?"

"Oh . . ."

I found I was looking at her, although I had no memory of turning around. But she was no longer looking at me. Her eyes had a remote inward look, as if she were peering back into the distant past.

"Some while," she said at last. "I didn't tell you because I thought you'd be upset. I know you always liked my old-fashioned ideas about liquor."

She looked at me directly for no more than two seconds, but in that one brief glance the truth stood revealed between us. When two people have lived together for a long time and loved one another deeply, there are certain circumstances where no concealment is possible.

"Well, you go right on drinking Scotch," I said. "What right have I to stop you?"

She thought for a moment. Then she said, "I no longer have any desire for it," and walked quickly from the room.

II

I SPENT all night trying to figure out how I could reopen the conversation with her, but of course this proved impossible. There was just no way the subject could be discussed. She was polite toward me but kept her distance. Once I almost shouted at her: "We've got to talk about it!" but I didn't. I was too afraid of what I might hear, and gradually I realized she too was afraid of where such a conversation might end. So we went on alone together, two people living in terror of wrecking the slender thread which still linked them, both mouthing courtesies, both clamping down on all emotion, and the pressure in me began to mount until I didn't see how I was going to avoid some violent, disastrous explosion.

III

". . . so IT's going to be a very big issue," said Jake, sipping his wine. "Not, I agree, as big as the General Motors spree last January, but still very sizable. There'll be a syndicate of two hundred and fifty investment-banking firms coast to coast. The big question—as usual— is how far the major stockholders will exercise their options."

"Sure."

We were having lunch at L'Aiglon two days after Sebastian had announced his engagement. Jake preferred to lunch midtown even though he knew I would have settled for a quiet corner of the partners' dining room; for the past twenty years he had refused to deviate from his opinion that it was impossible to find passable European cuisine south of Canal Street. That day he had ordered escargots, *filet de sole amandine,* and a bottle of French Chablis. I had prodded at half a grapefruit and was now looking at some plain poached bass. A waiter paused to refill my empty glass of wine. I had already drunk two martinis before leaving my office that morning.

"The biggest stockholder in Hammaco nowadays," said Jake, "is Pan-Pacific Harvester. Did you know that? I thought it was a rather intriguing piece of information. Apparently they own ten million shares, and assuming they exercise their options, they would have to pay out about forty million dollars—and of course that's a lot of money in any language."

"A lot, yes." Finding myself unable to look at him, I glanced around the restaurant at the smart clientele, the immaculate waiters, and the elegant room. Jake had been talking business ever since I had picked him up at Reischman's in my new mint-green Cadillac; we took it in turns to share the transport uptown.

"Right now we're building up the book of dealer-customers who'll take up the slack if Pan-Pacific Harvester drops out. Of course, it's a huge issue, but not, I think, unrealistic. It's very natural that Hammaco should seek to raise a hundred and twenty-five million to meet their additional plant needs. . . . Neil, are you listening to this?"

"Yes. One-twenty-five million. Additional plant needs." I managed to look at him. He was wearing a plain gray suit, and as always he exuded an air of low-keyed but elaborate self-confidence. It was hard to believe his great-grandfather had started life in America as a peddler. Devoid of that stereotyped, distorted image of Jewishness promulgated by the more ignorant Gentiles, his features still remained unmistakably Jewish to me. He had that fine-drawn, arresting elegance produced by considerable intelligence mingled with a highly controlled sensuality, a combination one sees sometimes in the old portraits of Sephardic Jews, although as far as I knew there was no Sephardic blood in the Reischman family. I had always accepted without question that he was attractive to women; certainly it was an image he had always taken care to promote.

". . . Rosenthal of PPH said he was worried about the market, but how he can be worried when steel's obviously going to hit a new peak in production, I just don't know."

I could not eat my fish. I motioned to the waiter to refill my wineglass.

". . . and then he started talking about the effects of consumer credit on the economy, and . . . Neil, is something wrong with that fish?"

"No. Nothing's wrong. I'm just bored with talking about business, that's all. Why do we always, always have to talk about business? Why can't we get personal for a change? I want to get personal. I think it's *time* we got personal."

Jake's fork hesitated for a second above his plate. "What do you mean? Is there some private matter you want to discuss?"

"Yes, as a matter of fact there is. Just how long have you been fucking my wife?"

The conversation droned on around us. A waiter nearby had embarked on the ritual of cooking a crepe suzette, and out of the corner of my eye I could see the flames leaping in the pan. My fingers tightened around the medication in my pocket, but my breathing was even, in, out . . . in, out, and my heart was pumping effortlessly in my lungs.

Jake put down his fork.

"Obviously there's been some mistake," he said, an aristocrat being forced to deal with some crude hobo who clearly had no idea how to behave in civilized surroundings. "I admire your wife very much, but she's always been entirely devoted to you."

"Who taught her to drink Johnnie Walker Black Label?"

Jake took a sip of wine, just a little sip, not because he wanted to drink but because it was necessary for him to make some fastidious gesture to show how utterly he disapproved of such boorishness. His face was very white.

"Oh, that," he said. "That was a very long time ago, a private joke between us. I'd almost forgotten it."

"Why, you—"

"I think we'd better leave," said Jake, signaling to the maître d'.

"I know what's going on! Why keep up the pretense? How dumb do you think I am? How long do you think I can be fobbed off with lies?"

"The check, please," said Jake to the maître d'.

"I'm so sorry, sir, was the meal not to your liking?"

"The check."

"Yes, sir, of course." He hurried away.

"I guess she told you all about our problems," said my voice. "I guess she told you everything. I guess there's nothing you don't know."

"I know nothing whatsoever," said Jake. "Nothing, nothing, and less than nothing."

"Your check, Mr. Reischman." The maître d' was hovering anxiously, still upset by our half-finished meal.

Jake signed his name. He managed to do that, but made a mess of adding the tip. He scratched out the figures twice, and he was still writing when I got up and walked out. My Cadillac was at the curb, but I paid it no attention. I just waited on the sidewalk, and when Jake emerged from the restaurant, I said tightly, "You leave her alone. You lay one finger on her again and I'll—"

Without warning, his nerve snapped.

"Fuck off!" he said in a low voice which shook with rage. "I've had enough of your shit! You've got the most wonderful wife in the whole damned world, and what do you do? You tell her to take a lover! And when she does take a lover—to salve *your* conscience—can you take it? No, you can't! Not only are you not man enough to make love to your wife, you're not man enough to face up to the consequences!"

For one long moment we stood there, the great-grandson of a German peddler facing the great-grandson of a poor dirt farmer from Ohio, and then three generations of education, culture, and refinement streamed right out of our blood into the gutter.

I went for him. I drove my fist into his face so hard the skin broke over my knuckles, but when he tried to hit me back my bodyguard stepped between us and restrained him. I moved in for another blow. I felt as if I were moving in a hot mist. There were tears in my eyes. My breath was coming in great sobbing gasps.

"Take it easy, sir," said my chauffeur, catching me by the wrist. "Take it easy."

I tried to fight him instead. When my bodyguard gently detached me, I turned on him too. I wanted to fight everyone, the whole world.

"Break it up, fellas! What the hell's going on round here?"

It was a cop. A crowd had gathered, and above us the sky was a steaming hazy blue, like that day long ago in 1933 when my dreams of a large family had come painfully to an end.

Another world had ended now. It was the end of an era which had begun in the nineteenth century when Paul Van Zale had applied for a position at the House of Reischman, and as I looked at Jake wiping the blood from his mouth, I saw also the last link severed with my precious Bar Harbor past.

There was blood on my hands, blood on my clothes, blood on the sidewalk. I stared at it dumbly. So much blood. I looked down at my hands again in bewilderment. Where had all the blood come from? How had it happened? How could I possibly have ended up in such a devastated arena? I felt as if I were choking on the blood. I wanted to vomit, but although I retched, nothing happened.

"This way, sir," said my bodyguard, easing me into the Cadillac as if I were severely disabled. My chauffeur had already slipped back behind the wheel.

"Hey, you!" called the cop. "Just you wait a minute!"

My bodyguard produced a fifty-dollar bill, the one he always kept for emergencies, and the last thing I saw as the car drove away was the cop's delighted face as he stowed the bill safely away in his uniform.

IV

I went home and shut myself up in my bedroom for a long time. When I emerged it was dark, and I didn't at first see the note that had been pushed halfway under the door. Stumbling over the envelope, I went back into the room to read the message inside.

Alicia had written: "I thought I might stay with Andrew and Lori for a few days. Would this perhaps be best? Tell me what you think I should do."

I ran downstairs. She wasn't there. In panic I ran back upstairs but found her in the television room. The television was off. She had a magazine in her hands, but it wasn't open. An empty glass stood on the table, but there was no bottle in sight.

"Don't go," I said. "Please."

"I just thought it might be easier—for a few days only."

"No. Please."

"All right."

"Do you want to go?"

"No."

"Do you want a . . ." But as usual, the word "divorce" got stuck in my throat.

"Of course not."

"Oh. I thought maybe . . . since he obviously thinks very highly of you . . ."

"Oh, that's all quite finished," said Alicia. She opened her magazine and started to flick through the pages.

"Since when?"

"Sunday night. When I realized you knew. Then I called him and ended it. Of course. Naturally."

"But . . ." I struggled for words. She went on flicking through the pages of her magazine. "What did he say?" I asked at last.

"He didn't believe me. He thought I was imagining that you knew. Then he called me this afternoon to say he was wrong. He wanted to meet, but I refused. I saw no point in it. Then I had the idea that I might go away—from him, not from you. I wanted to make some gesture he would understand. But it doesn't matter. I think he must understand now how I feel."

She stopped speaking, but I went on listening as if I could hear the explanation she had omitted. At last I said, "Well, I guess you'll find someone else."

"After this? Are you mad? Do you think I'd ever want to go through the last forty-eight hours again?"

"I'm sorry." To my misery I saw that because of my selfish, stupid behavior I had cut off all her secret opportunities for happiness and had locked her once more into an empty marriage. I felt numb with shame as I realized she must despise me as much as Jake did.

"We'll get divorced," I said in a rush. "It's the only answer. Too much mess . . . and pain . . . not fair to ask you to endure it any longer."

"Oh, no!" she said fiercely. "No divorce! Not after all I've been through! If I lose you now, it'll mean that I've been through all this for nothing, and I'm sorry, but I can't accept that. If you try to divorce me, I'll—"

"I don't want a divorce."

"Then why drag the subject up?" She tossed the magazine aside and rose to her feet. "I think I will go to Andrew and Lori after all," she said. "I'll go for a week, and when I come back, I don't want to discuss this again *ever*, do you understand? We'll just go on as we were and pretend this never happened. It's better that way. People talk a lot of trash about how awful hypocrisy is, but they just don't know a damn thing. Hypocrisy saves one's sanity. It's the shield you hide behind when the truth is too terrible to face. How many people really have the courage to live wholly in the truth? Not me, that's for sure. And not you either. It's easier to live with the way things ought to be, not to crucify yourself by living with the way things really are. Good night, Cornelius. I have to go to bed now. I'm very tired. Excuse me. . . ."

V

I WENT to the library and sat alone there for a long while. I wondered whether to call Scott, but I had no desire to play chess and I could hardly talk to Scott about my personal life. Scott and I talked about either business or eternity, and there was no halfway house. I remembered Bede's lighted hall and thought: It's not so well-lit as Bede believed; the shadows get darker and darker as one moves toward the far end.

I remembered the last of the Stuyvesants, dying alone after years of isolation in his Fifth Avenue mansion. But that wouldn't happen to me. There would always be one person I could turn to no matter what happened. There would always be one person in the world who would keep the isolation at bay.

I wrote "VICKY" on my notepad and drew a circle around the letters.

I knew then that I had to get her back. I didn't know what price I'd have to pay, but I didn't care. I wanted Vicky back home in America with me, and no one, not even Sam Keller, was going to stand in my way.

VI

THE KELLERS were unable to join us at Bar Harbor that August, as Sam was pulling off an impressive business coup and needed Vicky with him to organize the important dinner parties, but I suggested that they return to New York in November for a family Thanksgiving.

Vicky's reply literally transformed my life. She wrote to say how wonderful it would be not to have to scour Fortnum & Mason for imported cranberry sauce and how she couldn't wait to taste real American pumpkin pie.

She was homesick at last.

The tide was on the turn.

When I next spoke to Sam on the transatlantic phone, he started talking about Germany again, but I shut him up.

"I can't think about that at the moment. I've got enough problems here trying to maintain our relationship with Reischman's—I told you, didn't I, about that godawful row I had with Jake as a result of all the anti-Semitic talk that got bandied around when Sebastian and Elsa announced their engagement?"

"Christ, isn't that papered over yet?"

"It's not paper we need, it's cement. The rift's a big one. I may even have to recall you to New York, Sam."

"But—"

"Okay, stay in England, but just forget Germany for the time being. I don't want to hear about it."

There was a furious silence. Then he started reminding me that I had promised to let him open a German office in 1956, but I interrupted him.

"Vicky sounds excited about the prospect of coming home for Thanksgiving!" I said casually. "Is it my imagination, or has she been getting kind of homesick lately?"

There was a pause before Sam said abruptly, "She only gets homesick when she's depressed, and she only gets depressed as a result of pregnancy. It's not unusual, the doctor says."

"Uh-huh."

There was another pause. I waited for him to mention Germany again, but he didn't, and I realized then with enormous satisfaction that my suspicions had been correct. The balance of power had finally tilted back in my favor. I now had him exactly where I wanted him.

However, before I could make any move to terminate his European idyll, Vicky called me from London. She was calling me more often nowadays.

"More exciting news, Daddy—I'm having another baby next summer! I hope it's another girl, to keep Samantha company!"

"Why, that's wonderful news!" I said with alacrity, but I saw to my disappointment that I would have to postpone my final epic tussle with Sam until after the new baby was born. I didn't want to upset Vicky when she was pregnant, particularly since she had become pregnant so soon after giving birth to Samantha. I remembered Sam's talk of postpartum blues and felt anxious about her. "How are you feeling, sweetheart?" I said on an impulse. "Is everything okay?"

"Of course! How could everything not be okay when I'm so lucky and have everything a girl could possibly want? Why, sometimes I lie awake at night just thinking over and over again how lucky I am!"

I decided she would be luckier still if I could bring her back to New York for good, but I said no more in order to avoid burdening her with the worry of my approaching power struggle with her husband. Women shouldn't be involved in their husbands' businesses anyway. Women should stick to managing their homes and children, and I considered that I had a moral duty—a *real* moral duty—to protect Vicky from the seamy world of power struggles so that she could go right on being the perfect wife and mother. I was beginning to think the one genuine triumph of my personal life was how well Vicky had turned out.

I thought of Sam with a sigh, but I didn't feel too sorry for him. Probably he would have hated the reality of living permanently in Germany. I knew he thought of himself as a German yearning to return to his native land, but I was prepared to bet that the Germans would have no hesitation in treating him as an American expatriate—which he would have been, of course; the Germans are no fools—and then disillusionment would have followed as inevitably as night follows day. In fact, by recalling Sam to New York I'd be saving him a lot of grief—or so I told myself, but of course I was well aware that Sam was hardly going to see my decision in that light. I would have to tread very carefully. The balance of power might well be tilting slightly in my favor, but Sam was a dangerous opponent, easily capable of bashing the balance back in his direction if I put a foot wrong in the negotiations. I was going to need all the diplomatic skill and all the bargaining power I could lay my hands on if I was going to succeed in hauling him home across the Atlantic; in fact, it was going to be the rockiest of rocky rides.

Chapter Seven

I

THE FOLLOWING May Vicky gave birth to another daughter, who was named Kristin (an Americanization of yet another German name), and after the happy transatlantic phone calls had been exchanged, Sam wrote me a long memorandum from the Van Zale office in London. He said he had postponed his German plans long enough, and he suggested a three-week reconnaissance in Bonn in June, a conference in New York in September, and the opening of a German office in January 1957.

I saw that he had decided to attack in the hope that I'd still be unwilling to force a showdown. I smiled sadly and shook my head. It was by this time abundantly clear to me that Vicky had had enough of Europe, and although she never said so, I sensed she was longing to come home.

I wrote Sam the most exquisite reply. Ruefully I confessed that I had decided not to open a German office since I believed an additional branch would make Van Zale's too unwieldy for me to supervise in the manner to which everyone had long become accustomed. With shameless enthusiasm I lauded him for his achievements in London. Then I stated I was planning a reshuffle at One Willow Street and wanted him home.

His cable in reply read: "ARRIVING IDLEWILD 1430 HOURS WEDNESDAY TO DISCUSS FUTURE STOP SAM."

Wednesday was the next day. I sent a Cadillac to the airport to meet him but made sure it was last year's model.

He called from the Pierre. "Thanks for fixing me up with this wonderful suite!" he exclaimed, so skillfully acknowledging the lack of an invitation to Fifth Avenue that he neutralized the chill of my reception. "I'll just catch up on some sleep, and then maybe we can meet for dinner this evening."

I really couldn't let that pass. If I let him dictate the timetable of our confrontation a second longer, I'd be putting myself in a weak position.

"I'll see you here in half an hour," I said, and cut him off.

He was on time. Evidently he had decided it wasn't worth the risk of antagonizing me further by being late.

When he was ushered into my office I looked him up and down, much as a boxer might measure his opponent in the ring, and noticed details I had overlooked on previous rushed business meetings and busy family reunions. His dark hair was now quite gray, and the lines were deeper on his face. No doubt I too had aged, but fair people somehow weather the years better; my hair was a duller shade of yellow, but the silver strands were not noticeable at a distance, and although my face was lined, there were no pouches under my eyes and no slack flesh around my jaw. Regular exercise and no smoking had kept me in good condition despite my respiratory problems, and I had cut back the drinking that had followed my discovery of Alicia's affair. Sam looked in bad shape, and as soon as we were seated after the ritual performance of an affectionate welcome, he had to light a cigarette to steady his nerves.

Of course I knew approximately what was going to happen; the draft of the script had been hammered out long ago. Sam had been clever enough to set himself up in a position where he could tell me with truth that there were solid attractive reasons for the further expansion into Europe. He could have tried strong-arming me without bothering to set himself up in this persuasive position, but he knew me well enough to realize his best policy was not to beat me over the head to get what he wanted but to lure me gently on until I had no valid reason for refusing his demands. Obviously for Vicky's sake he had to make some effort to handle me with kid gloves and avoid antagonizing me needlessly.

One can lead a horse to water; twenty cannot make him drink. Having coaxed me to the water's edge and demonstrated what a magnificent drink he was offering me, Sam would be justified in losing patience if I subbornly refused to be a sensible horse and slake my thirst, and I could all too easily visualize him threatening to resign. What I found hard to visualize was him actually tendering his resignation. The weakness of his position was that he must surely be reluctant to quit; he wouldn't want to upset Vicky by alienating me for good, and he wouldn't want to diminsh his sons' prospects by cutting them off from the Van Zale fortune. If Sam threatened to resign and I called his bluff, I foresaw he would immediately be in trouble.

I smiled to show him how confident I felt, but he wasn't looking at me. He was still messing around with his unpleasant cigarette.

"Let's keep this strictly a business discussion, shall we?" he said, shaking out the match. "If we get personal, we always get overemotional."

Any business discussion could have only one result: he would be able to demonstrate with humiliating ease just how obtuse, irrational, and myopic I was being by refusing to sanction a German expansion. He would have the latest facts and figures at his fingertips, and within five minutes he would have made me look a complete fool.

"Oh, hell, Sam!" I said in a good-natured voice. "Give me a break, can't you? Change the record! I don't want to hear your reasons for opening a German office—I know them all so well I probably recite them in my sleep! The British are finished, you say, they can't work, they sit around drinking tea, they've been living in a fool's paradise ever since Macmillan told them they'd never had it so good. But meanwhile the Germans are working like blacks, crawling out of the gutter, and pulling themselves up by the straps of their jackboots. The mark's steadily rising. Soon the pound won't be worth a plugged nickel. If I open an office in Germany now, I'll make so much money I'll be able to buy up England and turn it into a Coney Island East for tourists—oh, Christ, Sam, I could go on reciting this forever, but can't we skip the crap and get down to what's really bothering us? And what's really bothering us, of course, has nothing to do with business."

"I refuse to get into an argument with you over Vicky."

"It looks as if you may have to. Let's talk about the way things really are. I didn't send you to Europe primarily to make money for Van Zale's. I sent you there because Vicky had a problem back in 1952 and needed to take a break from America."

"That's true. But—"

"And now," I said, sitting back in my swivel chair and rocking myself gently to and fro, "now Vicky's got over her problem. Now

Vicky wants to come home again. And why not? She's had four years in Europe and it's been a wonderful experience, but now she wants to see the Stars and Stripes flying everywhere instead of the Union Jack—she wants genuine Thanksgiving dinners and Walter Cronkite on TV and a charge account at Saks and an American accent for her children. And let me tell you something, Sam. I think she's right. I've no patience with expatriates who think America's not worth living in."

There was a silence. Presently Sam took off his glasses and polished them. "I hoped it wouldn't have to come to this, Cornelius," he said, and the sound of the name he never used signaled to me that he was picking up the gauntlet I'd flung down at his feet. "This is a sad end to a thirty-year-old friendship."

"What's that supposed to mean?" I said, knowing he was busy setting up the grand illusion that he intended to resign.

"What the hell do you think?" he said, fencing with me, but I knew this was no fencing match. This was stud poker and we were tripling our stakes at each twist of the bidding. "Neil, I wonder very much if you truly know what you're doing. To put it bluntly, you're trying to bust up my marriage. I want to stay in Europe, and I have a right to expect my wife to support me in any decision that involves my career, yet you're trying to muscle in, exploit Vicky's temporary homesickness, and assert that we'll all live happily ever after so long as Vicky comes home to Daddy! Well, I'm sorry, but I'm not prepared to take that kind of interference in my private life. If you're not prepared to act like a sane, rational businessman by sanctioning the German office, I quit. My reputation's very high in Europe and there are others who'll back me if you won't."

"And what are you going to say to Vicky?" I said lazily, still swinging to and fro in my chair.

He just looked at me. Then he said, "That's got nothing to do with you. That's *my* business."

This refusal to face reality annoyed me. I stopped swinging in my chair. "In other words, you're going to go right on making my daughter unhappy."

He sprang to his feet. "Look, pal—"

"Sit down, Sam, for God's sake, and let's not get overheated about this."

"Shut up. I think it's time you woke up and faced the cold hard facts of life. Vicky's my wife. She loves me and she's not about to leave me to run home to you. I'm the boss in my own home, and if I say we're going to Germany to live, then we go to Germany to live. And if you cut yourself off from me, then you cut yourself off from her."

Of course he was only bluffing, but it was amazing how convincing he sounded. I began to feel uncomfortable. I was breathing evenly, but my hands were sweating and my mouth was dry. I had an overwhelming desire to terminate the interview so that I could relax in peace with my victory. I didn't like living with this illusion that I could be defeated at any minute.

"Oh, stop trying to con me, Sam!" I said irritably. "You're not about to quit Van Zale's! You've got to think of your sons! Suppose I disinherited them?"

"I'm beginning to think that's the best thing that could possibly happen to them."

I had a moment of complete panic. This was no bluff. He really was going to quit. He'd just torn up my trump cards. He was going to take Vicky to Germany. I wasn't going to get her back. I was going to lose. I was going to wind up in isolation.

"Now, wait a minute," I said. "Just wait a minute. Surely we can get together on this. I mean, things don't have to be so acrimonious, do they? For Christ's sake! Surely we can work something out here. Uh . . . I can see now I've presented this all wrong. You see, the truth is, Sam, that I really need you in New York. That was what I said in my letter, wasn't it? Yes, well, I decided I wouldn't push that angle when I saw you, because I didn't think you'd agree to abandon Germany just because I needed you in New York. So I got involved in this argument about Vicky and the boys, and that was wrong—I see that now, and you were right to get mad at me. I'm very sorry. Of course she's your wife and I absolutely acknowledge I have no right to interfere in your marriage. And of course I'd never cut out those boys. You know how much they mean to me. I'm sorry I threatened you like that, it was stupid of me, but the truth is, Sam"—I paused for air and inspiration—"the real truth is, I'm in such a jam over this Reischman mess, the repercussions, the awkwardness, the impossibility of reasonable negotiations with Jake on areas where we've traditionally had mutual interests . . . I can't negotiate with him myself anymore, but all the other partners are useless, they can't stand up to him, I send them out onto the battlefield and they come back like packaged ground beef. . . . I know you and Jake are no longer friends, but at least you can stand up to him, at least he respects your abilities, at least you won't come back from a Reischman meeting in pieces. . . ."

I continued in this vein for some time, mixing fact and fiction as skillfully as I could to impress upon him that he was now indispensable to me, and all the time I kept waiting for him to interrupt. But he didn't. He just sat there letting me talk. Presently he even lit a cigarette, as if he were in no hurry to go. At first I was too sick with relief to question the unexpected withdrawal of the heavy artillery, but eventually I became puzzled, and finally I was fascinated. I talked on and on, and Sam listened and nodded until suddenly the truth hit me with such a jolt that I nearly passed out. This was no exaggeration. I ran out of breath, and my diaphragm felt as if it had been handcuffed to my rib cage.

Without a word Sam got me a glass of water and waited by the window till the asthmatic spasm had passed.

"So you do see, don't you," I whispered as soon as speech was possible again. "You do understand why I'm so anxious for you to come back."

"Yes," said Sam. He sat down again. There was a pause. Then he said slowly, "I'm not saying I can't imagine a situation in which it would be more attractive for me to return to New York than to go to Germany. But it does take a lot of imagination. Maybe you can give my imagination a helping hand."

"Oh, sure," I said. "I'm very imaginative. Let me see. Well, of course there'd be extra money, but that goes without saying, doesn't it? I wouldn't expect you to give up your German dreams without considerable financial compensation—"

"Joint senior partner."

"Pardon me?"

"I'll come back to New York if you'll make me joint senior partner."

"Oh . . . well . . . uh . . . yes, why not? I mean, I don't think I could *quite* split everything fifty-fifty, but certainly the title . . ."

"That'll do for a start. I'm sure you'll find you'll have plenty of opportunities to be generous later."

"Oh, yes," I said, "I'm sure they'll come along very fast."

We looked at each other. There was a long, long silence. I wondered why he had let me win just when defeat seemed to be staring me in the face, but I knew better than to push him further by trying to find out. I'd won. That was all that mattered. I'd won, and Vicky was coming home.

"Sure you still want me back?" said Sam.

"One-hundred-percent sure, yes."

There was another pause. Then Sam said in a low voice, "Neil, I don't know what kind of problems you have, but believe me, this solution isn't the answer to them."

"Well, why don't we at least try it and find out?" I said, relaxing at last with a smile, but even as I spoke, I was wondering if my triumph would turn out to be a Pyrrhic victory.

II

IT WAS still six months before I saw Vicky again. Sam's successor had to be chosen, dispatched to London, and introduced to all the clients; Sam himself had to wind up his unfinished business, and Vicky once more had to face the complexity of an intercontinental move. After the house had been sold, the staff paid off, and the furniture removed for shipment, I was hardly surprised when she wrote to say she was longing for five days' peace at sea.

She arrived in New York a week before Christmas with Sam, the four children, and the two nurses, and naturally I was in the front row of the crowd waiting at the pier as the passengers disembarked from the *Queen Elizabeth* and progressed through the customs hall. Sam's personal assistant was dealing with the mountain of luggage, so there were no delays. Vicky was almost the first person I saw, and as soon as she saw me she started running toward the barrier.

She looked lovelier than ever. She was wearing a Persian-lamb coat with a matching hat, and from a distance I was unexpectedly reminded of Vivienne, whose figure she had inherited. After she had left her Westchester apartment two years before, Vivienne had rented a house on the English south coast, and Sam had generously allowed her to visit her grandchildren once a month. Whether she would now return to New York, I had no idea, but I hoped her financial circumstances would convince her that life in Europe had more to offer than an impoverished existence in New York. I certainly intended to tell Sam that in my opinion he had done enough for her and that there was no longer any need for <u>him</u> to underwrite her maternal instincts.

"Daddy!" cried my girl joyously, rushing past the barrier into my arms.

I thought of Scott asking: "Has it all been worth it?" and a voice in my head answered: Yes, yes, and again yes. I was no longer alone. Nothing mattered except that.

When I finally relinquished Vicky to Alicia, the first person I saw was Sam.

"Hi," he said.

"Hi," I whispered, still recovering from my emotion.

The little boys clustered shyly behind him, and beyond them the two nurses were holding the little girls. All the children had grown very much in the year since I had last seen them, and Kristin, now seven months old, was already a large baby. I noticed that like the others she had inherited Sam's brown eyes.

"Come on, kids!" said Sam, giving Eric a slight push. "Wake up!"

Eric was six, still blond like Vicky but somehow not so like her as he had once been. In response to his father's cue he stepped forward and politely offered me his hand to shake. "Hello, Granddad," he said with his stiff little British accent.

"That's better," said Sam, who had obviously rehearsed the scene several times. "Now, come on, Paul! Speak up!"

Paul, who had resembled Sam since infancy, was now a plain stout three-year-old apparently incapable of speech.

A bright little thing danced up to me. "Hello!" it said, and jumped up and down like a puppy waiting to be patted.

I picked up Samantha and gave her a hug. She wore a little pink dress and a pink bow in her wavy fair hair, and I was immediately reminded of Vicky. "Hi—who are you?" I said, pretending I didn't know, and thought how odd it was that all four children had inherited Sam's eyes.

"Samantha's cute," I said to Vicky as we traveled crosstown in my new maroon Cadillac, and tried to stop myself thinking: But Samantha can't take over the bank.

I attempted to talk to my grandsons but soon gave up. If they were an example of a British upbringing, it was no wonder Britain was heading for the rocks.

"Please don't mind the boys being shy, Daddy," said Vicky awkwardly later when we were all relaxing in the Rembrandt Room after lunch. "It's just that everything's so new and strange to them."

I at once hated myself for failing to conceal my feelings. "Honey, of course I don't mind them being shy! Why, I was shy myself when I was small."

"They're really very sweet," said Vicky, and suddenly for no reason she began to cry.

I was shocked. "Sweetheart, they're wonderful! How could you ever think—"

"I've tried so hard to give you what you wanted," she interrupted, the tears streaming down her face. "I've tried so hard to be the sort of daughter you wanted me to be, I've tried so hard to make up for not being a boy."

"Vicky!" I was paralyzed. At the far end of the room Sam left Alicia and moved toward us. "Vicky, I love you the way you are— I've never wanted you to be any different! Vicky, I'd rather have you than all the sons in the world!"

"Okay, Neil," said Sam quietly. "I'll handle this. Come along, honey. You're very tired. I'll take you upstairs to rest."

Still weeping, she allowed him to lead her away. The nurses took the children off to the nursery, but I barely noticed. I went on sitting in my chair until at last Alicia came over to me.

"What happened, Cornelius?" she asked, puzzled.

"I don't understand," my voice said. "She can't truly believe . . ." I broke off again, then repeated, "I don't understand."

"I shouldn't worry. She's probably just overwrought. The last six months must have been very exhausting for her."

"But what did she mean? She said . . . Alicia, during all the years we've been married, have I ever once said to you that I wished Vicky was a boy?"

"No. But I expect you thought it occasionally."

"Never!" I felt very upset. "I loved her exactly as she was!"

"But who was she, Cornelius? We all know you've always loved her, but who have you really been loving? Was it Vicky? Or was it some ideal image that exists only in your mind? And if it really is Vicky you love, then who *is* Vicky, Cornelius? I'm not at all sure I know the answer. After all these years, I guess I can finally admit to you that Vicky's an enigma to me. I've never understood her and I doubt now if I ever shall."

We were silent, but at last she said, not unkindly, but with sympathetic concern, "Well, Cornelius? Be honest. How well do you really know your own daughter?"

"You're talking nonsense," I said roughly, and turned away.

III

"DADDY," SAID Vicky the next morning when we went for a stroll together in the garden after breakfast, "I do apologize for that ghastly scene yesterday. I think all the upheaval of moving must have finally unhinged me! Please can we treat the scene as if it had never happened?"

I thought of Alicia saying eighteen months before: "We'll pretend this never happened. . . . How many people really have the courage to live wholly in the truth? Not me, that's for sure. And not you either."

Automatically I heard my voice say, "Vicky, you've got to be truthful with me. You're the most important person in my life, and if something's wrong, I want to know about it so that I can help put things right. Aren't you happy with Sam?"

"But of course I am! Darling Sam, he's been an absolute angel—truly, Daddy, I couldn't have a more patient, kind, understanding husband. I'm so lucky, you see . . . always so lucky."

"Are you upset by Sam's decision to buy a house in Westchester? Is that the problem? Are you worried about settling down in the suburbs?"

"No, no, I'm sure it'll be best for the children—I'm sure Sam's right. Sam's always right. He's so wonderful, making all the big decisions and saving me from so much worry and anxiety. I just don't know what I'd do without him."

"You really mean that?"

She looked at me with her clear candid gray eyes. "Of course I mean it!" she insisted impatiently, and then she kissed me, slipped her hand into mine, and exclaimed, laughing, "Oh, Daddy, *please* stop asking such silly questions. . . ."

IV

WE HAD another fourteen months to go before the catastrophe, but the fourteen months passed with increasing speed. At first Vicky was occupied with house-hunting, and later, when Sam had approved her choice, she had the task of arranging the alterations which were necessary before the furniture could be moved in. I saw less of her than I saw of the grandchildren, who remained at my house on Fifth Avenue during this period of domestic upheaval. Meanwhile Sam had asked Alicia if she could help Vicky, and whenever Alicia wasn't occupied with my family she was busy with her own. Sebastian, who had married Elsa the previous spring, had quickly become a father, while Andrew and Lori were reproducing themselves with monotonous regularity. Alicia might no longer have a lover, but she could hardly complain that time hung heavily on her hands.

Sam and I were occupied too: with each other. After he had demanded to be joint senior partner I had hardly expected him to slip back into his old subservient role of right-hand man, but I was jolted when he revealed not only a taste for autocracy but a determination to persecute me until the title "joint senior partner" was accurately reflected in the articles of partnership. Before his return from Europe I was indisputably the boss of my own firm, but after Sam started throwing his weight around, I found I had to make concession after concession, until I felt I was carving up my kingdom in order to keep the enemy at bay.

Chilled, I watched him hire as many aides as I had and demand equal office space; he even had the nerve to suggest I should split my office in two and give him the better half with access to the patio. There were, it was true, prewar precedents for this demand from a joint senior partner, but never when the reigning senior partner had been omnipotent for twenty years. Rejecting his proposal, I bit the bullet and allowed him equal office space elsewhere. Biting the bullet yet again, I authorized the lavish expenditure he ordered on the latest office equipment and electronic gadgets.

The bullet began to seem harder and harder. I had taken a huge cut in my share of the partnership profits in order to meet Sam's extortionate financial demands without upsetting the other partners, but like all extortionists, Sam was never satisfied; soon he was agitating again for an increase in money that would have put his share on a par with mine.

Meanwhile, he had started demanding a portion of the prestige trips I made to Washington to see the secretary of the treasury and (occasionally) the president. He dealt with Morgan's on a major issue without consulting me. He insisted on two business trips a year to Europe to check up on the London office. He tried to tell Scott how to negotiate with Hammaco. It was rumored he even tried to dictate to Jake, and only backed off when Jake started dealing with him through a Reischman partner who had survived Dachau. I couldn't help admiring Jake. He was obviously the only man left in all New York who could keep my monster of a partner under control.

By this time I was in a constant state of rage, anxiety, and nervous exhaustion, but the bitter truth, as I had known all along, was that if I wanted to keep Vicky in New York I had to keep Sam happy. He had let me beat him back from Europe once—for reasons which still puzzled me; I supposed he had been unable to resist the opportunity to become a joint senior partner of Van Zale's—but Sam wasn't a martyr by nature, and I knew that if I failed to treat him royally, he would resign and take Vicky back to Europe. And Vicky, naturally, would go with him. She loved her husband and children, she was the perfect wife and mother, and no other option would be open to her.

Nineteen-fifty-seven was a terrible year.

Nineteen-fifty-eight looked like being even worse, and when in February Sam asked if he could meet me after work at the St. Regis, I immediately suspected some new mayhem was about to explode before my eyes.

I kept my face expressionless, but maybe I turned pale, for Sam said dryly, "There's no need to get excited—I'm not planning another coup d'etat. God knows I'm much too sick of the bank to want to talk about it."

Nothing he said could have alarmed me more. Sam losing interest in the bank was like God getting bored halfway through the Creation; it just didn't happen.

I had a meeting midtown that afternoon with the president of our commercial bank, the Van Zale Manhattan Trust, but by five-thirty I was at the St. Regis. Sam was already waiting for me in a quiet corner of the King Cole Bar with a half-finished martini in front of him.

"Have a martini with me," he said.

"Will I need it?"

"Yes."

The waiter delivered my martini.

"What's the problem?" I said, hardly daring to ask.

"I just don't know how to tell you."

Taking a sip of my martini, I tried to breathe as if nothing were wrong. "Is it the office?" I said.

"No."

For a sickening moment I remembered a former Van Zale partner who had fallen so deeply into trouble that he had conspired to commit a murder. "Christ, Sam, is it money?"

"No, Neil, it's not money."

"Your health?" I hazarded wildly. Thoughts of lung cancer flashed through my mind. He smoked far too much.

"Not my health," he said. "Vicky's. She's having another baby, Neil, and I just don't know what to do. I feel as if I'm going out of my mind."

I was transfixed. "She's in danger?"

"No, it's our marriage that's in danger. Neil, can I really talk to you about this, or is it better not? Can we ever get back to the days when we were friends who confided in each other—the days before I found you with Teresa? I know I've given you hell this past year, but I was so goddamned mad when I saw how ready you were to abuse your power at my expense that I just couldn't resist giving you some of your own medicine in return."

"I know. I understand. Yes, of course we can talk again. Sure we can." I was so shattered I hardly knew what I was saying. I had just realized he was on the brink of going to pieces and that he had picked me for the job of holding him together. I tried to take control of the conversation. "Now, calm down, Sam, and start at the beginning. Why is this new pregnancy a disaster?"

"Every pregnancy's a disaster. Scenes, tears, locked bedroom doors, you name it. Then after the baby's born, we just manage to get back to normal when—wham! Another pregnancy. Now, don't get me wrong. This isn't one long gripe about getting no sex. I can deal with that problem—I *have* dealt with it. I may not always have dealt with it in the smartest possible way, but at least I've always dealt with it without upsetting Vicky. Unfortunately, Vicky's all shot to hell anyway."

"Obviously she must see a psychiatrist."

"Christ, we've been knee-deep in psychiatrists for years! She saw every top psychiatrist in London!"

"You mean . . ." It was hard to speak. "All these years . . . How long has this been going on?"

"Since we moved to England, and it's just got worse and worse. Why do you think I let you beat me back here in the end? It was because I was worried to death about Vicky. I thought she might improve if she came home, and so she did for a time, but now everything's worse than ever. My biggest fear is that one day she'll walk out on me."

"*What!*" I half-rose to my feet, then sank back in my chair. My breathing was ragged. I fumbled in my pocket for my medication.

"Believe me, Neil, when I say the marriage is on the rocks, I don't mean *I'm* tempted to walk out on *her*. Do you think I'd be here talking to you if I was? I'm here because I'm crazy about her and I've got to talk to someone, and I figure you can't be too hard on me once you know how much I love her. I didn't love her before we were married, I admit that, but afterward I . . . she was just so lovely and so sweet and so young, and . . . I . . ."

He was going to break down. The scene was a nightmare. I found a handkerchief, put a hand on his arm to comfort him. "Take it easy, Sam." My ineffectual words dropped emptily into the huge sea of his grief. I doubt if he even heard them. I knew I had to be terse and unsentimental in order to get the conversation back on an even keel, so I knew it was vital not to think of the source of his unhappiness as Vicky. I tried to think of her as just some woman I knew socially, a partner's wife, no one special.

"Let's get back to the present problem, Sam. This new baby that's on the way—I guess that was an accident?"

"Jesus, they've all been accidents since Paul. I used rubbers before that because I didn't think she was old enough to cope with birth control, but after Paul was born, she said she wanted a diaphragm, so I said okay, if you want, give it a try. Well, it didn't seem to work too well, and we got a bit careless and . . . Samantha came. Well, afterward I said hell, don't go back to the diaphragm, we'll try the rubbers again, and she said okay, but then she thought she couldn't get pregnant if she nursed the baby—she'd never tried nursing before, but she read something about mothers in India spacing their families by breast feeding, so she tried breast feeding, but it didn't seem to work out too well . . . and she got pregnant anyway with Kristin. Boy, I had a rough time of it. Then she heard about some experimental pill she could take, but the doctor wouldn't prescribe it, said it caused cancer, so okay, I took no chances and used rubbers again from the very first time we got together after Kristin's birth."

I wanted to ask why she was apparently so set against him using rubbers, but I couldn't. It was because I knew that "she" was Vicky. I couldn't ask a question like that. I didn't even want to think about it.

"Well," said Sam, "that was okay. We got along all right until
. . . hell, you know what it's like when you're forty-nine—or maybe
you don't. I know nothing about your sex life nowadays. But I was
working too hard trying to handle all the new power I'd beaten out
of you at the office, and I started drinking in order to keep going,
and although I still wanted sex, I found I couldn't make it like I used
to. And then one night I really wanted it but it just didn't seem to
work with the rubber on . . ."

I thought: Just a wife, just an acquaintance, no one I know well.

". . . so I took off the rubber and then I made a mess of things
and didn't get out in time and . . . oh, Christ, it was bad luck to be
caught out like that—no, it was worse than bad luck, it was hell, it
was the biggest possible disaster, it was like some terrible punishment . . ."

I said in my most clinical voice, "Sam, it's absurd to suffer like
this. It's bad for both Vicky's mental health and yours. Obviously the
pregnancy should be terminated."

"Right. Just what I said. God knows I've always spoken out
against abortion, but—"

"When is Vicky having the operation?"

"She's not having it."

"Not having it?" I thought I'd misheard him.

"No. It was all set up, but when she got to the hospital, she
couldn't go through with it. I took her home, and she cried all the
way."

"When was this?"

"Yesterday. Neil, I'm terrified she'll leave. I think she hates me. I
think she hates the kids. *And I don't know why,* Neil. If I knew, I
could do something, fix it somehow. And what makes the situation
even more nightmarish is that *I don't think Vicky knows either.* It's
mad. I think we're both going completely crazy."

"Well, it's obvious," I said, "that Vicky's undergoing some kind of
breakdown. She must be hospitalized, and if you weren't so close to
breakdown yourself, this would be obvious to you too. I'll talk to my
doctor and fix up something at the best sanatorium."

"She won't go into a sanatorium, and I couldn't possibly have her
committed. She may be having a breakdown, but it's not that kind of
breakdown—she's not seeing visions or feeling as if little green men
are out to get her. She's still coping. She puts on a front before the
children . . . and before you too, of course. Neil, whatever hap-

pens, you mustn't tell Vicky you know about all this. I think it would kill her. It's very, very important to her that you should think she's well and happy and that the marriage is grade-A."

I felt as if I were lost in some dark valley but above me on the hillside I could see the lights of a beautiful house, while inside, beyond the lighted windows, I could see all the people who were so far beyond my reach. I saw Emily and Alicia and Sebastian, even Andrew, and Kevin and Jake, and now Vicky was there too, her face pressed against the glass in a mute appeal for help. But I was cut off from her. I couldn't get out of the valley, and although I searched and searched for the driveway that would take me up to the house, I kept getting lost in the dark.

"Jesus, look at the time!" Sam was saying, perturbed. "I must go at once, in case Vicky needs me." Stubbing out his cigarette, he finished his martini before adding in a brave attempt at optimism, "Well, I guess we'll survive somehow—I love her, and that's the most important thing, isn't it? We'll lick this problem in the end."

"Sure. Sam, if there's anything else I can do . . ."

"No, not for the moment. I feel better now I've talked it out. I want to thank you for listening, Neil. It must have been hell, and I'm sorry."

"I'm glad we talked."

Outside, on Fifty-fifth Street, it was cold, and a bitter wind was blowing east from the frozen American hinterland as we paused beside our cars to shake hands.

He said suddenly, "It's okay now, isn't it?"

"Yes, Sam," I said. "It's okay."

"We'll play 'Alexander's Ragtime Band' again?"

"Yes. And talk. Like the old days."

"Great. I've missed you, Neil. It's been a long time. . . . By the way, do you still see Teresa?"

"I'm on my way to her right now."

"Funny how unimportant all that seems nowadays. . . . Well, be sure to tell her hello from me, won't you? I was always so fond of Teresa."

He got into the Mercedes, but as the car drew away from the curb he looked back at me and waved. I waved in return. Then I crawled into my Cadillac as painfully as if I had broken every bone in my body, and was swept crosstown to the Dakota.

V

TERESA AND I had come to resemble a certain type of married couple; we bickered occasionally, had sex as a matter of routine, spent our time outside the bedroom watching television, and secretly enjoyed our humdrum domesticity. Our relationship might have become a habit, but it was a hard habit to break, like smoking.

Teresa had changed since we had first met. Having finally reverted to her early, natural style of work, she painted less but better, and with her creative life in firmer control, her organization of her surroundings had improved. She kept the apartment clean, wore smart clothes when she wasn't working, and made serious efforts to control her weight. The left-wing books in the apartment had long since been replaced, first by romantic novelettes, then by popular books on psychology and dieting, and as she discarded bohemianism to embrace the trappings of middle-class life, I began to suspect that she enjoyed thinking of our relationship as an informal marriage rather than a love affair. I offered her a charge account at Saks, and she said she would prefer Bloomingdale's. I asked her to choose a present at Tiffany's, and she did not laugh with scorn but spent half an hour selecting a hideous gold pin. Once a year, on her birthday, I took her out to dinner. In the early years she would drag me to some cheap ethnic restaurant in the Village, but now we patronized the smart restaurants midtown.

Occasionally we discussed art together, but usually intelligent conversation was too much of an effort. We yawned over trivia, picked over desultory issues, and watched *Dragnet* together, or perhaps a rerun of *I Love Lucy,* now irrevocably tainted for me by the thought of Sebastian's exploits off the New Jersey Turnpike.

When I arrived at the apartment that evening, Teresa was wearing a smart red wool dress which displayed her breasts to advantage, a black chiffon scarf, and the gold pin from Tiffany's.

"Why the hell didn't you call to say you'd be late?" she said, aggrieved, as I walked through the door. "The chicken Kiev's been keeping hot in the oven for well over half an hour."

"Cut it out, Teresa, I've had the most godawful day." I pecked her cheek in lieu of a kiss, walked wearily into the living room, and sank down on the ugly orange couch which she had bought long ago to match an ugly orange lounge chair.

Without further questions she fixed me a drink, turned on the television, and said she would bring in dinner.

"Teresa, forgive me, but I don't think I could eat a mouthful. I've had a bad shock about Vicky, and I'm worried to death about her. I don't want to go into detail, and I must ask you to keep this in confidence, but it's turned out she's very unhappy."

Without expression Teresa said, "Poor kid," and switched off the television.

"I don't understand it, Teresa. I want to fix it, but I don't know how to."

"Write a check to someone. Come on, have your drink and you'll feel better."

"Teresa, please don't try to joke about this. This problem can't be solved just by writing a check."

"Then welcome to the club of the ninety-nine-point-nine percent of the world who can't solve their problems by writing checks! Okay, don't get me wrong—believe me, I'm sorry if that poor kid of yours is unhappy, but if you want me to be truthful, I can tell you it's no big surprise. This is a repeat pattern, isn't it? You've never told me much about your past when you and Sam were just two young kids scaring Wall Street shitless with your fifty million bucks, but I've kept in touch with Kevin over the years, and now and then he's told me a thing or two about the seamy side of your past. You gave the orders and Sam was the executioner, isn't that right? Well, here we go again. You gave the order for Vicky to be happy and Sam's busted his ass being a yes-man, but unfortunately for everyone concerned, it was the wrong order and Sam's done a hatchet job."

I tried to focus on what she was saying. "Teresa, you might as well be talking Chinese. What do you mean?"

"Vicky should never have married Sam. Hell, Sam was my lover for four months—I should know what I'm talking about! If Vicky had been grown-up, as I was, she might have survived, but she wasn't grown-up, was she? She was just a kid, running away from her parents and blundering, by a series of accidents (or *were* they accidents?), into the bed of a man who underneath all that smooth talk is very insecure with the opposite sex."

"Insecure? *Sam?* Why, he had women all over the place in the old days!"

"Yes, and the best ones all walked out on him, didn't they? Any woman with a mind of her own would walk out on Sam Keller—he has a very rigid idea of what a woman ought to be: sweet, willing, and submissive to his authority. But let's be honest—not all women can take that kind of nineteenth-century junk nowadays, some women don't want to spend their lives wrapping a man's ego in lamb's wool, some women have figured out there are more rewarding ways of occupying their time!"

"Teresa, just what the hell are you talking about?"

"I'm talking about the real world, Cornelius, the one you ride through every day in your insulated glass bubble of a Cadillac, the one you keep at arm's length by signing checks. I'm not talking about your masculine pipe dreams of the way women ought to be, I'm talking about the way women really are! Believe me, I'm fond of Sam, and if he wants a crying, walking, sleeping, eating, living doll for a wife, good luck to him—we all have our different tastes, and I'd be the first to say we're all entitled to them, but he should have picked a woman who *is* that way, a woman who *wants* to be that way, not a mixed-up little girl who doesn't know who she is or what she wants!"

I stared at her. Then I said rapidly, "Okay, maybe Vicky shouldn't have married him, but she still had to have a husband, didn't she? It was obviously best for her to marry young . . . all I've ever wanted was the best for her!"

"You'd have no idea what was best for any woman—you'd only know what was best for the bank in a multimillion-dollar business deal! And why should it have been best for her to marry young? No, don't give me that crap about her being an heiress who had to be protected from all the wicked gigolos! You just couldn't wait for her to marry because you have this psychological need to see her as the perfect wife and mother—you were desperate to begin weaving these fantasies that were obviously so necessary to you!"

"What garbage!" I burst out. "What absolute bullshit!"

"Is it? I've lived with you for nine years now, and, honey, I'm beginning to think I know you better than you know yourself. Your trouble is that you're fixated on, quote, being a success in life, unquote. Why do you go chasing after money and power the whole damn time? It's because way back when you were learning the facts of life, someone—Uncle Paul?—taught you that for fifty percent of the world's population—men—the only equation worth worrying about if you wanted to be happy and masculine was the one which read: money plus power equals success. And what about the other half of the world's population? What was the magic formula they had to learn in order to ensure happiness and femininity? Oh, yes! Marriage plus maternity equals perfect fulfillment for all females! Marriage plus maternity equals *success!* Never mind who taught you that —your mother? your sister?—because it doesn't matter. You could have picked it up anywhere. It's become one of the most popular fairy tales of our time."

I just managed to get my temper under control. Speaking in a voice that rang with a calm, measured logic, I said evenly, "I wanted Vicky to be happy. I thought she would be happy as a wife and mother. Therefore, if I thought finding such happiness constituted success, will you please tell me why I shouldn't have wanted that kind of success for my daughter?"

"Why? I'll tell you why! It's because you didn't want that kind of success for *her* sake, you wanted it for yours! You wanted—and still do want—a so-called successful daughter so that all the world can say in admiration: Gee, what a successful father he is to have such a successful daughter! Sam isn't the only guy around here who's not as confident as he seems to be, Cornelius, and he's not the only guy I've ever met who uses women to boost his ego!"

"Jesus Christ!" I shouted, but again I somehow got my temper under control. "Look, I've had just about enough of this pseudo-egghead crap you keep dishing out to me. Where did you get it all from? Those popular psychology books you picked up from the racks in the five-and-dime? Let's get back to the facts. I'm only interested in the facts. Fact number one: Vicky genuinely wanted to be a wife and mother. Fact number two: all women basically want to be wives and mothers—"

"No, honey, they don't. Sorry, but they just don't. My fifty percent of the human race isn't a bunch of identical plastic dolls. We're human beings and we're all different, and incredible though this may seem to you, we don't all want the same thing. In fact, the real rock-bottom truth is that we're as diverse as that other half of the human race, the half you take such arrogant pride in belonging to!"

I had a better grip on myself now, but I was still taut with rage. "I'm not denying the diversity of the human race! I'm talking about the basic instincts of mating and reproduction which are common to everyone! Of course there are different types of women. God knows, no one could be less like you than Vicky!"

"How can you possibly make such a statement? You don't know the first thing about me! You probably don't know the first thing about that daughter of yours either! You're all cut off and sewn up!"

"My God, how could I sleep with you for nine years and not know you? You're—"

"I'm Teresa Kowalewski and I need a canvas and room to paint and no money worries and—oh yes, a good fuck on a regular basis, I guess I'd miss that if I didn't have it, although it often seems more trouble than it's worth. However, knowing your talent for seeing women in only one light, you probably think we're just like a married couple—oh, I'm a little eccentric, sure, but basically I only live for your visits, when I can play house, cook you a nice meal, and pretend I'm just another happy middle-class housewife. Well, I've got news for you, honey. I've got a whole big meaningful life which exists quite independently of you, and although I'm content for you to stop by now and then, all you really are to me is a checkbook and a hard-on. That's the real world, Cornelius. That's the way things really are. Am I getting through to you at all, or am I still talking Chinese?"

The doorbell rang.

We went on staring at each other. The doorbell rang again.

"Shit," said Teresa. "I guess I'd better see who that is."

She moved into the hall.

I went on sitting on the couch and looking at my untasted glass of Scotch, but dimly I became aware of voices.

"I'm sorry. I've got to see him."

"Hey, wait a minute! What the hell—"

"Excuse me, please."

My two separate worlds were grinding crazily against each other. The park had ceased to exist. Fifth Avenue was streaming alongside Central Park West in a great roaring freeway, and I was trapped on a concrete strip in the middle.

I was on my feet as Alicia appeared in the doorway, and as I stared, not understanding, Teresa pushed past her into the room.

"What the hell's going on? Look, if you two are going to have some big bust-up, would you mind not doing it in my apartment?"

Alicia's eyes met mine. My heart began to beat quietly, like the sea thudding far away in the distance.

"Cornelius, if Alicia's going to make some shitty scene, could you for God's sake get her out of here right away?"

Alicia's face was still but shadowed with grief. My heart began to thump a little louder, surf pounding more insistently on some deserted shore.

"Jesus Christ, what is it? Why the hell doesn't someone say something? What *is* it, for God's sake?"

We were still halfway across Bede's lighted hall, but someone had slipped out ahead of time into the dark.

"It's Sam, Cornelius," said Alicia.

The sea rushed toward me, and all was lost in the roar of the undertow.

"What about Sam?" said Teresa suspiciously. "What's he done?"

I did not answer, for I was way back in another era, and as the years cartwheeled away before my eyes, I saw the tall homely boy hold out his hand at Bar Harbor and exclaim: "Hi, good to meet you!" The kaleidoscope of time revolved. I was at Willow and Wall after Paul's murderers had shot themselves to death, and Sam was shaking with me as we helped Steve Sullivan to his feet. I was on Fifth Avenue in the great golden summer of 1929 when it seemed the good times would never end. I was dancing with long-forgotten girls, I was drunk on bathtub gin, I was having the time of my life with the best friend I would ever have, and far away in the distance I could hear Miff Mole and his Molers playing "Alexander's Ragtime Band."

"He had a heart attack when he was halfway home," said Alicia. "The chauffeur drove at once to the nearest hospital, but it was too late. He died almost at once."

I thought again of Scott saying: "Has it all been worth it?" and now, when I looked back at my struggles with Sam, I saw at once that they were meaningless. Everything was meaningless, all our schemes for revenge and counterrevenge, all our empty preoccupations with power—even power itself was ultimately meaningless, because when you reached the end of that lighted hall there was no power on earth that could save you from the dark.

My whole world tilted on its axis and then shattered as if it had been blown to bits in some huge crucible. If all power was ultimately meaningless, then it no longer mattered whether or not I had the power to father children. In the end it made no difference whether I had one daughter or ten sons. In the end, sterile or fertile, we all had to die.

The one unalterable fact of life was death, and as I allowed myself to look my death squarely in the face for the first time, I realized I would have to find some way of living with that death's unendurable relevance. I had to find an antidote to negate the horror of nonbeing, and the opposite of nonbeing was surely to *be*—I had to be, I had to live, but not in the old sterile way of communicating with people through power. Power had only cut me off from people, but now I had to reach them, I had to break out of that steel-lined room my power had welded around me, I had to communicate with others if I were to avoid isolation's living death.

I looked at Alicia and saw her actor's mask had been broken. I saw past her immaculate self-control then, past all her defenses, past all the grief and suffering that had separated us for so long. I looked at her and saw that she grieved for me, that the pity which I had always resented so fiercely wasn't pity at all, but something far finer, a compassion incapable of contempt and an unselfishness rendering no sacrifice too great to endure. I looked at her and saw the past transformed.

Jake no longer mattered, just as Teresa no longer mattered. I did not need to be told now why she had rejected him as soon as I had discovered the affair; I knew it was because she loved me too much to force me into the role of complaisant husband and too much to hurt me again by turning to someone else. She had always loved me, just as I had always loved her, and by some miracle almost too great to grasp, I looked at her and saw she loved me still.

Teresa was whispering in a hushed voice, "But that's terrible news . . . terrible. He was so young—was he even fifty? Why, I can't believe it. . . . Sam . . ."

I heard her, but I never saw her. My eyes saw only Alicia. I began to walk across the soft carpet.

Teresa was saying, "Honey, I'm so sorry—it must be terrible for you. But you hadn't been close to Sam for years, had you? You weren't truly friends anymore."

Alicia said clearly in her crispest voice, "Miss Kowalewski, can't you see what this means to Cornelius? It's as if he's lost a limb. Can't you see how completely alone he is?"

But I wasn't alone after all. I went on walking, one step in front of the other, past the ugly orange couch, past the ugly orange chair, and as I walked, I thought: I've got to get there. I've got to make it.

Yet in the end I didn't have to go all the way. Alicia came to meet me. She stepped forward, holding out her arms, and the next moment, when I reached her, our long nightmare came at last to an end. Her tears were wet against my cheeks. Closing my eyes, I held her in the dark, and all I said as the great wasteland of our troubles disintegrated was: "Take me home."

PART FOUR

Sebastian: 1958–1960

FEBRUARY 12, 1958. Sam Keller dies but I'm reborn because I now have a second chance to get what I want, and this time I'm going to succeed.

I see Cornelius, who looks like a tubercular wraith. I don't know what to say. In the end I mutter, "Sorry." He looks at me as if I'm some kind of ape, but he's in such a state of shock that he takes my condolences at their face value.

He'll never know how much I always disliked Sam.

February 17. Sam Keller's funeral. Bright colors glowing against the wintry background of the godawful Westchester cemetery. Cornelius has made room in the Van Zale family plot for his brother by unofficial adoption. Sam's mother died last year, and he had no other blood relatives.

The sun shines. Crowds of mourners cram round the grave. Sam alienated a lot of people at Willow and Wall during the last year of his life, when he was crashing around trying to be a bigger son of a bitch than Cornelius, but that's all forgotten now and people can only remember how popular he once was; everyone talks of that famous Keller charm.

The riot of flowers glows obscenely against the frozen background. The repulsive ceremony progresses inch by inch. Horrible. Why can't we dispose of our dead better? In ancient Rome they had the right idea: a big funeral pyre and a lavish dignified oration. Even the Celts were more natural with their keenings and their wakes. Some of the Germanic tribes once cremated their dead in style, but once those Angles and those Saxons got together for keeps they developed this nauseous tradition of stealthily scraping little holes˙in the earth for their dead and then stealthily scraping the earth back again over the corpses, like cats burying a mess. Disgusting. I wonder what the Reischmans think of all these closed Anglo-Saxon faces striving to maintain an impassive silence. I haven't been to a Jewish funeral yet. A treat in store. Oh, God.

I see Mother with her face like a marble effigy. Why doesn't she cry? Why does no one cry? It's so unnatural. We should be yelling and screaming and tearing our hair in a rage against the horror of death. Now, *that* would be an interesting scene. Dali would paint it well: a lot of tortured faces with funeral wreaths spewing out of their mouths, all set against a desert to express the sterility of repressed emotion. Or maybe Bosch would have painted it better: a canvas dotted with little creatures suffering, and dark horrors lurking in the background.

I see Andrew in uniform, and Lori, looking glamorous, beside him. The eldest child is only three, so they've left the kids behind in Manhattan, but I think children should come to funerals no matter how old they are; they could teach the adults how to behave more naturally. I must talk to Andrew, but it's difficult. What goes on in Andrew's head? Can he conceivably be quite so happy as he appears to be? Probably, yes. He may be bright enough to learn how to drive a plane without crashing it, but even the dumbest animals can be taught clever tricks, and there's something very dumb about Andrew. Dumb people are the lucky ones, of course. They haven't the brains to grasp how godawful life really is. I like Lori, though. Wonder what she's like in bed. Oh, well.

I see Aunt Emily, looking like a virgin, and Rose, who undoubtedly is and always will be a virgin, standing beside her. Rose is like Aunt Emily, sexless, not dumb, but like someone with restricted vision, a first-class horse in blinkers. I guess I like Aunt Emily, and Rose too, but I can't connect with them. Nothing to say.

I see the Van Zale partners, the stuffed shirts, all dumber than me except Scott. I like Scott. I especially notice Scott with his black hair and black eyes and white taut face. Wycliffe probably looked like Scott—all the medieval heretics probably looked like Scott as they went to the stake prepared to die for something that exists purely on a cerebral level. There's something very strange about Scott. Spooky. But he plays a good game of squash and he's smart on the job. The other day he figured out that Coastal Aluminum issue like a master chef boning a sole.

I see the Bar Harbor Brotherhood, gray middle-aged men in black, their faces beaten with grief. Cornelius and Jake stand some way apart, but Kevin is right beside Cornelius, and when they met before the service they shook hands and talked for a while. I like Kevin Daly but I don't know him well. Probably I never shall. How I wish I were like Kevin Daly, so sparkling always, never at a loss for something to say, always so full of charm—but not charm like Sam Keller's celebrated mannerisms, which to me always reeked of artificiality. Sam's charm was like water spewing out of a faucet, but Kevin's charm is like water bubbling up from a spring. Yes, I admire Kevin Daly and I like his plays. He's better than Williams, although I like Williams' plays' Southern sex and neurotic tension. Kevin writes about sex and neurosis too, though he's not so interested in sexual mechanics. He's more interested in sex as a form of communication, which can range so astoundingly from blissful perfection to hellish failure. Sometimes I think Kevin's as good as Miller, although I don't believe there's an American playwright alive who could surpass *Death of a Salesman*.

Yes, Kevin's a gifted guy. . . . Wonder what it's like to do it with boys. Maybe I should have tried that, but no, I'd miss all the things that women have. Funny about Kevin's sexual tastes. He looks so obviously like that segment of the American male population that Kinsey was generous enough—or dumb enough—to describe as normal.

Kevin's the only one of the Bar Harbor Brotherhood that I can look at without wanting to smash something. Jake looks sick, the old hypocrite, although he hated Sam for being one of the Master Race. But it must be a bad jolt when one of your contemporaries drops dead, even if the contemporary happens to be an ex-Nazi who always made you want to throw up. God, how the Jews suffered in the war.

I see Cornelius looking like a corpse. One day he *will* be a corpse, and then where will I be? In clover, with any luck—the clover field of the senior partner's office at Willow and Wall. I don't like Cornelius and he doesn't like me, but I respect him. I think he respects me a little too. He's going to respect me more. I think Cornelius knows that he's going to respect me more. There's one thing I have to admit about Cornelius: although he's extraordinarily dumb in many ways, he's no fool as soon as he crosses that threshold at Willow and Wall. In fact, as far as survival on Wall Street's concerned, he's the smartest guy I know. It takes a certain effort to admire a man who seldom opens a book and who thinks of art primarily in terms of financial investment, but it's worth making the effort, because it doesn't pay to underestimate Cornelius. We all know that at Willow and Wall, because the unemployment rate among those who forget is always one hundred percent.

I see more bankers; I see brokers, lawyers, and politicians; I see endless rows of blank faces. Everyone's come to the sordid cemetery to breathe the air polluted by those nauseous flowers—everyone except the most important person of all, the girl who's going to belong to me someday, the heroine I'm going to save. Vicky's in the hospital suffering from nervous exhaustion. Three doctors swore she was incapable of attending her husband's funeral.

I love Vicky. There's a line by John Donne: "For God's sake hold your tongue, and let me love." If Vicky would only stop talking and listen to my silences, she would learn so much. I have no words for all I want to say, but if I were given the chance, I could so easily prove how much I love her. What a stupid system language is. How strange that we should all communicate by opening our mouths and flapping our tongues and uttering little sounds. There should be a more concise way of communicating; we should have lights on our foreheads or hands with fifty fingers all tapping out some faultlessly unambiguous code. If there is a God, which I doubt, he fell down very badly on the communications front.

"Oh, Sebastian!" sighs my wife, Elsa, as we walk away. "Wasn't it a lovely funeral?"

I like Elsa. She's stupid but I like her anyway. At first I thought she was clever because her designs are so good, but the designs are a freak. I read once about a mental defective who couldn't write his name but could calculate logarithms in his head. That's like Elsa. She does these highly original designs of human eyes on richly patterned backgrounds, but there's nothing else there. I used to take her to New Jersey because I found it such an amusingly eerie reflection of our abominable culture, but although Elsa laughed with me, she secretly liked it. I discovered that when I asked her where she wanted to go for our honeymoon. "Las Vegas," she said, and she was serious. I offered her the whole of South America—I'd temporarily had Europe up to the eyeballs after my mandatory period of slavery as an army officer in Germany—I offered her Rio de Janeiro, all the Inca relics of Peru, even the chic coastal resorts of Chile, but she said no, Las Vegas, and please could we stay in a motel. Well, we did, and I have to concede it sure made New Jersey look tame. God, what a culture we have. It'll all get wiped out one day, of course. I give it fifty years. Of all the great empires the world has known, ours will be the shortest. Two hundred years of chasing the godalmighty dollar, and what do we produce? The A-bomb and *I Love Lucy*.

But I didn't mind Las Vegas because Elsa was so cute, dumb but cute, and I liked looking after her. I'd never had anyone to take care of before, because Cornelius always takes care of the people in our family. I liked having sex anytime I wanted it, too. Elsa never said no, and I was so pleased that she never seemed to mind that we saw little in Las Vegas except our motel bedroom. But after all, that's what honeymoons are for.

When we got settled in our new East Side apartment, I suggested we might as well have a baby and she said okay, so we did. No problems. I liked her being pregnant and I was pleased when the baby was a boy. I would have been pleased with a girl too, but I always think it's best to have the boy first so that he can take care of his sisters later. However, it turned out this boy was destined to have no sisters, because not long after the birth, something went wrong with Elsa's ovaries and the doctor said sorry, no more children. That was a pity. I liked this baby. It was red with black hair and it kept its eyes closed most of the time. It interested me. Probably I loved it, although the emotion I felt didn't feel like love in the usual sense. However, if anyone had tried to take the baby away I would have gone after the thief without thinking twice, clubbed him to pieces, and grabbed the baby back. Elsa moaned about how painful breast-feeding was and how her hemorrhoids were killing her, but the little baby lay snug in his crib, saying nothing stupid, a minute individual with a mind of his own. Smart, clever baby. Dumb, stupid Elsa. Poor Elsa. I was fond of her in many ways.

Half the trouble with Elsa was that her culture remained foreign to me. I tried hard to study it, but I found nothing to tie me emotionally to those Oriental aspects, and all the time I was conscious that I would always remain an outsider, the Gentile who had had the outrageous nerve to marry into the great House of Reischman. I was conscious too how different the Jews were, not inferior, not superior, but just different, different, different. They looked at the world from a different angle, saw history from a different point of view, and had different defense mechanisms for dealing with their vast collective consciousness of suffering and pain.

Of course it's misleading nowadays to make any generalizations about racial, cultural, and religious groups. In the old days when the groups were clearly defined, there was some excuse for it; Celts were redheads who wore mustaches, Anglo-Saxons were huge blonds, and so on, and such was the homogeneity which existed within each group that it was possible for an outsider to make certain intelligent generalizations that had a hope of being accurate. (Even so, one wonders about some of the more prejudiced remarks of historians like Caesar and Tacitus.) But nowadays we're all so intermarried that any generalization must surely be garbage, and any form of prejudice must be untenable from an anthropological as well as a moral point of view. However, that didn't stop the Reischmans from treating me as if I were a member of an inferior species, and that didn't stop me from beginning to wonder in despair if they were right.

My mother-in-law was no problem (I think she found me sexually attractive), but my father-in-law was a disaster. At first I thought he would make some effort to be pleasant to me, since Cornelius was one of his oldest friends, but evidently he had taken offense somewhere along the line around the time Elsa and I became engaged, and he behaved like a man who couldn't bear to set eyes on me because I reminded him of some deep personal hurt. Mother's rampant anti-Semitism had probably got to him in the end, and remembering some of the remarks she had handed out to me at my engagement, I wasn't one bit surprised.

With few exceptions the rest of the Reischmans were equally tough. Elsa had a younger brother, a good kid who found the home scene just as stultifying as I did, but the married sister in New Jersey was as dreary as her mother, and the Reischman relations were appalling. I'm not being anti-Semitic. Some of my Foxworth relations are appalling too, but at least I feel I can handle them because I know I'm just as good as they are.

I decided I had to learn to handle the Reischmans, and automatically I turned to my culture to sustain me. If the Jews could glorify the Passover and the Irish could swoon over Brian Boru in order to sustain them in hostile environments, surely I could discover some appropriate Anglo-Saxon skeleton in the closet! It was only then I realized I knew next to nothing about my remote ancestors. Having walloped Western civilization and come out on top, the Anglo-Saxons have no need to be interested in their early origins; why waste time picking over tribal myths when you can spend that time enjoying your position as top of the heap? Besides, the exquisitely civilized present, crammed as it is with privilege, snobbery, and power, is so much more entertaining than the violent, savage, distinctly murky past. Ah yes, I knew exactly what it was like to be a member of a privileged minority! But what the Reischmans succeeded in teaching me against all the odds was what hell it is to be a member of a persecuted race, and within six months of my marriage they had reduced me to a constantly simmering state of humiliation, mortification, and rage.

No wonder I felt I had to do something drastic. I fought back. Scott recommended a couple of books to me, and still livid that anyone should treat me as a second-class citizen, I embarked on some research. At this point I quickly forgot my rage. In fact I even felt grateful to my in-laws for propelling me into a study of the ancient races of the world and rekindling my interest in history.

I was sorry to discover that the Anglo-Saxons weren't entirely the villains their enemies would have everyone believe, but once I'd recovered from the disappointment of learning that they weren't just a bunch of lice-ridden louts who burned every Roman villa in sight, I enjoyed making their acquaintance. I was particularly excited by the story of King Alfred, the greatest Saxon of them all. He was the youngest of four sons, and when he was a kid he did nothing but shit at the wrong moment, so people probably thought he was dumb, but Alfred, underestimated Alfred, battled away against the invading Danes until he emerged not just king of Wessex, his own homestead, but king of England, king of the whole damned heap. He admired culture, taught himself to read at thirty-eight, and developed intellectual tastes which would have put most Americans to shame. Yes, I liked Alfred. I liked him very much, and in my new role of persecuted Anglo-Saxon I clung to the memory of his glory.

When my son was born I was informed by the Reischmans without so much as a "by your leave" or an "if you don't mind" that the baby was to be named Jacob Isaac.

"Forget it," I said. I probably sounded like a Nazi, but I wasn't. I'd married a Jewish girl willingly and had been delighted to do so.

It's true I don't care for the names Jacob and Isaac but I like the name Jake very much despite all my father-in-law's attempts to transform it into a dirty word. However, no one on earth, Jewish or Gentile, is going to wave the flag of prejudice in front of my eyes by dictating to me what I should call my son.

"His name's going to be Alfred," I said firmly at the inevitable interview with Jake Reischman.

"Alfred?" said the proud grandfather in disbelief. "*Alfred?* But what kind of a name's that?"

"Saxon," I said. "This is a matter of cultural, religious, and racial pride."

I thought he was going to have apoplexy. Jake is a pale man with eyes the color of blue ice, but he went bright red. At last he spluttered, "Is this some kind of joke?"

"No, sir. I come from a great race and I want my son to be proud of it. Alfred triumphed over the heathen Danes to keep England Christian. He was a great guy."

"My people," said Jake, maddened into making a big mistake, "were cultured when Alfred's forebears were illiterate savages shouting insults at Caesar across the Rhine."

"Your people," I said, "were itinerant parasites. Mine built the world."

"Why, you—"

"Exactly!" I said violently. "Now you know how I feel when you treat me like dirt! I feel mad and want to say all kinds of dumb obscenities like that remark, which we both know is the most disgusting bullshit. I would never have said it if you hadn't looked down on the name Alfred. Now, you listen to me. I'm willing to respect your culture but I'm damned if this respect is going to be a one-sided affair. You've got to give me some respect too, and you can start by respecting the fact that I'm the father of this baby. I'll call him Jacob as well as Alfred, but only on condition you treat me with the respect I deserve."

There was a silence before Jake said, "And his religion?"

"Christian. It's my right to choose, not yours."

"Elsa—"

"Elsa," I said, "will do as I say." I paused to let this sink in before I added, "If all goes well and I'm finally made to feel welcome in this house, I'll see he gets proper instruction in the Jewish culture. If not, forget it. You'll have a totally Gentile grandson whom you won't see too often."

There was another silence, but at last Jake said pleasantly, "I see. Yes. Ah, I've just remembered that one of the Seligmans was called Alfred—and of course there was Alfred Heidelbach of Heidelbach, Ickelheimer . . . A good German name! What are we quarreling about? What a tempest in a teapot!"

Jake was a smart old bastard and he had my measure then, all right. He probably had me figured out better than Cornelius did, although Cornelius was getting there slowly, groping his way along. After that incident Jake and I got along much better, because he respected me for standing up to him. You've got to stand up to that kind of people, and when I say "that kind of people" I don't mean the Jews. I mean people like the Bar Harbor Brotherhood, men Paul Van Zale marked for worldly success. You've got to talk to those people in their own language, but I can speak that language when I want to, and all the words are right there in my head.

They say Paul Van Zale often picked out unlikely protégés, people others would have overlooked.

I think he would have picked out someone like Alfred of Wessex.

I think he would have picked out me.

February 26. I go to see Vicky. She's been in the hospital two weeks and she's due to leave tomorrow, which is why I picked tonight to call. I've stayed away until now. I didn't want to see her with a load of other visitors, but I figure no one will be around just before she's discharged. They'll all wait till she goes home.

Vicky has a private room at Doctors Hospital and it's full of brightly colored flowers, as if people were determined to compensate her for the nauseous riot she missed at the funeral. I like flowers, but they should be in gardens where they belong—or if not in gardens, they should at least be out-of-doors, like the magnolia tree in the back patio at One Willow Street. That magnolia blossom's beautiful in the spring.

Like Vicky.

Vicky's wearing a white nightgown trimmed with white lace and her hair is held back from her face by a white band. She's very surprised to see me and not one bit pleased, although she pretends she is, to be polite.

"Sebastian! How sweet of you to come, but you needn't have bothered."

"Right." I pull up a chair and sit down by the bed. I don't ask her how she is. That's a stupid question. Obviously she's miserable. I don't say I'm sorry about Sam. She probably feels ready to scream by this time if one more person says that to her, and anyway I wrote her a note the day he died. "Dear Vicky: I'm very sorry. Sam will be missed by many people. Best, Sebastian."

I give her a little book of John Donne's poems. No flowers or chocolates or magazines. I wouldn't bring Vicky what everyone else brings, because unlike everyone else, I've spent great care choosing the gift and taken time to ensure it's not meaningless.

"Know Donne?" I say to her.

"I've heard of him, of course," she says carelessly. "Yes, I think I read a couple of his poems ages ago."

"They should read Donne more in school instead of going on and on and on about Shakespeare. I met a guy once who had had to spend two years in school studying *Hamlet*. Such things should be banned by law. Two years of picking over *Hamlet* would make even Shakespeare hate *Hamlet*. The class could have been reading Donne for part of those two years instead. Nowadays when you say 'poet' you think of some sloppy beatnik bumming around California, but in those days the word 'poet' really meant something. You said 'literature' and what you meant was poetry, and poetry was communication. Donne communicated. As a writer he's strong and tough with a terrific grasp of syntax and a mind which has triumphed over the inadequacies of language. Language is hell, and most people are incapable of expressing their feelings verbally, but Donne made language the mirror of his mind. Language isn't futile with Donne. Language lives."

She looks at me with wide gray eyes. I've never seen Vicky look so astonished. She thinks I'm a gorilla, unable to string more than a couple of sentences together. She thinks I really do like drive-in movies about werewolves.

"Oh," she says awkwardly at last. "That sounds great. Thanks. I'll read the book."

I look at the magazine on the table. There's a book there too, a spy novel, a modern fairy tale for people bent on escape from the hell of being modern.

"Kevin Daly's got a new play coming on Broadway next month," I said. "You like Kevin's plays, don't you?"

"Yes, most of them."

"Want to see the new play? I'll take you, if you like."

She looks wary. "With Elsa?"

"No, Elsa doesn't understand Kevin's plays. She thinks they're just about married couples being polite to each other when they should be having a fight."

"But wouldn't it look odd if you took me without Elsa?"

"No. Why shouldn't I give my stepsister an evening out after she's been through all this hell, and if she wants to go to a play Elsa wouldn't enjoy, what's wrong with Elsa staying home?"

I see her swallow hastily at this reminder of her bereavement. I at once blot out the image of her going to bed with Sam—an easy exercise in willpower for me, since I've had nine years' hard practice at perfecting the art—but I still look at her and wonder what kind of a mess he made of her life. If I could open up Vicky's head and take a look inside, I suspect I'd be reminded of a ball of wool which has been pushed around for hours by a couple of cats. Before the ball of wool is fit for use again, the whole complicated muddle has to be unraveled and rewound correctly by someone who cares enough to produce the patience needed for the job, but Sam Keller was not a patient man. He just hadn't the time. He was too busy trying to prove things both to himself and to other people; he tried to prove he was smarter than Cornelius (he wasn't) and just as tough as any blue-blooded Eastern Seaboard aristocrat (he was) and just as anti-Hitler as Churchill, FDR, and Uncle Joe Stalin (he didn't fool me), but the truth was he was just a hardworking son of a bitch with no imagination, no intellectual interests, no independence (Cornelius had bought him lock, stock, and barrel years before), and no taste for unraveling balls of wool. He used to boast about how he could reassemble television sets ("It takes a machine to make a machine," quipped some wag at the office in the days before ethnic jokes became repugnant to me), but I suspected that when it came to reassembling his own wife, he wouldn't have had any idea where to begin.

"Well," Vicky's saying doubtfully, "it's nice of you to want to take me to the theater, of course, Sebastian, but—"

The door opens. In walks Cornelius. I might have guessed he couldn't let even one evening go by without treating Vicky as if she were Electra. Those Greeks knew what went on in families, all right. I admire the Greeks. Too bad they got so civilized they fell to pieces, but that seems to be the destiny of man no matter whether he's part of a superb classical civilization or a modern junk culture: work hard, get rich, wallow in luxury, and go to pieces. Cornelius, that arch-representative of our materialistic society, certainly looks as if he's about to fall apart, although as we all know at One Willow Street, you couldn't dent him with a diamond cutter. But he's probably the last of his line to escape decadence. Vicky's sons will grow up to become disciples of Jack Kerouac—or whatever *Time* magazine will call the Beat Generation of the late '60s. The name will change but the scenery won't: a lot of drugs and inertia and everyone dying all over the place of boredom.

"Hi," says Cornelius to me after he's slobbered over Vicky.

"Hi."

He waits for me to leave. I stay. We all think automatically of that stupid incident years ago at Bar Harbor when he made such a disgusting scene. I was sitting in the sun by the pool and reading a book, Eliot's *The Waste Land* it was—I remember because I was far too young and ignorant to grasp all the allusions—and I was just looking up at the view when Vicky came down from the house for a swim. I didn't swim anymore in daylight by that time because I hated people noticing how hairy I was. I don't mind being hairy, but I hate people staring. One of the nicest things about Elsa is that she likes me being hairy. She says it's sexy. No one ever said that to me before or behaved as if it could possibly be true.

Vicky's wearing a navy-blue swimsuit, all in one piece, but it's too small for her now and she flows over the top of it. She's beautiful, fourteen years old, like Juliet, and I know just how that poor bastard Romeo must have felt.

Well, she sits down with her back to me as if I don't exist, dangles her legs in the water, and gazes out to sea. I have an erection and it's damned uncomfortable, so I unbutton my pants and shift around trying to adjust myself and the wicker chair squeaks and Vicky glances over her shoulder to see what all the fuss is about.

Disaster. Tears and scenes. Mother looks at me as if men's genitals were the most disgusting thing ever invented, but she tries to stand up for me. Fat chance. Cornelius has hysterics and treats me like a rapist, and I have to spend the rest of the summer with some Foxworth cousins whom I loathe. Finally Cornelius calms down, realizes he's been behaving like a Freudian casebook, and makes us all swear to put the incident behind us. Except, of course, we never do.

Vicky's mixed up about sex, that's for sure, but it wasn't me who made her that way. Any normal girl, confronted with her stepbrother messing around with his fly in a fever of embarrassment, would just have said, irritated, "What on earth are you doing?" Or maybe, if she was shy, she would have averted her eyes and pretended not to notice. But to have hysterics and run sobbing to Daddy is not normal, and when I look back on the incident again now, it makes me wonder afresh how she really got along with Sam Keller. Everyone keeps saying what a fantastic marriage they had and how they were such an advertisement for married bliss, but I wonder. I wonder very much.

"Well, thanks for stopping by, Sebastian," says Vicky, giving me the brush-off—not because she wants to be rid of me but because she can see Daddy wants to be alone with her, and Vicky always tries to give Daddy what he wants. "And thanks for the book. That was sweet of you."

I'm tempted to kiss her, just to scare Cornelius, but I don't. I touch her left hand, which is lying on top of the sheet, and say, "So long."

I don't bother to ask her what she's going to do when she leaves the hospital. I know what's going to happen. Cornelius is going to sell the Kellers' home in Westchester, ship all four kids and the nurses downtown to Fifth Avenue, and rake Vicky back into the family compound. Cornelius is going to take over as usual and go right on making a mess of his daughter's life.

But I love Vicky and I'm going to save her. Cornelius thinks he has the whole problem sewn up because I'm safely married off, but he's wrong. Cornelius is a smart guy, but where Vicky's concerned, his head's so buzzing with Greek drama that he can't think straight.

But I think straight. You're living in a fool's paradise, Cornelius. Your problem's only just beginning.

March 6. Cornelius says, "Scott's lunching with Jake today to straighten out that muddle over Pan-Pacific Harvester."

Something's happened between Jake and Cornelius, but no one knows what it is. For various pragmatic financial reasons, Reischman's and Van Zale's still do business together, but anyone can see the old informal partnership is dying on its feet for lack of sentimental affection. Jake and Cornelius will no longer deal with each

other in person, and whenever they meet by some unfortunate accident at a social occasion, they're exquisitely quiet and polite, like two
old Chinese mandarins. Rumor's rife about the cause of the rift, but
so far no one's improved on my theory that the trouble began with
my engagement to Elsa. The anti-Semitic talk that got flung around
then had to be heard to be believed, and knowing the Reischmans,
I'll bet there was plenty of unforgivable anti-Gentile talk being flung
around at the same time.

"Jake himself is having lunch with Scott?" I say to Cornelius.
Jake, whose reputation as a difficult man increases daily on Wall
Street, can be guaranteed to find fault with any of Cornelius' deputies, and after a couple of meetings he always appoints deputies of
his own to deal with them. The last I heard, he had refused to deal
with Scott (appointed after Sam's death to be the liaison man with
Reischman's) on the grounds that Scott was too young. Anyone
would think Scott was a vacuous teenager, but Scott is almost thirty-
nine, and very, very experienced. "I thought Jake had appointed Phil
to deal with Scott," I say, surprised.

"Jake fired Phil."

"Tough on Phil," I say laconically, picturing the head rolling into
the basket. "What did he do?"

Cornelius shrugs. Purges are of no interest to him unless he's signing the death warrant.

But he and Jake are a dying breed. Major private investment-
banking houses are becoming an institution of the past because nowadays it pays to incorporate the firm for tax purposes, and although
the new corporation president will try to be just as dictatorial as he
was when he was senior partner, he's held in better check by the
board. People's attitudes have changed, too; the war and a changing
employment picture have encouraged a man to think twice before he
places his career in the hands of an autocrat, and the board of a corporation offers not only a greater degree of security to the postwar
banker but a bigger slice of the pie.

"The point is," Cornelius is saying, "that Jake's obviously decided
to give Scott a second chance. And not only that, he's taking Scott to
lunch and he's suggested that you come along as well. He knows
you've been helping Scott over this PPH mess."

"Okay," I say, still laconic, but I'm excited, because Jake normally never lunches with anyone who's not a full partner. This invitation is a big step up for me, and Cornelius knows it—he knows Jake

would never have bothered with me, even though I'm his son-in-law, unless he believed I was worth bothering about.

I decide it's time to soft-pedal a few facts that Cornelius may have overlooked.

"Jake knows I'll be thirty next year," I said. "He knows I'm not just a kid anymore."

"Uh-huh."

"Jake told me he was made a partner in Reischman's on his thirtieth birthday."

"I remember it well!" Cornelius pretends to be nostalgic, but underneath, he's thinking hard. "And that reminds me, Sebastian—I was planning on discussing this with you later, but since the subject's come up . . ."

I'm offered a partnership. I accept.

"Well done!" says Scott, who's ten years my senior and has been a partner for some time.

He seems genuinely pleased, but what are you after, Scott? You're just about the smartest guy in the bank, aside from me and Cornelius, and Cornelius likes you very much, far more than he likes me. I like you too, but there's something strange about you, Scott Sullivan. It's not just that you don't drink, don't smoke, and live alone in some hermit's cell which no one is ever invited to see, and it's not just that you're so obsessed with medieval literature that you turn up your nose when I try to introduce you to a twentieth-century masterpiece like the *Four Quartets*. I'm not disturbed by your asceticism, because you're never priggish enough to flaunt your questionable virtues, and I'm certainly not disturbed by your intellectual tastes, eccentric though they may be, because they make it possible for me to communicate with you. In fact, it's a treat for me to talk to someone who's not excruciatingly dumb, but much as I like you, I'm becoming increasingly aware that there's something about you that doesn't add up. For instance, you sit around talking garbage about chastity giving a man superhuman strength, but you never explain the root of this unhealthy fascination with abstinence, never explain why you feel this superhuman strength is so necessary to you. Anyway, I don't believe you're chaste. I think that when you go on your vacations to Mexico, California, or Alaska you let off steam in the biggest possible way. Do I believe this just because I myself find celibacy inconceivable? Maybe, but I don't think so. I notice the spark in you when you return from your vacations, and I doubt if that's solely generated by lying in the sun.

But what does all this mean?

I don't know, but I do know that I've begun to watch you, Scott Sullivan. I'm watching you, and I'm going to find out.

Easter, 1958. Something's going on between Mother and Cornelius. They keep touching each other and exchanging little smiles. If the woman was anyone else but Mother, I'd say Cornelius was getting a piece of some very exciting action. Can two people pushing fifty who have been married for nearly thirty years possibly have anything approaching an exciting sex life—or indeed any sex life at all? It seems incredible, but what am I to think? There he goes, smiling at her again as if she's the sexiest woman since Mae West batted her eyelashes at Cary Grant, although God knows my mother is the last person to remind me of Mae West. Mother looks as if men's genitals might possibly be a good invention after all. How inconceivable it is to think of one's parents having sex. Surely Mother must be frigid, but now I'm probably the one who's being Freudian, playing Oedipus to Mother's Jocasta—or should it be Orestes to Mother's Clytemnestra? At least when Oedipus got so screwed up he didn't know Jocasta was his mother. I must get hold of a translation of Aeschylus and reread the *Oresteia,* along with the Theban plays of Sophocles. I might learn something.

Vicky's a bit out in the cold because of this raging love affair which is going on between our parents. She's quiet, probably appreciating the chance to relax. I take a look at her kids as the Easter celebrations roar on around us. There's a very cute little girl called Samantha whom everyone spoils shamelessly. The other girl, Kristin, is plain like Sam but cheerful. The two boys, who arrived back in the States too shy to say a word, are now noisy and ill-behaved, but Cornelius seems to think they should be allowed to scuffle in corners, break precious porcelain, and eat with their fingers at table. "Boys will be boys!" says Cornelius cheerfully. He never said that when Andrew and I knocked one of his Kandinskys off a wall during a fight. I wonder if he's going to be silly about these grandsons, so silly that he'll act out of his shrewd tough character. No, I'll pay Cornelius the compliment of saying that it would be impossible for him to be really stupid where the bank's concerned. If the boys are a dead loss, he'll write them off.

What are the boys like? Impossible to tell. They ought to be bright if heredity means anything. Eric might make the grade; the blond curls give him a vague resemblance to Vicky. But Paul might be smarter. Have to wait and see.

Vicky's having another baby, Mother says. Damn. That means Vicky will be wrapped up in reproduction till the end of summer. But maybe that's okay; it means it'll be considered harmless for me to take her out. Nobody goes around seducing pregnant women—except Cornelius, of course, when he took Mother away from Dad, but then, we all know Cornelius is capable of anything.

Easter isn't usually such a big family scene as Thanksgiving, but this year Andrew's got extra leave for some reason, so he and Lori have brought the kids east again for a vacation. The kids are all happy and normal, just like Andrew, and Lori's normal too, discussing fashion with Mother and telling her about the course she's taking in French cooking. Can people conceivably be that normal? Apparently.

"How are you doing?" I say skeptically to Andrew after everyone's stuffed themselves with roast turkey at lunch on Easter Sunday and heaved themselves out of the dining room.

"Swell. There's this fantastic new plane . . ."

God, Andrew's boring. He probably thinks I'm boring too.

"And how are you doing, old buddy?" he says cheerily, clapping me on the shoulder. "Still bumming around counting nickels and dimes?"

Andrew's grown up in this celebrated banking family and yet I do believe he still thinks Van Zale's is a commercial bank. There *is* a commercial Van Zale's, the Van Zale Manhattan Trust, and the two banks work hand in glove but I'm an investment banker channeling the public's capital into long-term investment for the benefit of the great corporations, not a teller cashing checks for some two-bit client on a weekly wage.

"I'm okay," I say to Andrew. What else can one say to someone so dumb? How does one communicate with such mindlessness?

He starts talking about some Foxworth cousins of ours. All the Foxworths love Andrew. I guess Andrew takes after Dad, and that's why he fits in so well with Dad's family. Dad must have been a fool too, giving up banking for politics, exchanging the fascinating world of economics for the plastic world of vote-catching in pursuit of a power that is largely illusory. Power attracts me, I have to admit it, but not a politician's power. That kind of power is puny when compared with the power wielded by the top members of the financial community who run this country's economy.

However, I'm not in banking just for the power, like Cornelius, and I'm certainly not in it just for the money and social status, like Sam Keller. My maternal grandfather left me a pile of money and I was born into what used to be described as the Yankee aristocracy. I'm in banking because I like it. I like figures. I like the challenge of working out a complicated deal. And I'm good at it. I may not have Sam Keller's synthetic charm or Cornelius' brutal streak, but I have something which I suspect neither of them ever had, a true financial brain.

If I say I like money, that conveys the wrong impression; one thinks of a miser hoarding coins under the bed or some materialistic hero of our modern culture chasing the godalmighty dollar, but I like the abstract nature of money and its mathematical properties, I like the absorbing variations of economic theory, and last but not least I like the challenges which few people in our rich plastic society care to confront: the endless confrontations between money and morality, battles which can only increase one's philosophical speculations on the ultimate value, purpose, and even reality of immense wealth as it exists today in the black chaotic doomsday world of our appalling twentieth century.

I'm not a philosopher. But philosophy interests me. (Only people like Cornelius call it a parlor game for eggheads.) And I'm no dehumanized ape. I'm tired of watching billions of dollars being spent on ways to make people die. I'm tired of watching the privileged citizens of the richest country in the world wallowing in mindless luxury while millions live in a poverty-stricken hell. I wouldn't say so out loud, of course; people would call me an "idealist," class me as "irresponsible," and ensure my career ended "tragically" (generous severance pay after inevitable nervous breakdown), but sometimes I dream of being president of a bank which tries to channel wealth not only into the poor countries but also to the people below the poverty line right here in America, *my* America, the America I love all the time I'm hating it, the America I care for enough to criticize, the America not of the A-bomb and *I Love Lucy* but the America of the Marshall Plan.

"My, you're quiet today!" says my noisy brother, clapping me on the back jovially again as if he were a candidate in an upcoming election and I were a recalcitrant voter. Again I'm reminded of my father. I guess my father was fond of me, but primarily he only made such a fuss about getting custody because he wanted to pay Mother back for running off with Cornelius, and he used to get irritated when I missed her so much. Mother loved me when no one else did, I'll say that for her. I love Mother too, deep down, but she drives me crazy. Mothers should guard against becoming obsessed with their children, but poor Mother, I can't get angry with her just because she uses me to fill some emotional lack in her life. Marriage with Cornelius can't always be a bed of roses. Mother thinks she understands me, but she doesn't, and I don't truly understand her either, although I sense she's often unhappy and that makes me automatically mad at Cornelius. Mother and I aren't alike, although once she said I did take after her side of the family. She said I reminded her of her father, Dean Blaise, who was once head of the investment-banking firm of Blaise, Bailey, Ludlow, and Adams. He died when I was six, but I remember him clearly. He used to sit glowering at his dinner guests, and if anyone was reckless enough to make some dumb remark, he would growl, "Damn stupid hogwash!" He was a big man on Wall Street. They say he was one of the few men who could give Paul Van Zale as good as he got. A tough guy. Smart. Hope I'm like him.

"So when are you and Elsa going to have number two?" Andrew's saying brightly.

"Mind your own business."

"Okay, okay, okay! Jesus, you're as prickly as an old grizzly! I just wanted to show some interest, that's all. Say, isn't it great being a father? I just love it! I like playing cowboys and Indians again and fixing up Chuck's train set . . ."

Scott comes to rescue me. He's part of the family as Aunt Emily's stepson, and he always takes at least one main meal with us during these family gatherings.

He talks to Andrew. He asks Andrew how he feels when he's cruising at twenty thousand feet.

"Great!" says Andrew happily. "I look at the ground and think, gee! Somewhere down there Chuck's playing with his train set and Lori's preparing some wonderful French meal, and Nurse is changing the baby's diaper . . ."

Scott somehow manages to keep the conversation going. How he does it, I don't know. God, Scott's a smart guy.

382

"You ought to get married, Scott!" says Andrew with enthusiasm. "It's just wonderful!"

Mother, slinking up behind him, stands on tiptoe to give him a kiss. "It's lovely you're so happy, darling!"

They stand there, thinking how wonderful marriage is, while I wonder again what the hell's happened between her and Cornelius to trigger this marital renaissance. I wish Mother wouldn't dye her hair. Elsa joins us with the baby. Poor Scott must be feeling wiped out by all this marital bliss.

"Hi," I say to Elsa, giving her a reassuring smile. Easter at the Van Zale mansion makes Elsa feel like an outsider, so I try not to feel irritated when she follows me around as if she's terrified to let me out of her sight. "Hi, Alfred!" I add, giving him my finger to clasp. Alfred's seven months old and he flays around making noises as he attempts to get what he wants. Alfred's trying to communicate and he's discovered how dumb most adults are. It must be hell to be a baby. Everyone thinks it must be so wonderful to do nothing except eat, sleep, and play, but think how traumatic it must be when you have so much trouble making yourself understood.

Alfred's wriggling in Elsa's arms. He pushes my fingers away.

"Put him down, Elsa. He wants to be free."

Alfred tries hard to crawl away across the floor.

"Boy, he's cute!" says Andrew good-naturedly.

Cute! Alfred's smarter than all Andrew's kids put together.

Vicky's sitting on the couch at the far end of the long room, well away from all the kids who are running around trying to kill each other. I stroll over to her just as Mother tells the nurses to remove everyone under ten to the nursery.

"Getting sick of the big family occasion?" I say.

Vicky looks up. Suddenly she smiles. My guts feel weak, as if I were responding to some folk memory of King Alfred's uncertain bowels. "Of course not!" she says. "It's lovely to see the family together."

She means just the opposite. It's exhausting, boring, and irrelevant to the true meaning of Easter. She knows that as well as I do, but she's locked up in the classic social dilemma of feeling obliged to say one thing while she privately thinks another. I try to bust through her psychological shackles by saying, "I've got tickets for Kevin's new play. It'll do you good to get out of this place and defrost those brains you've been keeping on ice for so long."

She smiles uncertainly. "Maybe it would. Thanks. Daddy said only the other day that it would do me good to get out—he even asked me to join him and Alicia for dinner at the Colony, but I didn't want to go. I felt it would be . . . well, an intrusion."

"Noticed, have you?"

"Of course! It's so obvious. But why do I also feel it's so bizarre?"

"I'm just rereading Sophocles and Aeschylus to find out. Have supper with me after the theater and I'll tell you why we can't stand the sight of our parents frolicking around as if sex had just been invented."

She laughs. My guts feel weaker than ever.

"Okay," she says. "I'll be looking forward to it."

The play interests me. It's about an Irish-American political boss at the turn of the century, and I guess it must be based on Kevin's father, who pulled a lot of political strings in Massachusetts in those days.

Luxuriating in the trappings of power, the boss is appalled to discover that the road to power is the road to isolation—and finally to a death of the spirit, a death in life, the ultimate human hell. This guy can only communicate through exercising his power, but paradoxically, the exercise of his power precludes true communication. He loses his friends, his wife, and eventually the election. The last scene shows him with his mistress and ends not with words but with silence.

"Why doesn't he say something?" says some moron in the row behind us.

I have a terrible feeling the play will be a box-office flop. A large proportion of the Broadway-theater audience can only handle musicals and farces, and perhaps a large proportion of them too dislike being reminded of their own emotional failures, which Kevin dissects with such honesty. The critics may go on praising Kevin, but some impresario who holds the purse strings will probably tell him to stop writing in blank verse and throw in a happy ending to keep the morons happy.

I wish I could tell Kevin how great an instrument his verse is. I wish I could tell him not only to stand up to the impresario but to those critics who say that such twentieth-century conversation as "Have you a light for my cigarette?" inevitably renders blank verse bathetic and obsolete. Kevin's not Eliot and he's not Fry, but he's one of the few English-speaking dramatists who dare to strive for literary elegance by shouldering the discipline of meter. He should be encouraged over and over again. He should be cheered on by all those who care about twentieth-century drama.

By one of those strange coincidences which make one almost believe in idiotic words like "destiny" and "fate," we bump into Kevin himself outside the theater. He's with some handsome young actor and they're on their way to Sardi's. I know I have only a few seconds to express myself, so I grope for the words to thank him for all those hours and hours he must have spent toiling over his play. Just to say "thank you" would be inane, of course. To say "I liked your play very much" would sound as if I really hated it but wanted to be polite. I've got to praise it but I can't just say something meaningless like "It was great!" I've got to say something no one else would think of saying; I've got to pull something electrifying out of my vocabulary. It doesn't matter if I exaggerate. So long as I hit the right original note, he'll see straight through to the core of what I want to say.

"It was a triumph over language," I say. "You remind me of John Donne."

"My God!" gasps Kevin. "Why the hell aren't you the theater critic of the *New York Times!*"

The actor's laughing, but Kevin, sparkling as ever, just exclaims, "Pay no attention to him! He probably thinks John Donne was one of the signers of the Declaration of Independence—perhaps related to Thomas Jefferson on the distaff side! Look, for God's sake join us for a drink—Vicky, persuade Sebastian!"

"We'll take a rain check," I say, smiling at him, "because we're on our way to eat. But thanks, Kevin."

"Then come down to the Village and see me sometime," says Kevin urgently over his shoulder, and the actor looks annoyed, but he doesn't understand. The actor's like Elsa. He'll never understand how exciting it is for Kevin to be compared with a poet who's been dead for over three hundred years.

We've communicated.

"Kevin's so attractive!" sighs Vicky. "What a waste!"

"It's love itself that's important," I say. "It doesn't matter how you love or whom you love, just so long as you're capable of loving, because if you're incapable of loving, you die. That's an Ingmar Bergman theme. Have you seen any Bergman movies?"

"No. Sam only liked westerns and thrillers."

We go to Le Chanteclair on East Forty-ninth Street and have onion soup, *ris de veau,* and a bottle of white burgundy.

"It's so nice to have French wine," says Vicky, remembering all the years of hock with Sam and California hooch with Cornelius.

We talk about our parents.

"What do you think happened?"

"We'll never know."

"Isn't it *odd!*"

"Maybe it's not so odd," I say. "We know so little of what goes on in other people's lives."

"True." She looks nervous suddenly.

"Everyone puts up such a front."

"Yes," she says, her eyes dark with memory. "They do."

I quickly switch the conversation back to the play, and I soon realize she's understood every line of it. It's wonderful to be able to talk to a woman whose conversation isn't confined to her home, her kids, and the latest mink she's picked up at Bergdorf Goodman.

I take her home. I don't touch her.

"Say, Vicky, let's do this again. It was fun."

"Well, I . . . Sebastian, this evening was just great, such a change, but—"

"It's okay, isn't it?" I say carelessly. "I'm just the stepbrother safely married off. You're the pregnant widow. If Cornelius reads into this what he read into that goddamned idiotic scene at Bar Harbor, he'd need to be certified."

"Oh . . ." She's embarrassed. "Well . . ."

"Of course I'll bet you don't give a damn now what happened all those years ago," I say swiftly. "You've lived with a man for nine years and you know how easily men get aroused by the sight of pretty girls in swimsuits. And you know too, just as I know, that it wasn't you that aroused me—I mean *you*—Vicky. It was just the sight of a female body seminude. It was certainly no big deal, no bigger than the sight of a fat lady salivating outside a bake-shop window, and you couldn't have less of a big deal than that."

Her serious strained expression suddenly fades. She laughs. "You mean I was no more important than a sugared doughnut?"

"No, you've always been important to me, Vicky. It was the incident itself which was so breathtakingly trivial."

She thinks it over carefully. She probably hasn't allowed herself to face the memory in its entirety since she was fourteen. I wait. I don't rush her. This is very important.

"Yes, I guess you're right," she says offhandedly at last. She can't quite bring herself to look at me, but her voice is calm. "What a fuss about nothing, wasn't it?"

These are brave words, a splendid funeral oration over a corpse we can now duly bury and smother with flowers. I still don't touch her, but I want to very much. I want to let her know how much I care about her. But I don't want to let her know that my one desire at this very moment is to undress her and kiss her and make love to her all night.

Vicky needs time, and I'm going to give it to her. I want her to know I have all the patience in the world.

"Okay, Vicky," I say casually as I leave her at her father's house. "So long. I'll call you." But underneath those casual words I'm very, very excited. The foundations of my dreams have just been hammered into a base of granite, and now at last I can start to visualize the house I've wanted so long to build.

At home Elsa's sitting humped up in bed and looking like the wrath of God—her God, the one who's so mean the whole damned time, the God who sent ten plagues one after the other to make life hell for the Egyptians. The older I get the sorrier I feel for Pharaoh.

"So where were you?" she says, staring at me with her father's pale eyes. "What happened?"

"Where do you think I was? In bed knocking up a pregnant woman?"

"Sex is all you think about," she says, wiping away a tear.

"Sex is all you want me to think about," I say, and slam away until she's too breathless to complain anymore.

"Oh, Sebastian!" she says, cuddling up to me afterward. "Sorry I was so mad at you."

I like Elsa. She's warm and soft and cozy. I like her best of all when I'm in bed with her, and she probably likes me best of all there too. I'm not talking about sex exactly, or love, but just that good comfortable feeling you get when you're close to someone you know is your friend.

Elsa goes to sleep, large body still pressing against mine and reminding me how soft and warm and feminine she is. I lie awake in the dark. I see no conflict in the future. I'm not interested in marrying Vicky. Marriage is just part of the front you put up for society. It took me awhile to realize that, but Cornelius spelled it out for me in the end. "I don't pick my partners from maladjusted neurotics who are incapable of leading normal lives," he said. I got the message. To get on in life you have to make everyone believe you're normal and well-adjusted. Of course, practically no one is, particularly on Wall Street, but that's not the point. The point is that everyone has to pretend that everyone outside a mental home is some kind of robot with "NORMAL" stamped on its forehead. When you get married you're flashing a sign saying "NORMAL, NORMAL!" and everyone stops worrying about you. You settle down, provide your wife with a nice home, start a family, and order champagne and flowers on each wedding anniversary. "NORMAL, NORMAL!" trill the little signals, communicating to the world that you're a regular guy.

I shift closer to Elsa in the dark and think how nice she is. We'll be married forever, Elsa and I, no fuss, no mess. There couldn't be any fuss, because if there was, the Reischmans would grab Alfred.

Nobody's taking Alfred away from me.

But Vicky's going to be part of my life too. Vicky won't want marriage. Vicky's had marriage, had it up to the hilt. I know Vicky and I understand her better than anyone else does.

We'll have what in the old days would have been described as a liaison. That's a good word. It conjures up images of brilliant women reclining on couches, like Madame Récamier. Paul Van Zale had a liaison for about thirty years with a woman called Elizabeth Clayton, who's dead now. His wife knew about it, and so did her husband, but everyone accepted the arrangement and lived with it. It wasn't normal, but they all worked so hard to make their marriages look respectable that the abnormality was overlooked.

My marriage will always be very presentable. Elsa won't like the liaison at first. There'll be tears and scenes, but she'll never get around the fact that she's a fat homely girl who's unlikely to attract another man, so although she'll be furious for a while, she'll calm down once she realizes I intend to stay with her and put up an acceptable facade to the world. We'll go on sending out those little signals trilling "NORMAL, NORMAL!" and nobody will look at her askance.

Vicky will go on living with Daddy so that Daddy can fulfill his ambition to take over the kids, but I'll lease an apartment somewhere, Sutton Place maybe, and she'll meet me there whenever we want to be alone. We'll fix up the apartment ourselves. We'll have a bed with black satin sheets in a room with a white furry carpet. I like black and white together. Erotic. I'll try to find a couple of Beardsley drawings, black and white, for the walls. No, not Beardsley. Too decadent. Something with a good clear line, something pure. A Japanese woodcut, perhaps. Or a sketch of a naked woman by Picasso.

Vicky can fix up the living room, but we'll choose the books together. Lots of poetry. All the usual people plus *Beowulf* in the original. It doesn't matter that neither of us can read Anglo-Saxon and that *Beowulf* is one of the most difficult poems ever created. We'll have it on our bookshelf for the same reason that the Romans kept busts of their ancestors in the atrium. And we must bring in Bede too, to keep Beowulf company. I still have the translation Scott recommended when I was feeling like a member of a persecuted race. I wonder if Vicky knows that famous passage about the sparrow in the lighted hall.

I think of Scott, talking about Bede.

Scott's the great anomaly, of course. He's the exception that proves the rule about people having to get married to prove how normal they are. He gets away with breaking the rule because he somehow manages to give the impression that he's as normal as all-American apple pie, but he's not normal, not by a long shot. The more I think about Scott, the more brilliant I think he is. In fact he's so brilliant he makes my scalp prickle. He's everything Cornelius detests: one, unmarried; two, an intellectual; three, celibate (mostly); and four, Steve Sullivan's son. Yet Cornelius thinks Scott's the cat's whiskers.

I don't like that at all. It's creepy. But is it dangerous to me? I don't see how it can be. Cornelius is never going to give a controlling interest in the bank to any son of his old enemy Steve Sullivan, so my future ought to be as safe as a diamond in a vault stuffed with security guards, but all the same I don't like Scott being the cat's whiskers at the bank. Maybe I should let Cornelius realize that, but no, it would be better to keep my mouth shut. If I try to clip the cat's whiskers at this stage, someone might try to clip my wings.

What's Cornelius going to think of my liaison with Vicky? He won't like it, but Mother will. Mother'll love it, and Cornelius will want to keep Mother happy, particularly as they're now having themselves such a ball again in the bedroom.

God, that's weird.

Elsa moans softly in her sleep, and I put my arm around her comfortingly. I like you, Elsa, I'm lucky to have you. Thanks for making everyone think I'm such a nice normal regular guy. . . .

Saturday, June 7, 1958. Scott and I play squash at the club, and I win. We shower and I have a couple of beers while he drinks Coke.

". . . so the question is," says Scott, "does the English legend of Childe Roland really have any connection with Charlemagne's nephew Roland, the hero of the famous *Chanson de Geste?*"

"How can there not be a connection? If you read Browning's poem—"

Scott sweeps aside Robert Browning, who missed being born in the Middle Ages by a good three hundred years. "According to Dorothy Sayers, there's no connection. She says . . ." Dorothy Sayers, as a writer of twentieth-century detective stories, is, like Browning, beneath Scott's notice, but as an eminent medieval scholar she's earned his respect.

I listen politely and decide that Scott Sullivan and I have spent enough of our spare time picking over the bones of the Middle Ages. I think it's time we climbed down out of our ivory tower of medieval scholarship and explored the darker reaches of the twentieth-century jungle where we spend our daily lives.

"Talking of Roland and the dark tower and other medieval structures," I say idly, "how's life at Mallingham these days?"

Mallingham is the medieval Norfolk village where Scott's father, Steve, is buried and where Cornelius' archenemy Dinah Slade was once lady of the manor. I know very little about Dinah Slade except that in addition to busting up Steve's marriage to Aunt Emily she piled up a lot of money, made life damned uncomfortable for Cornelius, and died a heroine's death at Dunkirk.

"Oh, all's well at Mallingham," says Scott sociably, just a nice normal regular guy discussing his family. "Elfrida's entirely wrapped in running the school—she's had more to do than ever since Edred quit. But Edred's decision to take the job with the orchestra was probably for the best. Elfrida didn't like the way he taught music, and there were rows."

Edred and Elfrida are Scott's half-brother and half-sister, the children Steve and Dinah produced long before they decided to marry. Only the youngest child, George, had the luck to arrive after the wedding.

"Nice of Cornelius to fund Elfrida like that, wasn't it?" I say innocently.

Scott's smile broadens. "Sheer Christian charity!" he says, making me laugh.

I pause for a moment to consider my next move. We all know at One Willow Street that Cornelius and Steve fought to the death back in the thirties, just as we all know it was probably the dirtiest of struggles, with plenty of punches below the belt, but no one knows the exact details of the grand slam—or if they do, they're not talking. Certainly I've never managed to find out the whole story, although I doubt if it would shock me if I did. Where Cornelius is concerned, I always believe the worst, because the worst is usually true.

But what does Scott believe? Surely with his brains and his experience of Cornelius he can't possibly fall for Cornelius' official view of the past; he can't possibly believe that Steve was crashing around being a menace and Cornelius, poor meek innocent little Cornelius, was driven to strike back in self-defense. I can accept that Scott was alienated from his father—buccaneers like Steve Sullivan all too often live at such a pace that their children get lost somewhere along the line—but just how deep did the alienation really go? I have no memory of Steve Sullivan, who left America for good in 1933, but I can remember Scott's brother Tony telling me once about the tree house his father had built for him by the beach of their Long Island home back in the twenties.

I remember saying to Tony enviously, "How great to have a father who spent so much time with you!"

And I remember Tony saying with that naive honesty which made dissimulation so difficult for him, "He was the best father in the whole world."

That testimonial was remarkable and it became all the more remarkable when set beside Cornelius' regular pronouncements that Steve was totally unfit to be a father and had made a despicable mess of his paternal duties. (Cornelius had a Victorian fondness for the word "duty" and treated it as a talisman which would invariably clinch any moral argument.)

But had Scott ever shared Tony's persistent loyalty to his father? He and Tony were very different both in temperament and in intelligence, and they had been estranged for some years before Tony's death. Tony's mind had been open and transparent. Scott's was closed and opaque. Were those two minds linked by an identical view of the past or not? Impossible to tell, impossible to guess.

Looking at Scott, I feel an intense desire to open up that shuttered enigmatic mind.

"Do you think Cornelius funded Elfrida out of guilt, Scott?" I say suddenly. "Do you think he was trying to make amends for wiping your father off the map back in the thirties?"

"I doubt it," says Scott, quite unfazed, effortlessly casual. "I can see him acting out of expediency ('Let me get rid of this girl by giving her what she wants!'), I can see him acting out of common sense ('If I'm nice to her she'll cause me less trouble!'), and I can see him acting out of his famous Christian charity ('If I help her I'll feel good about it afterward!')—but I can't see him saying to himself, 'Oh, God, let me atone for my sins by giving this girl a school!' "

I burst out laughing, and I can't help being impressed; this clear-eyed unsentimental analysis of Cornelius' motives rings so true and the good-humored affection in Scott's voice sounds so obviously genuine that I begin to think I've been suffering from paranoia by imagining treachery where no treachery exists. I remind myself that it's perfectly possible that Scott's rejected his father one hundred percent, perfectly possible that he's fond of Cornelius even though he has no illusions about him. One of the things I found so confusing when I was growing up was that although I detest Cornelius, there are those occasional times when I like him very much, and even, God help me, admire him too. I liked him when he gave me that rabble-rousing lecture on condoms when I left for Groton, and I liked him when he not only approved of my marriage but backed me staunchly all the way to the altar. And I admire how tough he is about his asthma, fighting it all the time, never complaining, never sinking into self-pity. I'd love to hate him one hundred percent, but I can't, and if I can confess to some occasional twinge of affection for Cornelius, why shouldn't Scott share my feelings? Scott's okay. He has to be. He's just a regular guy with some eccentric habits, and that mind of his isn't so opaque and sinister after all.

Or is it? Why do I keep feeling that somehow against all the odds Scott's acting out some medieval allegory in which he plays Retribution stalking Evil in pursuit of the Holy Grail of Justice? Yes, I must definitely be succumbing to paranoia. All this medieval crap Scott keeps dishing out must have finally reached me. I must pull myself together before I give way to the urge to embroider *The Canterbury Tales*.

"What was your father like, Scott?" I say suddenly, taking myself by surprise. "Everyone talks of him as if he was just another flamboyant hard-drinking Irishman, but he must have been far more complicated than that."

"He was no Irishman. He saw the world through Anglo-Saxon eyes and considered it was no more than an accident that he had an Irish name."

We're moving onto familiar ground here. When I first married Elsa and felt like a member of a persecuted race, Scott and I spent some time discussing the ancient races of the world.

"But didn't your father have any Celtic characteristics?" I ask idly, preparing to enjoy yet another foray into ancient ethnic territory.

"Hell, no!" says Scott, relaxing with me. "He knew only one world and one time and one reality—the view the Anglo-Saxons call 'logical' and 'commonsense' and 'pragmatic,' the view that dominates the Western world today."

"*My* view," I say, smiling at him.

"Your view, yes. But not mine."

He's done it. It's incredible, but he's done it. He's made a mistake. The shutters have slipped a fraction and I have a lightning glimpse into that opaque enigmatic mind.

"Why, listen to me!" he's exclaiming in amusement. "How crazy that sounds! Let me take that back. We both know that I'm no more a Celt than you're an Anglo-Saxon—we're just two Americans living in the great melting pot of New York, and to imply we're anything else would be pure fantasy!"

"Pure fantasy," I say soothingly. "Sure."

"And besides," says Scott, still furiously trying to get the shutters back in position, "didn't you tell me how senseless it is to make distinctions about race nowadays, since we're all so thoroughly intermarried and mixed up?"

"I did say that, yes. And I still believe it to be true," I say to reassure him, but part of my mind is already recalling Jung saying we are not of today, nor of yesterday; we are of an immense age.

So you identify with the Celts, do you, Scott Sullivan? That's very interesting. Thanks for giving me the missing key to your personality. You can be sure I'll make good use of it.

I remember all about the Celts. I came across them again and again when I was doing research into the Anglo-Saxons. The Celts' enemies never understood them; such logical, practical, down-to-earth people as the Romans and the Anglo-Saxons must have been baffled by a race whose outlook on life was so radically dissimilar to their own. The Celts were mystical and alien. Their literature revealed worlds within worlds, the supernatural mingling freely with reality in an eerie dislocation of time and space. Since they believed in an afterlife, death held no terrors for them; in fact, their society was suffused by death, for over and above all the other hallmarks of the Celts which their structured, disciplined enemies found so barbarous, towered the mighty tradition of the blood feud, which meant that the Celts continually killed each other as well as all the enemies who stood in their way.

If you were a Celt and someone killed your father, you couldn't rest until you'd killed him in return. Your whole honor would be at stake. "Forgive and forget," would have sounded a ridiculous piece of Christian folly to pagan Celtic ears, not only because forgiveness was unthinkable but because forgetting was impossible. The Celts never forgot the past. It was always part of the living present, kept effortlessly alive by the Celtic refusal to see time as their enemies saw it. Past, present, and future existed simultaneously in their looking-glass world, where death, the one reality, was treated as a myth which enabled them to waste their lives without regret in pursuit of a just revenge.

"Still thinking of all those extinct Celts and Anglo-Saxons?" says Scott, laughing.

"Extinct! What about the Irish-Americans and the WASPs? Say, have you ever met Jack Kennedy during any of your trips to Washington?"

We talk about the Kennedys, as tribal and hierarchical as all the best Celtic families, dedicated to having their revenge on all the White Anglo-Saxon Protestant aristocrats who once treated them like dirt, but all the time I'm thinking of Scott crowning his inborn folk memory of the blood feud with the intellectual trappings of medieval legend.

For Scott's Holy Grail is revenge. I'm sure of that now, just as I'm sure Scott's forgiven his father for the wrongs committed long ago. But that's all I'm sure of; although I've made enormous progress, I'm still up against a brick wall because I can't for the life of me figure out what Scott's planning to do. What *can* he do? Can he be mad enough to believe he could ever grab the bank, when we all know Cornelius can smell a whiff of treachery at fifty paces and cut down his opponent without even pausing for breath? It doesn't make sense. But if Scott's not planning some spectacular double-cross, just what the hell's he up to?

It beats me. But one thing's certain. I've got to find out. If we're all playing cards for high stakes and Scott's got the ace of spades stashed up his sleeve, the least I can do to protect myself is to find out the other cards in his hand. Scott could be dangerous not just to Cornelius but to me too.

For the first time in my life I see Scott not as a friend but as a rival.

July 4, 1958. Another godawful family reunion, but not such a large one. Andrew and Lori whoop it up on their air-force base, while Rose, who teaches English at an all-female boarding school near Velletria, has gone to Europe to pick over educational theories with Elfrida. Aunt Emily almost goes to Andrew and Lori but comes to Fifth Avenue instead. I think Mother's signaled that she's worried about Vicky, and Aunt Emily loves to help people in distress.

Vicky's all right, just bored with being pregnant and being treated like some priceless vase from the Tang dynasty. Naturally she gets scratchy with nothing to occupy her. God knows I'd be climbing the walls if I had to live in that place with the four children wrecking everything in sight and Cornelius and Mother still carrying on their torrid love affair whenever they think no one's looking. I bring Vicky a new translation of Cicero's letters. They make Cicero so real that you fully expect to see him alive and well and fussing around the Knickerbocker Club. It seems impossible to believe he's not holding a press conference somewhere and thundering about some morally offensive new batch of Wall Street shenanigans. I like the passage where he says he fears Caesar as he fears the shining surface of the sea. Yes, Caesar was deep. Caesar played his cards close to his chest.

Like Scott.

My favorite occupation at the moment is trying to put myself in Scott's shoes and figure out what I would do if I wanted to avenge my father. The obvious goal would be to gain control of the bank—and perhaps change the bank's name from Van Zale's to Sullivan's in order to draw a veil over Cornelius' reign and create a memorial to Steve. That would avenge Steve neatly and rewrite a disastrous past; or, as T. S. Eliot might have said, it ensures that what might have been has assumed a reality equal to that which actually exists. Bearing this in mind, I don't see how I can be wrong in assuming Scott aims to take over from Cornelius; the theory's irresistible. The only trouble is that it just won't stand up.

Scott can't get that bank. He might be able to grab it somehow if it were a corporation run by an oligarchy, but it's not. It's a dictatorship run by Cornelius, and Scott can't possibly wrest the controlling interest in the partnership from him.

So we're back at first base again with the knowledge that if Cornelius can't be forced to give up the bank, he would have to surrender it voluntarily, and if there's one thing that's certain on this earth it's that he's never going to donate his life's work to Steve Sullivan's son.

I sit back with a sigh of relief, but the funny thing is that I don't feel genuinely relieved at all, and after a while I feel more nervous than ever. *Is* Cornelius psychologically capable of handing the bank to Steve's son on a silver platter? Surely not! What about the grandsons? But they're still very young and may not add up to much later. Even so, Cornelius would surely try to stay around until Eric was eighteen. . . . But will he be able to stay around? Maybe his health will finally fail him. And while on the subject of staying around, what about that incredibly sentimental speech he made recently on his fiftieth birthday when he said there were more important things in life than wielding power and making money? He even said he was thinking of retiring early and going off to live with Mother in Arizona! The whole speech was such a laugh I didn't take it seriously, but maybe I should have. Maybe it was a mistake to sit back stifling my mirth at the thought of Cornelius wandering off into the desert like some kind of holy man to contemplate the evils of materialism.

I consider it seriously. If Cornelius takes an early retirement—or drops dead—while the grandsons are still minors, the bank should go either to me, his saintly, dutiful, long-suffering, goddamned efficient stepson with the true financial brain (the obvious choice), or to Scott, the only other guy in the bank who's as smart as I am. But it won't go to Scott because he's his father's son. And do I really believe that Cornelius meant all those moist-eyed remarks about turning over a new leaf? No, I don't. He was probably still unhinged by Sam's death and he'd just succeeded in falling in love with Mother all over again and he was temporarily not responsible for his actions when he made that speech. People may evolve as the years go by, but they don't fundamentally change, so any overnight conversion to a so-called "new life" should be viewed with extreme skepticism. Cornelius may believe he would be happy abdicating his powerful position and sinking into idleness Arizona-style, but he's fooling himself. This particular leopard's never going to change his spots.

Yet Scott must be banking on Cornelius retiring soon. He must know he'd never get the chance of grabbing the bank once the grandsons are grown up.

Maybe Scott's been working on Cornelius, persuading him to retire early. It's hard to believe Cornelius could ever be the victim of undue influence, but if he's suffering from some middle-aged softening of the brain, anything could happen. God alone knows what goes on at those late-night chess sessions. Scott says they talk about eternity. Christ, any man who can get Cornelius interested in eternity almost deserves to win the bank. Still, the thought of Scott assuming the role of Rasputin in addition to the role of cat's whiskers bothers me very much. I'll have to find out more about what's going on. I'll have to keep talking to Scott in the hope that he'll slip up again and drop another intellectual clue at an unguarded moment.

"Are you still talking about eternity in those late-night chess sessions?" I say to Scott at the end of July. We've just finished a game of tennis on the court of Cornelius' summer home in Maine, and we're drinking Coke together in the shade of the patio. As soon as I've asked the question I know it's a mistake, much too direct, much too obvious. Scott will sidestep the implications with the panache of an experienced matador.

"Oh, we've moved on from theological speculation," says Scott, uncapping another Coke. "We're pondering on philosophy now."

"Philosophy? *Cornelius?* Christ, Scott, what a miracle—I don't know how you do it!"

"It's no miracle. Why shouldn't Cornelius start to do some serious thinking now that he's approaching old age? And wouldn't it be so much less irritating if instead of beginning a sentence by saying, 'I consider it my moral duty to do such-and-such,' he said, 'I consider it would be more in accord with Plato's theory of absolute good if I did this, that, and the other!' "

"Oh, my God! Uh . . . peddling Plato to him, are you, Scott? And what does Cornelius think of Plato?"

"He thought he was just fine at first. But then he found out Plato was a homosexual, so he lost interest."

We laugh heartily together. As anticipated, the matador has

swirled his cape with a nonchalant flourish and easily sidestepped the rash charge of the bull. I wait, biding my time before making charge number two.

"As a matter of fact," says Scott, "I think Cornelius is more in tune with Descartes. I get the feeling he's questioning everything, experimenting with new theories, testing all his old values. His fiftieth birthday obviously had a profound effect on him."

"Sam's death, more likely."

"Perhaps. Anyway, the two together have certainly shaken him up."

"How long's it going to last?"

Scott looks dreamily up at the sky. "Who knows? His horizons may have expanded permanently. I've always thought you underestimate Cornelius, Sebastian—no, not at the bank. In his private life. If you strip away his despotic mannerisms and his tough-guy poses, he can be surprisingly sensitive. And he's very lonely."

"Scott, you have to be kidding! He's a power-crazed egomaniac!"

"At the bank, yes. But he's a very different man in front of a chessboard at one o'clock in the morning."

"I'll take your word for it. If I had to face Cornelius regularly over a chessboard at one in the morning, I'd be round the bend in no time flat. So what's going to happen, Scott?" (I seem to be unable to stop asking direct questions, but this one seems natural enough in the context of the conversation, so maybe it doesn't matter.) "Is Cornelius really going to retire within the next five years and wander off to Arizona for keeps?"

"I think he'd be bored to tears after one week in Arizona, but don't tell him I said so. As for his retirement . . . again, who knows? I don't. I just sit and listen to him speculating."

I'm puzzled by this apparent lack of interest in Cornelius' early-retirement plans. If Scott's ever going to get anywhere, Cornelius has to retire young.

"I thought you sat and lectured him on Plato!"

"Only when I'm asked!" He smiles lazily, so cool, so serene, so confident. It's as if he knew beyond any shadow of doubt that he was going to get the bank in the end. It's as if he feels he's safe whatever happens; I'm irrelevant, the grandsons are irrelevant, the rest of the partners are irrelevant, because Scott and Cornelius are playing chess for the bank and Scott's figured out exactly how he can call checkmate.

This time the matador's not only swirled his cape but flung dust in my eyes. I can't see a thing. I'm baffled and bamboozled.

"Oh, well," I said, giving up and preparing to retire from the ring, "in fifty years' time we'll all be dead anyway, so what the hell. It reminds me of that line from *East Coker* in the *Four Quartets*—gee, I wish I could convert you to T. S. Eliot, Scott—"

"I converted myself recently. I can't think now why I always found him so unreadable. Which line in *East Coker?*"

"The one about death. 'O dark dark dark. They all go into the dark, the vacant interstellar spaces, the vacant into the vacant, the captains—' "

" '—merchant bankers'!" he says with me, and we both break off to laugh. That's what they call investment bankers in England. Eliot was a banker once.

"Well, that's life!" I comment phlegmatically. "Even Cornelius has to go into the dark one day."

"Yes, and I think he's finally figured out the best way he can handle that tough Midwestern God of his when he reaches the end of the lighted hall."

That's it. I know that's it. I don't know exactly what "it" is, but I'll figure that out later. Meanwhile, keep talking, act naturally, and don't let him see I know.

"Oh, he'll fix God, all right, no problem," I say glibly, "and then he'll go right up that primrose path to the big bank waiting in the sky."

Scott shouts with laughter and spills Coke all down his tennis shirt. "Now, look what you've done, Sebastian!"

"Me?"

"Yes, you! No one else can make me laugh the way you can!"

Nice conversation between two old friends. Complicated conversation between two new rivals who could wind up very serious enemies. I wait till he goes off to change his shirt and then I go on sitting in the patio and think and think and think.

I think that Cornelius, starting to consider his own death, has finally begun to feel guilty about his past. Is someone as amoral as Cornelius capable of feeling guilty? Yes. Never mind whether he's amoral or immoral. The plain fact is that with his strict religious upbringing he's probably riddled with guilt by this time. Anyway, those people who act as if they don't know the meaning of the word "guilt" are so often the ones that suffer guilt most acutely. Their guilt is so enormous that they can't even bear to acknowledge its existence.

I'll bet that Cornelius is tempted to give the bank to Scott in order to assuage his guilt about Steve. He'd see it as the only way he could fix that tough Midwestern God of his, the only way he could face the dark at the end of the lighted hall.

Scott's been working for years to achieve this frame of mind, of course. He's been dedicated, disciplined, fanatical. He's out for justice—"natural justice," he would call it, implying an inexorable force which may or may not be controlled by God. But will he succeed in getting this justice of his? I wonder. Several things could happen to upset his plans. For instance, Cornelius could get his guilt under control and lose interest in Scott. Or Cornelius could merely resist the idea of retirement and live a very long time, longer than Scott, who's only eleven years his junior.

What will Scott do if natural justice doesn't pan out quite the way he thinks it should? And for that matter, what *is* natural justice in this situation? Will I think it's just if Scott snatches the bank from under my nose? I most certainly will not.

Natural justice may well exist. God may well exist. I don't know. I'm not so intellectually arrogant that I think I know all the answers. But one thing I do know. If there is a God, I firmly believe he helps those who help themselves.

I've every intention of helping myself. What's more, I think Scott will too if the going gets rough, and the scary part is that he might well be in a winning position. For Scott's slipped Cornelius into an emotional vise way, way back, that's quite obvious, and one day when Cornelius is old and tired and vulnerable, Scott's going to start tightening the screws.

The next day Scott and I play tennis again, and he wins. It seems like a bad omen, and afterward, when we sit drinking Coke in the shade of the patio, I'm more silent than usual.

What do I do about Scott? If I can prove to Cornelius how dangerous Scott is, I would immediately dispose of my rival, but I don't see how I can ever obtain concrete proof of what's going on in Scott's head. Also, I can't believe that Cornelius, with his enormous talent for survival, hasn't a notion of Scott's long-term ambitions. Hasn't Cornelius sensed that he's like a laboratory guinea pig being watched by some highly dedicated scientist? Scott must have neutralized him somehow, but how he's done it beats me. It's not like Cornelius to turn a blind eye to someone who could be dangerous to him. As soon as someone's potentially dangerous he's fired. So why hasn't Cornelius fired Scott? Why has he persisted in turning a blind eye in Scott's direction?

I try to figure out what's going on in Cornelius' head. Perhaps it's not a question of a blind eye but of an autocrat's distorted vision. Cornelius has been omnipotent for so long that perhaps he can't conceive of a situation in which Scott could be too hot to handle.

But I can.

Suppose Scott gets tired of waiting and decides to give natural justice a helping hand. Suppose Cornelius gets sick, really sick, so sick that he has to delegate most of his power and can do no more than sign his name where Scott tells him to. Suppose Scott does a secret deal with the other partners, who all have a stake in denting Cornelius' autocracy, and forces Cornelius into incorporating the firm. Scott would be president of the new corporation, of course, and Cornelius, weakened by ill health, would be kicked upstairs to be chairman of the board. It couldn't happen if, as I originally thought, Cornelius was at heart firmly prejudiced against Scott as Steve's son. But it could happen if, as I now think, Cornelius has lost sight of Steve in the murky past and has managed to persuade himself, for reasons which I still don't fully understand, that Scott can never be a threat to him.

I consider my options. I can keep my mouth shut. Or if I open it, I can try spelling out to Cornelius in bloodcurdling detail what might happen if Scott decides to give natural justice a helping hand.

Would Cornelius listen to me? No, he wouldn't. If he's managed to convince himself that Scott's just a sycophantic court jester instead of the hostile joker in the pack, he'll only laugh at my description of doomsday.

No, on second thought, he won't laugh; he'll be angry. He'll think: sour old Sebastian, jealous of Scott and making trouble by dreaming up these preposterous, paranoid, unproven theories. Sebastian, my cross, my burden, my pain in the neck. To hell with Sebastian, Cornelius will say to himself, and draw closer to Scott than ever.

I'll have to play a waiting game. There's no alternative except to watch and listen and hope that somehow, somewhere along the line, I'll stumble across the proof I need.

"God, it's hot, isn't it?" says Scott.

"Yeah."

"But that sea breeze is nice."

"Uh-huh."

Nothing going on there, just an exchange of words, and that's bad. I've got to keep the lines of communication open so that he doesn't get suspicious.

Scott's stalking Cornelius. And I'm stalking Scott.

Spooky.

August 11, 1958. Vicky has the baby. Another boy who might grow up to make life awkward for me at the bank. I smile politely and say, "That's nice."

Vicky won't commit herself to choosing a name and only refers to the baby as Postumus. I know why, although no one else does. Two weeks ago at Bar Harbor during a discussion of Cicero's letters I remarked to Vicky how sensible the Romans were about naming their children. You had no more than a dozen names to choose from if the baby was a boy, and if it was a girl you didn't even have the bother of choosing; she was automatically called by the female form of her father's patronymic unless you wanted to distinguish her from her sisters by tagging on a label like Tertia. A male born after his father's death might simply receive his father's name with the additional description "Postumus." Modern parents who agonize for days over books of names might well pause to envy the Romans their supreme lack of creative imagination on the subject of this potential family battleground.

"Little Keller Postumus," says Vicky, clear-eyed, not thinking of Sam, not thinking of anything except the ordeal of surviving this baby's birth and emerging at last from the long shadow of her marriage. "Poor little Postumus."

Five days after the birth she calls me at the bank. "Sebastian, can you be here during visiting hours this evening, and if I start to scream could you lock everyone out?"

"Sure."

You can visit this hospital at any time, but Vicky has asked her doctor to restrict visiting hours. Visitors are tiring, particularly when those visitors are Mother and Cornelius, still behaving like newlyweds.

Vicky has a couple of old friends paying court when I arrive, so I loaf around by the window and watch the sludge flow down the East

River. Then Cornelius and Mother arrive with the kids plus chief nurse, and the friends stage a tactful withdrawal.

Eric and Paul try to murder each other as usual and upset a bowl of fruit.

"Take them out, please," says Mother crisply to their nurse. "Vicky, I told them beforehand that they had to behave if they came."

"Yes, Alicia," says Vicky mechanically.

Little Samantha jumps up and down and pipes, "Mommy, can I see Postumus?"

Everyone laughs because she's so cute.

"Baby's name isn't truly Postumus, darling!" says Vicky. She loves Samantha.

"Well, what's the name going to be, sweetheart?" says Cornelius. "You know, I was thinking that my father had a good American name. I don't mean my stepfather, Wade Blackett, who brought me up, but my real father, who died when I was four. Why don't you call the baby—?"

"No," says Vicky strongly, "you're not going to choose a name. I sat by in silence for years while you and Sam decided what to call my children, but I'm not sitting by passively any longer. This is my baby and no one's going to name him except me. Postumus is going to be called Benjamin."

"*Benjamin?*" chorus the grandparents aghast.

"But that's Jewish!" adds Mother—predictably.

"I wouldn't care if it was Chinese!" says Vicky. "I wouldn't even care if it was Martian! It's the name I like best. Sebastian understands, don't you, Sebastian? You wouldn't let Jake and Amy tell you what to call Alfred."

"Right," I say, moving in. "You call Postumus Benjamin. Good choice."

Cornelius and Mother swivel to face me. I can see them recognizing that some sort of change has occurred in the family structure. This is the first time that Vicky and I have ever ganged up on them.

"Well, Sebastian," says Mother, nettled, "I don't see what this has to do with you."

"It's got nothing to do with you and Cornelius either, Mother. This is Vicky's decision and no one else has the right to make it for her."

Mother and Cornelius look astounded. I stand guard by Vicky's
bed like a pillar from Stonehenge. Vicky rings the bell.

"Oh, nurse, could you bring the baby in, please?" she says, a little
breathless after her triumphant victory.

This is the first independent step Vicky's ever taken as an adult.
It's a big step forward, and in taking it she's launched herself at last
on her voyage of self-discovery.

On an impulse I kiss her cheek to tell her I'm with her all the way.
She looks up startled, but she smiles, and when I glance at our
parents I see they're wide-eyed with wonder.

Vicky and Sebastian. Sebastian and Vicky. Could they . . . could
they possibly . . . ?

I can almost see Mother's thoughts racing around in her head like
a bunch of whippets chasing an electric hare.

Cornelius is transfixed with fascination.

"Here's Postumus, Mrs. Keller," says the nurse, bringing in the
new bundle.

It's surprising how catchy that old Roman tag is. I think we might
find it unexpectedly difficult to call him Benjamin.

August 28. Vicky's mother arrives unexpectedly from England,
where she now lives, and asks to see her new grandson. Vicky calls
me in hysterics and says she can't see her, Sam forced her to be nice
to her mother but she can't pretend anymore, her mother makes her
ill, her mother's a witch and a whore and evil personified.

"Okay," I say laconically, picturing a twentieth-century version of
Grendel's Mother in *Beowulf*. "I'll fix her."

Vicky's mother's name is Vivienne Diaconi, and she's staying at a
hotel which looks as if it should be on the Bowery. It's six o'clock
and I've arranged to meet Vivienne in the lobby.

I look around for Grendel's Mother and see this cute little old
lady, all dyed and manicured and dolled up, and I discover she has a
low whispery voice and a sexy walk which would have stopped even
Beowulf dead in his tracks.

"Hi," I say. "I'm Sebastian Foxworth."

"Well, hello there!" She looks me up and down as if I'm the
sexiest piece she's seen in a month of Sundays, and I find myself
wondering who's nuts: me, Vicky, Vivienne, or Cornelius. The only
offense this little old lady could possibly commit is cradle-robbing.

"Can I buy you a drink someplace?" I offer politely.

"Darling, how lovely of you to suggest it! I'd just adore some champagne at the Plaza."

Well, that's okay. I like little old ladies who know what they want. We take a cab to the Plaza and sit in the Palm Court and I order a bottle of champagne. Meanwhile she's talking continuously about how wicked Cornelius is, unhinging Vicky so that Vicky gets upset at the sight of her own mother.

"Yeah," I say when she pauses to drink her champagne. "Okay. Well, that's the past. How about the future? You didn't come to New York just to bitch to me about Cornelius. Now, I can arrange for Nurse to bring all the children, including Benjamin, to see you, but I think it would be easier if you weren't staying at that hotel."

She says that's no problem. The Plaza will suit her very nicely, thank you, and please could her suite overlook the park.

"Sure," I said. "I'll fix that before I leave."

She says I'm sweet. I give her a look, but it's no good, I can't keep a straight face, and when I laugh, she laughs too.

I've become friends with Grendel's Mother.

"I guess you want to come back to New York to live in order to be near your grandchildren again," I say as we down the champagne, but beneath the mask of makeup the little face stiffens. "I don't want to upset my girl anymore," she says. "I've moved from Florida to New York and from New York to England to be near her, but it's never worked out. I can't keep following her and upsetting her. I can only wait now in the hope that someday she'll change. I feel so strongly that if only she could get away from Cornelius' influence—"

"Can you give me some idea of Vicky's problem," I interrupt, "without mentioning the word 'Cornelius'?"

But she can't. Cornelius is part of her personal myth. She's got to blame someone for the fact that after a lifetime of glamour she's just a little old lady facing old age alone, and it's easier to blame him than to blame herself.

She says Cornelius deliberately did everything he could to turn Vicky against her. She says she and Vicky used to get along beautifully. She says she knows she got in kind of a mess with Danny Diaconi, but at least she put it all right by marrying him. Besides, Danny was sweet. Such a family man. She, Vicky, and Danny had all been so happy before Cornelius muscled in, smashing up their happy home.

I wonder how I can steer her away from this Cornelius-the-arch-villain tack, but she's no fool; she's seen I'm bored with her one-sided view of the past, so she says, "To get back to the present . . ."

"Sure, yes."

"You seem to speak of Vicky in a special way. Would you be . . . could you be . . . ?"

"Yes, I'm in love with her. Of course I am."

"Darling, how wonderful!"

I offer her a cigarette and she leans forward stylishly for a light. She must have been a real sensation thirty years ago. No wonder Cornelius became so infatuated with her that he didn't realize till afterward that he'd been married for his money.

"And does Vicky love you?" she was asking eagerly, her voice husky with the thought of romance.

"I'm working on it."

Vivienne flutters her eyelashes and says she'd just love me for a son-in-law someday.

I don't tell her that Vicky and I will never marry and I don't attempt to explain my idea of the liaison. Instead I settle her in the most expensive suite available, order up six bottles of champagne to keep her happy, and tell her I'm glad she's now in the right environment because her kind of glamour is wasted outside of a Plaza suite decorated with champagne bottles.

Her eyes soften mistily. She says she just loves strong silent men with hearts of gold.

I ride the elevator downstairs to the reception desk and tell the cashier to bill the suite to Cornelius.

Vivienne stays two weeks and sees the grandchildren every day. She asks me if she can borrow a hundred dollars to cover expenses like Plaza tips, and I give her two hundred and tell her not to bother to pay me back. Then I book her a first-class cabin on the *Queen Mary* and arrange for champagne to be waiting for her as soon as she arrives on board.

Vicky, who's summoned the nerve to face her mother twice during the two weeks, makes a supreme effort and takes the children down to the pier to see the ship leave.

We discuss Vivienne later. We don't say much because Vicky can't discuss her mother rationally, but I think she should try to talk about her to someone; I think that when a relationship between a parent and child goes very wrong the problem should be gently aired now and then instead of being swept under the rug of the subconscious to fester at leisure. I'm reminded of our disastrous Romeo-and-Juliet scene at Bar Harbor. The worst thing we could possibly have done was to swear to Cornelius that we would never refer to the incident again.

Of course by this time I'm feeling totally baffled by the nonrelationship between Vicky and her mother. Vivienne obviously cares about her daughter. Equally obviously she was once a femme fatale, but that doesn't automatically mean she was incapable of being a good mother. I can see she was probably dumb to have got involved with a member of the Diaconi family, who mass-produce gangsters out west, but it's not as if she met the Diaconis during the course of a life of crime; she met Danny through her cousin Greg Da Costa, who used to work for Danny's father in a legitimate hotel business in California. So why does Vicky talk as if her mother's a vice queen, the wicked villainess who must always be kept at arm's length? It makes no sense at all.

"Your mother means well," I say vaguely, using a vacuous phrase to defuse the tension surrounding the subject.

"Perhaps. But she still revolts me."

"Why? She's no big deal, just a little old lady with a lot of oomph and pep. I think she's cute!"

Vicky shudders but says nothing.

"What really happened, Vicky, back when your father got custody of you? Did Danny make some kind of pass at you, and your mother got so mad she kicked you off to live with Cornelius?"

"Sebastian!" She's genuinely appalled by my lurid imagination. Obviously I'm way off the mark here. "Of course not! What a thing to say! Heavens, I was only ten years old!"

"Some men like little girls. Read Nabokov."

"Well, Danny was no Humbert. And I was no Lolita."

"Then I don't get it," I said frankly. "There's a piece missing from this puzzle somewhere. Did you like Danny?"

"Yes, at first, although not later, when he started getting angry with Daddy. He was cute. He was years younger than Mother and looked a bit like Elvis Presley. I kind of like Elvis," she added as an afterthought, "although I can't think why."

I can. Elvis is safe. He's confined to a movie screen so that Vicky can enjoy his sexuality without feeling threatened by it. I'm now one-hundred-percent certain that her marriage with Sam ended in a sexual disaster, and I wish so much I could unlock the door of Vicky's psyche and let all those mixed-up feelings out. What did he do to make her scared of sex? No, wait a moment, maybe I'm jumping to conclusions. I've now got the message that the thought of sex is repugnant to her, but disliking sex and being scared of it aren't necessarily the same thing. And the crazy part is that even though sex is repugnant to her, she's still interested enough in it to feel a sneaking liking for Elvis. So she can't quite be a hopeless case. If she really thought sex was a hobby of the devil, she'd go around insisting that Elvis should be crucified on Capitol Hill for his sex appeal.

If I'm ever to get anywhere with Vicky, I've got to try to sort out this muddle and make sense of it. Think, think, think.

Obviously Vicky was originally scared to death by the thought of sex; our Romeo-and-Juliet scene at Bar Harbor proved that, and in the light of my new knowledge, I'm now beginning to think that she spent her adolescence terrified that she might grow up like her mother. That would explain why she married young, why she was a virgin when she married, why there's never been any kind of hint that she wasn't one-hundred-percent faithful to Sam. Girls as pretty as Vicky have lots of opportunities, but Vicky's been too scared to take advantage of any of them. Maybe when she caught me with my pants down at Bar Harbor (roughly speaking) she had hysterics not because she was horrified by the sight of my unattractive adolescent body but because, on the contrary, she found the experience riveting and was terrified this meant that she was evolving into a junior version of her mother, the ogress.

Yes, this is an attractive theory for explaining the early Vicky, but it hardly explains the present-day Vicky, who's now far away from Bar Harbor, virginity, and teenage anxiety about sex. I think she got over this fear of her sexuality by channeling her sex drive toward marriage. For Vicky at that stage, marriage was the only answer. With her mother in the front of her mind, she must have thought: extramarital sex is horrific and condemns me to eternal damnation, but marital sex is fine, marital sex is okay, marital sex means I can relax and enjoy myself. Cornelius probably spelled that out to her once. I can just hear him saying it. I'll bet Vicky wasn't the only one in that house on Fifth Avenue who was terrified she'd turn out like her mother.

We still haven't figured out why she's determined to regard her mother as an ogress, but let's forget that for now; let's put Vivienne aside for a moment and think of Cornelius. Of course it goes without saying that Vicky's father-fixated, but most girls are in one way or another, and it needn't necessarily spell disaster. Anyway, marrying a father figure probably helped her come to terms with the malign effects of that particular situation, because she would have had the chance to act out and neutralize all those theoretical (and maybe nonexistent) Oedipal fantasies. God, Oedipus has had a bad press! Freud did a real hatchet job there. Poor Oedipus. For Christ's sake, how the hell was he to know Jocasta was his mother when he hadn't seen her since he was a baby? What lousy luck some guys have. . . .

"Sebastian," says Vicky, "these silences of yours are so unnerving. What are you thinking about now? No, don't tell me, let me guess. You're thinking I'm nuts."

"That's right. I'm delighted you're nuts. I don't like normal people. Normal people are usually boring and dumb. If there were more abnormal people like us around, the world would be a far better place."

She laughs. "But I'm not abnormal, Sebastian!"

Oh, yes you are, Vicky, but you can't admit it. You're abnormal in the best possible sense, you're original, you're different, you're not dumb, boring, and run-of-the-mill. That's why I like you so much. That's why I love you. And that's why I'm going to do my very best to extricate you from this prison of normality where you've been locked up so unjustly for so long.

Where had I got to before I started getting so worked up about Oedipus? I seem to have reached the horrible conclusion that Vicky's marriage to Sam Keller was probably for the best. It enabled her to come to terms with her sexuality and it allowed her to work off her father complex. So everything in the garden should have been lovely. Except, of course, it wasn't. I think the first year was all right, though. Anyone could see she was in the seventh heaven of marital bliss then, so the sex must have been fine at first. So what happened? What went so very, very wrong?

"You're not listening, Sebastian!" Vicky's saying crossly. "I said I'm *not* abnormal!"

"All right. Maybe abnormal's the wrong word. How about 'unconventional'?"

"What can be more conventional than being a wife and mother? Anyway, I don't want to be unconventional. We've all got to conform, haven't we, if we're going to fit into society and do well in life?

And I want to do well in life. I want to be a success, not an embarrassing failure."

"The most successful thing you can do in life," I say, "is to figure out who you are and then be yourself. It's a big mistake to try to be someone you're not. It's the equivalent of murder—you're murdering your true self. That's no road to bliss. That's the road to depression and despair."

Her eyes widen. I've reached her. Finally she blurts out, "But supposing you don't like your true self? Supposing it's socially unacceptable?"

"Well, if you go around breaking the law, I agree you've got a problem, but assuming you're a law-abiding citizen with a reasonable level of intelligence and a tolerably humane outlook, why the hell shouldn't you like yourself? If other people criticize you and make you think you're no good, why should you automatically assume they're right? What gives them the right to lay down the rules anyway? What gives them the right to judge you? And just who the hell do they think they are?"

She thinks. We're silent for a time, but at last she says, "I'm not even sure if I know my true self. Sometimes I think I don't know who I really am. But I know the way I ought to be, and that way's the easy way, Sebastian, it's all safe and clearly marked out, and I know the people I love will approve of me if I try to live up to their expectations."

"No, Vicky," I say gently. "That way's not the easy way. That way's the way that's nearly killed you. Anyway, to coin one of our father's most well-worn maxims, I'm not interested in the way you ought to be. I'm interested in the way you really are."

September 7, 1958. Alfred is one. He crawls very fast, with his head lowered like a miniature bull, but he can't walk yet. He knows who I am. He smiles when he sees me, and since I'm not demonstrative I guess no one can figure out why he should be so pleased, but Alfred knows I always understand what he wants.

Alfred and I communicate.

Alfred is dark-haired and large like me. He sits gloating at the one candle on his birthday cake, his pale blue eyes misty with dreams of future triumphs. Elsa cuddles him, all the Reischman relations coo nauseatingly, Mother looks as if she's about to burst with pride.

Leave him alone, all you stupid people. Can't you see he wants to dream a little?

Vicky's at the birthday party with all the kids. Eric and Paul are trying to murder each other, as usual. Too bad they never succeed. Little Postumus sleeps. Newborn babies are so smart.

"Sebastian . . ."

It's Vicky, looking desperate. Kristin's been sick on the carpet, Samantha's throwing a tantrum, and the boys are crashing around in the nearest toilet. No sign of Nurse. She's either passed out or walked out, and who can blame her?

"Sebastian, I can't cope!" No tears, just a tense brittle gaiety, the lull before the storm.

"Go to the bathroom beyond the master bedroom and lock yourself in." I hook Mother out of the crowd of Alfred worshipers. "Mother, do you still love children?"

"Darling, what an extraordinary question! Of course I do!"

"Then take charge of your husband's granddaughters."

That fixes Kristin and Samantha. Taking a deep breath, I locate the boys, seize them by the scruffs of their little necks, and threaten to beat the hide off them unless they shape up. Children like to be yelled at occasionally. It's good for them. They gaze at me open-mouthed, and I realize nobody's ever spoken to them like that before.

Vicky's going to have trouble with those boys. Cornelius will probably pull himself together to perform his surrogate-father act when they're past puberty, but right now he's too much the doting grandfather to be any use.

I bang on the bathroom door. "Vicky! All clear!"

"Oh, God!" She staggers out, no hysteria, just genuine laughter. Lightly touching her arm, I draw her farther into the master bedroom.

"Sit down for a moment and relax."

"And to think this is only Alfred's first birthday!" She sinks down on the edge of the bed. "How are we going to survive the others? Is Elsa livid at all the damage?"

"I don't care about Elsa." I sit down with her on the edge of the bed. At once she shifts away.

"It's okay," I say before I can stop myself. "I'll wait."

"Sebastian, I don't want it to get like this. . . ."

"Okay."

"I just don't think I could ever bear to go to bed with anyone again."

"Sure."

She sits there in a lilac dress, her lovely breasts full and lush. I wonder if she's nursing Postumus.

"Was it really bad with Sam?" I say. I know I shouldn't ask, but I just can't help myself. Although I want to have the patience of a saint, I'm only a human being a long way from canonization.

"It was terrible at the end," she says, fighting back her tears.

"Okay at first?" I say, taking no notice of her tears as usual. Vicky has enough people slobbering over her when she cries.

"Yes, it was nice. I loved Sam. He was so sweet, so kind, so understanding . . ."

I grit my teeth but somehow manage not to grind them. Meanwhile she's mastered her tears, but I give her my handkerchief anyway as a friendly gesture.

"That was why it was all so awful," she says, staring down at the handkerchief. "I loved him, yet at the end I couldn't bear him near me. . . . Oh, I feel so guilty, just thinking about it! Why couldn't I love him properly anymore? What went wrong?"

I have a revelation, but it's not a mystical flash of intuitive brilliance. It's the result of commonsense logic. I'm trying to reconcile her picture of sweet, kind, understanding Sam with the tough self-centered machine I remember, but I'm having trouble. Human beings are often complex but Jekyll-and-Hyde types, who keep two distinct personalities in watertight compartments, are mercifully rare. Sam may well have kept the sweet, kind, understanding side of his nature under lock and key as soon as he crossed the threshold of One Willow Street, but do I really believe he stopped being a tough self-centered machine as soon as he crossed the threshold of his own home?

No.

"How could you possibly go on loving someone who treated you so selfishly?" I demand. My revelation expands. I can now grasp the whole panorama of her marriage at a glance. I feel weak, though whether from horror, relief, or sheer mental effort, I'm not sure. "Just think, Vicky—think of all those years of exile you endured in order that he could pursue *his* ambitions, all those philosophy classes you never went to in order to attend to *his* needs, all those pregnancies you endured to boost *his* ego . . ."

But it's no good. I'm going too fast and too far and she can't handle that kind of panorama, not yet. She has to believe in this mythical figure, Saint Sam, because she feels so guilty about her failure to be the model wife and she wants to punish herself. As soon as I mention the word "pregnancies," she starts to say, "I love my children, Sebastian." At least she can still console herself by pretending she's the model mother.

"Yes, I know you love them, Vicky," I answer, and think: You love them as I love my mother—genuine devotion encased in a constant nagging exasperation, like toothache. I want to ask her how many of those children she really wanted and how far they make her feel either happy or fulfilled, but I can't. I've gone too far already and it would be dangerous to tear down all these illusions at once. The illusions are necessary to her at the moment; they're her crutch as she hobbles down the road to recovery, and you don't take an injured man's crutch away from him. You just help him along until he's ready to throw the crutch away himself.

I've no illusions about motherhood. Maybe that's because I'm a man and can view the subject without getting emotional, but no, men often get more emotional on the subject than women (back to poor Oedipus). Maybe it's because my mother wasn't around much when I was young, so that I grew up not taking her for granted and walking all over her but seeing her with enough detachment to realize how damned lucky I was to be the son of a woman who really wanted to be a mother. There are plenty of those women around, and they should be encouraged to have as many children as they like. What shouldn't be encouraged is motherhood for motherhood's sake.

You don't have to be a social worker with personal experience of deprived children to realize there will always be women who should never be mothers—and I'm not just talking about the impoverished alcoholic child-beaters at the bottom of the social ladder. When I was growing up, I saw all too clearly that some of my mother's richest friends treated their offspring as something to be exhibited, like a new mink coat, and then sent back to the nursery for storage. I appreciated my own mother then. I wasn't a fool and I knew when I was well off.

I hated it when Mother tried to explain to Andrew and me once why she left us for Cornelius. She got so upset and it was so unnecessary. Just because she was temporarily deranged, it didn't mean that she stopped loving us. Anyone could see she always loved her children. It was so obvious. Poor Mother. I guess one day I ought to say to her how much I appreciate the way she's always been such a loving, caring mother, but I never will because (a) Mother would cry and I couldn't stand it, (b) I'd be sure to sound repulsively mawkish, and (c) as the result of (b) I'd feel like throwing up. How goddamned difficult the mother-son relationship is—but then, the truth is, any parent-child relationship is fraught with difficulty and that's why no one, *no one,* should take on parenthood until he knows exactly what's involved and honestly feels he can handle the responsibilities.

"I don't know what I'd do without the children," says Vicky, leaning heavily on those psychological crutches of hers, but the next moment she unexpectedly has a timid try at standing upright without them. "But the awful thing is that I don't know what I'm to do *with* them, either. I just don't know how I'm going to manage on my own —that's why I keep putting off making any big decision about the future."

"Very sensible. You need lots of time."

"I certainly need something. I feel so inadequate. Daddy keeps saying cheerfully: 'Never mind, sweetheart, at least you don't have to worry about money,' but that doesn't make things easier. It just makes things different."

"Money solves a lot of problems and creates a whole lot of new ones to take their place."

"Yes. Of course I know I'm terribly lucky not to have to worry about money. I know I'm terribly lucky to be able to afford help with the children. But the more employees I have, the more complicated life seems to become, and also—God, I hate to admit this, because it sounds so feeble, but it does happen to be the truth—also I just don't know how to run a household. Sam always organized everything, you see. He and his secretary and his aides were always around to pay the bills, hire and fire the staff, make all the big decisions. Daddy says I can have secretaries too, as many as I want, but he's missing the whole point. I hate all those people milling around under my nose, I hate them all thinking I'm so feeble and stupid, I hate not even being able to sneeze without someone looking on. . . ."

"It must be hell. I've often wondered how on earth Louis XIV survived at Versailles."

"I feel I want to simplify my life, not complicate it, but how can I simplify it with five children? At first I thought the easiest thing was to live with Daddy because it cut out all the awfulness of setting up an independent household, but now I'm not so sure that was the right thing to do. I just can't take life in that house on Fifth Avenue anymore. I don't know why. It's not your mother. Alicia and I get along surprisingly well nowadays. I think the problem must be Daddy, although don't ask me to define it, because I can't. He makes me feel claustrophobic—as if I'm all laced up in a straitjacket. Can you understand what I mean?"

"Christ, Vicky, it's the story of my life! Look, let me tell you what I think. Stay based at Fifth Avenue for a while longer—you mustn't take on too much too soon or you'll crack up. But don't stay at Fifth Avenue all the time. Get yourself a little apartment—maybe around Sutton Place—somewhere with a view of the river. You need a place where you can be *you*—not just Sam's widow or Cornelius' daughter or the kids' mother. You need to think. Thinking's very important. Anyone with brains needs to be alone to think occasionally. Then, when you feel stronger, you can tackle this mammoth task of setting up an independent household for yourself and the kids."

"Oh, how clearly you see everything, Sebastian! What a good idea! But I don't think I'll tell Daddy. He'd be hurt. He wants me to stay at Fifth Avenue until I remarry. Sometimes I think he talks about all those secretaries and staff I'll need in an independent home just to scare me into staying with him."

"Vicky, you must definitely—and I mean *definitely*—have an apartment where you can lead some kind of a life of your own. I'll find one for you, if you like. Then when I've signed the lease you can help me pick out the furnishings."

Her eyes brighten. "I'd like that," she says wistfully. "I wanted to furnish the house in London by myself, but Sam said we had to have the top interior decorator to make sure it was done right. . . ." Her voice trails away. Then suddenly she says, "I was very unhappy in Europe at the end. You were right just now when you said I was exiled. London was fun at first, but I was terrified of going to Germany. I'm no good at languages . . . I was afraid of letting Sam down . . . disappointing him . . ."

"Did Sam never ask you," says my voice, "whether you wanted to go home? When you said dutifully, 'Gee, Sam, I want whatever you want,' did he never once sit down beside you and say, 'Look, what do *you* want? And where do *you* want to live?'"

"Yes, he did," she says, "at the end. After Kristin was born, I took an overdose of sleeping pills. I didn't mean to kill myself. I just wanted to . . . well, to communicate with him, I guess, but it was a wicked thing to do. Poor Sam—he was frantic. I felt so guilty and so ashamed."

I feel guilty and ashamed too—for selfish son of a bitch Sam Keller driving his wife to the brink of suicide and loading her with a guilt that has nearly crushed her to pulp.

"The hell with him!" I mutter, very unwisely. It's always asking for trouble to criticize one's rival to a woman who feels morally obliged to defend him.

"But he loved me," she says earnestly. "He really did. He loved me very much, and he was so sweet, so kind, so . . ."

It's teeth-gritting time again, and God knows how I control myself, but I do. "Yeah. Well . . . but that's all over now, isn't it, Vicky?" I manage to say calmly. "That's all over, and you've got a whole new life just waiting to begin."

"What a heavenly apartment!" cries Vicky. "And how wonderful to have a place where I can be on my own with no one breathing down my neck! Look at the dear little kitchen! Sebastian, I'm going to learn to cook. Will you come to my first dinner party?"

"What do I get? Soft-boiled egg?"

I've taken some time to find the apartment, because I wanted to make sure I found the right one. It's north of Sutton Place and both the living room and the one bedroom face the river. The building is postwar, well-run, spotless. I open all the closets but there's not a roach in sight. The appliances are new. The floors are parquet. The heat works. There's air conditioning.

"Sebastian, I dread to think what would happen if Daddy ever found out about this place. After he'd got over feeling hurt, he'd be hiring decorators for me and giving me pictures from his art collection, and I think I'd go mad. I'm just so excited at the idea of us fixing it up by ourselves. . . . When can we go shopping for furniture? Next weekend?"

"Okay. You pick it out, I'll charge it, and you can pay me back."

"Will it be expensive?"

"Yes. You've got to learn about money, Vicky."

"I want to learn, Sebastian," she says. "I've always wanted to learn."

Vicky's a case of arrested development. She may be almost twenty-eight, but after nine years of Sam protecting her from everything under the sun except childbirth, the one thing she should have been protected from, she often seems no more than eighteen.

"Don't worry about it," I say comfortably. "I'll teach you."

"Oh, Sebastian, this is such fun! How great the living room looks— like a real home, not a museum! And how sweet of you to have bought all those lovely books in order to make the room look lived in!"

"Don't be dumb, I bought them in order to read! Say, I know it's your apartment, but could I come around here sometimes and read them?"

"Of course! Anytime. Now, Sebastian, how are we going to fix up the bedroom?"

"Tell you what: you leave it all to me and I'll give you a big surprise."

"How exciting! I'll keep the door closed and the room'll be like Pandora's box!"

"Do me a favor, Vicky, and don't come here for three days till I get everything fixed. Okay?" I have everything waiting to be delivered, but she doesn't know.

"Okay, Sebastian. Thanks a million. . . ."

Elsa goes to a hen party at the apartment of one of her friends. I take Vicky to dinner at the Colony. We have oysters Rockefeller, lobster, and champagne.

"To celebrate the new apartment!" I say, raising my glass.

"Can't wait to see the bedroom, Sebastian!"

We laugh sociably. For dessert we order strawberry mousse, black coffee, and Courvoisier.

"Gee, Sebastian, I feel kind of loaded. I'm not used to drinking so much."

"Does that mean Postumus gets drunk tomorrow morning?"

"I'm not nursing Postumus. Oh, stop calling Postumus Postumus!"

We laugh again. I wonder why she's not nursing Postumus. Breast-feeding's interesting. Considering how far we are from the natural order in this plastic society, it's a wonder any function like breast-feeding survives. It gives one hope for the future. Maybe natural man will survive the plastic society after all, instead of degenerating into a computerized robot.

We return to our apartment, and the living room's beautiful, the best of W. & J. Sloane offset with thick dark blue rugs and plenty of glass and a watercolor which Vicky picked up for five dollars in Greenwich Village for no other reason than that she liked it. It's a view of snowcapped mountains across water, a scene which reminds me of Tahoe in Nevada, but on the back the artist has written, "The South Island seen from the coast near Wellington," and we figure the location is New Zealand, a beautiful country a long way away, somewhere to aim for someday, like heaven.

I have more champagne in the refrigerator, so I whip into the kitchen to pull the cork.

"Sebastian, *no!* I can't drink another drop!"

"Just one glass!"

We take our glasses to the bedroom door.

"Okay," I announce. "Sound the trumpets! Hey, presto!"

Opening the bedroom door, I switch on the light. A black-and-white pattern dances before my eyes. Chiaroscuro. Erotic. My guts feel as if they might melt. I drink my champagne very quickly.

"My God!" says Vicky in awe. She tiptoes unsteadily toward the Picasso drawing on the wall. "Sebastian, is this an original?"

"Of course not. I think it's obscene to spend thousands of dollars on overpriced originals. That's a first-class print and it cost twenty dollars, which in my opinion is exactly what that drawing's worth. But it's nice, isn't it? I like the long line of her neck and back."

"It's beautiful. The whole room's gorgeous." Vicky subsides weakly onto the bed, but she's not watching her glass and the champagne spills on the floor. "Oh, no! The white carpet! Quick, where's a cloth?"

I get two cloths, one for each of us, and sinking onto all fours, we sponge furiously at the pile.

"I think it's going to be all right," says Vicky seriously at last.

"I know it is," I say, looking straight at her.

She hears the note in my voice and shrinks against the bed at her back.

We're silent. At last she says, "What a fool I've been."

"No, Vicky. You're not that much of a fool. You wanted it all the time but you've been pretending to yourself that you haven't because the thought of it makes you angry—not frightened, but angry—and you don't want to be angry with me. But Vicky, I'm not going to treat you as you were treated in the past. I love you and I respect you and it's all going to be very different."

418

She says without hesitation, "I don't know what you're talking about. I'm not angry. Nobody's made me angry. Nobody's treated me badly."

I get up, retrieve the champagne bottle from the kitchen, refill our glasses, and knock back as much champagne as I can manage without pausing for breath. Then I say in a remote academic voice worthy of a college professor who's trying to get through to an intelligent but obstinate student, "Okay. You're not angry. You just don't like sex anymore. So what? A lot of people don't like sex. There's a whole industry built around people who don't like sex. People aren't breaking the law if they don't like sex. This is a great big wonderful country, and you don't have to like sex the way you have to like your mother, the flag, and apple pie. But why don't you give poor old sex a break for once? Why not give poor old sex another chance? After all, you've got all that first-class equipment for free, and it seems a shame not to use it occasionally. Have you ever read the plays of Middleton?"

I've thrown her off balance. "Who?"

"Thomas Middleton. He was a contemporary of John Webster and Cyril Tourneur. He wrote about our sort of situation, although he laced it with a lot of seventeenth-century melodrama. The villain pursues the heroine. The heroine repulses him. The villain somehow gets her to give in, and then—surprise! The heroine finds she likes it after all." I touch her lightly with my index finger and she doesn't draw back. "I won't hurt you, Vicky," I say urgently, moving a little closer. She still doesn't shrink away. My hand glides to her thigh. My guts must look like full house at the snake pit. I want to take off my clothes. "It'll be okay," I insist in a low voice. "I'm not like Sam. All men are different. No one makes love quite the same way. Like handwriting." I've got closer. My hand's on her hip, then on her left breast. I kiss her neck. My blood feels molten, like some new liquid metal cooking in a surrealist fantasy. "I want to make love to *you*, Vicky," I say. "Not just a female body with the right vital statistics, but *you*, the person who listens to Kevin's plays with me and knows what they mean, the person who knows that Cicero was a philosopher as well as an orator, the person whose favorite color is blue and who likes oysters and bright lights reflected on wet sidewalks and the fountain in front of the Plaza and Frank Sinatra's singing and Gervase de Peyer on the clarinet. You, you, you."

She lets me kiss her. She says nothing. I must be sweating at every pore. I don't want to take off my clothes with the light on, because that might bring back the inhibiting memory of our Romeo-and-Juliet scene at Bar Harbor. I unbutton her dress instead. She lets me. My fingers don't work properly, can't connect with my brain. Can't unhook her bra. Oh, hell. Mustn't be clumsy. Please, please, God, make me be smooth and calm and confident like Frank Sinatra's voice, another form of liquid metal flowing effortlessly out of the phonograph.

I get rid of all the clothes. She never moves, never speaks. I kiss her all over in the hope that she might respond, but she doesn't, and suddenly I realize I just can't wait anymore. Pulling back the bedcovers, I ease her onto the black satin sheets. Jesus Christ. I try to turn out the lamp, but I knock it over and it goes out by itself. That was dumb. I've got to cool off. But I can't. Everything's molten now, not just me but everything, as if I'm in the midst of the white glowing lava which burst out of Vesuvius to inundate Pompeii in A.D. 79. In the darkness I strip off my clothes and find the satin sheets are like ice; there ought to be a sizzling sound, white-hot lava streaming into subzero water, but no, there's just Vicky, firm, round, beautiful, perfect. . . .

There must be a God somewhere, must be, because I'm in heaven. I'm in heaven and still alive. The ultimate triumph.

She screams.

I tell her it's okay. I don't know what I'm saying. I don't know anything except that I can't stop.

She claws my back, tries to push me off.

Maybe she's afraid she'll get pregnant, but don't worry, Vicky, I'm no dumb kid, I know what I'm doing even when I'm almost out of control, almost, almost . . . Jesus, that was a close call. But I made it. I got out in time.

Next time I'll wear a rubber, but this time was special. This time it had to be just you and me with nothing between us.

Oh, God. Oh, God. Oh, God, I'm so happy.

I lie breathing very fast on the satin sheets, but Vicky pulls away from me, runs to the bathroom, and locks herself in.

I hear her sobbing. Getting up at once, I pound on the bathroom door. My legs feel weak.

"Vicky, are you okay?" Dumb question. Obviously she's not. I rattle the handle. "Vicky, let me in, please."

I hear the hiss of the shower. She's washing off everything, my kisses, semen, the whole paraphernalia. Question: Does she always do this, or is it because I've revolted her?

Don't know. Have to hope for the best. I turn on the light in the bedroom and scramble into my clothes. I don't want her to be more repulsed by seeing me with no clothes on. Then I pour myself another glass of champagne and drink it right away.

I wait.

After a long time she comes out wrapped in a red towel. I want to communicate, but I can't think of the right words.

She's unnerved by my silence, although she needn't be. Averting her swollen eyes, she says, "It's all right. It's always hell the first time after childbirth. It doesn't matter."

I want to take her in my arms and hold her gently, but I know she'd push me away. I'm just a sweating, hairy, slobbering beast who hurts her inside. God, what hell women go through sometimes, and what hell men go through when women go through hell.

"I love you," I say at last.

"Yes," she says wearily, but she doesn't understand.

I haven't communicated.

I must try to think of something that will fix the pain. If she knows I'm concerned about her pain, I'll communicate.

"I'll buy a lubricant," I say.

She doesn't answer. She's thinking of something else, or maybe she's in some kind of shock. She picks up her clothes and goes back to the bathroom to dress. I hear the lock turn again on the door.

I drink some more champagne. I hate champagne now. It seems like an offbeat lemonade, a perverted 7-Up. Finishing the bottle, I chuck it into the garbage can.

When she leaves the bathroom she looks fresh and tidy, but her eyes are still swollen.

"I want to go home now," she says.

"Okay."

I take her home.

" 'Night," she says when the cab stops.

" 'Night."

We don't touch, don't kiss. I'm alone, she's alone, but we're both in hell.

I go home to Elsa and pass out with all the drink just as she's screaming to know where on earth I've been.

January 15, 1959. I write Vicky a note because I can't talk to her. "Dear Vicky: I love you very much. I want to make everything right. Please let me try to fix it. Sebastian. P.S. I want to see the latest Ingmar Bergman movie, *The Seventh Seal,* for the third time. Will you come with me? We don't have to go to bed afterward. I just want to be with you."

She calls me at the office. "Thanks for the letter."

"Okay. How about the movie?"

"All right. If you want."

"Uh-huh. Vicky . . ."

"Yes?"

"What movie do *you* want to see?"

There's a pause. Then she says, "Elvis Presley in *Jailhouse Rock.*"

"Right. Let's go."

It's not a new film, but Sam said it was junk when it first came out shortly before his death, and he refused to take Vicky to see it. I'll bet it's junk too, but I don't care. If it makes Vicky happy, that's good enough for me, so we set off downtown to where the movie's showing in some incredible dump on Avenue B.

I'm right. Sam was right. It's junk. We're back in the plastic culture again, stooping to the lowest common denominator, but that's okay, it's a laugh—we both laugh. The only defense against a plastic culture is to enjoy its awfulness or else it'll send you completely up the wall. Vicky knows that too, and suddenly we're together again, splitting our sides with mirth as Presley swivels across an elaborate set and rasps about the party he's attending in the county jail. *Jailhouse Rock* is in black and white. Chiaroscuro. Exciting.

When I clasp Vicky's hand, she doesn't pull it away, and afterward she agrees when I suggest we stop for hamburgers and malteds at a Greenwich Village coffee shop.

"Can we go to our apartment, Vicky?" I dare to say at last. "Or don't you want to?"

"Okay."

We get to the apartment, and it's a wonderful surprise because she's cleaned it up and there's a present for me on the table.

I'm so overwhelmed I can't speak. I unwrap the package clumsily and find an edition of two of Middleton's plays: *The Changeling* and *Women Beware Women.*

I kiss her and kiss her. Finally we go to bed. I'm in better control this time, and I cling to the control for all I'm worth, because I know

I'm damned lucky to get a second chance. I don't push too hard and I've got a packet of Trojans and enough lubricant to polish a ballroom floor.

She doesn't scream.

I'd like to shower with her, but I don't want her to see me with the light on. Maybe later when I'm more secure. We get dressed and I have a Scotch while she drinks Coke. We sit on the couch in the living room and look at the lights twinkling beyond the window. I'm much better. I don't dare to be happy yet, but I think I might be soon.

"How's Postumus?" I say after a long silence, but Vicky seems to accept my silences at last, so I don't have to worry about them.

"Postumus is sweet. He smiles beautifully now."

"I like Postumus," I say. "Sometimes I feel as if he's mine."

Vicky considers this. "Because you stood up for me about calling him Benjamin?"

"Uh-huh. And because after he was born you asked me for help. Because I loved you all the while you were pregnant, and afterward. Because there was no Sam around to remind me Postumus isn't mine after all."

She asks if Elsa wants more children.

"She can't have any more. Pity. Still, we've got Alfred."

"Sebastian . . . what exactly *is* the situation with Elsa?"

I explain my concept of the liaison. "You're not interested in marriage, are you, Vicky?" I add, just to make sure.

"No," she says automatically, but adds with great haste, "I mean, not at the moment. Of course, I know I should get married again someday for the children's sake."

"And what about your sake, Vicky?"

"Oh, that too, of course! There's no other acceptable alternative."

"There's the alternative we've got going for us right now."

"Yes, but marriage is—"

"Marriage is just a code word for society's attempt to make order out of the chaos between the sexes. It's like philosophers talking of the Absolute and the One in their attempts to make order out of a chaotic universe. But you can philosophize without referring to the Absolute and you can love someone without referring to marriage."

"You talk as if there's no such thing as morality. This liaison of ours may suit us very well, but what about poor Elsa? How can you morally justify your behavior with me when you're going to make her unhappy?"

"She won't be unhappy! It takes very little to keep Elsa happy, just a nice home and the right charge accounts and Alfred and a bit of bed now and then. . . . Uh, you don't mind if I still sleep with Elsa sometimes to keep her happy, do you, Vicky?"

"Yes, I do mind. Very much."

My jaw sags. I quickly clamp my mouth shut, but I'm speechless.

"I think it's wrong to run two women at once," says Vicky strongly. "The Moslems get away with it, but look at their women! Anonymous bundles in yashmaks! But women aren't just anonymous objects, Sebastian! They're people who can get hurt."

"Christ, Vicky, you don't have to tell me that! Other men may think of women as a load of cattle, but I could never be that dumb!"

"Then why can't you see that Elsa's an individual, not some anonymous lump labeled 'wife'? She has feelings, just like anyone else."

"And I'm respecting them!" I protest. Vicky's picking up her coat and I'm moving after her rapidly to the door. "I'm going to go on taking care of her!"

"You're going to humiliate her!" Vicky's now very angry. We leave the apartment and I follow her as she sweeps down the corridor to the elevator.

"Look, Vicky—"

"Okay, go ahead! Humiliate her! Your marriage is none of my business!"

"Say, you sound as if you're jealous!" I say, knowing she's not but trying to neutralize the anger in the conversation with a dash of humor.

She gives me a scornful look as the elevator hits the lobby. "Good night, Sebastian. I'll go home by myself, thank you."

I put her in a cab and watch it drive away.

Oh, hell. Oh, damn. Oh, *shit*.

March 15, 1959. Alfred looks at me with pale pleased eyes and says, satisfied, "Daddy!"

Smart little kid. He knows who understands him. I pick him up and he cuffs me around the ear. Don't be sentimental, you big bastard, he thinks, don't be stupid. As if I don't have enough of that kind of junk already.

I put him back in his playpen. I watch him play. He has a little xylophone which he bashes, and I watch his face, tense with concentration, as he tries to figure out which keys to hit.

A shadow falls across the sunlit nursery. Elsa.

"Alfred, my precious, my angel . . ." She scoops him up, tears him away from the xylophone, and bombards him with baby talk. Alfred screams with rage.

"Put him down, Elsa, for God's sake!"

She glares at me with her father's icy blue eyes. "I want to talk to you."

Alfred is dumped back in his playpen, but he's upset. He still screams in indignation. Nurse scampers in and picks him up again. More screams. Poor Alfred. Only one person understands.

Elsa and I go to our bedroom, and Elsa slams the door.

"You're sleeping with her, aren't you?" she says.

Oh, God, here we go, but I guess it had to come sooner or later. I may as well tackle it now and get it over.

"How do you figure that?" I say to give myself time to shore up my equilibrium.

"Because I only get it once a week nowadays and that leaves six days of the week totally unaccounted for!"

Vicky and I have only made love five times in the last two months, because each time we get to bed we end up having a tiff, which allows her to keep me at a distance for a few days. But I'm patient and I'm willing to wait until Vicky's more settled and can face sex more often. She doesn't hate it. If she did, I wouldn't force myself on her, but she can't yet accept the idea that it could be fun. At present it's just something she's willing to do to be polite and friendly, like drinking pink champagne provided for you by a very old friend who should know better. But I accept that a change of attitude takes time, and meanwhile even making love to her occasionally is paradise compared with all those years when I never made love to her at all. I've been trying, but I just can't maintain my interest in Elsa. This liaison, imperfect though it still is, seems to be impinging on my marriage to a degree I never anticipated.

"You bastard!" says Elsa furiously, making me jump.

I pull myself together. "Okay," I say, "I'm sleeping with her, but there's no need to get upset—I've no intention of leaving you! I'll stay with you and be a good husband, but the truth is, there are precious few good husbands who are faithful to their wives—ask your father, if you don't believe me. Your father's always taken care of his family as a good husband should, but it's common knowledge he's always had a lot of other women—"

"My father," said Elsa, "is a goddamned hypocrite." She sits down suddenly on the stool before the vanity and looks at herself in the glass. She's cool, calm, and collected. No tears, no hysterics, no panic.

This is odd. Something's not right. This scene's not going according to plan.

"My mother's taken too damn much from my father over the years," says Elsa, still looking at her fat homely face in the mirror. "Poor Mama, she had no choice. She was a victim of her class and her culture and her times. But I'm not like my mother and I'm not living in her times. I'm not going to let you treat me as my father treated her. You think I'm just a lump who weighs one-sixty-five and has no mind of her own, but you're wrong, Sebastian. You're just so wrong."

I get hot under the collar—literally. I have to run a finger under my collar to unstick it. I feel very, very uneasy. Can this be Elsa talking? Can this conceivably be poor dumb cute little Elsa who snuggles up to me in bed and says how wonderful I am? Something's gone astray somewhere. I've missed some vital connection. I've miscalculated.

"Look, buster," says Elsa, suddenly as tough as a James Cagney movie and a true chip off the granite Reischman block, "let me lay this on the line. Marriage is marriage. You stood up before witnesses and promised me fidelity, and I'm holding you to that promise. If you weren't prepared to keep it, then you shouldn't have married me. I'm your wife and I'm not sharing you with anyone, least of all with Vicky. You've got to choose, Sebastian. Either you come home, stay home, sleep by my side all night long, and act like a real husband, or else I'm seeing my lawyer and suing the pants off you for divorce."

I try to wake up, but no, this is no horrible nightmare, this is reality, and I'm sweating right here in the middle of it. I try to call her bluff. "You won't divorce me! You know damned well you'd never get another man!"

She looks at me coldly. "Wanna bet?"

I'm dumb—dumb meaning stupid and dumb meaning speechless. "But you couldn't . . . wouldn't dare divorce me!" I splutter.

"Try me," says Elsa, blue eyes almost frosting the glass of the mirror.

I turn on my heel and walk out. Or, to be accurate, I stumble away. I grope my way into the living room, pour myself a triple Scotch, and drink it.

There's a photograph of Alfred on the table by the window, smart little Alfred aged six months, sitting up and glaring, knowing his privacy's being invaded by some dumb grown-up who's cooing to make him smile for the camera.

When the Scotch is gone, I go back to the bedroom, but Elsa's not there. I go to the nursery and find she's stuffing Alfred into a new skip suit for his Sunday-afternoon visit to her mother. Nurse is away getting his coat and boots.

We don't speak, just look at each other.

"Daddy!" says Alfred, pleased, and points his little finger at me.

I want to smash something. I want to break all the dishes in the kitchen and beat Elsa up. But I don't. What's more, I never will. Once I did lose my temper with a woman and gave her such a shove that she knocked herself out on the edge of a nightstand, but I vowed afterward I'd never stoop to violence again. Violence is wrong. Violence is sick. Violence, not sex, is the real obscenity in our culture.

Wiping all violent thoughts from my mind, I pick up Alfred and say to Elsa without expression, "Let's all go on that visit to your mother."

I call Vicky. "Vicky, I've got to see you." I never call Vicky "darling," or "sweetheart" or "honey." She's had enough of those endearments from people who have never understood her.

We meet in the apartment.

"I'm in a big mess," I say, and tell her about Elsa. I'm drinking Scotch as if the distilleries have ceased production. "We can't continue to meet here in case she has me watched," I add. "We'll have to meet at Fifth Avenue. The detectives can follow me to your father's house until they wear out their shoes, but they can never prove I didn't go there just to see my mother."

"Heavens, I can imagine nothing more inhibiting than creeping around that old mausoleum trying to avoid Daddy and Alicia! I wonder what on earth they'll think."

"They'll like it. It'll give them a vicarious thrill."

"Sebastian, dear, they don't need vicarious thrills. They've got real live thrills of their own."

"Jesus, is that still going on?"

We discuss our situation further and make some plans.

"The worst result of this crisis," Vicky says at last with a sigh, "is that we won't dare go out to the movies or the theater anymore. We'll be like an updated version of *Back Street*—although anything less like a back street than Fifth Avenue would be hard to imagine. It's a bleak prospect, isn't it?"

I move over to her. "Vicky, I'd leave Elsa tomorrow, but—"

"I know. Alfred. I understand."

I want to make love to her, but she says no, it's the wrong time of the month. I seldom take any notice of that with Elsa, but I respect Vicky's wish to be private, so I kiss her and leave. But I'm worried, worried sick, and all I can think as I drag myself home is that I'm not at the bottom of this mess yet, not by a long shot.

We start meeting once a week after work in the unused west wing of the Van Zale mansion, and it's not as bad as we'd feared. We take over one of the remote bedrooms and Vicky produces a phonograph and her collection of Frank Sinatra records while I bring my masterpieces by Mozart, including Gervase de Peyer soloing triumphantly on my favorite clarinet concerto. I try to introduce Vicky to Wagner's music, but she can't bear it. Pity. I stick to the safe things by Beethoven instead and slip in a bit of Brahms occasionally, but I draw another blank with Bruckner, while Mahler sends her right out to buy a Presley classic that tells me I'm nothing but a hound dog.

It's odd going to bed together beneath Cornelius' roof; it makes us feel as if we're committing incest, but we dress up the bed with our black satin sheets and then we start enjoying ourselves again. At least I do, and I don't think it can be so tedious for Vicky either, because soon she lets me make love to her twice a week. I'm much encouraged by this, but I can't help wishing I knew how to make her enjoy it more. It's difficult to discuss the mechanics of sex without sounding like either a fool or an Elaine May/Mike Nichols satire, but at last I do say casually, "Let me know if there's something special I can do to make things work well for you."

She looks suspicious. "What do you mean?"

"Well . . ." I know I'm skating on thin ice and I can now see it won't support my weight. I try to back off. "I don't mean to imply that human existence is incomplete without the occasional orgasm, but—"

"Never mention that word!" she yells at me. "Never, never mention it again!" And she jumps out of bed in a rage and locks herself in the bathroom next door to cool off under the shower.

I get dressed, fix us both large drinks, and when she reappears I do my best to unravel the mystery. Apparently this is a problem Sam encountered, but being Sam Keller, he just tells her all women have orgasms at some time or another and if Vicky doesn't, she must have some kind of offbeat problem and should see a psychiatrist.

"And what did the psychiatrist say?" I ask politely.

"He didn't say anything much. I could never really talk to any of the psychiatrists I saw. I thought once I might have been able to talk more easily to a woman, but Sam said all the best psychiatrists were men."

"Yeah," I say, grabbing the bottle of Scotch by the neck and pouring myself a double. "That figures. And what did he say when all those wonderful psychiatrists of his failed to cure you?"

"Oh, but he thought they did. I pretended to be cured in the end. It seemed the easiest way out. I didn't want Sam to go on being worried and unhappy because I wasn't normal."

"I see. Yes. So you assumed all the guilt, all the worry, and all the unhappiness on his behalf. That's great! Lucky old Sam! I salute him!" I raise my glass and drink.

She stares at me. "What are you trying to say?"

"I'm trying to say it takes two to make love, Vicky, and if you could never make it then, maybe—just maybe—that husband of yours was partly responsible. And even if he wasn't, even if he was all hell in bed and you were still unable to tune in, he should have made more effort to put things right than to palm you off on a string of psychiatrists whom you couldn't relate to!"

"But Sam was so wonderful, so sweet, so kind . . ."

I've had it. I just can't stand by gritting my teeth one second longer, and setting my glass down with a crash, I swing to face her. "Vicky, Sam may well have been all those things to you at some time or another, but if he allowed you to carry the full guilt of all your marital problems, he's not such a hero as you think he is. He may still not be a villain, but believe me, he's no hero."

"But—"

I take her by the shoulders and give her a sharp jerk to show her how important it is that she should see Sam without the halo her guilt has nailed to his memory. "Don't canonize Sam," I say strongly. "That would be a very big mistake. Sam wasn't a saint, Vicky. He

was human and he had his faults, just as we all have, but he covered
them up so efficiently with that notorious Keller charm that you
probably weren't aware of them. You've got a right to be very angry
with Sam about some things, just as you've got a right to love him for
others. Well, be angry! Get mad! Don't just say, 'Oh, it was all my
fault . . . I was a wife who failed her husband.' Don't turn the anger
in on yourself! Try saying instead, 'That son of a bitch Sam Keller—
he turned his back on me when I needed him, he was a husband who
failed his wife!' That still may not be the exact truth, but I'll bet my
bottom dollar it's one hell of a lot closer to the truth than this myth
of failure and inadequacy you've been carting around on your back
for so long!"

She stares at me until I feel I'm a mirror, one of those mirrors you
see in horror movies which reflects a death's-head instead of the
human being before the glass. I pour her some more Scotch and
shove the tumbler into her hand.

"Sorry," I mutter.

"No," she says. "Don't say sorry, and don't—"

"And don't say 'orgasm' either? Okay, Vicky, whatever you want.
Unlike Sam, I'm not about to get upset just because you don't thrash
around in bed like some acolyte performing the rites of Dionysus. To
be truthful, I don't give a damn what you do so long as I'm not making you miserable. Am I making you miserable?"

She kisses me. "No. You make me very, very happy. You make
me believe . . ." She stops.

"In yourself? Do I make you believe in that neglected long-lost
person who exists under the neurotic misfit who hated being a showpiece wife and a model mother and doing the things which all women
without exception are supposed to find totally satisfying and rewarding? Do I make you feel less guilty for not enjoying the suppression
of your own personality in order to sacrifice yourself for your husband? And have I finally convinced you that any meaningful relationship between a man and a woman should be a matter of give and
take, and not all take on the one side and all submissive, self-effac-
ing, soul-destroying give on the other?"

She doesn't answer. Tears are streaming down her face. Finally
she says, "It was all so wrong, wasn't it? It shouldn't have been like
that. I was like those POWs in Korea. The ones who were
brainwashed."

I put my arms around her and hold her close. There's another long silence, but when she says, "I think I'm beginning to feel angry," I know that she's put her crutches aside at last and begun her long uphill walk back from the far side of hell toward a new life not yet begun.

I'm in F. A. O. Schwarz buying a present for Postumus. Last year Alfred was given a useful string of colored beads which he could chew without poisoning himself, and I think Postumus would enjoy the gift as much as Alfred did.

When I leave F. A. O. Schwarz I grab a cab uptown but suddenly I remember I'm out of Trojans. Hell. Where's the nearest drugstore? I lean toward the driver.

"Go over to Madison."

The driver thinks I'm nuts, but we go over to Madison and all I see is a series of little shops with one dress in each window and no price tag in sight.

"Go over to Lexington."

"What are you looking for, buddy?"

"Drugstore."

"Why didn't you say so?" The driver swoops on uptown on Madison for three blocks and halts outside a drugstore on the corner. Telling him to wait, I run in.

No Trojans. I buy another brand and race back to the cab, which swings over to Fifth Avenue. That's wasted time, and I have to be home by eight, otherwise Elsa won't believe I'm working late.

Mother meets me in the hall. Damn.

"Oh, darling, I thought you were Cornelius! Come and join us for a drink. He should be home any minute now."

"I've brought a present for Benjamin. Maybe—"

"Hi, Sebastian!" calls Vicky from the top of the stairs as she tries to figure out how to rescue me. "A present for Benjamin, did you say? What a nice surprise—come up to the nursery!"

Cornelius walks in. "Sebastian! Come and have a drink!"

I usually make a special effort to arrive before the drinking invitations, but the combination of F. A. O. Schwarz and the contraceptive hunt has disrupted the schedule.

"Come and tell us the latest news of Alfred!" says Mother. She really does want to see me, and I feel guilty because I spend so much time sneaking up the west-wing stairs to see Vicky.

We all go to the Gold Room for drinks. Cornelius and Mother sit on the couch and hold hands. Vicky and I sit opposite each other and try to look chaste. The air is thick with a sexual miasma. Even the Greeks would have found it hard to take.

When we finally escape, we forget Postumus and race to our distant bedroom.

"I've got to leave in ten minutes!" I mutter.

"Is it worth going to bed? Why don't we just have another drink and chat?"

"I'd be awake all night thinking of you."

We rush to bed and for a few precious minutes all's well, but then there's one of those freak accidents, the kind which always happen to other people, usually to young kids who rely for their supply of contraceptives on the slot machines in men's rooms. This batch of rubbers shouldn't have left the factory. Quality Control made a mistake.

I say nothing except a private prayer. Vicky says nothing either, and after I flush the disaster down the toilet, she slips past me for her shower.

However, we're both in luck for once, because this particular accident has no consequences. Ten days later Vicky says it's the wrong time of the month again. I guess my face must have sagged with relief, for she adds, "Look, Sebastian, why don't I take charge of the birth control for a change? I used a diaphragm for a short while once, and I'm willing to try it again."

"You're sure?"

"Very sure."

She gives the diaphragm a fresh try, and as far as I'm concerned, it's a great improvement. I ask her three times if she's happy with the change, and she says she's not crazy about it but she feels safer than when I was using rubbers.

That's when I realize she doesn't trust birth control when it's provided by her partner, and on reflection I'm not one bit surprised. It would be just like Sam Keller to practice birth control like a suicidal gambler practicing Russian roulette. She even tells me fiercely that I've got to let her use the diaphragm every time, and when I assure her that Russian roulette has never been one of my favorite pastimes, her eyes fill with tears. Horrific vistas into the past open up. I take her in my arms and hold her close to block them off.

I'm not Sam Keller and I'll never, never, never stand in his shoes.

June 12, 1959. In the nursery Postumus chews his beads and smiles speculatively at his nice kind Uncle Sebastian. His two brothers are smart enough to keep out of sight when I'm around, but little Samantha flirts with me and Kristin gives me Sam Keller's smile.

At home Elsa adopts a polite neutral manner toward me, has her hair tinted a lighter blond, and buys a book about dieting. Alfred runs around dragging his beat-up xylophone after him and tries to redecorate the hallway with Elsa's nail polish, but I smack him hard on the backside. Yells and screams. Elsa calls me a brute. But Alfred looks up at me with fierce pale eyes and respects me. Alfred won't do that again.

Everything seems to be jogging along satisfactorily, but as the summer days pass a little cloud appears on the horizon, and as more days pass, that cloud grows bigger and bigger.

Vicky and I are waiting for the wrong time of the month, but the time always seems to be right, and slowly we realize we're waiting in vain.

It's disaster time again.

She's pregnant.

"How the hell did it happen?"

"The doctor said I should have had the diaphragm refitted."

"But . . ." It's hard to find the words to express my horrified incredulity. "Didn't you get a new one?" I say dumfoundedly at last.

"Yes, I did. I had a look at my old one, but the rubber part seemed odd, so I got a new one over the counter at one of those huge discount drugstores midtown—I didn't want to ask my doctor for a new diaphragm when he knows I've got no husband at the moment. He might have given me a lecture."

"He might have *what?*"

"Oh, doctors are always giving women lectures—you've no idea what it's like. When I thought I might have Postumus aborted, they went on and on and on at me. I just couldn't take it, I hated all doctors after that, particularly gynecologists—"

"Okay. Hold it. I understand. Doctors are fundamentalist preachers trained in KGB interrogation techniques who lie in wait for women around Park Avenue. But there are clinics where everyone thinks it's the most normal thing in the world to issue a diaphragm to a woman under thirty with five children! Why didn't you—?"

"You don't understand. You're missing the whole point. I didn't think it was *necessary* to go through the whole performance of being fitted for a diaphragm again. I knew the size I took and I thought one stayed the same size for life—just as one stays the same size in shoes. After all, one doesn't have one's feet measured once a year to see if they've got bigger or smaller."

"But *someone* must have told you!"

"No. No one. You see, I only used a diaphragm for a short time when I was married, less than a year. When the doctor gave it to me he did say I was to be sure to have it checked every year, but he didn't say why, and I just assumed he wanted to make sure it wasn't broken. But then I got pregnant, and later Sam insisted on taking control of the contraception again—"

"—with all the fervor of a man gearing himself up to appear in a fertility ad. Okay, now, let's just think about this. We're upset enough as it is, so let's not make ourselves more upset by resurrecting the disastrous past. Let's just focus on the present." I give her a handkerchief for her tears and mentally kick off Sam Keller's shoes, which seem to be trying to slide their way onto my feet. I do this by telling myself firmly that I'm not just an innocent bystander here; I can't just sit back and announce that none of this is my fault. I know all too well that Vicky, thanks to Sam, has led a sheltered existence protected from the facts of life, and you don't entrust sole responsibility for birth control to such a fundamentally innocent person without a thorough discussion of the entire subject to make sure there are no potentially lethal areas of ignorance. Vicky may have made a mistake, but I've made a big mistake too, and it's now up to me to step forward, stand by her, and stave off tragedy as best I can.

I fix us both large drinks, put my arm around her, and say, "Vicky, I'm not going to dictate to you about this. You had nine years of Sam dictating to you, and I'm not going to be like Sam. This is our joint mistake, and I assume full responsibility, but when all's said and done, it's your body. You have the burden of carrying this child for nine months. You have the ordeal of giving birth. You must decide what you're going to do, but before you decide, I'll say this: whatever your decision is, I'll back you up. The decision must be yours, but you won't have to deal with the consequences alone. That at least I can promise you."

She kisses me on the mouth. "I love you," she says.

I'm holding her tightly as I kiss her in return. Nothing else matters, nothing in the world. I want to speak but can't. As I kiss her again, I grope in my vocabulary until at last I'm able to say, "Do you know what you want to do, Vicky? Have you any idea?"

"I want to marry you," she says.

Willow and Wall. I go to Cornelius. Cornelius sits behind a big desk in a sterile room which could be beautiful but isn't because he's filled it with all the wrong things. Imagine hanging a Kandinsky over an Adam fireplace. Typical.

"Sir"—I usually call him "sir" at the office in an attempt to crawl out from the shadow of nepotism—"I've come to ask for a three-month leave of absence. I apologize for the inconvenience."

Cornelius, scenting trouble, looks watchful. "Why do you need such a leave of absence?"

"I want to go to Reno, sir, to establish Nevada residency. I've decided to get a divorce."

"Sit down, Sebastian." He's chilly. Divorce is not normal. It happens, of course, but it's not standard behavior. This has to be handled carefully if people are to be prevented from forming unfortunate opinions. Tiresome old Sebastian, he's thinking, always a thorn in my side. "Sebastian, I blame myself very much for not having had a frank talk with you earlier about this. Of course I'm not unaware of what's been going on, but I haven't interfered, partly because you've been very discreet and partly because . . ." He gets stuck.

This is difficult for Cornelius. He knows Mother is thrilled that Vicky and I have gotten together at last, and he wants Mother to be happy. But he hates the thought of Vicky in bed with anyone but her lawfully wedded husband, and even a lawfully wedded husband might be hard for Cornelius to contemplate with equanimity. However, on top of this emotional muddle lies the iron control of his pragmatism, and as usual with Cornelius, pragmatism triumphs.

"Don't misunderstand me," he says carefully. "I disapprove of the immorality, but how can I deny Vicky a little happiness with someone who cares for her? That would be wrong . . . and unnecessarily inflexible. I've no intention of criticizing you, Sebastian, but I do think you shouldn't let your current success with Vicky jettison you into a rash decision. Wouldn't it be better to keep the status quo for a while?"

I decide I've had enough of him preaching to me without full knowledge of the facts, so I fire the truth at point-blank range.

"Vicky's having a baby," I say tersely. "We'll marry in Reno as soon as I have my divorce."

Cornelius looks incredulous; he can't believe I would be dumb enough to get Vicky pregnant out of wedlock. Then he looks furious; I'm the bastard who's knocked up his little girl. But finally an expression of unwilling fascination creeps into his eyes. Against all the odds, Mother's soap-opera dreams are coming true. He and Mother will have a mutual grandchild at last. Forget Eric, Paul, and Benjamin. They're just Sam's sons. Vicky and Sebastian are going to produce the son he and Mother never had, and everyone is going to wallow in domestic bliss from here to eternity.

Cornelius is suddenly pulsating with excitement. "I see," he says, trying to keep calm. "Yes . . . yes, obviously you must marry!" He gropes for his customary practical outlook. "How much do the Reischmans know?"

He's nervous about Jake. This may be the final nail in the coffin of the informal partnership between the House of Reischman and the House of Van Zale.

"Elsa's already threatened me with divorce," I say, "although since time's important to Vicky, I don't want to hang around here while Elsa activates the messy, unpleasant New York State divorce law. Moreover, I think Elsa will be glad if I go to Reno and wind the whole thing up as swiftly as possible. Elsa's being very tough-minded about this, and that's one of the reasons why I don't think Jake will be too upset when he hears the news. It'd be different if Elsa were as wrecked as Vicky was when Sam died, but she's not. She's in good shape, already chalking the marriage up to experience and looking around for someone new. She'll be just as pleased as Jake to get rid of me."

Cornelius is much impressed by this reassuring analysis. He's already planning instructions to Scott on how to handle Jake with kid gloves. "Well, that doesn't sound so bad," he says, relaxed. "Good. I'm sure it's all for the best. When are you going?"

"Tomorrow at noon, if you approve the leave of absence."

Cornelius approves. He's beside himself with excitement by this time, and as soon as I turn to leave the room, he's picking up the phone to call Mother.

September 29, 1959. I pretend to go to the office but sneak back to pack my suitcases. Elsa always has a hair appointment on Tuesday mornings and meets a girlfriend afterward for lunch.

When my bags are packed I go to the nursery.

Alfred is trying to figure out how to put different-sized cubes into the right holes of a bright red box. Nurse is in his bedroom next door while she puts away some clean clothes.

I watch Alfred for a while.

There's a line by John Donne which begins: "Wilt thou forgive me?" and I try to remember the rest of the poem but I can't. Will you forgive me, Alfred? No, probably not. "Damn bastard!" you'll say when you're big enough. You'll turn your back on me and I won't be able to explain that I'm incapable of turning my back on you. It may look as if I'm turning my back, but I'll be facing both ways, for I'll be watching you always in my memory, watching you pick up those little cubes and drop them into the right slots of that gaily painted box.

"Smart kid," I say aloud.

Alfred looks up. "Daddy!" he says, and hurls a cube at me. I pick it up and show him which hole to put it in.

He drops the cube and beams up at me.

Alfred and I have communicated for the last time.

I want to take him to Reno, I want to take him to Mother, but what's the point? The Reischmans'll get him. Elsa's an innocent deserted wife and she'll be awarded custody. I'm not going to battle for Alfred either. I'll let him go—and not only because I know I've no hope of winning a legal struggle. I'll let him go because I can remember how it feels to be a child trapped between two parents fighting for custody, but my son's not going to have that kind of memories, not if I can help it.

I'll probably get good access in time. Elsa will shed forty pounds and when she remarries she'll be generous, just as my father eventually abandoned his bitterness when he remarried.

I'll see Alfred later. It's the end of something, but it's not the end of the world.

It feels like it, though. It sure feels like the end of the world. Worse.

I pick up Alfred and hug him. Then I put him down again, run out of the nursery, grab the picture of six-month-old Alfred from the living room, shove it in one of my suitcases, and blunder outside. I hail a yellow car but it's not a cab.

Can't see properly.

Stupid. I hate stupid things. Tears are stupid, permissible only for women and every other race on earth except Anglo-Saxons.

Maybe I'm not such an Anglo-Saxon after all.

We go to Reno and wallow in plastic culture for six weeks. When my residency is established I file for a divorce and bribe everyone to push the proceedings along as quickly as possible. Elsa signs the appropriate papers, and the day after the divorce is granted Vicky and I marry in a marriage parlor crammed with plastic flowers.

That afternoon we leave for Los Angeles, and the next day fly to Hawaii for a week.

I look forward to the honeymoon, but sex hurts Vicky now, so I just go for walks by myself along beautiful beaches, very romantic, and I listen to the sea and try not to think too much about Alfred. Vicky and I talk a little, but she remains tense. Finally we decide it's the wrong time for a honeymoon, so we fly home to New York, and Vicky can hardly wait to reach Fifth Avenue to see the kids.

I watch the joyful reunions and think of Alfred. Presently I say hello to Postumus, who's over a year old now, with thick reddish-brown hair, blue eyes, and an impudent look. He smiles at me chirpily and I smile back, trying to pretend he's mine, but he's not; he's Sam Keller's son, and brother to those two little horrors Eric and Paul. The thought of being stepfather to Eric and Paul is not one bit exciting. Soon we'll be looking around for a brownstone large enough to accommodate the family and all the servants we'll need to keep the domestic wheels turning, but I wish we could leave the four eldest kids with Mother and Cornelius and just take Postumus. I think Vicky would prefer that too, but she'll never do it—and not just because she loves those children of hers. She'll never leave them because she knows she could never handle the resulting guilt.

Vicky and I aren't meant to have a bunch of kids. Some couples are, some couples aren't. Elsa and I could have managed six kids and enjoyed them; Elsa slobbers over Alfred only because she knows she can't have more children, and if she had a large family she'd soon pull herself together to play the role of materfamilias to perfection.

But Vicky is incapable of being a materfamilias. Her children are a mystery to her. She showers them with affection, which is good, but beyond this she seems to have no idea how a mother should behave. If there are unpleasant scenes, she retreats behind Nurse; she not only can't face the squabbles endemic in any large family, but she can't face up to the fact that if you really love your children you'll lay down the law occasionally in order to help them understand they can't gallop through life trampling everyone underfoot as they grab what they want. Perhaps her desperate concern to demonstrate love by lavish kisses and misguided permissiveness springs from a subconscious knowledge that she doesn't, in truth, love them as she should. But she'll go to any lengths to conceal this from them, from the world, and from herself, so she beats her brains out trying to be what she thinks is a good mother, with the result that the little pests, spoiled rotten, walk all over her. This in turn destroys her confidence in herself, and the less confidence she has, the more she craves their love and the more she spoils them rotten in the mistaken belief that this will transform them into devoted sons and daughters.

There's only one ray of hope that I can see on the horizon, but it's not much of a ray and it may be a mirage created by my intense longing to view the future with optimism. It's possible, just remotely possible, that Vicky, contrary to most parents, may be able to handle those kids better when they're teenagers. I think she has the potential ability to look back clear-eyed at her own adolescence and draw some honest, sensible conclusions. However, meanwhile she has five children under ten and she's useless.

With an understanding and supportive husband, Vicky could possibly manage one child. Two would put a strain on the marriage, but with additional luck and the same understanding, supportive husband, she could probably still manage. But five children is a disaster and six is a plain invitation to tragedy. How we're going to survive, I don't know, but all we can do is try.

Vicky and I could probably manage Postumus and the new baby. We could without doubt manage the new baby alone. But the truth is, we should be a childless couple. I always sensed this, I think, and that's why the liaison seemed such a good idea. Mother and Cornelius may be dewy-eyed at the thought of the new baby, but Vicky and I deep down are running scared.

These are taboo thoughts. Not wanting children is abnormal. Acknowledging that some couples are better childless is offensive to society. So Vicky and I keep our doubts to ourselves and pretend we're pleased, a married couple signaling "NORMAL, NORMAL!" to everyone we meet.

"You're sure you don't want an abortion?" I say to Vicky more than once.

"I couldn't. I believe women should always have the right to choose whether they want an abortion or not, but I don't think I could ever face it unless the pregnancy was the result of rape or the doctors swore the child would be born a monster. It's the guilt. It frightens me. I'd be too terrified of cracking up."

She's right. Vicky's been overloaded with guilt for so long that even though I've helped her shed some of it, she's still in no fit state to risk taking on more. Of course some women see no need to feel guilty about having an abortion, but if you're guilt-prone or if you've been reduced to the brink of suicide in the past because you feel so inadequate and ashamed, you don't go asking for trouble by aborting a fetus. That's common sense, and if Vicky can see that, then surely I can see it too.

"You want me to have an abortion, don't you, Sebastian?"

"No, I want whatever's best for you, and as far as I can see, you've made the only possible decision under the circumstances. But I had to make sure you didn't want to change your mind while there was still time."

"I couldn't . . . couldn't . . ."

"Then don't. You're right. I'm glad. We'll manage."

"I'll love him when he comes," says Vicky, falling back on a platitude to keep our distress at arm's length.

"So will I."

It's true. We'll love him. But that doesn't alter the fact that his conception was a big mistake which is bound to have far-reaching and perhaps disastrous consequences.

We decide not to set up a home of our own before the baby comes, so we stay on at Fifth Avenue, and whenever we can't stand life in the Van Zale mansion a second longer, we escape to the blessed privacy of our apartment.

It's good to be back there again. Vicky's pleased too, but soon she's miserable, knowing I want sex, feeling inadequate because she can't face it, crashing emotionally from inadequacy to guilt to shame.

"Look," I say, "it's okay. I'll get along. I'm not going to die. I had to live a celibate life at school, and I'll live a celibate life again for a while, that's all. It's no big deal. Don't feel there's any pressure on you."

She looks at me with troubled gray eyes and says, "Will you be unfaithful?"

"Not interested. Other women don't exist."

"But how will you manage?"

She's so innocent sometimes that I'm reminded of the diaphragm disaster. I explain how I'll manage behind a locked bathroom door.

"Sam probably did the same and didn't tell you," I say, shrugging it off to show her how unimportant the subject is, but even as I reassure her, I'm thinking that it would be just like Sam Keller, smart-aleck man-of-the-world Sam Keller, to kid himself that her aversion gave him a legitimate excuse to two-time her.

I can feel Sam's shoes sliding onto my feet again, and this time they're pinching a bit, but with an effort I can still kick them off. I'll not stand in Sam Keller's shoes because I love Vicky, and no matter what happens, I'm going to save her; I'm going to give her back that life which Sam went so far to destroy.

I call Elsa. It's stupid, but I can't help myself. I've got to know how Alfred is. Mother says he's fine, but she hasn't seen him since Vicky and I went to Reno, because Amy Reischman took Elsa and Alfred on a trip to Europe and they've only just returned.

"Hi," I say. "Don't hang up. How is he?"

"Fine." She hangs up.

I get mad. Anger's healthy. I call back.

"I want to see him."

"Huh! What a hope!" is her first reaction, but then she relents and I see Alfred. He remembers. His little face lights up. He runs over and chatters to me. He still doesn't talk too clearly yet, but I can understand what he's saying. I stay ten minutes and watch him play. I never see Elsa. Nurse meets me when I walk in, and Nurse shows me out when I leave.

I feel much better after seeing Alfred.

Christmas comes and goes. The new decade dawns. Vicky and I no longer attempt sex, but one good aspect of our marriage is that we can now go out frequently without having to worry about Elsa's detectives. We go to plays, galleries, and concerts—even to Presley's most recent movie, *King Creole,* which keeps reappearing to give sustenance to all the Elvis fans gasping for their drafted hero's next venture on the screen. We have a lot of laughs, a lot of interesting conversation, a lot of fun. It almost makes up for the sex being hopeless, but even that should pick up after the baby's born. All I have to do is endure a schoolboy's sex life until March—no, April or early

May. The baby's due in March, but Vicky'll need time to recover
from the birth.

God, it seems a long time to wait.

March 21, 1960. Vicky gives birth to our son. I feel happy, but
Cornelius and Mother are happier. I hope they don't upset Vicky,
who's looking pale and tired.

"I'm all right," she says when I see her, but she's not. Something's
going on in her mind. She's thinking, thinking, thinking. She's a million miles away.

I've taught her how to think. I've shown her the view from a
different window on the world. I've encouraged her to believe she's
an individual with a mind of her own. Is the ultimate irony going to
be . . . ?

But no, I can't let myself consider that. I won't.

Come back, Vicky. Please come back. I love you and I truly believe we can make it together.

Maybe Sam Keller said those words once. I'm right back in his
shoes again, but this time they're stuck and I can't kick them off.
Have I really done no better than Sam Keller? Maybe not.

But surely I must have done better! Because I love Vicky I can see
her with such vivid clarity that I can not only identify her suffering
but also unhesitatingly locate its source. I understand her. I know exactly what she's been through and I've helped her survive. How
could I improve on that?

Yet something's wrong. Perhaps after all it's I, not Elsa, who
resemble the "idiot savant" who can't write his name although he can
calculate logarithms in his head. I may be an expert on Vicky, but
I'm no expert on women in general—the way I underestimated Elsa
proves that. In certain favorable circumstances I can show prodigious
talent as an amateur analyst, but what's really going on at the back
of my mind behind the overwhelming drive of my love and sympathy
and concern?

Perhaps I want to cure Vicky not so much for her sake as for
mine. Perhaps, like Sam, I'm trying to make her over into what I
want her to be—an intellectual companion, an exciting partner in
bed, a mistress who can enable me to enjoy life to the full. But what
does Vicky want? I think she would have enjoyed the role I wanted
to assign to her; I think the liaison could have worked very well. But
that's not the point. The point is, first, that Vicky's still not running

her own life, and second, that the liaison itself is no more. Vicky's no longer my mistress. She's my wife, and I don't think she's any more suited to be a wife than Sam Keller was suited to be a husband.

Do I seriously think Vicky's going to enjoy running a big household and dealing with a shoal of kids any more now than she did when she was married to Sam? No, I don't. And do I seriously think that after performing these herculean domestic duties she'll have any more energy left over for me than she had left over for Sam? No, I don't. And never mind me, either—forget me for a moment. The truth is, Vicky won't even have enough energy left over to live any kind of life of her own, the one destiny I've advocated for her all along. She'll just be getting bogged down all over again in the kind of life she's not at heart interested in, and she'll never have the chance to find out what kind of life might suit her better. In other words, despite all I've done, she'll be right back at first base.

If only we could have maintained the liaison! I can see more clearly than ever now that we were meant to be lovers, not a married couple as defined by our plastic society, and yet here we are, a married couple with a baby plus five other kids waiting in the wings, and it's all wrong for both of us, and both of us secretly know it.

I'm in such pain that I can't analyze the situation further, can't work out what the answer is—if there's an answer at all, which I doubt. All I know is that the trouble's getting bigger, like the pain, and our relationship's falling apart.

I begin to doubt if the pain can get any worse, but it does.

The baby becomes sick. We've decided to call him Edward John. He weighs eight pounds, two ounces and is pink and white with no hair. I like him very, very much and when he's sick I'm very, very upset. He lies in an incubator fighting for breath.

The doctors say it's cystic fibrosis.

Babies don't live if they develop cystic fibrosis.

Edward John dies after six days in the world.

I'm drinking too much. I've asked Mother if she could take the kids away for a while, and she and Cornelius somehow pull themselves together sufficiently to ship everyone, including themselves, to Arizona. Cornelius has recently bought a winter home there, not only because the air is good for his asthma but because he's still kidding himself that he's building up to an early retirement among the cacti.

I sit alone at Fifth Avenue and drink. Presently I have to see a social worker at the hospital, and with her help I organize a very, very small funeral for that very, very small coffin. I'm the only mourner, and the service is over in minutes. Then I drink some more and go to the hospital to see Vicky.

Difficult to talk, but I must try.

"It's been hell, hasn't it?" I say. "What do you think's the best way out? I can take you away somewhere . . . or we can stay at the apartment if you don't want to travel."

She stares down at the sheet. Finally she manages to say, "I want to be alone, Sebastian."

This is what I've been afraid of.

"To think?"

"Yes. To think."

"Okay." Sam Keller's shoes are nailed to my feet and they're the tightest possible fit. I'm hurting all over. I don't know how I'll live with the pain.

I take her to the apartment.

"Call whenever you feel ready to see me," I say, kissing her briefly on the cheek.

She nods. I go away.

I return to the Van Zale mansion and wonder how long I'll have to wait.

She calls. She's been alone for two weeks. Cornelius keeps phoning in a frenzy from Arizona to say she's been mentally unhinged by the loss of her child and may kill herself. Since it's impossible for me to hold a rational conversation with him, I ask Mother to explain that Vicky wishes to be alone and that no one, least of all Cornelius, has any right to intrude. To her great credit Mother appears to understand and promises me she'll restrain Cornelius from rushing to Vicky's side.

I'm about to leave the bank when Vicky calls.

"Sebastian, can you meet me at the Plaza?"

When I arrive she's waiting in the lobby. She's wearing a drab coat and she hasn't set her hair, so that there are no curls, only waves. This makes her look younger, and unexpectedly I remember her as she used to look long ago before she unconsciously played Juliet to my disastrous Romeo at Bar Harbor.

We have a drink in the Oak Bar.

"How are you doing?" I say to her.

"Better. Everything seems clearer at last."

We're sitting in a corner and I'm drinking Scotch too fast while she's stirring but not touching a Tom Collins. Her voice is calm and her eyes are dry, but she keeps stirring and stirring and stirring. She can't look at me.

"It was terrible about the baby, wasn't it?" she says at last. "It seemed so pointless to put a baby in the world just for six days. The pointlessness upset me. I felt there had to be a point. I just couldn't believe we went through all that for nothing."

"Yes. Futile. No God. Obvious. It makes me mad." I drink nearly all my Scotch and signal for another. "But it doesn't matter now—nothing matters so long as we can get back together again." I don't mean to say that, but it slips out, and now I'm the one who stares down at my glass and can't look anyone in the eye.

I hear her voice. "Sebastian, I do love you in many ways, and I'll never forget how much I owe you for standing by me when I was in despair, but—"

"Don't say it. Don't. Please."

"I've got to," she says. "I've got to face up to the way things really are. It's a question of survival."

I look at her, and for the first time in my life I see Cornelius behind her eyes. She's never reminded me of him before. There's a physical resemblance, but nothing in her character or personality has ever reflected him to me, and for a second I see the new Vicky—no, not the new Vicky but the real Vicky, the person no one, not even I myself, has truly tried to know.

"I could go on kidding myself," she says. "I could say Edward John lived and died to bring us together in holy matrimony so that we could live happily ever after. I did say that for a time, because otherwise his life and death seemed so pointless, but then gradually I began to realize the point was *not* to encourage me to go on living the same old lies. The point of his life and death was to bring me face to face with the truth, and the truth is, of course—"

"I know we should never have had Edward John, but—"

"No, probably not, but that's not the main issue. The main issue is that I should never have married you. It's true I've had a much more successful relationship with you than I ever had with Sam, but that hasn't stopped us from ending up in exactly the same mess, has it? You're so sweet and kind and understanding that I let you make love to me not because I want to but because I feel I ought to—can't you see the familiar pattern recurring? And let's be honest—our sex life's been a disaster, hasn't it? You probably had better times with Elsa than you ever had with me."

"No, Vicky. The most wonderful times of my life were with you." My new drink arrives. I take a big gulp of it but can hardly swallow. "Vicky, I think we can get this to work. I'm sure we can solve our problems. We've got so much else going for us."

"Yes," she says, "we have, but the sex is just no good. There are two reasons for this, not just one. If there was only one, maybe we could work something out, but . . ."

"I don't know what you mean," I say. But I do.

"Well, the obvious reason is the physical one—we just don't seem to fit together well. You must know this—you can't be unaware of it. We're physically mismatched."

"Only in your mind, Vicky."

"But—"

"What you're saying is anatomically impossible. It's just one of those old sex myths which everyone believes but which has no basis in medical fact."

She shrugs. "If you want to take that line, I can't stop you."

I have another gulp of Scotch. She still hasn't touched her drink. I'm reminded of Cornelius toying with a sherry glass the size of a thimble while he conducts an interview requiring all his skill and concentration. "If you want to take that line, I can't stop you." I hear the pragmatism echoing behind the terse, ruthless monosyllables, and again I glimpse the stranger who's so unnervingly familiar to me, the stranger with a mind of her own.

"Vicky . . ."

"All right, you disagree. Then let me give you the other reason why the sex is just no good. It's because my motives for going to bed with you are all wrong. They were all wrong with Sam too. What I was really saying to you both was: 'Help me, take care of me, I can't handle life on my own.' I said that to you when I got pregnant and panicked, although the words which came out were: 'I want to marry you.' Sebastian, I've got to learn to stand alone. If I keep seeking out men to take care of me, I'm always going to end up in the same mess, can't you see, because what I'm really doing is trading my body in return for paternal care. I'm prostituting myself all the time—

no wonder I so often suffer from a revulsion toward sex! It's a miracle I can bring myself to go to bed with anyone at all. So I've got to end this cycle, Sebastian. I've got to get out and set myself free."

I don't answer, can't answer. She's probably right, I know she's right, but where does that leave me? How do I survive in a world where Vicky never wants me to make love to her again?

"I didn't always hurt you, did I, Vicky?"

"Usually."

"No pleasure? None at all?"

"None."

How brutal the truth can be. No wonder we all spend so much time lying to each other and deceiving ourselves. It's dangerous to look directly at the sun with the naked eye. The sun can blind you. You can be maimed for life.

"Sebastian . . ."

"No, don't say any more. No point."

What more is there to say? I love her; I'll love her always, and perhaps one day she'll come back to me. But meanwhile all that matters is that I can no longer help her and that if I love her I'll let her go.

I take a five-dollar bill out of my pocket and leave it on the table for the waiter.

Suddenly she starts to cry, and then she's the old Vicky again, lost, muddled, and unhappy, turning to the nearest protective male for the care she's been mainlining on for years. That's some habit Cornelius gave her, and I know now I've got to do all I can to help her break it.

"Forgive me, Sebastian—I hate hurting you like this . . . I do love you very much. . . . Oh, Sebastian, I didn't mean it, let's go to the apartment, let's try again. . . ."

"Then Edward John would have lived and died for nothing." Now it's my turn to present the brutal truth. "Sure you love me, Vicky—like a sister loves a brother. Let's leave it at that, shall we?" I get up. I don't touch her. I don't kiss her good-bye. But I say quietly in my firmest voice, "Good luck, Vicky. Lots of luck, all the luck in the world. And remember—wherever you are and whatever happens to you, I'm with you all the way."

She can't speak, just covers her face with her hands.

I leave.

I'm blind with pain. I walk but don't know where I'm walking. Once I stop in a bar, but I can't drink. I want to talk to someone, but there are no words.

Should I go back to Elsa? No, she'd never have me back. I'd swallow my pride to be with Alfred again, but Elsa's all Reischman and she'll never forgive me for walking out on her.

I wonder what I'll do about women in the future. I guess I'll eventually make it with someone again, although at present this seems inconceivable. I've no desire. I'm dead from the waist down.

I walk and walk and I know it's late because I see fewer people on the streets. I must go home, but where's home? There's Elsa's place and Vicky's place and Mother's place, but none of them feels like home to me now. I must get a place of my own. A studio apartment. I'd like to live in one room, like a monk. I wonder who lives in Kevin Daly's attic nowadays.

I'd like to talk to Kevin Daly. I'd like to talk to the man who understands that two people can love each other yet still be cut off from true communication; I'd like to talk to the man who knows that love doesn't necessarily conquer all.

But Kevin's so famous, so popular, so busy. Better not to bother him.

Where the hell am I? I stop to look around. I seem to be on Eighth Street west of Fifth Avenue. Not far from Kevin.

I find a pay phone and get the number from the operator. Kevin's listed under the pseudonym Q. X. O'Daly. I remember Vicky and I laughing about that once, long ago.

The phone rings.

"Hello?" says Kevin.

"Hi," I say. It's so hard to speak, but I manage to tell him my name.

"Ah!" says Kevin, sparkling as ever. "The man who compared me with John Donne! When are you going to come and see me?"

I want to be polite and diplomatic, but it's beyond me. I just say, "Now?"

"Okay. You know the address, don't you?"

"Yes." I say good-bye. Then I hang up and glance at my watch. It's half-past one in the morning.

Kevin's wearing plain blue pajamas with a white robe on top. He opens the door and says he's making coffee. Would I mind sitting in the kitchen?

I try to apologize, but he waves that aside and somehow succeeds in making me feel welcome. His kitchen is warm and unpretentious. I tell him so, and he's pleased.

We sit down with our coffee. I'm not sure what to say—I don't even know if I want to say anything—but I like sitting in a well-lit room with someone friendly. It's better than being alone in the dark.

"Well, how are you, Kevin?" I say, feeling that I must make some effort to talk, since he's been so kind to me.

"Frightful," says Kevin. "My personal life's like Hiroshima after the bomb. How are you?"

He's probably lying, but it doesn't matter, because he's signaling a message which has nothing to do with the surface meaning of this extravagant declaration. He's seen that I'm wrecked. He's agreeing how hellish life can be. He's saying that if I want to talk he'll listen.

I talk a little, but not much, because I'm afraid of not behaving like an Anglo-Saxon.

"Christ, this coffee's terrible!" says Kevin. "Have a drink."

He's writing a prescription to help me along.

"Okay."

"Mind what you have?"

"No."

Kevin produces a bottle with a picture of a bird on it, and soon talking gets a little easier. I can't tell him everything, but it doesn't matter, because Kevin picks up my disjointed sentences and reads meaning into them as no one else would.

We have another drink.

"I keep asking myself what will happen to her," I say at last. "Will she in fact ever be able to stand alone? And if and when she does, will she like her new life any better than the old life she's rejecting? What does independence mean for a woman anyway? Isn't it a contradiction in terms? How can a woman reconcile the concept of independence with the biological fact that in most male-female relationships both parties are more comfortable if they feel the man's the dominant partner?"

"Ah, but is it biological?" says Kevin quickly. "Or is it just social conditioning? I remember discussing this point once with my sister, Anne, and she said—did anyone ever tell you about my sister, Anne?"

"I don't think so."

"No, I don't talk much about her nowadays. Well, Anne called this problem the classic feminine dilemma, and years ago, after her husband died—or was it after she left him? the two events were almost simultaneous—we sat down right here at this table and debated the subject together. I took the optimistic view: I thought that if only a woman would have the courage to be herself she'd have much more of a chance of finding a man with the courage to accept her as an independent person, even if she didn't live up to our society's concept of the ideal woman. But my sister Anne said I was deluding myself. She said this was sheer romantic idealism."

"Your sister Anne sounds a depressing cynic."

"My sister Anne is beautiful, intelligent, witty, and talented. But she said any woman who wanted to be independent automatically cut herself off from men in the male-oriented society we live in today because this society ensured that men could only cope with their own plastic fantasies of womankind; she said that by the time our society had raised these poor guys to fight wars and chase the godalmighty dollar, they just had no energy left to face any woman smarter than an animated doll. Anne said that until society changed, men's attitudes to women wouldn't change, but she saw no hope of change while the world was preoccupied with war and materialism. She told me to pray for a better world."

"And did you?"

"No, I decided to leave it all to her. She's a nun now, although whether she became a nun to pray for a better world or because she thought no man was good enough for her, I'm damned if I can decide. Every Christmas I go up to Massachusetts to see her, and every Christmas I get drunk out of my mind with rage. Anne says I'm jealous of God. Maybe she's right. Christ! Have another drink."

"Okay. Kevin, this sister of yours . . ."

"Oh, yes, it's just another one of those run-of-the-mill till-death-do-us-part sibling relationships, nothing unusual, nothing sensational, but I was so pleased when her marriage broke up—it was after the war, and I'd bought this house and she was going to come and live with me, I had the attic all fixed up. She used to paint—Christ, I liked her paintings, I wanted Neil to buy one, but you know Neil, he probably thought it wasn't a good investment."

"Yeah. He would."

"Then Anne went into the convent, so there I was with the attic fully converted for artistic use and no artist to put in it. That was when I embarked on my illustrious line of caretakers. I didn't need a caretaker, of course, but no one seemed to think my behavior in the least extraordinary. It just shows that if you act with enough confidence people accept your actions without questioning them. Incredible. Did *no one* find it odd that I kept a caretaker? Apparently not. . . . I can't think why I'm telling you all this. I usually keep my mouth shut about my more bizarre behavior."

"I don't think it's bizarre. Did you ever find anyone who measured up to Anne?"

"No, of course not. And even if I had, I'd have been incapable of doing anything except treating her as a sister. God, isn't life hell! More ice?"

"Thanks. Say, Kevin, talking of your caretakers, is anyone using your attic at the moment?"

"No, as a matter of fact I've just had the most godawful crisis. My last caretaker fell in love with me. I can't tell you what a mess it was. I had someone living here at the time—a most unusual departure from routine, because I can't stand anyone getting under my feet when I'm trying to write—and in a reckless moment I went to bed with both of them. Not together, of course, I'm much too old for orgies, but then, goddammit, the two of them got together and compared notes and all hell broke loose. The stupid thing was that Betty, my caretaker, was the one I really enjoyed living with—or not living with, if you follow me—but of course it was no good in bed, while my other house guest . . . Well, you can guess the rest. The truth of the whole matter is that I'm incapable of sustaining a close personal relationship with either sex. It's a defect of my communications system. I communicate by writing, not by loving. My so-called talent's just a profitable way of handling a huge inadequacy."

"Christ, Kevin, if everyone inadequate wrote your kind of plays, I'd go down on my knees and pray for a whole lot more inadequate people in the world!"

"What shameless flattery! I love it. Have another drink."

I laugh and he laughs with me. Can I really be laughing? Yes, I am. I mustn't think of Vicky, though, or I'll start hurting again. Oh, God.

"Now, tell me why you wanted to know whether the attic was free," says Kevin, filling our glasses again.

"I was wondering if I could rent it from you for a while. I've nowhere to go. I promise I'll keep myself to myself and not be a nuisance."

"That's okay, I'll heave you out if you get tiresome. Yes, of course you can have the attic. Stay as long as you want. I think I may have reached the end of my long line of caretakers."

"How much rent shall I pay you?"

"Don't be ridiculous. Buy me a bottle of bourbon occasionally to replace the ones your stepfather drinks."

"How often does Cornelius come here?"

"About once a month. After Sam died, Neil and I decided we both found it comforting to talk occasionally to an old friend of well over thirty years' standing. One gets appallingly sentimental, you know, once one's past fifty."

"Christ, I wonder what Cornelius will think when he hears I've moved in here!"

"The worst, of course," says Kevin, poker-faced.

We laugh again, and again I'm amazed that laughter's possible. I feel very grateful to Kevin, but I don't know how to show it except by not outstaying my welcome. I get up to leave.

"Where are you off to now?" says Kevin, surprised. "I thought you said you had nowhere to go."

"Well, there's Fifth Avenue . . ."

"Forget it. You'd cut your throat in despair before you were halfway across the threshold. The attic's in a mess at the moment, but I do have two guest rooms. Use one."

I use one. I sit down alone and think that communication's like love. It doesn't matter where, how, or with whom you do it so long as you do it because if you don't do it you die.

I'm going to live.

I lie on the bed and think: I won't sleep.

But I do.

PART FIVE

Scott: 1960–1963

Chapter One

I

THE TELEPHONE rang.

"Scott? Cornelius. The latest development in this godawful crisis is that Sebastian says he wants to go and work in the London office—he thinks it would be better if he went right away for a while, and personally so do I, I'm all for it, I don't want him sulking around here and upsetting Vicky, but of course Alicia's hysterical at the thought of Sebastian going to live so far away and she's been saying some very harsh things about Vicky which I just can't accept. . . .

"Life's tough at home at the moment, let me tell you, and I'm beginning to feel like I'm going crazy. It would all be so much easier if Alicia and I knew *why* this marriage has collapsed, but nobody explains, nobody tells us anything, and we're just supposed to make guesses as if it was same damned quiz show. . . .

"Do you think it's got something to do with sex? I mean, if two people get on real well together yet still feel they've got to live apart, wouldn't that imply there was some overriding sexual problem? Christ, that oaf Sebastian! First he walks out on Elsa, now he walks out on Vicky—the man's obviously sexually unstable. I never told you this before, Scott, but there were a couple of incidents years ago, one at Bar Harbor and one right here in New York . . . What was that you said? Yes, yes, I know it's Vicky who's walked out, I know it looks as if Sebastian's not the guilty party, but what else could my little girl do after winding up married to a sex pervert? . . . What did you say? . . . Oh, cut it out, for Christ's sake! What do you know about marriage anyway? You're just a forty-one-year-old bachelor who never gets involved! . . . The hell with you!" yelled Cornelius, having whipped himself into a rage, and slammed down the receiver.

II

THE PHONE rang again five minutes later.

"Hi, Scott, it's me again. Look, I'm sorry I bawled you out just now—the truth is I'm so miserable I can't think straight. Vicky's gone to that apartment of hers on Sutton Place, Alicia's not talking to me, and I've given up trying to confide in Kevin because he's on Sebastian's side and just says stupid things like, 'Neil, fuck off, for God's sake, and mind your own business.' But it *is* my business! It was my grandson who died, wasn't it, and my daughter whose heart's been broken, and my wife who . . . well, let's not talk about Alicia. I tried to tell Kevin all that, but he hung up, and then I just felt so down and so upset that I automatically dialed your number. . . . What was that? . . . Chess? Well, I hate to ask you, Scott, because I know how late it is, but . . . You will? That's wonderful of you, Scott—many, many thanks. God, sometimes I wonder what I'd ever do without you. . . ."

III

"THIS IS about the last private house left on Fifth Avenue, isn't it?" said the cabdriver five minutes later. "Gee, the taxes must be sky-high! How does the old guy afford to live there? If I was him I'd sell out to the real-estate guys and go live in Miami Beach someplace and sit in the sun all day long. . ."

The driver chattered on, unthinking, unfeeling, unaware that he was no more than a microscopic speck imprisoned in the straitjacket of time. Scott lived in time too, but *I* was beyond it. Scott saw the shabby interior of the cab and heard the driver's Hispanic accent, but *I* saw the great gates of the Van Zale mansion and thought as I had so often thought before: "Childe Roland to the Dark Tower came."

It was Scott too who entered the house when the door was opened, but *I* was right there with him, just as I always was, and in my impregnable invisibility I watched his world with detachment from behind his smiling eyes.

"Scott! I sure appreciate you coming . . ." Cornelius, wearing three sweaters, was hunched over an electric fire at one end of the library while he read a book by Harold Robbins. The temperature in the room was probably ninety degrees. "What are you drinking, Scott? Coke? Seven-Up? Root beer?"

Cornelius was reminding me again of Masaccio's portrait of St. John in his painting *The Tribute Money*. According to Masaccio, St. John is beautiful. He has curling golden hair, gray eyes, and exquisitely molded features, but despite these dazzling looks the face remains hard, the eyelids lowered at a sinister angle. Masaccio had caught the humanism of the Renaissance but had ruthlessly tainted his idealistic vision with the ferocious despotism of the Medicis.

"It's cold, isn't it? Makes me wish I was in Arizona, but God only knows when I'll see Arizona again. Alicia now tells me flatly that she hates it and has no intention of spending more than two weeks a year down there in future, so it looks like my dream of an early retirement and going to live at the ranch isn't going to come to anything. . . .

"But that doesn't matter. I'd just about decided anyway that God didn't intend me to live in Tucson, Arizona, any more than he intended me to live in Velletria, Ohio. The truth is, I don't know what I'd do down there to keep myself occupied. I guess I could start an art museum, but I can't see it ever being as much fun as the one here in New York—in fact, I can't see anything down there being as much fun as anything in New York, and besides . . . what would I do without the bank? I don't think, after all, I'm cut out for an early retirement. . . .

"Yes, I admit that when Sam died all I wanted was to work myself into a position where I could give up everything and live a quiet, peaceful, domestic life with my wife somewhere a long way from New York, but I think I was in some kind of shock or something, I don't think I was being realistic. If my asthma forces me to retire eventually, okay, so be it. But until that happens . . .

"Oh, sure, I know that money and power are really very important, but banking's my whole life, and goddammit, *someone's* got to run the country's banks, and if God didn't mean me to be a banker, why did he make me the way I am? If God gives us specific gifts, isn't it up to us to utilize them to the best of our ability? It seems to me I've got a kind of moral duty to keep working."

"Cornelius, your mind never ceases to amaze me once you start to wrap it around metaphysical problems! Let's get going on our game of chess."

Half an hour passed. Two bottles of Coca-Cola were emptied, and the soft glow of the lamp illuminated the ivory figures edging toward one another across the board.

"Are you mad at me, Scott?"

"Why should I be mad at you, Cornelius?"

"For postponing my retirement."

"No. Obviously you want to do what's best for you and best for the bank. I could hardly expect you to do other than that."

"Well, I still want to be fair. I still want . . . Scott, I'm going to be just about this, and generous. I want to make everyone happy."

"That seems like a praiseworthy aim!"

"No, seriously, Scott! I mean it. Look, this is the way I see it: I'm fifty-two, and unless my health gets much worse, I think I can go on working till I'm sixty. Then I'll cut down my workload, retire from banking, and just keep on with the Fine Arts Foundation and the charities—the 'good' things, if you follow me . . ."

"Uh-huh."

"And I'll turn the bank over to you. When I'm sixty you'll still only be forty-nine. The only proviso I'd make would be that you'd pass the bank eventually to my grandsons, but that's okay, isn't it? You've got no sons of your own, and you can make them your heirs, just as I've made you my heir. I see you as a kind of benign caretaker during a Van Zale interregnum . . . but it's the right solution, isn't it? You approve?"

"I approve. Your move, Cornelius."

The knight sprang forward and sideways. A pawn slipped forward to protect the queen.

"The real truth of the matter is," said Cornelius, "that although I wanted to quit directly after Sam died, it just wasn't possible. You realized that, didn't you? I had to get the best man to take care of the bank for my grandsons, but when Sam died, there was a power vacuum—he *was* the best man. And even when you emerged top of the heap in the ensuing maneuvers among the partners, my hands were still tied because there was no way I could pass over Sebastian without wrecking all my new happiness with Alicia. There would have been no problem if only he'd been a fool, but of course, as we both know, he's not. He's very competent and able. Until now I just haven't had an excuse for passing him over, but now . . ." Cornelius made an insignificant movement with his rook. ". . . now it'll be easier."

"I understand."

"I'll keep Sebastian in Europe, give him a large expense account and a lot of freedom, and Alicia won't even realize he's been railroaded. In the end I can even give her the illusion he's been promoted, but it'll all take time, Scott, and that's why I need these extra years so badly. I've got to be able to wrap up Sebastian securely before I can pass control to you. You will be patient, won't you? It's in your best interests as well as mine."

"Of course."

"You've been clever with Sebastian, Scott. I've noticed what care you've always taken to get on well with him. Your move."

"This may surprise you, Cornelius, but I genuinely like Sebastian."

Cornelius laughed good-naturedly at such a fantastic possibility, and said with affection, "God, Scott, you're a smart guy!" I was aware of his fingers curling toward the palms of his hands as he stealthily waited for me to make the error which would give him the upper hand in the game.

More time slipped away. Dawn broke over Central Park, and beyond the chink in the heavy drapes the sky changed from black to navy to azure, and finally to a very pale duck-egg blue. Cornelius' fine delicate skin was faintly flushed with excitement; the light glinted on the silver in his hair and was reflected in his shining eyes.

"Checkmate! I've got you, Scott!"

"Shit!"

Laughter. The king crashed sideways on the board.

"The moment of truth!" said Cornelius gleefully.

"Yes. 'Childe Roland to the Dark Tower came.'"

"I never did understand that story," said Cornelius, uncapping two final bottles of Coke. "Tell it to me again. This knight Roland was on a quest, you say, although the reader of the poem is never told what the quest is. Now, isn't it kind of annoying that we don't know exactly what he's after? Then he reaches the Dark Tower and he thinks: 'This is it!' and he sees his ex-companions watching him from the hillside, but they're all dead. Which is kind of morbid, if you ask me. So he puts his horn to his lips and blows, and that's that. But why does Browning end the poem there? I don't get it at all."

"Roland met his destiny by raising the horn to his lips."

"But what was his destiny?"

"Life or death. Perhaps death. When Galahad reached the end of his quest, he died. According to T. H. White, when you reach perfection you die because there's nothing else left to achieve."

"Huh! More metaphysical garbage. You're death-obsessed, Scott— that's your trouble!"

"Isn't everyone, consciously or subconsciously? After all, as Spenser said, 'All things do decay and to their end draw near.' "

"And that's a goddamned depressing thing to say! I don't like it when you talk like that—it's as if there's someone else there who's borrowed your voice . . . my God, listen to me! What a crazy thing to say—you must have infected me with that morbid streak of yours! Okay, Scott, we'd better both go and snatch some sleep now, but thanks again for coming, I truly appreciate it. So long."

"So long, Cornelius," I said from behind Scott's eyes, and as I left I thought of that future when I would call on Cornelius again, I the president of the newly incorporated Sullivan empire, he the retired senior partner hunched in his wheelchair, his grandsons sacked and scattered among the Wall Street unemployed. "Good morning, Scott," he would say to me, but in his mind he would call me by my father's name, for I would be my father's ghost waiting to usher him from the lighted hall of life, and in his doomed future he would see the past I had rewritten, my father's defeat transformed into a mighty victory and his own triumph erased by the fierce flames of a cataclysmic fire.

IV

THE SUNLIGHT streamed through the hospital window onto the bed where Emily lay recovering from an operation for gallstones. Emily's hair was wholly gray now, her face lined and bony through loss of weight.

"Scott, dearest, how sweet of you to come all the way to Velletria for the weekend—I do appreciate it! I'm sorry I sounded so depressed to you on the phone before I went into the hospital. It was strange, but I had this strong premonition that I'd come here to die, but of course that was just me being silly because I do so hate being in the hospital . . . well, I mustn't think about death anymore. Tell me your news. Dare I ask how things are in New York?"

"Better. Sebastian's left for Europe and Alicia seems to be accepting at last that there's nothing she can do to patch up his marriage. Vicky's decided she must have a home of her own, so she's looking for an apartment big enough to house all the kids and staff."

"I wish I could do something to help that girl, but she seems to be beyond my reach nowadays, just like Cornelius. However, I mustn't get depressed thinking of Cornelius. I've done my best for him, and there's nothing more I can do. But I wish I could do more for Vicky . . . and for you too, Scott. Oh, yes! I often feel I failed you in the past."

"Failed me? You? I've never heard such nonsense in all my life!"

"If only I'd been older when I married Steve, old enough for you to regard me as a mother! But you never saw me as a mother, did you? I was always the fairy-tale princess, just a few years your senior, and when Steve left, I was transformed overnight into the jilted heroine. I should have said something then, I should have talked to you, I should have sat down with you and had at least one honest conversation—"

"Emily, please! Stop crucifying yourself!"

"—but I said nothing. I left it all to Cornelius. I was weak and cowardly and self-absorbed with my own unhappiness, and I let Cornelius use you to fill the lack in his own life."

"Well, why speak of that as though it's some great tragedy? It's all ended happily enough."

"It hasn't ended. It's still going on, forcing you to lead this abnormal life. Oh, don't think I don't realize what's going on! As soon as I read Tony's letter—"

"Oh, forget the letter, for Christ's sake!"

"But it made me realize just how you must feel toward Cornelius!"

"I doubt that very much. Emily, my feelings for Cornelius are really very unimportant."

"You must forgive him, you must! Otherwise you'll never be at peace with yourself, never be able to lead a normal life . . ."

"Emily, I hate to say this, but you understand absolutely nothing here."

There was a silence. Then she shrugged listlessly and turned her face to the wall. "If you can't be honest with me, I guess there's no use talking to you."

"It's the truth. The driving force in my life isn't a hatred of your brother. The situation's much more complex than your simple reading of the facts would make it appear."

"I don't understand."

There was another silence.

"Can't you explain?"

The silence persisted.

"Oh, Scott!" she said in despair. "How I wish you could talk to me! Is there no one you can talk to? I hate to think of you so horribly cut off and alone."

"But I enjoy my solitude!"

"That's not solitude," she said. "That's isolation. That's a living death."

"Well, that's your opinion, Emily, and I'm sure you're entitled to it, but your opinion doesn't happen to be mine. Now, please—why don't we talk about something more cheerful?"

V

EMILY DIED a week later of a pulmonary embolism, and there was a big family funeral in Velletria. Cornelius wept. There was no longer anyone alive now who was part of his remote past, and so it was as if a part of him too was being buried with Emily that day in the Midwestern suburb he had always detested.

"Ashes to ashes," said the minister. "Dust to dust."

Memories stirred, memories of a golden-haired, much-loved Emily transforming a desolate household long ago, happy memories, memories of times long gone but not long forgotten, when death was as remote as snow on midsummer's day and all pain was obliterated by peace.

The cold wind blew again. Scott's eyes saw the sunshine of that cool day in early spring, but in my eyes it was dark and a great clock was striking noon. In Scott's world the minister was reading the Christian service, but although I heard those words, they meant nothing to me for I was beyond them in time, far, far back in the remotest corner of the blueprint inherited from my father, and in my folk memory of forgotten summers I knew a different moral code. Blood calls for blood, violence for violence; Christianity is a mere veneer, civilization is only skin-deep, and beneath it all is the timeless chaotic ecstasy of the dark.

Scott stood at the graveside, black-suited, head bowed, united with the other grieving mourners, but I was apart from Scott now, I was escaping from my grief, I was drifting away from him into that other world, the world of my solitude, the world of my dreams.

VI

I USED to dream that I was the knight in Bergman's film *The Seventh Seal*. The knight played chess with the hooded figure of Death on a beautiful deserted shore, and before Death could complete his inevitable victory, the knight begged him for additional time in which to live.

I often felt that I too was begging Death for extra time. I was so afraid of dying before I could achieve my ambition—or before I could "complete my quest" as I used to say in my dreams once I had discarded the personality of Bergman's knight and become the legendary figure of Roland, the hero of the poem which I had attempted to explain to Cornelius. Sometimes, even when I was awake, I would feel as if I were living out a myth, the myth of the medieval knight who devotes his life to the pursuit and attainment of some great spiritual goal, and although I kept my mythical vision of myself and my consciousness of my own reality in two separate mental compartments, I was aware of them meeting in my dreams, and I thought that perhaps one day they would meet and merge in my waking hours. Part of my fascination with Browning's Roland could be attributed to my growing conviction that one day I would have to face my own version of Roland's Dark Tower and would, like Roland raising the horn to his lips, be forced to make some grand gesture which would enable me to meet my destiny and complete my quest.

But these were *my* fantasies, and the world of my solitude, the world of my dreams was a long way from the world of Scott Sullivan, the prosaic meticulous banker who carefully remembered his sisters' birthdays, patiently listened to Cornelius worrying over Vicky's increasingly checkered private life, and dutifully attended all the family reunions which took place on national holidays.

"Hello, Scott, this is Alicia. Will you be joining us for Thanksgiving as usual this year?"

". . . joining us for Christmas . . ."

". . . Easter . . ."

". . . Fourth of July . . ."

The holidays marched by. The years trudged on. The crisis of 1960, when Vicky had left Sebastian, was receding further and further into the past. 1961 dragged by. Then 1962. And in 1963 . . .

"Hi, Vicky! How are you doing?"

"Hi, Scott! How are you?"

Empty words exchanged by two strangers distantly acquainted for decades. Looking at Vicky through Scott's eyes I saw only Cornelius Van Zale's daughter, a restless, discontented woman who had ruthlessly divorced the man who loved her and was now idling her life away in the smart nightspots of Manhattan. Cornelius had given up reading all newspapers which carried a gossip column, and recently, to my profound relief, had decided he could no longer discuss his daughter with me.

"How's Daddy?" she said. "I haven't seen him lately."

"He's just fine."

After several months of upheaval, Cornelius had moved to a triplex on the twentieth floor of a new apartment building on Fifth Avenue. He had made the move partly out of pique, because Vicky had refused to live with him in the Van Zale mansion, and partly because of a pragmatic recognition of the fact that it no longer made any economic sense to maintain a private Fifth Avenue fiefdom; I also suspected that Alicia had wanted a change and Cornelius had been anxious to appease her after the trouble created by Sebastian's departure for Europe. The Van Zale mansion, now unoccupied except for the security guards, was being administered by the Van Zale Fine Arts Foundation and was shortly to be opened to the public. It was rumored that Mrs. John F. Kennedy was to preside over the opening.

"I think Cornelius and Alicia have been enjoying fixing up the new apartment," I said to Vicky.

"Yes, but they're bound to make a mess of it—Daddy's taste is so frightful. Have you seen that appalling new chess set of his in which every pawn's an astronaut? He specially commissioned it to commemorate the president's speech about getting a man on the moon."

"I've not only seen the set, I've even played chess with it! Well, if you'll excuse me, Vicky . . ."

The party droned on, boring to a nondrinker, a waste of time and effort and money, but long after I had left, I still remembered Vicky laughing amidst a crowd of men as the host put yet another martini in her outstretched hand.

Chapter Two

I

"IT AMUSES me how Kevin keeps running off to Washington to pay court to the Kennedys in their latter-day version of Camelot," said Jake Reischman, winding up the small talk which always had to precede our business discussions. "In fact, it amuses me to think of the Kennedys acting like royalty. I remember in my young days when Joe Kennedy was making the fastest buck on Wall Street—no, I ordered half a bottle of wine, not a full bottle, and bring another ginger ale for this gentleman here. What's the matter with this restaurant nowadays? Can't you get an order right? And these clams are tough—take them away."

It was a fetish of Jake's to hold business lunches in the smart midtown restaurants where he had a wider scope for his tyranny than in his own partners' dining room or in one of the clubs which were burdened with his membership. A fat, balding, middle-aged man, he effortlessly succeeded in exuding an aura of icy discontent.

"I see nothing strange in the Kennedys' desire to inject a shot of culture into Washington, Jake. When the Celts get to power, they always turn to the arts. That's why writers and artists have always had the highest status in a Celtic society."

"You mean I should be charitable and say what a welcome change the Kennedys are from all the Anglo-Saxon philistines who have previously occupied the White House. Very well, I'll be charitable. But in my opinion there's nothing behind that carefully marketed

Celtic image except a set of typical American preoccupations with wealth and power. And talking of the godalmighty dollar . . ."

I prepared to settle down to business.

". . . I must tell you, Scott, that I'm seriously concerned yet again about the future relationship between our two houses. I'm referring, as you must know, to the activities of your London office."

Jake wore a suit as gray as the sky beyond the long windows of the restaurant, and his eyes looked gray too, although this was an illusion of the light; his eyes were normally a pale color resembling wet stones of a bluish sheen. His short ugly fingers were busy destroying a roll of bread as he spoke; his voice, butter-smooth with a steel edge, could make even a compliment sound threatening.

"It's three years now since Neil packed Sebastian off to London, and what's happened? Sebastian hacks his way into the top spot—a maneuver stage-managed by Neil, I've no doubt, to keep Alicia happy—and then, before I know where I am, Sebastian's doing his best to see my new London office has as many setbacks as possible! Well, you can tell your boss I've had just about enough of Sebastian Foxworth poaching my clients. I'm very angry."

"I agree there was one unfortunate incident—"

"Don't give me that crap. There's been a whole string of catastrophes. You tell Neil I want Sebastian recalled to New York where he can be permanently muzzled. I know it's useless expecting Neil to fire him. God, who would have thought Neil could turn into such a henpecked husband!"

The maître d' reappeared with half a bottle of wine and a glass of ginger ale, while a waiter ran behind him with a fresh dish of clams. Jake broke off his tirade long enough to sample the clams, but was unable to fault them; the maître d' closed his eyes with relief and withdrew.

"I concede Cornelius is always anxious to please Alicia, Jake, but I would hardly describe him as a—"

"Oh, forget it, I don't give a damn, I'm not interested in their marriage, the hell with it, we're talking about that son of a bitch Sebastian. The truth is that Neil wants Sebastian in London because he can't stand him but doesn't dare fire him for fear of upsetting Alicia—"

"Jake, it's you, not me, who keeps dragging up the Van Zale marriage!"

"—And *you* want Sebastian in London too because Sebastian's absence gives you the chance to build up your power as Neil's right-hand man. You're cherishing this grand illusion that if you can play your cards right Neil will hand you the bank on a silver platter, but don't kid yourself, Scott! He doesn't have any intention of giving you the bank. The only reason why he's kept you in the firm this long is to enable you to act as a counterweight to Sebastian's inevitably increasing power—so long as he can play the two of you off against each other, he's free to carry on for as long as possible in order to hand the bank directly to his grandsons. Those grandsons will get the bank in the end, believe me. Blood's always thicker than water, and the blood running in your veins, Scott, is all the wrong kind for a transfusion."

The ginger ale was a pale gold, and the tall glass reflected the shifting lights of the fountain playing in the middle of the room. Silver knives gleamed upon the surgical white of the tablecloth.

"What's all this leading up to, Jake? As far as I can make out, you're telling me I'm wasting my time keeping Sebastian at bay in London because even though I may be the best man to take over eventually from Cornelius, Cornelius himself will somehow be dumb enough not to pick the best man for the job."

"I'm telling you that you'd do better to wash your hands of both Sebastian and Cornelius and throw in your lot with me."

"I'm sorry, I think I misheard you. Did you say—?"

"Yes, I did. You've heard, of course, that I'm planning to incorporate? Well, I've decided that my last act of despotism is going to be to screw all my incompetent partners who hope to crawl into the shoes I leave behind when I go upstairs to be chairman of the board. I'm going to bring in a president from outside the firm, and I'm going to bring in the best man I can get, Jewish or Gentile. In other words, I want someone who has all your father's virtues and none of his vices. Name your price. The job's yours."

"Well, I . . . I'm flattered, of course . . ."

"You can even have your name on the masthead. Reischman and Sullivan. How does that sound to you? Does that compensate you for your father's spectacular failure back in the thirties? Oh, don't think I don't have you figured out! I've been watching you closely for a long time, and I'm one-hundred-percent sure you're just the man I want to be my successor."

"To screw your partners? Or to screw Cornelius? What are you really after, Jake? And while we're on the subject, just what did go wrong between you and Cornelius back in 1955? Was it something to do with Alicia?"

Jake raised a cynical eyebrow, looked at me as if he profoundly pitied anyone who could indulge in such fantasies, and said shortly, "If Neil's never been stupid enough to tell you what went wrong, I'm certainly not going to be stupid enough to embark on unnecessary explanations which are none of your business. Let's return to the subject under discussion. Well? What do you say? Will you consider the offer?"

"Of course. It's a very generous offer and I'm certainly interested. If I may take time to think it over . . ."

"We'll have lunch again when you come back from your vacation. Oh, and meanwhile, do make it clear to Neil, please, that something has to be done to curtail Sebastian's activities in London. I may be wrong, but I think Neil's still anxious enough about the relationship between our two houses to treat the exhaustion of my patience with the respect it undoubtedly deserves."

II

"JAKE'S CUTTING up rough, Cornelius, about the way Sebastian's been smart-assing around in London."

"Frankly, I'm not surprised. What the hell do you think Sebastian's up to, Scott?"

"Well, it may not be a personal vendetta against the House of Reischman, but it's sure beginning to look like it."

"This is embarrassing to me. I don't want a confrontation with Jake over this."

"Do you want me to go to London to investigate? I can cancel my vacation."

"Certainly not. You work very hard and you deserve a break. But I'll get Sebastian over here, and when you return to the office, we'll have a full inquiry to find out why he's been playing brinkmanship with Reischman's. . . . Okay, now, let me see . . . is there anything else we should straighten out before you go on vacation?"

"Well, that wraps up Reischman's. But I'd like to talk to you for a moment about a potential client, a young man called Donald Shine. . . ."

III

"HI, SCOTT! Good to see you! You're looking great! How are you doing?"

Donald Shine was twenty-two years old and had a heap of freshly washed dark hair, wide innocent brown eyes, and a dubious taste in clothes. He spoke in an exuberant voice garnished with a Brooklyn accent.

"Hi, Don! Take a seat."

Donald Shine sat down, still smiling, still exuding exuberance, still convinced he would be a multimillionaire well before he was thirty.

"I've had a word with Mr. Van Zale and he's willing to see you, but I should warn you that he's one of the old school and a little suspicious of modern technology. His attitude to your scheme to lease computers is likely to be either 'There's no market for it' or 'Let's leave it all to IBM.' Keep your spiel short and reasonable, and whatever you do, don't get too excited and make some overly enthusiastic scene. Mr. Van Zale just wants the facts, not a sales pitch or a one-man show."

"I get it. I behave like a WASP stuffed shirt, not like a Yiddishe momma. Okay, no problem."

"It's just possible you might feel more comfortable with a less conservative house . . ."

"Look, Scott, like I told you, I've set my heart on seeing Mr. Van Zale because I figure that since he made it big by the time he was twenty-two he won't dismiss me on account of how I'm only just through college. Besides, I don't want to waste time. If I've got to deal with investment bankers, I want to deal with the best—forget the second-rate money men! Forget everything second-rate! Time's ticking by, for God's sake, and I want to get this scheme off the ground before my hair turns white, I don't want to wait years and years for success, I want it *now!*"

"Uh-huh. Okay, I appreciate the rush, but could you just pause long enough now to let me give you a word of advice on your appearance? Before you see Mr. Van Zale, get a haircut and a dark suit —oh, and a tie too, if you don't have one—and hide those sandals in a closet and wear plain black socks with conventional black shoes. And make sure your shirt's white—got it? W-h-i-t-e. If you want to join forces with the Eastern Seaboard establishment, you've got to look as if you've never heard of the line 'The old order changeth, giving way to the new.'"

"Well, that's no problem, I never have. Who said that? Ed Murrow? Hey, Scott, it was a lucky day for me when I bulldozed my way past your secretary into your office! I wish now I could just do business with you instead of having to go bullshitting around with an old square like Van Zale! How about you yourself giving me the couple of million I need to get my scheme off its ass?"

"Tempting though that suggestion is, Don, I'm afraid it's a temptation I'll have to resist. I don't want Mr. Van Zale turning round on me later and saying, 'Just who the hell is this wunderkind Donald Shine and why did I never get the chance to meet him?' I'd rather play safe and exhibit you right away. I need hardly tell you how different you are from our usual type of client."

"Brother, it's the age of youth! Investment bankers nowadays are backing people like me in the record business, in the garment business, in advertising, in—"

"Second-rank investment-banking houses are, of course, entitled to take dubious risks. Front-rank houses like Van Zale's are usually too busy. Three o'clock tomorrow, Don, and remember the white shirt."

IV

"HAVE YOU gone out of your mind?" said Cornelius in a rage. "Or do you think I've gone out of mine? Do you seriously think I'd take on a long-haired kid like that who comes to an interview in a suit which looked as if it had been snitched from a Lower East Side street market, and who talks a lot of junk about how there's a market for leasing computers when everyone knows computer technology is changing so rapidly that the only hope you have of keeping up-to-date is to get the latest model from IBM? I concede the kid might make a good salesman—a used-car salesman on a fifth-rate lot in Brooklyn—but as for suggesting we should underwrite his fantasy of becoming a tycoon—"

"Just a minute, Cornelius. This kid is brash, I agree. He comes from a background which you have trouble even imagining, let alone relating to, and his clothes have to be seen to be believed. But this is

a bright boy, Cornelius. I know he only went to a local college, bu
he does have a college education and he's made the most of it. He
knows the subject of computers inside out—he probably knows jus·
as much as anyone at IBM—and I think he's hit on an idea whose
time has come. Let's take the chance and back him."

"We don't need that kind of client, Scott. I know we all have to
compete for clients nowadays, but there are still some clients who
aren't worth competing for."

"You're making a mistake. What's your problem? Is it his youth?
You weren't always fifty-five yourself, remember! Besides, times are·
changing—"

"Yes, and not for the better! I'm sorry, Scott, but I'm not financ-
ing any kid who looks like a no-good beatnik and talks like a Jewish
joke, and that's my last word on the subject."

V

"JAKE, WOULD you be interested in an unusual client whom I think
has great potential but whom Cornelius has just refused to deal
with?"

"I could be. Tell me about him."

"He's a twenty-two-year-old college-educated computer expert,
and his name is Donald Shine . . ."

VI

"WHAT DID you think of him, Jake?"

"Donald Shine? I thought he was an appalling young man. Of
course I took him on." Jake sighed and looked out the window of his
office. "He'll make money. Whatever he does, he'll make money.
He'll have to be closely watched, but then so do some of my older,
more conventional clients."

"You were smart not to be prejudiced against him."

"I was very prejudiced against him," said Jake in an ironic echo of
Cornelius. "How could I not be prejudiced against a long-haired
youth who looked like a Seventh Avenue messenger boy and talked
like a bad satirical joke? But after all, one must try to make allow-

ances. We can't all be born with silver spoons in our mouths. . . .
Why are you smiling?"

"I was just thinking that Marx was right after all. It's not race that
ultimately divides men, and it's not religion, either; it's class."

VII

"HIYA, SCOTT, I'm just calling to say a big thank-you for all your
help. I thought Jake Reischman was just a swell guy. I could relate
to him you know, we got along real good. Hey, can I buy you lunch
sometime next week in token of my appreciation?"

"Thanks, Don, but I'm about to go on vacation. Can I take a rain
check?"

"Sure! Where are you going? Europe?"

"The Caribbean."

"I'm jealous! Well, have a great time around all those schmaltzy
palm trees, and we'll get together later. Oh, and Scott . . . give my
regards to that son of a bitch Van Zale and tell him I'll wipe the floor
with him someday," said Donald Shine, and laughed not altogether
good-naturedly as he hung up the phone.

VIII

CONVERSATIONS.

Words spoken through Scott's mouth. Scenes watched by Scott's
eyes. But Scott doesn't exist except in the minds of other people, for
Scott is a mere shadow projected by the power of the will, the will
that belongs to me, the individual behind the shadow—and the individual as the medieval philosopher William of Ockham wrote long
ago, is the sole reality.

Scott told everyone he was going on vacation, but that was a lie.
Scott never left New York. It was always *I* who left the city, just as it
was always *I* who relaxed in his apartment after Scott had arrived
home each day from work.

Scott came home on that November day in 1963, and as usual
when the front door closed, he ceased to exist, and *I* was the one
who went into the bedroom and looked at myself in the mirror. Then
I took off Scott's clothes, the dark suit, the white shirt, and the plain

tie, emblems of a life I despised, and showered to remove the slime of his life from my body, and when I was clean again I put on *my* clothes, the white slacks, the silver-buckled belt, and the brilliant blue shirt, which I left unbuttoned, but in the kitchen I fixed myself not the drink I was always tempted to try when I was myself, but Scott's drink, which I knew would never harm me, the tall dark Coke with a dash of lemon juice added to kill the sweetness as the liquid foamed noisily over the ice.

With my drink in my hand I sat down in the recliner, swung my feet up onto the ottoman, and expelled my breath slowly in relief. The mountaineer had made it back to base camp again after yet another grueling climb on the mountain. Two weeks of rest and recuperation stretched enticingly before me in my mind's eye.

I glanced around my apartment. I lived opposite Carl Schurz Park on the Upper East Side, but I worked such long hours at the bank that I seldom saw the view of the East River in daylight. But on weekends I would watch the sunlight sparkling on the water while I drank my breakfast of black coffee. The river was filthy but in the morning sunlight it looked beautiful, reminding me of the ideal seascape where I longed to live in peace once my quest had been completed. I had never found this perfect seascape, although I could see the scene so clearly in my mind's eye, the beautiful deserted shore bordering a dark and glassy sea. The sands were clean and white and pure, and I thought there were mountains in the background, although it was hard to be sure.

I never entertained visitors in my apartment, since I needed every moment of my leisure hours to recuperate from the strain of being Scott, and so I had never bothered to acquire more than the essential items of furniture. The recliner and ottoman stood alone on the carpet. The walls were lined with books, and in one corner wider shelves supported my stereo and record collection. There was no television. As I spent most of my days with the trivial and the meaningless, I hardly wanted to recreate that environment in my leisure hours. Instead of watching television, I read a great deal, not following, as everyone believed, an unrelieved diet of medieval literature, but selecting novels, history, some psychology, anthropology, and philosophy. On weekends I played squash and took long walks, but sometimes when the gap between vacations seemed uncomfortably long, I'd take a plane somewhere—to Bermuda or Canada or even merely to another big American city—and spend the weekend in the pursuit of an alternative physical activity.

After the war, when I had given up alcohol, I had soon realized I needed another escape route when stress made life intolerable, and although I regarded all escape routes as potential threats to my self-discipline, I had worked out a set of rules to ensure the risk of trouble was minimal. My aim was always to cut short an involvement before it had the chance to develop into an unfortunate obsession, so I kept my affairs brief and made sure they only took place a long way from home.

This recipe for self-indulgence might have seemed unsatisfactory to many people, but the truth was I never enjoyed sex much. If I merely wanted to relieve sexual tension, I preferred to seek relief by myself, since if there was no other person involved I could safely set aside my fear of losing control for a few minutes, but I sought more than a physical release when I took my trips to those distant cities. I liked the fun of the chase and the contact, no matter how brief, with another human being; it was the mental, not the physical, release which meant so much to me, the chance to escape temporarily from the burden of my isolation.

Even before the postwar decision that had altered my life, I had never managed to sustain an affair beyond the first few dates. The idea of falling in love horrified me. I had been fourteen years old when my father had walked out on Emily in 1933 to pursue his obsession for Dinah Slade, and I saw all too clearly that such obsessions caused nothing but suffering and unhappiness to the innocent people left behind. After the catastrophe of my father's desertion I trusted no women but my beloved Emily, and for many years I lied regularly to Cornelius when he made discreet paternal inquiries about my private life, but in the navy I was afraid to be the odd one out in case I was labeled homosexual, so I got drunk one night during a shore leave and finally managed to conform to the normal pattern of masculine behavior. After that incident I at least never worried that I was a homosexual, although I knew that Cornelius, who firmly believed that every normal man should have intercourse at least three times a week in order to conform to the Kinsey Report, often worried that I showed no interest in marriage.

The idea of marriage had always seemed remote to me, but after the war, when I decided what I was going to do with my life, the idea seemed not merely remote but inconceivable. In fact, I was so opposed to any long-term relationship either in or out of wedlock that I was hardly surprised when women sensed this revulsion and reacted accordingly. With my ambitions shrouded in secrecy and a veil drawn over the unhappy past, I presented an enigma which they found both baffling and, ultimately, when my reserve proved impenetrable, repellent. I knew very well that if I ever made the mistake of trying to prolong a relationship the woman would soon make some excuse to walk away.

Yet the big irony of my situation was that despite the fact I had so little to offer, I was never short of partners. Once I had been amazed that women should be anxious to go to bed with me, for I was neither as good-looking nor as personable as my brother Tony, but eventually I had come to accept that there was no accounting for feminine taste and that I might as well make the most of this unexpected advantage. So when I periodically traveled my escape route, I always tried to have as many women as possible, but this led to yet another irony in my offbeat private life: I couldn't take full advantage of my good fortune. I was much too afraid of losing control.

I'd been all right in the navy. With my fear of involvement anesthetized by alcohol, I had had no trouble producing a sexual performance which even the great Kinsey would have certified as normal, but after the war, when I had abandoned alcohol and had become steadily more absorbed in the need for self-discipline, matters had changed. For years now I had suffered from a chronic inability to complete the sexual act in the normal manner, although fortunately—and this was the crowning irony of my ironic private life—most women never realized the extent of my limitation and assumed with profound gratitude that I was prolonging the act for their sake.

Sometimes I used to get upset, but not often. There are worse sexual problems. Why complain when most women think one's some kind of supremely considerate stud? I had enough common sense to realize I must see the humorous side of the situation, so whenever I found myself getting upset, I'd smile to myself and shrug my shoulders and pretend the failure was very unimportant. So long as I kept up the appearance that I was successful with women, what did the reality matter?

But reality was waking up alone in a hotel room in a city far from home. Reality was touching people yet making no contact. Reality was a chase which never ended and a longing which no one satisfied and a freedom from fear which was always beyond my reach. Reality was isolation, a lifeless life, or, as Emily had said before she died, a living death.

I sat in the dark thinking of Emily for a long time, but eventually I stood up and moved back into the kitchen to open another bottle of Coca-Cola. I was determined not to be depressed that night. Later, when my vacation was over, I could allow myself a few minutes of self-indulgent gloom, but not now when my vacation lay ahead of me and I had the chance of traveling a two-week escape route from Scott's life at Willow and Wall.

Thinking of the bank reminded me of Cornelius, and I looked up at the picture on the wall. I had only one picture in the apartment, and I kept it above the kitchen sink because it would have been an intrusion in the bedroom or living room. It was the detail from *The Tribute Money,* an enlargement of Masaccio's sinister portrait of St. John. I wondered if Cornelius would have seen himself in that picture, but I thought not. We never see ourselves as others see us.

Switching on the gooseneck lamp in the living room, I picked up my copy of *JFK: The Man and the Myth,* but Victor Lasky's critical assessment of Kennedy irritated me and I soon put the book aside. It was fashionable nowadays to knock Kennedy, but I was determined to have no part of it. We were almost the same age, Jack Kennedy and I, and sometimes I thought his courage and his glamour and his supreme fulfillment of all his father's dreams gave me the will to go on with my quest. He was the living proof that all the sacrifices were worthwhile; he proved that if one had enough ambition one could go on and on and on to the very end of one's dreams.

I put on a record, soft jazz by Dave Brubeck, and thought about my dreams.

I was satisfied with my progress. My position was excellent. Of course there was no possibility that I would accept Jake's offer, but it would be politic to flatter him by taking a long time to turn the offer down. Later I would tell Cornelius about it and we would laugh together. That would make Cornelius happy, and his confidence in me would reach new heights. Jake had the situation summed up entirely wrong, but that was hardly surprising, since he was only an outsider, trying to decipher a complicated situation from a long way away.

Unless I either went mad or made some incredible mistake, I was going to get that bank. Cornelius' guilt, which I had exploited so carefully for so long, would never let him rest until he had conceded more power to me than he could afford, and once that happened, I could wrap up my quest in double-quick time. Nineteen-sixty-eight, the year he had promised to retire in my favor, was still five years away, but I often wondered if he would last that long. He was fifty-five years old now, and his asthma was becoming an increasing burden. He had already outlived my father by three years.

I thought about my father for a while. I did not consciously think of him often, but he was with me always, a shadow on the mind, a weight on the soul, a memory burned on the brain, and so completely had I absorbed all essence of him into my personality that usually I *was* him, although sometimes I could stand apart and view him dispassionately as a separate entity. I wished I could have understood more clearly what he had seen in Dinah Slade. I could now accept that he had been out of his mind as the result of a sexual obsession, but the irrationality of his action still upset me. "Dinah was the love of his life," my brother Tony had written in his famous letter which had given Cornelius such a fright, but I had read those words and felt more baffled than ever. *Dinah Slade?* I remembered a large plain woman with an irritating English accent. I had forgiven my father, but even now I was still a long way from understanding him.

I meditated again on the extraordinary phenomenon of sexual attraction, and the next moment I was remembering Sebastian, wrecking his career by pursuing his irrational obsession with Vicky. *Vicky?* I couldn't think what he saw in her. It was true she was pretty, but her mind was as limited as her father's, and her frivolous personality should have been far too shallow to attract a man of Sebastian's caliber. His infatuation with her was as incredible as my father's infatuation with Dinah, and made me wonder again how any sane person could believe that falling in love was a romantic dream. Falling in love was no romantic dream. Falling in love was a nightmare.

I sighed as I thought of Sebastian. I missed him. I thought: If Sebastian were here we could talk about the Greek concept of Eros and contrast it with the medieval convention of chivalrous love, and Sebastian would say chivalry was all a myth, and then we would debate whether myth was superior to reality: I would argue in favor of myth, citing the legends of Finn Mac Cool and Cuchulain, but because Sebastian thought Celtic legends were incomprehensible, he would dredge up all his Anglo-Saxon heroes to argue that reality was always superior; he would exclaim: "Give me Alfred any day

. . . or Edwin . . . or Oswald carrying his great cross into battle—they were *real* people!" and we would laugh together and be the friends we were meant to be instead of rivals becoming gradually more divided by our ambition.

I got up restlessly, moved to the window, and tilted the slats of the blinds so that I could stare across the dark park to the lights of Queens. The thought of my ambition had reminded me of Cornelius again. What did I feel toward Cornelius now? An exasperated dislike? No, not even that. Once long ago I had hated him, but that white-hot hatred had burned up all emotion and left only the scorched scars of indifference. Scott had made sure of that. Scott had understood that a man makes mistakes when he's under the influence of hatred, just as he makes mistakes when he's under the influence of love. Scott had made it clear to me that there was no room in my life for the violent extremes of emotion, and anyway, Scott was fond of Cornelius and found him amusing. Cornelius had been very good to Scott, a fact which meant nothing to me, but of course it was not surprising that Scott should feel grateful.

The truth was, Cornelius was just an object to me now, a little ivory figure retreating before me upon the chessboard, and one day soon I'd be able to reach across that board, pick him up, and toss him into the garbage can along with his grandsons. Would I then feel some emotion? Yes, I'd probably feel the most acute relief that the long game had finally been concluded, and then . . . *Then* I'd be able to set aside my fear of death at last, then I'd be able to lead a normal life—

The telephone rang.

"Hi, Scott. Cornelius . . . no, relax! I'm not about to haul you over here for a game of chess—I know you're getting ready for your vacation. I just wanted to say have a good time and send me a card if you get the chance, and . . . say, how about telling me where you're going? You're always so closemouthed about your vacations!"

"California." I often lied to Cornelius about my destination because I didn't want him dragging me back to the office if some unforeseen crisis arose.

"That sounds nice! And November's a good time to go chasing the sun."

"Right."

"Okay. Well . . . that's all, I guess. So long and good luck."

Scott said good-bye and vanished. I hung up the phone and wondered with a detached intellectual curiosity whether it was abnormal to feel such an absence of emotion. Then I decided that abnormal or not, lack of emotion was safe. It merely proved I was totally in control of my life.

I went to bed and dreamed I was halfway through a bottle of Scotch and smashing a bloodstained faceless head against a wall.

IX

I was alive. I had cast aside the deadweight of Scott's persona and my spirits were soaring as high as the Pan Am 707 which swept me off the tarmac in New York and climbed up and up and up into the coruscating sunlight of my liberation. The bank was far away now, as far away as the recluse's life I had to lead off-duty to recuperate from my working hours, and as far away as the Middle Ages where myth and reality had mingled so effortlessly in that war-torn, plague-infested, death-ridden landscape. I was in the twentieth-century present, surrounded by twentieth-century technology. I was a twentieth-century American with *Time* magazine in my hands and a pretty young stewardess at my elbow.

"Can I get you a drink now, sir?"

I smiled at her, and as she turned a delicious shade of pink, I suddenly wanted all the pleasure I could get; I wanted champagne foaming from a gold-necked bottle, I wanted caviar, I wanted a king-sized bed with a mirror above it in the ceiling, I wanted six women one after the other, I wanted to spend a thousand dollars a minute for twenty-four hours straight, I wanted each one of the seven deadly sins gift-wrapped in gilt and garnished with a scarlet bow.

I laughed at myself, and the pretty stewardess laughed with me, not understanding but responding instinctively to my mood.

"How about that champagne?" she said, remembering I had declined champagne earlier.

"Make it a ginger ale. Say, how long's your stopover in Puerto Rico?"

It was six o'clock that evening when I reached the Sheraton Hotel in San Juan and checked into a suite overlooking the ocean. The entryway, bedroom, and bathroom covered a bigger area than my New York apartment. After a shower I toweled myself down by the windows facing the sea and thought how much ascetic, intellectual Scott would have detested the plush American hotels overseas, but I was entertained by their twentieth-century opulence and the brash vulgarity of those guests celebrating life as crudely as they knew how.

I went downstairs to the bar.

A brunette of uncertain age but certain obvious charms was killing time drinking daiquiris before heading to the airport to take a plane home to New Orleans. I offered to pick up the tab for the drinks and was accepted. Two hours later, after I had seen her into a cab, I only just had time to run back to my room to straighten the bed before the pretty stewardess called me from the lobby on the house phone.

The stewardess had to leave me by nine o'clock the next morning, but by nine-thirty I was sunning myself by the pool. I wore my tightest, whitest pair of swimming shorts, but I needn't have troubled to make myself so noticeable. All I had to do was lie on my chaise in the sun and admire the originality of all the women who devised ways of striking up a conversation.

I spent the day much as I had spent the night, and spent the following night much as I had spent the previous day. Then I checked out of the Sheraton and checked into the Hilton so that I had a change of pool and a new chaise. By this time I had convinced myself I was in the midst of a highly enjoyable vacation. So far all the women had complimented me, and whenever it had become necessary to gloss over my imperfections, I had delivered my word-perfect excuse with a smoothness any con man would have envied.

"I believe in conserving my energy . . . I don't want to wind up worn out before I'm halfway through my vacation . . ."

The absurd words would have made me laugh if the situation had been less awkward, and when every woman accepted the absurdity unquestioningly, I often did laugh, particularly when admiring remarks followed about my technique and stamina and consideration for my partner; one woman even asked if I had any tips she could pass on to her lover back home. However, when I laughed, the women just thought I was being modest, so I got away with my deception time after time and emerged from each encounter with nothing worse than a well-exercised body and a vague incredulity that so many women could be so easily deceived.

And then one afternoon I found myself in bed with a chaste-looking schoolteacher—I was always more attracted to the ones who looked chaste—and within minutes I knew not only that her chastity was as much an illusion as my competence, but that she was quite sharp enough to laugh outright at any garbage I might try to hand her when the time came for an explanation.

It was not an unknown situation for me to find myself in, but it was a situation which never failed to appall me. No con man ever enjoys being unmasked. The disaster would no doubt have reduced many men to impotence, but on me it had exactly the opposite effect. As soon as I realized I was on the brink of being found out, my extreme tension not only made a climax out of the question but made me afraid to withdraw for fear my lack of satisfaction would be so obvious.

"What's your problem?" said the woman when she was well-satisfied and had obviously had enough.

"No problem. I . . ." I couldn't make up my mind what to do. With a less-experienced woman I could have tried faking it; that usually worked, although the women had probably speculated afterward about the physical evidence—or the lack of it. Then I wondered if I could have some convenient attack of sciatica, or perhaps trouble with a disk which slipped at inconvenient moments. I lay there propped on my elbows, sweating profusely, breathing rapidly and no doubt looking as thoroughly ridiculous as I felt, and then before I could make up my mind how I should extricate myself from the mess, the woman herself took charge of the situation.

"Let's call it a day, shall we?" she said, pushing two competent hands firmly against my chest. "I've met guys like you before. You're not interested in your partner—you don't have the time. You're too busy worrying over your ego and wondering why the hell you can't get all the fancy equipment to work properly."

I somehow managed to pull out and drag the sheet up to cover myself, but I was trembling and it was hard to make even the simplest movements. I was also in considerable physical discomfort. I managed to say without looking at her, "I'm satisfied with the equipment. If you're not, shop around," and then I blundered away into the bathroom to relieve myself. It was several minutes before I could summon the nerve to go back into the bedroom, but when I eventually opened the door, I saw the bed was empty and I knew I was alone again in yet another hotel room a long way from home, unbearably alone, unbearably humiliated, unbearably conscious of an unbearable failure.

I wanted to rest, but I couldn't. I got dressed and went right down to the nearest bar and picked up another woman. Then I went through the whole performance again, except that this time the woman went away happy and unsuspecting. But I was still alone, still a failure. I said aloud to myself: "It doesn't matter. It just doesn't matter." But I knew that it did. I wanted to get drunk then, but I knew that was the one escape route I must never try, so I went down to the casino instead and dropped a thousand dollars at the tables. It took me all night to lose the money, but I didn't mind that, because I didn't want to go back to that empty room.

I felt glad I was due to leave the hotel the next morning to join my cruise ship at the docks. As I knew from past experience, it was almost impossible to feel alone on a cruise ship. That was one of the reasons why I so often spent my vacations at sea; the other reason, of course, was that a cruise provided unlimited opportunities for casual sexual connections.

Blotting out the memory of my disastrous encounter with the schoolteacher, I checked out of the hotel, took a cab to the docks, and boarded the snow-white European ship with a determination to recapture my high spirits and salvage my vacation.

My stateroom on A deck seemed more than adequate for nocturnal adventures. Checking the stewardess, I found her unattractive, but undaunted, I unpacked my suitcase and strolled back to the promenade deck to inspect the public rooms. The bars where I would be consuming vast amounts of ginger ale were plush, the ballroom large but not cavernous, the inevitable casino well-appointed but discreet. The passengers as always would be an unknown quantity, but since the cruise was short, it was likely that a high percentage of them would be young; I always avoided the longer cruises dominated by the geriatric set.

I had just decided with satisfaction that I could spend ten entertaining days and ten equally rewarding nights aboard this particular ship when a brace of well-manicured college girls asked me the way to the aft bar and I had to pause to get my bearings. Ahead of me I could see the main hall, and after I had dispatched the girls up the nearest stairway, I moved on toward the purser's office with the idea of cashing a traveler's check.

The main hall was crowded, as passengers were still boarding, and as I stepped sideways to avoid a seaman wheeling a baggage cart, I bumped into a woman who was standing in front of a notice board with her back to me. Her huge straw hat was tipped askew by the collision, and as the strap of her bag slipped off her shoulder, she turned with annoyance to face me.

"Excuse me!" I exclaimed. "I . . ."

The words died.

Scott tried to step in front of me, but Scott was in New York and there was no summoning him. I stood there, stripped of my protective persona, and felt as defenseless as if I'd been staked stark naked to an anthill.

"Scott!" The familiar voice was appalled.

Like the snap of a hypnotist's fingers, the sound of his name jolted me into action. It was useless even to pretend to be Scott. Scott would never set foot on a cruise ship, never wear bright, tight casual clothes or a silver medallion, never find himself face to face with the wrong woman in the wrong place at the wrong time.

"Scott? Scott, it *is* you, isn't it? Or is it your double?"

"Of course it's me!" I said, laughing, but as she spoke, I realized with astonishment that she was just as disoriented as I was. For she had left Vicky behind in New York, just as I had left Scott behind, and like me, she had come to the ship in her other identity to pursue that twentieth-century chastity: pleasure without involvement, total abstention from a commitment of any kind.

"Why, what a surprise to see you, Vicky!" I heard myself say smoothly. "Welcome to good times!"

Chapter Three

I

SHE WORE a dusky-orange sundress, cut low, and a thin gold pendant round her neck. Her short bright hair was barely visible beneath the huge hat. She already had a delicate tan. Her wide gray eyes remained dismayed.

"But what in heaven's name are you doing here, Scott?"

"Guess!"

I had never seen her look so baffled.

"Relax, Vicky, there's no problem! We'll make a pact. You go your way and I'll go mine and neither of us will say one word afterward to either Cornelius or anyone else in New York. Okay?"

"Okay. . . . You mean you're not exactly a eunuch after all?"

I just laughed.

She blushed. "I'm sorry, I know I'm behaving stupidly, but it was just such a shock to see you like this . . ."

"Then I'll leave you alone to recover. So long, Vicky—enjoy yourself."

I moved on through the crowd, but when I reached the purser's office and glanced back I saw she had remained motionless, the bemused expression still in her eyes but a faint smile curving the corners of her father's firm, familiar mouth.

II

THE SHIP departed for St. Thomas, and soon the passengers had sloughed off the polite mannerisms of twentieth-century convention and had adopted the bawdy camaraderie displayed by Chaucer's pilgrims on their immortal journey to Canterbury. Abandoning all memory of Scott in his New York role of the Clerk of Oxenford, I adopted the role of the Knight and set out to see the world with my own code of chivalry stamped well in the forefront of my mind. I saw a young girl I liked, but rejected her as too vulnerable; I met someone older but rejected her as too neurotic. I had no wish to hurt them. However, within hours I had found a widow of my own age from Atlanta, and once I had discovered that her attitude to vacations coincided with mine, we were soon busy proving our mutual theory that cruises had more to offer than vacations ashore.

I did my best to avoid Vicky, but on a ship it's hard, if not impossible, to overlook a glamorous young divorcée who attracts more than her fair share of attention. Resplendent in their white uniforms, the officers fluttered around her as soon as the sun sank into the sea; the cruise staff, personable young men hired to look after the passengers, recklessly ditched their attentive wallflowers to dance with her. At first it seemed Vicky preferred the cruise staff because the majority of them were uninterested in smothering her with sexual attention, but presently she eyed the officers and selected the chief engineer. The captain, an inscrutable man who operated with great discretion, had probably signaled that he was willing to wait.

I enjoyed my widow from Atlanta, but of course I had to move on; the disaster in San Juan had only enhanced my dread that my incompetence would be discovered unless I changed partners regularly. But it was with genuine regret that I edged away, trying a quick fling with another widow before making a fleeting connection with a B-deck stewardess who turned out to be frigid. I was just beginning to feel depressed again when on the approach to Martinique I spotted an interesting-looking woman who was sharing a cabin with an individual soon known to one and all as "Old Blue-Rinse." The interesting woman, who was plain but with an excellent figure, proved to be a poor relation of this formidable Miami matron, and had been offered a free cruise on condition that she wait on her benefactor daily from dawn till dusk.

I circled the pair warily. First I decided that an unmarried, obviously chaste woman in her mid-thirties would expect too much if I started paying her attention, but then I changed my mind. The sheer misery of life as Old Blue-Rinse's lackey would hardly have encouraged the woman to hold high expectations of the cruise, and any encounter, no matter how fleeting, was likely to be gratefully received.

I rashly decided to give her a voyage to remember.

"Hi, Judy!" I said one afternoon when we met by chance outside the library. "Are you free for shuffleboard?"

It was hardly a brilliant opening, but on cruises even the most unoriginal proposal will suffice.

Judy was obviously pleased to be noticed, but she declined the invitation. Having just taken a book from the library, she was on her way back to the tyrant for the afternoon reading session.

"How about a drink this evening?" I persisted, spelling out the proposition in letters a yard high.

"Gee, I'd love to, but . . ." Judy was entranced by the offer but terrified of Old Blue-Rinse.

"I can wait," I said, "until after Mrs. Miami Beach is stashed in bed in her curlers."

"Oh! Well . . ."

"Think about it," I said kindly, moving past her into the library doorway. "I'll be in the forward bar."

Judy stammered her thanks and rushed off in confusion to her jailer. Feeling somewhat as Santa Claus might feel after paying a pre-Christmas visit to a deserving child, I strolled on into the library to cast a glance over the shelves.

Sitting just inside the door, her feet tucked up beneath her on the couch, was Vicky.

"Hi!" I said. "Reading something mindless?"

"Deliciously banal!" She showed me the title of the costume romance and we laughed together.

I was more at ease with this other Vicky now because I had trained myself to think of her as someone entirely different from the Vicky that Scott knew in New York. That Vicky had a narrow, uneducated mind and irritated Scott by her phony intellectual poses. This Vicky was smart enough to know poses were a waste of time. The New York Vicky, surrounded by children, servants, and a doting husband or father, was distracted and moody, totally encased in a rich spoiled woman's discontent. This Vicky was as direct and relaxed as her father when Scott met him at night for a game of chess.

I looked at the costume romance in her hands and thought of Cornelius reading a book by Harold Robbins. It was odd that Vicky should remind me of Cornelius, not Emily, but I had long known that Vicky was radically different from her aunt, just as I had long realized the great irony implicit in Cornelius' relationship with his daughter. He had wanted a daughter who was the mirror image of the sister who had personified all the traditional virtues of womanhood to him, but instead he had produced a daughter who was far too like him for him to dare to accept her as she was.

If Cornelius had been able to see his daughter as she was, he would hardly have wasted time worrying about whether she was drinking, drugging, or sleeping herself into an early grave. This woman was a survivor. She had that same frail delicate look which Cornelius had perfected to fool his enemies, but I wasn't fooled for a minute. In my detachment I saw so clearly that this was a woman who had endured a broken home, two unfortunate marriages, five children, the Van Zale fortune, even the efforts of Cornelius himself to bend her into Emily's image—and yet still she had emerged from the wreckage with enough strength to carve out a new life of her own. I was reminded of Cornelius enduring a secluded childhood, poor health, a domineering mother, years of stupefying middle-class boredom in Velletria—and yet still managing not only to escape but to grab the Van Zale bank and the grudging respect of everyone who had previously written him off as a nonentity.

Yet no matter how admirable their survival record, survivors should always be treated with care. They're tenacious, going after what they want and clinging on till they get it, and such single-mindedness can be dangerous; having long ago bracketed Vicky with her father as a survivor, I had simultaneously resolved to keep her at arm's length at all times.

"Aren't cruises extraordinary?" she was remarking, amused. "I've never before stepped into such an unreal world!"

"I don't see anything unreal about everyone running around submitting to their basic instincts. You could even argue that this is a more real world than the world we know in New York."

"Some reality! Say, Scott, I sure hope Judy can escape tonight. If I were in her shoes, I'd have murdered that old bag on the first day out of San Juan!"

"I believe you!" I drifted away again, reflecting idly on the difference between Judy's vacation and Vicky's. Vicky had discarded the chief engineer after Martinique and to everyone's astonishment had annexed the chief officer before Barbados. The captain was still waiting discreetly in the wings. I guessed he'd make his move as we sailed out of Curaçao on the last section of the voyage back to Puerto Rico.

Returning to my cabin, I took a nap to catch up on all the sleep I was missing and crawled off my bed to dress for dinner. A couple of envelopes had been pushed under the door while I slept. One was an invitation to a party, but the other was a note which read: "Hi! I'd love to see you this evening, but please not in the bar in case word gets back to Mrs. B. Could we get together in your cabin? Mrs. B. will be asleep by 11:30, so I could slip away around midnight. If this is okay, please wear a white carnation in your buttonhole at dinner this evening. Judy. P.S. Please could the cabin be *totally dark* because I don't usually do this kind of thing and I am *very shy*."

I whistled my appreciation. It was true that Old Blue-Rinse would have driven even the nicest woman to a clandestine assignation with a stranger, and it was also true that on board ship anything can happen, but I was still impressed by the panache of the girl's counterproposal. A white carnation at dinner followed by a midnight rendezvous—without any boring preliminaries—between the sheets! I was not only greatly entertained by this odd combination of the romantic and the bawdy; my palate, which by this time was becoming jaded, even showed signs of being titillated. I certainly forgot about my depression, and after buying a very large white carnation at the florist's, I ran down to dinner with unprecedented eagerness. If I had been a drinker, I would have ordered champagne for everyone at my table.

I smiled at Judy across the dining room, and Judy smiled at me.

After idling away the evening in the casino without losing too much money, I retreated to my stateroom, and by midnight I was tucked up in bed with the lights out. To say I was excited would have been the understatement of the year.

The door opened.

I could not see it, for my cabin was L-shaped, the door opening into a tiny corridor which connected the bathroom with the rectangular bedroom. Since the bed was in the far corner, all I could see of the corridor was the beginning of the row of closets which ran along one wall, and when the door of the stateroom opened stealthily, it was not the door I saw but the shaft of light which filtered in from the main passage outside.

The door closed. The light died. There was a silence while we both held our breath.

"Hi!" I called softly at last. "Can you see anything? Sure you wouldn't like some light?"

"No, I'm okay," she whispered. "No lights. Please. I wouldn't know where to look."

"Relax! I admire your guts in getting away for some fun! You're wonderful!"

This seemed to give her the encouragement she needed, for she groped her way to the bed and I heard the rustle as she discarded her dress. Static from the hot nylon flashed in the dark, but apart from an anonymous moving shadow I could see nothing.

She slipped between the sheets into my arms.

Since the circumstances were unique, even in my broad experience of cruises, and since I sincerely felt that she deserved the best possible reward for her originality, I decided I must do everything I could to make the occasion memorable for her. So I took the time to linger over each caress, and as my hands moved across her body I discovered to my surprise that her figure was even better than I had supposed.

Her response was silent but avid. We twisted together with increasing fervor for some minutes, and then when I felt at last that I had completed my outside reconnaissance, I unleashed my most urgent inclinations and went in.

It was the most remarkable visit.

The most erotic part of all was that she was completely silent. I had never before made love to such a silent woman, but I knew from the movements of her body and the texture of her hidden flesh that the experience was as exceptional for her as it certainly was for me.

She was breathing swiftly, but still not even a whisper passed her lips, and suddenly the anonymity of her silence smoothed away all tension from my mind. I began to feel as if I were making love not to a specific woman but to an entire world which I had been forbidden to enter, and yet I found myself enrapt by it, drawn on and on until the word "forbidden" was meaningless and all that mattered was the magnetic light of that other world, the world which existed in a dimension where death had no part to play. And with the distractions of speech excluded and all trace of my shackled personality smoothed away, I was free to bend both mind and body toward celebrating my escape from the shadow of the death I feared so much; I was free to pass beyond my dread that one false step would lead me to the grave with my life's ambition unrealized; I was free to be free, free to be myself, and free, free, free at last from my fear of losing control. . . .

III

"OH, GOD!" cried the woman beneath me, rocketing me back into the other world, and the involuntary thrust of her body shoved us both violently against the wall alongside the bed.

The shock streaked through me like a high-voltage explosion. I knew that voice and it didn't belong to Judy.

I punched on the light.

She screamed.

For a second we both had to shield our eyes against the glare, but as we let our hands fall we stared at each other, each of us unable to look away. Her pupils were utterly opaque. The irises were a petrified pristine gray.

Neither of us spoke.

A second later I was moving. I had kicked aside the tangled lump of sheet and was on my feet. The floor felt cold. I was so dizzy that I had to put out a hand to steady myself against the wall, but at last I reached the sanctuary of the bathroom and rammed home the bolt as soon as I had slammed shut the door.

IV

VICKY TAPPED timidly on the panel. "Scott?"

I did not answer. I was trying to turn on the cold tap, but my fingers had no strength in them. I tried again, using both hands, and the next moment the cold water was burning my hands like dry ice. After dowsing my face, I nerved myself to look in the mirror, but the reflection there was the one I wanted to see, and I knew I was safe. I'd been afraid I would see Scott. That would have been very serious, but Scott was evidently still back in New York along with the New York Vicky, and I was still myself, emerging from yet another one-night stand with just another chance acquaintance. That was a manageable situation. That was something I could handle with one hand tied behind my back. That was something I could control.

I grabbed a towel, tucked it around my waist, and unlocked the door.

She was there. She had pulled on one of my shirts to hide her nakedness and was hugging it tightly to her body. Her bright hair was disheveled. She looked sick with fright.

"Oh, Scott . . ."

"You want to use the bathroom? Go ahead. Sorry I was so long." I stepped past her, and as the door closed quietly I began to make the bed as if I could somehow unmake what had happened there. Halfway through straightening the blankets, I had to sit down. I felt exhausted, and suddenly I was aware of the soiled sheets, the smell of sex, the satiation in the groin, the danger, the horror, the fear . . . The shock reached me at last, and I was stupefied. I felt no joy, no triumph, no excitement. Now that I knew who she was, the success would never be repeated. And now that I knew who she was, the success was no longer a success but an unbelievable lapse in self-discipline.

The shock deepened. I abandoned the idea of making the bed and began to grope around for my clothes. I could no longer think clearly. I hardly knew what I was doing.

The bathroom door opened.

"Scott . . . No, please! Let me speak! I must tell you how very sorry I am—I must at least ask you to forgive me! It was a cheap, sick, decadent trick, and . . . Oh, God, I'll never go on another cruise again, never, never, never . . ."

She stopped. I knew instinctively, like some masterly actor faced with a world-famous speech by Shakespeare, that this was where I showed my years of training, experience, and class. I groped for my identity—but which identity? Not Scott. He would never have got himself into such a mess. That left myself, the cripple who conned his partners he was uncrippled, and I saw at once with the most violent self-loathing that even though I had just proved I need not be crippled, I would still have to go right on living my crippled life. The only way to extricate myself from danger was to continue to play the con man. I had to go right on being a liar, a loser, and a cheat.

"Relax, Vicky!" my voice said, laughing. "Spare me the great soul-searching agony! What's the big deal? It was fun! Sure it was a trick you'd never dream of pulling on shore, but so what? Half the fun of a cruise is that you do all the things you'd never dare do anywhere else! Now, let's be honest—it was a brilliant maneuver superbly executed and we both had a great time. So why don't we celebrate? Let me take you to the aft bar for a drink so that we can toast each other's health before we go our separate ways!"

After a pause she said levelly, "Sure. Okay. Why not?" and gave me a passable smile.

So far, so good, but I was sweating with tension. It had never seemed more difficult to assume the role of playboy; and it had never seemed more unpleasant. The effort of continuing to speak in character was so great that I could hardly get the words out, but I managed to say smoothly enough at last, "You want to shower with me before we get dressed?"

"You bet!" she said, and the slang sounded odd, making a mockery of her attempt to sound spontaneous and sophisticated.

We stood looking at each other. She was still wearing my shirt. I had at some stage scrambled into my shorts, but now, groping again for the playboy image, I shed them carelessly and strolled toward the bathroom.

She never moved. I walked right up to her, but she still blocked my path, and it was then that I realized she was as disoriented as I was—and just as trapped in a role she had no wish to play.

I put aside all pretense. It was no conscious decision, but merely the overwhelming urge to be myself, and as I looked at her I knew I couldn't just tear up my pass to a world which had been transformed.

We never did get as far as the shower. Nor did we get as far as the aft bar for our phony celebration drink. We couldn't even get as far as the bed. I stepped forward at the exact moment that she held out her arms, and as the light glowed softly behind us I slammed her hard against me and took her against the wall.

V

IN THE dawn light we began to talk.

"Do you have a mistress in New York?"

"No, I'm different there."

"So am I. I can't live the way I really want to live."

"Who can? Freedom's a grand illusion. We do what we have to do and there's no escape."

"And what is it you have to do, Scott?"

"I'd have thought that was obvious. I'm under a compulsion to make amends for my father's failure and get to the top of my profession. No doubt any analyst would see my behavior as only too predictable."

There was a pause. Then she said, "Is it really that simple?"

"Why should you say that?"

"Because life so seldom is. What do you truly think of my father?"

"Vicky, there's no need for you to feel, as I'm sure Sebastian often felt, that I'm privately wrapped up in some titanic drama of revenge. The truth's a lot more complicated than that."

"But what *is* the truth?"

I was silent. But then I said, "I wish I could tell you. I think I would tell you if I thought you would ever understand. Maybe one day . . ."

VI

LATER, WHEN the sun was streaming through the porthole and the sea was a pure translucent blue, she said, "And do you really have no time or energy for a personal life in New York?"

"Is that so hard to understand?"

"No, only too easy. I'm in much the same boat. The family life I'm obliged to lead leaves me no time or energy for a real life of my own. But I'm not fueled by ambition, as you are. I'm fueled by guilt."

I got up and went over to the porthole. It was suddenly impossible to speak.

"I don't think we do what we have to do," she said. "I think we do what guilt makes us do."

I still couldn't speak.

"Sometimes you can't just put your guilt aside," she said, conscientiously explaining herself. "You want to but you can't. It's nailed to you and if you try to tear it out you bleed to death and innocent people suffer. So you go on doing what your guilt dictates you should do, and the only escape is to construct a sort of double life—to divide your personality in two. That's a terrible burden too, of course, but it's less of a burden than living daily with a guilt you can't endure."

Speech was still beyond me. There was a hotness behind my eyes, a blurring of the vision.

"Sorry," she said. "You must think I'm talking garbage. Forget it."

"Vicky . . ."

"It doesn't matter. Come back to bed."

VII

LATER STILL, she was the one standing by the porthole and I saw that the skin below the line of her delicate tan was as pale as ivory.

"We're approaching Curaçao," she said. "I guess now's the time I have to face slipping back to my cabin in broad daylight in full evening dress. . . . What are you thinking about?"

"I'm thinking you look as Maeve and Grainne ought to have looked but probably never did."

"Who the hell are they? No, don't answer that, I'm not in the mood to be educated. Look, why don't we go ashore together once the ship docks? I'm supposed to be lunching with the captain, but I'll get out of that."

"No, I . . . won't be going ashore."

Her eyes widened in disappointment. "Why not?"

"I'm tired. I'm not Superman. I've got to have some rest. And Curaçao's nothing special, just an island left behind by the Dutch on one of their off-days."

"Oh, but . . . Well, okay, if that's the way you feel. Maybe I'll rest too, and then this evening . . ." She paused.

"This evening," I said. "Yes. I'll call you."

She smiled. I watched her dress. When she was ready, she didn't touch me but merely blew me a kiss from the doorway.

"Till later!" Her eyes glowed. She was radiant. I wanted to push past her, lock the door, and toss the key out of the porthole, but I didn't. I was paralyzed by the conflict in my mind, torn between the dream of living a normal life and the reality of the compulsion to complete my quest, but as soon as I was alone I realized I had no choice except to pull myself together and face reality. The dream was over; I was a survivor and I had to protect myself; I had to escape home to Scott without delay.

By the time we docked at Curaçao I had already made my arrangements with the purser, and soon after the gangway had been lowered I left the ship and set off on my return journey to New York.

VIII

IN THE first letter which I intended to leave for her I wrote: "My dearest Vicky: First I want to thank you for seducing me with such remarkable originality—how you would have delighted Chaucer! I can imagine him writing 'The Wyf of New York's Tale' and greatly improving on 'The Miller's Tale,' where all kinds of couplings took place under cover of darkness. If you can imagine Chaucer writing 'The Investment Banker's Tale'—or perhaps he would have called me 'The Rich Lombard'—I hope you believe he would have described me as generously as he would undoubtedly have described you.

"So much for the Middle Ages.

"Unfortunately, since we have to live in the present, I see no way we can continue to act out our latter-day version of *The Canterbury Tales*. Having taken many cruises, I know very well that the reality which exists on board ship never survives the reality of the return to shore, so since our new relationship, enjoyable though it is, has no future, I see no point in extending it to the end of the cruise. Better to have a single memory of one perfect night than a painful recollection of the kind of emotional mess which I'm sure both of us want to avoid.

"I wish you a safe trip home and the best of luck in the future, Scott."

It was only when I wrote his name that I realized I had been trying to write in his voice. I reread the letter and was struck at once not by the coldness, the priggishness, and the stylized intellectual detachment, though they were all present, but by the falseness which permeated the letter from beginning to end. What I had written had nothing to do with what was really going on in my mind.

I folded the letter but realized I couldn't send it. I tore it up. By this time the ship was within minutes of docking and my time was running out, but I knew I could not leave the ship without also leaving some word for her. Finally, since an explanation was impossible and an apology would have made me seem not only a coward but a heel, I wrote: "Vicky: I just have to cut this encounter short. I don't want to, but I must. If we go on, I see nothing ahead of us but insoluble problems, so the only sane course has to be to stay uninvolved. But believe me when I say I'll remember you always as you were last night when you made the myth of romance live, no matter how briefly, in reality."

I did not want to sign Scott's name so I wrote no more. Sealing the envelope, I left it at the purser's office for delivery, and tried not to imagine how she would feel when she opened the letter and found I had kicked shut the door she had so magically opened between us.

IX

I HAD a four-hour wait at the airport for the one direct flight to New York. As soon as my bags were checked, I bought some magazines, but when I tried to read them, I found it hard to concentrate. Eventually I set them aside and just sat thinking about her. I told myself the incident had been no more than a chemical reaction between two people who under bizarre circumstances had seen each other in an irresistibly attractive light, but I remained unconvinced that our meeting could be summed up so easily. I couldn't understand why my discovery of her identity hadn't destroyed the chemistry. How could I have continued to make love to her successfully once I knew who she was? In panic I tried to find a rational explanation of my behavior. I was beginning to feel as if my entire sanity was on the line.

Her words echoed in my mind.

"Do you have a mistress in New York?"

"No, I'm different there."

She hadn't even asked me what I meant. She had known I wasn't Scott. She had recognized me as myself, and more important still, she had accepted me as I was. And I knew and accepted who she was, too. Not Cornelius Van Zale's daughter or Sebastian's ex-wife, or the harassed mother of all those noisy ill-behaved kids. This was a fellow survivor juggling with the double life. This was a fellow traveler tormented by the demands of self-discipline and driven by motives no one understood. This was the companion I'd always wanted to put an end to my isolation. This was the woman I'd long since decided I'd never be able to find.

I couldn't even regret that she was someone who knew Scott's world so well. That only added to the understanding between us, because there was no need to explain Scott to her. She knew exactly who Scott was, so we were immediately beyond all the boring questions other women found they had to ask: Where do you live, what do you do, have you ever been married . . . ? I thought of all those dreary questions and reveled in their absence. Then I remembered saying to her at some time during the night: "But Tony was the good-looking one—how could you possibly think I was more attractive than he was?" And she had said idly: "Yes, he was nice, but he was kind of boring, I always thought, like Andrew." And amidst all my gratification I had suddenly thought how wonderful it was that she *knew* Andrew and Tony and that there was no need for me to embark on turgid explanations.

So Vicky could ease the weight of my reserve merely by sharing so much of my background, and when I thought more about that background I saw yet another of Vicky's advantages: She had no interest in how much money I made and what kind of life I could afford. Since she herself was rich, she could see me so clearly because my own wealth didn't stand in her way. That fact alone was enough to make her very different from most of the women I met in the course of my travels.

I found I wanted very much to see her again.

I was on my feet in a second. I was wide-awake, yet obviously I was still living in a dream. I had apparently become entangled in a fantasy which bore no relation to the reality of my New York life, but I was appalled to discover that now it was my New York life which seemed a fantasy, while Vicky was the one reality in a confused, disordered world. I sat down again, forced myself to be calm. I was, of course, very disturbed. That was why I was having so much trouble distinguishing between fantasy and reality, and that was why my instinct for self-preservation was beating me back to New York, where Scott could reestablish his control over my life.

Or was Scott a fantasy?

No, Scott might be a myth, but he was still part of my reality, for unlike fantasy, myths were only different dimensions of the truth. That was why myths could be just as important as reality, and that was why in the most successful lives they were not in conflict with reality but complementing it, so that both myth and reality streamed side by side in time.

I looked down at the magazine and saw the photo of Jack Kennedy. He had gone to Florida to make assurances that he was not "against business" and he was now on his way to Texas on a similar mission. That was the reality, but the myth was there too, streaming side by side through his life, the legend of JFK, the man who had followed his father's ambition on and on and on to the very end of his dreams. One day, too, my myth and my reality would merge forever and I could begin to live as I really wanted to live, but first I had to complete my game of chess with Death; I had to outflank him and survive.

Tonight I would be in New York. Tomorrow President Kennedy would be in Dallas, Texas. That was reality. But at the end of ambition's road was light and life, and as I looked down once more at Jack Kennedy's smiling face, I thought that Death had never seemed so far away.

"Eastern Airlines announces the departure of their flight to New York. . . ."

I forced myself to board the plane.

"Can I get you a drink, sir?" said the pretty stewardess at my elbow.

I wanted to reply but was too afraid I might order the wrong drink. I felt very tense. The man next to me had ordered a Scotch.

"Some coffee, maybe?"

As I nodded, it occurred to me that I was in an even worse state than I'd imagined, and that the sooner I reached New York the better. Scott would hold out the straitjacket, I would slip thankfully inside, and then there would be an end to all my dangerous delusions and a welcome return to sanity.

The plane flew steadily on to New York.

X

As soon as I reached New York I started looking for him. I went to the men's room and checked the mirror as I washed my hands, but I saw only my own face, shadowed with fatigue, and my own eyes, underlining my confusion to me. Later, when the cabdriver waited for instructions, I expected to hear Scott's confident voice giving him the familiar address, but all I heard was my own voice saying worried: "Manhattan, Eighty-fifth and York," as if I were a stranger and my one friend in town had failed to meet my flight.

I saw the Manhattan skyline, looking oddly distorted by the new Pan Am Building, and the alteration of the familiar landscape dislocated the vertical structure of time and bent it into a curve in my mind. I saw the skyscrapers as giant dolmens arranged in patterns as sinister as any megalithic stone circle on the edge of Europe, and I knew I was moving into some macabre sacred grove where human lives were daily sacrificed to appease insatiable gods. For a second it seemed to me that the dolmens glittered with blood, but of course that was an illusion, the reflection of the setting sun on the glass windows.

"Home sweet home!" cried the driver cheerily as the car sped over the Fifty-ninth Street Bridge.

But this was no home of mine. I could no longer accept that my home lay among those bloodstained dolmens where my life was drained from me daily within the prison of Scott's personality.

"Okay, pal?" said the driver as he drew up outside Scott's apartment building.

I was so disturbed that I couldn't answer him. Thrusting a twenty-dollar bill into his hand, I ran into the building without waiting for change and rode the elevator to the twelfth floor. By this time I was panic-stricken, and as soon as the elevator doors opened I ran all the way down the corridor to the door of my apartment. The key slipped as I rammed it into the lock. I dropped it, picked it up, tried again. The door opened. Flinging it wide, I burst across the threshold.

There was a musty smell in the apartment, as if someone had died and been efficiently embalmed. I closed the door. The sound seemed to echo and reecho through the dim, funereal rooms, but I didn't stop to listen to it. I was on my way to the bathroom to check the mirror.

He wasn't there. Blundering into the kitchen, I fixed him his favorite drink, a tall Coke on ice with a dash of concentrated lemon juice, but I was the one who drank the drink and I was the one who abandoned the empty glass in the kitchen. In the bedroom I dressed in his clothes, the dark suit, white shirt, and sober tie; I even took one of his favorite books from the living-room shelves, but it was I who sat down in the recliner, and it was I who waited and waited for the man who never came.

The truth crept into my mind then, as I sat there dumbly with *Piers Plowman* in my hands. Scott wasn't there and he wasn't going to come back.

Scott was dead.

I was on my own.

Chapter Four

I

I WAS in the bathroom again, but this time the mirror was blank. The shock of not seeing any reflection, even my own, was so violent that I found myself fighting for breath, but when I realized the hallucination had been triggered not by mental confusion but by physical exhaustion, this essentially sane diagnosis produced the required chemical reaction in my brain and I saw my own reflection in the mirror as soon as I stopped rubbing my eyes. I looked not only ill but also scared out of my wits, so I laughed to give myself courage and said aloud to my reflection, "What you need is a drink."

That made me feel more frightened than ever, so I shut myself in the bedroom, where there was no telephone directory to give me the number of the nearest liquor store, and picked up the pad and pen I kept by the phone on the nightstand. I thought if I behaved as much like Scott as possible and made a list of the chores that had to be done I might achieve some semblance of normality.

I wrote: "1. Unpack. 2. Get food. 3. Sort out laundry. 4. Eat." Then I tore up the list, wrote "SLEEP" in giant letters on the page beneath, and pulled loose my tie.

So acute was my exhaustion that I blacked out a second after my head touched the pillow. One moment I was thinking: I'll survive without him somehow, and the next moment the lights were flashing before my eyes as I fell from the top of the Pan Am Building into the river of blood countless floors below.

II

WHEN I awoke, I felt better. I had slept for fourteen hours, a fact which made me realize how exhausted I had been, for I seldom needed more than six hours' sleep a night. In the bathroom I looked at myself carefully in the mirror but shaved with a steady hand. Then I put on a pair of jeans and a T-shirt and padded hungrily to the kitchen, only to be reminded I had no fresh food, so I called the nearest delicatessen and placed an order. Half an hour later when I had fixed myself eggs, bacon, toast, and coffee, I was feeling not only more organized but also more optimistic. Scott might be dead, but was he such a great loss? I was already figuring out how I could adapt to my new situation without putting my ambition in jeopardy.

Scott would have told me to forget about Vicky, but Scott had been a priggish intellectual bore who never took a single risk that would have made his life worth living. The hell with Scott! Naturally I couldn't give up my ambition; that was out of the question, but I wasn't going to give up Vicky, either. That was out of the question too.

Of course Cornelius would start to wonder about me again, but so long as I made my intentions clear, I saw no reason why he should conclude I intended to deprive him of his family by marrying his daughter. I had no intention of marrying Vicky or of depriving him of all those detestable grandchildren of his.

I didn't believe in marriage. The best marriages never lasted, the rest just limped unattractively along toward the cemetery gates. Marriage caused suffering and grief; I could remember that all too well.

Nor did I believe in cohabitation. I needed a certain amount of solitude in order to recuperate from the strain of my Wall Street life, and this inevitably made me ill-suited for any kind of domestic life either inside or outside marriage. I could not afford to introduce still more strain into my private life by attempting to live in a way that was alien to me. I already lived under pressures which often seemed more than I could bear.

But of course. I wanted to see Vicky regularly and of course I wanted to sleep with her, and fortunately I saw no reason why I shouldn't get exactly what I wanted. I thought Vicky would be more than willing to settle for what I had to offer, since she needed a further strain on her double life no more than I did, and was probably by this time as reluctant as I was to risk outright cohabitation.

My thoughts turned back to Cornelius. Why should he object if Vicky and I confined ourselves to a discreet affair which wouldn't impinge either on her life with her children or my life at the bank? Vicky was obviously going to sleep with someone, and after the gigolos and the jet-setters of the past three years, Cornelius would probably gasp with relief that I had decided to keep Vicky happy for a while. Cornelius would trust me to do nothing stupid, and I would soon prove I had no intention of disappointing him.

Closing my mind abruptly against all thought of Cornelius, I put on a sweater and my leather jacket and left the apartment to buy a paper, but I didn't buy the paper immediately. Deciding a short walk would do me good, I drifted crosstown on Eighty-sixth Street, and then just as I reached the traffic lights on Lexington, a stranger, white-faced and clearly in a state of shock, accosted me with the words "Have you heard the news?"

"What news?"

"He's been shot."

"Who's been shot?"

"Kennedy."

"Who?"

"The president. John F. Kennedy has been shot in Dallas, Texas."

"That can't be true."

"He's dying."

A car drew up beside us at the lights, and the driver leaned out. "Is it true?"

People were getting out of their cars. I looked around the sidewalk and saw people had stopped walking.

"Is he dead? Is it true? Is he dying? Is it true? Is it true, is it true, is it true . . . ?"

The terrible questions were repeated like a Bach fugue, and far back in my memory I remembered Emily playing part of the St. Matthew Passion on her phonograph at Easter, remembered listening to the moment when the twelve apostles learn from Christ that one of them will betray him and sing in a beautiful unearthly counter-point: "Is it I? Is it I? Is it I?"

Terrible questions. Terrible answers. A terrible, hideous truth.

I was in a bar saying "Kennedy's been shot," but they already knew. The television was showing an appalling reality in black and white, and someone was talking brokenly into a microphone and the barman just looked at me and said, "He's dead."

"Give the man a drink, Paddy," said the Irishman at my side, and I realized I was in an Irish bar. There were painted shamrocks decorating the mirrors, and posters of Ireland on the walls, and when I saw those pictures of the Cliffs of Moher and the Ring of Kerry and the Twelve Bens of Connemara, I saw in my mind's eye the beautiful landscape of legend where Jack Kennedy's myth drowned in blood and drained away into the dark.

The glass of Irish whiskey was standing in front of me on the bar, but the vomit was in my throat. I turned, ran outside, and threw up into the gutter.

"Have you heard . . . is it true . . . ? He's dead . . . dead . . . dead . . ."

I was walking. I walked and walked and walked. I didn't stop in case I went into another bar, but I passed liquor store after liquor store, and I saw all the bottles, row upon row, display upon display—I saw Beefeater gin and Cinzano French and Tanqueray and J & B and Hennessy cognac and Grand Marnier and Ronrico rum and Drambuie and Remy Martin and Cutty Sark and Harvey's Bristol Cream and Lancers *vin rosé* and Kahlua and Pernod and John Jameson and Dubonnet and vodka—and *crème de menthe* had never looked so green and Chartreuse had never looked so yellow and Johnnie Walker's labels had never looked so red, so black, and all the time I walked on and on and on.

Gradually I was aware of the voices changing around me. I heard people saying, "Where was his protection?" and, "What kind of a madman would do a thing like that?" and, "Those damned Texans, no better than wild animals," and finally, in full recognition of the horror, "That he should have traveled all over the world, only to be killed in his own country—killed here by one of us. . . ." And I saw at last the dark underside of the myth which everyone had overlooked. Arthur had not lived happily ever after at Camelot. He had been killed by one of his own men, and everything Camelot represented had streamed away with him into the dark.

I was on Fifth Avenue, and in the window of Best's stood an American flag with black crepe on its staff. At Saks a photograph of Kennedy was flanked by urns of red roses. And all the while as I walked, the office workers were swarming out of the buildings, all talking in soft shattered voices, and as their whispers filled the air,

the great bell of St. Patrick's began to toll for America and the great
doors swung wide as the crowds streamed up the steps into the nave.
"How could this have happened to us? What did we do?" I heard
the people saying, and I went with them up the cathedral steps as if I
too believed there was some answer within to the unanswerable questions, and I stood for a long time in the shadows of that great church
built by the Irish to give their dreaming myths the reality of stone
and glass, and I waited and waited without knowing what I was waiting for, until suddenly there was a hiatus in the spontaneous service,
a magical silence followed by the huge dramatic sound of thousands
of voices raised in unison. The bishop had called on the congregation
to sing the national anthem.

Later I was walking again, walking westward crosstown as the
darkness fell, and in Times Square people were weeping and the famous bar of the Astor was silent and still.

"Yes, sir?" said the barman.

"Give me a Coke."

"A *Coke?*"

I turned and walked out, but when I emerged from the hotel I
stopped dead. The lights were going out in Times Square. I watched
transfixed, and in my memory I heard the famous words of Sir Edward Grey: "The lamps are going out all over Europe; we shall not
see them lit again in our lifetime." And I saw with my inner eye
America turning some huge corner, pausing for a moment to grieve
for the passing of an innocent uncomplicated past, and then moving
on into the uncharted, infinitely more complex world which lay
ahead.

The last light went out. I began to walk home, but with me as always walked Death, my familiar companion, and in my mind I said
to him over and over again: Not yet. I must have more time.

But time had run out for John Kennedy at Dallas. And time had
proved that at the end of ambition's road lay nothing but the bullet
and the grave.

Nothing else.

Nothing, nothing, nothing. . . .

III

THE NEXT day I bought a television and spent the day watching it. All the usual programming had been canceled, and in the uninterrupted coverage Kennedy's death became not a remote world event but a very personal bereavement. Occasionally I got up, resolved to watch no more, but I could never bring myself to turn off the set. I found myself torn between the urge not to hear any more and an uncontrollable hunger to obtain the latest information. I drank steadily—Coca-Cola, root beer, ginger ale, even grape soda. I spent a long time mixing each drink and dressing it with slices of lemon or maraschino cherries, and I avoided drinking quickly by never taking more than three sips at a time from my glass. For long periods I forgot to eat, but occasionally I made myself a slice of toast. Later I went out, but Times Square was still in darkness and the city was like a morgue.

The day ended, the new day began, and the curtain went up on more violence. Ruby assassinated Oswald. I watched the murder live on television, but the events on the screen seemed so like the fantasy of some profoundly sick mind that I began to wonder if I had imagined the entire episode. It was a relief to go out and discover people were talking about this new assassination; amidst all the horror, it was still a relief to know that I wasn't hallucinating, that this was America on November 24, 1963, that the president had been assassinated and now someone had killed the killer. I walked in Central Park past the people who were listening to their radios, and then, unable to stay away any longer, I returned home once more to the television.

The day passed. Monday dawned. New York was like a vast church, and like a church it was hushed and somber. Everyone was watching television; everyone was at the funeral.

I began to watch too, but then, unable to endure my apartment any longer, I went out. But still I could not escape from the television. Thousands of people stood silently watching a huge screen in Grand Central Terminal, and although I again tried to watch, it was impossible; I couldn't endure the sight of that riderless horse, so I left the terminal and walked west on Forty-second Street.

At noon the police halted all traffic in Times Square, and as everyone on the sidewalks bowed their heads, we heard the military bugle sounding from the top of the Astor's marquee.

The sun was brilliant in a cloudless sky. It was a beautiful day. I stood in that sunlight and wished I could believe that death was a mere pause between this world and that other world where everyone was eternally young and beautiful and the sun always shone, but the twentieth century must have worked a mutation into the blueprint of my heredity, for I could not believe in an afterlife. I did believe in that other world, but I believed too that it existed only in the mind's eye.

I went home and drank my way through a six-pack of Coke, dressing each measure up differently and using an original assortment of glasses. The television droned on, but at last I was able to switch it off. Kennedy was dead, Oswald was dead, even Scott was dead, but I could no longer endure to look Death straight in the eye. Death was still there, facing me across the chessboard, but now I could turn my back on him for a while and think only of life, for today was the day Vicky had planned to return from the Caribbean. Glancing at my watch, I uncapped a bottle of 7-Up and then dialed the airport to inquire about flight arrivals from Puerto Rico.

IV

"MRS. FOXWORTH, please," I said to the doorman.

It was half-past seven on Monday evening, and I had calculated that Vicky would have been home for three hours, long enough to have surmounted the family reunion and be longing for a quiet, secluded dinner. I had half-thought she might call me, but I had been disappointed. The phone had rung only once; Cornelius, knowing I had been due to return from my vacation late on Sunday night, had called early on Monday morning to gossip about the assassination. Normally I would have seen him that day at the bank, but Kennedy's funeral had closed all offices nationwide.

"And the name, sir?" said the doorman in the lobby of the building where Vicky had her two apartments.

"Sullivan."

The doorman turned to the intercom but was told by the housekeeper of the duplex that Mrs. Foxworth had just departed for her smaller apartment on the third floor. The doorman tried again and this time succeeded in reaching Vicky, but when he announced my name, the connection was severed so abruptly that he jumped.

"I guess Mrs. Foxworth isn't receiving any visitors right now, Mr. Sullivan."

I handed him twenty dollars to silence him and headed for the elevator.

I had never been to Vicky's private apartment, and as far as I knew, not even Cornelius had managed to cross the threshold. It was popularly supposed that Vicky invited no one to her apartment except her lovers.

I rang the bell. I had to wait some time, but at last there was a small scratchy sound as she slipped back the cover on the spyhole.

"Sorry," she called through the door, "casual sex isn't available here tonight, but there's a very high-class call girl in apartment 5G. Why don't you check and see if she has a cancellation?"

"I'm not interested in call girls," I said in a neutral voice from which all trace of my thoughtless arrogance had been meticulously eliminated. "My name is Peter Abelard and I'm looking for Héloise."

I had spent the entire ride in the elevator cursing myself for being so stupid as to imagine she would welcome me with open arms after the way I had walked out on her in Curaçao. Then I had waited an entire minute in the third-floor hallway while I worked out how I could best approach her. Knowing she had long fancied herself interested in philosophy, I figured the reference to Abelard might appeal to her, but as the silence now lengthened, I wondered with a sinking heart if this purported interest in philosophy had been no more than an empty pose.

"Vicky—" I began tentatively, but she interrupted me.

"Yes," she said coolly. "Well, I'm sorry, but casual sex isn't available even to you, Peter Abelard, but if you have anything useful to say about the conflict between the Augustinian and the Aristotelian systems, you may, of course, come in."

The door opened a crack. We looked at each other. The ache in my body tightened into a solid swelling pain.

"Thank you," I said as she opened the door wider. "I seem to be suffering from an uncontrollable urge to demonstrate my skill in dialectic."

I crossed the threshold and we stood facing each other four feet apart in the small hallway. She wore a white sweater, a black skirt, and high-heeled black shoes. The Caribbean sun had lightened her hair and peppered her nose with freckles beneath the pale golden tan. She wore no makeup.

"Wasn't it an appalling day," she said abruptly as if she felt speech could dissolve the tension of our silence. "Imagine the sun shining like that! And I couldn't bear the way Washington looked so beautiful, like a dream city with its buildings so classical, so impossibly white—a background like that made the procession seem all the more macabre. . . . Oh, it was unbearable, I couldn't stand that restless riderless horse pawing the ground in anguish . . . God, what a nightmare! How can you bear to be sober? Don't you want to drink?"

I wanted to take her in my arms, but I knew she was using the conversation to keep me at arm's length, and before I could open my mouth to answer her, she had turned away.

"You'd better come into the living room," she said tersely, moving through the open doorway beyond the hall.

I followed her. "So you saw the funeral?" I said, bending my whole will to sustain this discussion of the day's events. "You must have come home earlier than I thought."

"I flew home on Saturday as soon as the ship docked in San Juan. Do you think I could have lingered there enjoying myself after what happened last Friday in Dallas?"

"I—"

"Oh, don't let's talk about that anymore! I'm sick of hearing about murder and violence, sick of it—I had such an odd feeling when I saw Jackie with the blood on her clothes. I felt as if it were all happening to *me,* not to her, and I became so horribly frightened. . . . So now I want to put it all behind me. I can't take any more of this gruesome reality. I want to talk about something utterly remote and cerebral like medieval philosophy, and that's the reason why I invited you across this theshold, so go ahead, Abelard. Talk to me."

"Okay," I said. "Let's talk about William of Ockham."

She threw me a contemptuous look. "I don't think you could, Abelard. You died long before he was born."

I stopped. She laughed. "What do you think I do in this place?" she said. "Hold orgies? Ask any mother of five children and she'll tell you that all she wants at the end of an average day isn't sex but just peace and quiet. I come here to be alone. I come here to recu-

perate from the kind of life I'm not well-equipped to lead. And I
read. I read a lot of things, mostly junk, but just occasionally, if I'm
feeling particularly brilliant and ambitious—which isn't often—I read
about the people you think I've never heard of, people like Peter
Abelard and William of Ockham and—"

"Johannes Scotus Erigena?"

"Ah, the Irishman! Okay, I'll talk about Johannes Scotus. He was,
of course, a Neoplatonist—"

"—shaped by his knowledge of Greek." For the first time I could
relax sufficiently to be aware of my surroundings and I saw that like
Cornelius, Vicky had dispensed with the antiques that had surrounded her for so much of her life and had furnished the apartment
in an ultramodern style. Long low couches upholstered in white
vinyl reminded me of the departure lounges of airport terminals.
Two pink fish swam in an aquarium by the window, and three modern paintings, all geometrical abstracts, adorned the plain white
walls. Above the aquarium someone had taped a primitive drawing
of a fat woman with yellow hair, and stepping closer I saw the artist
had written in black crayon: "MY MOM by SAMANTHA KELLER,
aged 8."

"Johannes Scotus Erigena," I heard myself saying casually as
Vicky stooped to take a cigarette from the box on the glass-topped
coffee table, "held that man in his fallen state had lost his power of
direct insight into the truth and that man was able to know the truth
only through the experience of the senses . . . and that leads me exactly to what I came here to say—"

"My God, you're a smooth operator!"

"—which was this: Vicky, from my experience of the senses with
you I've reached a truth which I was completely wrong to deny in
that letter I left for you—"

"Do you have a light?"

"Of course not, I don't smoke."

She snapped the cigarette box shut and walked out of the room.
When she returned with the cigarette burning between her fingers I
tried to resume my speech, but she cut me off.

"Look, Scott, I have enough problems of my own without having
to deal with your problems, too. If you choose to run away to avoid
any kind of emotional commitment, you go right ahead, and good
luck to you. That's your problem and I'm not mad enough to believe
I could ever solve it. But don't, please, try to intrude in my life any

further. I don't want to get involved with someone who doesn't want to get involved. I can think of no bigger waste of my time and energy."

"I thought . . . on board ship . . . you weren't interested in permanent involvements."

"That was one world," said Vicky, "but this is another. I couldn't live here as I lived on board ship. It's too self-destructive. I've tried it and I know. In New York I want a commitment, I want someone supportive, I want someone who's more than just a good lay. You don't fit the bill. Sorry. It was great, but it's over. It has to be. You said it all in that letter, and now there's nothing else to say."

"But you misunderstand! The situation's far more complicated than it at first seemed on board ship! I assure you I didn't come here just to go to bed with you—"

She laughed in my face. "Oh yeah?"

The telephone rang.

"Let it ring!" I said, exasperated by the interruption.

She immediately grabbed the receiver. "Hello?"

There was a pause, and as I watched I saw a softer expression creep into her eyes, while the hard line of her mouth relaxed. She turned away to block me from her vision.

"Oh, hi. . . . Yes, Alicia told me you were arriving today. . . . Recovering from the flight? I sympathize. I had a hellish flight back from Puerto Rico last Saturday. . . . Oh, just a vacation. Lots of humidity and frightful people—I never want to see another palm tree again. . . . What was that? A present for Postumus? Oh, he *will* be pleased! You must come over tomorrow. . . . Oh, anytime. Postumus gets up at five-thirty, six on his good days, and goes to kindergarten at a quarter of nine. Then he comes home at eleven-thirty, gives Nurse hell till four, and afterward watches TV until he has to be forcibly removed. . . . Yes, they're all well, thanks. Eric goes to Choate next year—isn't it amazing how time flies? Well, listen, dearest, I . . . Dinner tomorrow? I'm not sure. . . . Would it be a good idea? We'd probably get overemotional, and then . . . Okay, you stop by with the present for Postumus and then we'll see how we feel. . . . Yes, it was terrible about the president. Look, I have to go now—something's boiling over on the stove. . . . Okay. 'Bye." She hung up and stood looking at the phone.

"Sebastian?" I said at last. "What's he doing back in town?"

She looked at me in surprise. "I thought you'd know about it. Alicia said it was a business trip."

I had a distant memory of Cornelius promising to recall Sebastian to discuss the trouble in London with Reischman's. "Why, yes, I remember now. It'd gone clean out of my mind."

She moved to the sideboard and started to fix herself a drink. "Can you go now, please?" she said over her shoulder. "I've had enough of you prowling around the room like a character out of a Tennessee Williams play. Why the hell do you have to look so sexy? I thought you were always sexless celibate Scott as soon as you set foot in New York!"

"Scott died."

The martini spilled. She spun round to face me, and we stared at each other, but she never asked me what I meant.

I moved to the aquarium where the pink fish were chasing each other in an obscure courtship ritual, but when I turned to look at her again, all she said was, "That statement has no relation to reality. It's just words."

"But what is reality?" I said without a second's hesitation. "We seem to have come full circle back to William of Ockham. He believed the individual was the sole reality. He believed that everything else existed only in the intellect. He believed"—I found myself right beside her at the liquor cabinet—"he believed in the power of the will."

"The power of the will," she said. "Yes."

Her clear eyes were brilliant with some powerful emotion which refused to be checked, and suddenly I realized the emotion was mine, projected into her thoughts and reflected at me by the mirror of her mind. The impression of an electric current running between us was so strong that I even hesitated to touch her for fear I might trigger some explosive force beyond my control.

"The hell with you!" she exclaimed suddenly. "Walking out on me like that and then expecting me to—"

"We all make mistakes."

"You bet we do, and I'm just about to make the biggest mistake of my life, you . . . you . . . you . . ."

Words failed her. She was shaking with rage.

". . . son of a bitch!" she finally shouted through her tears as I drew her into my arms, and then the next moment she was pulling my face down to hers and kissing me violently on the mouth.

Chapter Five

"MOM!" SHOUTED a clear, fierce treble far away, and I heard the short sharp burst of an electric drill.

At first I thought the interruption came from my brother Tony. I could see him clearly, six years old, with my father's curly hair and blue eyes, and I knew he was up to his usual tricks, borrowing my toys and breaking them, endlessly getting under my feet and in my way. It was a severe burden for any civilized nine-year-old to have such an untamed younger brother.

"*Mom!*" came the fierce treble again, and I knew there was something wrong, because my mother had always insisted that we called her "Mother" as soon as we were old enough to pronounce the *th* without lisping. The electric drill buzzed again, and suddenly I knew it was no drill, but a doorbell; suddenly I was wide-awake, sitting bolt upright in bed in Vicky's apartment while Vicky herself was struggling frantically into her robe.

"What the hell. . . . ?"

"It's okay. It's just Benjamin stopping by to say hello on his way to kindergarten." She ran out, banging the bedroom door so clumsily that it rebounded from its frame, and I automatically jumped out of bed to make sure the view of the bedroom was cut off from anyone entering the hall. But before I could close the door completely, Benjamin had galloped into the hall and was piping, "Hi, Mom! Surprise! Here's Uncle Sebastian!"

I froze. A few feet away from me, Vicky was speechless. Eventually Sebastian said in typically monosyllabic fashion, "Hi. Looks like I goofed. Dumb of me. I'll come back when you're dressed. 'Bye."

"No . . . wait, Sebastian! I'm sorry, I was just so surprised . . . I didn't expect—"

"I've been awake since five. Jet lag. Then I remembered Postumus got up early, so I thought I'd pay you an early visit."

"Of course. Yes. Well . . ."

"Hey, Mom!" shrilled Benjamin, interrupting this awkward exchange. "Look at the great present Uncle Sebastian's brought me! It's a tank that shoots real bullets!"

"Oh, Sebastian, do you really approve of war toys for children?" She was making the mistake of prolonging the conversation while making no effort to invite him across the threshold. Sebastian was going to guess she was not alone in the apartment—if he hadn't guessed as much already. I wondered why she didn't behave more naturally by inviting him into the living room, but the answer hit me as I backed noiselessly away from the door and looked around for something to put on. My clothes were missing. They were littering the floor of the living room, where Vicky and I had first made love on the couch under the baleful gaze of the pink fish.

"War's a fact of life, isn't it?" Sebastian was saying. "Do you want Postumus to grow up without a sound knowledge of what goes on in the world?"

"*Don't call me Postumus, Uncle Sebastian!* Mom, can I take the tank to school?"

"Sebastian, that thing doesn't really fire bullets, does it?"

"Of course not! What a question!"

"Mom, can I . . . ?"

"Well, I don't know if—"

"*Oh, Mom!*"

"Oh, okay, yes, take it to school. Sebastian, let me call you later when I've had time to wake up properly and get myself together. Right now I—"

"Hey, Mom, can I feed the fish?"

"You'll be late for school!"

"Oh, *please!*"

"But they don't need feeding just yet!"

"*Oh, Mom!*"

"Hey," said Sebastian, "you make a lot of noise for a little kid your size. Tone it down."

"Uncle Sebastian, come and see the fish! They're called Don and Phil after the Everly Brothers!"

"Ben, wait . . . Ben, I've got some lovely new cookies here in the kitchen—"

"Gee, Mom, what are all these clothes doing all over the living-room floor?"

"Ben, will you do as you're told and come out of there at once! Oh, there's Nurse calling! Now, here you are, darling, here's a nice chocolate-chip cookie—"

"Can I have two?"

"Well . . ."

"Oh, Mom!"

"Oh, *all right!* Anything for a quiet life. Now, run along, darling."

"Vicky, does that kid always get exactly what he wants?"

"Oh shut up, Sebastian! I can't cope with both of you harassing me. Now, *out,* Benjamin, before I get *real* mad! Oh, and don't forget to thank Uncle Sebastian for—"

The door slammed as Benjamin made a triumphant exit with a tank and two cookies.

There was a silence. Unable to stop myself, I moved back to the door and looked through the crack between the hinges. Sebastian was standing on the threshold of the living room, and as I watched, he picked something up from the table that stood just beyond the door.

"This is nice," he said politely, to Vicky. "Where did you get it?"

It was my silver medallion from Ireland.

"Mexico," said Vicky after a pause.

"Yeah? It looks Celtic." He put it back on the table, took another casual look around the disordered living room, and then turned aside as if what he saw was of no importance to him.

"Sebastian . . ."

"Okay, I'm going—you don't have to throw me out. Sorry I embarrassed you by walking in at the wrong time."

"Sebastian, I just want to say—"

"Don't bother. It's not my business whose clothes you pick to decorate your living room. Don't think much of his taste, by the way. Levi's and a black leather jacket, for God's sake! Looks like you finally tempted Elvis Presley to swivel right out of the silver screen! No, don't answer that. Forget it. Dinner okay for this evening? No, I promise I won't get emotional—there won't be time, because I'll have so much to talk about. There's going to be a big scene at the bank today, and I think I'm going to be able to blitz Cornelius into recalling me from Europe. He doesn't want to, of course, but I've deliberately made London too hot to hold me, and since he can't fire me in case Mother takes offense and starts locking her bedroom door—"

"Sebastian, I'm sorry, but I just can't cope with all this right now. Would you mind . . ."

"Okay, I'm on my way. So long. See you. Sorry." The front door closed abruptly. Footsteps retreated into the distance. Sitting down on the bed, I waited in silence for her to return to the room.

She came. My clothes and my silver medallion were dumped on the floor at my feet. I looked up, but she had already turned away.

"Vicky, I'm sorry. I can see you're upset. But he must surely realize you haven't lived like a nun since the divorce!"

"Making commonsense assumptions is one thing; seeing the sordid evidence to confirm those assumptions is quite another. Could you please go?"

I said in a voice which I tried hard to keep neutral, "Sounds as if you still love him."

She spun round to face me. "Yes," she said, "I love him. I'll always love Sebastian. He picked me up when I was down and out and he saved my life—I mean that. I'm not exaggerating. Before that I just existed. I was no one, just an adjunct to various people who made me over into whatever they wanted me to be. Now, will you please leave and allow me some privacy? You've already overstayed your welcome by approximately six hours."

"What do you mean?" I said, startled.

"I didn't invite you to stay the night, did I?"

"Well, I naturally assumed—"

"Yes," she said, "you would. That's the trouble with men who are too successful with women—they can't imagine there are times when they're resistible!"

"Now, wait a minute—"

"No, I won't! I feel mean and shabby and upset, and I want to be alone! For God's sake, are you completely insensitive?" shouted Vicky, in a great rage by this time, and slammed the bathroom door in my face. A second later the hiss of the shower drowned all future attempts at conversation.

I stood there stark naked and was aware of a wide range of emotions, none of them happy, elbowing for a place in my mind. I was angry, hurt, irritated, and jealous. I also felt in some obscure way guilty, although I told myself this was unnecessary, since Vicky was no longer married to Sebastian. Struggling into my shorts, I pulled on my T-shirt and told myself Vicky was behaving unreasonably, but this only made me feel more angry, more hurt, more irritated, and more jealous. This onslaught of violent emotion confused me. I was unused to it and found it hard to handle.

I was just thinking how horrified Scott would have been by my disordered feelings when I caught sight of the clock on the nightstand, and the next moment all my introspective thoughts were wiped out by panic. It was after nine o'clock. I was supposed to be at the office. Scott would have been at the office, because Scott was never late for work, and if I were late now, it would be a disastrous start to my new career as an actor playing Scott's role.

Dragging on the rest of my clothes with lightning speed, I ran back to the bathroom door. "Honey, I'm sorry for everything!" I shouted. "I'm truly sorry, I swear it! I'll call you later, okay?"

There was no answer, but I thought I heard the shower increase in volume to drown the sound of my voice.

I dashed to the front door and then remembered what Sebastian had said about maneuvering his return from Europe. That had to rank as valuable information, and if I used it skillfully I'd score. I dashed back into the bedroom, grabbed the phone, and dialed the Van Zale triplex, but of course Cornelius wasn't there; he had already left for work. I ran a hand distractedly through my hair and wondered if I was going out of my mind. This was no time to go crashing around and making a mess of everything. I had to calm down and be Scott, but I wasn't Scott, not anymore, and although I tried to be calm, I only felt more distracted than ever.

I ran out of the apartment, fretted by the shaft when the elevator failed to arrive promptly, and was just about to dive down the fire stairs when the red light flashed above the doors to signal that the elevator had at last reached my floor. I dashed inside. After an eternity it reached the ground. By this time the sweat of impatience was streaming down my back, and as soon as the doors opened I began to sprint across the lobby.

The next moment every muscle in my body snapped taut. I stopped. The shock dropped like lead to the pit of my stomach. Sebastian was standing by the doorman's desk.

I started to back away, but it was too late. He had been watching the elevators for the first sign of a man wearing the offbeat clothes

Scott would never have worn and making all the mistakes Scott would never have made. He saw me immediately.

We both stood transfixed. Other people from the elevator walked past me, said good morning to the doorman, and walked outside onto Seventy-ninth Street, and every time the doors opened, the reflected sunlight shone on the silver medallion Sebastian had examined with such care. No error of identification was possible. In three seconds I saw him try, convict, and sentence me, and in three seconds our long friendship came brutally to an end.

There was nothing to say, so neither of us spoke. He must have been just as shocked as I was, but in the end it was he who turned his back on me and walked out. I arrived on the sidewalk just in time to hear him say to the nearest cabdriver, "Willow and Wall."

I had one thought, and one thought only. I had to get to Cornelius first. For a long moment I stared at the slow-moving rush-hour traffic, and then I ran all the way to the corner of the block and dashed down the steps to the subway.

II

HALFWAY DOWN the subway steps I realized I was once more out of my mind. I could hardly turn up for work unshaven and wearing denim and black leather. Bolting back up the steps into the street, I grabbed a cab for the six-block ride uptown to my apartment, and as I sat on the edge of the seat I thought not of Cornelius but of Sam Keller bawling me out years ago because I had turned up disheveled in his office after falling asleep at my desk the night before.

The memory of Sam Keller, the man who had sent my father down the last mile of his road to self-destruction, always made me clench my fists, but this time they were clenched already. I felt like a passenger in a plane which was about to crash.

"Go faster, can't you?" I said to the driver.

"What's this—a suicide mission?"

I dropped a five-dollar bill onto the seat beside him. "Move it."

Horns blared as we jumped the lights and another driver leaned out to yell obscenities at us as our cab screeched off down the block.

In my apartment the water from the shower stung my skin and the towel was rough against my face. I shaved, seized some fresh underclothes, and reached for the phone.

"Is he there yet?" I said to Cornelius' secretary, the phone tucked between my ear and my shoulder as I pulled on my shorts.

"Not yet. The traffic's very heavy this morning. Is there a message, Mr. Sullivan?"

"No. Yes. Wait a minute, let me think." The truth was, the situation was so far beyond my control that panic was propelling me into a series of rash moves, each one more unfortunate than the last. It was time I stopped to consider the facts I couldn't alter. There was no way I could arrive at the office before Sebastian, just as there was no way I could stop Sebastian denouncing me to Cornelius, but even so, my situation might still not be beyond redemption. Cornelius disliked Sebastian, he disliked any criticism of me, his favorite partner, and he disliked being reminded that his daughter was neither married nor chaste. If I summoned all my nerve, stopped crashing around like a guilt-ridden playboy, and made a strong counterattack, the odds were that I could stave off disaster by talking my way out of trouble.

My silver medallion, symbol of a silver-tongued race, lay on the nightstand beside the phone. I said to the secretary in my smoothest, most charming voice, "Could you tell Mr. Van Zale, please, that I've been unexpectedly delayed but I'll be with him as soon as possible. Thanks very much! And perhaps you could suggest to him that the meeting about the London office be put back till ten-thirty? Thank you."

I hung up, glanced at my watch, and decided that since I'd bought myself some extra time I might as well make the most of it. After I was dressed I lingered over some black coffee, but finally, when the moment could be postponed no longer, I set off, feeling as naked as any ancient Celt who had rushed screaming into battle, and made my silent, well-dressed, immaculately controlled way downtown to Wall Street to fight for my professional life.

III

THE SUN shone as I walked down the street past Morgan's to the corner of Willow and Wall. The doorman at the bank greeted me with a smile, and I forced myself to make a leisurely progress down the great hall as I exchanged a few words with my partners who worked there. In the back lobby I moved swiftly past the closed doors of Cornelius' office and ran up the back stairs, but before I entered my room I made sure I was breathing evenly. This was going to be my dress rehearsal. I had to practice being as casual and relaxed as any other carefree bachelor just returned from a successful vacation in the Caribbean.

I flung open the door. My secretary and personal assistant were standing by my desk like victims awaiting a firing squad, and I remembered belatedly that Scott never discussed his vacations but immediately got on with the job of packing twenty-five hours' work into a twenty-four-hour day.

"Hi!" I said, thinking what hell Scott must have been to work for. "How are things?"

They gaped at me but decided my cheerful inquiry was just a temporary aberration.

"Scott, Mr. Van Zale wants to see you right away—"

"—and there's a crisis at Hammaco—"

"—and the computer's broken down—"

"—and there are urgent messages from—"

I thought: What a boring life Scott had, dealing daily with all this crap. "Hold it!" I protested. "Relax! Let them all wait! How have you two been doing?"

They stared at me openmouthed.

"Well," said my secretary at last, "I guess we're still recovering from the assassination. Scott, hadn't you better call Mr. Van Zale? He did say 'right away.' "

The phone rang.

"I'm not in yet," I said, taking off my coat.

My secretary got rid of the caller.

"Who was that?" I said, glancing vaguely at my accumulated correspondence.

"Donald Shine."

"Donald who?"

This time both my secretary and my personal assistant looked at me as if I were certifiable.

"Donald Shine! Don't tell us you've forgotten the young kid from Brooklyn who wants to start a computer-leasing business! He wanted to know when you could have lunch with him."

"Oh, Donald Shine! Sure, call him back and fix something. Where's that new beautiful blond from the typing pool with my coffee?"

Their gasps were audible. My secretary even dropped her notepad.

I was still laughing at them when the red phone jangled, making me jump. I took care to let it ring three times, and then, sitting down on the edge of my desk, I picked up the receiver and said cheerfully, "Sullivan!"

There was a pause. That was when I remembered that Scott always just said "Yes?" or "Hi!" when he answered the red phone.

"Cornelius!" I said swiftly.

"Scott?" He sounded odd. The inflection in his voice turned my name into a question.

"Who else?"

There was another pause. Then he said in his politest voice, "Could I see you right away, please?"

"Sure, I'll be right down." I replaced the receiver and stood up. "Okay, you two, I'll see you later. Keep the home fires burning."

They gazed at me speechlessly as I left the room.

It was only when I reached the back lobby that my nerve failed me and I had to pause. I am appalled to realize I was scared—and not just of the approaching battle, which I still felt confident I could win. I was frightened of Cornelius. I was no longer passionless, steel-nerved Scott who could regard him without emotion. I could only think that since Scott was dead it was *I* who now had to confront this man who had twisted my life in ways which Scott had never permitted me to dwell upon. I dwelt upon them. I wanted to vomit. I felt not only frightened but physically ill with my horror and revulsion.

I opened the door. He was there. I walked into the room. I felt I should be shaking, even shuddering, but I moved as smoothly as if I hadn't a care in the world, and Cornelius was moving smoothly too, standing up and coming around his desk to meet me. Beyond him the sun was shining palely on the gaunt branches of the magnolia tree in the patio, and above the fireplace the violent reds and blacks of the Kandinsky masterpiece looked like a mutilated corpse painted by a madman. The folding doors which divided the double chamber were closed, and the effect was to make the room infinitely more sinister and confined.

I stopped, but Cornelius moved on. He walked up to me with his hand outstretched and gave me his warmest smile.

"Hi!" he said. "Welcome back! It's good to see you again!"

I shook his hand without a word. I felt as muddled as I had felt in my teens when he had been so kind to me all the while he was brainwashing me against my father. I had forgotten what it was like to feel so intolerably confused. Scott had protected me from Cornelius with that wall of emotional detachment, but now the wall was in ruins and all the old wounds were breaking open in my mind. I didn't know it was possible to live with such pain and still remain conscious. I had a craving for brandy, a lot of brandy, poured neat into a huge glass.

"Are you okay?" said Cornelius.

I thought of my father dying while drunk. The desire for brandy died. And so did my fear. Looking at the man before me, I felt nothing but the darkest, most primitive rage.

I clamped down on it, struggled, somehow got it under control. It was perhaps the most supreme effort of will I had ever made. Then I said in a pleasant voice, "I'm just fine, Cornelius, but I admit it's been a hell of a morning. However, I don't want to bore you with all the trials and tribulations of my private life. I know you've always disapproved strongly of partners airing their private lives at the office."

"That's right. I have," he said, smiling at me to signal his approval of my good sense, and turned toward the doors which divided the two rooms. "By the way, I've postponed that meeting on the London office," he added over his shoulder. "Under the circumstances I thought a preliminary discussion would be helpful."

"A preliminary discussion?" I said, surprised. "Okay, sure. Just as you like."

He had opened the doors, and now he gestured to me to precede him into the other half of the room. I walked past him and stopped.

The notorious digital clock was still standing on the mantelshelf. The equally notorious Scandinavian couch was still standing before the hearth like an empty slab at the morgue. And Sebastian was standing by the window.

IV

"SEBASTIAN'S BEEN talking to me," said Cornelius, breaking the silence as he idly tested the mantel for dust with his finger and watched us both in the mirror above the fireplace. "Sebastian's been propounding a number of dramatic and interesting theories. I think you ought to hear these theories, Scott. Because, believe it or not, they're all about you."

"Great!" I said at once. "Well, I've got some theories too, and believe it or not, they're all about Sebastian. Why don't we have an exchange of information?"

"Why not?" agreed Cornelius sociably. "But before we start, let me make one point clear: Vicky's name is not to be mentioned in this discussion. Her private life is her own affair, and I've long since vowed never to interfere with it again. So if either of you have plans to use Vicky as a pawn in your games with each other, you can forget them. I'm not interested in who happens to be her current lover. It's immaterial to me."

"Wait a minute," said Sebastian.

I jumped, but he wasn't looking at me. He was looking at his stepfather, and Cornelius was assuming his most patient, long-suffering expression.

"Is this an act?" said Sebastian. "I find it hard to believe you could really be this dumb. This guy's screwing you all along the line, Cornelius! And when he's finally succeeded in screwing you all the way off the map, it won't be your portrait he'll hang on the wall of this office after he's changed the bank's name to Sullivan's—it'll be his father's!"

Cornelius sighed, leaned wearily against the mantel, and turned to me with resignation. "Okay, Scott, your turn. You want to answer that? Go ahead. You do it so well—I've always admired the way you have the perfect answer for all these awkward accusations that crop up from time to time."

"And I've always admired the way you've been smart enough to see the truth, Cornelius! Sebastian, if you think I'm motivated by revenge, you understand absolutely nothing—"

"Never mind what motivates you!" shouted Sebastian. "You're so mixed up and creepy and just plain odd that your motivation doesn't matter. What matters is that you want this bank, and once it's yours, you'll wipe out all trace of Cornelius as efficiently as he wiped out all trace of your father! It's all so goddamned obvious—"

"Sure it's obvious—to a man who's out of his mind with jealousy!"

"Why, you . . ."

I swung round on Cornelius, who was watching us as if he were a latter-day Zeus on Olympus, an all-powerful god casting an interested eye on the squabble of two minor deities. "There are no prizes for guessing what motivates Sebastian, Cornelius—his motives, at least, are crystal clear! He knows you'll never recall him from Europe, so he's maneuvered himself into a position where you have no choice but to bring him back, and once he's back, he'll use his mother's influence over you to get what he wants here at Willow and Wall. And once he gets what he wants, Cornelius, do you really think he'll raise a finger later to help your grandsons, whom he's always detested? And do you really think he'll keep the bank's name Van Zale's in memory of a man he's always secretly despised? He's the one you want to watch, Cornelius! He's the one who's out to make trouble! My conduct in New York has always been exemplary, but can you say as much for his recent conduct in London?"

"Okay, okay, okay," said Cornelius. "Nicely said, very impressive, I take your point. Now let's calm down, shall we, boys, and discuss this rationally. I'm not interested in watching the two of you conducting an overheated slanging match. Sebastian, what's all this nonsense about you feeling you had to engineer your recall from Europe? It was your decision to go to London back in 1960, remember, and it was a very unpopular decision with your mother. If you wanted to return to New York, all you had to do was ask."

"You goddamned hypocrite!" blazed Sebastian with such force that Cornelius recoiled. "It might have been my decision to go to London for a while, but you were delighted—you couldn't wait to get rid of me! And you didn't just want to get rid of me because you thought—getting the wrong end of the stick as usual where Vicky's concerned—that I'd messed up your daughter's life! You wanted me out of the way because my absence meant you'd have Mother's undivided attention. Christ, and to think you have the nerve to stand by and let this creep accuse *me* of jealousy! You've been jealous of my place in Mother's life for as long as I can remember!"

Cornelius moved to the folding doors. "This discussion is terminated. I've no time to waste listening to such irrational hysteria."

"This is no irrational hysteria, Cornelius—this is known as calling a spade a spade! Okay, let me call your bluff. Bring me back here from London! If all I have to do is ask, then okay, I'll ask. But I'll tell you one thing: if I come back, *he* has to go. You may be content to sit back and let him screw your bank and screw your daughter, but—"

Cornelius said simply, "You're fired," and walking into the main half of his office, he opened the French doors and stepped out into the patio without a backward glance.

There was a silence. Sebastian and I were struck dumb. Beyond the patio doors, Cornelius had found the packet of seed he kept for the birds and was busy feeding a couple of pigeons.

Finally Sebastian moved, bumping awkwardly against the desk and banging wide one of the French doors.

"You're crazy. You can't do this. You just can't do it."

"I'm senior partner of this bank, with absolute authority to hire and fire as I please, and no man, not even my wife's favorite son, tells me how to run my firm." Cornelius replaced the packet of birdseed in the ornamental urn, dusted his hands, and stepped back into the room.

Sebastian followed him. I still hadn't moved.

"Get out, would you," said Cornelius as he sat down at his desk and casually rustled a stack of papers. "I doubt if there's anything you can usefully add to the conversation."

"But Scott—what about Scott?"

"Scott's no concern of yours, not anymore."

"But—"

Cornelius rose to his feet so swiftly that Sebastian backed away. Then, leaning forward with both hands on his desk, he said in his clearest voice, "This conversation, like your career at Van Zale's, is now absolutely at an end. Got it? It's over. It's finished. I have nothing else to say."

Sebastian went very white. Without a word he stumbled to the door, but before he left the room, he looked back. "I hope he screws you into the grave, you bastard!" he said in a shaking voice. "But if you're still alive after he's finished with you, don't you come crawling to me for help in putting your life's work back together again—not unless you offer me the senior partnership and your own resignation from power!"

The door slammed. Cornelius sat down, loosened his tie, and took a pill from a small gold box. I waited. Finally he looked at me. It was a remote, cold, empty look.

"And so," he said, "we come to you. Can you give me one good reason why I shouldn't now fire you right along with Sebastian, as you so obviously and so richly deserve?"

V

"YOU'VE LEFT it too damned late," I said. "You fire me, and I go up the street to Reischman's and take all your top clients with me. Jake's already offered me the presidency of the new Reischman corporation. I've got it in my power now to slice you to ribbons, and don't you forget it."

A second after I had finished speaking, I realized I had made a horrific mistake. Scott had built his whole success on convincing Cornelius that although he wanted the bank one day he wasn't fundamentally hostile; he had let it be known that so long as Cornelius was generous enough to give him what he wanted, he in turn would be generous enough to keep the bank's name unchanged and look after the grandsons. This was the story Cornelius had wanted so much to believe, and this was the story Scott had dedicated himself to propagating. Yet by one short brutal speech spoken straight from the heart, I had shattered the enticing illusion Scott had taken years to build. Cornelius flinched, and as I saw him stare at me appalled, I knew he was recognizing me as my father's son and looking for one terrible moment deep into an intolerable past.

"Ah, the hell with it!" I said suddenly, knowing my whole survival was on the line and grabbing every ounce of nerve I still possessed. "Why are we talking to one another like this? Why are we behaving as if we're enemies? I think the shock of that godawful scene just now must have driven us both out of our minds!"

I paused but heard only silence. Cornelius seemed to grow a little smaller, a little older. He fidgeted with his tie again and took another pill. He was no longer looking at me.

"Look," I said, somehow finding a level, reasonable tone of voice, "I'm sorry. I know Sebastian put his own head in the noose and gave you no choice but to fire him, but I concede I was to blame by upsetting Sebastian in the first place. I encroached on territory which he obviously still regards as his, but Cornelius, believe me, Sebastian was the last person I ever wanted to know about the latest developments in my private life! It was all a terrible accident!"

"I thought you didn't have a private life."

"Well, no . . . that's true, but—"

"This was the exception that proves the rule? Okay, forget it. It doesn't matter. I'm not interested in your private life."

"Perhaps I should take this opportunity to stress to you—"

"Don't bother."

"—that I'm not out to marry Vicky—"

"Marry Vicky? *You?* Take on a divorcée with five kids? Don't make me laugh!"

"Well, I can see that you may now be feeling worried about Vicky, but—"

"No, I'm not worried about Vicky," said Cornelius unexpectedly. "Vicky's not so dumb as people think she is. I'm worried about you."

"I assure you there's no need—"

"Don't hand me any more of that garbage."

"Goddammit, I'm not interested in going to Rieschman's! I only said that because you were so hostile!"

"But Jake's offered you that job."

"Yes, but—"

"And you could make life hell for me if I now fired you."

"Christ almighty, Cornelius, just calm down, would you? I don't want to make your life hell! I'm not Dracula, I'm not Frankenstein, I'm not Jack the—"

"I know who you are," said Cornelius.

"Then in that case stop behaving as if I was some kind of hired assassin! Now, please—let's try to straighten things out so that we can both stop being so upset. The situation's simply this: I want to stay in the firm for reasons which we both know inside out. I've always done a good job here, and I'll continue to do a good job if I stay—there's no reason why you should doubt my ultimate loyalty just because Jake offers me a job, I stupidly lose my temper with you, and Sebastian throws a neurotic scene. Listen, let me make a gesture of good faith to show you how anxious I am to preserve the status quo and maintain the good relationship we've always had with each other; let me offer to make amends for my contribution to this disastrous scene with Sebastian. What shall I do? You tell me. Just give me the order and I'll carry it out to the very best of my ability."

"Great," said Cornelius. "Thanks. You can go to Europe and pick up the pieces Sebastian's left behind."

"Sure. How soon do you want me to go?"

"As soon as you damned well can."

"Okay. And when I come back—"

"You won't be coming back."

I felt as if I'd been slugged below the belt. "You mean . . ."

"I mean that this is no brief two-week vacation in London. We'll make it a four-year assignment—let's say until the first of January 1968. That's going to be a crucial year, because that's when I'm sixty and that's when I want to sew up the future by making some far-reaching decisions. You go to London, and if you care about your future, just you use those four years to convince me you still have one. That's all I have to say."

I hesitated. What would Scott have done now? I didn't know, and it didn't matter. I knew what I had to do. There was no choice. I was being edged toward a wooden box, and the nearer I got, the more plainly I could see it was a coffin.

"Cornelius . . ." I said.

He looked at me with those empty gray eyes.

"I'm very willing to go to London," I said. "I'm very willing to stay there four years and do a first-class job. But I'm afraid there must be a written guarantee in the articles of partnership that I'll be recalled here to Willow and Wall by the first of January 1968. I'm not going to have you railroad me as you railroaded my father."

Cornelius' fair delicate skin now had an almost transparent sheen. He said nothing.

"I'd rather resign," I said, "than go off to Europe with no guarantee I'll be recalled."

Another silence. At the far end of the room the digital clock flickered on in scarlet. I could see the rapid light out of the corner of my eye.

"I won't press you for any other guarantees about the future," I said, "because I'm confident I can convince you I'm still the best partner you have, but this particular guarantee I must have. I've got to safeguard myself against this apparent—and I hope temporary—hostility of yours. I don't want you suffering a burst of insecurity and firing me in my absence . . . or perhaps a touch of paranoia which persuades you to keep me in Europe after the dawn of 1968. Am I being so unreasonable? I don't think so. Wouldn't you want a similar guarantee if you were in my shoes?"

"If I were in your shoes," said Cornelius, "the one thing I'd never do is resign. That's an empty threat if ever I heard one."

"Then call my bluff and try to send me to Europe without that guarantee. Naturally, I'd prefer to stay here at Van Zale's, but please don't make the mistake of underestimating Jake's offer. Jake's gone out of his way to make the proposition attractive. He's even offered to change the firm's name to include my own. Generous of him, wasn't it? And of course the financial rewards would be very substantial."

Nothing. More scarlet flickers from the right. Shallow little breaths from Cornelius. Sweat crawling down my spine.

"Hm," said Cornelius at last, "well, okay . . . why have we worked up such an atmosphere here? What you say is reasonable enough, I guess, although as you know, I hate anyone trying to give me orders and displaying unnecessary muscle. However, we'll overlook that, as you now seem to be making an effort to appear respectful and obliging, and I like that, that's the sort of behavior which should be encouraged. So why don't we have a businesslike discussion instead of an emotional exchange of melodramatic opinions? I like businesslike discussions. They're sane, soothing, and rational. They help the participants keep a sense of proportion, and that's what we want now, isn't it, Scott? A sense of proportion. A preoccupation with the present, not the past or the future. The present is all we need concern ourselves with right now."

"I agree."

"Good. Now, here's what I'm going to do: I'll get the lawyers over and revise the articles of partnership to exclude Sebastian from the firm and give you your guarantee that you'll be recalled no later than the first of January 1968. I'll also guarantee that I can't fire you during that time without the consent of every single one of our partners."

"Without—"

"Be reasonable, Scott! This is where *you* have to make a concession! Supposing you misbehave yourself in Europe? I've got to have some kind of safeguard!"

"Okay. But it's got to be all the partners."

"Didn't I just say every single one?"

"I want this clause to spell out that I can't be fired, even with the consent of all the partners, unless I've been guilty of behavior which endangers the welfare of the firm."

"Okay. That guards you against the fact that all the partners tend to be yes-men when I'm around. No dismissal without valid cause. . . . Is that all? Can we relax now? Or are you going to change your mind and go after more guarantees?"

"No, not now that I've guaranteed my security until 1968. Of course I'd like more guarantees, but you needn't worry. I won't press you for them."

"Such as?"

"I'd like a guarantee that if you decide to incorporate the firm before 1968 I'll get the presidency of the new corporation. And I wouldn't mind a guarantee that if you drop dead while I'm in Europe I'll get your share of the partnership—with the proviso, of course, that I pass control of the bank eventually to your grandsons. In other words, Cornelius, I wouldn't mind a guarantee that I'm going to get what you've been promising me for a long time. I wouldn't mind being reassured that Sebastian hasn't scared you so shitless that you're tempted to double-cross me at the last moment."

Cornelius smiled a very passable smile, neither radiant nor friendly but pleasant and amused. "It takes more than Sebastian to scare me shitless!"

"I hope so."

"You can still trust me, Scott—if you can convince me I can still trust you."

"Just watch me in London!"

"I'll be watching." He smiled at me again. I wondered what he was really thinking. I thought I'd got him, but I wasn't sure. I knew he wanted to trust me again. If only I could find the appropriate wool, I thought he himself would reach out to pull it over his eyes, but although I was searching feverishly, the wool was proving elusive.

"You know what really scares me, Scott?"

At first I thought this was a rhetorical question, but then I realized he expected a reply. "I . . . won't even attempt to guess," I said uneasily, but I knew. I'd guessed. I realized exactly what was coming.

"Then I'll tell you," said Cornelius. "What scares me, Scott, is the sight of you bucketing around playing your father's ghost. Only, I'm not scared for myself, you understand, I'm scared for you. Your father made some very bad decisions, Scott. I'd hate to think of you trying to equal them."

There was a pause. Then I said, "That's not very likely to happen, is it? After all, I wasn't trained by my father. I was trained by you and Sam."

We looked at each other, and then suddenly Cornelius laughed. "That's supposed to make me feel relieved?" he said, laughing again, and the wry humor which was one of the more attractive elements in his personality sparkled before me, effortlessly defusing the tension between us. "Well, why not?" He smiled, shrugged, made a small gesture of dismissal with his hands. "Hell, what are we really talking about here? Nothing's changed, has it, except that we've both got rid of Sebastian, and that's something you and I have both wanted for years. I admit I was upset at first, because this is sure to mean trouble with Alicia, but maybe it'll be worth the trouble; maybe this whole scene this morning was a blessing in disguise."

"I hope so. Sure."

"And I admit I was a little disturbed to hear you've become interested in Vicky, but I guess that was just me being overprotective as usual. After all, Vicky can take care of herself now, and nothing catastrophic's going to happen. Why should it? I've every confidence that you can both conduct an affair discreetly without going off the rails."

"That's right. And I can promise you, Cornelius, that you won't be disappointed."

"And I'm sorry about London, Scott, but from a practical point of view I do think it's for the best. God knows what kind of mess that office is in at the moment. It'll certainly need a man of your caliber to straighten it out."

"Well, you know you can rely on me to pull it together."

"I know I can, yes. You won't consider it a demotion in any way, will you? I'll authorize an upgrading of the expense account to make sure you're really comfortable, and while we're revising the articles of partnership I'll increase your share of the profits to compensate you for having to leave America."

"That's very generous. Thank you."

"Well, I want to be generous, Scott. I've always wanted to be generous. . . . You're not really worried about those extra guarantees, are you—what happens if I drop dead before '68, all that kind of thing?"

This was the test. If I showed I distrusted him, he would be sure to keep right on distrusting me. I had to set his mind at rest. Grabbing the wool with relief, I prepared to pull it safely down over his eyes.

"No, Cornelius, I'm not worried. I only brought up the subject of extra guarantees because I was feeling hurt that I was being kicked off to London, but since you're now going to such lengths to make London attractive . . ." If he dropped dead, I'd still scoop the board somehow; none of the other partners had the muscle to stop me. And even if he tried to incorporate before 1968, he could hardly do it behind my back, and once I heard the news, I'd move immediately to safeguard my interests. Besides, he wasn't going to incorporate before 1968. He'd cling to his power for as long as he could. ". . . and by the way, Cornelius," I added as an afterthought, "you haven't yet spelled out exactly when you want me to leave."

"How about a week from today?"

"A week! So soon?"

"Well, there's no problem, is there? You're just a bachelor with no ties, and a pint-sized apartment. I realize you have a . . . romantic interest in your life right now, but that's nothing serious, is it? That's just a passing diversion—on both sides! Oh, don't think I can't understand. I'm not such a square as everyone here seems to think I am! I mean . . . well, that's the way it is, isn't it, Scott? I'm not wrong."

"No, you're not wrong. That's the way it is."

That was the way it ought to be. One week. Only one week. Oh, my God . . .

"Worried about something, Scott?"

"Only about my work. There's a lot to be done before I go."

"Have lunch with me today and we'll discuss how we can best take care of it."

"Okay. Thanks."

"Uh . . . Scott . . ."

"Yes?"

"I know it's none of my business . . . and of course you don't have to tell me anything . . . but . . . well, just why in God's name did you suddenly decide to seduce Vicky?"

"But I didn't seduce her," I said. "She seduced me."

He gaped at me. He was flabbergasted. I had had the last word in the conversation, but he had certainly arranged matters so that he could have the last laugh. Excusing myself from his presence, I somehow found my way back to my office, and then I collapsed exhausted in the nearest chair.

Chapter Six

WHEN I finally reached my apartment that evening, the telephone was ringing. I was so tired I could hardly reach it. Rubbing my neck where the muscles were aching, I slumped down on the recliner and picked up the receiver.

"Yes."

"Scott?"

It was Vicky. Dimly I remembered that I had promised to phone her. I tried to picture her, but she seemed too far away for me to see her clearly. I closed my eyes in an effort to bring her back into focus.

"Are you mad at me for being so upset this morning?" she said nervously.

"No."

"Oh. I thought that maybe that was why you hadn't called."

"To be honest, I hadn't even thought about it. I've had a bad day at the office."

"Oh, I see. Well, I've had a bad day at home, too—could we recuperate together this evening?"

My blurred memories sharpened abruptly at the thought of the nights we had shared.

"Fine," I said. "There's nothing I'd like better than to switch off my mind, get into bed, and make love. But I've just got to be alone for a while first. Get into your best negligee, turn down the bed, and I'll try to be with you around ten."

She hung up with a bang which jolted me out of my exhausted

stupor and made me curse out loud in exasperation. I had openly displayed an attitude which women never failed to find offensive. For a moment I wished we were back on board ship where the need for sex was treated as natural and not as some obscure practice requiring the maximum camouflage.

I called her back. She allowed the phone to ring eighteen times before she picked up the receiver.

"Yes?" she said coldly, mirroring my own opening response in the previous conversation.

"Look, I'm sorry I implied you were no more than a bedroom amenity like some fully automated electric blanket. Why don't we have a quiet dinner someplace? I can pick you up in half an hour. At least . . . Aren't you having dinner with Sebastian?"

"He canceled."

"Do you know why?"

"I guess he just thought better of the idea. I was out when he called, and my housekeeper took the message."

"Uh-huh." Now was definitely not the moment to explain what had happened to Sebastian. "Well, in that case—"

"Scott, I'd love to have dinner with you, but there's a complication. I've got tickets for the new play by Kevin Daly—I bought them today as a surprise for Sebastian, but since I shan't be seeing him . . ." She paused, and when I said nothing, she added in a rush, "What's the matter? Don't you feel in the mood for the theater?"

I wanted to tell her I felt in the mood for one thing and one thing only, but all I said was a cautious "I don't like Kevin Daly's plays."

"Don't you?" She sounded astonished.

There was an awkward silence. I realized I had put a foot wrong again, and again I was exasperated with myself. With a great effort I made a new attempt to please her.

"But maybe I'll like this latest play," I said quickly. "It's a comedy, isn't it? Great! I feel in the mood for something which requires no intellectual effort. I'll pick you up at your apartment as soon as possible—let's say in twenty minutes' time. We don't want to miss more of the first act than we have to."

She was waiting in the lobby of her apartment building when I arrived half an hour later. She wore a white mink coat, a sky-blue dress cut too low, thin-heeled shoes stacked too high, and a careless assortment of diamonds.

"I thought you were going to stand me up!" she said lightly. She was clutching her purse so hard that her skin was bone white around the scarlet nails. "I was just about to get mad."

"I'm sorry, I had trouble getting a cab." I gave her a kiss, and knowing I should make some compliment about her appearance, I glanced again at the fur and jewelry I detested.

"You're looking very Hollywood tonight!" I said with a smile.

She was immediately tense with anxiety. "I've worn all the wrong things, haven't I?"

"Well, it's a great neckline," I said, still smiling at her, "and who cares about anything else?"

She flushed unexpectedly and pulled the facings of her mink coat together to hide her breasts. "Let's go."

"Hey, I'm sorry, I didn't mean—"

"No, it's okay!" She smiled too in a frantic attempt to dispel the awkwardness between us, and as I searched without success for the words which would enable us to relax, I thought how bizarre it was that we should be forcing ourselves to adopt a program for the evening which was so much at odds with the intimate privacy we both wanted. However, I was determined not to alienate her by refusing to play the game as she apparently felt it had to be played. It was better to sit through a Daly play and a late-night supper at some overpriced restaurant than risk ending up in bed alone when the evening came to an end.

The trouble with Kevin Daly's work was that he had nothing to say. He used to conceal the vacuum behind the lines of his plays by writing in an antiquated meter which appealed to those intellectuals who believe that a play written in verse must necessarily be worthy of critical acclaim, but this latest play was in prose. As far as I could judge, it was pointless, and I could well understand why it had been panned by the intellectuals who had finally been able to see how far they had been conned. I paid little attention to the story, which concerned a rich successful businessman who fell violently in love with his secretary and abandoned his fame and fortune to live happily ever after in impoverished obscurity, but the audience around me listened avidly and laughed a good deal. It occurred to me that this kind of comedy probably represented the limit of Kevin's theatrical talent. He did have a certain facile wit and a knack of writing bright dialogue, even though he was incapable of achieving any creative depth on stage.

I stifled yawns, allowed my thigh to press hard against Vicky's, and finally allowed my mind to drift away toward the future. I had Cornelius sewn up again even though we'd both scared each other out of our wits before I had managed to thread the needle and start stitching, and the truth was that so long as I went to London obediently, behaved impeccably, and displayed nothing but the most faultless loyalty for the next four years, I ran no danger of having my throat cut. All Cornelius needed was reassurance. He no more wanted to believe ill of me than he wanted to fire me. I was much too valuable to him from both a professional and a personal point of view.

I glanced surreptitiously at Vicky in the darkened theater and asked myself if Cornelius was glad he had had the chance to break up the affair. Almost certainly the answer was yes. If he trusted me, he could probably have accepted any relationship I might have with his daughter, but now that his trust had been temporarily undermined, he had no doubt decided it would be best if Vicky and I were kept apart.

However, fortunately for Vicky and myself, Cornelius had miscalculated the distance across the Atlantic in this new age of jets. He might pride himself on not being "square," but if he thought sending me to London would automatically terminate my affair with Vicky, he was obviously out of touch with the facts of modern life. What was a few thousand miles these days between two lovers with money to burn? I would be returning to New York regularly on business, and there was no reason why she couldn't pay equally regular visits to London. And then perhaps her visits would get longer and longer . . . Cornelius and Alicia would be on hand to take care of the children . . . Despite my initial fear that we might be heading for trouble, I now saw that, on the contrary, the future looked very promising.

I took Vicky's hand in mine and under cover of the darkness I allowed it to graze lightly against my body. The pleasure was exquisite. When the lights went up a second later at the end of the first act, I felt as if I had been interrupted at a crucial point in the act of intercourse.

"Do you want to go?" said Vicky in a low voice.

"Yes, why don't we?" I said before I could stop myself, but luckily she had misunderstood the cause of my restlessness.

"I don't like the play much either," she said as we moved up the aisle to the lobby. "I don't think frothy comedy is Kevin's métier."

"At least the play wasn't pretentious. All the other plays pretended to be so deep, but the truth was, their message was as blank as the verse."

She stopped to stare at me. "But you're missing the whole point!" she said. "I know very often the characters seemed to have nothing to say to each other, but Kevin was writing about the void of noncommunication!"

"So the critics said, yes. But I couldn't see it myself." We were outside in the street. The air was cold, and to our left the arid neon desert of Broadway lit the tawdry landscape in a harsh glare. I felt myself sinking into a wasteland, the wasteland which Browning's hero Roland had journeyed through for years during his endless quest, and suddenly the isolation seemed more than I could endure. Taking her hand again, I held it tightly in my own. "Let's go back to your place."

"Don't I get anything to eat?"

"Sure! I'm sorry. I often forget about eating." I looked at her mink and diamonds and wondered where I could possibly take her. I felt like stopping at Nedick's for a hot dog and an orange juice.

A cab halted in response to my signal. "The Four Seasons, please," I said as I opened the door for Vicky.

"Wonderful!" exclaimed Vicky. "I just love the Four Seasons! What a great idea!"

At last I seemed to have done something right.

When we reached the restaurant Vicky had a large martini, which made her relax sufficiently to face first oysters and then a Dover sole. She also drank half a bottle of champagne. I had some soda water with a lime twist, half a plain grapefruit, and a filet mignon with a green salad. I found eating difficult.

I was just wondering if we could leave without lingering over dessert when I was aware of someone approaching our table, and the next moment Vicky gave an exclamation of delight.

"Kevin, what a lovely surprise!"

"Vicky darling, how incredibly glamorous you look!" He glanced in my direction and gave me a brief nod.

I nodded back. Kevin and I had never had much to say to each other. He had long ago sensed that I was unimpressed by his work, and naturally his vanity had been wounded. Sometimes he still made catty remarks about me to Cornelius. I knew this because Cornelius always repeated them to me in the correct belief that I would be

amused rather than upset by this childish display of pique. In a way I
felt sorry for him. It couldn't be much fun to be an elderly homosexual, and he now looked and acted just like the aging queer that he
was.

"How are you, Kevin?" Vicky was saying affectionately. "What's
your news?"

"Darling, I'm so glad you asked that question. I'm so outrageously
happy that everyone takes one look at me and turns away in disgust.
Life begins at fifty-five, my dear, and don't let anyone tell you
you're all washed up at twenty-one—or however old you happen to
be these days! Come over to my table for a moment and meet
Charles. He's a British friend of mine and he's over from London for
a couple of weeks on business. By a most extraordinary coincidence,
I met him through Sebastian when I was visiting London last summer, and . . . Hell, that reminds me, listen, I was just wiped out by
Sebastian's news. I think Neil must have finally taken leave of his
senses."

I was on my feet at once. "Vicky, it's time we were on our way.
Excuse us, please, Kevin."

"But, Scott . . . wait a minute!" Vicky was baffled. She turned
back to Kevin. "What's all this? What's happened?"

Kevin looked surprised. "Hasn't Scott told you? I thought that
since he was one of the principal actors in the morning's drama at
Willow and Wall—"

"What drama?"

I stepped forward. "I was planning to tell you later," I said to
Vicky. I tried to hide my anger, but it was difficult. "I didn't want to
spoil our evening."

"Tell me what? What is this? For God's sake, what's happened?"
Vicky was now both alarmed and upset.

I turned angrily to Kevin. "You tell her. It's obvious you can
hardly wait to do so. I don't know why guys like you are always so
addicted to gossip."

"Guys like me?" said Kevin. "You mean guys who have a genuine
concern for people as opposed to guys like you who are all wrapped
up in a world from which people have been deliberately excluded?"

I lost my temper. I had had a grueling day, my patience was
stretched to its limits as I waited for the moment when Vicky and I
could be alone together, and at that point Kevin's malign interference
was more than I could tolerate.

"No," I said, "I mean guys like you who can't fuck properly and get vicarious thrills listening to stories about the guys who can."

"Scott!" gasped Vicky.

"God, what fun!" exclaimed Kevin. "How can I possibly resist such a challenge? Let me buy you some soda water or something, Scott—soda water at the Four Seasons! How chic can you get!—And then you really must explain to me how you would define the word 'properly' when used in conjunction with the word 'fuck.'"

"Some other time." I was already furious with myself for playing into his hands. Tossing some bills on the table, I moved closer to Vicky. "Come along, honey," I said, putting my hand on her arm. "I'll take you home."

Vicky wrenched her arm away. "I want to know what's happened to Sebastian."

I kept a tight hold on my self-control and said neutrally, "He was fired today from Van Zale's. It was his own fault. He tried to tell your father how to run the firm."

"Oh, pardon me," said Kevin, smooth as glass, "but don't you think Vicky should know the whole truth instead of your highly biased version of the facts?"

I whirled round on him. "You stay out of this! What the hell do you know about the truth of this particular situation anyway?"

"Damned nearly all there is to know, I'd say. Sebastian and Neil visited me in rapid succession today and drank me clean out of Wild Turkey bourbon."

"Then in that case you're probably too drunk to listen to my side of the story!"

"I'm never too drunk to listen, but I suspect you'll always be too buttoned up to talk. A pity. I feel sorry for you in a way. Vicky darling, do you fully realize what kind of problems you've taken on along with this guy?"

"Why, you goddamned bastard—"

"Scott, please! Kevin—"

"This guy's trouble, darling. He's too mixed up to relate properly to anyone—all he can relate to is his ambition. If he weren't so dangerous he'd be pathetic."

"You bastard, you son of a bitch, you miserable *fucking* queer—"

"Let's skip the sex angle, shall we? It's so boringly irrelevant."

"What gives you the right to sit in judgment of me? What makes you think you've got some God-given gift for analyzing people and making an unqualified, pseudopsychological diagnosis when you're not even in possession of all the facts? You know nothing about me, and nothing, nothing, *nothing* about my situation! Now, get the hell out of my way and leave us alone or I swear I'll knock your teeth down your throat and smash your face to pulp!"

I had been speaking in a low voice, but gradually it sounded louder and louder, and when I stopped talking at last, I realized why. Our quarrel had called attention to our corner, and everyone had turned to stare at us. The maître d', fearing trouble, was watching us with dread.

There was a silence. I had a fleeting impression of Vicky's gray eyes dark in her white tense face, but I was only wholly aware of Kevin. I could see now what a long way he was from being sober, but he held his liquor so well that there were no obvious signs of drunkenness. He was motionless; there was no swaying on his feet. His speech was clear and incisive; there were no slurred consonants. Only his manner betrayed him; his characteristic debonair spontaneity had fallen apart to reveal the tough-as-nails bitchy bedrock of his personality, and for a moment this bizarre unveiling was revealed in his face. The dimple in his chin seemed very deep, his long-lashed, liquid brown eyes very bright, his square jaw very hard. He looked ready to take a swing at me, but I knew he never would. That kind of guy never does.

"But how violent!" said Kevin at last in a pleasant voice, retreating behind the veil again. "I detest violence. But perhaps violent behavior makes you feel more masculine. Good night, Vicky. I'll withdraw before Scott can turn the scene into a barroom brawl. I'm sorry if we've upset you."

He walked away. I sat down abruptly.

"Some dessert, sir?" murmured the maître d', anxious that the scene should immediately return to normal. "Coffee? Brandy?"

Brandy. Courvoisier, Remy Martin, Hennessy. Dark brown brandy, warm brown brandy, rich bitter brandy, I could smell it, taste it on my tongue, and suddenly I was back in that Mediterranean port again and the gray warship was waiting in the bay for me to return from shore leave. I saw the smashed bottles and the smashed furniture; I heard the ship's captain saying, "Guys like you are always trouble"; I felt the pain as the ship's doctor dressed the cut on my head; and worst of all I remembered the shame of waking next morning and telling myself I was unfit to live.

"No brandy," I said aloud in that smart New York restaurant twenty years later. "Nothing."

"No beer," I had said to the landlord of the pub at Mallingham after I had visited my father's grave in 1946. "Just ginger ale."

Vicky was standing up. "I want to go now, please," she said in the Four Seasons in 1963.

"Take all the time you want," said Death to Bergman's knight in the world of my fantasies, "but if you take one false step, I'll be waiting for you."

So vivid was that image of Death that I found myself looking around for him, but all I saw was the blazing hulk of the Pan Am Building as we stepped out onto Park Avenue, and the next moment I was flagging down a cab, opening the door, hesitating over the address.

"Will you come to my place?" I heard myself say to Vicky.

"*Your* place!" she said in a hard offhand voice. "God, I thought no one ever got invited there!"

"I want you to see it."

Her eyes filled with tears, but all she said was, "Thank you. I'd like that," and when I reached for her hand again she didn't draw it away.

The cab set off uptown. For some time we were silent, but at last I said, "I'm sorry. Forgive me. I don't know what happened. It's been such a terrible day."

"Is that all you're going to say?"

"I . . ."

"Was Kevin right? Are you always going to be too buttoned up to talk?"

"Well, I . . . Vicky, you mustn't listen to him. . . ."

"No, you're the one I want to listen to. I'm listening right now. But I can't hear anything."

"I . . . Look . . ."

"Yes?"

"I want to talk," I said. "I do want to. That's why I invited you to my place. I . . . didn't want to be alone there anymore . . . cut off . . ."

"Yes, I understand that. It's all right. I do understand. Let's wait till we get there."

I kissed her, and then in a moment of panic, which was all the more terrifying because it was so unexpected, I wondered if I'd be crippled again once we got to bed. Kevin seemed to have severed Vicky from me, with the result that she was now drifting steadily beyond my reach. I felt desperate, knew I would do anything to get her back. The thought of being forced back into my former isolated half-life was now far more than I could endure.

The quality of the silence in the cab changed abruptly, and I realized with a shock that the driver had switched off his engine. His next words confirmed that we had been stationary for some time outside my apartment building.

"Do you folks want to get out?" he inquired. "Or should I get some blankets and pillows to make you comfortable?"

I paid him and without a word took Vicky up to my apartment.

II

YET IN the end it was Vicky, not I, who halted the drift and brought us back together again. I couldn't have done it. For a while I thought she couldn't do it either, but when I saw how determined she was, I became determined too, and my determination gave me the strength to help her.

She began to talk as soon as we entered the apartment.

"Kevin was wrong, wasn't he?" she said. "He was wrong to imply the driving force in your life was your ambition—as if you only cared about money and power and success. You don't really care about all that, do you?"

"No."

"And Sebastian was wrong too, wasn't he, when he decided the driving force in your life was the desire for revenge. You're not a hero in a play by Middleton or Tourneur."

"Right."

We were standing by the window of the living room, and before us stretched the lights of Queens. I was holding her hand very tightly and wishing I could talk more, but my throat hurt too much and my head was throbbing with pain.

"Nobody's ever understood, have they?"

I shook my head.

"It's guilt, isn't it?"

The lights of Queens began to blur.

"You're like me," said Vicky. "I recognized the likeness in the end. The driving force in your life is guilt. You feel horribly, over-poweringly guilty. But why? What did you do? Can you tell me about it?"

I nodded. She waited. But I was dumb.

"Something happened back in the thirties?"

I nodded again.

"Between you and my father?"

I shook my head. Then I said, "My father." A second later I wasn't sure whether I had spoken the words aloud, so I said them again. "My father," I said. "Mine."

"Something happened between you and your father? I see. What was it?"

"I . . ."

"Yes?"

"I was an accessory . . ."

"An *accessory?*"

". . . before the fact . . ."

"*Before the fact?* What fact?"

". . . of his murder," I said. "Of course. What else?" And slump-ing down on the ottoman I buried my face in my hands.

III

"BUT YOUR father wasn't murdered," said Vicky.

"Yes, he was. He was driven into alcoholism and harassed to his death. And I stood by and let it happen. I turned away from my fa-ther. I was loyal only to the man who killed him."

"But your father walked out on you!"

"No, he always wanted me and Tony to live with him. He walked out on Emily but not on us."

"Yes, but—"

"I was upset because I loved Emily so much. I was only fourteen and I didn't understand anything. Then Cornelius stepped in and took me over. I shouldn't have let him, but I did. It was a terrible thing to do. I turned my back on my father and made up my mind to have nothing more to do with him."

She was appalled. "Are you trying to tell me that my fa-ther . . . ?"

"Your father's not really an issue here. Don't get sidetracked. The main issue's between me and my father. Your father's just a figure on a chessboard whom I have to manipulate in order to reach my father and make amends to him. I have to make amends, you see. It's my one justification for being alive. I wouldn't be fit to live otherwise. I did such a terrible thing, siding with his murderer, conniving at his guilt. . . . How can people do such terrible things and survive? My father died, my brother died, my mother died—and yet *I lived*. It seems so wrong, and that's why I've got to justify myself, I can't die now till I've justified my survival. If I can bend my undeserved life to rewriting an undeserved past . . . You understand, don't you? You do understand?"

"You couldn't have treated your father that badly! You were so young, you were mixed up, this has all got exaggerated in your mind . . ."

"My father loved me. I hated him and hoped he would die. When he did die, I was glad. I actually said to Cornelius, 'Thank God he won't be around to bother us anymore.' Can you imagine that? I actually said—"

"This is all Daddy's fault, I know it is. It's utterly wrong that you should blame yourself like this."

"I shouldn't have let myself be influenced by Cornelius. Tony wasn't influenced. He always saw straight through him."

"Tony's position was probably different from yours. He was younger, at a less vulnerable age. And Daddy never liked Tony, did he? Tony was probably not subjected to the same influence. You shouldn't compare your behavior with Tony's."

"I even turned my back on Tony, and later I never had the chance to make it up with him. I never had the chance to make it up with my father, either. They died and I was left with no way of unloading my guilt—no way except one way, and that was the way I had to take. . . . God, can't you see the kind of past I had to live with as soon as I read Tony's last letter to me and realized exactly what I'd done? Well, of course, the truth was I couldn't live with it. I saw at once I had to rewrite it through Cornelius and the bank. There was no choice. There was nothing else for me to do. I did think of killing myself, but—"

"Scott!"

"Well, of course I did! Of course! And if I fail to rewrite the past, I'll think of it again, because then I wouldn't want to live anymore."

"You mustn't talk like this! It's wicked! It's wrong!"

"Why? Death and I are old acquaintances—I think about him often, I live with him all the time. Sometimes I see him watching me when I look in the mirror, and then I go to the bathroom and get the razor, and sometimes I even run the water in the bath. . . . The Romans committed suicide that way—a hot bath, the severed veins, and then death comes without pain, very peacefully, you just drift into unconsciousness, but always I've thought, no, I can't die yet, I can't die until I've completed my quest and succeeded where my father failed. . . ."

"Scott . . . Scott, listen . . . Scott, please . . ."

"Ah, Vicky, Vicky, you never knew my father, but he was such a wonderful guy, so full of life—yes, that's what I remember best, I remember how full of life he was, and that's why I've got to go on, Vicky, that's why I live the way I do, that's why nothing matters to me but to rewrite the past, to bring him back from the dead, and *to make him live again.* . . ."

IV

I WAS in the kitchen in the dark. My body was racked with silent sobs and my eyes were burning with pain. I was so unused to crying that I couldn't begin to handle such humiliation. I could only give way and wait for it to pass.

"Scott . . ." She was in the lighted living room beyond the doorway. Her voice was gentle.

I tried to say: "I'm okay," but I couldn't.

"Do you want to be alone?" she said. "Shall I go?"

I was so sure I could say "no." It was such a simple word, one of the first words a child learns. But I couldn't say it.

"Don't hurry to answer," she said. "Take your time."

She moved farther back into the living room and I was left to battle with my humiliation in private. I tried to remember when I had last cried. I thought it must have been after my mother's death, when I was ten, but then Emily had been there and Emily had expected children deprived of their mother to cry, so I had cried. In fact, I had seen little of my mother. Tony and I had been brought up by a succession of nurses, and the one permanent feature of my childhood had been not my mother, who was always so busy with her social activities, but my father. My father had worked hard all week in the city, but every weekend he had come home to Long Island to play with us and take us on expeditions.

I opened the door of the refrigerator and looked at all the bottles inside.

"God, I could use a drink," I said, and astonished myself by sounding normal. Perhaps the road to recovery lay in making trivial observations.

"Then why don't you have one?" called Vicky casually. "You're not an alcoholic, are you?"

"No, I was never an alcoholic. But drink didn't suit me," I said, uncapping a bottle of Coke with clumsy fingers. "I felt better when I'd given it up."

"I envy your strength of mind. I know I drink too much at the moment."

"I doubt very much if you know what those words can mean."

"Well, naturally I don't go on binges! But I always have two martinis a day, and in my opinion, that's at least one too many. . . . Would you mind if I had some coffee? I'll make it myself, if you like."

"No, I'll make it." I switched on the light and filled the kettle. The gas flared on the stove. I put the kettle down and stood watching the steady flame.

"I meant to go on the wagon years ago," said Vicky, watching the flame with me. "But somehow I never seemed to be able to get through the day without a martini to help me along."

"Plus the occasional playboy?"

"Oh, them! They never mattered. I was just trying to prove to myself that I wasn't frigid."

"Frigid?" For the first time I was able to look at her directly. I prayed my eyes weren't bloodshot after the tears. "You? I don't believe it!"

She laughed. "If I told you the real truth about my supposedly glamorous private life, your head would be so swollen you wouldn't be able to walk through that doorway!"

I tried to figure this out. I was feeling better, but still confused. I had to make a great effort to concentrate. "And if I told you the real truth about *my* supposedly glamorous private life," I said, "your head would immediately be as swollen as mine." That seemed like a neat thing to say. I had a sudden picture of us effortlessly swapping bright, brittle remarks as we stood kettle-watching in the kitchen.

"You make it sound as if we both suffered from the same problem," said Vicky, surprised. "But men don't have that kind of problem . . . or do they?"

"Men have all kinds of problems, believe me."

"You mean you couldn't get it up?"

"No, that was easy."

"I see. So in that case you must mean you couldn't . . ."

"Yes. Of course, it was all very trivial."

"Of course. But don't you think it's so often the trivialities of life which cause the most misery, once their cumulative effect becomes a back-breaking burden?"

"Christ, you can say that again." The kettle was starting to boil. I groped for her hand and found it.

"I often think sex is like money," said Vicky. "When you've got it, you never think about it, and when you haven't got it, you think of nothing else."

I squeezed her hand tightly and kept my eyes on the kettle. "What would someone like you know about having no money!"

"What an insulting remark! Do you think I'm totally devoid of intelligence and imagination? Do you think I've never wondered what it's like to live in poverty on a diet of rice with ten children under ten and no birth control?"

"Incidentally . . ."

"Yes, I was wondering when you were going to ask. I take a little pink pill. No fuss, no mess, no mistakes. Sebastian would no doubt call it the ultimate product of our plastic society."

"And what do you call it?"

"Liberation."

We had our coffee in the living room. By her own choice she sat on the ottoman and I sat opposite her on the recliner, but after a while that didn't feel right, so we sat side by side on the floor with our backs to the wall and held hands again.

"What did I do in bed that everyone else didn't?" I said curiously at last.

"I don't think you did anything in particular. Oh, God, sorry! That's not very complimentary, is it? Of course you were great. That goes without saying, but what I really meant was—"

"It was the anonymity, wasn't it? The secret was that I thought you were someone else. It set you free to be yourself."

"Yes. That's it exactly. And later . . ."

"You'd established a new identity and didn't feel a prisoner anymore."

"Later," corrected Vicky firmly, "I realized you were the sexiest man I'd ever met."

"I'm flattered! But please don't feel you have to anesthetize me with compliments."

"I don't. But since we're being so frank with each other . . ."

"God, yes. It's more of a relief than you could ever imagine."

"You'd be surprised what I can imagine. I know all about being buttoned up in a straitjacket with my mouth gagged and my hands tied behind my back."

I kissed her.

"Do you want to go to bed now?" said Vicky later.

"Yes, very much. But I'm still so shook-up I'll probably be no good."

"Well, we don't have to do anything, do we? We're not circus performers. No one's watching, so who do we have to impress?"

"My God, what a marvelous woman you are!" I said, and took her to the bedroom.

"I can't think what you were worried about," she said later as I lit her cigarette.

"Neither can I." I went to the kitchen and brought back two more bottles of Coke.

"Scott . . ."

"Uh-huh?"

"If this question upsets you, don't answer it, but did my father make a real effort to turn you against your father? I mean, it wasn't a few careless remarks here and there, was it? It was an all-out, deliberate brainwashing?"

"Yes."

"How horrible. And how *wicked*. Are you speaking the truth when you say he's so unimportant to you nowadays? Surely you must loathe and detest him!"

"You can't live daily with violent emotion, Vicky. To survive, you have to distance yourself from it. Besides, it's unlikely Cornelius deliberately set out to be wicked. Knowing him, I'd say it was more likely that he'd conned himself into believing he was acting with the purest possible motives."

"But that makes him all the more repulsive! How could you ever have worked at his bank day after day and allowed him to treat you as a substitute son?"

"But I didn't," I said. "I just stayed home. It was Scott who went to the bank and dealt with Cornelius."

She switched on the light. We were very close on my narrow single bed, and I had felt the frisson which had made her whole body rigid in my arms.

"Sorry," I said. "Big mistake. Now you think I'm crazy."

"No. I just feel frightened to think of the kind of strain you must have been living under."

"But don't you see? Scott was my solution to all the strain . . . Scott was my way of distancing myself from all those violent emotions which I couldn't live with on a daily basis!"

"But didn't you tell me yesterday," she said, "that Scott had died?"

"Yes, he had to die. There would have been no room for you in Scott's life. I had to choose between the two of you, and I chose you."

"I see. Yes. And may I ask how you're now going to manage without him?"

"I'll get along. At least I have you. I'll be all right."

"Great. And what happens about my father? Has he received news of Scott's death yet?"

"You're laughing at me!"

"I assure you I'm not. It's no laughing matter, is it?"

I was reassured. "Yes, your father knows."

"An unpleasant shock for him?"

"Yes. He'd just got rid of Sebastian and he suddenly found himself locked up with a tiger in a rapidly shrinking cage."

"Tell me what happened. Everything. I've got to know."

I talked for some time while Vicky smoked her way through another cigarette. In the end all she said was, "Poor Sebastian."

"He'll be okay. He'll easily walk into another top job somewhere else."

"He only cared about Van Zale's."

"I appreciate that. I'm sorry for him too, but he was asking for trouble. He behaved very foolishly."

"So what happens next?"

"We recuperate from the explosion and get back to normal. I think if I'm very careful now, I'll still be able to weather this storm."

"Good. I want you to get the bank. I'm sure it's the only just solution after the way Daddy's behaved in the past, and I'm all for justice. . . . What will you do when you finally get control? Put the name Sullivan in the title alongside Van Zale? That would be justice too, wouldn't it?"

"Well . . ."

"I can't see why Daddy wouldn't agree to that. The bank will go back into the Van Zale family eventually, as you've no sons of your own, so why shouldn't he be generous to you?"

"Hm."

"Funnily enough, Eric's anxious to be a banker. I can't imagine why, but I'm glad for Daddy's sake. Poor Daddy. I can't help feeling sorry for him in spite of everything. Is that guilt too? I wonder. Maybe it is. I always feel his life would have been quite different if he'd had a son instead of a daughter."

"I doubt that very much. Cornelius has glamorized the idea of having a son. We always glamorize what we don't have. A real son would almost certainly have been a disappointment to him."

"Perhaps. . . . I wish I could convince you not to think of yourself as a disappointment to Steve. Surely, Scott, if he was the wonderful father you say he was, he would have forgiven you for all those mistakes you made?"

"That only makes the burden of my guilt more intolerable. If he would have forgiven me in spite of everything—can't you see how that would make me feel all the more ashamed of myself?"

"But you must try to see this from a different point of view. You'll never have any peace otherwise. You'll just stay trapped in this terrible cycle . . ."

"Once I get the bank, I'll be at peace."

"I wonder about that. I wonder very much."

I sat up in bed. "What do you mean?"

"Well, I have this unpleasant suspicion that no matter what you do to make amends to your father, you'll find it's never enough. I suspect this quest, as you call it, has no real end."

"No, no, you're wrong! Once I've rewritten the past—"

"Oh, Scott, those are such empty words—that phrase has no real meaning! You can't rewrite the past. The past is over, the past is done, and to talk of a past recaptured is, if I may say so, just classic *fin-de-siècle* romanticism with no valid root in reality!"

"You don't see time as I see it," I said. "My time is different from yours."

"But that's absolute . . ." She checked herself. Then she exclaimed passionately, "Scott, can't you see your situation as it really is? You're wasting your whole life doing something you don't really want to do in pursuit of a release from a pain which is largely a self-inflicted illusion! You've bound yourself to some kind of nightmarish wheel, but you don't have to stay there, you don't have to go round and round—that's all an illusion too! If you could only forgive yourself, you could step off the wheel, you could free yourself of all these illusions, you could start at last to live the kind of life you really want to live!"

"I wouldn't want to live. I'm sorry you see the situation that way. I'm sorry you don't understand." I started to get out of bed, but she grabbed me and pulled me back.

"I'm sorry," she said rapidly. "Don't be angry. I love you. Don't cut yourself off from me. I'm trying so hard to understand, I want so much to understand. Please believe me."

"Shhh." I extinguished her cigarette and started kissing her. "Let's not talk anymore. We've both talked more than enough, and there's so little time."

The words were out of my mouth before I'd realized what I'd said. I saw her eyes widen, heard her sharp intake of breath, and I cursed myself for triggering the big scene I'd made up my mind to postpone.

"What do you mean?" she said. "Why do we have so little time?"

And it was then, with the greatest reluctance, I told her that her father was transferring me to London.

V

"GET OFF that wheel," said Vicky. "Quit. Now's the time to wash your hands of this mess and start a new life. You don't want to go to London, do you?"

"I guess you're thinking of us. Well, I agree it'll be inconvenient, but—"

"Inconvenient? Did you say *inconvenient?*"

"But we'll still see each other! I'll be coming back to New York regularly on business, and of course you can come to London as often as you can make it."

"An intercontinental love affair—yes, I see," said Vicky. "How wonderful. How glamorous. What more could I possibly want?" She started to cry.

"Vicky—"

"Oh, shut up! You just don't live in the real world at all!" She struggled out of bed and groped for her clothes.

I was groping too—for an understanding of what was going on in her mind. Belatedly I remembered that she had talked of wanting someone who was more than just an uncommitted lover, and I realized I had to give her the reassurance she needed. To offer an intercontinental love affair was not enough. I had to convince her I wanted more than just a part-time relationship; I had to make her an offer which would help her feel more secure.

"Come to London with me," I said abruptly. "We'll live together. I don't want us to be apart any more than you do."

She stopped crying and looked at me. "But what about the children?"

"Well . . ." I suddenly found I had no idea what to say. "Well, I'm sure you love your kids, Vicky, but I somehow thought . . . if there was an alternative way of life available to you . . . I'm sure Cornelius would be happy to help you out."

"Let's get this straight," said Vicky. "I'm not leaving my children. Where I go, they go."

"But I thought you implied on board ship that you hated your life here and only stayed with your children out of guilt!"

"That's true. I do feel guilty. I brought those children into the world when I didn't want them, and what could be more thoroughly wrong than that? The very least I can do to make amends is to stand by them and make some sort of attempt, no matter how inadequate, to show them I care."

"But if you don't care, isn't that just being hypocritical?"

"My God, it's easy to tell you're a childless bachelor! I do care about my children. I love them very much. I love them all the while I'm hating them for messing up my life and draining me emotionally day after day after day. But if you can't give up the life your guilt makes you lead, why should you expect me to give up mine?"

I got out of bed, went to the bathroom, and spent three minutes doing some hard thinking. Then I flushed the toilet to provide myself with an excuse for my absence and returned to the bedroom. She was still wearing only her underclothes, but she had lit another cigarette and was standing tensely by the window.

I put on my robe and knotted the cord. "Let's have some more coffee."

We sat at the kitchen counter and drank Sanka in silence. Finally I said, "There's got to be a way we can work this out. I respect how you feel, but please try to understand my difficulty. I'm not used to children. I'm not even used to living with anyone. I'd like to be able to tell you I could handle all of you with one hand tied behind my back, but if I told you that, I'd be a liar. I've got to take this a step at a time."

"But time is the one thing we don't have!"

"Yes, but if we can keep on seeing each other . . . I accept that you can't cut off your life here in order to live with me full-time in London, but—"

"The trouble is," she interrupted, "that an intercontinental love affair with all the jet-set trimmings would suit you right down to the ground. You're used to long periods of celibacy punctuated by bursts of high-powered activity, and if I consented to adopt that pattern with you, why should you ever settle for anything different?"

"When I return to New York—"

"But that's four years away! I'm sorry, you may be able to live that kind of life for four years, but I couldn't. I'd crack up. I couldn't stand all the strain and the tension and the awful partings and the frustration of you never being around when I most wanted you—God, can't you see how hopeless it would be? Anyway, I have enough strain in my private life, and I'm just not equipped to take on any more."

There was a silence. We finished our coffee. She stubbed out her cigarette.

"Well," she said, "so much for the insoluble future. And we've certainly had more than enough tonight of the intolerable past. That leaves the present. It's not much, but it seems to be all we've got."

"I can't accept that."

"Oh, Scott, neither can I. . . ."

She was in my arms. My robe parted. She shoved aside her clothes. Within ten seconds we were in bed together, and then time ceased to matter at last as the night exploded brilliantly before our eyes.

VI

SHE CALLED me at nine the next evening when I was dictating the last memo into the machine. My head was aching and the light from the desk lamp hurt my eyes. The jangling of the call coming through on my outside line was so loud I winced.

"Hi," she said. "How are you doing?"

"Badly. Sorry I haven't called."

"Do you want to come to my place when you're finished?"

"You know I do. But I'm very tired. I'll be poor company."

"Have you eaten anything today?"

"No. Yes, wait a minute, I had half a hot dog at my desk, but I never got the chance to finish it. There's so much to do to clear the way for my departure."

"Get out of that horrible place and come here right away."

I left.

When I arrived at her apartment she was wearing a white quilted robe and no makeup and her bright hair was smooth and soft beneath my fingers.

"I've got some barbecued chicken and French fries from the takeout joint around the corner," she said, "and a six-pack of Coke. I thought we needed a contrast to the Four Seasons."

We ate all the chicken and all the French fries and drank all the Coke.

"Feeling better?"

"Like a new person."

We went to bed.

"Got anything else to drink?" I said later.

"I've got some quinine water, the stuff the British call tonic and drink with gin. If you're going to London, you'd better practice drinking it."

Without a word I got out of bed and went to the kitchen. The quinine water was on the bottom shelf in the refrigerator door.

"I'll cut you a slice of lemon to go with it," she said.

I still said nothing.

"I'm sorry," she said. "I shouldn't have mentioned the word 'London,' but I couldn't help myself. I've been thinking about the future all day."

I took a sip of the quinine water and decided it was drinkable. I took another sip.

"Is there no chance that Daddy could change his mind about this decision?"

"None."

"But he'll miss you so much! Who will he play chess with in the evenings?"

I said nothing.

"Things are hell for him at the moment," she said. "Alicia's not speaking to him because of Sebastian. Poor Daddy's absolutely miserable."

"That's tough." I poured myself a little more quinine water and added another ice cube.

"Might he recall you, do you think, after a few months?"

"Not a chance."

"Supposing . . . supposing . . ."

"Yes?"

"Supposing you just flatly refuse to go. Would he fire you? He couldn't, could he, because you told me he was terrified of what might happen if you became president of Reischman's."

"No, he wouldn't fire me now. He'd fire me later, as soon as he had the chance to do so."

"But he might have forgiven you by then!"

"No. Never. No man, not even me, defies Cornelius to that extent and gets away with it."

"But supposing . . . supposing . . . Scott, supposing we got married."

I turned away and watched the two pink fish floating dreamily in their aquarium.

"Don't you see?" said Vicky in a trembling voice. "If you marry me, you're certain to stay in the firm and get what you want. How could Daddy pass you over if you were his son-in-law?"

I drank the quinine water and went on watching the pink fish.

"I know you dislike children, but—"

"I don't dislike them," I said, suppressing the memory of Rose and Lori taking up too much of Emily's time in the past.

"—but Eric and Paul will both be away at school for most of the year soon, and the girls are so little trouble—girls are much easier than boys—and that leaves Benjamin, but Benjamin's really very sweet, and I can manage him. I wouldn't let him bother you in any way . . ."

She stopped. Then she laughed awkwardly and said, "I don't usually propose to men like this, believe me, but it's the only solution to our problems that I can come up with."

I knew I had to choose my next words with great care. "It's a very attractive solution," I said warmly, giving her a kiss. "And in theory it's a great idea."

"In theory? Not in practice? You don't think it would work?"

"No. The timing's all wrong." I knew better than to try to kiss her again then, but I took her hands in mine and held them tightly. "Vicky, listen. The truth is that if I marry you now and get out of going to London, Cornelius is going to be very upset. He won't believe I'm marrying you because I love you. He'll immediately convince himself that I'm marrying you just to secure my future, and who could blame him for jumping to that conclusion in the circumstances?"

"Oh, screw Daddy! I'll fix him!"

"I doubt that. You may have a lot of influence with him, but not where the bank's concerned."

"I see. So you haven't the guts to marry me because you're afraid of upsetting Daddy!" She jerked her hands away and stood up.

"It's not so simple as that. Supposing we did marry now and couldn't get the marriage to work. It's possible. We have a lot going for us, but marriage is never a bed of roses, and we could run into trouble. And then where would I be? I agree I'd have Cornelius where I want him if I were his son-in-law, but where would I be if I was his ex-son-in-law by the time we come to his magic date of the first of January 1968? I'd be washed up and out in the cold."

"I see what Kevin meant now," she said. "I'm beginning to think he was right after all. You can't relate properly to people. You can only relate to your ambition."

"Now, wait a minute—hear me out! I'm not saying we should never marry! I want to marry you very much. All I'm saying is that it would be a mistake to rush into marriage now. I think we ought to give our relationship a thorough trial over a long period of time so we can iron out all the difficulties that are certain to crop up. I think we should marry when I return to New York in 1968."

"Wonderful," she said. "That, of course, would be the perfect moment to nail down your future once and for all without alienating

Daddy. He can hardly object to the legalization of an affair which has been going on for four years."

"But Vicky, I just feel in all sincerity—"

"You feel nothing. You don't care about me. All you care about is that damned bank. What's going on here can be summed up in four words: you don't love me."

"But I do love you!" I shouted. "I'm crazy about you! You're the one who's not in love. If you loved me, you wouldn't let me go to London alone! You'd come with me. When a woman's really in love, she doesn't care about anything except being with her lover—she doesn't even care about her kids! Look what happened when Alicia met Cornelius!"

"I don't have to look at what happened," she said. "I lived with it for years. I was one of the victims."

"Yes, but—"

"Okay, maybe I *don't* love you! Perhaps you're right! Perhaps I just like the way you make love! The truth is, I'm so upset and confused and hurt and rejected and just plain goddamned unhappy that I don't know anything anymore. Would you mind going now, please? I don't want to make love to you again. I couldn't bear it."

"Vicky . . ." I was in despair. "Look, we'll work this out, I know we will."

"Oh, face reality, Scott, for God's sake! This is no fairy tale! It's been a wonderful affair, but now it's over. It has to be over. There's nowhere else for it to go."

"But, honey . . . sweetheart . . ."

She looked up at me with fierce gray eyes. Tears were streaming down her face, but she was unaware of them. "I wish I was with Sebastian!" she said brutally. "He really loved me! And he never called me any of those stupid, meaningless, empty names!"

The jealousy hit me with such violence that I felt dizzy. I stumbled back a pace, jarred the coffee table; the quinine water splashed turbulently in the glass.

"Okay, go back to him," I said. "Why don't you?" I found my way to the bedroom and pulled on my clothes. "If he solves all your problems," I shouted, "you go back. Fine. Great. Good luck to you."

I heard muffled sobs. I knotted my tie, pushed back my hair with a shaking hand, and found myself once more in the living room. She was slumped on the couch with her hands covering her face.

"So what's your problem?" I said. "Maybe Sebastian doesn't have too much finesse in bed, but why should that bother you now? If ever you want a good fuck, just jet into London and maybe if I'm not too busy I'll spare you a couple of hours of my time. That's all you wanted out of me anyway, wasn't it? You were just using me to prove something to yourself, and now that you've got the proof you need, you don't want me anymore!"

She raised a blotched tearstained face swollen with weeping. I had a sickening memory of Emily grieving for my father.

"Vicky, I'm sorry. Forgive me—I didn't mean that."

"Shut up!" she screamed. "Get out! You've messed up my life quite enough. Leave me alone! Christ, and to think you have the nerve to accuse *me* of using *you!* You've been using me all the way along the line! You can't treat women in any other way! You're sick! It doesn't matter how good you are in bed—you'll always end up a failure with women because you'll never be any better than an emotional cripple!"

I picked up the glass of quinine water and hurled it against the wall. Vicky screamed. Fragments of glass burst across the carpet. I turned. I was by the liquor cabinet. I picked up the bottle of gin and flung that too after the glass. There was another crash, another scream, then the sickening reek of alcohol.

"No!" shouted Vicky. "No! I'll call the police! No!"

I looked down. I had a bottle of Scotch in my hand. I replaced it slowly in the liquor cabinet and rubbed the back of my hand across my eyes. "I'm sorry," I said, dazed. "I don't know what happened. I've never done that before when I was sober."

She backed away from me. I could tell she was frightened.

"Please go now," she said in a high voice.

"I'm very sorry. Forgive me . . ."

"Just go."

"I'll call you."

She did not answer, and I did not look back. Groping my way to the front door, I left the apartment and somehow found my way out of the lighted corridors into the darkness which lay waiting for me beyond.

Chapter Seven

I

"ARE YOU okay?" said Cornelius.

"Just fine."

"Still think you'll be ready to leave on Tuesday?"

"My secretary's made the plane reservation."

"Good. . . . No problems?"

"None."

I called her as soon as I returned to my office. I had intended to wait until the evening, but I now knew waiting was impossible. I had to talk to her at once.

There was no answer from the apartment, so I called the duplex and spoke to the housekeeper.

"Mrs. Foxworth's gone away for a few days, sir. She left an hour ago."

"Where's she gone?"

"I don't know, but she's left an address with her father in case there was an emergency. I'm sure if you asked Mr. Van Zale—"

I hung up. No wonder Cornelius had been inquiring so tenderly after my health. I called his houses in Arizona and Bar Harbor, but no one was expecting her to arrive. Later in the day I called them again, but she wasn't there.

I somehow got through the rest of the day, and when I reached home late that evening I found a letter which had arrived for me by special delivery. She had written: "I don't want to see you again before you leave and I don't want you to call me from London. I've no doubt we'll eventually meet again, but meanwhile I must have time to get over all this. I do sincerely hope you'll be happy in London and that you'll get whatever it is you want out of life. I've quite accepted the fact that it isn't me."

I switched on the television to distract myself, but no distraction was possible. I switched off the set and read the letter again. I began to be afraid I might call the liquor store to place an order, so I immediately fixed myself a tall Coke with a heavy twist of lemon, but to my alarm I drank it in seconds. That was bad. I always tried to drink slowly. I decided I had to get some quinine water. I wouldn't want to drink that fast. Did the supermarket carry quinine water? I couldn't remember. I decided to inquire at the nearest liquor store.

I got to the liquor store, but then it occurred to me that it would be easier—not smarter, not wiser, just easier—if I visited the supermarket instead, so I went in and bought a six-pack of 7-Up.

Back home again I fixed myself a fake Tom Collins and drank it very slowly while I found some notepaper and sat down at the kitchen counter.

I wrote: "Dear Vicky," but that seemed so cold, so I tore off the sheet and tried again. No words came. I was remembering how Vicky had said: "Get off that wheel!" and suddenly I thought how wonderful it would be to be free. What would I do with myself? I decided I would like to live with Vicky on a boat somewhere a long way away. I loved the sea and I was a good sailor. My father had had a yacht, and every weekend in the summer he had taken me sailing on Long Island Sound.

I got up abruptly. My glass was empty. Fixing myself another fake Tom Collins, I used the notepad to make a list of matters which still had to be settled before I went to Europe. Then I called the superintendent of the building to arrange for my apartment to be sublet; I examined the Yellow Pages to find a firm who would remove and store my meager possessions; and I made a list of the books and records which I wanted to have crated and air-freighted to London. That used up some time. I fixed myself a hamburger but couldn't eat it. That took another quarter of an hour, but the night still stretched endlessly ahead of me. Pushing my glass aside, I tried to write to Vicky again.

This time I was more successful. I wrote: "Vicky, I love you very much. I think you've been too hasty in insisting that we're through, and I know I was wrong in making no effort to compromise. Will you at least see me one more time before I leave to see if we can't figure something out? I'm sure you were right to bring up the subject of marriage, and I'm sorry I mishandled the conversation so badly. Please, give me one more chance to put matters right. It's very lonely here without you. All my love, Scott."

II

I FELT MUCH more optimistic about the future once that letter was written. I thought that if only I could engineer a reconciliation she would agree to take a vacation in London in the new year, and once we had been together for a brief period there, the way would have been paved for future visits. I would, of course, give her an engagement ring to reassure her that I was committed to the idea of marriage, and once she knew I had committed myself, I thought she would find it easier to accept the idea of a long engagement. I was willing to concede that a long engagement wasn't an ideal situation, but on the other hand it was neither unknown nor unmanageable. In the navy I had often met men who, engaged for years, only saw their fiancées at irregular intervals, and nobody had thought the situation in the least odd.

"Could you have this letter mailed to Vicky, please?" I said to Cornelius later. "It's very important and I know you have her address."

It was Thanksgiving, and the bank was officially closed, but I was about to go downtown to get on with my work. I had already excused myself from the family's Thanksgiving dinner. When I called at the Van Zale triplex, I found Cornelius had finished eating his breakfast but was lingering in the dining room with a final cup of coffee.

He gave me a hard look. "She didn't want to be bothered by anyone. She was very upset."

"I realize that. The aim of this letter is to make her less upset. You want to read the letter? Go ahead. I'll open the envelope."

"Good God, no, of course I don't want to read your private correspondence! What happens between you and Vicky has nothing to do with me."

"Then you'll forward the letter."

"Okay." He eyed the envelope coldly.

I sat down with him at the breakfast table. "I'm sorry about all this trouble, Cornelius."

"So you damn well should be. You've spoiled my entire Thanksgiving. I was counting on Vicky to be here. Alicia's gone off to stay with Andrew and Lori, and I don't know when she'll be back."

"I'm . . . sure she won't be away long."

"No, probably not, but all the same . . . You just don't know what's been going on here. I've had another row with Sebastian."

"Another row? For God's sake, what about?"

"Well, I . . . you know I never go back on an important decision, but . . ."

"You offered to reinstate him?" I tried not to look appalled.

"Yes, well, you see, Alicia was so upset, and . . . well, I figured maybe I'd been a bit hasty, and . . . oh, the hell with it, what does it matter! Sebastian rejected the idea anyway, so we're all back at first base again."

"Sebastian refused your offer to reinstate him?" This time I couldn't stop myself looking incredulous.

"That's right. 'I meant every word I said when you fired me,' he says. 'I'm not coming back unless you resign and make me senior partner.' So then I get so mad I threaten to see he doesn't get another job on the Street, and you know what he says then? 'Save your energy!' he says. 'I'm quitting banking. I've had it. Do your damnedest,' he says, 'and see if I care. I'm going off to Europe. It's the only civilized place to live. I'm through with the savages and the philistines and the plastic society.' "

"He's crazy!" I thought how much Sebastian loved New York. "He can't mean it!"

"Just what I said to him. 'You can't do this!' I said to him. 'What about your mother? You can't go off to live thousands of miles away from her! What's she going to do?' 'That's your problem,' he says, 'and I hope you enjoy solving it.' And he walks out. My God! I tell you, it's been a terrible forty-eight hours!"

"I'm sorry . . . very sorry. I know it must seem as if it's all my fault . . ."

"That's right. But maybe we'll have a bit of peace once you ship yourself off to Europe. Thank God you're going soon," said Cornelius, slipping Vicky's letter into his pocket, and walked out of the room without another word.

III

ON FRIDAY my possessions were taken away to be stored or crated, and vacating my apartment, I checked into the Carlyle Hotel for the remainder of my time in New York. However, since I spent the weekend working, I saw little of the hotel, and by the time I had wound up my business affairs on Monday night I was so exhausted I wondered how I could summon the strength to get back to my suite. I was just about to leave the office for the last time when the red phone rang on my desk.

Apparently Cornelius had also worked late, perhaps to postpone the moment when he had to return to his deserted triplex. Alicia was still in California and Vicky had not responded to my letter. I was almost sure now she had never received it.

"Yes?" I said abruptly into the red phone.

"Will you be much longer?"

"I'm just leaving."

"Okay, I'll give you a ride uptown."

In the Cadillac we sat in silence for some time, but somewhere north of Canal Street he said, "Did you hear from Vicky?"

"No."

"Oh. I forwarded the letter. I guess now you think I didn't."

"Right."

"Well, you're wrong."

"Okay, I'm wrong."

We rode uptown a little farther.

"Sorry I was so mad at you the other day," said Cornelius. "I enjoyed Thanksgiving in the end. I get a lot of pleasure out of those kids. I'm damned lucky to have five grandchildren."

The Cadillac stopped at some lights. I looked out of the window at the wasteland, and in my weariness it had never seemed so ugly to me.

"But of course they're very young still," said Cornelius. "They're great, but I can't really talk to them, you know, I can't really . . . I'm not sure how to put it. I tried to teach Eric and Paul to play chess, but they didn't seem to want to learn. Uh . . . Scott . . . how about a quick game of chess tonight? Just one last game before you go?"

I saw only one answer which wouldn't imply hostility. "Okay."

"Well, we won't play if you're too tired," he said anxiously. "But have some dinner and a couple of Cokes with me."

"All right." I pulled myself together with an effort. "Thanks."

In the triplex Cornelius uncapped our Cokes while we waited for our steaks to be broiled. "What do you think of this Southeast Asia business?" he said. "I wonder if Johnson's right to keep on with Kennedy's policies there. Still, war's good for big business. Remember Korea."

"Right."

"Hope Andrew doesn't get posted there. I've done my best to keep him out of it, but now he says he wants to go. That would be the last straw for Alicia, of course. Christ, this has been a terrible year. By the way, what do you think of the latest developments on the assassination? Of course, it's all a communist conspiracy. I said to Sam back in 1949 . . ."

I mentally switched off, and as Cornelius went on talking, I looked at the ugly furniture in the room, the abstract paintings all hinting obscurely at violence, the shelves of unread books, the barren trappings of a barren life.

We ate our steaks in silence. Cornelius unexpectedly opened half a bottle of red wine and drank every drop of it. Finally he said, "I can see you're very tired. I'm sorry, I guess I was being selfish, dragging you back here for dinner. But the truth is, I'm not looking forward to losing you tomorrow. I'm going to miss you a lot."

"Your choice, Cornelius. Not mine."

"Choice? What choice? No, don't answer that. Scott . . . we're parting friends, aren't we?"

"Of course."

"That's good. Please understand that I'm truly grateful to you for stepping into the breach like this in London—and don't think I've forgotten how to express my gratitude in a meaningful way when the time's right."

After a slight pause I said, "Thank you. I don't think you'll find my performance in London a disappointment."

"I've every confidence in you. Good. I'm glad we understand each other again."

When we had finished dinner, he saw me out into the hall.

"Well, I guess this is it, then," he said. "This is where we say good-bye." And he held out his hand shyly.

I looked at the hand. Then I took it, shook it, and dropped it. "So long."

He looked at me. His eyes were bright with tears. I assumed the wine had made him uncharacteristically maudlin, and I found this display of emotion highly unpleasant.

"You'll always be my boy, Scott," he said, "no matter what happens. Remember that."

I thought of him murdering my father and I wanted to vomit in his face, I wanted to beat him to a pulp, I wanted to take him by the neck and squeeze the life out of him very slowly so that he would know the full horror of dying by inches. But I never moved. I just thought remotely: I'll wipe him out in the end, and aloud I just said, "I'll remember."

Then I left him and walked back to the Carlyle.

IV

THERE WAS still no letter from Vicky waiting for me, and although I called her housekeeper, there was no message. I knew now that Vicky was determined to break with me, and I wondered if I could delay my departure, confront her on her return to the city, and persuade her to change her mind. Then I decided it would be dangerous to postpone my flight. If I postponed it once, I might be tempted to postpone it again. My nerve might crack. Already I felt as if I were on an emotional rack from which I might not emerge alive.

The night wore on. I sensed Death was very close. I was thinking continuously of Vicky, wondering how I would survive if she insisted on ending the affair.

The possibility of survival was suddenly a mere fragile thread which could snap at any moment, and as I watched the dawn break at last over the East River, I saw Death begin to walk toward me across the chessboard by the sea.

V

AND SO at last my fantasy merged with reality and I found myself acting out the myth which had mesmerized me for so long. As I stepped into the BOAC section of the departures building at John F.

Kennedy International Airport, I stepped into the desolate landscape of Roland's quest, and when I saw that blighted desert of concrete and glass, I recognized it as the wasteland which guarded the Dark Tower.

I stopped as the recognition engulfed me. I knew there would be a sign then, a sign which pointed the way to the inevitable moment when I would have to make the decision sealing my future, and as I spun round I saw the departures board and read the letters that spelled London.

Instantly I visualized the plane which would take me to England. I saw it as clearly as Roland had seen his Dark Tower, and suddenly I knew that *this was the time,* this was the place, this was where I had to choose whether to pursue my ambition or abandon it, this was where Roland had been forced to meet his destiny by raising the magic horn to his lips.

Someone called my name. I looked back and found *she was there,* dressed in white in contrast to the black hooded figure of my fantasies, and the palomino mink was draped very tightly around her as if to ward off the chill of death. And as she ran toward me, weaving in and out of the crowds, she held out her arms and cried, "Scott! Don't go!"

Then a voice said remotely far above us, "British Overseas Airways announces the departure of their flight 510 to London . . ."

"Vicky," I whispered. "Vicky."

She was in my arms. For a moment nothing mattered but that, and I saw so clearly then what I had to do.

"Oh, Scott, please—you mustn't go, you mustn't! Can't you see what's happening? Can't you understand?"

". . . and will all passengers in possession of boarding passes please proceed to . . ."

"I'd give up everything, I'd go to London with you, but it would be pointless, because the central problem crippling you would still be unsolved, and so long as that problem exists, there'll never be enough room for me in your life . . ."

". . . Air France announces the departure of their flight to Paris, Rome, Beirut . . ."

"Forgive yourself, forgive my father, end it, let go, stay, survive— I'll help you, I swear it, stay with me and I know we can make it together, I know we can, I know it."

I knew it too. The sane rational part of my brain knew it. The part that loved Vicky knew it. I looked down at the passport in my hand, I looked down at the boarding pass, I took the boarding pass between my fingers to tear it in two, but then the past stepped in to paralyze me and my fingers never moved.

The magic horn was at my lips but the fanfare of life was never sounded, and as I struggled in vain for the one breath that would set me free, I saw not the destiny I wanted but the destiny I could not avoid move forward to encircle my life and draw me on to the Dark Tower.

"I can't stay," I whispered. "I want to but I can't. I can't, I can't, I can't."

She recoiled from me. "Then I can do no more. I can't help you. I can't reach you. And I can never see you again."

We said nothing else. She looked at me numbly, too appalled to show deep emotion, too spent to attempt the futility of rational argument, but finally she stumbled away from me toward the exit.

"This is the final call for British Overseas Airways flight 510 to London . . ."

I walked through the great hall, I walked to the farthest reaches of that wasteland of concrete and glass, I walked with Roland and as Roland to the very end of that myth I had made my own, I walked to the Dark Tower and went inside.

"First class, sir? This way, please. The seat by the window. . . . May I take your coat?"

I sat down and waited, and after a while someone started talking to me again.

"Would you like a drink, sir, before we take off?" said the pretty stewardess at my side.

I looked at her and longed for death. The pain of living was more than I could endure.

"Yes," I said, "I'll have a drink. Bring me a double martini on the rocks."

PART SIX

Vicky:
1963–1967

Chapter One

I

"GOOD MORNING," said the disembodied voice. "This is Mr. Van Zale's private wire. May I help you?"

"This is Mrs. Foxworth," I said. "Get him."

There was a shocked silence. Even frivolous society women were supposed to know how to address a very important executive secretary with respect.

"I'm sorry, Mrs. Foxworth, but Mr. Van Zale is in a meeting—"

"Get him out, please."

"But—"

"*Get him out!*"

She gasped. Then the hold button was pressed and the line went dead. After lighting another cigarette, I found a second dime to use if the operator demanded more money, but the silence remained uninterrupted until the line was reopened and my father said breathlessly, "Vicky? Sweetheart, what's happened? Where are you calling from? Are you still up in Boston at the Ritz Carlton?"

"I'm at Kennedy airport."

"But what's happened? Is it Scott? Did his plane crash? Is he—?"

"Scott's on his way to London," I said, "and now I think it's time you started picking up the pieces of the mess you've made of his life and mine. Get out here right away, please. I'll be waiting in the hall of the International Arrivals Building."

"But, sweetheart . . . honey . . . sure I understand that you must be very upset, and of course I'll come out to you just as soon as I can, but I'm in the middle of a very important meeting, and—"

"Screw the meeting! This is *my life* we're talking about! You get out here right away or I'm taking the very next plane to London."

II

THREE-QUARTERS of an hour later my father's Cadillac halted by the curb and my father, flanked by two aides and a bodyguard, was assisted out onto the sidewalk by his chauffeur. I was waiting, the mink coat slung over my arm like a deadweight. I had had some coffee since concluding the phone call and had put on fresh makeup to disguise how much I'd cried earlier.

The chief aide darted over to me. "Perhaps the VIP lounge, Mrs. Foxworth . . ."

"Totally unnecessary. We'll sit in the bar."

"His asthma—"

"Oh, don't hand me all that garbage about his asthma! Come along, Father, I'll buy you a brandy and you'll soon feel better."

My father just looked at me with furious eyes and began to wheeze something in his best asthmatic whisper, but I interrupted him.

"Wait in the car, please, both of you," I said to the aides, and to the bodyguard I added, "You can come with us, but you're to sit on the other side of the room."

The three men looked at me as if I'd grown horns and a tail. Then they looked at my father. He nodded painfully. He was a grayish color, and his breathing was unpleasantly audible.

"Come along, Father," I said, gripping his arm. "This way."

We reached the bar and I settled him in a corner before I bought a martini and a double brandy. The bodyguard withdrew with a glass of beer to a distant table. We were alone.

"I shouldn't drink this," whispered my father. But he drank it. He took a small sip, then a larger one, and finally started fussing around, dusting his cuffs, clearing his throat, and fingering a spot on the table. When he had finally decided on an appropriate speech, he said meekly, not looking at me, "I'm sorry if you're upset about Scott. Of course I don't approve of you calling up in hysterics, dragging me out of a vital meeting, and hauling me over here to the airport, but I do understand that women often behave neurotically when they're crossed in love, and I'm prepared to make allowances for you. But now it's important that you calm down, behave sensibly, and see this business in proportion. I guess you think I sent Scott to London to bust up your affair with him. Well, that's not true. I was motivated purely by business considerations. I never interfere with your private life nowadays. I fully accept that you're a grown woman and entitled to live as you please."

He stopped and looked at me directly. His eyes were clear and candid, his expression sincere. Earnestness permeated every inflection of his voice. I was nauseated.

I said, "Have you quite finished?"

"But, sweetheart—"

"Don't you 'sweetheart' me!" I shouted. "What you're really saying is that having messed up Scott's life to the point where he's incapable of behaving rationally, you now intend to wash your hands, like Pontius Pilate, and say piously, 'I'm innocent! All this has nothing to do with me!'"

"I don't understand what you're talking about."

"You don't understand that we're all living with the consequences of what you've done?"

"But I've done nothing wrong! All I've ever wanted was the best for you and Scott!"

"Then why did you brainwash Scott into hating the father who loved him?"

"Oh, but—"

"You're going to deny it?"

"You don't understand! You see, that's not the way it was at all."

"That *was* the way it was, Father. It wasn't the way it ought to have been. But that was the way it really was."

"I was justified. Steve didn't deserve Scott. He'd forfeited his rights."

"I don't believe that. That's what you wanted to believe at the time, but—"

"Steve didn't care. Why should he? He was always fathering children all over the place—what was it to him whether he had one son more or less? Anyway, Scott needed to be taken care of. I thought it was justice. I thought it was as if God intended—"

"You and your God!" I cried. "Don't you talk to me about your view of God and morality! You did a selfish, wicked thing, and it's time someone came right out and told you so! Don't you realize what you've done? You've crippled Scott so that he's incapable of leading a normal life! You've maimed him!"

"Sheer feminine nonsense. You pull yourself together, please, and stop being so hysterical. Scott's a brilliantly successful man."

"*Success?* You call that *success?*"

"Certainly I do!"

"Well, what a price to pay!"

"Now, look here, Vicky—"

"You've ruined him, Father. That's the truth. It's a truth you're apparently unable to face, but that doesn't stop it from being true. You've ruined him."

"How can I have ruined him?" shouted my father. "All I ever wanted—"

"Don't repeat that crap about wanting the best for him. All you ever wanted was the best for you. But tell me this: if you wanted a son so much back in the thirties, why the hell didn't you go out and get one of your own? Why did you stay married year after year to that cold bitch of a wife who always made you so unhappy?"

My father flinched. He made no attempt to explain, but misery radiated from him, creating an aura of shame and despair which made me recoil appalled.

"Ah, Vicky," he said. "If only you knew. If only you knew."

But I did know. I saw it all, every detail of the landscape he had moved through during his marriage. I knew it so well. I'd been there myself.

All my rage vanished and only the love remained.

III

"YOU WOULDN'T understand," he said. "I felt so guilty, so useless, such a failure. I was the inadequate partner in a wonderful marriage. I had to watch things fall apart and know that it was all my fault. You wouldn't know what that was like. You wouldn't understand."

"*I wouldn't understand?* Daddy, have you no idea, no idea at all, of what happened in my two marriages?"

We stared at each other. We stared for a long, long time. Then he said, faltering over his words, "Then you'll understand . . . the way things really were."

"The more of a failure you felt, the more important it was that there should be people in your life—preferably children—who should go on loving you and thinking of you as a hero."

"Yes."

"That was why you stopped at nothing to get Scott away from Steve."

"Yes."

"You knew it was wrong, but you couldn't help yourself."

"Yes."

"You figured that so long as you were the best possible father to Scott, everything would come right in the end and no one would be hurt."

"Yes. That was it. That was the way things ought to have been. I moved heaven and earth to make things come out that way. I don't know, don't really understand what happened . . . I did try so very hard."

I finished my martini and rose to my feet.

"Where are you going?" said my father in panic.

"To get another round of drinks."

When I returned he was sitting very still, a slight delicate figure hunched in his black overcoat, no longer a monster but merely the kind of failure he himself had always so openly despised, pathetic and pitiable, miserable and misguided. I neither criticized nor condemned; I was too conscious of my own failures. Even with Scott I had failed in the end. I had failed to keep him, failed to cure him, failed perhaps to love him enough. . . . Tears pricked my eyes again, but then I remembered Sebastian saying: "Be angry! Get mad!" and I told myself fiercely: No. It wasn't I who had failed Scott. It was he who had failed me.

I looked at my father and wondered how much he knew. "How well do you understand Scott, Daddy?" I said abruptly.

My father's tired face seemed to age still further before my eyes. "Too well," he said.

"Are you sure?" I took a sip of the new martini. "What I can't understand is why you allowed yourself to be manipulated by him for so long."

"He wasn't manipulating me."

"But—"

"You've got it all wrong, Vicky, just like everyone else. Scott wasn't manipulating me. I was manipulating him. I fooled everyone, even Scott himself, all the way along the line."

IV

I WAS SHATTERED. I stared at him. "What on earth are you talking about?"

"Are you still unable to see the way things really were?"

"I think we must be talking at cross-purposes . . . or perhaps there's been some sort of fundamental misunderstanding . . ."

"I doubt that, but let's just recheck the situation from Scott's point of view to make sure neither of us has missed a trick. Scott thought, didn't he, that if he went into the bank, worked like a slave, and dedicated himself to being indispensable to me, he'd achieve the apparently impossible feat of coaxing me to hand over the bank to him in the end. He had this extraordinary theory, which he implied to me over numerous late-night chess sessions, that I'd eventually feel compelled to give him the bank out of guilt; I was supposed to make a grand gesture of atonement when the time came for me to retire . . . Why are you looking at me like that? Don't you agree with me?"

All I could say was, "So you knew. You knew everything."

"Of course! Scott made himself perfectly clear in his own indirect mystical way. Funny what garbage these intellectuals dream up when they put their minds to it. They have these weaknesses for high-flown theories which exist only in the imagination, and of course Scott loves all that kind of thing—myth, allegory, medieval junk, general hocus-pocus. . . . I never could see the attraction myself, but if he wanted to pull the medieval wool over his eyes, who was I to stop him?"

I felt sick. I just said, "Go on."

"I won't say I don't feel guilty about the past," said my father. "That would be a lie. Steve and I had the dirtiest of fights, and I didn't win it by being a pillar of chivalry, but there are two points which ought to be remembered here before anyone starts calling me a villain . . . or before I start setting up the cross of a guilty conscience to ensure my crucifixion. Number one: if I hadn't cut Steve's throat, he would certainly have cut mine. And number two: since Paul had clearly marked me as his successor, I had more right to that bank than Steve Sullivan. Those two facts always seem to get lost in the shuffle. I can't think why. They're very important. They're the reason why, although I feel guilty about some aspects of the past, I can't bring myself to regret what I did. Certainly I could never feel so riddled with guilt that I'd have some kind of nervous breakdown and carelessly toss my whole life's work away to soothe my conscience. . . . Are you still with me? And are you beginning to see the situation not from Scott's point of view but from mine?"

I couldn't speak, but I nodded.

"Good," said my father, "because now we come to the heart of the matter, which is this: I'd never pass the bank to a man of whom I fundamentally disapproved, but when all was said and done, I didn't fundamentally disapprove of Scott. In other words, when all was said and done, I didn't need the kind of unreal convoluted intellectual motivation that Scott was always trying to foster in me."

"You mean you wanted . . . you wanted always . . ."

"Yes," said my father. "Always. I always wanted Scott to have the bank."

I stared at him. My mouth was bone dry. "Daddy, you must never, never let him know that. You must never tell him that he's spent all these years dedicating himself to giving his father's enemy what that enemy's wanted most. If he knew his quest was nothing but a grand illusion, it would destroy him."

"Do you think so? I wonder. Scott's very tough. I've always admired how tough he is. . . . You do understand now, though, don't you? I wasn't motivated by guilt. Guilt just didn't enter into it. I wanted Scott to have the bank because—"

"Because he was the younger brother you never had and the son you always wanted, and you thought of him as belonging entirely to you. As far as you were concerned, his connection with Steve was just a biological accident."

"That's right," said my father. "I wanted Scott to have the bank because I loved him. Strange how simple it sounds when I say it outright like that. I've never said it out loud before—I hardly even liked to acknowledge it to myself, because I was so afraid I might later betray just how I felt."

"You mean you had to cover up the truth."

"Why, yes, if I was ever going to get what I wanted, I couldn't afford to let the truth get out! You can see, can't you, what a difficult situation I was in? First of all I had to think of Alicia, who naturally wanted me to make Sebastian my heir. I could hardly let her know I wanted to pass over Sebastian and in fact didn't care much for either of her sons. However, Alicia was really just a side issue. The main problem, I saw from the start, was going to be Scott himself."

"I suppose," I said slowly, "you were afraid he'd walk out on you and disappear into the blue if he knew his ambition consisted in giving you what you wanted."

"No, you're going too far too fast. You're overlooking the crucial fact that for years and years I didn't realize Scott was hostile to me. We'd grown very close before the war, and after the war when he came home he gave me no indication whatsoever that his feelings for me might have changed. No, the problem as I saw it then was not that he might cut himself off from me and disappear into the blue if he found out the truth; I just thought that if he knew he could get the bank comparatively effortlessly, he would lose interest in being a banker and turn to some other profession to prove to himself that he was a better, smarter, and wiser man than his father ever was."

"I think I understand. You're saying Scott needed a struggle. He needed to punish himself by taking on some back-breaking task."

"Well, I'm no expert on psychology, and I didn't put him in deep analysis, but instinct told me that he wanted to believe—had to believe—we were engaged in some big mythological battle, and that if I was ever to get what I wanted I'd have to play along with him. I had to let Scott jump through these self-imposed imaginary hoops—and why not? They didn't strike me at the time as being sinister. They were entirely compatible with my theory that he was mixed up about his father and this was his way of straightening himself out. Let me repeat that he never showed any sign of hostility, never. He was as efficient at deceiving me, you see, as I was at deceiving him."

"When did you start to see through him?"

"Nineteen-fifty-five. Up till then everything had worked out just fine, although looking back, I'm surprised how effectively I succeeded in creating this illusion that I couldn't possibly regard Scott as my successor. There were two clues which provided a complete giveaway of the way things really were. The first was that I did take Scott into the firm. People like Emily thought it was sheer Christian charity, but of course that was nonsense—I'd never have hired him unless I wanted him. And the second clue was that I never fired him. Sam wanted him fired. A lot of people have wanted Scott out of the way at some time or other, but I kept him safe and helped him through every stage of the game—until in the end, of course, I realized I'd been digging my own grave."

My father stopped talking. He was breathing better now, and his face, although pale and drawn, was less gray. He drank some more brandy, and around us I could hear the hum of the airport, the shuffle of people coming and going, the murmur of conversation and the drone of the announcements from the public-address system.

I said, "What happened in 1955?"

"I discovered Tony Sullivan had left behind a posthumous letter." My father thought for a moment before adding carefully, "It presented Steve's view of the past. Of course I'd raised Scott on mine."

"But why should Scott have rejected your view and adopted Steve's?"

"Tony's letter was very convincing." My father paused as if to reconsider this statement but finally confirmed it by repeating, "Very convincing. It was biased and inaccurate, naturally, but—"

"Was it? But Tony was always so honest! I'd have thought he would have been the last person to invent a web of lies!"

"That's true, and of course that's why the letter would have influenced Scott so much. However, there are different ways of looking at the truth, and as I've already said, although I admit I had a rough fight with Steve, I've never at heart regretted it because I've always considered my actions were justified."

"Scott believes you killed Steve."

My father went white. "He told you that? But . . ."

"Don't worry, I didn't take that too seriously. Scott's neurotic about his father, and it's so obvious that he's got the past out of proportion." I sighed and made an effort to turn the conversation back to the present. Steve's death might have been a tragedy, but as far as I was concerned there was no reason why I should now dwell on all the sordid details. I was interested in Scott, not his father. "When did Scott see this letter of Tony's?" I demanded abruptly.

"After Tony was killed in 1944, but unfortunately I didn't realize the letter existed till 1955. However, as soon as I saw the letter, I knew Scott was certain to be hostile to me—I knew I had to fire him."

"But then why didn't you? What happened?"

"Well, you see, Vicky," said my father, suddenly looking very old and tired, "I'm not really as tough as I always want to believe I am. In fact, sometimes I'm so weak I just can't face the truth at all. Scott wasn't the only one here who found a certain course of action psychologically necessary to him."

"In other words, you couldn't face firing him."

"Oh, I faced it! I always fire partners as soon as I no longer trust them one hundred percent—it's a reflex action, and so much quicker and cleaner than keeping them on and agonizing over them until they make another attempt to stab me in the back. No, I faced firing Scott, but I convinced myself it was unnecessary. I thought I could handle him. It was probably the worst decision I've ever made."

"But I still don't understand why—"

"I was going through a bad time in my private life, and I just couldn't bear the thought that I wouldn't have Scott around anymore. Anyway, I still thought he was fond of me. I had to believe that, you see. That was *my* myth. It was necessary to me. It protected me from a reality I couldn't bear to face."

"But you knew he was hostile!"

"I knew he wanted the bank not just to straighten himself out but to avenge his father. I knew he was out for justice, but I thought: Okay, so he wants a little justice, and why not? And I figured I could still work out a solution that would keep everyone happy. I had this idea that he could be a caretaker for the bank in between the time when I retired and the time when my grandsons were old enough to take charge. I still didn't really see him as hostile. Maybe a little antagonistic . . . tough-minded . . . difficult . . . but not actively *hostile*. Right up to the end I believed he was fond of me in his own way, despite everything."

"And then came the end."

"Yes," said my father. "Then came the end."

"It came a week ago, didn't it? When he returned to the office after his vacation."

"Yes. He tore up my myth and flung it in my face. It was as if Scott, the Scott I'd known for years, had died and someone violent and dangerous had taken his place. It was the violence which shocked me most. He controlled it, of course, but it was there, it was obvious, as obvious as the fact that he hated me. I can't describe to you how I felt then. I didn't know how I was going to get to the end of the interview. I didn't see how I could survive till the end."

"But you did, didn't you? You pulled yourself together, tied Scott up, and prepared to airmail him to Europe!"

"What else could I have done? I couldn't have fired him or he'd have turned Reischman's into a hatchet to swing in my direction. I couldn't have kept him in New York—I'd never have had a moment's peace. All I could do was try to insulate myself for a while so that I could reorganize my defenses."

"Daddy . . ."

"Yes?"

"Daddy, you won't fire him, will you, as soon as you can risk doing so? I mean, despite all that's happened, you wouldn't . . . couldn't . . ."

"I can't fire him before 1968. There's a written agreement."

"But even after 1968 . . . Daddy, if you care anything for Scott at all . . ."

"Of course I care for him. He'll always be my boy, whatever happens. I told him so before he left." My father had begun to look at me very warily. "I'm beginning to think you haven't faced up to the implications of Scott's hostility to me."

"Yes, I have! He may be hostile, but he's not basically concerned with you. His main aim is to get the bank in order to 'make his father live again,' as he puts it, and so long as you give him what he wants, I don't think you'll find him hostile. On the contrary, I think you'll find then that he'll at last be able to forgive you and be reconciled."

After a pause my father said, "I'm sorry, Vicky, but that's just sheer feminine romanticism."

"No, it's not! How dare you say that! What an insulting thing to say!"

"Has it never occurred to you that he might want to wipe me out, change the bank's name to Sullivan's, and make sure my grandsons never cross the threshold of Willow and Wall?"

"What an idiotic suggestion! And what a typically masculine fantasy, chockful of power and aggression!"

"Okay, okay," said my father rapidly, "don't let's get upset over this. We've both been doing so well. Now, sweetheart, don't you worry about anything—I know you're fond of Scott and this is highly disturbing for you, but just relax, I'll work something out here, you'll see. Scott and I just need a little time to cool off, that's all, but eventually we'll establish a new modus vivendi, and everything'll work out fine . . . if he's sensible. My one dread is that he'll try using you to double-cross me."

"You would think that, wouldn't you? Another fantasy!"

"I agree he's made no attempt to do so up till now, and I can assure you that's been a very big relief. Naturally, as soon as I heard he'd involved himself with you, I couldn't help thinking—"

"Father," I said, "get this straight: when Scott first slept with me, he didn't even know who I was."

My father boggled. "What the hell do you mean?"

"Just what I say. My God, have you still not grasped the fact that I'm not the fairy-tale princess of your dreams?" I said, in a fine rage again by this time, and it was then that we had our first honest conversation about my disastrously mismanaged past.

V

"POOR SAM," I said. I was calmer now, my voice remote and detached. "That marriage was a disaster for him, wasn't it, as well as for me. He was so unhappy already, and I only made him unhappier. What a wasted life he had, longing for all those dreams which never came true, but I guess he'd have been no happier with Teresa. . . . Daddy, whatever happened to Teresa in the end? I often wanted to ask but never quite had the nerve. I liked her when I met her at the exhibitions."

My father looked astonished, but all he said was, "She shacked up with some rich Mexican and went to live in Acapulco. She now paints pictures in the style of Diego Rivera. They're terrible. I won't exhibit them." He stared gloomily at the rain streaming down on the highway.

By this time we were traveling in his Cadillac, the new orange one, with the bodyguard sitting in the front seat beside the chauffeur and the two aides following in a cab. My father was holding my hand and I was too lightheaded to care; I had eaten nothing all day except the olives from my martinis.

"I've told you far more than I should have," said my father. "The more I talk about it, the more clearly I can see what an unforgivable role I played in promoting your first marriage. I should have kept my mouth shut."

"Daddy, you couldn't be more wrong. Don't you think that after fourteen years I have the right to know why Sam decided to marry me?"

"Yes, but you must feel so angry!"

"On the contrary, my predominant feeling is one of huge relief. I've sorted it all out at last. I don't have to feel angry anymore."

"I don't think I understand. You mean . . ."

"I mean now that I know that the marriage was obviously doomed from the start, I'll find it much easier to come to terms with its failure. I won't have to keep agonizing over its memory and saying: 'Maybe if I'd done this,' or 'Maybe if I'd done that.' I can just say: 'It would have failed anyway, no matter what I might have done,' and that'll be that."

"No more guilt?"

"No. Sadness, yes. But no guilt. I'll be able to remember Sam now and think of the happy times. For years I've been trying not to think of him because I've been too afraid of what I might remember."

There was a silence as the car drove on through the rain, but eventually my father said, "Vicky, I wish we could now discuss you and Scott as sensibly and dispassionately as we've just discussed you and Sam. Tell me, what exactly did you mean just now when you said—"

"I don't think you'd really like to know, Daddy," I said, withdrawing my hand abruptly. "Not really. I know we've just spent some time discussing my total failure to become a replica of Aunt Emily, but nevertheless—"

"How very glad I am now," said my father, "that you're not a replica of Emily!"

"But I thought that was what you always wanted!"

"Yes, but it was all a mistake, like wishing occasionally you were a boy. I can't think how I could have been so stupid. If you'd been a boy, just imagine where we'd be now! You'd be bossing me around, trying to strong-arm me into an early retirement and generally giving me hell, and I'd be white-haired, ready to sink into an early grave! Christ, I feel weak at the thought of it. What a lucky escape I've had! How incredibly fortunate I've been!"

The car began its approach to the Midtown Tunnel.

"Am I to understand," I said cautiously, "that this hymn of thanksgiving means you like me just the way I am?"

"Yes, but the big question now is, can you say as much for me? God knows what you must think of me after all this frank talking. I guess I can't possibly expect you to feel the same way about me anymore."

"Maybe not, but would that be such a bad thing? Our previous relationship doesn't strike me as being any great loss, based as it was on illusions and platitudes."

"But at least you loved me!" said my father, determined to be maudlin. If his despair hadn't been so obviously genuine, I might have succumbed to the temptation to push this sentimentality aside with a couple of tart comments, but instead I said patiently, "I loved the man I thought you were, just as you loved the girl you wanted me to be. We were both of us loving people who didn't exist, and what's so great about that? I'd rather have a genuine relationship with a real person, not a fantasy link with a figment of my imagination."

"But how can you ever accept me as I am?" said my poor father, somehow managing to sound both pathetic and exasperating, very old yet curiously childlike, world-weary but naive.

"Daddy," I said, "if you've got the guts to accept *me* as *I am,* why shouldn't I have the guts to accept you as you are?"

The car plunged into the tunnel, and the quality of sound in the car changed. We looked at each other warily in the dim artificial light.

"What do you truly feel, Vicky?"

"I don't know. I just hated you this morning after I discovered how damaged Scott was."

"Yes."

"But to tell the truth, I feel too confused now to indulge in a simple straightforward hatred. All these honest conversations should have helped, shouldn't they, but I think I just feel more mixed up than ever. Where does that leave us?"

"Well," said my father shyly, like some reticent student philosopher proposing a revolutionary new theory, "perhaps we might manage to be friends."

"That ought to be impossible. Why do I have this terrible suspicion that you may be right?"

"Because nothing's impossible if you want it badly enough," said my father.

The car shot out of the tunnel into the wet shining streets of Manhattan.

"I don't know whether I can be friends with you," I said, taking his hand in mine again. "I don't know whether parents and children can ever be friends in the accepted sense of the word. There's nearly always too much love and hate going on. But perhaps we can make a better job of just coexisting."

"How magnificently pragmatic!" said my father admiringly. "I think we shall have a very successful coexistence."

VI

HE REFUSED to go back to Wall Street.

"I don't want to keep you from your work," I said.

"Forget the work. You come first."

"I'm all right."

"You're not. You're starting to cry again."

We went up to his triplex and sat in the library, that beautiful airy room full of glass and space-age furniture which gave it a resemblance to the set of a science-fiction movie. Central Park floated below us in a misty haze. It was still raining.

My father mixed me a martini which tasted like four parts of vermouth to one part of gin, and served it in a liqueur glass. I was so exhausted that I didn't even have the strength to complain. I merely accepted the glass thankfully as he sat down beside me on the couch.

"I'd still like to be convinced that Scott didn't engineer this affair of yours," he said. "I know it's none of my business. I know I mustn't pry. But I'm just so anxious for you to put my mind at rest. I wish I could persuade you that I'm quite unshockable."

"This would shock you. It even shocked me after I'd done it. That's why I don't want to tell you. I'm not afraid of offending your nonexistent sensibilities. I'm afraid of being ashamed all over again, except I'm not ashamed, not really, I'm glad it all happened the way it did, I'm glad I took the initiative into my own hands."

"Vicky, you're driving me crazy with all these hints and allusions! Either tell me or don't tell me, for God's sake!"

"Okay, I'll tell you. I'm too exhausted to care. I'll tell you everything, and if you don't like it, just remember that it was you who asked for it."

I embarked on the saga of my Caribbean cruise. Predictable exclamations such as: "My God!" and "Christ!" and "You didn't!" emanated regularly from my father.

"Well?" I said wearily when I faced him at last and saw his expression. "Are you ready to disinherit me?"

"Was I looking horrified?" said my father. "I was only thinking of all those wasted vacations on my private yacht. I could have been on a cruise ship being seduced by pretty women!"

I laughed, then started crying, then decided to laugh again. "Daddy, I think that's the nicest thing you've ever said to me."

"There, there, sweetheart . . ."

"Now, don't spoil it! God, I hated that cruise. It wasn't funny really, Daddy. It was a disgusting atmosphere on that ship, with everyone aboard running around and copulating like animals."

"Disgusting," said my father.

I looked at him suspiciously, but he was poker-faced.

"It was!" I said defiantly.

"Am I arguing?"

"Hypocrite!"

My father patted my hand soothingly. "Okay, you've convinced me that Scott didn't initiate the affair. But how soon did he try to take advantage of this new relationship?"

"He didn't. At first he thought it was a disaster. In the end it simply became an obstruction to his ambition, and I had to be cut out of his life."

"If he felt that, why did he persist in continuing the affair once the cruise was over?"

"He realized I was the one woman in a million for him, just as he was the one man in a million for me."

"Vicky, listen to yourself! Spare me, please! That's the kind of line Alicia lives for in her daytime serials!"

"I can't help that. I'm just stating the facts. You asked me a question and I gave you a truthful answer. If it's too romantic for you, that's your problem, not mine."

"It just seems . . ."

"As a matter of fact it's got very little to do with romance and more to do with the facts of life."

"Sex, you mean? Are you trying to tell me Scott shot you a line about some kind of problem and then said only you could solve it?"

"I did solve it."

"Well, I'll be . . . You mean he was impotent?"

"Oh, Daddy, you haven't understood anything!"

"Some malformation of the genitals perhaps . . ."

"Of course not! He was just the same size as Sebastian, which was most extraordinary, because I always thought—"

"Wait a minute," said my father. "I don't think fathers and

daughters ought to talk about this kind of thing. Hasn't this conversation wandered a little far from the point?"

"I was only trying to explain—"

"Okay, you explained. Now, tell me exactly what Scott said to you about me."

I summarized Scott's long confession after the clash with Kevin at the Four Seasons. "That's why I know for a fact that he's not as hostile as you seem to think," I said defiantly. "He never said anything about erasing the name Van Zale and keeping Eric out of the bank."

"Vicky, that's a very naive remark for a woman of your intelligence."

"And that's a very cynical remark, even for a man who prides himself on his cynicism! Wake up, Daddy—be rational! Come down out of those cynical clouds! I wish I could convince you that Scott would never harm me by harming my family. If only we could marry—"

"*Marry!* Who said anything about marriage?"

"I did. I want to marry him. He's the only man in the world, as far as I'm concerned."

"You're not serious," said my father. He had gone very white. "You can't be serious. I was given to understand this was just a casual affair."

"*A casual affair?* Well, I guess you were entitled to think that after listening to my account of its bizarre beginning, but Daddy, I told you Scott was the one man in a million for me!"

"Yes, but that was just sex. For God's sake, Vicky, what's come over you? I don't believe you're in love with him. You can't be!"

"Daddy, I'm hopelessly, horribly and wholly in love with him! Do you think I'd want to marry him if I wasn't?"

"But . . ." My father was struck dumb for a moment. Then he stammered, "But Scott's not interested in marriage! You'll never get what you want there!"

"Oh?" I said. "But didn't you just tell me that anything's possible if you want it badly enough?" Tears began to stream down my cheeks again, and I gave up trying to check them. "Daddy, I can't help it, I'm crazy about him, I know it should be no good, but I can't accept that, I know how damaged he is but I think I can cure him, I think I can fix the damage somehow. God, if I thought it would do any good, I'd run after him, I'd go to London to live with him, I'd even leave the children—"

"I'm dreaming this conversation," said my father. "It's not happening. It's a nightmare. I'll wake up in a moment, or maybe you'll wake up and reassure me you haven't gone clean out of your mind. Did you really say you'd even leave the children?"

"Yes, but if Scott thinks there's a chance I'll live with him without the children, he'll never marry me. That's why I stood firm when he tried to persuade me to go to London with him. Also, I thought that if I stood firm he'd give way, but . . . he didn't. Oh, Christ, he didn't. He called my bluff and left me. I was so sure he wouldn't, so sure that in the end he'd choose me, but he didn't—he *couldn't* . . . crippled . . . couldn't help himself . . . not his fault . . ." I broke down altogether and could say no more.

My father gave me a handkerchief, patted me on the shoulder, and sat like a statue at my side until I was more composed.

"I'm sorry," I whispered at last. "I must pull myself together."

"Right," said my father, and the brutal note in his voice made me jump. "You must. Face the facts. He's left you. You've backed a losing horse. That man's never going to marry anyone. As far as he's concerned, you're just a good lay."

"No!" I screamed. "That's not the way it is, it's not!"

"Yes, Vicky, that's the way it is, although I see no way of proving it to you except to say okay, you go ahead, you go to London and live with him and get him clean out of your system. I'll take care of the kids. It wouldn't be for long anyway—the affair would be burned out inside of six months. We could invent some story for the kids so that they'd never know, and then you can come back easily when it's all over and pick up the threads of your normal life again."

There was a long silence. Then I dried my eyes, finished my martini, and said, "No. That's a good recipe for handling an inconvenient love affair, but this isn't just an inconvenient love affair. I want to marry him and I've got to handle this right. I'm not going to run after him to London and I'm not going to fall swooning into his arms as soon as he comes back here on his first business trip. He's got to realize that he can't just turn our relationship into an intercontinental love affair, and besides . . ." I set down my empty glass abruptly. "Besides, I couldn't really leave those children. I wouldn't be able to bear it in the end. I'd despise myself too much."

My father was very quiet. Some time passed.

"I do love him, Daddy, I really do. . . ."

"Oh, forget him, Vicky—give him up, for Christ's sake! My God,

I'd even prefer you to remarry Sebastian! No chance of that happening, I guess, but . . ."

"None. I could never go to bed again with any man except Scott. He's the one I want. And he's the one I'm going to have. I'm sorry, Daddy. That may not be the way things ought to be. But that's the way things really are."

Chapter Two

I

"DEAR VICKY: I hope it's okay if I write. If it's not, say so and I won't. How are you doing? Since you're there and he's here, maybe things aren't so good for you. I won't say anything about him, but I'm sorry if you're not happy.

"I've decided not to live in London after all, as the people I know here are mostly connected with banking, and I want to get clear away from that particular scene. I've decided to live in Cambridge. I came here as a tourist a couple of years back and bumped into Elfrida Sullivan in King's College Chapel and she showed me around. She was at college in Cambridge and she knows it well. It's a very, very nice place. I like it. It's a very, very long way from the plastic society. Thank God my grandfather left me some money so I don't have to waste my time doing something stupid, like banking, in order to earn a living.

"I'm going to write a book. I don't want to write a book, but the research will be fun. Maybe I won't even have to write the book—I'll just go on and on doing research. Elfrida Sullivan says the world is crying out for the definitive economic history of Roman Britain, and why don't I do it. I kind of like Elfrida Sullivan. She's very smart. But I think she's a lesbian. Your friend, S. Foxworth."

II

"Vicky, darling," said my cousin Lori, "you look just awful. Is anything wrong?"

I looked at her and thought of Scott. There was no marked physical resemblance between them, but now I could see so clearly that they had shared the same father. There seemed to be nothing of Aunt Emily about her. Lori was smart, sexy, and tough as nails beneath her perfect California suntan, and she had her life effortlessly well-organized. Her children were bright, attractive, clean, and courteous; her husband, now away in Vietnam, had always basked in uxorious bliss; the PTA, the essential charities, and the required women's organizations were managed with incomparable flair and zest. Lori was a huge success in life and knew it. Her attitude toward me ranged from the critical to the patronizing. I detested her.

"I'm fine, Lori," I said. "Just fine."

"You shouldn't drink those martinis, Vicky," said Lori's sister, Rose, who was becoming more and more like Aunt Emily every day. Rose was a hugely successful schoolteacher at a hugely successful Midwestern boarding school for girls. All her pupils seemed to win scholarships to the best colleges. She was looking at me now as if I were an object who deserved all the Christian charity she could lay her hands on. I wanted to slap her.

"Shut up," I said. "I'll drink what I like. Why don't you drink martinis occasionally? They might improve you."

"Ah, come now, darling!" said Lori, exerting her forceful Sullivan charm. "No quarrels at Christmas! Personally, I don't like martinis—they've got such a godawful taste. *Crème de menthe* is kind of nice, I'm just crazy for that mint flavor, but personally I can't think why people drink every day—life's so wonderful, so glorious, why blot it into a fuzzy blur? It's a mystery to me, but I guess if one's unhappy or something . . . Vicky, forgive me for getting personal, but don't you think it might help if you did something constructive, not charity work necessarily, because, let's be honest, a lot of charity is just bullshit—whoops! sorry, Rose, darling—but there are all kinds of interesting things you can do in New York City. Maybe if you took a course in flower arranging . . ."

"Lori, when I want your advice about how to run my life, I'll ask for it. Meanwhile, cut it out."

"Well, I only wanted to help!"

"We're just so concerned about you—"

"*Shut up!*" I yelled at the pair of them, and bolted headlong from the room.

III

"WHAT'S WRONG with Vicky, Cornelius? She seems very depressed, much more so than usual. Don't you think you should say something to her? I do think it's a pity she can't put up more of a front when the children are around."

"Alicia, that's just the kind of criticism Vicky doesn't need right now."

"Well, I'm sorry, but I think it's disgraceful that after wrecking my son's life she should be allowed to go on wrecking her own and making everyone around her miserable."

"She hasn't wrecked Sebastian's life! Sebastian chose of his own free will to retire from banking, even though I offered to reinstate him, and he chose of his own free will to go to England to live. And Vicky doesn't make everyone around her miserable! She doesn't make *me* miserable. You leave her alone!"

"Shhh, here she is. . . . Hello, dear, how are you?"

"Hello, Alicia. Just fine. Hi, Daddy."

"Hi."

There was a pause before I said politely, "Thank you for having the children for me today. I hope Nurse kept them in order and they weren't too much trouble."

"No, dear, of course not."

Another pause.

"Vicky," said my father impulsively, "come and see me after dinner tonight. I'll teach you to play chess."

"Oh, Daddy, I'm so tired, so exhausted, so . . . Did you say chess? But you always told me chess was a man's game!"

"Did I ever say that?" said my father. "The older I get, the more amazed I am by the dumb things I used to say when I was too young to know better. Chess is a wonderful game and takes your mind off almost everything. Everyone should play."

"But I'm so stupid. I'd never learn."

"Who do you think you're kidding? You're no dumb blond. Don't be so feeble, and don't be so selfish! None of my present aides can give me a decent game, and I've no one to play with at the moment. If you had an ounce of filial feeling for your poor old father . . ."

"Daddy, you're monstrous, worse than Benjamin. He always gets his own way, too. All right, I'll try to learn. If you say it's my moral duty, I'm not going to argue with you, but I'm sure you'll find teaching me a complete waste of time."

IV

"Mom," said Eric, "can you get Paul to turn down that godawful phonograph? I can't stand it any longer!"

"But he's playing the Beatles!" said Samantha with shining eyes. "And they're fab!"

"I wouldn't care if he was playing the 'Hallelujah Chorus' sung by God. If he doesn't turn that thing down, I swear I'll get a meat ax and—"

"Christ, what a great day it'll be when you go off to Choate!" yelled Paul from the doorway. "I can't wait to be rid of you!"

"Oh, don't fight, don't fight!" wept little Kristin. "I can't bear it when everyone fights!"

"Mom," said Benjamin, "my white mice have escaped."

"Mommy, I don't want everyone fighting."

"Paul, play the one Ringo sings—the one about wanting money."

"You play one more track from that shitty record and I'll—"

"That's not Ringo! It's John Lennon who solos on 'Money'!"

"Mrs. Foxworth, Mrs. Foxworth, there are white mice all over the kitchen!"

"Mom, can I have a cookie?"

"Mrs. Foxworth—"

"Christ, I hate living cooped up in a city apartment with a bunch of morons. Mom, why can't we move back to Westchester like when Dad was alive? I want a garden, I want room to breathe, I want someplace where I can escape from that godawful phonograph—"

"Mom, Cook's killed my favorite mouse!"

"Mrs. Foxworth, I'm quitting, I just can't take no more, ma'am."

"Oh, Mommy, poor mouscy . . ."

"Mommy . . ."
"Mom, you're not listening!"
"Mom, *Mom,* MOM . . ."

V

"FUNDAMENTALLY THE problem that Kierkegaard raised in his works was, 'What is the point of man's life?' 'What sense can he make out of human existence?' 'What is the purpose of human events?' Kierkegaard attempted in his literary works to reveal an image of human life as anguished and absurd, harrowing and meaningless."

I closed the book. It was midnight, and I was in the small apartment which I kept for my private use, the retreat I resorted to when I could no longer bear the sound of voices, the precious haven where I had made love to Scott.

I wanted to think about him but I knew I mustn't. I wanted to have a drink but I knew I mustn't do that either. I had become disturbed about my drinking, not because I thought I was descending into alcoholism but because I was gaining weight, and so I was rationing myself to a glass of wine a day. Surprisingly, giving up the martinis had been easy. Then I had tried to cut down on my smoking, but that had been hard. I checked the timetable I had made for myself and found, as I already knew, that I had one last cigarette to smoke that day. I smoked it and wondered if I could cheat and have another. I decided I couldn't. I had to do something else very fast so that I wouldn't have time to think of the cigarette I wasn't smoking.

I wished I were a creative person. If I were, I could immerse myself in producing something worthwhile, but instead I could do nothing which could be described as meaningful. I could no longer even concentrate on serious reading. My lack of talent made me feel so useless, yet I felt so sure there was no need for me to lead such an inadequate existence if only I could decide what I wanted to do with myself; I felt my intelligence was like a pair of crossed eyes that might have provided good sight if only they could have been able to focus correctly. But I was still trying to get my world into focus, still looking for a way of life that would enable me to wake up every morning with pleasure instead of with dread and apathy. I was now beginning to think I would never get the world into focus. I was no longer young and my life still seemed to resemble a sheet of water cascading down a drain.

"I feel so guilty," I had said once to Sebastian. "Why should I feel like this when I have everything a woman could possibly want?"

"You mean you have everything that some women could possibly want," Sebastian had said. "But what do *you* want, Vicky?"

It seemed such an anticlimax to hang my head in shame and say I didn't know.

"It doesn't matter anyway," I said. "Even if I knew what I wanted to do, I couldn't do it. The children take all the energy I have."

When I did have time to myself, I was usually too exhausted to do more than slump in the nearest chair and stare at the wall.

"I'm nearly thirty," I said to Sebastian in 1960, "and I've done nothing and everyone thinks I'm stupid and frivolous and shallow, and even *I* think I'm stupid and frivolous and shallow, and yet I know there's something there if only I can track it down."

"Caesar did nothing till he was forty," said Sebastian. "He was rich and handsome and everyone wrote him off as an effete society rake. Yet not long after he was forty he went off to Gaul, and ten years later he had conquered the world. Not bad for a man everyone had dismissed as stupid, frivolous, and shallow!"

I thought of Sebastian saying that. I could remember the occasion as clearly as if it had been yesterday, and suddenly I cried out loud to the silent room: "Oh, I do so miss you, Sebastian!" And I thought, though did not say: And I miss you especially on days like today when everything goes wrong at home and Kierkegaard tells me life is harrowing and absurd and I can do nothing but think what a failure I am at everything I undertake.

I stood up abruptly. Self-pity would get me nowhere. Finding pen and paper, I sat down at my desk with the letter Sebastian had sent some weeks before and began at last to attempt a reply.

VI

"DEAR VICKY: Reading about Kierkegaard would drive anyone up the wall. Give philosophy a rest for a while. Are you really getting anything out of it? You sound too low to concentrate properly on all those does-life-have-a-meaning-and-if-it-does-what-the-hell-is-it kind of questions, which are about as mind-grabbing as a wet blanket when you're in a low state.

"Why not do some *real* reading? Read something violent and bloody and brutal like *Wuthering Heights* (how did the myth that this is a romantic novel ever get around, I wonder?), but if you feel this death-obsessed work of genius won't after all make you feel how wonderful it is to be alive and surviving in mid-twentieth-century America, may I recommend instead that you try a more modern masterpiece, the *Four Quartets* by T. S. Eliot. Yes, it's poetry. No, don't be frightened of it. It's written in very simple clear language which a child could understand. The catch is that Eliot's writing of things which exist only on the periphery of human thought. Maybe it would appeal to your philosophical curiosity. I challenge you to read it. Don't dare tell me later that you chickened out and chose Heathcliff.

"You'll find my old copy of the *Four Quartets* in the second guest room of your father's repulsive triplex, fourth book from the right on the top shelf. Your friend and mentor, Sebastian. P.S. I regard Cornelius' offer to teach you chess with grave suspicion. *Don't let him try to take you over again.* You're not his mirror image in female form (thank God). You are *you*. Never forget that. S."

VII

"HE'S COMING back," said my father, toying with an astronaut pawn. "Your move."

The chessboard at once became a senseless pattern which hurt my eyes. I looked away. "When?"

"In two weeks. He'll be staying at the Carlyle. Why don't you change your mind and see him while he's here? I doubt if he could make you more miserable than you've been since he left."

"Daddy, I never thought I'd see the day when you urged me to go to bed with a man who's not my husband." I pushed my rook roughly toward him.

"Stupid move," said my father, capturing it with his bishop. I was always forgetting that bishops moved diagonally. "Well, Vicky, you know how I feel about the situation. Morals aren't much use here. Better to get him out of your system."

"Morals don't exist merely to be useful. What are you doing?"

"I'm giving you back your rook. You weren't thinking when you made that last move. Try again."

"Certainly not! I lost the rook and I'm not taking it back!"

My father sighed and moved a remote, apparently insignificant pawn on the edge of the board. "Don't say I haven't tried to help."

"I don't need your help. God, with you for a friend, who needs enemies?"

"But, sweetheart—"

"Oh, shut up, Daddy, and let me think. You're deliberately putting me off my game."

VIII

I WOKE up to the knowledge that Scott was in New York. Scrambling out of bed, I ran to the window, and when I pulled the drapes, the spring sunshine blazed into the room from a cloudless sky. The Carlyle was five minutes' walk from my apartment.

I dressed with great care in case he decided to stop by without phoning, just as he had after Kennedy's funeral, and when the children had departed for school, I hurried downstairs to my private apartment to wait by the phone.

I had already decided not to go to bed with him that night. He had to realize that he couldn't sail back effortlessly into my life, but of course we'd have dinner together, and of course he'd be *there*, only inches away from me, and nothing, least of all the past six months, would matter anymore. I thought of the secret weeping in my room, the exhausting effort of pretending to be happy whenever I was with the children, my cousins' pitying criticisms, Alicia's ill-concealed resentment, by stupid friends calling up about nothing and not realizing, not even beginning to comprehend the hell I was going through, but then I pushed those memories aside. I was going to see Scott again. The future would be very different.

I had long since decided that I had been too inflexible when I had resolved to sever all communication with him while he was in Europe. It was only common sense to see him occasionally to remind him I existed. Women were hardly about to leave him alone so that he could keep my memory evergreen, and since he'd found one woman who satisfied him completely, there was no reason why he shouldn't find another, particularly if he believed I no longer cared for him. It was very clear to me now that if I was ever to marry Scott, I had to keep the affair going on a limited basis. I would still refuse to dash over to London at regular intervals, but I was fully prepared to take up residence at the Carlyle whenever he returned to New York on business.

I waited by the phone.

The day seemed endless. Finally it occurred to me that he was probably too busy at the office to make personal calls, and I decided I would be unlikely to hear from him before the evening.

After returning upstairs to the duplex to check on the children, I began my vigil by the phone in my bedroom. Dinnertime came, but I was unable to eat. I was even unable to face a martini. I told everyone I had a migraine. Hour after hour I waited in my room, but an uninterrupted night followed an uninterrupted day, and I remained alone.

The next morning I called the Carlyle, but he had already left for the office.

"Is there a message?" said the clerk.

"No. No message."

I called the bank at Willow and Wall.

"Van Zale and Company," droned the operator. "Good morning, can I help you?"

After a long pause I said, "Sorry, wrong number," and hung up. I was trembling. I told myself I had to give him more time before I started running after him; once I started running, the reconciliation would be far easier than he deserved. I had to display a dignified self-restraint, not a breathless self-abasement which he would eventually come to despise.

I began another vigil by the phone. I wondered if he was delaying calling for fear of being rebuffed, but no, men like Scott Sullivan found it hard to imagine being rebuffed, because the women they wanted always yielded with gratitude to even the most careless of their advances. I thought of poor Judy, whose place I had taken in Scott's bed aboard the cruise ship. How pathetically grateful she had been when he had noticed her, and how pathetically upset she must have been when she found she had been stood up! I glanced at myself in the mirror. Perhaps in the end I was going to be no luckier than Judy. And perhaps in the end Scott was going to care no more for me than he had cared for her.

Hours later I could no longer avoid the truth that was staring me in the face. Scott wasn't going to call. The truth was that nothing had changed since we had parted the previous November—except that he had probably become even more determined to eliminate me from his life. My father had been right in telling me I'd backed a losing horse, and now that the race was indisputably over, I could see my mistake all too clearly.

Covering my face with my hands, I wondered in dumb misery how I was ever going to cut my losses and move on.

IX

"So HOW was the bastard?" I said to my father as we sat down at the chessboard for the first time in two weeks. "He didn't call."

"Yes, he made it clear he considered his affair with you was finished. I'm sorry, but I couldn't help feeling relieved."

"What a fool I've made of myself, haven't I? But at least I managed to stop myself hitting rock bottom by calling him up and begging for a meeting! Well? Aren't you going to tell me how the two of you got along? Are you bosom friends again, with everything forgiven and forgotten?"

"That's the way he wanted to play it, and I saw no reason to discourage him."

"How nauseating! Thank God he's washed his hands of me! And how was he? It sounds as if he's quite his old self again after his temporary lapse last November."

My father gave a small neutral smile. "Maybe. But one thing's changed. He's drinking."

"Drinking! I don't believe it! But is he all right? Can he handle it?"

"Apparently. I never saw him have more than two Scotches on any one occasion, and I certainly never saw him drunk. As a matter of fact, I thought liquor suited him—he was much more relaxed and entertaining."

"I see. Well, obviously he's now in perfect control of his life again after his temporary madness. How wonderful. I envy him. Can I have a martini, please?"

"Vicky," said my father, "I think the time has come when you have to do more than drink martinis and play chess with me. Why don't you—"

"Don't you start dictating to me, because I won't stand for it, not anymore!"

"—get off your ass, get a new interest, get a job, get laid—"

"Daddy!" I was deeply shocked.

"—get out of this rut, for Christ's sake! You've had six months of hell, don't think I don't realize that, but now you've just got to pull yourself together—no, I'm not trying to dictate to you! Nor am I trying to make you over into someone else altogether. I'm just trying to help you live a happier life as you are. Now, listen. I've been making some inquiries, and I've found out there's a good summer course on economics at the New School . . ."

"Forget it."

"Okay, how about a course in philosophy?"

"If it's just a summer course, I probably know most of it already."

"Then why not take a full college course?"

"Daddy, it's a beautiful dream, but you just don't even begin to realize how impossible it is. It's a question of mental energy. I doubt if I could even complete a summer course. Probably I couldn't even complete a weekend seminar. I'm too old, too harassed, too bogged down. I've had it. I accept now that my chance for an academic life is absolutely gone, so why should I make myself miserable by taking courses which would only remind me of the kind of life I've failed to achieve?"

"Aren't you being a bit negative?"

"No. Just realistic. I'd be better off taking a job than trying to live an academic life, but what kind of job could I possibly get? I'm unemployable, and even if I wasn't, I suspect I couldn't handle the pace. No one who's not a mother of five children could ever realize—"

"But you have help with the children! You're so fortunate! What would you do if you were one of those mothers who had no choice but to go out to work to support her family?"

"I couldn't have done it. I often think how different my life would have been if I'd been poor."

"You'd have managed somehow!"

"Who can say? All I know is that I'm not like Lori, who can run a home, husband, children, and God knows what else with one hand tied behind her back. Whenever I try to be superwoman, I go to pieces."

"Perhaps I could find you a little job in the Fine Arts Foundation, nothing very demanding, but just something which would take you out of yourself and help you not to get so depressed."

"Yes, I guess a tame little sinecure might be better than nothing, but not right now, Daddy. Later. I can't just switch Scott off and immediately zip into a rewarding new life. You've got to give me another chance to get over this mess I'm in. You've got to give me more time."

X

A LETTER came from my accountant with some information about a new stock which my broker had bought for me. I chucked the letter in the trash basket. Then, having nothing better to do, I retrieved the letter and read it more carefully. My accountant had known me since I was a little girl, and his tone was faintly patronizing. I didn't like it. I thought: Damned men, messing me around, thinking they're God, taking me for a fool. I'll show them.

I read the letter again. Then I went out, bought *The Wall Street Journal,* and decided to take a course on the stock market.

XI

Time present and time past
Are both perhaps present in time future,
And time future contained in time past.
If all time is eternally present
All time is unredeemable.

I thought immediately of Scott, obsessed by time and bending the past to encircle the future.

The phone rang.

"Hi, sweetheart, did you enjoy your first class? What was it like? How many people were there?"

"I didn't go. Nurse is sick, Nora insisted on taking her day off, and the doctor says Kristin's got chickenpox. Daddy, can I call you back?"

What might have been is an abstraction
Remaining a perpetual possibility
Only in a world of speculation.

What might have been and what has been
Point to one end which is always present.

   The door opened.

"Mommy, Samantha hit me and I think my arm's broken in three places and I've got a huge bruise on my leg and my knee's streaming blood."

"Hm. Just a minute."

"Mommeeee!"

"Oh, do be quiet, Ben! Are you referring to that scratch which I can't see properly without the aid of a magnifying glass? Run off and apologize to Samantha. You must have done something awful if she tried to beat you up."

"Well, I kind of accidentally sat on her best picture of the Beatles . . ."

Footfalls echo in the memory
Down the passage which we did not take
Towards the door we never opened
Into the rose-garden . . .

   I stopped, then read that passage again. I read it a third time and a fourth. I thought of my years at college studying philosophy, and suddenly I could hear the footfalls echoing in *my* memory down the passage I had not taken toward the door I had never opened into my own personal rose-garden.

   I read on. The simple pellucid words expressing their complex thoughts slipped silently into my mind to tantalize me. I understood yet did not understand. Then I wondered if in fact I understood anything. Or was the truth simply that I did understand but had no words to express the understanding which crept across my consciousness? Finally I no longer cared whether I understood or not. I merely continued reading, pausing only to savor random phrases. "The roses had the look of flowers that are looked at . . . Only in time can the moment in the rose-garden be remembered . . . Only through time time is conquered."

   I stopped again. I had read the first of T. S. Eliot's *Four Quartets.* Closing the book, I sat down at my desk and began to write to Sebastian.

XII

"DEAR VICKY: Don't worry about dropping out of that course on the stock market. They'd probably have told you nothing you can't pick up for yourself. I like your idea of lighting a fire under your financial advisers. Stick with it and give 'em hell.

"Is Eliot saying that no opportunity is ever really lost? you ask. Is it possible to go back, to walk down the passage you never took, through the door you never opened into the rose-garden? Maybe. According to one of the commentaries, what Eliot is saying in *Burnt Norton* is that there are moments when what has been and what might have been actually *are*. Work *that* one out in between your martinis! Incidentally, I'm sending you airmail a copy of Eliot's play *The Family Reunion,* which has more references to rose-gardens, including the possibility of actually making it through the door that was never opened into the . . . etc., etc. Glad you like Eliot. I consider it my moral duty (ha-ha) to raise your mind far above your father's level (no big deal, since his level is rock bottom).

"I'm okay, thanks. I've got this house which would fit into one wing of your father's triplex, and no servants except for a housekeeper (a toothless hag) who comes in daily. I've started doing some research. I finally decided to write—wait for it—a history of investment banking. It seems I'm more hooked on the subject than I ever realized, but I remain, your happy exile from the plastic society, S. Foxworth, Esquire. P.S. Tell Postumus hello, and don't let him walk all over you."

XIII

And what did not happen is as true as what did happen
O my dear, and *you walked through the little door*
And I ran to meet you in the rose-garden . . .

The phone rang, and putting aside my well-thumbed copy of *The Family Reunion,* I picked up the receiver.

"Vicky?" said my father. "Listen, I've just been talking to Kingsley Donahue, and he tells me you've fired not only your accountants but your brokers as well! Sweetheart, was that wise? Are you sure you know what you're doing? Kingsley's real hurt!"

"That's tough," I said, "but he'll live."

"But I don't understand why you've done this!"

"Oh, Daddy, they were so conservative, so boring, and I think that if one's got a bit of money, the stock market should be exciting and interesting! Jake's recommended a nice go-ahead young broker called Jordan Salomon, and I've decided to give him a try."

"Jake! What are you doing talking to him? I thought he still held it against you for busting up his daughter's marriage!"

"Now Elsa's remarried, he doesn't care about that anymore, and anyway, his new mistress is an old schoolfriend of mine. He was very friendly when I met him at one of her parties the other day."

"A party? So you're going out again! Sweetheart, I'm very pleased to hear it. Maybe you'll meet someone new."

"Oh, I'm always meeting someone new," I said. "The fortune hunters, the gigolos, the female-flesh fanciers, the trite, the boring, and the inane. The world's full of new people all gasping to meet me. It's a great life."

"Now, sweetheart, don't get too cynical."

"And don't you start talking junk. Good night, Daddy. I hate being interrupted when I'm reading T. S. Eliot. I'll talk to you some other time."

XIV

I AWOKE and knew at once it was a very special day. Edward John would have been five years old. I watched the sun slanting through the drapes and pictured him effortlessly, fair-haired and gray-eyed, looking like a little choirboy, not rude and rowdy like the real children, the ones who had lived, but docile and sweet-natured, gentle and loving. I had a vivid picture of him running toward me across the rose-garden with his arms outstretched, and suddenly it seemed unbearable that I had no way of opening the door and rushing into the rose-garden to embrace him.

A bell jangled at my bedside. I reached for the receiver of the phone.

"I have a call for a Mrs. Foxworth from Cambridge, England."

"Oh! Yes . . . yes, speaking."

"Go ahead, caller."

"Hi, Vicky."

"Hi." I was sitting bolt upright in bed. "How are you?"

"Okay. I just thought I'd give you a call."

"Yes . . . thanks."

There was an awkward pause.

"Made any money lately?" said Sebastian at last.

"As a matter of fact, I have. I'm giving it to a charity which cares for Vietnamese war orphans. I think I've finally found the kind of charity work I like best."

"Great. The market's on the upswing, isn't it, enjoying a boom . . . I get *The Wall Street Journal* airmail."

"Oh, Sebastian, how homesick you sound!"

"No, I just like to know what's going on. Where did you make your killing in the market?"

"I backed a client of Jake's. Have you ever heard of a young man called Donald Shine?"

"Sure. Computer leasing. Boy, you're smart, Vicky! Fired any more dumb brokers lately?"

We laughed. I at last began to feel less tense.

"How's your book going?"

"Okay, but I'll be taking a rest from it soon, because I've got Alfred coming to stay for two weeks. Elsa's all sweetness and light since she remarried. What's the new husband like, do you know? The man must be some kind of a saint to marry into that family!"

"Well, he's Jewish, so he won't have the problems you had. I haven't met him, but I've heard he's charming. Of course Elsa herself looks terrific nowadays. I saw her in Tiffany's the other day—I was slumming around at the back ordering notepaper, and she was queening it at the front trying on diamonds. She looked like a movie star."

"Christ, isn't it odd the way things turn out."

"Odd, yes."

We were silent, and I knew we were both thinking of Edward John.

"Well, thanks for calling, Sebastian . . ."

"Found the rose-garden yet?"

"Not yet. I know it's there, but I can't find the way. I even think that if I did find the way I might not recognize the rose-garden when I reached it, because I still don't have a clear idea of what it is."

"It'll be like an elephant. Hard to describe but instantly recognizable."

"Maybe."

"Don't give up, Vicky. Just keep on surviving those kids and giving your broker hell and keeping a lot of Vietnamese orphans in rice. Nobody could ask more of you just now."

"Yes. Right. Well . . ."

"Okay, so long. Take care. Don't worry—I won't start pestering you with transatlantic phone calls. I just wanted to speak to you today because . . ."

"Yes," I said as he stopped. My eyes filled with tears. "I'm so glad you called. Thank you. 'Bye."

" 'Bye."

We replaced our receivers, and I pictured him, thousands of miles away, staring at his phone as I was staring at mine. In the end I did manage not to cry, but for a long time I remained motionless, thinking of Sebastian, thinking of Edward John, thinking with unbearable clarity of a world that might have been.

XV

"VICKY, MY dear," said Jake Reischman at the cocktail party, "allow me to introduce you to my client Donald Shine."

I saw a tall rangy young man with long thick sideburns and hair that curled well down on his collar. He wore a pink shirt, a matching pink flowered tie, and a suit which looked as if it had just crossed the Atlantic from Carnaby Street.

"Hello," I said. "Congratulations on your takeover of Syntax Data Processing!"

"Well, thank you! I hope you made a lot of money out of it—Jake tells me you've been following my fortunes!" He offered me a warm, firm friendly hand and flashed me a frank winning smile.

I could almost feel his personality wrap itself around me in order to extract every ounce of admiration and salt it away for future use.

"I'm certainly curious to know what your next venture's going to be," I said. "Or is that a state secret?"

"Well, everyone must know by now that I've got great plans," said Donald Shine, masking his arrogance with his buoyant enthusiasm, so that he achieved the impossible and sounded modest. "The way I see it, I reckon the corporate financial structure of this country could use a real vigorous shake-up to bring it all the way into the age of Aquarius."

I tried not to look too amazed. Could this man be the financial sensation of the year? He seemed to be more like some hip DJ incapable of discussing any subject beyond *Billboard*'s top hundred, and as I continued to regard him with disbelief, I saw exactly why sober, staid, conservative Wall Street was so appalled and affronted by his success.

". . . so I'll have to see what opportunities come my way," he was saying. "Hey, Jake's a great guy, isn't he? How did you meet him?"

"He's an old friend of my father's."

"Who's your father?"

"Cornelius Van Zale."

Donald Shine burst out laughing. "No kidding!"

"You know my father?"

"Sure. He took me to the cleaner's once. I was cleaned, pressed, starched, packaged, and tossed out into the street in less than thirty seconds. I've never forgotten that," said Donald Shine, flashing me his winning smile again, "and I'll bet I never will."

I was embarrassed. "I'm sorry you don't have happier memories of my father," I said. "But no doubt my father's now busy wishing he'd made a better impression."

"Could be!" He laughed again and shrugged his shoulders. "He's no different from a lot of other guys I've had dealings with. Never trust anyone over thirty, that's my motto."

"It's obviously my exit line. If you'll excuse me . . ."

"Hey, don't get mad just because I'm not a member of your father's fan club! Are you really over thirty? You look so gorgeous I figured we were totally, like, contemporary!"

"Vicky," said Jake, swooping back to rescue me, "I'd like you to meet another friend of mine—excuse us, Don . . ."

I escaped thankfully through the throng.

"What an amazing man!" I said to Jake. I felt dazed, as if someone had picked me up and shaken me till my teeth rattled.

Jake's thin aristocratic mouth curled contemptuously at the corners, but all he said was, "My dear, keep buying his shares."

608

XVI

"I'M VERY sorry, Jordan, but I can't go through with this. I thought I could, but I can't. Anyway, I'm not sure it's a good idea for a woman to sleep with her broker."

"Is it because I'm still married? My divorce is coming up very soon."

"It's got nothing to do with your divorce."

"Is it because I'm younger than you are?"

"No, Jordan. Anyway, you're only two years younger. Stop talking as if I were a senior citizen!"

"Is it because—?"

"Stop! I refuse to let this conversation degenerate into a parody of a daytime quiz show!"

"But what's your hang-up?"

"I'm frigid, of course. Isn't everyone?"

"Frigid! Why didn't you say so? Listen, Vicky, I know this really great technique . . ."

"I'm sorry, I don't smoke pot. I have enough trouble with cigarettes and alcohol."

"Pot! Vicky, I'm a respectable broker! What I meant was, I have this fantastic sex manual . . ."

"Jordan, darling, could you please get the hell out before I throw up?"

"You mean you're not feeling well? Why didn't you say so? Okay, I'll give you a call tomorrow."

"Don't bother. You'd be wasting your time."

"You can't know that for sure!"

"I know it," I said. "Believe me, I know it."

"But—"

"Good night, Jordan."

I got rid of him and slammed the door.

Then I went to bed and thought of Scott.

I had come a long, long way since the November of 1963, and I was now adept at going through the motions of my new life without him, but the thought of sharing that life with another man was still intolerable.

It was over three years now since I had seen him. He came to New

York three or four times a year, but I always took care to be away from the city during his visits in case I was ever mad enough to give way to my most self-destructive impulse and rush to the Carlyle to grovel at his feet. When I returned to the city from my enforced vacations I would always inquire politely about his welfare, and my father would reply equally politely that everything was just fine. I had conscientiously willed myself to think of him as if he were dead, but every spring I knew he was alive, and as the trees burst into leaf in the park and the New York skies became that rare pristine spring blue, I would think of him and live hour after hour with my memories.

It was spring again by this time, the spring of 1967. Eric was seventeen, doing well at Choate, and had started to wear glasses which transformed him into a younger, very serious version of Sam. Paul refused to cut his hair and was now devoted to the torrid nihilism of the Rolling Stones, while Samantha, more obsessed with boys than ever, pestered me for lushly padded bras and kept a poster of Mick Jagger over her bed. Kristin had other problems; she was constantly at the bottom of her class and cried daily at the prospect of school. Benjamin continued his career as infant monster; one day I caught him sniffing glue in a closet and I spanked him so hard he was quiet for two days.

My father told me sternly I should lecture the children about the evils of drugs, but I replied that although I advised, I refused to lecture, because lectures might only have the disastrous effect of severing the already slender lines of communication. During a family discussion of the Younger Generation, Rose told me it was all quite different in the Midwest, where no one burned their draft cards and slouched around smoking marijuana, while Lori announced she had complete confidence that none of her wonderful children would get into trouble, and implied it was a pity I obviously couldn't say as much for mine. Alicia commented wanly that we were living in terrible times, and I knew she was thinking of Andrew, who, having survived one tour of duty in Vietnam, had returned for another and was again writing regular letters home about the war.

The grass had grown over John Kennedy's grave, but the blood was still flowing in America, and the escalating violence seemed to permeate the very air we breathed.

"What's new?" I said, arriving at the breakfast table on that pristine spring morning in 1967.

"Nothing much," said Paul, barely glancing up from the *World-Journal-Tribune.* "There's going to be a parade next week to *support* the troops in Vietnam—can you imagine? The body count's up again. There's been another mass murder inspired by that guy in Chicago who knocked off eight nurses last year. Oh, and there's been another riot somewhere, and another black's called for total revolution. In other words, it's just the same old daily garbage, nothing new."

"My God," I said, "sometimes I wake up and think America's gone mad. Maybe Sebastian was smart to get out and go to England."

"England!" breathed Samantha. "The Stones! Mick! Wow!"

"Oh, cut it out!" said Paul. "It's so boring living in the same apartment as a sex-crazed twelve-year-old."

"You only say that because you're a spotty lump of fourteen and daren't ask any girl to go out with you!"

"Paul, Samantha . . . please! I can't take this at breakfast before I've had my first cup of coffee!"

The phone rang.

"I'll get it!" shrieked Samantha, who had recently run up a phone bill of three hundred dollars talking to a male classmate who had moved to California.

"If it's Billy," I shouted after her, "you make damn sure he's not calling collect!" Billy's parents had caught on to these coast-to-coast calls quicker than I had.

There was a pause, a blessed moment of peace while Paul read the sports page in silence and I sipped my coffee. Kristin and Benjamin were with Nurse somewhere in a remote corner of the duplex. I could hear Benjamin shrieking, but I paid no attention.

"Mom . . . for you." Samantha sounded cross.

"Okay." I levered myself reluctantly to my feet. "Who is it, do you know?"

"I guess it's Uncle Sebastian. The operator said it was a call from England."

"Heavens!" In great surprise I hurried to my room to take the call. Sebastian never called except on Edward John's birthday. I hoped nothing was wrong.

"Hello?" I said anxiously into the phone. "Sebastian? What a nice surprise! Is everything all right?"

There was a silence broken only by the hum of the transatlantic wire.

"Hello?" I said. "Hello, can you hear me?" I suddenly felt faint. My heart had begun to beat much too fast.

"Go ahead, London," said the operator.

"Hello?" I said. "Hello . . ."

"Hello, Vicky," said Scott. "Don't hang up. I've got to talk to you."

Chapter Three

I

I HAD forgotten the exact timbre of his voice, but immediately he spoke I felt as if I had remembered it daily since our last meeting. His flat neutral Eastern Seaboard accent was neither attractive nor remarkable, but he had the trick of speaking without hesitating, and this gave him an air of authority which made it easy to believe in his determination to get what he wanted at all times.

"Vicky?" He sounded crisp, confident, and cold.

"Yes, I'm here." My skin was crawling with heat. I rubbed my eyes, and when I opened them again the room seemed no longer blurred with shock but blindingly clear, the bright colors glowing and the softer shades heightened to a brilliant gleam.

"Listen, I'm calling about your mother."

I tried to focus on what he was saying, but this was hard, because I never liked thinking about my mother. My mother was seventy-four years old and lived in London. I did not write to her, but every Christmas I sent her the year's photographs of the children and every January she wrote back to say how pleased she was to be able to keep her album up-to-date.

"Vicky? This is a terrible line! Did you hear what I said?"

"About my mother, yes. What's happened? Is she dead?"

"She's had an accident. She's been hospitalized with a broken hip."

"Oh." In my mind I was back in bed with him. I could feel the tensed muscles of his chest and hear the rasp of his breath as wave after wave of pent-up emotion exploded between us. I began to feel dizzy again.

"I've got her out of a Dickensian ward in some National Health nightmare of a hospital, and put her in the London Clinic. The authorities called me, you understand, after she'd had the accident, because in her purse she had one of those cards giving a number to call in case of an emergency, and for some reason she'd put down the number of the bank in the City. She appears to have no friends and of course there are no relatives here. She's also short of money. Apparently rising prices have taken a toll on her fixed income, and she's been living in some dump south of the river."

I was jolted abruptly out of the past. "I'm sorry," I said, "but could you please repeat that last sentence?"

He repeated it and added, "Let me get the operator—this line's impossible."

"No, I can hear you. But I don't understand. Why didn't she ask me for money?"

"She said she didn't want to be a burden to you anymore."

"Oh, but I would have considered it my moral duty . . ."

"Yes, she said she knew just how you felt about her. Look, you'd better come over and sort this out. How soon can you get a plane?"

"Oh, but . . . I don't think I could possibly . . . I'll wire money, of course, but—"

"Vicky, I have this pathetic old senior citizen here who's asking for you. Like it or not, she's your mother. She looked after you for the first ten years of your life, so presumably you must owe her something, no matter what unforgivable mistakes she made later. And are you sure those mistakes were really so unforgivable? And just out of interest, can I ask if you turned around and began to hate your mother all by yourself? Or were you aided and abetted by someone else, someone I don't need to name?"

I couldn't speak, but a voice inside me was screaming: No, it couldn't be, it wasn't, he didn't, he *couldn't have*.

I felt as if I were on the rack. Again I tried to speak, but again no words came.

"Cable me your arrival time," said Scott, "and I'll send a car to meet you at Heathrow and make a reservation for you at the Savoy. There's no need for us to meet if you'd find that distasteful."

"Distasteful?"

There was a pause. Then: "I'm not entirely unaware of what's going on in New York," said Scott, "and I hear from more than one source that you have a new romantic interest in your life. In those circumstances I fully understand that you've no wish to be reminded of a past you'd prefer to forget."

"Are you referring to Jordan Salomon? But—"

"It's not important. All that's important at the moment is that you should cable me at your convenience so that I can make the appropriate arrangements. I'll hope to hear from you as soon as possible. Good-bye."

"Scott . . ." I gasped, but he had hung up. I sat there trembling from head to toe, the receiver still in my hand, and whispered, "Scott . . . Scott . . . Scott . . ." until the operator came back onto the line and asked if the call had been cut off.

I replaced the receiver but went on sitting on the edge of the bed. I decided not to think about my mother. There was some sort of apocalyptic truth hidden in that situation, but that was all right, I had learned long ago to shove that to the back of my mind so that I wouldn't have to think about it. Eliminating her effortlessly from my thoughts as usual, I found myself free to think entirely of Scott.

Suddenly I noticed that light was streaming into the room, and when I went to the window, I found I was taut with excitement. Beyond the window the world basked in brilliant sunshine, and suddenly I no longer felt as if I were on the verge of middle age. My despair was gone. So was my sense of futility and waste. For I was thirty-six years old, in the very prime of life, and the one man I wanted had obviously made up his mind that we should soon be face to face again.

II

I DECIDED to say nothing to my father. Since he thought I had fully recovered from my affair with Scott, I had no intention of disappointing him, and although he had urged me to continue the affair in 1963 when it must have seemed I was in the grip of a temporary infatuation, I suspected he would take a very different view of the situation now in 1967 if the affair were to revive long after it should have died a natural death.

It was also only a matter of months until Scott was recalled permanently to New York. I could well imagine my father growing nervous, tying himself in knots over his Machiavellian power games and attributing all kinds of sinister motives to Scott if the affair were revived, but I saw now so clearly that I could not expect rational behavior from either my father or Scott where the bank was concerned. Obviously I was going to have to mediate between them. They would never trust each other sufficiently to reach a satisfactory truce unless I imposed a solution which would end their ridiculous power games once and for all.

It occurred to me, not for the first time, how very childish and stupid men could be. It was small wonder that the world, run by men, was in such a shambles, when they persisted in locking themselves into tight corners from which they could escape only by making some violent demonstration. It seemed extraordinary that they never fully comprehended the futility of aggression. If it weren't for women, men would have been extinct long ago, demolished by their own stupidity, but of course women were stupid too, letting men get away with their nihilistic behavior and accepting their violent behavior as inevitable.

I had no intention of accepting this particular violent conflict as inevitable. During the past three years I had tried not to think too much about Scott's future, but as time passed and I realized he was giving a typically impeccable performance as a banker in London, I had thought it probable that he would eventually reach some new understanding with my father which would enable them to maintain their close business relationship even though they might remain privately estranged. I didn't seriously believe that my father, loving Scott as he did, would take any blatantly destructive step against him, and I didn't seriously believe that Scott would ever be a threat to my father so long as he was treated fairly. If I could somehow end their private estrangement, I thought that their business relationship, no longer fueled by bitterness and suspicion, would eventually take care of itself. All they needed was the chance to return to a normal rational coexistence without either side believing he was being conned, and I was going to provide that chance. Those two men were going to be reconciled. A reconciliation was what I wanted, and a reconciliation was what I was going to get, because this was a situation where for once in my life *I* was in control.

Power blazed through me like an aphrodisiac. At last I felt strong enough to conquer the world, and smiling at Sebastian's description of the effete Julius Caesar who had become the toughest man in town, I dialed Pan American Airways and booked my flight to London.

III

I ANNOUNCED to my family that I had received an unexpected invitation to spend a few days with an old schoolfriend in Virginia, and the only person I took into my confidence was Nurse. It was essential that she should know where I was in case an emergency arose, but I told her I was keeping the visit to England secret because I didn't want the children to worry about their grandmother.

I packed carefully, remembering that English springs could be cold. I also remembered that Scott liked women to be chastely dressed, like Aunt Emily, so in addition to the skirts and sweaters I took one dress with a high neckline. Then I consulted the calendar, realized I had no time to waste, and hurried to the nearest clinic for a new supply of the pill. I had abandoned the pill when Scott had abandoned me, but I had once resumed taking it for a short while when it seemed I might have an affair with Jordan.

I went to the airport. I boarded the plane. I set off on that long journey east into another world. We seemed to fly endlessly above the hazy sea far below, but after the long twilight darkness fell, the plane began its measured descent and finally the neon glow of London stretched ahead of us as far as the eye could see.

IV

I KNEW he was somewhere nearby as soon as I walked out of the customs hall. I stared feverishly at the crowds hanging over the barriers, but beyond the blur of unknown faces there was no sign that he had come to meet me.

Then I saw him. I had moved around the edge of the crowd and was just looking back across the hall when he walked through the doors from the sidewalk. He was thirty yards away.

He gave his smallest, politest smile and raised his hand in greeting.

I tried to move forward to meet him, but nothing happened. I just stood there, my suitcase in my hand, and was at once immensely aware not of time standing still but of time moving on at last after some intolerable hiatus.

I forgot my clear-eyed analysis of the future in which I solved everyone's problems with such matchless efficiency. I forgot the frustration of the present in which I felt shackled by my past mistakes. And I certainly forgot the pain of the past, when I had daily wondered how I was going to survive on my own. In that second when I saw him again, my mind focused itself on his presence with such intensity that every move he made seemed like a revelation of some spellbinding truth and every detail of his appearance assumed a blinding significance.

His hair was grayer at the sides, and also longer, to conform with current masculine fashion. I had never realized until I saw him then how short he had kept his hair before. At first glance I thought he was still clean-shaven, but a second later I saw he now had a pair of slim, trim sideburns. He had put on some weight too, but that suited him, for he had always been too thin. His eyes were a bright black, like polished volcanic rock. His walk was rapid but very smooth, very confident. He wore an immaculately tailored dark suit with a discreetly striped blue-and-white shirt. His tie was navy-blue silk. His shoes gleamed. His cufflinks were silver. I wanted him so much I could barely stand.

"Hi," he said. "How are you? Good trip? Okay, let me take your case. The car's outside." And he began to walk away from me with my case in his hand.

I just managed to stumble along in his wake. My breath was coming unevenly and I felt unbearably hot. All rational thought was impossible.

Outside, a policeman, an English policeman with a helmet and no gun, was chatting sociably with the chauffeur of a milk-white Rolls-Royce, but when we left the building he turned to face us, and the chauffeur sprang forward to open the passenger door.

Scott set the suitcase down on the pavement. "Sorry, officer, we're just going."

"Very good, sir, but perhaps you'd be so kind as to ask your chauffeur to use the car park next time, if you please."

I remembered that I was now a foreigner in a land where even threats were wrapped up in inscrutable politeness, and looking around dazedly, I saw the malformed little cars with their displaced steering wheels, the shabby people in raincoats, the soft drizzle falling steadily from the alien neon sky.

I suddenly realized they were all waiting for me, so I crawled into the Rolls and collapsed on the upholstery. Scott sat on the back seat beside me. We didn't speak, just waited while the chauffeur placed the suitcase in the trunk and returned to his position behind the wheel.

The car drew away from the curb.

"I spoke to your mother on the phone today," said Scott effortlessly while I was still racking my brains for the appropriate small talk. "She's much better. I don't think she'll have to stay in the Clinic long. I'm having my secretary find out about convalescent homes on the south coast."

"Oh. Yes. What a good idea. Thank you so much." The car was heading for the tunnel which led out of the airport.

"She's looking forward to seeing you, of course."

"Yes. Oh, yes. Good." I didn't dare look at him in case I lost control of myself and did something stupid which would upset him. His lack of emotion made it obvious that the last thing he wanted from me was an embarrassing display of passion.

We traveled on in silence, but at last, feeling that even the most mundane question would be preferable to this appalling lack of conversation, I said, "Do you like living in London?"

"Not much."

"Oh? Why's that?"

"You're three thousand miles away."

I looked at him before I could stop myself, but not a muscle of his face had moved. And then, very slowly, he smiled.

"Christ, Vicky," he said, "it's been such a long time."

"Oh, God, Scott . . . I . . . Oh, God . . ."

"I'm sorry about what happened. I don't expect you to forgive me, but—"

"Oh yes, you do!" I blazed. "You turn on the charm and expect me to grovel at your feet, you egoist, you son of a bitch, you . . ."

He started to laugh. "All I did was offer you an apology!"

"I'll tell you what you can do with your apology!" I said, but I never did. I raised my face to his as he leaned over to kiss me, and the next moment his hair was coarse beneath my fingers, his hands were hard upon my body, and his mouth was dry as my tongue slipped past his lips.

The Rolls-Royce swept serenely on toward London.

V

"ALL RIGHT, you bastard, level with me. Why didn't you call?"

"I had nothing to offer you. What right had I to reopen all the old wounds when I was still no closer to solving the problems that had divided us back in '63?"

"But were you never tempted—?"

"Tempted! Of course I was tempted! I nearly called you lots of times to offer you another ride down the same dead-end street, but I always felt I just couldn't do that to you. I cared too much. Then later your father said—"

"If he lied, I'll kill him. I will! I've had enough of him lying to you and wrecking everything!"

Scott laughed. "This time we can't blame your father. Other people besides Cornelius told me you'd made a new life for yourself, taking an active interest in the stock market, supervising your own portfolio, going out to parties, making new friends, even—"

"No," I said, "you can forget the gossip you heard about Jordan."

"Well, of course there must have been others. I fully realize that."

"No."

"No?"

"No, I was sick of meaningless sex and I didn't want anyone but you. My God, why on earth did I have to tell you that? I must be mad. The last thing your ego needs is a woman confessing she's slept alone for three and a half years because she couldn't get you out of her mind."

"Vicky . . . Don't be so hard on yourself."

"What choice do I have? It seems I'm constitutionally incapable of being hard on you. More fool me."

"Shhh." He started kissing me again. "It's all going to come right, Vicky. Our dead-end street's going to be opening into a freeway. It's only a matter of months now till I'm back in New York, and then—"

"The Savoy, sir," said the chauffeur, opening the door.

We exchanged one more kiss. Then Scott dismissed both car and chauffeur and followed me into the hotel.

VI

"OKAY," I said, "I've been frank with you—much too frank—and now I'd like a little frankness in return. Tell me all about your show-stopping private life during the past three and a half years."

Scott smiled. We were propped up against a huge mound of pillows and drinking a bottle of champagne which he had found in the refrigerated liquor cabinet in the living room of my suite. For Scott, living on European time, it was two o'clock in the morning, but for me it was only nine o'clock at night. I felt alert, bright, and euphoric.

I glanced at him. The soft light from the bedside lamp glowed on the tousled bed, where the upper sheet, limp and creased, wound its way over my feet across his thighs and back again over my stomach. My breasts were a delicate shade of mottled pink, as if the recent unfamiliar events had proved shocking to them; dragging the sheet upward to cover their absurd color, I deprived Scott of the scanty covering on his thighs and at once I was aware of his strength, his solidity, and the pattern of hair on his chest, stomach, and groin.

"Well?" I said. "Aren't you going to tell me you've been having a whole string of glamorous affairs?" I was smiling too to show him I didn't care what he'd done, but we both knew I cared very much. The rational part of my brain knew he must have had other women, but the irrational part made me feel jealous and hurt. I couldn't bear to think of him with anyone else. But neither could I bear the thought of him lying to spare my feelings. "I want the truth!" I said fiercely, no longer looking at him. "I deserve it! You owe it to me!"

"Sure." He took my hand in his and stroked the back of it gently with his index finger. "I was in bad shape when I got to England," he said at last, "and I thought my only hope was to try to replace you as soon as possible. I had an affair with a librarian. She wasn't pretty but she was smart and I liked her. It seemed like some kind of answer. We lived together for six weeks. Then she left."

I waited for an explanation, but when none came, I said cautiously, "She found someone else?"

"No, she just found me impossible to live with. I . . . was drinking a lot at the time." He looked down at the glass of champagne in his hand, and I noticed for the first time that he had barely touched it. "However, I got that problem straightened out by moving out of the apartment I'd rented and moving into a town house, where I had to hire servants. When I was obliged to maintain a certain standard of behavior at home as well as at the office, I found it easier to keep my drinking under control."

"I see." For some reason I didn't like to question him further about his drinking. "And did the next girl last longer?"

"Next girl? Oh, after the disaster with the librarian I didn't like to risk living with anyone else. I did try my old game of one-night stands for a short time, but that didn't work out either. I was too afraid of my old problem coming back, and soon I found I couldn't face a woman until I'd had too much to drink—another recipe for disaster, as I discovered all too quickly. Well, I knew I had to keep the drinking under control, so I thought, hell, why bother with women, why go to all the trouble, why try to use sex to relax when the result is so far from relaxing?" He laughed at himself, mocking his situation as if he were merely shrugging off past absurdities. His eyes shone with pain. "So finally," he said, making a great business of turning away from me and setting down his glass of champagne, "sanity prevailed, common sense triumphed, and my show-stopping private life drew to its ignominious close. No doubt you're now thinking I got exactly what I deserved after the way I treated you in New York. That's certainly my opinion, and you're very welcome to share it."

I put my hand over his and held it. He turned out the light so that he no longer had to make the effort to hide his expression. We lay side by side in the comforting darkness for some time.

Finally he said, "I think I'm going to survive after all. I didn't know how I was going to get through these years away from you. I often thought I wasn't going to make it."

I put my fingers softly against his mouth. Then I kissed him. Later I said, "I would have come to London. I'd have done anything. If only—"

"No," he said. "No 'if onlys.' If you'd come to London to live with me, it would have solved some problems but created others— and those others might well have made life just as intolerable. Do you think I didn't consider every option? Do you think I didn't go over the situation time after time after time? The only solution I could see was to survive in London alone somehow and pray for a miracle which would leave you free and willing to see me again when the time was right." He switched on the light once more and finished his champagne with an effort. "It's strange," he said, looking into his glass, "but I don't even like liquor much. I drink Scotch because I'm never tempted to have more than two shots—I don't care for the taste. The drink I like is vodka. You can dress that up and never know you're taking alcohol . . . but perhaps that too has its disadvantages. I got into bad trouble in the navy once or twice because . . . But those days don't matter anymore now that I've got my drinking under control, so why resurrect them? Let's talk of something else." He leaned over me with a smile and began to run his fingers slowly through my hair. "I like you with your hair long."

"Good. Alicia thinks I look like mutton dressed as lamb."

"Alicia's jealous of you, as usual!"

"Yes, but it doesn't bother me anymore. I don't give a damn."

"How are she and Cornelius getting along nowadays?"

"It's hard to tell. I used to think they were on the verge of divorce again, but now I think they're just very, very married. I've come to the reluctant conclusion that in their own peculiar way they're a remarkable couple and that I should stop sneering at their marriage and start admiring it instead. Do you realize that they've now been married thirty-six years? That's no mean feat, is it? My God! What on earth can it be like to have been married to the same person for thirty-six years!"

"Shall we try it and find out?"

I spilled champagne all over the bed. "Is that a proposal?"

"What did you think it was? An invitation to a scientific experiment?"

"Oh, Scott . . . darling . . ."

All pain was over. He started laughing, I laughed with him, and in a haze of joyous relief we fell clumsily into each other's arms.

VII

"ARE YOU sure you want to marry me?" I said anxiously sometime later. "I know you've always felt you were unsuited for marriage."

"All I know is," said Scott, "that I'm unsuited for a life without you. So long as we can be together, I don't care whether I'm married, living in sin, or in residence at a zoo."

"In this case, you'll have both marriage *and* the zoo! Oh, Scott, are you sure you don't mind about the children? I know how you feel about—"

"Let's stop talking about how I feel and talk about how you feel. I know how much your children mean to you. I know you want a permanent relationship with a man you can rely on, and obviously in your circumstances it's better if that man's your husband and not just your lover. None of this is unreasonable. In fact, it could hardly be more natural. I hope you don't think I'm so emotionally disturbed that I can't understand your position, respect it, and go along with it."

"Well, of course I don't think you're emotionally disturbed, but—"

"I'll do my best with the kids, Vicky, I promise. It may not be a very good best at the beginning, but I'll work at it. I love you and I'd do anything to make you happy. You mustn't worry about the kids anymore."

Tears filled my eyes because this assurance was so exactly what I had wanted to hear. I whispered my thanks and kissed him lightly on the cheek.

We were silent for a while. By this time it was very late and I was feeling sleepy.

"Of course," said Scott at last, "your father's not going to like this very much."

I was suddenly wide-awake. I noticed for the first time that there was an oval molding on the ceiling around the center light, and matching moldings in the ceiling's four corners.

"Your father and I are getting on very well at the moment," said Scott. "I think we've managed to paper over all those cracks that developed in our relationship back in 1963. Even so, he's bound to regard this marriage of ours with extreme suspicion. You do realize that, don't you? I hope he won't make you too upset."

"I'd just like to see him try!" I went on watching the ceiling. The soft light from the bedside lamp was reflected in the glass of the chandelier.

"You've got much closer to him, haven't you?" said Scott. "I could tell from the way he talked about you."

"Oh, we get along. It's no big deal."

"If he should try to turn you against me . . ."

"Scott, I'm thirty-six years old and my own mistress, and no man tells me how to run my life anymore."

"Okay. Fine. I just thought I should warn you . . ."

"All right, you've warned me. Now, let's drop it. It makes me angry to think of you and my father playing murky, messy, destructive games with each other. Thank God that'll all be over when we get married! You can hardly go on shadowboxing with each other when I'm planted firmly between you with an olive branch in one hand and a white flag in the other!"

I heard him laugh. "The referee in the ring?"

"Well, why not?" I finally stopped watching the ceiling and turned my head to look at him. "It's about time somebody tried to drill some sense into the pair of you!"

He smiled at me. "Well, don't look so fierce! I'm willing enough for a truce! It's your father who's going to be the problem!"

"You leave him to me," I said. "I'll fix him."

VIII

LATER, MUCH later, I opened my eyes to find him stooping over me as he stood fully dressed by the bed. The light was on in the little hallway which linked the sitting room with the bedroom of my suite.

"I have to go home now, Vicky. I have to shave and change before I go to the office. Call me later, after you've seen your mother, and we'll fix something for this evening."

"Mmmm . . ." I nodded, still drugged with sleep.

His lips brushed mine. I was aware of his shadow moving away, and a moment later the light clicked off in the hall.

"Good luck with your mother."

"Hm."

"I love you very much."

The door closed softly far, far away.

I slept.

IX

I DREAMED I was the child I had been long ago, the child with the custom-made dresses, the English nurse, the closets full of toys, the carefully selected playmates, the part-time bodyguard (the Lindbergh kidnapping had made a deep impression on my mother), and the miniature mink coat. I was very rich and very happy, although my nurse did her best to ensure I wasn't also very spoiled. However, she must often have thought she was fighting a losing battle.

My mother used to worry in case Nanny was too strict with me, but in fact I enjoyed my well-regulated hours in Nanny's company because they made the time spent being spoiled by my parents so much more wicked and exciting. If I'd been spoiled continuously I've no doubt I'd have been very unhappy. It was a lesson I was to remember when I had children of my own, and from the moment I knew I was pregnant I had made up my mind to employ an English nurse so that there would always be at least one person in my household who refused to indulge my children in every one of their whims. I reasoned that wealth would later give them far too many opportunities to have exactly what they wanted; the least I could do for them when they were young was to try to protect them from the undermining influence of a large income for as long as possible.

I lived in a Spanish-style mansion by the sea in Palm Beach, and my mother, a fairy godmother who flitted around in gorgeous clothes and smoked cigarettes from diamond-encrusted cigarette holders, lived with me. My mother called me "Darling," never "Vicky," and was so proud of me that I was regularly exhibited at her smart parties, where I became famous for my "cute" remarks. (It was the age of Shirley Temple.) Nanny somehow saved me from developing too inflated an idea of my own importance, but I still grew up believing that my mother had only to wave her magic wand to keep all misfortune at bay.

Then Danny arrived. My mother had met him years before in California, and one day in 1940 when Danny came to Florida on vacation he called to renew the acquaintance.

Danny was tall and slender, with sad dark eyes and excellent manners. He spoke without a foreign accent but once when he talked to his father on the phone he had spoken fluently in Italian.

"Such a pretty language!" sighed my mother, an incurable romantic. She was flushed with triumph at capturing Danny, who was ten years her junior, and soon, as he lingered on and on at Palm Beach—it was apparently unnecessary for him to work for a living—it was no longer I who was the prime exhibit at my mother's smart parties; I had to take second place to Danny.

I didn't like this at all, and neither did my father.

The custody struggle broke out afresh. I always enjoyed the custody battles. They made me feel important, and it was always so gratifying to know that my parents were constantly fighting for the privilege of my company. I never considered myself the product of a broken home; since the home had been broken even before I had entered the world, I had no memory of it, and relations between my parents were always so bad that it never occurred to me that they might one day be reconciled. All that mattered to me was that I loved my parents and that they loved me. I didn't care if they lived in separate houses. I didn't even care if they hated each other, although occasionally I did think it was a pity that the two people I loved best couldn't be good friends. However, since I had no memory of them being anything but unpleasant to each other, I accepted their antagonism as a fact of life which could never ultimately harm me, since I knew they both loved me so much.

Regarding the approaching custody battle with equanimity, I began to discuss what I should wear when I went before the judge in his rooms for the customary chat to discuss the situation.

"It's nothing to worry about, sugar," said Danny, giving me a fresh box of chocolates. "I'm going to marry your mother and bury your father in orange blossoms. He's only cutting up rough because he figures I'm a no-good wop battening on your mother's alimony, but I got money, I got prospects he doesn't know about, and the hell with the alimony, I don't care about it, it means nothing to me. And once Viv and I are married, she'll be all respectable again and your father's demand for custody will fall flat on its face, just you wait and see. Then your son of a bitch of a father can go kiss a concrete block for all the good it'll do him."

With that short concluding sentence Danny made his fatal mistake. After those ill-chosen words I ceased to see him as a generous supplier of candy whose only fault was that he claimed too much of my mother's attention, and saw him instead as my father's enemy. Only my mother was allowed to call my father a son of a bitch. That was her privilege as his ex-wife. But no one else was allowed to abuse him in front of me. Ever.

I decided that Danny would have to go. I considered it my moral duty, as a sophisticated intelligent ten-year-old, to save my poor mother from a disastrous marriage.

"Well, let me give it to you straight," I said to the judge as we chatted together in his room. "I'm real worried about this situation. I've never worried about my mother's boyfriends before, but this is different. I think he'll break her heart. I think that after they're married he'll go chasing other ladies. I think"—I summoned my most worldly smile—"I think he might even chase *me*. He's always giving me boxes of chocolates and cuddling me when Mommy's not looking."

I remember sailing out of the room and thinking serenely: That'll fix him. The judge would tell my mother that marriage with Danny was out of the question if she wanted to retain custody of me, and that would be that. On reflection I was proud of the way I had handled the situation by so skillfully embroidering the facts of life. I knew, of course, all about the famous facts of life. If you were a woman you eventually fell madly in love with the man of your dreams, went to bed with him, kissed him on the mouth in a frenzy of passion, and were immediately transported into rapturous bliss. My mother said it was as good as being in heaven. I could hardly wait to have the opportunity to sample such delights, and spent much time yearning for the onset of puberty.

"But how could you tell the judge such disgusting lies?" screamed my mother to me after the judge had delivered his verdict consigning me to my father.

Her rage took me aback. I had expected sorrow, not anger. It wiped out my triumph and left me feeling frightened.

"Danny said some disgusting things about Daddy!" I screamed back. "So why shouldn't I say some disgusting things about him?"

"But you stupid little girl, don't you realize what you've done?" My mother collapsed in a storm of weeping.

The tears reassured me. I had fully expected her to cry at the prospect of losing Danny, so I felt that everything was at last going according to plan. "Don't worry, Mommy, it'll all be all right in the end, and once Danny's gone, we'll live happily together ever after."

"Gone?" said my mother. "But he's not going! I'm not giving him up!"

And she didn't. In the end, I was the one who had to go away.

"I won't give you up!" said my mother fiercely. "I won't give up Danny and I won't give you up either. We'll go back to the judge and say there's been a mistake."

More custody hearings followed, but they were no longer amusing. I found I couldn't eat and didn't care what clothes I wore when I went to see the judge. Finally I broke down and cried in front of him. I was so ashamed.

The judge said, "The child is clearly disturbed. I'm afraid this situation can't be allowed to continue."

My mother had hysterics and lay for hours in a darkened room until I thought not only that she was dying but also that I was responsible. Finally, unable to endure my misery any longer, I burst into her room and shouted, "I want my daddy! He loves me even if you don't!"—which was a stupid thing to say, because it made my mother hysterical again, with the result that I became more terrified than ever.

"But, darling, I do love you, I do, I do, but you just don't understand, I *can't* give up Danny! The man I love . . . Oh, darling, you just don't know what it's like, you can't imagine how a woman feels when she's approaching fifty, you've no idea of the sheer horror of growing old and knowing that soon most men won't care anymore, and, oh, I can't bear it, I'm so terrified of ending up alone and unloved—"

"But *I* love you, Mommy!"

"Oh, darling, you're lovely, you're sweet, you're the most adorable little girl in the world, but . . ."

"This is all to do with those facts of life you told me about," I said. "They're all that really matters to you. You don't care about me at all. You'll be glad to send me off to Daddy, because then you'll be able to spend all your time playing facts-of-life with Danny."

"Vicky, no! Darling . . . my precious . . . oh, God, I can't bear it, I can't be torn in two like this any longer, I'll do it, I'll give him up—"

"Don't bother," I said. "Forget it. I don't care anymore. I'm going to live with my daddy, and I never want to see you again."

I got my daddy. But I also got a huge cold new home in New York and two stepbrothers I detested and a stepmother who fired my beloved nanny because she thought it was better for me to have "a fresh start" and who gave all my favorite clothes to charity because she said they were "unsuitable." My father loved me, of course, but since I had only seen him sporadically in the past, I had never realized before how hard he worked and how much time he spent away from home. In my dreams of a new life there had always been just the two of us: my father and I. In the reality of my new life there were also just the two of us: Alicia and I. Sebastian and Andrew soon went away to school, and then I was alone day in and day out with my stepmother in that echoing mansion on Fifth Avenue.

The puberty for which I had longed during my precocious sun-drenched early years finally arrived on a dark morning when the snow was falling. I did not want it. Alicia gave me conscientious lectures about sanitary napkins and the way I could expect boys to behave now that I was growing up. I was revolted. She also told me the real facts of life, not the romantic misconceptions I had acquired from my mother. I was appalled. I thought: So it was all worse, much, much worse than I believed it to be. My mother wanted to give me up in order to do *that*. It wasn't just kissing and cuddling. It was *that*. Unbelievable. Disgusting. Obscene.

Yet I knew all the time that my mother hadn't wanted to give me up. I knew she had loved me. And I knew the whole mess was my fault. I had told lies to the judge, and now, not only was I being punished, but my mother was being punished as well. Sometimes I thought I would die of the guilt. Sometimes I thought I could hardly bear to live with the shame.

But then my daddy came to my rescue, wonderful Daddy, always so good with children, so kind and patient and concerned, and of course *he* soon realized something was wrong; *he* knew I was unhappy.

"Tell me all about it, sweetheart," he said, and I did. I poured out the whole story to him and he nodded and listened and held me close.

Then he made it all come right. He said, "Sweetheart, it's all wrong that you should blame yourself for what happened. This was your mother's fault from beginning to end. If she hadn't been messing around with a gangster like Danny Diaconi, you'd never have been forced to act as you did. Your mother's a wicked, unprincipled, immoral woman and she's not fit to bring up an innocent little girl like you." And he went on telling me how immoral my mother was, sleeping with man after man, and all the while my father was talking, I felt so much better because I began to feel I wasn't to blame after all for the events which had brought me to New York. I began to believe that my mother really had been setting me a terrible example and that my father had been completely justified to press for my custody long after I had recanted and begged the judge to be allowed to stay with my mother.

It all seemed so clear to me then. If I hated my mother, I wouldn't have to feel guilty for what I'd done, and if I believed her to be wicked, then I could never resent my beloved daddy for dividing me from her.

"I never want to grow up like her!" I sobbed. "Never!"

"Of course you won't grow up like her, sweetheart," said my father. "You'll be a good girl always, and when you fall in love you'll get married and be the perfect wife and mother and live happily ever after. That's what you want, isn't it? You're a good girl and you want to make me proud of you."

And of course he was right. That was exactly what I wanted, for I loved my daddy, my wonderful daddy who had ridden up on his white horse to save me when I had been in despair, and all through the years that followed I did everything I could to show him how much he was loved. For if I hadn't loved him so much, I might have started loving my mother again, and once I started loving my mother again, I mightn't have been able to go on believing she was as evil as I'd been told she was, and once I admitted those kinds of doubts to myself, I might even start to wonder whether it had been *my mother* who had been so wicked and unprincipled all those years ago, but of course those terrible dilemmas could never arise because I would never give them life by acknowledging that they could exist. So long as I went on loving my father and hating my mother, I'd be safe, and that was why any variation in my attitude toward my parents had become literally unthinkable . . . unthinkable . . . unthinkable . . .

X

"Unthinkable!" I shouted, and woke with a gasp to find myself in my suite at the Savoy.

It was only five o'clock in New York, but in England the morning was already well advanced and I had to get up. I knew I could eat no breakfast, so I only ordered coffee. Afterward, when I was dressed, I phoned the London Clinic and was told I could visit Mrs. Diaconi at any time, since she was so much better.

I went on sitting on the edge of my bed. I felt sluggish, full of a vague dread which made me want to shut myself up in the suite for the remainder of the day. Presently I realized with surprise that I was thinking of Danny. He had been killed in a shooting incident at one of his father's Las Vegas casinos. I supposed my mother had been very upset. They had been married for five years, but of course I had

known nothing of their marriage, because my father had always refused to let me visit them.

I left the hotel abruptly and took a cab to the clinic.

London slipped past me beyond the window. I had a fleeting impression of gray skies, gray buildings, gray people, and gray pigeons.
The red buses made a welcome splash of color in that forbidding
landscape, but the city still seemed chillingly alien, reminding me of
the last unhappy years with Sam. I wondered how Scott could have
tolerated his years of exile, but then I found I could no longer think
of him. All I could think about now was my mother.

"Can you stop at a flower shop, please?"

Thank God I had remembered flowers. One always took flowers to
hospitals. I could remember everyone bringing armfuls of flowers to
me in the hospital after Sam's death, everyone except Sebastian, who
had brought me a book of poetry.

We reached the London Clinic. I was feeling very sick by this
time, so I just thrust a five-pound note at the cabdriver and ran inside without waiting for change. At the reception desk I was directed
to the appropriate floor, but I had to force myself to follow the directions.

"Oh, Mrs. Diaconi will be *so* pleased to see you. . . . All the way
from New York? Oh, she *will* be thrilled! Not a very nice day, is it?
But they say the sun's going to shine later. . . ."

The nurse's English platitudes washed over me, but I barely heard
them. We were walking down a long corridor, and seconds later she
was opening the door at the far end.

"Good morning, Mrs. Diaconi! Now, here's a *lovely* surprise for
you!"

The room was light and airy, freshly decorated, spotlessly clean.
Scott's secretary had organized the appropriate flowers, chocolates,
and magazines, and making an immense effort, I managed to look
past these trappings of illness to the occupant of the bed.

I had not seen her since 1959 when she had paid her last visit to
New York and Sebastian had helped me to cope with her. I remembered a woman with dyed black hair, a mask of makeup, and a
nauseating range of false small talk and affected mannerisms. Her
parody of various Hollywood sex symbols had become more repulsive with her increasing years, and by that time had made her gro-
tesque. Just to look at her had revolted me.

Fully prepared to feel revolted again, I faced her, but nothing hap-

632

pened. For I was no longer the same woman I had been eight years ago in New York—and neither was she.

An old woman with dull gray hair, a creased face, and a soft shapeless body was lying propped up in bed against the pillows. Only her eyes were unchanged, the blue eyes which I had always refused to admit had been inherited by Benjamin. She looked at me, and those eyes softened with love.

"Oh, Vicky," she said, "how very, very good of you to come."

And suddenly all I could hear was my father's voice echoing down the years, and I remembered with terrible clarity that scene at Kennedy airport after Scott had left for Europe. I remembered my father's confessions about his desolate private life. I remembered saying to him: "That's why you stopped at nothing to take Scott away from Steve," and instantly, before I could blot the thought from my mind I heard myself add the words which had never been spoken; I heard myself say: "And that's why you stopped at nothing to take me away from my mother."

I saw then exactly what he had done.

He knew I had loved my mother. He had been afraid I might want to go back to her when I had become so unhappy at his unhappy home on Fifth Avenue, so he had distorted the truth, bent it and rent it with his lies, so that I would wind up hating my mother and loving him more than ever.

I went on looking at the mother who loved me and had gone on loving me through all the years of my neglect, and at last—at long, long last—I was able to see her as she really was: no monster, no obscene personification of unmentionable vices, but just a foolish woman who had made mistakes and paid for them, just another mother not as good as some but better than others, just one more of my father's many victims.

XI

MY FATHER was at the airport when I returned to New York four days later after a long weekend spent with Scott. I had cabled my father and told him to be there. Later he had tried calling the top London hotels to locate me, but I had refused to accept his call when it reached the Savoy.

Walking out of the customs hall I saw him looking frail and anxious behind the barrier. As usual he had three or four satellites in orbit around him, but I took no notice. I just walked up to him and said, "I want to talk to you."

"Vicky, what were you doing in London? What happened? What's the trouble?"

I walked past him without replying, and he hurried after me frantically. Outside the building, his latest Cadillac, an unpleasant piece of engineering in pale cream, was waiting at the curb.

"Vicky . . ." He was gasping for breath. He stumbled as he crawled into the backseat beside me, and when I turned to look at him I saw his hands were trembling as he opened his pillbox. "You must tell me . . . please . . ."

I tested the partition that separated us from the chauffeur and bodyguard, but it was tightly closed and I knew that any conversation we had would be inaudible to anyone in the front seat. My father always soundproofed his Cadillacs, as he often spent the journeys to and from the bank in confidential discussions with his aides.

"My mother's been ill," I said shortly. "I had to go to London to make arrangements for her convalescence. I saw Scott too, but we'll get to him later. Right now I want to talk to you about my mother. I'm bringing her back to New York to live. She's going to have an apartment at the Pierre and you're going to pay for it."

"Me?" said my father, wheezing and gasping. He was ashen. "I don't understand."

"Oh yes, you do! You took me away from my mother and poisoned my mind against her!"

"Oh, but . . . Vicky, surely you realize how things were? Your mother just didn't deserve to have a wonderful little girl like you."

"You're the one who didn't deserve me! I loved my mother and she loved me, but you wiped her out of my life—Christ, it was as if you murdered her!"

"But I had to take action for your sake. All those men . . . the immorality . . ."

"Oh, don't hand me all that crap anymore! My mother was a sexy woman without too much brain who got herself in a mess. Yes, of course she had affairs after she divorced you—she wasn't a nun! But she always hoped to remarry, and after years of waiting to make sure she didn't make the same mistake she made when she married you, she found someone she felt could make her happy, and that someone was Danny Diaconi. Okay, so maybe he was a gangster. But maybe he wasn't; the Diaconi hotel chain was legitimate. Maybe it was just easy to think of him as a gangster because he was Italian and his father had had shady connections, but what does a word like 'gangster' mean anyway? When I look at you, I think maybe you're more of a gangster than Danny Diaconi ever was!"

"But Vicky, you hated Danny!"

"I was jealous of him. I was a mixed-up little girl, a fact which you capitalized on and exploited to separate me from my mother and keep me all to yourself!"

"But I honestly believed it was in your best interests!"

"How could you? How could it have been best for me to have been subjected to such brainwashing? I used to feel ill whenever my mother's name was mentioned! You've caused immense suffering not only to my mother but to me as well!"

"Well, I . . . Look, I . . . Vicky, don't be angry, please forgive me, I just couldn't bear it if . . . Listen, just give me one chance to make amends. The Pierre, you say? Okay, I'll get the best apartment they have."

"You bet you will, and that's just the beginning. Now, you listen to me. I never want to hear you say another word about my mother for as long as you live. You're to treat her with decency and respect; you're to treat her like a human being. Got it? Okay, then get this, too: if you ever do such a wicked thing again, we'll be through. And I mean that. You can't be allowed to think you can get away with smashing up people's lives time after time in order to further your own selfish sordid ends. You're my father, and despite all I've just said, I still love you—probably I'll always love you, no matter what you do—but there comes a time when one has to take a stand, even against those you love, and that time has come, Father, this is it, this is where I draw the line. You're on the brink. Stay there or retreat, and I see no reason why we shouldn't continue our peaceful coexistence. But you take one step beyond that line, and I'll wash my hands of you for good. I've forgiven you for what you've done to Scott. I've forgiven you—just—for what you've done to me. But I can't go on forgiving you like this, Father. I'm no saint, I'm your daughter, and this is the very last chance I'm giving you to change your ways."

I stopped. There was a long silence.

"Well, Father?"

"Okay."

"Got it?"

"Got it."

We looked at each other. He was sweating lightly, and there was a sick expression in his eyes.

"Are you in pain from the asthma?"

"Hm."

"Does this repulsive car have a bar? I'll get you some brandy."

But there was no bar and no brandy. I looked at him again and saw he had put his right hand on the seat midway between us. I eyed that hand for a while, then picked it up and held it. His fingers curled gratefully, lovingly in mine.

We said nothing else for the remainder of the journey, but when we reached my apartment building I invited him in—not to the duplex, but to my private apartment where we could be alone.

"You want to say something else to me?" whispered my father, frightened as he followed me across the threshold.

"Yes," I said, heading for the liquor cabinet and pouring him a double brandy. "I want to talk to you about Scott."

Chapter Four

I

"SCOTT AND I are getting married," I said. "We're having a very quiet wedding next month in London."

I had half-thought my father might collapse, but of course he didn't. Neither did he panic, lose his temper, drain the brandy in a single gulp, or exhibit any other sign of weakness. On the contrary, he showed all the signs of pulling himself together with remarkable rapidity. My disclosures about my mother had been the real shock; my announcement about Scott was something he must have feared in 1963, and as I watched him take a small sip from his glass to play for time, I wondered if he was trying to remember his part of a dialogue he had mentally rehearsed long ago.

"Well, what a surprise!" he said. "I always thought Scott was so set against marriage. How pleasant that I've been proved wrong!"

I regarded him with extreme suspicion and said nothing. My father made a new effort. "Do you have an engagement ring?" he inquired guilelessly.

I drew off my glove and showed him the diamonds.

"Very nice!" said my father. "Congratulations—you must be very pleased and excited. . . . A bit sudden, wasn't it? Or have you been secretly in touch for some time?"

I explained the sequence of events.

We were sitting on the long white couch, he at one end, I at the other, with a considerable space between us. By the window my latest two pink fish, tended by Benjamin in my absence, were swimming dreamily in their aquarium. The room was cool and shadowed.

"Father, I know exactly what you're thinking, but—"

"Vicky, please don't call me Father. It's so cold. If you don't want to call me Daddy anymore, you can call me Cornelius."

"Certainly not! I disapprove strongly of children calling their parents by their first names! Oh, Daddy, please try to be rational about this."

"Am I hysterical? Am I gibbering unintelligible protests? Haven't I just offered you my sincere congratulations?"

I had the terrible suspicion I was being outclassed and outmaneuvered. "Were they sincere?" was all I could say.

"Of course. Any woman who can get Scott Sullivan to consider a trip to the altar has earned the most sincere congratulations I can offer."

"You think he's manipulating me, don't you?" I burst out. "You think he's got all kinds of ulterior motives!"

"I just think he's wrong for you," said my father simply, "but so what? It's none of my business. It's your life." He stood up.

I was caught off-balance. "You're going?"

"I've got to get to the office. Important meetings. But let me take you out to dinner tonight to reassure you I've no intention of being unpleasant or making any attempt to stand in your way."

"Oh," I said, floundering in my surprise. "Well, thank you . . . but perhaps not tonight. I'll be too tired—jet lag—how about lunch tomorrow?"

"Sure." He looked around my quiet room as if admiring its peace and privacy. "Could we eat here? I get so tired of eating lunch at expensive restaurants—although of course if you want a smart lunch, I'd be only too happy to—"

"No, I've just had a string of smart lunches in London. I like your idea of an informal meal. What do you want to eat? I'll get a takeout order from Hamburger Heaven."

My father considered this carefully. "One hamburger medium-well, with everything except onion rings. French fries and a large Coke." His face brightened. "What a treat that'll be!"

I found myself smiling at him as I rose to my feet. "I must go upstairs and see if the children are home from school."

Outside in the hallway we paused together by the elevator shaft.

"All I want's your happiness, Vicky, believe me."

"Don't scare me, Daddy. You were doing so nicely before."

We embraced with a laugh, and although I tried to maintain my skepticism, I couldn't help thinking with huge relief: It's all going to work out, everything's going to come right, I'm going to win in the end.

II

"A DOUBLE order of French fries!" said my father happily. He dipped one in his plastic container of ketchup. "Delicious! Thank you, sweetheart."

"My pleasure. And now perhaps you'll tell me the real reason why you wanted this very private lunch."

My father's face altered subtly, emptying itself of expression so that the fine bone structure of his face stood more clearly revealed. His slim figure and extreme good looks made him look uncannily young once he had his back to the light, and his hair, still copious though now a pale indeterminate color, heightened this illusion of youth. His eyes were a peculiarly clear, starry gray.

"I wanted to discuss your good news a little further, Vicky."

"I thought so."

"Unfortunately I can't pretend it's going to be an easy discussion."

"That doesn't surprise me in the least."

"I hope we can discuss the subject sensibly, without getting upset."

"I hope so too."

We stared at each other politely for a moment. Then my father started fussing with his hamburger, rearranging a lettuce leaf, toying with a tomato slice, examining the pickle. "I meant what I said yesterday," he said. "You go ahead and marry him. I'm not going to make a fuss, and afterward I'll do my very best to welcome him into the family as my son-in-law."

"Great. Thanks."

"However, I would just like to make one small suggestion. Of course you're under no obligation to listen to it."

"Of course."

My father sighed, took a bite of hamburger, munched it, swallowed it, and filled his glass of Coke. I had had two French fries and had just realized I couldn't eat another mouthful. Abandoning the Coke, I went to the liquor cabinet to fix myself a martini.

"I want to appeal to your maturity and common sense," said my father.

"How attractive that sounds. I hope my maturity and common sense can rise to the challenge."

"I hope so too. Vicky, don't rush into this marriage. Go to England next month and spend the summer with him, but live there as his mistress, not his wife."

I said nothing.

"You didn't mention it yesterday, but I presume you were intending to spend the summer with him while the children are up at Bar Harbor as usual."

"Yes. I thought he should have the chance to adjust to a wife before he returns to New York and has to adjust to five stepchildren."

"Fine. Yes, that was what I figured. But why not marry in the new year after he's returned to New York for good? Look, Vicky, let's just forget for a moment that this man's Scott. The fact that he's Scott only confuses the issue. I'd give you this same advice no matter who you planned to marry. You've got two marriages behind you now, and neither was an unqualified success. Or, to put it bluntly, you've lived with two men, and each time the relationship ended up in ruins. You can't afford a third mistake right now. It would be bad for you and for the children. If you do marry again, you've got to be sure it'll work, and that's why I think you'd be a fool not to have a trial marriage before you risk everything on a third trip to the altar."

I sipped my martini and sat looking at my untouched hamburger. Presently my father started talking again.

"I've no intention of making any pertinent observations, about Scott's potential ability—or inability—to adapt to married life, but I'll just say this: as far as I know, Scott's never made a success of living with anyone. Don't you think it would be only fair to him to live with him first before you wrap him up legally in a relationship which—although he may have the best will in the world—he may find himself unable to handle? It seems to me not only the sensible, prudent thing to do; it also seems to me to be the kindest and most considerate."

He paused again, but I was still unable to reply. I revolved the stem of my martini glass round and round between my thumb and forefinger.

"Live with him this summer in London," said my father. "Spend the fall in New York preparing for the wedding. Then marry him in the new year—"

"—after you've fired him."

My father grimaced. "Don't be stupid, Vicky. I'm not going to do anything which could possibly alienate you. Now, pull yourself together. The situation's awkward enough without you trying to cast me as the villain of the piece."

"Can you promise me you won't fire him once he's my husband?"

"Well, naturally! Do you think I don't care whether or not we remain on speaking terms?"

"I want to hear you promise."

"All right. I promise I won't fire him once he's your husband. As you know, I can't fire him before 1968 unless he's been proved guilty of some gross professional misconduct, and even then I have to have the consent of all the partners. So marry him before January the first if you're so nervous of me."

"Don't worry, I've every intention of marrying him before then. And what of the future? Are you retiring next year? And if you are, what happens?"

"I was afraid you'd ask me that," said my father. He rearranged the lettuce leaf again on his plate. "And now, Vicky, I'm afraid we must come to the most difficult part of this interview, the part where I have to give you the news you don't want to hear. The truth is that whether you marry Scott or not, I've made up my mind that he's never, under any circumstances, going to obtain control of the bank."

III

THERE WAS a dead silence. Then I felt so frightened that I drank the rest of my martini and rose to my feet to mix myself another.

"Now, don't panic," said my father. "This isn't the catastrophe you think it is. You can't see Scott clearly anymore because you're in love with him, but I see him very clearly indeed, and I've got everything figured out—yes, put down that martini. You won't need it, and even if you did need it, you shouldn't have it. The first thing you should always remember when you're in the middle of a difficult interview is to leave the liquor alone."

"Shut up." But I left the martini alone and sat down again opposite him at the table.

My father poured me some Coke. Then he said, "I'm going to stay on until I can hand the reins directly to Eric. My asthma's no better, but it's certainly no worse. I reckon I can make it. I've got to make it. No choice. I wouldn't trust any of my other partners to help me out. If Scott has to stay in the firm, he'd turn them inside out in no time flat once I was out of the way."

"Daddy—"

"No, let me finish. I'll be good to Scott. And I'll be kind to him. I won't tell him outright that he's not going to get what he wants. I'll let him realize the truth painlessly over a period of years. I'll keep postponing and postponing my retirement; I'll keep refusing to commit myself to any definite plan for the future. I'll let him down easy, I promise, and he'll adjust and survive, I know he will. Scott's one hell of a lot tougher than you think."

"No," I said. "He's more vulnerable than you could ever imagine."

"In some ways, perhaps—in certain areas of his private life. But in his business life he's damned close to being impregnable, and that's why if I keep him in the firm—and I will, if that's what you want— I've got to take certain precautions. For example, I couldn't have him here in New York. I won't send him back to Europe, because I'm sure you'd both regard that as exile, but I thought I might have him open an office in California. How do you like the idea of a few years in San Francisco? It's only a few hours away by plane, and you'd still be in America, still be home in your own country. How pleased Sylvia would be if you moved to San Francisco! She's over eighty now, but still very active—"

"Daddy, please . . . please . . ."

"I'm sorry. I knew this would upset you, but it's a question of options. I won't fire Scott. But if I keep him in the firm, it has to be on my terms. If he can't accept them, then of course he's free to go to another house."

"He's not free. He's never been free. He's locked up in the past and you're refusing to produce the key that would let him out!"

"I'm afraid I don't see the situation as dramatically as that," said my father politely. "I suspect the truth is much more prosaic. Scott had this very understandable ambition to get the bank. He's not going to get it, but he's had a first-class career as a banker and he's certainly proved to everyone he's a far better man than his father ever was—and that, if you want my opinion, is the crux of the matter. So long as he's proved that—and he has—I think he'll find in the end that life isn't such a disappointment. Particularly if he has you to keep him happy. In fact, you'll play a very important role in his readjustment. You'll fill the void and give him something new to live for. He'll be all right. It'll all end happily, you wait and see."

"But I can't think why you're so set against trusting him! Surely after Scott and I are married you can trust him to do nothing that would hurt me?"

"Why should I? Husbands hurt their wives regularly. Scott's father nearly annihilated my sister. Scott himself may be capable of annihilating you. I can't give him control of the bank just because he'll have had the remarkable foresight to marry you and save himself from being fired."

I jumped to my feet. "You bastard!" I shouted at him. "How dare you imply that! How dare you twist everything and distort everything and *pollute* everything—"

"Not this time, Vicky. This river's already polluted. All I'm doing is analyzing the muddy waters. Thank you for the lunch. I'm sorry this should have been such a difficult conversation, and please don't make me regret that I paid you the compliment of speaking plainly. I hope you'll still consider my earlier advice, even if you choose to ignore my last comments."

He moved into the hall and opened the front door before glancing back. "So long, Vicky. Call me later when you've had a chance to think over what I've said."

The front door closed gently in my face.

I stood there listening to his quiet footsteps receding down the corridor, and then, rubbing my eyes as if to erase a vision I found intolerable, I picked up the phone to call Scott.

IV

"Hi!" SAID Scott. "Coincidence—I was just about to call you!"

"You were?"

"Yes, it looks as if I'll be in New York the week after next. Something came up today, and I'll have to have a conference with Cornelius."

"Wonderful!" I tried to think clearly. "That's great news!"

"How are you feeling?"

"Well, now that you mention it, I feel as if I've been beaten over the head. Is it my imagination or does jet lag really get worse as one gets older?"

"For one bad moment I thought you meant you'd been engaged in hand-to-hand combat with your father! How did he take our news?"

"Not badly. In fact, very well. That's why I was calling, but now I know you're coming over, I'll save the full details for when we meet. But you needn't worry, darling. He accepts the idea of the marriage and he's demonstrated that he has no intention of making himself unpleasant."

"Pragmatic as ever! My God, Cornelius is a smart guy!"

There was a pause.

"Vicky? Are you still there?"

"Yes," I said. "Oh, yes, I'm here. Darling, I won't keep you from your work. I'll talk to you again soon."

He told me he loved me and hung up.

I went on sitting by the silent phone.

V

"DADDY, I'M sorry to call you at the office, but I thought you'd want to know that I've decided to take your advice about the trial marriage and postpone the wedding until my birthday on Christmas Eve. After eloping to Maryland with Sam and Reno with Sebastian, I decided it was about time I had a normal family wedding in New York —no circus, nothing grand, just a low-key family occasion with all the children present."

All my father said was, "I'm glad. I'm sure you're doing the right thing. Thank you, Vicky. . . . Have you told Scott?"

"I'm waiting till he comes to New York."

"I hope he doesn't get angry and accuse me of manipulating you."

"Don't be silly, Daddy, Scott knows I have a mind of my own."

VI

Two weeks later I was with Scott at the Carlyle. It was early evening. His plane had arrived on time, and after meeting him at the airport I had driven to the hotel in my car, not the station wagon I used for ferrying the children around, but the little British sports car which I so seldom had the chance to use. Scott, a nervous passenger, had emerged wan but unscathed at the journey's end.

"Do you want to rest for a while?" I asked anxiously, but he made a rapid recovery and invited me up to his suite.

Later, much later, he stretched himself luxuriously beside me on the bed and exclaimed with a new burst of energy, "Let's go out and have a celebration drink!"

"Okay." I was propped up on one elbow as I dreamily smoked a cigarette and watched the light glint on the silver in his sideburns. As he put his hands behind his head, I feasted my eyes on the lines of his shoulders and ribs, and reaching forward, I trailed my index finger lightly from his mouth to his navel and from his navel to the taut muscles of his thighs.

"Where would you like to go to celebrate?" I said.

"Let's take a few more minutes to think about that," he said, smiling at me with hot sleepy black eyes, and drew me back to him for another kiss.

I noticed the thickness of the hair at the nape of his neck as I caught it between my fingers, and I was again aware of the roughness of his cheek, which betrayed how much time had elapsed since his morning shave in London. His sideburns, seen at close range, weren't slim and trim but shaggy and thick, the hairs a complex mixture of black and silver. His teeth, unstained by nicotine, were very white; I always forgot unless I looked closely at his mouth that they weren't quite even, the eyeteeth being a fraction out of alignment. His mouth, sensual when relaxed, was normally hard and obstinate, his full lower lip held in check by the thin upper lip's unyielding pressure. Fine lines marked the corners of his eyes and hinted at past suffering harshly suppressed. It was a strong face but not a happy one.

He started to make love. His intense concentration should have seemed unpleasantly self-absorbed, but I always found it hypnotically exciting, although I was unsure why I should have been so consistently mesmerized. Part of his success could probably be attributed to his looks, but not all; it's an unfortunate fact of life that strikingly attractive men aren't necessarily mesmerizing in bed. Perhaps the truth lay closer to the fact that I wanted to be mesmerized and knew Scott could achieve this triumph of making me relax completely. With him I knew there would be no awkwardness which might reduce the scene to an embarrassing mess, and so his smooth, accomplished, apparently indestructible competence, which might well have chilled many women, was exactly what I needed to help me overcome my terror of making a false move and blighting the encounter by my inadequacy. I put my trust in this machinelike control time after time and was never disappointed, yet in the final analysis it wasn't this mercifully impersonal competence which I found so erotic; it was the powerful release of all his pent-up emotions, the opening of that closed, unreadable, infinitely mysterious mind.

"Come on, Mr. Mystery Man," I said. "Let's go out and have that drink."

"Why am I so mysterious?"

"You're so different. If we were characters in a science-fiction movie, you'd be the alien in human guise."

"If we were characters in a science-fiction movie, I strongly suspect I'd be the only human and everyone else would be aliens disguised as robots!"

We laughed, dressed, and made our way leisurely downstairs.

"I'm beginning to feel like a tourist in this city," said Scott, hailing a cab outside the hotel, "so let's pretend to be tourists at Beekman Tower and watch the sun set behind the Manhattan skyline."

"Lovely, but we don't need a cab, do we? What's wrong with my sports car?"

"Please! I don't want to start the evening drinking brandy to revive me!" he said, and we laughed and tumbled into the cab and spent the journey crosstown kissing in the backseat like a couple of teenagers while the driver watched us in the mirror with a jaundiced eye.

High above First Avenue in the cocktail lounge at the top of the Beekman Tower, we found a table by one of the windows which faced west to the shining towers of Manhattan, already silhouetted against an impossibly crimson sky.

"The lady'll have a martini, straight up, with an olive," said Scott to the waiter, "and I'll have . . ." He paused as his mind roamed among the vast choices available. Then: "Give me vodka," he said, "on the rocks with a lemon twist. And make that a double." He saw me looking at him and added with a smile, "I've got to have something to wake me up! It's almost midnight by European time, and I've had a busy day."

"I don't know how you're in such good shape. That westward flight across the Atlantic's a real killer." I was about to say something else when I glimpsed a dark young man sitting at a table nearby. He was with a glamorous brunette who in the old days would have worked in Hollywood but who was now more likely to be earning a living in a New York recording studio. "Good heavens!" I exclaimed, surprised. "There's Donald Shine."

Scott swiveled in his chair, but the young man didn't see us. He was too busy listening to his companion.

"You never told me you knew Donald Shine!"

"Didn't I? I met him at a party Jake gave about two years ago. It was just after Shine had taken over that data-processing company."

Scott smiled wryly. "He's come a long way since then."

This was undeniable. Donald Shine had just taken over Stamford-Hartford Reliance, one of the biggest and oldest insurance corporations in the country, and had afterward announced that his company was in future to be known as Shine & General, a conglomerate specializing in financial services. Wall Street was now watching him with the fearful fascination of a bunch of elderly rabbits cornered by a hungry young cobra.

"Your father nearly had apoplexy when Stam-Hart Reliance fell to Shine," said Scott as the waiter arrived with our drinks. "I had him on the phone for a full hour talking about the horrors of a kid from Brooklyn giving orders to middle-aged, white Anglo-Saxon Protestant, Ivy League elder statesmen. The incident gave him a magnificent opportunity to sound off on all the evils afflicting the country, and you know what your father's like when he gets going on draft dodgers, black anarchists, and teenage drug addicts. . . . Incidentally, since we're talking of your father, tell me how he reacted to the news of our engagement. I was relieved he'd decided not to be openly hostile."

"Yes. . . . You may find this hard to believe, but he even came up with some sensible advice. At least I thought it was sensible. I hope you will too."

"Did he ask you to postpone the wedding?"

I was startled. "Yes, he did."

"My God, don't tell me you gave in to him!"

"I wouldn't put it that way," I said. I could feel my face becoming hot. "There are several advantages to marrying at Christmas. I thought—"

"In other words, to cut a long story short, Cornelius has manipulated you into postponing your commitment to me." He knocked back his drink and flagged down the nearest waiter. "Another double vodka."

"That's untrue and unfair." I felt very upset. "Quite apart from the fact that I'd like a quiet family wedding in New York when you're finally through with Europe, I think we owe it to ourselves to try a real affair instead of these unreal jet-set interludes! I want to marry you more than anything else in the world, but I don't want you turning around later and accusing me of pressuring you into marriage while we were still strangers!"

"Strangers!"

"Yes, strangers! We've had one week in New York in 1963. We've had one long weekend in London earlier this year, and now we'll have a few more days in New York. Well, that's wonderful, that's exciting, that's glamorous, but it's so far removed from normal married life that it could be a mating practice on another planet! My father wants us to live together in London this summer and try to create a relationship which bears more of a resemblance to marriage. A trial marriage can never be exactly the same as a real marriage, but at least afterward we may have more idea than we have now about what our marriage is going to be like. I'm sorry, but I think my father's right. It's got nothing to do with manipulation. It's my own independent decision."

"Your father's playing for time. He's betting on you tiring of me and breaking the engagement—or maybe just postponing it into the new year when he'll have a chance to fire me—"

"Oh, I get so tired of this paranoid suspicion you two men display toward each other! Scott, you can relax. Daddy's given me his word he'll never fire you, and I believe him. He'd never do anything that would permanently alienate me."

"Where the bank's concerned," said Scott, "there's nothing Cornelius wouldn't do. Okay, what else did he promise you?"

I looked blank. "What do you mean?"

"You know what I mean! If Cornelius promised he'd never fire me, that means you must have discussed my future at Van Zale's. When's he going to retire and name me as his successor?"

"I . . . I didn't like to ask him about that."

"Ah, come on, Vicky! Don't hand me that kind of crap! You asked and he told you!"

"No, for me it was enough to know he had no intention of firing you."

"You don't really think I'm going to believe that, do you? Why are you lying to me like this? Whose side are you on here, for Christ's sake?"

The waiter arrived with another double vodka.

"Scott," I said, "if you're going to lose your temper and talk to me like this, you'll only succeed in strengthening my conviction that we should have a trial marriage. And please—is it necessary to drink so fast and so heavily? You've always told me that kind of drinking never suited you."

He picked up his glass and again drank all the vodka straight off. I stood up. "I'd like to go now, please."

He said nothing. He was looking down at his empty glass with a surprised, shocked expression, as if he had found himself in an unpleasant position but had no memory of how he had arrived there. Then he set down the glass carefully, rested his hands on the table as if to steady himself, and said with a humility that moved me because it was so obviously genuine: "I'm sorry. Forgive me. That was a very stupid thing to do."

I sat down, but during the silence which followed, I was aware that my movements had attracted the attention of Donald Shine. I did not look directly at him, but out of the corner of my eye I could see him turning to stare at our table.

"I can think of only one reason why you should be so reluctant to tell me what your father said," Scott was saying evenly. "He must have decided to cut me out. He won't fire me—he'll keep me in the firm in order to maintain good relations with you, but he'll see I'm railroaded to some place where I can't bother him. Where did he suggest? Europe again? No, he'd never be content to see you disappear for a second time into Europe—always assuming, of course, that his luck deserts him and he fails to stop our marriage. Boston? No, too near. He'd never be able to sleep at night if he knew I was only an hour away on the LaGuardia shuttle. How about California?

Banking's booming on the West Coast, and he knows you've always admired San Francisco—"

"Well, look who's here!"

We both jumped as the long shadow fell across our table.

It was Donald Shine.

"Scott Sullivan! Hey, how are you doing? Great to see you! Are you still battling the British, or are you back in town for keeps?" He turned to me with his broadest smile, his extraordinary exuberance wrapping itself around me as if he could strong-arm me into liking him. "Hi, beautiful. I forget your name, but I remember you—once seen, never forgotten! You're Cornelius Van Zale's daughter."

"Vicky Foxworth. Hello, Mr. Shine."

"Congratulations, Don!" said Scott, smiling at him.

"For what? Oh, that old insurance racket up in Connecticut! Yeah, they're still picking up the shit I knocked out of them, but hell, that's all past history now, and who's interested in the past? This is the Now generation! Hey, Scott, are you in the city for long? Let me buy you lunch tomorrow!" He turned to me, his long hair flopping engagingly over his ears as he gave me another of his broadest smiles. "You may not know this," he said, "but I've got a soft spot for this guy here. He was the one who gave me my first big break when I was just a kid in jeans and sneakers." Laughing at the memory, he swung back to Scott. "How about it, pal? Twelve-thirty tomorrow at Twenty-One—come on, say yes!"

Scott looked up at him for a long moment. I saw his fingers tighten around his empty glass of vodka. Then suddenly he laughed too and said carelessly, "Sure, why not? Thanks."

"Great! Seeya!" He paused long enough to wink at me. "'Bye, beautiful."

He was gone, and suddenly, miraculously, so was our tension. We looked at each other and tried to stifle our mirth.

"Isn't he awful!" I whispered.

"Don't be such a snob! Personally I've always liked Donald Shine. I admire anyone who can go after what he wants with such single-mindedness!"

"Yes, he goes after what he wants, all right—with the restraint of a pack of wolves and the delicacy of a tank on maneuvers! Maybe I'm getting conservative in my old age, but for once I agree with Daddy— I don't like Donald Shine converting Wall Street into a hip playground for the Now generation. . . . Oh, God, why did I have to mention Daddy again? Scott—"

"Relax. You're right, and I was being paranoid. If you yourself independently believe we should wait awhile before marrying, that's okay by me."

"Are you sure? You really mean that? Oh, Scott, you mustn't worry about anything—I'm sure it's all going to work out in the end."

"Of course," he said soothingly. "Of course." His hand closed over mine and held it tightly. "I'm sorry I behaved so stupidly just now. I guess I must be more tired than I realized."

"Let's go back to the hotel."

Halfway across town, as our cab paused at some lights, he said idly to me, "Was I right?"

"About what?"

"California."

There was a long silence. Finally, seeing no reason not to admit the truth when we had both agreed that I could ultimately persuade my father to change his mind, I said, "Yes, San Francisco."

Scott's arm tightened reassuringly around my shoulders. "I'll bet he still doesn't believe we'll ever get married! I'm going to get a great kick out of proving him wrong!"

"Scott, I'll marry you tomorrow if that's what you really want. You've only got to say the word, you know that."

"No, let's call his bluff and wait till December. Let him realize this is one game of chess he's not going to win."

"Darling, you do believe, don't you, that I'll be able to straighten everything out with my father in the end? Promise me you believe it!"

"When you look at me like that, I'll believe anything!" he said with a good humor which made me feel faint with happiness and relief, and the next moment he was kissing me very silkily on the mouth.

Chapter Five

I

"Dear Vicky: My mother tells me you'll be visiting London soon. Any chance of you stopping by in Cambridge while you're in England? It's less than a couple of hours from London by train, so you could make it a day trip. I'll show you around and buy you lunch. I promise not to commit indecent exposure, rape, or any other social faux pas. We can talk about Eliot, Elvis, and Eternity. Love, Sebastian. P.S. It's okay, I know you'll be staying with Scott."

II

"Vicky darling, Neil has just told me during the course of a hopelessly extravagant transatlantic phone call (God, how these bankers simply *squander* money!) that you're going to be in London this summer, and I thought I'd write at once to issue you an invitation to dinner to celebrate your engagement. Be sure to give me a call as soon as you arrive so that we can fix a date.

"Well, I've been in London over a year now, and I can't tell you what a wonderful change it is from that junk heap at the mouth of the Hudson. At the risk of sounding like one of those dreary old bores one always yearns to avoid at parties, I must say I think New York's not what it used to be—'Gone to the dogs, m'dear!' as the Anglo-Indian colonels always say in the Agatha Christie novels—and that reminds me, if you bring me over a bottle of Wild Turkey bourbon I'll give you a treat and take you to see *The Mousetrap,* which is something of a theatrical institution here.

"Anyway, I'm so enrapt with this magnificently *civilized* city (believe it or not, they don't know what the word 'mugging' means) that I'm thinking of selling my house in Greenwich Village, but the trouble is, I don't think I could bear to part with the kitchen. Charles thinks I'm mad but being British, he's too polite to say so. I know you didn't meet Charles that night when I crashed over to your table at the Four Seasons and needled Scott into making some bitchy remarks about homosexuals, but did you meet him later? My memory is obviously disintegrating with terror at the thought of being sixty next year! Anyway, darling, enough idle chatter—come to London and be reborn in the great creative renaissance which is sweeping the country! I look forward to seeing you. All love, Kevin. P.S. It's wonderful to be writing novels again after abandoning Broadway to Neil Simon! P.P.S. Bring Scott to dinner too, of course. I'm not a man to harbor grudges."

III

"DEAR VICKY: This letter will come as a surprise, when we've never exactly been the best of friends, but I hope you'll accept it as a peace offering. I'm writing of course, to offer you my best wishes on your engagement. I hope you and Scott will be very happy. Although Scott's my half-brother, I really know him so imperfectly, first because he's so much older than I am, second because I hardly ever saw him when I was a child, and third because he was—and is—a difficult person to know well. Even now, after his three years in London and his frequent visits to Mallingham, I still feel he's somewhat of a stranger to me, but I do believe he's a worthwhile person who now genuinely feels the need for someone who can share his life with him. Clever you, persuading him to give up the bachelor life at last! And lucky you, too—I've always thought Scott was one of the most attractive men I've ever met. Yours, Elfrida. P.S. Edred and George are also writing to you, but you may have to wait some time for their letters, as they're hopeless correspondents."

IV

"DEAR SEBASTIAN: Thanks for the letter and invitation—let me call you from London. Love, Vicky. P.S. Elfrida Sullivan is definitely not a lesbian."

V

"MOM!"

"Married!"

"Again? Aren't you getting a little old for that kind of thing?"

"Certainly not, Paul! Don't be so rude! Now, this may come as a great surprise to you all, but the man I've decided to marry is Scott."

"*Scott!*"

"Scott who?"

"Scott Sullivan? But why?"

"I don't like Scott," said Benjamin. "He never gives me anything. Mom, why don't you marry Uncle Sebastian again? Uncle Sebastian gives me real groovy presents!"

"Scott's never taken the slightest interest in any of us," said Eric, who was home from Choate for the weekend. "Mom, I don't want to sound rude, but are you sure you know what you're doing?"

"Why do you always have to marry men you've known for years and years? Why can't you marry a stranger for a change?"

"That's an interesting question, Samantha. I think it's been no accident that I've always married men I've known for a long time, because those men are the only men who are capable of seeing past my looks and my checkbook to the person I really am. I'm afraid that when you grow older, you'll come to realize—"

"When are you getting married?"

"Next Christmas. But I've decided I must spend the summer in London so that—"

"You're going to live with him?" said Samantha, lynx-eyed.

"That's kind of immoral, isn't it?" said Paul. "If you spend your summer having sex and swilling martinis, why can't I spend my summer smoking pot?"

"Sex and martinis aren't against the law. Smoking pot is."

"But it's a ridiculous law!"

"So are a lot of laws," I said. "Ask any woman. But that's not the point. The point is that we have to obey the law or we end up in a mess. If you don't like the laws, then work to change them, but don't bore the pants off everyone by moaning about injustice. Now, look here, kids—"

"Mom, does this mean you approve of premarital sex?"

"I think any sex, marital or premarital, is something you should always approach with care, concern, love, and respect. It's not something you can toss off for cheap thrills, like an ice-cream sundae. Now—"

"But, Mom—"

"*Quiet!* I've had enough of you walking all over me! Just let me hear myself think for a moment! Right. Thank you. Now, what I was going to say was—"

"What's premarital sex?" said Benjamin.

"Mommy, I don't understand why you have to go to London," said Kristin, starting to cry.

"*Oh, Mom!*" bawled Benjamin, trying to sob louder than Kristin as usual.

"Kristin, darling, that was exactly what I wanted to explain, except that no one would let me get a word in edgeways. *Be quiet, Benjamin!* That's better. Now, the fact is, Scott and I have a lot of things to discuss before we get married at Christmas. Also we have to get used to spending a lot of time in each other's company, and that's not always so easy as you might think."

"So you *are* going to live with him!" said Samantha, enthralled. "That's cool, Mom! I think Scott's dreamy!"

"You're mad!" Paul said to her in disgust. "You're a sex maniac! You're obscene!"

"Huh! You're just jealous because you know you can't compete with a tall, dark, handsome, glamorous, sexy *older man!*"

"And that's another thing," said Paul. "Scott's so chronically *old!* I'll bet he's never even heard of the Rolling Stones!"

"Lucky Scott," said Eric, rising to his feet to make his escape.

"Mommy, oh, Mommy, how are we all going to live without you for the whole summer? Maybe we'll die!" said Benjamin, and greatly intrigued by this possibility, he added, "Then you'll be sorry!"

"Take no notice, Mom," said Eric. "The little pest forgets all about you once he gets to Bar Harbor. He's so busy being spoiled rotten by Granddad he never even mentions your name."

"*You big creep!*" shrieked Benjamin.

"Mom, what kind of birth control are you going to use?"

"Samantha, my personal hygiene is none of your business, but I'll say this: I'm almost thirty-seven and I try to live my life as a responsible woman who believes that it's important to have certain standards in life. I don't always succeed in living up to those standards, I'm not a saint, I'm not perfect, but I keep trying. Neither you nor anyone else has the right to cross-examine me about my private life, but if I live with Scott and practice birth control, it's because I'm doing my best to live responsibly and pave the way for a happy, successful marriage, and not, as I said a moment ago, because I'm out for cheap thrills. Okay, any more questions, or can I call Scott to tell him what time he can come to dinner tonight? I want him to see you all before he goes back to London tomorrow."

"Mom, just one more question about premarital sex . . ."

"Christ!" said Eric. "For once in my life I agree with Paul. Is there anything more tedious than a twelve-year-old girl in the full flush of puberty?"

"You bet!" said Samantha. "The conversation of a seventeen-year-old boy who's never had a girlfriend, apparently doesn't want one, and spends all his spare time talking to a bunch of plants! Just what kind of freak are you, for God's sake?"

"What's puberty?" said Benjamin.

"Mommy," said Kristin, "how many times a day will you call us from England?"

"Well, darling, naturally I'll call as often as possible . . ."

"I'm going to water my plants."

"I think he makes love to the chrysanthemums," said Samantha to Paul. "Get it? Freud. 'Mum' is short for 'chrysanthemum,' and 'Mum' is also English for 'Mom.' "

"Are you kidding? What would Eric want to make love to Mom for?"

"Mommy, will you *promise* to call us every single day?"

"*Mom, what's puberty?*"

VI

"How DID Scott get on with the kids?" said my father after Scott had flown back to London.

"I thought he was wonderful with them—particularly with Samantha and Kristin. I guess he can draw on his experience with Rose and Lori when they were little. He did his best with the boys, but Eric's still so shy and Paul never has a word to say to anyone over twenty-five. Benjamin was monstrous as usual. He got jealous when Scott paid so much attention to the girls."

"Sebastian's the only one who could ever handle Benjamin."

I said nothing.

"Will you be seeing Sebastian in England?"

"Maybe."

There was another pause.

"It's a funny thing," said my father tentatively at last, "and I never thought the day would come when I'd hear myself say this, but sometimes I kind of miss Sebastian."

But I didn't reply. I was too busy counting the days till I left New York, too busy longing to be with Scott again in London.

VII

SCOTT LIVED in a town house on the borders of Knightsbridge and Belgravia, a tall slim white house rising for three floors above the basement apartment where his chauffeur and housekeeper lived. The dining room and library flanked the hall at street level, but above them was the fine living room where Scott held the parties which his position as senior partner in London made it necessary for him to give. In New York he had lived as a recluse, entertaining clients only in restaurants, but in New York his position had been subordinate to my father, who had naturally assumed the duty of entertaining clients at home.

I wondered how well Scott had adjusted to this new social life, which must have been so unappealing to him. I knew he needed seclusion in order to maintain the equilibrium which his demanding job must so often have undermined, but nowadays his opportunities for seclusion had been reduced, and I found myself speculating how far he had come to depend on alcohol to help him endure his boredom and distaste. Although I tried not to admit it, I had been disturbed by the double vodkas at the Beekman Tower.

Scott had no interest in interior decoration, no interest in possessions such as pictures and antiques, and no real interest in his home so long as it provided him with a roof over his head and the minimum of inconvenience. He was the most nomadic person I had ever met, and his home, decorated by experts and startlingly impersonal, reflected this indifference to his surroundings. Unlike Sam, who had been sensitive about his nationality to the point of neurosis, and unlike my father, who became irrationally xenophobic whenever he left the United States, Scott merely accepted his surroundings, adapted to them, and took the rough with the smooth without fuss. No doubt he was able to do this because, living so much in his mind, he was less dependent than most people on the society in which he lived, but this strange nomadic ability to settle easily in a strange place without making any deep connection with it struck me as not only odd but unnatural.

The word "home" and all that it implied was very important to me. "I'm a New Yorker," I would say, and what I was really saying was that New York was home, a place where I could relax and feel that mysterious inner comfort of belonging to a certain culture, a certain society, a certain way of life. I might be capable of settling in other countries for a short time, and even enjoying a new life there, but no matter how long I stayed away, New York would always be home. Yet for Scott, the nomad, home was inside himself; home was a state of mind. "I'm a New Yorker," he might say unhesitatingly, but he had none of that cynical, exasperated, passionate devotion which a true New Yorker feels for his city. New York was just the background of his life, the place where he was obliged to live and work, and now that he found himself in London, it seemed nothing had changed for him but the scenery. The landscape of his mind was more real to him than any city which existed in the world around him.

I had spent long hours trying to work out how I could live successfully with someone who was not only a loner but who saw the world in a way which was alien to me, and on the morning after my arrival in London when we were drinking coffee together in the patio of the back garden, I said to him carefully, "Scott, you mustn't feel you have to be with me all the time in order to keep me constantly entertained. I know you'll be working long hours and I know you'll want a certain amount of time to yourself, and I certainly don't expect you to change. It's up to me, not you, to neutralize this potentially aggravating situation by taking steps to see that my whole life doesn't revolve around waiting for those phone calls which tell me you're going to be late home from the office, so I've decided I must build some small life of my own while I'm here. I'm going to enroll in a course."

"A course?"

"Yes, now that I don't have the children buzzing around me like a swarm of bees, I think I might be capable of some form of mental activity. I've always looked down on summer courses, but that was probably because I knew I didn't have the time or the energy to face them. However, right now I do have the time and I ought to have the energy, so I'm going to make the effort. I think it's time I found out just how stupid and addled by martinis my brain really is."

"Okay," said Scott.

I waited, but he said nothing else. I wondered if he were upset, if he could possibly be one of those men who resented their wives pursuing any activity outside the home, but he seemed tranquil and unconcerned. It then occurred to me that this was exactly why his reaction was so off-key: he was unconcerned. What I did with my time was of no importance to him so long as I was available when he needed me.

Reminding myself that he was unaccustomed to sharing his life with anyone, I tried not to be hurt. "Well, you might show some interest!" I protested with a smile. "I shall be interested in your work, so why shouldn't you be interested in mine?"

"Oh, I never talk about my work," said Scott. "Once I leave the office, that's that. The last thing I'll ever want to do when I come home at night is tell you what I've been doing all day."

I was so taken aback that I couldn't at first decide what to say. Neither Sam nor Sebastian had regaled me with the details of issues, bids, mergers, and all the other delights of investment banking; it had been left to my father, confiding in me through many an evening during the past three years, to give me that kind of information about the world where my husbands had spent so much of their lives, but Sebastian had been full of amusing anecdotes about the mundane side of office life, and Sam had talked interminably about the importance of the people he advised. Sometimes I had been interested, sometimes I had been bored, but always I had been aware that they had been making some attempt, no matter how limited, to share with me the huge segment of their lives from which I was excluded. The thought of Scott living an existence to which I had no access was like pulling the drapes on a sunny morning only to find that the window had been walled up during the night.

"I probably know more about banking than you think I do," I said hesitantly at last. "And I enjoy following the stock market."

"Great," said Scott. "That kind of small talk will come in useful when I have to give these goddamned dinner parties. I hope you won't find them too boring."

There seemed to be nothing else to do but drop the subject. Taking a sip of coffee, I looked vaguely around the patio as I tried to think of another topic of conversation. It was cool in the garden, probably no more than sixty-five degrees, but the lack of humidity was so pleasant that I didn't miss the heat of New York. Huge white clouds billowed across the midsummer sky, little English robins sang fleetingly from the top of the mellow brick wall, and beyond the white wrought-iron table where we were sitting, the miniature roses glowed scarlet in their tubs. It was a Saturday morning.

"I've never cared much for London," I said at last, "but I can see the attraction of the serene, leisurely English way of life. Kevin certainly seems very happy here. . . . By the way, Kevin wants us to have dinner with him. Is that okay?"

Scott shrugged. "If he can make the effort to invite me, I guess I can make the effort to go."

This was hardly encouraging. "Maybe I'll call him and suggest he and I have lunch *à deux.*"

"That would probably be better, yes."

I decided that this would be the wrong moment to mention Sebastian. Abruptly I began to talk of our afternoon plans to see my mother, now happily installed in a luxurious south-coast hotel which catered to convalescents. I had decided to sail home to New York with her at the end of August.

"My mother's taken to you in a big way!" I said, smiling at him. "She's thrilled we're going to be spending the summer together. . . . Scott, there won't be any difficulty, will there, about me being here like this? I know we're in so-called swinging London, but will all those poker-faced businessmen from the City and their impeccably dressed wives approve of us living together without the blessing of the Church of England?"

"The important thing is that you must never attempt to explain just what you're doing here—never even refer to it. The British can accept almost anything from a couple who have the good taste to behave like hermaphrodites."

We laughed.

"And besides," said Scott, "we're not going to spend all our time in London surrounded by businessmen and their wives. I want to take you down to Mallingham to see Elfrida. You've never been to Mallingham, have you? It's an interesting place. I'm sure you'd like it."

I was silent. Mallingham was the one place I never wanted to visit. Mallingham was where Steve Sullivan was buried and where there was a memorial commemorating Scott's brother Tony. Mallingham represented the past that was still trying to prise Scott apart from the future he deserved. Mallingham summed up in one word everything which threatened our happiness. I wanted to keep it at arm's length.

"What's so special about Mallingham?" I said, trying not to sound hostile.

"The time there is time out of mind."

There was a pause. I groped for a reply. I had a sudden picture of our two minds forming two circles which touched but never intersected.

"I'm not sure what you mean by that," I said.

He looked apologetic, as if he had committed some faux pas by speaking in a language I couldn't understand.

"I just mean it's very old there and very peaceful."

"Oh, I see."

"As a matter of fact, my own personal vision of time out of mind is a seascape, a dark sea breaking on white sands with blue mountains beyond. Mallingham's very different. It's set in a flat marshy landscape about a mile and a half from the coast, yet still there's this absence of time there; I've always thought of it as a place where perhaps for one brief moment one can step out of time altogether and be conscious of the vastness where time doesn't exist. I'm glad my father's buried at Mallingham. It's right. For him it's a true home where he can rest in peace. A true home can't exist in time, because time destroys everything. A true home can only exist beyond time in places like Mallingham."

I had never before been so intensely aware of how inflexible my mind was. As I cautiously tried to bend it to meet his, I saw exactly why he had always seemed so mysterious to me. His world wasn't bounded by logic and common sense as mine was. His world opened into other worlds limited only by the scope of his intellect and imagination.

"You mean Mallingham for you," I said slowly, "is a little like T. S. Eliot's rose-garden, a magic place where everything comes together, and . . . what might have been and what has been coexist and . . . *are.*" The very effort of expressing such thoughts, which for me were so far from normality, made me feel limp.

"That's right," said Scott casually, the gifted bilingual who switched effortlessly back and forth between his two languages. "Mallingham's like Burnt Norton." Then suddenly he was back in my world again, speaking my language. "Hey, you never told me you'd read T. S. Eliot!"

"Oh, I'm not such a philistine as you think I am!" I retorted with spirit, but although we were at ease with each other again, I never told him who had introduced me to Eliot's *Four Quartets.*

Somehow it seemed so much more comfortable not to mention Sebastian's name.

VIII

I WAS appalled even though I wasn't surprised by how hard he worked. However, since I had anticipated the late returns in the evenings, the exhaustion, and the desire for solitude in order to recuperate, I didn't complain or press him into conversation as soon as he arrived home from work. Instead I let him rest by himself for a while in the library, which was his retreat, the one room I seldom entered. He would have two drinks there by himself and read for half an hour. I privately wished we could have shared at least one evening drink together, but Scott said no, what he liked was to have two drinks on his own. Remembering the magazine articles on alcoholism which I regularly read in order to give myself a healthy fright, I was at once suspicious and started checking the levels of the liquor bottles every day, but contrary to the know-it-alls who swore that to drink alone was the road to ruin, Scott never seemed to have more than two drinks during these solitary sessions. Finally with relief I decided that he liked to drink alone simply because he liked to be alone, and that this particular preference was no more sinister than his taste for reading alone or listening to music by himself.

Sometime around nine-thirty we would have dinner together. Scott, who was uninterested in food, apparently never suffered from hunger pangs, but I would be starving by early evening and I soon arranged with the housekeeper that I could have access to the kitchen at seven o'clock in order to fix myself a low-calorie snack. After dinner, during which Scott never drank, although I often secretly yearned for wine, we would either read in the living room or listen to records, but we never watched television because Scott had no set. To be fair to Scott, I must admit he offered to rent a set for me, but I decided it would do me no harm to live without television for a couple of months.

At midnight we would go to bed, and very often that was all we did: undress, get into bed, and fall asleep. This prosaic end to the day disturbed me at first, but since Scott wanted to do little else on weekends except make love, I soon stopped regretting the uneventful evenings during the working week. Presently, to my surprise, I even began to enjoy this unexpected pattern of our private life, with its extremes of abstinence and excess. The abstinence made the excess more exciting and heightened the electrical tension which was always present between us but which rose to an almost unbearable pitch toward the end of the week.

"Maybe those Victorians weren't so dumb about sex as we now think they were," I remarked once to Scott. "Think how exciting sex must have been when everyone postponed it endlessly until they almost went out of their minds!"

"Marriage was postponed," said Scott, "but sex wasn't. It's a myth that the Victorians kept sex at arm's length. The reality was prostitutes and pornography, with everyone being scared out of their wits by venereal disease."

"Yes, but . . ." I sighed. Scott often made me feel hopelessly ignorant. He didn't mean to; he drew on the well of his superior education automatically, but the effect was still depressing. Once I tried to talk about the course I was taking—I had selected an extramural London University course on existentialism in modern literature—but Scott's knowledge of literature and philosophy only made me realize how vast the two subjects were and how little I knew about them. However, I was determined not to feel depressed when I had every reason to be happy, so I reminded myself how boring it had been to live with a man like Sam, whose favorite hobby had been dismantling television sets, and how lucky I was now to be able to live with a man like Scott, who could stretch my brain and exercise it daily.

"I don't know how you can read that garbage, Vicky," said Scott, as he found me as usual at the breakfast table with my nose in the *Daily Express*.

"I like William Hickey's column. Anyway, darling, I must have some kind of light relief, particularly at breakfast! I can't live on an intellectual plane twenty-four hours a day!"

"I guess not," said Scott, opening the *Times*.

"Here's a picture of Elvis. Maybe he's made another of his frightful films."

"Who?"

"Elvis Presley."

"Oh."

I thought guiltily: I must call Sebastian, how awful not to have called before. But then I looked at Scott and thought: Later.

We still hadn't been to Mallingham. Elfrida, busy winding up her school's summer semester, had suggested we visit her later, but despite our postponed trip to Norfolk, our weekends had been busy, sailing in Sussex, walking in Surrey, and Shakespeare-watching at Stratford-on-Avon. Soon we became busier during the week. I found myself enjoying the dinner parties which bored Scott so much, and presently I made a couple of new friends and realized I was close to feeling at home in that alien city where I had been so unhappy in the past. Relaxing at last, I experimented with miniskirts behind my locked bedroom door, let my hair grow a little longer, and wondered how far I dared alter my eye makeup. Fortunately Scott's desire for me to be chastely and conservatively dressed made me no more than a closet follower of current British fashion trends, but even behind my locked bedroom door I still enjoyed myself enormously.

Then one day in August I suddenly thought: I can't put off this phone call one second longer. I've got to talk to Sebastian, and I've got to mention his name.

"Something wrong?" said Scott when we had finished making love after breakfast and were seriously thinking of getting up. It was a Sunday morning.

"No. I was just wondering if you'd mind if I went up to Cambridge for the day next week. Sebastian wrote to me way back with an invitation to lunch, and I just feel I can't spend the whole summer in England without making the effort to see him."

There was a silence. Then without a word Scott got out of bed and reached for his bathrobe.

"Scott, I didn't think it would be necessary for me to say this, but there's no need whatsoever for you to worry. Sebastian and I are just good friends. I know that sounds corny, but—"

"Not just corny," said Scott. "Inconceivable."

"But Scott—"

"Vicky, just who the hell do you think you're kidding? You lived with that man, you had a child by him, he was—and probably still is—obsessed by you. Believe me, the one thing you and Sebastian can never be is 'just good friends'! You've been much too deeply involved with each other."

"But you don't understand!"

"I understand too damned well! You stay away from him!"

"But surely you don't believe he'd make a pass at me when he knows I'm engaged to marry someone else!"

"Whether he behaves like a heel or a knight in shining armor is irrelevant. The point is, he'll upset you by raking up a past which is best forgotten."

"*You're* a fine one to give me lectures on the subject of forgetting the past!"

Scott's mouth hardened. I had a split-second impression of violent anger imprisoned behind the bleak blunt bones of his face.

"Okay," he said, "let's just check if I have this straight." He never raised his voice. On the contrary, his voice had a peculiarly lifeless quality, as if all emotion had been mercilessly excised from it, but he still managed to radiate an immense anger. "You're going to marry me. We're living right now in a trial marriage, and since this is so, I reckon I'm entitled to the rights of a trial husband; I reckon I'm entitled to tell you to stay away from a man whose one object in life is to get back into bed with you again."

"But what about me? Am I just a Kewpie doll with no mind of her own? Don't you attach any importance to what *I* want to do? I don't want to get back into bed with Sebastian! All I want is—"

"All you want, apparently, is to make a complete fool of yourself!"

"Look, Scott, if you'd ever been married, you'd know that marriage is more than issuing orders and talking about rights whenever you find yourself in a situation which is disagreeable to you. There are times when you have to trust your partner, times when there has to be give and take—"

"Yes, but this isn't one of those times. Excuse me."

The bathroom door slammed. I allowed myself a full minute to calm down, and then I went to the other bathroom to calm myself still further by taking a long hot bath. By the time I emerged, Scott had disappeared. After dressing quickly, I went downstairs to the library, but when no one answered my knock on the door, I assumed the room was empty. I turned away, but some instinct made me turn back, knock again, and look in.

He was standing by the window with a glass in his hand. The vodka bottle, one-quarter full, was standing uncapped on the table.

"Oh!" I said. I was so upset I could say nothing else. I went on standing stupidly in the doorway.

He glanced around. "I wanted to be alone. If you can't leave me alone, I'll get out."

"Sure. Okay. Sorry," I said, backing away, and closed the door very softly, as if I were afraid it might shatter beneath my fingertips. Upstairs in the living room I looked at the phone but made no attempt to call Sebastian. I merely sat down and waited, although what I was waiting for, I didn't know.

He went out ten minutes later. When I heard the front door close, I ran to the window and saw him walking swiftly away in the rain. In the library I found the vodka bottle. It was empty.

The clock on the mantel told me the time was eleven o'clock in the morning.

IX

I WAITED all day for him to come back. Once or twice I started crying, but I controlled my tears and forced myself to stay calm. I could neither eat nor drink. I just waited and waited, longing only for the opportunity to tell him that I wouldn't see Sebastian, not if it upset him, because nothing was more important to me than his belief that I loved him enough to prevent anyone dividing us.

It was after eleven o'clock that night when he returned. Upstairs in our bedroom I was sitting at the vanity as I brushed my hair, but as soon as I heard the front door close I jumped to my feet and ran to the head of the stairs.

I thought he might be drunk, reeling from side to side of the hall, perhaps even singing. But I was mistaken. There was no singing, no reeling. When I reached the head of the stairs I saw he was leaning nonchalantly against the panels of the front door, and it was only when I called his name and he glanced up that I saw how far removed he was from normality.

His eyes were like black holes. They saw me yet did not see me. Very slowly he stopped leaning against the door and straightened his back, but there was no swaying, no stumbling. As always, his self-control appeared to be immaculate, and thinking in relief that he was disturbed but sober, I rushed down the stairs to take him in my arms.

I got no farther than the fifth stair. Then I stopped. I think it was because he was so still. His extreme stillness made my scalp prickle, and then suddenly I could feel the violence vibrating across the yards which separated us and I knew that his immaculate self-control was an illusion, a facade which was already crumbling before my eyes.

I called out, "Just a minute—I'll be right with you," and my lips were so stiff that I could hardly speak. Darting back to the bedroom, I just had time to struggle into jeans and a sweater before he burst into the room.

What terrified me most was his incredible speed. Then, when I realized I was terrified, I was more terrified than ever. I tried to get a grip on my terror by telling myself that everything was going to be all right, but I knew now what my instinct had told me on the stairs. Everything wasn't going to be all right. Everything was going to be very, very wrong.

He swung the door wide, and then, using every ounce of strength in his body, he flung the door back into its frame. The wood cracked. The noise reverberated sickeningly in my ears. For a moment he wrestled with the lock, but the door must have dropped a fraction on its hinges, for the key refused to turn. In a rage he pulled the key out and hurled it across the room at the vanity. The mirror instantly smashed. The floor was strewn with glass, and my heart was hammering in my lungs.

I tried to be calm, tried to be rational. "Scott," I said gently, "I'm very sorry about—"

"Shut up!" he shouted at me. "Shut up, you fucking bitch!"

I could see now that he was blind drunk. The fact that it was so very far from obvious only heightened the horror; I had begun to think he had gone out of his mind unaided by alcohol, and I might have gone on believing that for some time if he hadn't blundered against the nightstand and betrayed his unsteadiness on his feet. The collision maddened him. Furious that anything should impede his progress, he picked up the lamp to smash it, but it slipped through his fingers to the floor, and when he started to curse, I heard the blurred consonants at last and knew that although he was using the full force of his will to obliterate the hallmarks of drunkenness, his will was slowly slipping as the poison invaded his brain.

I said in the most normal voice I could manage, "I'll go and fix you some coffee," and I tried to slip past him to the door.

He grabbed my wrist, twisted my arm behind my back so fiercely that I screamed, and shoved me away from him. I screamed again, tripped, fell across the bed.

"Scott—"

"You shut your mouth or I'll kill you."

I saw now that it was useless to be calm or to attempt to talk rationally. He was far beyond all words of love and comfort. There was nothing I could do for him. All I could do was get out.

If I could.

He took a step toward the bed. I somehow managed to roll away from him over to the far side, but that was very difficult, because my limbs felt like lumps of lead. He began to talk, but at first I could not hear him because the blood was pounding so fiercely in my ears, and then when he raised his voice and I did hear him I wished I could have gone on being deafened by my own terror. He said I wasn't to give him orders because he was the one in control; he was the one who gave the orders and dealt out the punishments. He said he hated everyone who hurt him, but that was all right, that was fine, because hatred kept a man alive. It was love that killed him.

"Do you hear what I'm saying?" he was shouting at me. "Why don't you answer? Can't you hear?"

"Yes, I can hear." I wanted to leave the bed, but I was afraid to stir in case any movement triggered some uncontrollable force in him, so I stayed motionless and listened to him talking about how love destroyed people, how women destroyed men, how women had to be punished, had to be beaten back, had to be smashed down, had to be . . .

I put my hands over my ears.

"No, you listen to me!" He was on top of me in an instant, wrenching my hands aside. "You listen to me! I'm going to teach you a lesson, I'm going to teach you a lesson you'll never forget, I'm going to . . ."

I didn't think he could possibly be capable of intercourse. What terrified me was what he would do when he found himself impotent.

By this time my thoughts were no longer flashing through my mind in inarticulate images, but rapping out short sharp messages in words. Had to distract his attention. Couldn't think how. He wouldn't notice. He couldn't see anything. He could barely see me. He was only seeing symbols. He was drowning in his own darkness, suffocating in his own blood.

He was cursing again as he struggled with his clothes and found he had lost control over his fingers. The zipper on his fly jammed, snapped free, then jammed again.

Mustn't display panic. Mustn't display fear. Terror would only turn him on.

"Darling, you're so sexy when you're like this!" I said. "But wait—don't bust the zipper. Here, let me fix it for you."

His hands automatically relaxed, leaving his body unguarded. I hit him as hard as I could, and then in a flash I was running, running, running, out of the door, down the stairs, lots of stairs, running, running, running across the hall, falling against the front door, scrabbling with the lock, and all the while he was running and shouting behind me, running, running, running with his demonic unnatural speed, and then the door was open and the night was dark and wet and cold, and I was running, running, running in my bare feet down the road, until suddenly there were bright lights and huge buildings and moving people and I was in Knightsbridge and a cab was cruising past and I shouted and it stopped and I fell inside.

"Where to?" said the driver, bored.

I whispered, "Anywhere. Just go."

He drove off. We circled Hyde Park Corner three times, but before we could embark on our fourth orbit, I knew where I wanted to be.

Ten minutes later, outside Kevin's Chelsea mews I was ringing the front doorbell with a trembling hand.

X

"HAVE A little Irish whiskey, my dear," said Kevin. "You'll love it after the first few hair-raising sips. No, don't keep on saying how late it is and how awful you feel about bothering me and what the hell can Charles be thinking. Charles is asleep and very unlikely to wake up, I don't give a damn how late it is, and I adore being bothered by beautiful women in distress. One gets so little of that kind of excitement at my age. . . . Did Scott kick you out?"

"I ran away," I said, and broke down, my body shaking with sobs, the tears streaming down my cheeks, the Irish whiskey spilling from my glass.

Kevin said, "That's better. That's much more natural." I felt his arm slip around me as he removed the glass from my hand. Then he said, "Let me get you a sweater and some socks. You're very cold."

I went on crying, but by the time he returned I had controlled the sobs and was wiping away the tears.

"Here you are," said Kevin. "Put these on and then wrap yourself in this blanket. I'll make you a hot drink."

He disappeared again, and clumsily I pulled on a pair of gray socks over my bare feet. That took some time, because my fingers were so stiff. Then I struggled into the thick blue sweater and huddled myself in the woolly blanket just as Kevin reappeared with a mug of dark sweet tea.

We sat for a while on the couch. Very slowly I began to feel warmer. Sipping my tea, I stared at the typically English faded elegance of that comfortable living room, the antiques lying casually around as if they had grown out of the floor decades ago, the jumbled collection of books on the shelves by the fireplace, the scattered papers on the desk, and on the table a Waterford crystal vase filled with yellow roses.

" 'And the roses had the look of flowers that are looked at,' " I thought, and suddenly realized I had spoken Eliot's words aloud.

"Ghastly, aren't they?" said Kevin. "Charles keeps on buying them, but I think their plastic splendor gives the room an air of total unreality. . . . Do you feel any closer to reality yet, or do you still feel as if you're struggling in a nightmare?"

"I'm feeling better. But . . ."

"But everything's still a nightmare? Tell me about it. A nightmare shared is often a nightmare pared down to manageable proportions. Besides, since I've never liked Scott, I'm unlikely to be either disillusioned or shocked."

"This'll shock you."

"Oh, good. I'm so tediously difficult to shock. It makes life so dull. Shock me."

I talked in disconnected sentences for some minutes, and when I broke off at last to look at Kevin, I saw he was indeed shocked.

"Kevin . . ."

"Yes. Sorry to be so blank. I was just trying to think. You realize, of course, that he's an alcoholic?"

"But, Kevin, that's what's so extraordinary! He's not! He has complete control over his drinking habits!"

"My dear," said Kevin, "if that's true, why are you here?"

"But this was just an isolated occasion!"

"Do you seriously believe this has never happened before?"

I thought of Scott talking of the abrupt termination of his affair with the librarian. I remembered him saying, "I got into bad trouble in the navy." I heard him confessing that he had given up casual affairs when he had found himself unable to face them without alcohol.

I couldn't speak.

"You can bet this wasn't the first time," said Kevin, "and you can bet it won't be the last, unless he and alcohol part company for good. God knows I'm a heavy drinker, but at least I don't make life intolerable for myself and the people around me by my drinking. Are you going back to him?"

"Oh, but I must!" I started to cry again. "I'm going to help him . . . save him—everything depends on me!"

"No, Vicky. Everything depends on him. My God, I hate to have to say this, but I'm going to have another drink. How frightful! I think I must be scared by you displaying all the symptoms of the redeemer complex. Don't get hung up on redemption, Vicky. It's a dead-end street."

"But I love him!"

"Yes, that seems obvious, but what's not so obvious is why. I can't really believe you're hung up on redemption. You don't strike me as being a masochist who falls in love with a man not in spite of his imperfections but because of them." Kevin sighed, added some soda water to the Irish whiskey in his glass, and returned to sit beside me on the couch. "In some ways you remind me of your father. You pick the great love of your life, and he or she—let's think of Scott and say he—turns out to be very buttoned up emotionally and not good at expressing his feelings. However, that doesn't faze you, because you have this very American attitude that anything damaged can be fixed. You take on the job of fixing the damage—of course it's an exercise in power—and then you have the shattering experience of discovering that you're not such an effective Mr. Fixit as you thought you were. Result: unhappiness, disillusionment, and grand passion on the rocks. Am I depressing you? Okay, try this alternative theory on for size: it's not love you feel for Scott, but guilt. You feel compelled to make amends for your father's mistakes."

"Oh, but . . ."

"No? Then let's make the theory even simpler and say this whole affair of yours is just one big act of rebellion against your father."

"Kevin . . ."

"Yes, home truths are loathsome, aren't they? Or am I perhaps very far from home?"

"You couldn't be further away. Scott's the only man I've ever really been able to relate to."

"What a diabolical coincidence. And what a diabolical phrase 'relate to' has become! Nowadays it seems to cover everything from a limp handshake to an orgasm, but of course we're hardly talking about limp handshakes here, are we? A pity. I only wish we were."

"We're not just talking about orgasms, either. Look, Kevin, why I love Scott doesn't matter . . ."

"Okay, I give up. You want to go back to him."

"Yes."

"When he's sober."

"Yes."

"And only if he swears to give up liquor for good."

"Yes."

"So be it. I've no right to meddle any further. Now, let me get the guest room ready for you—you must be exhausted."

I stopped him making up the bed. Crawling under a pile of blankets, I lay awake shivering for a long time, but at last the shivers stopped, my eyes closed against the dawn light, and I somehow managed to rest.

XI

"I'M SORRY," said Kevin, "but I'm not letting you go back to that house on your own. I'm sure that by now he'll have reached the stage where he's more interested in throwing up than in behaving like a psycho, but I'm taking no chances. I'm coming with you."

We were sitting by ourselves in the dining area of the old-fashioned kitchen. Charles, whom I seemed fated never to meet, had left for his office long before I had dragged myself out of bed at ten o'clock. I was feeling calm but was unable to eat.

"More coffee?" said Kevin.

"Thanks." I watched him reach for the coffeepot. The far side of middle age had made Kevin look less of a maverick and more like a distinguished man of letters. His hair, long at the nape of the neck but carefully trimmed, was the purest shade of white, and although he was much heavier than in his younger days, he had retained his trick of making casual clothes look elegant. His accent, formerly a curious mixture of Eastern prep school and Broadway theater, now leaned heavily toward the BBC. He wore glasses but kept taking them off, as if he suspected they made him look too elderly, and waving them around vaguely while he talked. The performance only added to his unexpected new air of distinction.

"We'll take a cab," he said as we left the house. "I've only driven once in this country, and it was a disaster. I have this incurable urge to drive on the right."

I could barely smile. I could think only of Scott. Anxiety gnawed at the pit of my stomach.

When we reached the house, I could hardly fit the key in the lock, and Kevin had to help me open the front door. We stepped into the hall. The housekeeper was vacuuming the living room upstairs, and the normality of the noise came as an immense relief and gave me the courage to tap on the library door.

"Scott?"

There was no answer. We looked at each other.

"My God," said Kevin, "is it possible that he was able to get himself to work this morning?"

Scott came out of the library.

He was freshly shaved and immaculately dressed, and when I realized the supreme effort he must have made to master his appearance, I felt the tears spring to my eyes. He looked very ill. His eyes were bloodshot and his face was bleached of color. He made no effort to speak, but merely stood looking at me, and the wordlessness of his pain drew me instinctively toward him.

"Scott . . . darling . . . we thought . . . we wondered . . ."

I saw him swallow, but still he was unable to speak. I turned to Kevin.

"It's all right now," I said. "Thanks so much for everything."

Kevin just said, "Call me later," and left quietly. The front door closed behind him.

The first words Scott said were, "Don't leave me. Please don't leave me. I couldn't bear it. I couldn't go on."

"Darling, I'm not leaving you. I'm not."

"I couldn't live if I didn't have you, I'd rather die. I wanted to die this morning when I realized what I'd done. I don't deserve to live. I do such terrible things."

"Shhh." I took him in my arms and stroked his hair as he clung to me.

"I thought you wouldn't come back," he said. "I thought it was all over. I even ran the bath and got the razor ready . . ."

"Come and sit down."

We went into the library and sat down quietly on the couch. Far away, as if in another world, the housekeeper continued to vacuum the living room.

"Scott," I said, "you must have help. Will you please see a doctor?"

He nodded vigorously. "I'll get some pills. They'll help me over the first few days. I'll never drink again, never, I swear it."

I kissed him and held him close. "I wasn't just referring to the liquor. I want you to have help in handling all those violent feelings that are buried inside you."

He looked puzzled. "So long as I don't drink, I have no violent feelings."

"Scott, alcohol isn't a creative force. It doesn't manufacture these violent feelings out of the blue. They're there all the time, but you keep them locked up. All alcohol does is open up your mind and let them out."

He sat thinking about this. Once he put his hand to his forehead as if his head was hurting so much that thinking was difficult, but he never complained of feeling ill. Finally he said, "Well, perhaps. Yes, maybe. But the cure doesn't lie with psychiatrists. It lies with me. Once I've repaid my father what I owe him, I'll be at peace with myself and then all my violence will be a thing of the past."

There was a slight pause. Then I said, "I think your father would have felt long ago that he'd been repaid. I think he would have wanted you to look after yourself now. If you were to talk to a doctor . . ."

"A psychiatrist, you mean."

"Yes. A psychiatrist. It's not that I think you're crazy—"

"I'll bet that's exactly what you think. And after last night, I don't blame you, either."

"It's not that I think you're crazy," I said again, as if he hadn't spoken. "But I do think you're living daily with too much pain, and why go on suffering when maybe, just maybe, a doctor could help alleviate the distress? Isn't seeking help at least worth a try?"

"Well, I'll do anything you want, of course," he said. "Anything at all. If you want me to see a psychiatrist, I'll see one."

I was very much aware that he was consenting to see a doctor for all the wrong reasons. I took a deep breath and made a new effort to reach him.

"You've got to want to be cured, Scott," I said. "If you don't, a psychiatrist can't help you."

"I do want to be cured. I've spent my whole postwar life trying to cure myself by the only method which is ever going to be successful."

We seemed to be going round and round in circles. With reluctance I decided I had no choice now but to be very blunt indeed.

"There's something you should understand," I said evenly. "If you can't control this violence, you won't be able to keep me. I used to think nothing could ever come between us, but that was just me being arrogant and thinking I was some kind of superwoman who could fix anything if she tried hard enough. But I'm not a superwoman . . . and I'm not a masochist, either. I loathe violence and I won't stand for it in my private life. I think you should know that. It'll help you to believe me when I say that if you ever try a rerun of that scene last night—"

"I promise you," he said, "I swear to you that last night's scene will never, never, never happen again."

"I know you'll give up liquor. I've every confidence in you as far as that's concerned."

"Then you can relax. You've got nothing else to worry about."
I was silent.

"I'll see a psychiatrist too, of course," he said after a pause, "but not here. I'll wait till I'm back in New York. I wouldn't trust a European psychiatrist to relate to my American background."

This I could understand. I thought of the psychiatrists I had seen years ago in London, and remembered how foreign they had all seemed. I had felt quite unable to communicate my feelings to them.

"All right," I said. "Fair enough. Wait till you come home."

He kissed me, and I held him close again as I stroked his hair. For a long while we were silent, but at last I heard him say in a low voice, "And now I want to say something about Sebastian."

I drew back sharply. "No," I said, "Sebastian's name is never to be mentioned between us again. I'll write and say I can't visit him."

"But that would be the greatest possible mistake!" Scott sounded on the verge of despair. "Of course we must inevitably refer to Sebastian from time to time, and of course you must go to see him while you're over here . . . yes, you must! I insist! There's no question about it! I'll never forgive myself for what happened last night, but at least it'll be easier to live with the memory if I know I didn't after all keep you from seeing someone who has such an important place in your life. Please call him right now and fix a day."

Tears filled my eyes again, because I sensed how hard he was straining to reach me. I felt his mind brushing clumsily against mine, reminding me of the two circles which met without intersecting, and I wanted to hold it in place and soothe it and stop it slipping away again into isolation.

I couldn't look at him, but I took him in my arms and at last I was able to say gently, "Okay. Thanks. I'll call him right away."

XII

"HERE'S MY car," said Sebastian. "Don't laugh."

I laughed. It was a mini, bright red with tiny wheels and a body like a lunchbox.

"How do you fit into it?"

"Jack's beanstalk's giant could fit into it. Hey, you're on the wrong side—unless you want to drive."

We scrambled in, Sebastian folding himself improbably behind the wheel, and as the car roared off at a fierce pace through the narrow streets of Cambridge, I saw rows of tiny houses and glimpses of green trees and distant spires.

"Oxford's okay," said Sebastian, "but this is better. We're not going through the main sightseeing areas at the moment, but later I'll take you around and you can clap your hands and say 'gee whiz' and make all the noises an American tourist is supposed to make."

Sebastian was dressed like an Englishman, in baggy gray flannels, which were clearly the relic of some bygone era, a shabby tweed jacket patched with leather at the elbows, and a sports shirt which might once have been white but had faded to a mild gray. He was going bald at the crown and made no effort to conceal it. He drove with great skill and cursed a lot under his breath whenever a bigger car forgot to give him a wide berth.

"How's New York?" he said. "I hear that kid Donald Shine's still busy terrorizing Wall Street. What's his next target going to be? Does anyone have any ideas?"

"The rumor is he'll go gunning for another insurance company, but nobody's sure." I was too busy admiring the scenery to talk of Donald Shine. Ahead of us a wide stretch of grass was reminding me of an English village green, and a second later Sebastian said as he navigated a traffic circle, "That's Midsummer Common and there's my house on the edge—the black one with the white front door."

The house, one of a row, was small and square, with a satisfying symmetrical facade. Since the tiny front garden bordered the common, we had to leave the car in the alley at the rear and approach the house through the backyard.

"What does Alfred think of it?" I couldn't help asking. Elsa had a fondness for large luxurious modern homes, and her new husband's taste obviously reflected her own. They had a mansion in Westchester and a fifteen-room penthouse in Manhattan.

"Alfred wants me to ship it all back to the States brick by brick. He wants it for a playhouse in his garden."

He took me into a snug little living room, and while he fixed the drinks I wandered around looking at his pictures, his prints, and his books. We were silent, but the silence was comfortable. I had long since become accustomed to Sebastian's silences.

"How's the book?" I asked as he handed me my martini.

"No good. I've decided that my style of writing isn't suited to a work about investment banking."

"You mean you're going to give it up?"

"Probably."

"What are you going to do with yourself instead?"

"Don't know. I think I'm going crazy. I find myself yearning not only for banking but also for the plastic society. Still . . ." He glanced out of the window at the pastoral tranquillity of Midsummer Common. ". . . it's been a great rebellion. Everyone ought to have at least one chance in life to quit and ride off into the blue like the hero of one of those old-time cowboy movies who's just lost the girl he loves to the guy who used to be his best friend. . . . I've often wondered since what happened to all those old-time cowboys. Did they die of a broken heart under some far-off cactus? No, probably not. I'll bet they ended up back on the range again, earning their living in the only way that appealed to them, and seeking out the only environment, repulsive though it might appear, which offered them the chance to be themselves."

"You're serious? You really want to leave here? But I thought you loved England!"

"And so I do. Yet I don't fit in here, Vicky. Maybe I'm just too young to sink into a quiet retirement in a civilized intellectual retreat. Or maybe I'm just too American. It's no bed of roses being a foreigner, even if you wind up in a country where the natives are reasonably friendly."

I smiled at him. "You'll be like a character out of an Orwell novel. Your epitaph will be: 'He came to love the plastic society!'"

"Maybe." Sebastian looked gloomy. Then he sighed and added wryly, "Henry James and T. S. Eliot came to Europe and were upset because it seemed so decadent. I come to Europe and I'm upset because it seems so goddamned dull. I have this craving to be back where the action is. The vicarious thrills I got from the latest Shine takeover could almost be classed as obscene. . . . Okay, let's go to lunch. There's this nice place right by the river . . ."

We drank white wine and ate herb omelets by the window of an upstairs restaurant which seemed to lean out over the water. Below us on the river young tourists drifted by in punts, and in the distance above the roofs and gables the college spires soared into the summer sky.

"Sebastian," I said on an impulse, "I'm doing this course on existentialism in literature, and although I only understand about one word in ten, I'm finding it very fascinating. Have you ever read the Sartre trilogy *Les Chemins de la Liberté?*"

"Loved the first, hated the second, never faced the third."

We wrangled happily about Sartre for some time, but when our omelets were finished and the waitress had arrived with our coffee, Sebastian brought the conversation back to earth by asking after the children. I told him I was worried about Eric because he didn't seem interested in girls and I was worried about Paul because I was afraid he was smoking pot on the sly and I was worried about Samantha because she was boy-crazy and I was worried about Kristin because she was so overshadowed by her pretty sister and I was worried about Benjamin because he was Benjamin. And Sebastian laughed and said how much more interesting it was to have children who were individuals instead of children who were well-regulated robots, like the offspring produced by Andrew and Lori, and somehow it was such a relief to talk to Sebastian about my family because he always made me feel I wasn't doing so badly as a parent and in fact might even be doing rather well.

After finishing our meal, we strolled outside.

"I'll take you down to the backs," said Sebastian, and drove us in his little red car down to the meadows at the back of the major colleges. We walked down an avenue of trees to the river. It was quiet and the fields were full of flowers. On Clare Bridge we both paused to lean on the parapet, watch the weeping willows, and admire the glow of the sun on the colleges' mellow walls.

"Imagine going to college in a town as beautiful as this!" I said enviously.

"The little devils probably take it all for granted. Come on, I'll show you King's College Chapel. It's a real tourist trap, but you can't possibly leave Cambridge without seeing it."

The chapel turned out to be not a chapel at all but a full-sized church, and as we drew nearer I saw the miracles of architecture which had made it so justly famous. I was still admiring the soaring walls and the long windows when I stopped dead. "My God!" I said in awe.

"What's the matter?"

"The roses! Sebastian, just look at those voluptuous stone roses—oh, and there's more of them over here! How did the stonemasons manage to carve them like that? They're magnificent!"

"The English today think they're vulgar," said Sebastian. "Elfrida

Sullivan referred to them as 'typical Tudor *nouveau riche* excess.' "

"I'd have slapped her. What did you say?"

"Said I'd rather have *nouveau riche* excess than *ancien régime* decadence. Elfrida said why settle for either and began talking about the temples of classical Greece."

"Elfrida was always such a know-it-all." I was gazing at the great vaulted ceiling, and it seemed to me that the slim columns supporting it were straining upward for some mystical attainment which could never be expressed in words. "It's lovely," I heard myself whisper inadequately. "Lovely."

"Yes, it's okay. Christ, here comes another coachload of Americans! August in Cambridge is like an extraterritorial meeting of the United Nations. Let's go and sit on the lawn overlooking the backs and pretend we've lived here all our lives."

Finding a bench facing the huge expanse of lawn which stretched from the river to the walls of King's College, we sat for a while in the sun. It was very quiet, very peaceful.

"I don't see how you could ever leave such a wonderful place, Sebastian."

"Crazy, isn't it? Why did I have to be a born banker with a built-in homing instinct for New York? It makes no sense."

"Well, I'm sure you'll have no trouble getting another good job on Wall Street."

"There's only one job I'd ever consider taking."

We went on sitting on the bench. The sun went on shining on the tranquil scene, but I shivered as I scrabbled in my purse for a cigarette.

"But that's okay," said Sebastian. "That's no problem, because of course in the end Cornelius will invite me back—and on my terms. Egged on by Mother, he'll swallow his pride and make another effort to come crawling back to me, and *that'll* be the justice Scott was always trying to find; Cornelius will have to hand over his life's work not to Scott, the guy he's always secretly liked, but to me, the guy he's always secretly loathed. Christ, what an irony! I'll be literally laughing all the way to the bank."

"And Scott?" said my voice.

Sebastian looked surprised. "What about him? Cornelius has obviously ruled out the possibility of making Scott his successor—why else would he have railroaded Scott to Europe for so long? If he's lucky, Scott may manage to hold on to his partnership, but he won't get any further. He's shot his bolt. Cornelius finally wised up. My guess is that Cornelius is just waiting for your affair with Scott to end and then he'll fire him."

"But I'm going to marry Scott, Sebastian. We don't plan on being engaged indefinitely. We're going to marry at Christmas."

There was a pause. A bell began to toll somewhere, and far away we could hear the sound of laughter from the people punting on the river.

"Uh-huh," said Sebastian at last. "Well, if that's what you want, good luck to you. I always told you to go after what you wanted, Vicky. I always told you to stop other people trying to run your life for you. And I always said that whatever happened, I'd be with you all the way."

I couldn't speak. I felt as if someone were revolving a knife round and round in my body, and in that single moment I felt more confused than at any time since we had agreed in the Oak Bar of the Plaza to end our marriage.

A group of tourists were wandering past us as we sat on the bench, and one of them, a little boy with fair hair and blue eyes, was skipping along ahead of his elders with a daisy chain in his hand.

"Same age as Edward John," said Sebastian, idly voicing what we were both thinking. "Funny to think of Edward John. I guess that by this time he'd be running around being a menace and giving us both hell, but I never think of him that way. I think of him saying 'please' and 'thank you' and giving you flowers on Mother's Day and running off to read *Treasure Island* in his spare time. How one sentimentalizes the dead! 'They shall grow not old, as we that are left grow old. . . .' By the way, I always thought Rupert Brooke wrote that line, but the other day I discovered the author was some guy called Binyon. I wish I had the time to take you to Rupert Brooke's Grantchester—it's only a couple of miles away, but I guess we'd better be getting back to the station. You don't want to miss your train."

We returned to the car in silence, and the silence persisted all the way to the station.

"I won't park the car and see you off," said Sebastian. "That sort of genteel masochism only belongs in dated British movies. So long. Thanks for coming. Good luck."

"Sebastian . . ."

"We do what we have to do. I know that. You don't have to explain."

"I wish so much—"

"No, don't. No point. Call me if ever you need me. Now, get the hell out, please, before you miss your train and everyone in London starts to think I've abducted you."

I struggled out of the car and blundered into the station. Amidst all my confusion I was acutely conscious that Scott had been justified in trying to stop me seeing Sebastian. He had prophesied the meeting would upset me, and now here I was, very upset indeed. I told myself I shouldn't have seen Sebastian, shouldn't have gone to Cambridge, shouldn't have put myself in such an unbearable position, but when I asked myself just what that position was, I found I was incapable of defining it.

I thought of Edward John and cried all the way to the end of the platform as I waited for the train.

Chapter Six

I

"I'M CALLING to offer you my best wishes, Vicky," said Jake Reischman. "I hear your engagement's now official."

It was September. The children were back in school and I was back in New York after crossing the Atlantic with my mother on the *Queen Elizabeth*. Scott was due to return to New York on business in October, so our separation was to be short, but I had still hated to leave him on his own. However, after a summer away from home I knew my children should now be my first priority, so with a great effort I had resisted the temptation to stay on in London.

"Why, Jake, how nice of you to phone." I was in my bedroom changing into a dress before I paid my weekly visit to my father for an evening's chess and gossip. By the telephone on the nightstand was my best framed photograph of Scott, and as I spoke to Jake I was remembering how the sea breeze had ruffled Scott's hair as he had smiled for my camera. We had been sailing off the Sussex coast at the time, and he had just given up liquor again. Out of sympathy I had joined him on the wagon and was delighted when I immediately lost weight and felt healthier. In fact, I had just decided that there was no reason why I should ever drink alcohol again when I had boarded the *Queen Elizabeth* with my mother, and within half an hour had been gasping for a martini. My mother had driven me to distraction during the voyage by flirting with a seventy-eight-year-old widower, drinking champagne from dawn till dusk, and reminiscing interminably (as old people will do) about the so-called "good old days."

"It's real nice of you to call, Jake," I repeated, trying to concentrate on the conversation as I watched Scott smiling at me from the photograph frame.

But Jake never mentioned Scott's name. Nor did he ask any questions about my impending marriage. All he said was, "I have a favor to ask you. When will you next be seeing your father?"

"I'm on my way to him right now."

"Then will you tell him, please, that it's most urgent that we talk? I've tried calling him, but I only get the young men he hires to pick up after him, and although I leave messages, he doesn't return my calls. I'd greatly appreciate it if you could help me."

"All right." I was annoyed that my engagement had merely provided him with an excuse to enlist me as a go-between, but since Jake had been good to me, forgiving me for my role in Elsa's failed marriage and remaining fond of me despite his long estrangement from my father, I made an effort to keep my annoyance hidden. "How are you, Jake?" I said politely. "I haven't seen you in a while."

"Unfortunately I'm not well, which is one of the reasons why I must speak to your father as soon as possible about this business matter which concerns us both. My ulcer's been making my life difficult again. I go into Mount Sinai tomorrow for an operation."

"Oh, I'm sorry to hear that." I was startled, my annoyance forgotten. "Well, I wish you lots of luck—and I'll make sure Daddy calls you this evening, I promise."

"Let me give you the number of my new apartment. He won't have it." He dictated the phone number rapidly and then added with that colorless air which autocratic men often assume when they try not to appear as if they're dictating orders: "Don't listen if he says he'll call me later, Vicky. Have him call me while you're there, and if he stalls, tell him . . ." He stopped for a moment, as if to choose his words with care. Then: "Tell him I've got sentimental in my old age. Tell him the Bar Harbor Brotherhood means more to me than the new generation controlling this decadent disastrous decade."

It suddenly occurred to me that he might be very ill indeed and anxious to heal past quarrels before he entrusted himself to his doctors.

"Don't worry, Jake," I said. "I give you my word that he'll call."

II

"LET ME show you my new toy!" said my father with enthusiasm. "A tape recorder which is activated by the sound of the human voice —how Sam would have enjoyed it! I'm going to have it installed in my office so that I can record every interview without fuss. Why, the clients won't even know they're being recorded! Isn't that clever? When I think of the old days when Sam had to mess around with the Vox Diktiermaschine and the Dailygraph—"

"Lovely, Daddy. Listen . . ."

"—but now all I have to do is instruct my secretary to make sure there's always a tape in the machine. Then even *I* can forget the interview's being recorded! There'll be no knobs to switch on, no buttons to press, no . . . Sorry, were you trying to say something?"

I told him what Jake had said.

We were in the library of my father's apartment, and beyond the windows the sun was setting behind the trees of Central Park. My father's new tape recorder lay on the coffee table alongside a copy of *The Economist*. The astronaut chessmen faced one another expectantly on the table by the steel bookstands, and beyond them above the television was the latest painting my father had acquired, a ketchup bottle by Andy Warhol.

My father had been stooping over his tape recorder, but as I spoke he straightened his back and looked out at the long sunset. His face was almost hidden from me, and the light, streaming through the windows behind him, made it still harder to see his expression.

"You'll call him, won't you, Daddy?" I said, putting Jake's number by the phone. "Please!"

He picked up the slip of paper, but I knew he was looking not at the numbers but at the tennis court at Bar Harbor and the four boys who had played and laughed together there long ago beneath cloudless summer skies.

Without a word he picked up the receiver and started to dial.

"Mr. Reischman, please. This is Cornelius Van Zale."

He had seated himself behind his desk, and as he waited, he picked up one of his silver ball-point pens and drew a pattern on the blotter. I had just realized that the series of rectangles formed a tennis court when he began to speak.

"Jake? Vicky gave me the message."

There was a long silence while Jake talked. My hand fidgeted with one of the pawns, but all the while I was watching my father, and as I watched, he slowly laid down his pen and turned his swivel chair away from me to face the window.

At last he said, "I see. Yes. Thank you." And after another silence: "I'm sorry to hear that. You must tell me if there's anything I can do." And finally: "Yes, I'll take care of it. Thank you again."

Swiveling the chair slowly back to face the desk, he replaced the receiver. His features were grave and somehow pure, as if they belonged to a statue whose sculptured features were incapable of expression. His fine eyes were a clear empty gray.

"Is he dying?" I heard myself ask.

"Yes. There's a fifty-percent chance he may die on the operating table tomorrow. If he survives, he'll have a year. Cancer. Someone said only the other day how thin he'd become."

I thought of the Uncle Jake I had known long ago, and felt the lump form in my throat.

We said nothing for a time. My father went on sitting at his desk and looking at the tennis court he had drawn on the blotter. I went on sitting in my chair and watching him. Finally I said, "Daddy, what went wrong between you and Jake?"

"It doesn't matter anymore."

The minutes slipped away, and still he didn't move. Eventually, as I began to recover, I realized he was still in shock.

"What was the business matter he wanted to discuss with you?"

My father was bone white. As he slowly swiveled his chair to face the window again, I noticed that the long sunset was over and darkness was falling at last on the city.

"Nothing," said my father. "Vicky, you'll excuse me, but I'm going to have to take a rain check on our game of chess."

"Of course." I was moved that he should have been so affected by the news of Jake's illness, and crossing the room, I stooped to kiss the top of his head as he sat in his chair. "Shall I stay longer so that we can just talk? Or would you rather be alone?"

"I have to be alone," he said. "I've got to think."

"Sure. Good night, then, Daddy," I said, giving him another kiss, and left him alone with his thoughts in the steadily darkening room.

686

III

JAKE SURVIVED his operation but for the first three days was allowed no visitors except the members of his immediate family. I heard that his elder daughter, Ruth, twice divorced and now living in Europe, flew to New York and visited him with Elsa, but Jake's son David, a California dropout, couldn't be traced, and his ex-wife Amy remained in Florida. When the ban on visitors was lifted, I felt reluctant to go to the hospital in case I met Elsa, but after a week of dithering I bought a small spray of flowers and ventured into the reception hall of Mount Sinai.

"I was wondering if I could see Mr. Jacob Reischman for a few minutes," I said after I'd been referred to the nurse in charge of the appropriate floor.

In the brief silence that followed, I noticed that she had blue eyes, finely lined at the corners, and soft dark hair beneath her cap. Then she said in a kind voice, "I'm sorry, but I must give you some bad news. Mr. Reischman had a relapse this morning and died half an hour ago. Would you be a member of the family?"

I said, "No." And then, "Yes. In a way. Excuse me." And turning away, I walked quickly down the corridor, avoided the elevators, and ran down the stairs to the lobby.

IV

ALICIA GREETED me in the hall of my father's apartment. As usual she was dressed, not dowdily, for her clothes were exquisitely cut, but dully, in a plain dark blue skirt and jacket with a white blouse and no jewelry. A small dark blue hat partially covered the dyed brown sweep of her hair.

"Hello, dear," she said. "I was just going out to lunch. Why, how very pale you look! Is anything the matter?"

"Oh, Alicia!" I said, the words tumbling out of my mouth. "I feel so sad. I've just been to the hospital, and they told me Jake died this morning. I don't know why I should feel so sad when I've seen little of him recently, but somehow he seemed to stand for the past—for something that's now gone forever . . ."

I stopped. It was the expression in her eyes. Her face remained still, her features composed in the passionless mask which had always alienated me, but her eyes were brilliant with memory, and I knew then, even before she spoke, that she had loved him.

V

"OF COURSE I never considered leaving your father," she said. "I've always loved him more than anyone else. But we've had our difficult times."

We were sitting by the window of her bedroom on the uncomfortable chaise longue which Alicia had for some reason cherished for years. Alicia was smoking a cigarette. The pitcher of martinis before us on the table was empty, but our glasses were still full.

". . . so you see what a mess it was," said this extraordinary woman I had never known. "It irritates me so much nowadays when adultery is depicted as if it were no more than an innocent date between teenagers. It's the fashion now, I know, to condemn hypocrisy, but all I can say is we're living in very dishonest times. We're not mechanical dolls programmed to copulate without emotion at the drop of a hat, and to pretend that we are—as most young people seem to today—strikes me as being not only dangerous but pitifully naive. How ironic that the chic word today is 'cool'! To dabble in other people's emotions isn't cool. It's lighting a fire and stepping into the flames."

There was a pause while she stubbed out her cigarette and I offered her another.

"Well, we all got burned," she said when the cigarette was alight, "but after Sam died, things got better. Cornelius gave up Teresa and I'd already given up Jake. I suspect Teresa was glad to go, but Jake . . . He wasn't the sort of man who quits easily. He approached me again after Sebastian was fired and matters were at a low ebb once more between myself and Cornelius, but of course there was no question of me resuming the affair, because by then I knew that Cornelius and I were capable of recapturing our past happiness no matter how deeply we might be estranged. We'd proved that after Sam died, and I thought that if only I waited long enough, we would prove it again."

"And did you?"

"No. I doubt if we ever will now. I've been waiting in vain . . . But don't misunderstand! We may not be close, but we don't quarrel and we're fond of each other, and that's more than most couples can say after thirty-six years of marriage. I'm content. I have my sons and my grandchildren, my health and my looks. On the whole, life's been very kind to me. It's only on days like today, when life seems so greatly diminished, that I want to cry for the past and the way life might have been."

"Alicia, I do wish we could have talked before."

"There was never anything to say. Our lives were like two parallel lines which never met. But I'm glad I've talked to you about Jake. I've wanted to talk to someone about him for years, but there was never anyone to tell." She looked over her shoulder at the silent phone. "I wonder if I should call your father. No, let him hear the news from someone else. It's better that way."

After a pause I said, "I'll call him," and began dialing the number of the bank at Willow and Wall.

VI

ON THE twenty-second of November, just a month after fifty thousand antiwar demonstrators had marched on Washington, the United States Army captured Hill 875 near Dak To after one of the bloodiest battles of the war in Vietnam, and the blood seemed to stream through my own living room as I watched the television news. That evening I wrote to Sebastian: "There's got to be an end to such pointless waste of life. Someone's just got to draw the line," but no one drew the line, so life went on with the daily body counts of the dead and the shattered, the daily promises of President Johnson to deliver his Great Society, the daily reminders of divisiveness and death. And as the drumbeat of violence rose in a steady crescendo, I was acutely aware of the accompanying music of the times shifting key as the songwriters moved away from innocent love songs and began instead to glamorize the increasingly fashionable drug scene.

"I draw the line at that kind of song," I said after I had been forced to listen to a certain hit record from beginning to end.

"Oh, Mom!"

"You can shriek all you like, but I'm not going to be soft and dishonest and pretend I think it's the greatest. You don't want me to be a hypocrite, do you?"

"But, Mom, you just don't know where it's at!"

"I know exactly where it's at. It's at the point where I draw the line and say this mindless retreat into passive drug-ridden introspection is just as sick as this mindless escalation of violence at home and overseas. God, I sometimes wonder how we'll survive this decadent disastrous decade!" I exclaimed passionately, and then realized with a shock that I was echoing the words Jake had used to reject a once-cherished culture which was now cracking apart at the seams.

"I'm sorry," I said to my children, "I don't mean to sound so hopelessly square, but try to see things for a moment from my point of view. It's hard for someone like me, who can remember better times, to stand by with a smile while the country undergoes this peculiarly unpleasant nervous breakdown. It's not easy to live through a national trauma without feeling rattled as all the old familiar landmarks of custom and behavior fall by the wayside, but perhaps the landmarks are still there after all, perhaps it's only on the surface that things have changed, perhaps young people today are in fact much as they've always been . . ."

"What's she talking about?"

"She's trying to tell us our generation's nothing unusual. What an insult! Everyone knows we're the unique product of the H-bomb and the postindustrial society—everyone knows there's never been a generation like us before in the whole history of mankind!"

"Mom knows all that—she's trying to be nice to us! Stop being so mean to her!"

"I'm not being mean to her! All I'm saying is that it's impossible for someone as old as she is to realize just how unique we are."

"Stop talking about me as if I'm senile!" I shouted. "And stop being so goddamned arrogant! You're right—this generation *is* unique! It's the first one insensitive enough to think good manners are unimportant!"

"Cool it, Mom. We don't mind you being old. We love you anyway."

"Those kids are driving me nuts," I said to my father that night as we sat down to play chess. "The whole younger generation's driving me nuts. Whenever I see anyone under twenty-five nowadays, I want to scream."

"I know how you feel." My father looked gloomy. "I fired two clerks today for peddling marijuana in the typing pool, but when I told Harry Morton during our lunch together up at the Trust, he just said that a lot of drug-taking was going on in the Wall Street lower echelons. Imagine that! I was shocked, but Harry just shrugged his shoulders and said it was a sign of the times."

Harry Morton was the president of the Van Zale Manhattan Trust, Van Zale's commercial bank, and was fifteen years younger than my father. My father had once tried to foster a romance between us, but men like Harry Morton, twice divorced, totally married to his job, and interested in nothing outside banking but the jet engine of his new private plane, had no appeal for me.

"Can't you do something to cheer your father up?" said Harry to me when we met at the end of November at one of my father's regular dinner parties. "He talks and acts as if the world's coming to an end!"

"Maybe it is," I said dryly, and sure enough, two days later came the first of a series of moves designed to end the world my father had controlled for over thirty years. A major article on the front page of *The Wall Street Journal* revealed that Donald Shine's notorious conglomerate Shine & General was planning to take over not another insurance company but Harry Morton's own Van Zale Manhattan Trust, the vital adjunct to my father's investment bank at Willow and Wall.

VII

"BUT I don't understand," said Eric. He and Paul had by this time returned to Choate after their noisy weekend at home that had left me with such an antipathy toward the younger generation, but as soon as the article had appeared in *The Wall Street Journal,* Eric phoned me from school. "How can this be a threat to Granddad? Isn't the Van Zale Manhattan Trust entirely separate from Van Zale's?"

"Legally, yes, but in practice, no. In practice it's as if they were one big bank. The Trust offers the banking services which Van Zale's used to offer before the Glass-Steagall Banking Act separated commercial and investment banking back in 1933. The two Van Zale banks are the two halves of the former single entity, and if one falls by the wayside, the other will be in trouble."

"But Shine could never take over Van Zale's!" protested Eric, horrified. "Van Zale's is a partnership still, not a corporation like the Trust! Surely Granddad has the power to exclude Shine indefinitely from Willow and Wall?"

"If the Trust falls to Donald Shine, Van Zale's days are numbered. Your grandfather may be able to hold things together till he dies or retires, but after that, Shine will move in. There'll be pressure to incorporate, the partners will sell out to become members of the new board, and then Shine can put his own man in the president's chair. That'll give him an investment bank as well as a commercial bank and an insurance company, and Shine & General will be a conglomerate specializing in a wide range of financial services, just as Shine's always planned."

"But surely . . . surely Shine's not going to succeed?"

"Well, Granddad seemed confident of winning, but I'm beginning to wonder if he's just putting up a front. Everyone else seems to think it'll be touch and go."

VIII

"ERIC CALLED," I said to my father, "and sent you his best wishes for the coming fight. How's it going? What's your next move?"

"We're figuring out a way we can attack Shine & General's stock and weaken Shine's artillery."

"But aren't bear raids illegal nowadays?"

My father gave me a cynical smile. "Of course," he said.

By this time I was beginning to have a clearer picture of what was happening. Camouflaging himself by funneling funds through a New Jersey bank, Donald Shine had embarked in October on a repeat performance of the takeover which had annihilated the Stamford-Hartford Reliance Insurance Corporation. Shine & General had begun to buy huge blocks of shares in the Van Zale Manhattan Trust, but unknown to Donald Shine, word had reached my father of his plans and his supposedly secret purchases had been observed and monitored. Shine and his lieutenants were still putting the finishing touches to their tender—the offer they believed the bank's stockholders would find irresistible—and were still continuing to buy the necessary shares when my father, acting through Harry Morton, forced Shine into the open by leaking the news to *The Wall Street Journal.*

Caught on the wrong foot, Shine made an ambiguous statement which only heightened the publicity, and the day after my father had cynically confirmed to me that "bear raids" were illegal, the stock of Shine & General started to fall.

"But how are you doing it?" I said, mystified, to my father. "Rumors of a takeover usually send the stock up, not down!"

"Shine & General's not as secure as everyone thinks it is. We've been secretly investigating it since early September, and it didn't take us long to find out that it's top-heavy and overextended. Donald Shine may be a bright boy, but all the information indicates he's bitten off more than he can chew. Youth," said my father with a sigh, "is so impetuous."

"But I still don't understand how you can make the stock fall!"

My father laughed. "It's a technique known as 'multiple flogging.' It's a new name for the old practice of bear raiding, and it's impossible for the authorities to detect it."

Two days later, disturbed by the publicity and his falling stock, Shine called Harry Morton and asked for a meeting. Paying lip service to the fact that Van Zale's and the Trust were separate entities, my father stayed away and only listened to the recording of the brief hostile encounter; Morton told Shine that he was an innocent if he thought he could get away with taking over an important commercial bank, but Shine insisted that he was well-intentioned and wanted only to improve the nation's banking services by making them more democratic.

A strategy meeting was then held at the offices of the Van Zale Manhattan Trust and was attended not only by my father and the board of the Trust but also by all the senior officers of the huge banks who had a stake in opposing Shine.

"For, after all," explained my father to me, "if Shine succeeds with us, who knows who his next target might be?"

Various strategies were discussed, even the extreme suggestion that the Trust should merge with some other computer-leasing firm; this would have created a situation in which Shine could no longer have acquired the bank without violating the antitrust laws. However, the strategy which found most favor was one involving the introduction of state and federal legislation to make such a takeover illegal. Meanwhile, Shine & General's stock had steadied on the

Exchange, and Shine was summoning his resources to move forward into the attack.

At this point my father invited Shine to lunch.

Shine accepted and was given a very plain meal (steak, baked potato, salad, no wine) in the partners' dining room at Willow and Wall.

My father talked about the detriment to the bank of a hostile takeover, pointed out that the top management would certainly resign, and forecast that the leading clients would take their business elsewhere. Shine protested that he had no intention of making a hostile takeover and repeated that all he wanted was to improve the bank by making it more responsive to its stockholders and enlarging the range of services available to its customers. My father suggested kindly that he was an ignorant young man who would be incapable of running a bank. Shine suggested that it was time the old guard moved over to make room for new blood. My father said he would offer him one last chance to withdraw gracefully before that new blood was splattered from one end of Wall Street to the other.

But Donald Shine just laughed and said, "That'll be the day!"

That same afternoon he began to receive calls from the leading investment banks, including Reischman's, to say that under no circumstances would they participate in any Shine & General tender for the Van Zale Manhattan Trust, and two days later Shine was informed that the Trust had retained the two leading proxy-soliciting firms to deny their services to his corporation.

Shine & General's stock began to fall again. It was now down to 120 and in full retreat, and in early December the Van Zale lawyers began to draft laws which could be passed by the Assembly in Albany to prevent the takeover of banks such as the Trust by conglomerates such as Shine & General. Meanwhile, in Washington the Department of Justice had written to Shine to say that although the antitrust laws were not apparently violated by his plans, the proposed merger did raise certain questions which they felt they should discuss with him.

Shine & General's stock slipped to 115.

When Shine went to Washington, he found not only the members of the Senate Banking and Currency Committee but also the majority of the Federal Reserve Board were adamantly opposed to the takeover; he also found himself regarded as a pirate, and realizing at last

694

that both big business and government were firmly set against him, he decided he had no choice but to surrender.

For the last time Shine and his lieutenants met Harry Morton and the task force of the Van Zale Manhattan Trust. Shine said he planned to issue a statement of withdrawal, and once his opponents had finished wringing one another's hands in an ecstasy of relief, the first man Harry called was my father at Willow and Wall.

IX

"Now THAT it's all over," said Harry to me the next day at my father's champagne reception, "I can admit it was a very close call. God only knows what would have happened if we hadn't had the time to investigate Shine & General thoroughly and force them into the open before they were fully prepared to launch their attack."

A passing footman refilled my glass. "You mean," I said, struggling to concentrate amidst the roar of a hundred guests in a celebration mood, "that you were damn lucky to have prior knowledge of Shine's plans. But, Harry . . ." I had to raise my voice as a group behind me burst out laughing at yet another anti-Shine wisecrack, "Harry, who tipped you off? Did one of Shine's lieutenants double-cross him?"

"My God, didn't your father tell you? It was Jake who tipped us off, Vicky! Jake Reischman!"

The room seemed to empty itself of noise. I was aware of the crowds around me, but now they were mere moving shadows and I was alone with Harry Morton on a bare chilling stage.

"You're kidding," I said.

Harry laughed. He was tall, almost as tall as Scott, and he had that brand of distinguished good looks which were so often found in the corporate boardrooms, where an impressive appearance is so useful in disguising less-attractive behavior. He had dark hair, well-silvered in the right places, frank blue eyes, and remarkably even teeth which were displayed whenever he smiled. They gave him a predatory look which his charm could never quite manage to annul. Sebastian had once described him as a barracuda.

"No, it's true, I promise you!" He laughed again. "Ironic, isn't it? Jake had Shine's full confidence because Shine looked up to him—respected him as the cream of American Jewry. But of course Jake detested him. Jake was a snob, one of the old school. Don't forget that when the Russian Jews streamed into New York at the turn of the century, it wasn't the Gentiles who flung up their hands in horror; it was the German Jews uptown."

I saw the tennis court drawn on my father's blotter, and in my memory I heard Jake talking wryly of the Bar Harbor Brotherhood. I tried to speak, but Harry's arm was already steering me into a quieter corner of my father's long living room and his voice was already saying idly, "That's better—now we can hear ourselves think. Are you truly so surprised about Jake? Cornelius said Jake used you as an intermediary."

"Yes, he did. But I didn't realize what was going on. My father hasn't been confiding in me." And a voice in my head immediately said: Why? But another voice answered just as swiftly: It doesn't matter because it's all over now.

"Well, I guess he felt it was strictly men's business," said Harry indulgently, "and not something you should have to bother your pretty head about. No, the real mystery is not who tipped *us* off. The real mystery is who tipped off Donald Shine."

I stared at him. "What do you mean?"

"Well, of course he was tipped off!"

"Why? What about? How?"

Harry was looking more indulgent than ever. "My dear, Shine had to have inside information about the Trust in order to work out exactly how he could best take it over, and everything indicates that his inside information was very comprehensive indeed. I hate to point the finger at any of the board, but Shine's knowledge seems to have been on a boardroom level, and beyond the board I can't think of anyone—except your father, of course, and a couple of his partners—who would be in a position to give Shine the briefing he needed."

"More champagne, sir?" said a passing footman.

The champagne was pale gold. I watched it sparkle in Harry's glass and listened as Harry's voice added, "There'll have to be a full investigation, of course, and that upsets me, it really does. Like your father, I'm just a nice well-intentioned guy who dislikes any unpleasantness."

I said abruptly, knifing through his nonsense, "When do you think Shine first got the idea of taking over the Trust?"

"I'd say last spring. Jake died in September, and by that time Shine seems to have had all the information he needed and was busy formulating his plan of attack. If we assume he'd been working on the idea for at least three months, that takes us back to June . . . or maybe May."

"The weather was lovely in May," I said. "I remember Scott and I watching the most wonderful sunset at Beekman Tower . . . but no, I don't remember it too well after all, not really, it's just a blur in my mind." I drank all the champagne in my glass and turned aside. "Excuse me, please, Harry."

Leaving him, I moved around the edge of the crowd toward the door, but all the time I was watching my father as he stood beneath the central chandelier with a bunch of his oldest friends. He saw me and smiled, and somehow I smiled back because I didn't want him to know anything was wrong. I didn't want anyone to know. I didn't even want myself to know, and the voice in my head spoke to me again, telling me that if I didn't think about Harry's disclosures they'd soon go away.

I went home and resolutely began to make more plans for my wedding on Christmas Eve.

X

"HI, HONEY, how are you doing over there?"

"Not so badly. How lovely to hear you! I've just got back from the most exhausting Bacchanalian revels at Daddy's place—everyone's gone berserk with relief, and I left them drinking champagne by the gallon. They'll be cursing Shine all over again tomorrow when they awake with their hangovers!"

Scott laughed. "So I've missed a good party!"

"No, all that wild glee was very boring, and besides . . . Oh, I'm just sick to death of Donald Shine! I don't want to talk about him anymore—he's just past history as far as I'm concerned, and all I care about right now is the future. Oh, darling, I can't wait to meet you at the airport! I'm having the MG specially overhauled for your arrival!"

"Forget it! Why don't you borrow a Cadillac and chauffeur from your father and put a double bed and pull-down shades in the back? Incidentally, is your father all right? He hasn't been in the office the last few times I called, but I guess he's been very tied up with the takeover."

"Oh, don't worry about Daddy! I haven't seen much of him lately either, but he's okay, he's fine, there's no need to worry about Daddy at all."

"Honey, is something wrong? You sound a bit . . ."

"No, I'm just going crazy because there's so much to do before the wedding, and I keep having these neurotic dreams—"

"Erotic? So do I! Couldn't get by without them!"

"No, neurotic—neurotic as in psycho and bananas and freaked-out. Darling, please don't get knocked down by a bus or crushed to death in an auto accident or killed in a plane crash, I mean, you will be careful, won't you, you promise me? I keep having these horrible dreams that we're never going to meet again."

"I hope that's not wishful thinking!"

"Oh, Scott—darling, if only you knew how much I love you and how I care about absolutely *nothing* but the future—our future . . ."

"Then relax. All you're suffering from is prewedding nerves. Aren't they supposed to be very common?"

"I . . . I guess they are. . . . Are you nervous too?"

"Yes—at the thought of that hair-raising little sports car! Can't you give it away to someone? Then we could look forward to a long and happy life together!"

I had to laugh. "I feel better now that I've talked to you."

"Honey, don't worry about anything. I've no intention of stepping under a bus, believe me. Just be at that airport and watch me walk through the custom area. I'll be there."

"I know you will," I said. "I know it."

"Everything's going to be all right," he said. "Everything's going to be just fine."

XI

"MOM," SAID Eric, "may I talk to you for a moment, please?"

It was the day before Scott was due to arrive in New York, and both Eric and Paul were now home from school for the Christmas recess. I was sitting at the desk in my bedroom as I worked out the servants' wages. Dinner was due in half an hour.

"Yes, of course, Eric. Come on in."

He sat down in the chair next to the desk and regarded me seriously. This was characteristic; he was a very serious young man.

He was as tall as Sam now, but thinner and more angular, and the blond hair which had given him a resemblance to me in his childhood had darkened to brown. His eyes were somber behind his glasses, and as he swallowed awkwardly I realized to my astonishment that he was nervous. The idea that any of my children could be nervous of me was so novel that it took me a moment to ask him what was wrong.

"Two of my best plants have died," he said.

"Oh, Eric, what a pity! And Nurse is usually so good with them while you're away."

"It's not Nurse's fault. It's the air. I'm sure the pollution's getting worse, and that's why I . . . I feel so strongly that more should be done to protect the environment. In fact, I've decided that when I go to college . . ." He stopped. He was looking white, and as I saw him struggle to tell me the truth he could no longer carry alone, I found myself leaning forward until I was sitting on the very edge of my chair.

"When you go to college . . ."

"When I go to college, I want to—*must*—major in something relevant. Mom, I'm very sorry, but I can't go on pretending anymore. I can't major in economics. I can't be a banker. I want to major in environmental studies and then get some kind of job in conservation."

I knew it was important that I should pull myself together, but it was hard to make the effort required of me. I felt too sad and too disappointed for my father.

Then I was taken by surprise. Eric leaned forward and said urgently, "Mom, try to understand. This so-called Great Society is laying waste this planet, and this society is fueled by money from institutions like Van Zale's, and that's why I *cannot* be a banker, not under any circumstances. I know I have a duty to Granddad, particularly since Paul obviously won't go near the bank, and it's hard to imagine Benjamin being anything except a pain in the neck, but I can't sell out my principles to work for something I don't believe in. Can't you see how wrong that would be? I'd be trying to be something I'm not, and then after a while I'm sure I'd hate myself and despise what I was doing and consider that I was wasting my life. . . . Don't try to make me over into what I'm not, Mom. Please . . . let me be myself! Let me do what I really want to do!"

So it was all very clear in the end, clearer than I had ever imagined, and of course I found the strength I needed to overcome my sadness, because I realized how very unimportant my disappointment was when compared with Eric's happiness. I'd been on the brink of making the mistake my father had made when he had tried to bend me into Emily's image, but I wasn't my father and I wasn't going to make his mistakes. I was myself, and when I spoke, it was with my own voice, not my father's. I said, "Of course you must do what you really want to do, Eric. I'm very proud of you for having the courage to speak out, and you can be sure I'll back you all the way."

He stumbled over to me and gave me a clumsy hug. I was moved because he was normally so reserved, and in a flash I understood why he had been withdrawn for so long. He had been living with his conflict ever since he had been old enough to understand that he was destined to succeed his grandfather at the bank.

"Mom, Granddad . . ."

"It's all right, I'll tell him. But I may not tell him just yet. I've got to pick the right moment."

He hugged me again, and I heard his muffled voice saying, "He'll never understand, will he?"

"No," I said, "probably not. But I think your father would have understood. He spent so much of his life doing something he didn't really want to do."

That made him feel less guilty. He said he wished he had known his father better, and we talked about Sam. Time passed. My housekeeper looked in to say that dinner was ready. We joined the rest of the family in the dining room. But that night I sat up long after all the children had gone to bed, and all I could ask myself was: How am I ever going to tell my father? How am I ever going to find the words to let him know?

Then just before dawn it occurred to me that Eric's decision would strengthen my position as peacemaker when the time came for me to engineer a truce between my father and Scott. If his grandsons were to have no part to play in the bank's future, my father might at last feel able to turn back to Scott and consent to a big reconciliation with his son by adoption.

It seemed not only a reasonable but a profoundly satisfying possibility.

I fell instantly into a dreamless sleep.

Chapter Seven

I

SCOTT WALKED out of the customs area and I ran to meet him. He was carrying a raincoat and a small case, but he dropped both to embrace me, and the familiar taste of his mouth made me feel dizzy with relief that nothing had kept us apart. Pushing my fingers blindly through the hair at the nape of his neck, I pressed his face again to mine and felt his arms tighten, crushing me against his ribs.

"Welcome home!" I whispered at last.

"You see?" he said, laughing. "I made it!"

A redcap was already wheeling away the rest of the luggage, and outside the building the chauffeur was waiting with my father's latest Cadillac.

"Pull-down shades and double bed?"

"Just tinted glass!"

"So you took me seriously about the sports car?"

"I began to be terrified I'd have an accident on the way to the airport."

"Why, you poor little thing!" he said, astonished, taking my neurotic fears seriously for the first time. "I'm sorry I laughed at you on the phone."

"It doesn't matter—nothing matters anymore now that you're here."

We sank into the backseat of the Cadillac and he pulled me into his arms.

Since it seemed likely that we would have to move to California in the new year in order to humor my father's paranoiac fear of working alongside Scott in New York, I had made no effort to set up a new home for us in the city, but had instead done my best to adapt the available space in my duplex to my new life as Scott's wife. I didn't foresee our stay in California as being a long one, but I thought if I played along with my father at first he in his turn would be more willing to play along with me later when I began pressuring for our recall to New York. Entangling myself in these necessary diplomatic maneuvers would be both exhausting and tiresome, but I felt I could tackle anything, even my father's paranoia, once I was Scott's wife and Scott was no longer separated from me by the Atlantic Ocean.

"How are the kids?" he was saying.

"Fine." With pubescent children on the premises, I had felt it would be a mistake to offer him my bedroom at the apartment before we were married, and Scott had agreed to spend the last days of his bachelor life at a suite at the Carlyle. I had offered him my private apartment, but Scott had preferred the convenience of the hotel's room service.

"And your father?"

"Oh, he's okay. Darling, I can't wait to show you the changes I've made in the apartment—I've had the master bedroom completely redecorated, and the dressing room has been converted into a retreat for you . . ." I was intertwining my fingers with his as I spoke; it was hard to believe he was so near. Every bone in his hand seemed important, and every movement of every finger seemed vital.

"It sounds wonderful!" he said, smiling at me. "I can't wait to see it all!"

I felt dizzy with relief again, although I wasn't sure why. "You're so relaxed," I said. "So calm. I think I expected you to be as tense as I am."

"But why? I've finished with Europe and you're almost my wife and here I am back in New York! If ever there was an occasion for relaxing, this is it!"

"Of course! How silly I'm being. . . . It's just that the last months have been so awful—the decorators running wild in the apartment, Donald Shine running wild on Wall Street . . ."

"Poor old Don!" said Scott indulgently. "So the Eastern Seaboard finally taught him that chutzpah doesn't necessarily conquer all—a bitter pill for him to swallow! I guess he became overconfident once he got Jake's support in the Trust takeover."

At first I thought I'd misheard him. "I'm sorry—could you say that last part again?"

He said it again. My heart started to thump against my ribs.

"But Scott," I said, "Jake wasn't supporting Shine."

"Why, sure he was! Shine needed to be thoroughly briefed about the Trust, and Jake was the obvious route to the information he needed. Jake knew all the board of the Trust, and there must have been at least one member he could have bent to suit his own purposes. Now that Jake's dead, I doubt if we'll ever know who that member was, but I guess Harry Morton has to be allowed his witch-hunt and his therapeutic purges. I must ask your father how the inquiry's going, although personally I think it's a waste of time . . . Hey, what's the matter? Why are you looking at me like that? What's wrong?"

I said unsteadily, "Just about everything. Jake was the informer, but he was on our side. That's why we won. He slipped the word to us way back in September that Shine was after the Trust."

There was a silence broken only by the remote hum of the Cadillac. We were leaving the airport and heading for the Van Wyck Expressway. Beyond the tinted windows the sky was a distorted gray.

"Did no one tell you?" I said. "No one at all?"

"No." He hesitated, but only for a moment. Then he said, "But that's not so odd. I was very cut off over there in London, and some things are better not discussed over the transatlantic phone. Also, I can hardly believe . . . Honey, are you sure you have your facts right? Jake was Shine's obvious ally. He'd hated your father for years."

"At the end, when he was dying, none of that mattered anymore."

"But even so . . . Are you sure—quite sure . . . ?"

"Scott, you've been away so long you've no idea how strongly the conservatives of Wall Street felt about a smart young operator like Shine muscling in on the financial community! Jake acted in character. Like all the old guard, he viewed Shine with prejudice, anger, and just plain revulsion."

"But then if Jake didn't brief Shine, who did?"

I shook my head, shrugged my shoulders. "I don't know. I don't think anyone knows. Isn't that why Harry's in the middle of this postmortem at the Trust?"

"God knows what Harry can be up to. I don't understand any of it, and I still can't believe this story about Jake. Where did you get it from?"

"Harry himself."

"Did he talk directly to Jake?"

"No."

"Well, there you are! The whole story's some kind of crazy rumor —you'd be amazed at the kind of rumors that get around after a crisis like this. I wonder where Harry picked up the story. I wouldn't have thought he'd have been so gullible."

"Harry got it from my father."

"*Your father?*"

"Jake talked to Daddy on the phone before he died."

"But that's impossible! They hadn't talked directly to each other for over ten years!"

"I was in the room when my father made the call. Jake used me to persuade my father to contact him. It's all true, Scott. It's no rumor. It's all true."

He stared at me. He said nothing. Then he turned to stare out of the window at the ugly Long Island suburbs.

"Of course," I said, "although I was in the room I couldn't hear a word Jake was saying over the phone, and my father gave nothing away. He was upset afterward, but I thought that was just because of Jake's illness. It never occurred to me at the time to think they were talking about . . . well, never mind what they were talking about, what does it matter now, I don't care. The Trust's safe and Shine's withdrawn and that's that. Oh, Scott, please! Let's forget the whole thing! Can't we talk about something else?"

"Sure." He was motionless, still staring out of the window. His face was without expression. At last he said, "Yes. I'm sorry . . . tell me more about the kids. What was Paul's final verdict on his first semester at Choate?"

I started to talk about Paul. I was wondering whether I should tell him about Eric's decision not to go into the bank, but in the end I was so loath to discuss any subject connected with One Willow Street that I said nothing. I talked instead about my plans for a family Christmas, and as I listened to my voice chattering on and on, I saw the jagged towers of Manhattan pierce the steel skies beyond the concrete ribbon of the freeway.

When we reached his suite at the Carlyle, all I wanted was to go to bed and bolt the door against the world for a few precious hours, but Scott merely said, "Why don't you order up some drinks while I take a shower?" and left me alone in the sitting room.

Dialing room service, I ordered six Cokes, a bucket of ice, and one double martini. Then I went on sitting in the living room and staring at the closed bedroom door. Some time passed, but eventually the bell of the telephone nearby stirred softly and I knew Scott had picked up the extension in the bedroom.

I told myself I wouldn't listen. But I did. I couldn't stop myself. A second later my burning cheek was pressing against the panels of the bedroom door and I heard Scott say abruptly, "Is he there, please? Okay, could you have him call Scott Sullivan at the Hotel Carlyle? Thanks." The receiver clicked, and by the time he was opening the door I was already some distance away by the window.

He had changed not into casual clothes but into another suit with a fresh shirt and tie, and I was just about to ask him in surprise why he felt he had to be so formal when the room-service waiter arrived with the drinks.

The telephone rang just as Scott had produced a tip.

"Shall I get it?" I said, but he was already reaching for the receiver.

"Hello?" he said, but evidently it was not the call he expected. I saw him relax for a moment, but suddenly he was tense again, and as I watched, he turned away as if to exclude me from the scene. "Sure," he said into the receiver. "I'll come right away. No problem. How are you doing, Cornelius?"

But the receiver went dead in his hand. He stood looking at it for a moment before turning back to face me with a shrug. "That was your father," he said. "Some new crisis. He wants to see me right away."

"Oh, but . . ." I ran out of breath. It was so odd. My lungs seemed to have forgotten how to work rhythmically. I wondered if I were belatedly developing my father's asthmatic weakness.

"Yes, of course he's being outrageous," said Scott quickly, "but what can you do with despots but humor them? I know better than to argue with your father once he decides to play the great dictator! Look, honey, I've no idea how long this'll take, but why don't you go home and I'll join you there as soon as possible?"

"Okay." I was breathing again, but every breath hurt. I sank slowly down on the edge of the couch. "You go ahead. I'll just have my drink."

"Sure." He stooped to kiss me, his lips brushing my forehead, and the next moment he was gone.

I drank my martini, but it seemed to make no difference to the tightness in my chest. I had just realized I'd never been so frightened in my life when the phone rang a second time at my side.

I was so terrified that several seconds passed before I could nerve myself to pick up the receiver.

"Hello?" I whispered.

A man's voice said cautiously, "Vicky?"

"Yes."

"Well, hi, beautiful—I thought it must be you! This is Donald Shine."

II

"HEY, IS Scott there?" he said. "I just checked with the office, and when I heard he'd called me, I realized I was only a couple of blocks from the Carlyle, so I decided to stop by. I'm downstairs right now in the lobby. Can I come up?"

In those brief moments while he spoke, I lived through an entire lifetime of love, hate, rage, and grief, but when I spoke, my voice was expressionless.

"Sure," I said. "Why not?" And then, cutting the connection, I went to the door to wait for him.

He was looking very smart in a well-cut dark green suit with an olive-green striped shirt and a color-coordinated patterned tie. His hair, still as bright and floppy as if it had been newly washed, was longer than ever and waved attractively over his ears. Despite his recent setbacks, his brown eyes had lost none of their zest, and as soon as he walked into the room I saw that his buoyant manner too was unchanged.

"Hi!" he said, sauntering across the threshold as if he had bought the entire hotel seconds earlier. "Where's Scott?"

"He's not here. But I wanted to talk to you."

"Oh, yeah?" said Donald Shine, swiveling abruptly to face me.

The pain had gone from my chest. Now that I knew the truth, I could no longer be paralyzed by my fear of facing unbearable facts, and suddenly it was easy to be cool, just as easy as it was to say in my politest voice, "Please sit down, Mr. Shine."

"Now, wait a minute! If you're going to bitch to me about the Trust, I think I'll keep on my toes! Look, the Trust is buried six feet deep as far as I'm concerned, and even if it wasn't, I wouldn't discuss it with you after the hand you dealt me!"

"The hand *I* dealt you? What the hell do you mean?"

"Well, it was you, wasn't it? You committed pillow talk, as Doris Day said to Rock Hudson before she lost her virginity. Or did she lose it? I don't think I ever saw that movie."

"Are you trying to tell me—"

"Ah, come on, Vicky! Come clean! Scott trusted you when he should have kept his mouth shut—right? And then you ran straight to Daddy with the bad news as soon as Scott's back was turned! How else would Cornelius Van Zale have found out about my plans so well in advance? Hell, I'm surprised Scott's still going with you, but I guess he figures you're the safety net—he's taken a bad fall on the high wire, but so long as he marries you, he'll still wind up president of an incorporated Van Zale's one day after the old man's kicked the bucket!"

"But . . ."

"And goddammit, why shouldn't he marry you? You're so pretty that even *I* can't feel mad at you anymore! Scott's a lucky s.o.b., and you can tell him I said so!" He smiled good-naturedly and moved back toward the door. "Well, if you'll excuse me . . ."

"I wasn't the one who tipped off my father," I said. "It was Jake Reischman."

As he swung round, I noticed that there were flecks of green in his dark eyes and that the pupils seemed to dilate as all the buoyancy drained from his face. He said, "You've got to be kidding."

"No. He told me personally that old friendships meant more to him than new business ties."

There was a long silence.

"Well, shit," said Donald Shine at last. "Well, *shit*." He pulled open the door, but then, overcome with the desire to express his rage, he shoved it shut again and spun to face me. "If that story's true," he said violently, "that lover of yours is in big trouble. Jake knew everything. He knew Scott suggested to me last May that my next target should be the Trust, and he knew Scott gave me all the information I needed. There was nothing I didn't tell Jake about the whole deal."

"Thank you," I said. "I'm sure that was exactly what Scott wanted to find out when he called you just now. Good-bye, Mr. Shine."

"And you can tell that father of yours—"

"The door's right behind you. Please go."

"The hell with you—the hell with the whole goddamned lot of you, you fucking snobs!" yelled Donald Shine as he walked out of my life, and then, as the door slammed, I found myself alone at last with all the terrible wreckage he had left behind.

III

BLUNDERING DOWNSTAIRS, I grabbed a cab and told the driver to take me to Willow and Wall. My moment of calm had passed, and now the fear was smothering me again, pushing me to the brink of panic. I knew nothing except that I had to get to Scott as soon as possible.

"Yes, ma'am?" said the new young security guard at the bank's entrance. "Can I help you?"

"I want to see Mr. Sullivan, one of the partners—a tall dark man in his forties—he would have arrived here about half an hour ago."

"Oh, he left, ma'am. He didn't stay long."

"Left? Left, did you say? Are you sure? All right, I'll see my father—Mr. Van Zale."

"Mr. Van Zale's left too, ma'am. He left in his car shortly after Mr. Sullivan."

"I see. I'm sorry, but I've got to sit down. I'm not feeling well. Is there a chair?"

He hastily showed me into the inner lobby, where I sank down on a chair facing the pillars which framed the great hall, but before I had time to fight my nausea, one of the partners rose from his desk in the distance and hurried over to me.

"Vicky! Are you okay?"

"Peter . . . No, I'm feeling awful. Is there any brandy some-where? Perhaps my father's office . . . I know he's left for the day, but perhaps if I could just sit in his room quietly for a while . . ."

"Sure. I'll take you there myself. Should I call a doctor?"

I somehow found the words to tell him this was unnecessary.

We were walking through the great hall and I was staring at the floor so that I didn't have to acknowledge the other partners whose desks I passed. My father's office lay off the back lobby, and once I was there I got rid of my escort, drank the brandy he had poured me, and slumped into the chair behind my father's desk. There were several phones on the desk. I tried the black one first and after some delay obtained an outside line.

The receptionist at the Carlyle said Scott had not yet returned, and although I dialed the hotel a second time five minutes later, there was still no answer from the suite. Then I dialed the number of my father's apartment.

He had just stepped into the hall.

"Vicky?" he said as the butler passed him the receiver.

"Yes." I couldn't go on.

"Where are you?"

"Willow and Wall."

"Have you talked to Scott?"

"No. To Donald Shine."

My father said curtly, "I'll come at once. Stay where you are, please. I'll be as quick as I can."

"Daddy . . ."

"How much do you know?"

"Everything. Oh, God, everything."

"Then you'll understand that I had no choice but to—"

"No . . . no, you didn't fire him . . . please, please say you didn't—"

"It wasn't just my decision, Vicky. I don't have the power on my own to fire Scott before the new year, but of course once all the partners knew just how grossly he'd misconducted himself, jeopardizing not only the Trust but the entire firm at Willow and Wall—"

"Daddy, you can't do this. You mustn't. You must reinstate him. It's all been the most terrible mistake—he would never have messed around with Shine if he hadn't been under this delusion that you intended to cut him out altogether!"

"Now, hold it, Vicky! Take it easy! The situation's not as bad as you think. Of course Scott realized I had no choice but to fire him— he came to me fully prepared for the worst, even resigned to it. There was no big melodramatic scene. Quite the contrary! We had a calm reasonable discussion and I offered to do everything in my power to see he was offered an equivalent partnership elsewhere. I

also made it clear that although it was impossible for me to retain
him as a partner, I was anxious for your sake that we should remain
on friendly terms. Things'll work out, Vicky. This has been a catastrophe, I won't deny that, but we're all going to get over it. Do you
hear me? Are you listening? We're all going to get over this, Vicky.
It's all going to—"

I hung up on him and dialed the Carlyle, but still no one picked
up the phone in Scott's suite. I knew I should rush there immediately,
but when I stood up, black spots danced before my eyes and I had to
sit down again. I poured myself some more brandy, and as I continued to sit numbly in my father's chair, one thought detached itself
from the jumble of impressions tormenting me and revolved round
and round in my mind. I thought: I don't believe my father. I don't
believe one single word he says.

I stared at the top of the desk. Presently I realized I was looking
for something, although what that something was, I didn't know.
There were some letters under a glass paperweight, a photograph of
Alicia, a photograph of me, a leather desk set, two slim files, and an
unexpectedly large silver cigarette box. My father never kept cigarettes for guests, never encouraged smoking in his presence.

Reaching forward, I raised the lid.

"Oh, God," I said, and in the box the spools of the exquisite little
tape recorder revolved automatically at the sound of my voice.

I had found my father's latest toy.

I fidgeted with it clumsily for a time, but at last the tape was rewound and I had discovered how to play it back. I pushed the button. The performance began.

For two minutes I listened to a one-sided phone conversation between my father and Harry Morton, but seconds after this ended a
woman's voice said over the intercom, "Mr. Sullivan's here to see
you, Mr. Van Zale."

"Show him in."

Another pause. The door opened. Scott's voice said pleasantly,
"Cornelius! Good to see you again!"

I waited, holding my breath, but all I heard was a silence broken
only by Scott saying abruptly, "Well, if you won't talk and won't
shake hands, perhaps I should ask for an explanation."

My father did speak then. He said as dispassionately as a chess
player winding up a difficult game with all his most consummate skill:
"Let me first fix you a drink."

IV

I LISTENED, a blind witness to carnage, while the little spools turned around and around in the shining box. The world was reduced to a desktop and the voices that after a while I failed to recognize because it seemed they could have no connection with the two people I loved. I told myself I was listening to a conversation between strangers; I told myself I was hallucinating, acting out the nightmares which had seized control of my subconscious mind; I told myself I was someone else in some other place and that eventually I would emerge from the world of illusion and be reclaimed once more by the world of reality.

But all the while I told myself these frantic lies, I knew that the revolving spools *were* reality and that I was right there watching them as they spun all my dreams far out of sight into oblivion.

"You've just wasted your entire life, Scott. You've ended up as big a failure as your father. And the greatest irony of all is that for years and years I wanted you to have the bank. In fact, although you didn't know it, you'd dedicated yourself to giving me what I wanted most."

"No!" I screamed. "Don't tell him that! Never, never tell him!"

But the spools never stopped for one instant, and my father's voice went on.

"But it wasn't enough for you to get the bank, was it? You're so mentally sick that nothing less than the destruction of everything I cared about would satisfy you, so you started messing around with my daughter and dividing me from the people I loved."

"No!" I sobbed. "No, no, no!"

"No!" shouted Scott. "It wasn't like that! You're the one who's sick, twisting everything around like this and making out I don't love Vicky!"

"Well, you can forget about Vicky now! She's through with you. She told me so herself. As soon as she heard the truth from Jake back in September, she saw at once how you were using her to guarantee your future!"

"That's a lie!"

"Is it? I tell you, she wanted to break off with you right then and there, but I persuaded her to hold on until I'd taken care of Shine. She didn't want to do it—she's scared of you. She's been scared of you for some time—haven't you noticed how tense and nervous she's become? She didn't even want to see you today, but I gave her my word I'd send for you as soon as you arrived at the hotel. I didn't want to run the risk of you harming her."

"But I'd never harm Vicky, never!"

"My God, you've got a hell of a nerve to say that—and to think you accuse *me* of lying! You must be even sicker than I thought!"

"I swear to you *I'd never hurt Vicky!*"

"Don't give me that crap. You wanted to kill her back in August."

I thought dimly: Kevin betrayed me. In the end, like Jake, he found his first loyalty was to that alliance formed years before I was born.

"She told me all about it. You tried to beat her up. You threatened to kill her. She never got over that, never, and she never will, but she was too frightened of you to break the engagement off right away. It was only when she got back to New York and learned the whole truth about your activities with Shine that she realized just how far she'd been used and abused!"

"You're lying to me, you're lying to me just as you once lied to me about my father!"

"You know I'm not. You know it's the truth. You just can't face up to it, that's all. You're too sick. You ought to be locked up. The very least I can do is make sure you never get another job in banking, and the very least I can do is stop you from terrorizing my daughter. I'm going to see all Wall Street knows about the way you double-crossed me with Donald Shine, and I've already got security guards keeping a twenty-four-hour watch on my family. You make one move—just one—to see Vicky again, and I'll see you nailed on an assault rap, and don't tell me I can't do it, because we both know damned well I can. You're finished. Got it? I don't want to know you, Vicky doesn't want to know you, nobody wants to know you anymore. You've failed. You're through. Now, get out of here and go somewhere a long way away and live with those truths—if you can. From now on I don't care what happens to you, because I never want to see you again. It's over. It's finished. I have nothing else to say."

I switched off the tape recorder. I said aloud, "I can't listen to such wickedness," but I was still speaking when I turned the recorder back on again. "I can't listen," I said. "I can't." But there was my father, talking with such poisonous credibility as he laid waste the life that was so precious to me, and there was Scott, shouting abuse until the room echoed with his disjointed sentences, and then my father's bodyguards entered the room and there was a scuffle and someone, surely not Scott, but someone very ill, was threatening violence, and my father said, "Make one more threat like that in front of witnesses and you'll be in the psychiatric block of the nearest jail before sunset tonight," and then, as Scott began to shout obscenities again, I switched off the recorder. But this time I didn't switch it back on. I looked at the little spools dumbly for a long time. Then I rewound the tape, removed it from the recorder, and slipped it into my purse. I was dry-eyed by that time, and my hands were steady.

I left the room. I walked the whole length of the great hall without looking either to right or to left, and when the doorman in the front lobby offered to find me a cab, I said, "Yes. Thank you, that would be nice," as if I were on my way to some social engagement.

Halfway uptown I almost asked the driver to stop at a pay phone, but I knew there was no point in calling the Carlyle again. Scott obviously wasn't answering the phone.

At the hotel I paid the driver and crossed the lobby to the elevators. I began to feel as if I were moving in a dream; the world looked bright but far away, as if seen through the wrong end of a telescope, and I could no longer hear what people were saying.

With my hand still steady I used my key to unlock the door of the suite, and walked in. There was, of course, a note. I believe there always is in such cases. The note said: "My darling Vicky: Believe nothing your father tells you. I shouldn't have involved myself with Shine, but I knew your father had become determined to cheat me out of what was justly mine, and Shine was my last chance to achieve that peace of mind which I've wanted so much for so long.

"However, I know now that there's no justice and no peace. I shall never make amends to my father for what I did to him, just as I shall never make amends to you for leading you to believe I could ever bring you the happiness you deserve. I realize now we were deceiving ourselves when we thought we could have a successful marriage. I'm unworthy of you, not fit to live. The violence just won't let me be.

"I've managed to go on all these years because I've turned the violence outward. By channeling it into my ambition, I was able to live with myself, but since my ambitions have been annihilated, I no longer have an outlet for the violence, so the violence has nowhere else to turn except inward upon myself. But perhaps after all, this is what I've always wanted. Sometimes the worst that can happen to a man isn't to die. It's to live with the consequences of what he's done —or what he's failed to do.

"I love you so much I can't quite believe you don't still love me, but if you don't love me anymore, please forgive me for all the pain and unhappiness I've brought you, and please believe me when I say that I'm going into the dark thinking of you and thanking you for all those wonderful sunlit hours we shared together. My love always, Scott."

I went into the bathroom and knelt down by the bloodred water. His body was still warm but he was quite dead. I laid my cheek against his for a long while, and as I stroked his hair I saw Kennedy dying in Dallas and Jackie's dress stained with blood, and the soiled mud of Vietnam, and the burning cities of America—I saw all those random images of violence blend to form the background of our affair, and then it seemed to me that Scott and I were no longer in the center of the stage but were dissolving in the blood which was gushing from the scenery to engulf us; it was as if the violence had moved to the center of the stage to dominate and destroy our lives.

I said aloud, "I must take him somewhere very peaceful," and suddenly I craved for peace and for an end to violence's intolerable suffering. I felt I had to get away, far, far away; I felt I had to make a new beginning, but that longing seemed so unattainable and conjured up yet another world seen through the wrong end of a telescope, and I didn't know how I was ever going to get there. I just went on kneeling by the bloodstained water and stroking his dark hair until at last I said, "I must do something now," and I went back into the living room. Then it occurred to me that I didn't want anyone interrupting us, so I put the "DO NOT DISTURB" notice on the outside of the door. After that there didn't seem to be anything else to do, so I sat down on the couch.

I sat there for some time. Outside, it began to get dark. I wondered if I should call the police, but I knew I couldn't talk to anyone. Normally I would have turned to my father, but of course I couldn't turn to my father, not anymore.

When it was dark, I switched on the light and moved toward the bathroom to sit with him again, but when I reached the bathroom door I found myself unable to open it. I heard my voice say, "Scott's dead," and suddenly I glimpsed myself in the long mirror, a woman in a blue coat, a woman a long way away in some private hell where no one could reach her, a woman suspended in time, impaled on the past, paralyzed by the present, unable to conceive of the future.

"Scott's dead," I said. "Dead." I remembered then that dead people had to have funerals, and I was glad when I remembered that, because I knew at once where I would have to take him. I wondered how I could arrange for the body to be transported to England. Probably it would all be very complicated. I decided I had to get help immediately, and once I'd made that decision, I felt much better, because I realized how sensible I was being. Moving to the phone, I asked for the international operator and placed a call to Sebastian's little house in Cambridge.

V

SEBASTIAN PICKED up the receiver on the second ring.

"Oh, hi," I said. "It's me. Look, I'm sorry to bother you, but Scott's dead—he's committed suicide—and I'm not sure what to do. I'm here with him now, and I just can't quite figure out how I'm going to cut through all the red tape in order to take him to Mallingham. What do you think I should do next? I can't ask my father. You do understand that, don't you, Sebastian? I can't ask my father."

"Wait."

I waited obediently.

"Okay, let's take this one step at a time. Are you sure he's dead?"

"Yes, of course."

"Have you called the police?"

"No, not yet."

"Where are you?"

"In Scott's suite at the Carlyle."

"Right. Now, here's what you do. Pick up your purse and anything else that belongs to you, but leave your key to the suite on the dresser in the bedroom. Got that? Okay, do it and come back to me."

I did as I was told.

"Great," said Sebastian when I returned to the phone. "Now, leave the hotel as casually as possible and walk home. Don't take a cab. The object of these instructions, as you may realize, is to leave no obvious trace of yourself at the Carlyle. If you can do that, then the police will be more likely to begin their inquiries at Willow and

Wall, and then your father will be able to take care of them before they can bother you."

"I see. Yes."

"Now, when you get home, look in the Yellow Pages under the entry 'Security' and hire two guards to sit outside your front door for the next thirty-six hours to keep everyone out. Insist that no one is to cross your threshold except your kids and staff. I'll call you as soon as I arrive. If I get the morning flight out of London, I'll be with you around four o'clock tomorrow afternoon. Have you got all that? Do you want me to repeat anything?"

"No, that's fine."

"One last thing: was there any blood?"

"Oh, yes," I said, surprised. "He cut his wrists. The bathwater's bright red."

There was a pause before Sebastian said, "Right. I get it. Yes. Okay, before you leave the suite, just check that you have no blood on your clothing. We don't want people noticing you on the way out."

"It's all right. The blood's all in the bath."

"Yes . . . I guess it would be. Vicky, when you get home, will you please call a doctor and get yourself treated for shock?"

"I'm okay, Sebastian. I feel much better now that I know what to do. All I needed was a little advice."

"Uh-huh. But call a doctor anyway, would you? Just as a favor to me?"

"Sure, if you like."

"Thanks. Remember, I'll be with you as soon as I can. Just try to hold on till I get there."

"No problem. Don't worry about me," I said, and only just managed to replace the receiver before I blacked out.

VI

I WAS unconscious for only a short time, but when I recovered I felt so ill that I thought at first I would be unable to leave the hotel. But I did. Following Sebastian's instructions, I went home, summoned a doctor, hired two security guards, and took myself off to bed. I told the children I suspected I was coming down with flu, and later I explained the guards' presence by saying I'd received a threat that someone intended to steal my jewelry. The telephone rang repeatedly, but I insisted I was too ill to speak to anyone.

When the doctor arrived, he prescribed a sedative, but I slept only briefly. Sometime during the night I vomited, but I didn't mind that because afterward I felt less ill. I drank a little water but could eat nothing.

The next morning the telephone continued ringing at regular intervals, and once I heard voices raised in the hall as someone tried to gain admittance to the apartment, but the security guards knew their business, and nobody disturbed me.

The police never came, but the letters did, letter after letter slipping under the front door into the hall. My father always dictated letters, which his secretaries typed, but these letters were handwritten. He had small neat handwriting which he wrote in straight well-spaced lines. There were no erasures. I wondered if he had sat up all night drafting and redrafting what he wanted to say.

"My darling Vicky: On failing to find you at the bank after our phone conversation, I went to the Carlyle to see if you were with Scott, but there was no reply from the suite. I then went home, but I was so worried when I still had no success in contacting either of you that I returned to the Carlyle and insisted that the manager open the door of the suite for me. What I found there was the most terrible shock, and since you're refusing to see me, I can only assume you not only know what has happened but somehow hold me partially to blame. Sweetheart, this is an appalling tragedy and one which I never for one moment anticipated—you mustn't, please, hold me in any way responsible. I promise you that I can explain everything if you'll just give me the chance. Meanwhile, don't worry about the police or the inquiries. I'll take care of everything, but please let me see you. All my love, Daddy."

"My dearest Vicky: Since you still refuse to see me, perhaps it would help if I set out the facts as plainly and unemotionally as possible, so that you can judge me on what actually happened and not on what you think might have happened between Scott and myself.

"As you know, I was devoted to Scott and it was a terrible shock to me back in November 1963 when I had to face up to the truth I should have acknowledged long before: that the devotion was in no way reciprocated and that he was out to extract the widest possible revenge for his father's death. I knew then that I should have to fire him as soon as I was free to do so, but of course Scott knew this too and so he resolved to outmaneuver me once and for all during the four-year reprieve he had engineered for himself in London.

"His plan involved you, since it was obvious that if he used you correctly my hands would again be tied when he returned to New York. I know it was your mother's accident which led to the revival of your affair, but you can be sure that even if your mother hadn't been ill Scott would have engineered a reconciliation by some other means. I'm not claiming he was entirely insincere. You're a charming and attractive woman and I'm sure he derived genuine pleasure from your company, but when he agreed to marry you I'm afraid he was motivated primarily by his ambition, which by this time could only be described as a dangerous obsession.

"Of course he thought originally that through you he could not only force me to retain him in the firm but also ultimately force me to hand over control of the bank. However, I did manage to communicate to him (through you—of course I knew you'd immediately tell him every word I said) that I'd made up my mind that control of the bank would never pass to him. I thought once he knew this he would back away from marrying you, but Scott was determined by this time to divide me not only from my bank but from you as well, and that was when he decided to use Donald Shine to help his plans along. If this scheme had worked, he would have got both you and the bank in the end. He might have had to wait awhile, but his future as the president of a reorganized Van Zale's within the Shine & General conglomerate would have been guaranteed.

"You were with me that September evening when Jake told me what Shine was planning and how Scott was in it with him up to the hilt. I doubt if I have to remind you how shocked I was and how I had to be alone afterward to recover from such a terrible blow.

"I decided I had to take Shine first. If I'd fired Scott immediately (as I was still entitled to do in view of his behavior—the other partners would without doubt have backed me up), it would have warned Shine that we were on his trail. So I kept Scott in ignorance—and that meant keeping you in ignorance too. I was sure you were just an innocent pawn in Scott's game, but I also had to allow for the possibility that you had sided with Scott and were secretly fighting with him against me. A woman in love can be capable of anything, and her judgment in such circumstances can lead her very far astray.

"Once I was rid of Shine I knew I had to keep Scott in ignorance until our final confrontation—he might have done too much damage otherwise, so I had Harry go through the motions of a full inquiry at the Trust and went on pretending no one knew who'd betrayed us to Shine. I can admit to you frankly that I was scared of Scott by this time. Obviously he was mentally unbalanced—I was horrified when Kevin told me about the incident in London last August. Don't be angry with Kevin for telling me. He truly felt he was acting in your best interests by keeping me informed of the situation, and he was seriously worried by the possibility of you marrying such a man. I know that by firing Scott I was destroying his motive for marrying you, and so you may well accuse me of interfering once more in your private life, but I must defend myself by saying that I had to fire him anyway for business reasons, and that in the long run you must surely be better off without such a dangerous, unstable man who used you as he did.

"However, I do understand that you loved him very much, and that's why you must believe me when I say I'm deeply distressed for your sake and want to do everything I can to ease your grief. You must realize that despite everything I too feel deeply bereaved. He was still *my boy,* as I always put it in my thoughts, and one of the most painful aspects of parenthood is that you go on loving your children no matter what they may do to hurt you.

"Please let me see you so that we can have the chance to comfort each other. I remain, as always, your loving and devoted father, CPVZ."

"Dear Vicky: I finally realized why you weren't answering my letters, and having just received confirmation that the last tape has disappeared from the machine in my office, I have decided with great reluctance that I must speak very plainly indeed.

"First, you must understand that I was deeply hurt by what Scott had done. I also felt bitterly angry with him, bitter enough and angry enough to lash out and say things that should never have been said. When someone hits you, your instinct is to hit them back. It may not be a very Christian response, but I venture to suggest it's a very human one.

"The truth is that I just couldn't handle the fact that Scott had rejected me so destructively—although this rejection is easier to handle now that I realize he couldn't help himself. He was sick. His suicide proves that. Remember: *sane people do not commit suicide.* They take their lives when their minds are disturbed. I'm convinced Scott's mind had been disturbed for a long time. Anyway, he'd certainly lost touch with reality. That much is obvious.

"I *couldn't* have let you marry such a man. You had to be protected from him. I was afraid that after I'd fired him he might kill you in some outburst of uncontrollable violence. That's why I had to lie and make sure he believed you no longer wanted him. I had to cut him out of not only my life but yours—*I had to,* Vicky, can't you see? I did it for your sake. I did it because I love you. *I did it all for you.*

"You've got to see me and we've got to talk. Stop hiding from me now, please, and let's meet face to face. CPVZ."

"Vicky: *Please.* I can't bear the way you're trying to shut me out like this. You mean more to me than anyone else in the world, and you're hurting me terribly. You know by now that although I have a lot of friends, there's no one I can really talk to except you and Kevin, and Kevin looks like he's settled in London for good, and I hardly ever get to see him nowadays. Of course I love Alicia, but we've nothing in common, and talking's so difficult. You're all I've got, Vicky, except the grandchildren, and they're wonderful, but the younger generation are so strange nowadays and often I find I don't know what to say to them. So we've got to put this tragedy behind us and face the future together. Why, we owe it to the kids not to remain estranged! I'm truly looking forward to taking Eric into the bank—I think I can hold on there till he's twenty-five and capable of carving out a position for himself. I'm very proud of Eric. He'll give everything meaning for me and make up for Scott's terrible rejection. It'll all come right in the end, you'll see, and you'll find someone else, the right man this time, and you'll be happy again one day, I swear it. Now, sweetheart, please do write or call me on the phone— I'll stand by you, I'll help you through this, I'll do anything, anything at all, to make things right. With all my love now and always, Daddy."

"Father: Eric will not be going into the bank. He'll major in environmental studies when he goes to college. This decision is final and I support it one hundred percent.

"In my opinion a meeting between us would serve no useful purpose. You killed the man I loved. What more can possibly be said? Vicky."

VII

SEBASTIAN ARRIVED, announced laconically, "I'll fix this," and set to work. He talked to the children and made arrangements with Nurse for them to follow me to Europe so that we could all spend Christmas together after the funeral. He even arranged for my mother to take a Christmas cruise so that she wouldn't be alone over the holidays. He talked to the police, the doctors, the bureaucrats. He organized the removal of Scott's body to Mallingham. He retained the security men so that I could remain in seclusion. He conferred with my father's aides to ensure that the inevitable publicity was kept to a minimum. He saw my father but he would not tell me what had been said. And finally he took me to England.

The English Sullivans were at the airport to meet us: Scott's half-brothers, Edred and George; Scott's half-sister, Elfrida. I had not seen them the previous summer. When Scott had given way to my reluctance to visit Mallingham, his English family, much annoyed, had refused to visit us in London and so my estrangement from them had persisted, but as soon as I saw them now I realized all animosity was at an end. I had to keep reminding myself how closely they were related to Scott. They seemed so alien with their English voices and English clothes and English manners, but they were kind in that understated way which was so typically English, and said how sorry they were and how I mustn't worry because all the funeral arrangements had been made and when I said a martini did I mean a dry martini cocktail or straight vermouth, and then they took me to a London hotel and there was a comfortable bed and I slept.

Rose arrived the next day from Velletria, but not Lori; Lori wasn't coming to the funeral. She had just heard that Andrew's plane was missing over Vietnam and her eldest son had been arrested on a drug charge and her psychiatrist had advised her against making the long journey to Europe.

"I just can't understand it," said Rose when she thought I couldn't hear. "There's Vicky's Eric, who's turned out so well, and there's

Lori's Chuck who's dropped out of school to peddle LSD. How could it possibly have happened? What did Lori do wrong?"

"Maybe Vicky did something right," said Sebastian. "Did you ever consider that?"

"The trouble with Lori," said Elfrida, the school principal, "is that she sees her children as two-dimensional figures who boost her ego and exist to decorate her beautiful home. I never trust any mother who boasts non-stop about how perfect her children are. It usually means she hasn't the faintest idea what's going on."

"Vicky knows what's going on," said Sebastian. "Vicky listens when the little monsters talk to her. Vicky communicates," he added, as if pronouncing the last word on the subject, but they must have thought this the most eccentric judgment, for of course I couldn't communicate then with anyone. I barely spoke, barely ate, barely breathed the air which Scott had ceased to breathe, but when I came at last to Mallingham I understood that time which he had described as time out of mind, and in seeing his world through his eyes I was able to step out of my grief and accept his death as he himself had accepted it, as an end to violence and a dissolution of the structure of time which had imprisoned him. Nothing mattered now except that he was to be at peace with his father in a place where the sea wind hummed over the marshes of a remote, ancient, beautiful land; nothing mattered now except that I had brought him home.

I was aware of the voices again, sometimes talking to me, sometimes talking past me, sometimes talking far away when they thought I couldn't hear.

"Vicky looks as if she's about to collapse."

"Will she ever get through the funeral?"

"Vicky, dear, don't you think you should go and lie down?"

"Maybe a doctor . . ."

"Vicky's going to be all right," said Sebastian. "Vicky's okay."

Voices, voices, voices, all floating on the air, and people wandering past like people in a dream, and all the while I looked past the lawn to the waters of the lake or leaned out of the window of my room to let the sea breeze cool my face, and always I thought how perfect, how peaceful, how right Scott was to want to come here.

"Now, Vicky," said Elfrida to me briskly when she found me wandering in the garden on the morning of the funeral, "I'm going to be very bossy and interfering and give you a piece of my mind, because I really think someone ought to say certain things to you. Please don't think I'm hostile, because nothing could be further from the truth. My experience as a headmistress has taught me that perfectly frightful parents can produce surprisingly nice children, so I'm certainly no longer prejudiced against you on account of your father—I judge you as you are and on your own merits.

"Now, you seem an intelligent woman with a reasonably pleasing personality, so there's no reason why, after all this is over, you shouldn't have a worthwhile, satisfying future. But you must pull yourself together and start making plans. Why don't you stay in England for a while and get right away from that dreadful New York? Sebastian says you've often toyed with the idea of taking a degree, so may I suggest that the time for toying is past? Now is just the time when you should take action! It would give you not only a new interest but also a new life, which seems to be exactly what you need in order to recover from this catastrophe. Why don't you take a degree at my old university, Cambridge? They do take elderly students with no qualifications except a reasonable intelligence and a strong desire to learn, and my former tutor's still there—I'll introduce you to her, and I know she'll do all she can to help. Also, Sebastian could be useful—he knows Cambridge well enough to help you set up a home there.

"Oh, yes, I know what you're going to say! You're going to say: 'I can't, I can't, the children need me!' Now, Vicky, you must be realistic about this. Your children are growing up, and unless you prepare for the future now, you're going to wake up one morning and find all the birds have flown from the nest and your life is completely empty, because after dedicating your life to your children you have no life of your own to sustain you once they're gone. I see this syndrome constantly recurring among the mothers of my pupils, and believe me, such mothers are much to be pitied.

"No, don't try to argue with me! Eric and Paul will obviously complete their education in America, but there's no reason why Samantha and Kristin shouldn't be at boarding school in England—heavens, I'll take them myself! We're not so far from Cambridge, and anyway, a happy boarding school like mine would be a painless way for them to settle in a new country and make plenty of friends. As for Benjamin, he's just the right age for English prep school . . . oh, yes! Don't say he's too young! Boys here always get sent away to school young if it's financially possible—the parents know it's better for them than being coddled at home. The English are sentimental about animals, but not children, and anyway, from what I hear about Benjamin, it's obvious he would thrive at prep school.

"So if all the children are away at school, this will leave you very much on your own, and while I do understand that this must be a horrifying prospect, I would suggest to you . . . Vicky, what is it? Why are you laughing? Oh, God, Vicky, you're not going to have hysterics, are you?"

I pulled myself together and reassured her I was not. Then, as if to prove both to her and to myself how calm and rational I could be, I set aside all thought of the children and made the request I had been nerving myself to make ever since I had read my father's attempt to justify the part he had played in Scott's death.

"Elfrida," I said, "do you still have your copy of your brother Tony's posthumous letter?"

VIII

I READ the letter twice, once with great speed, once very slowly, and afterward wondered how I could ever have dismissed the details of Steve's death as a series of past incidents which didn't concern me. I wondered too why I had automatically thought Scott neurotic when he had called my father a murderer, and why I had not questioned my father more closely when he had referred with such evasive reluctance to Tony's letter.

Then I remembered my old attitude to my mother. Perhaps I had known the truth subconsciously all along. Perhaps, repeating a well-worn defensive pattern, I had simply found it less painful to shut my mind against the facts I hadn't wanted to know.

I considered those facts. I considered them with the calm detachment which often follows in the wake of emotional exhaustion. I considered them for a long time.

As the result of my father's deliberate cold-blooded maneuverings in 1939, Steve Sullivan had got drunk, gone out, and smashed himself to death on an empty country road. The truth of the matter was that my father had pushed Steve toward that drunken car crash as violently as he had pushed Scott toward that bloodstained bath—and in both cases he had persisted in declaring that his unjustifiable crimes were justified.

I didn't like to think of such actions going unpunished. That didn't seem right at all, although I couldn't think what I could do about it. I was trembling and could no longer reason clearly, so I decided I would have to think about my father later, after the funeral.

I went downstairs to join the others, who were all waiting to set out for the church, and soon I heard the conversation droning around me again—voices, voices, voices, all talking of the future, the present, the past, but I was beyond them all with my memories of Scott, and as the moment of the funeral drew nearer, I was conscious again of seeing his world through his eyes and moving to meet him across the borders of time.

" 'To be conscious,' " I said, " 'is not to be in time.' "

"That's T. S. Eliot, isn't it?" said Rose. "A very overrated poet, I've always thought."

But Sebastian took my hand in his as we set out for the church, and Sebastian said, quoting from the *Four Quartets:* " 'What we call the beginning is often the end and to make an end is to make a beginning. The end is where we start from . . .' "

IX

THE SKY was gray above the square tower of Mallingham church, and the trees beyond the churchyard were bare. The Episcopal service was short. The coffin was lowered into the ground, the minister closed his book, and the chilly east wind from the sea ruffled the wreaths of flowers. I had ordered many flowers, not just for Scott but for Steve and Tony, for Dinah and her son, Alan, all either buried or commemorated beneath the boughs of the cherry tree which Dinah herself had planted to flower every spring.

I dried my eyes and stood watching all the flowers. They were chrysanthemums, bronze and yellow. I liked looking at the flowers, but presently Elfrida murmured, "Vicky . . ." and I knew it was time to go.

But Sebastian said, "She'd like to be alone for a moment."

They went away, and I was alone.

Instantly I was seeing through Scott's eyes again, and I was aware, as he would have been aware, of time bending so that past and present seemed to flow into each other in a long unbroken loop. I looked around the churchyard, and although the cherry tree was bare, by some miracle I could see it in full bloom. I glanced up at the church tower, and for a single second a thousand years coexisted simultaneously in a single chord of time.

The tears dried on my cheeks. I stood very still, afraid to move for fear of shattering the spell, but then I heard the lych-gate click far away and I knew at once that my father had entered the churchyard.

He came slowly toward me. He wore black and looked very neat and quiet and old.

"So you did come," I said as he halted. "They said you wouldn't. But I knew you would."

He was breathing evenly but audibly, as he often did after his asthma had been severe. "Yes," he said. "I had to come." He looked past me at the flowers, and suddenly his eyes shone with tears. "Vicky," he said, "Vicky, please . . . forgive me and come home. Please, Vicky. Please."

I looked at him, and when I saw myself reflected in his eyes I saw a justice which none of us, not even Scott, had even begun to imagine. I saw too that natural justice was terrible in its merciless purity, far more terrible than any justice engineered by man, and in that moment I knew not only what I had to do; I knew that I had no alternative. It was as if I were an instrument wielded by forces which could never be more than imperfectly understood. At the most I was merely an individual deprived by circumstances of any freedom of choice.

I said politely to my father, "We shan't meet again."

He began to struggle for breath. "But, Vicky . . . oh, God, Vicky . . . Vicky, please, you've got to listen to me . . ."

I could see his future so clearly. He would live on alone long after all his friends were dead; he would live on knowing that I lived too, though we might never meet; he would survive to a great age, for his punishment was not to be death; he was going to have to live with the consequences of what he had done.

"Vicky, you must forgive me, you've got to. . . ."

The moment had come. It was time to pass sentence, and as I listened, I heard myself say, annihilating him with the words he had so often used to annihilate others: "It's over. It's finished. I have nothing else to say."

X

LEAVING HIM among the graves, I walked away down the path, and as the church clock chimed the hour, I paused in the shadow of the lych-gate.

With the exception of my father's black limousine and Sebastian's red mini, all the cars had gone, and at first I thought there was no one in the lane. Then I saw Sebastian. He was some yards away, tugging a sprig of holly from its bush in the hedgerow.

It was only then that I noticed the branches of the wild roses, and suddenly I could see the hedgerow in spring as clearly as I had seen the cherry tree in the graveyard: I saw the whole lane in full bloom, rose after rose, spots of light in a dark incomprehensible universe, ravishing symbols of a triumph over time.

I called Sebastian's name. He turned, smiled, and walked toward me, the sprig of holly glowing in his hand.

The strength flowed back into me. Stretching out my hand, I raised the latch of the lych-gate and walked at last, through the door I had never opened, into the rose-garden.

Howatch   c.4 BRANCH

Sins of the fathers.